Tom Davies, a Welshman born and bred, trained as a journalist with the *Western Mail* and later worked for the *Sunday Times*, the *Sunday Telegraph* and the *Observer* where for three years he was the diarist Pendennis. Now a full-time writer, his previous books include MERLYN THE MAGICIAN AND THE PACIFIC COAST HIGHWAY, STAINED GLASS HOURS: A MODERN PILGRIM-AGE (both non-fiction works) and the novels ELECTRIC HARVEST and ONE WINTER OF THE HOLY SPIRIT (which is published by Futura).

Tom Davies is married and has three children.

Also by Tom Davies

ONE WINTER OF THE HOLY SPIRIT

TOM DAVIES

BLACK SUNLIGHT

Futura

A Futura Book

ISBN 0 7088 2998 8

Reproduced, printed and bound in Great Britain by
Hazell Watson & Viney Limited,
Member of the BPCC Group,
Aylesbury, Bucks

Futura Publications
A Division of
Macdonald & Co (Publishers) Ltd
Greater London House
Hampstead Road
London NW1 7QX
A BPCC plc Company

Author's Note

I went to live in Maerdy, home of the last pit in the Rhondda, to write and research this book and would like to thank Mrs Dilys Evans and Jeffrey for looking after me; the Rev. Andrew and Ros Morton for their companionship; Bob Reeves for the use of his fine poem *Gwaed* (which is Welsh for blood); Tim Shackleton and Richard Evans for their skilful advice; the marvellous miners of Maerdy with whom I spent many happy hours, both drinking and picketing, and my wife Liz who virtually gave me two years off to leave home and learn about the life of the Rhondda miner.

But Maerdy is not my fictional village of Bont and neither is the Valley herein the Rhondda. The characters and Valley of this book are entirely my own creation and through them I have sought to tell the story of the widespread betrayal and sad decline of the South Welsh Valleys over the last twenty years. It is to my beloved people of the Valleys that this book is dedicated with the quiet prayer that, one day, they will find cause to sing again.

Part One

The Ceremony of Innocence

Once I strode the green fields
On steel sprung thighs
My breath was the breath
Of mountains and I
Snorted fire in my pride.

I knew the heat of iron,
I knew the smell of sulphur,
Mine was the way of moles,
And I thought my pick had
Conquered coal when I shed
My sweat a mile below the sun.

Gwaed, Bob Reeves

Chapter One

It was early evening in Bont, the sun just hanging over the rim of the Valley.

A queue began forming outside the Miners' Welfare Hall for the Saturday night hop. The dance was not due to start until eight o'clock but many queued early so that they might claim their favourite seats – next to the bar perhaps, or the one in which they were once lucky in bingo. Madge Williams from the bakery, they said, had won the flyer seven times this year from her seat by the ladies.

From down in the village square came the long pained squeals of the brakes of the Western Welsh bus as it three-point turned around the clock tower.

The mining village of Bont was a raggle-taggle community scattered along the far end of the Glamorgan Valley, the heart of the South Wales coalfield. Completely enclosed by high, rock walls, it might have been sitting at the bottom of a volcano. A dozen or so streets ran at right angles to the main terrace; there were a few rundown streets around by the waste-paper factory, next to the river, and some slightly posher terraces, with foaming lace curtains cascading around coloured plastic flowers, right up the hill next to the severe grey shape of the Libanus Chapel and a row of rackety pigeon cotes perched dangerously on bandy-legged stilts.

About a mile away from the village were a reservoir, sitting right at the end of the Valley, three huge, black tips and the stern black geometry of the mine itself. As the miners walked or drove down from the pit at the end of their shifts they first came to the cavernous Welfare Hall, with its three lounges, four bars and dance hall. Then there was a long row of shops including the Co-op supermarket, a branch of Barclays

Bank (open three mornings a week), a fish and chip shop, a betting shop and Lee Hoo Wonk's Chinese takeaway. Plonked right at the end of the majestic curve of Bont Terrace was the village's small cinema, The Bug.

Beyond them, in turn, was the brown rocky bend in the Valley, which led to the next village, another world altogether.

Just full of itself was Bont in the early summer of 1966. Every morning cockerels could be heard bugling in the voluptuous dawns. As the sun rose high, cats stretched out on the corrugated roofs of the garden sheds, luxuriating in the glorious warmth of it all. Every afternoon was vibrant with doorstep gossip and the chimes of Gazzi's ice cream van dancing down the gullies. The boys on the bench in the square sat out, drinking cider and yarning. Come the night and lovers found their way down to the long grass on the river bank where they kissed and touched one another.

Every three hours, night and day, a pair of diesels throbbed up the railway line, past the tump, towing a brown rattling chain of empty wagons. Some three hours later they laboured back from the pit again, the wagons piled high with the finest Welsh anthracite. There was enough coal down that hole to blacken and heat the whole face of the world, the miners of Bont reckoned. There was certainly enough to keep Bont going for a hundred years and, when that time was up, they would worry about the matter again.

Back at the Welfare Hall, the doors had opened. Everyone duly paid their half crown entrance fee to Dai Fat in the glass kiosk and filed upstairs to the dance hall. The building was a gloomy warren of bubbling, flaking paint with the smell of stale beer trapped in the carpets. There were aluminium foil ash-trays on the tables, many made level with wodges of beer mats stuffed strategically under one leg or another. Down every corridor you could hear the bright, brittle music of the one-armed bandits or the echoing click of snooker balls. Even in the heat of the summer you could sniff the mildewed, slightly mushroomy damp.

Two women were standing on one of the concrete landings of the stairs and talking to one another in low tones of high urgency:

'I told her. And I do keep on telling her. But she gets proper craxy when you tell her anything at all.'

10

'What did you tell her then?'

'Poor dab I do feel awful sorry for her. I told her again last week but there's no shape on her. There's no grain in her washing. No shape on 'er in the 'ouse. No nothing.'

'So what did you tell her?'

'I told her to brighten her ideas up if she wanted her leg varnished with that stuff again.'

'What stuff was that?'

By far the largest room in the Welfare Hall was the dance floor, its curving, art deco balcony festooned with spotlights. Against a stage backdrop of giant gold and silver strips Smokey Evans was even now setting up his disco – Smokey Sounds – which attracted people from all over the Valleys. Smokey, a young and rather fetching Teddy boy from Pontypridd, had firmly set his back on all the Beatles music that was swamping every set of ears in the land. He still served up the driving hits of the Shirelles, the Crystals and the Ronettes.

He knew his audience well; Smokey's music, they said in the Valleys, was the greatest ever recorded. It might also have been the loudest. When Smokey started up his disco they said the miners started jiving together on the face of the Meadow Seam, a mile underground. For much of Saturday night the whole of Bont Terrace would shake to the nakedly primitive pounding of Phil Spector's Wall of Sound. Aunty Phyllis, in No. 3, would stuff up her ears with bits of Kleenex while Bomber Jones, in No. 9, before getting on with the slow business of dying of pneumonicosis on his brass-knobbed bedstead, would take out his rattling false teeth just as soon as the Ronettes started wailing about how awful it was when the one you loved ran off with your best friend.

The hop began, as usual, with five hands of bingo. Some veteran players marked up to six cards, though a few had difficulty with one card and kept calling bogey houses. A group of young miners, above all this, stood together in a pool of fluorescent light around the bar. Most of the bingo players were young girls, many dressed in the careful emblems of the American teenager – pony-tails, bright red neckerchiefs, tiny pleated skirts and white socks. Their brows furrowed in concentration and their mouths were quiet, for a change, as Walford James, the bingo caller, read out the all-important numbers from his tray of leaping, bouncing table tennis balls.

Seven and six — was she worth it? On its own — number five.
Legs — eleven. Downing Street — number ten. Top of the shop —
number eighty. Unlucky for some — thirteen ...

The one doing all the talking in the group of young miners
was Glynmor Jones, one nicotine-stained hand holding a pint
and the other in the trouser pocket of his mohair suit. 'Look
I'm telling you now, boys, and this is a fact, no lie, but on my
mother's life, this piece — a smart piece she was an' all — this
piece said that his dick was so big he did wash his back with it.
Isn't that right Jampots?'

'That's what she said, aye.' Glynmor always looked for
confirmation from his best butty, an even smaller youth with a
haggard pale face and a taste for ill-fitting suits and rolling his
own cigarettes.

'How can you wash your back with your dick?'

'That's a fact that is,' Glynmor affirmed again with a nod.
'She said 'e was the only man she'd ever met who could crawl
on all fours and leave five trails. It's monstrous. Just like some
bastard python. Isn't that right Jampots?'

'Correct.'

'They said it was so big that, when he had a bad back, he
had a doctor's note so that he didn't have to take it out when he
wanted a piss.'

'You're having me on, mun.'

'That's a fact that is. Isn't that right Jampots?'

Glynmor was a short, broad-shouldered man with dark,
Welsh good looks. His eyes were blacker than the coal he mined
and he had thick eyebrows and a square jaw. But it was his
smile that always got the girls going, a broad, laughingest smile
which was always there, sitting well with the consistent crudity
of his language. Rarely without a Capstan full-strength in his
hand and a dirty joke in his mouth he approached every
problem with an open mouth did our Glynmor. It was said he
could talk the robin off a packet of starch. He had, as they say
around 'ere, a bell on every tooth.

After the bingo had finished — with Madge Williams
calling the flyer *again* — Smokey began slipping on his golden
oldies, orchestrating the pace of the dance with the cunning
peculiar to many of the natives of Pontypridd, content, for the
while anyway, just to let the girls jive together with their
handbags placed near their feet for safety. Sparkly coloured

12

lights bounced off the huge mirrored ball suspended from the ceiling, chasing and streaming over the largely empty dance floor in flashing lights of reds, blues and greens. Now the Ronettes were at it. *Why don't you beeeeeeeeeeeeeee myyyyyy babeeeeeeeeeee* ... Soon Smokey would have the whole place bouncing. He was one of the first disc jockeys to have his own light show too – a weird and wonderful collection of winking orange and red lights, mainly stolen from traffic signals and parking bollards up and down the Valley.

But no matter how hard Smokey worked, the only boy who ever danced through choice, from very early until very late, was Biscuits, who worked in the stores down the pit. He had not, it seemed, stopped dancing since seeing *Rock Around the Clock* (thirty-four times). The girls all agreed that Biscuits was the best dancer in the Valleys. Indeed, he was not overmuch bothered who he danced with either, merely wandering into the thickest clump of girls and grabbing the nearest hand to jive with. Then all eyes feasted on this fabulous dancer who, dressed entirely in black, had all the elegance and slime of a Brylcreemed tarantula, his hands held out carefully as the quiff of his Tony Curtis haircut dangled down on his forehead and bounced up and down to the beat.

It was from her table, three away from the stage and just next to the Emergency Exit, that Maggie Evans sat with her friends watching Glynmor's every move. Even as she sat discussing such important matters as how much of a bra strap it was proper and sexy to show, or who Betty Sugarlump was knocking off that week, Maggie watched Glynmor even more carefully than a hawk. As far as she was concerned he was the only ship on the seven seas. The poor girl was just crazy about him, even carrying his photograph around in her locket.

Glynmor, alas, was not exactly crazy about her. But if he'd had enough beer and no other piece sparkled his fancy, he usually came over for the final few dances with Maggie.

Whether Maggie Evans was really classy or not was always debated hotly by the boys in the bar. Her face was a perfect etching of a Welsh beauty, with long bobbed hair and lashings of black eye-liner and mascara, in the style favoured by the Crystals. Her mouth was as full as the reservoir after the rain and so was her bosom. Perfect, said some; they didn't like 'em skinny and titless in the Valleys. A bit fat, said others, the girls especially. She could lose half a stone easy, they said, and she knew it. She was very conscious of her figure was Maggie.

Such pneumatic arguments aside, many of the boys were very taken by Maggie, largely because of Glynmor's persistent lurid lies of how she was always desperate for it. Tales of how she would tear off her knickers and beg him to ravish her had entered the mythology of the Valley. As the dance went on, and the alcohol flowed ever more freely in the blood, a whole string of randy and hopeful boys would come over to her table offering a drink or a dance.

But she refused all offers. Just like a bloody fool, said the girls. Her eyes were only ever for Glynmor who never so much as bought her a drink before getting drunk himself and coming over for the last few dances, arms wide apart and one of those silly bloodshot smiles on his chops. Then the soft cow was just putty in his hands.

The girls always despaired of this surrender. It just wasn't right. She wasn't a doormat was she? You're not a bloody doormat, are you? They were always advising Maggie to start being a bit of a girl, to try and play hard to get. At the very least, she should dance with some other boy. But she just couldn't do it. The soft cow just couldn't. She just wasn't interested in any other boy and that was that.

The dopey cow was happy to be putty in his hands. She'd wipe his arse for him if she could. When did a girl ever get anyone acting like that? The soft sod deserved all she got, didn't she?

By ten o'clock more and more dancers were crowding onto the floor. Smokey was turning the musical screws a bit but still Glynmor did not seem to want to come over. He seemed happy to let Maggie fret over her vodka and lime. Oh sure she pretended that she was having a great time, laughing loud along with the girls' quips and even making a few of her own, but her belly was the tightest knot of pain and her big black eyes locked like radar onto Glynmor's every move.

See, now he's left his butty Jampots and gone over to talk to that horrible piece from Penrhos. Now he's moved on again, joking with some old slag in an ocelot dress. An ocelot dress! Only prostitutes down in Bute Street in Cardiff wear ocelot dresses. Come to think of it that one looks like a tart on the beat. She's putting her hand around the back of his neck and

14

playing with his curls, the old slag. And look at the way she walks. You'd think her arse was chewing a toffee. Well she'd open her legs for him fast enough no doubt. Perhaps she would have to give in one day. But someone like Glynmor would immediately get fed up and go somewhere else. Boys like him are only ever interested if there was a challenge. Give in and they're off.

She sipped her drink, then brought the glass down hard onto the table. Oh, why did he do this to her? It was true enough what the girls said: he was a right bastard was our Glynmor. But you never went for the tidy ones did you? That wasn't the way it worked at all. You always fell for bastards like Glynmor who treated you like shit and were always playing you up. And to think she could have had that manager of the shoe shop down in Pontypridd just like that. He wouldn't have mucked her around like this. He was a proper gentleman that one, exactly what her Mam had always wanted for her too.

Smokey was playing the slow numbers now and Dave Berry was singing how he knew all there was to know about the crying game. She watched Glynmor go to the bar and buy a drink for the slag in the ocelot dress. When did he ever buy anyone a drink? She must have promised him a bit of a rub. Now they were laughing secretively together. Making jokes about her no doubt and how she was so fat an' all. He was probably telling her the story of how her backside got wedged in the hand-rails of the slide on the children's playground. He was always telling people lies about her like that. Glynmor must have been the biggest bastard that ever drew breath. *I knoooooooooow all there is to knoooooooooooooow ...*

The girls were talking of the days when they had live acts here – Maggie, do you remember the night David Whitfield came and we had to go out and get him some chips? – and now the flames of jealousy and betrayal were burning big holes inside her. She stood up, indicating to the girls that they should pick up their handbags. It was time to convene a special emergency conference in the lavatory.

Maggie you've got to stop acting like this init? If he knows what he's doing to you he'll only make it worse. Dance with Biscuits. Try and make Glynmor jealous isn't it? No, not Biscuits. When did anyone ever get jealous of Biscuits? Give us a squirt of that will you? What about Danny? Oh him. He's with that piece that works for Polikoff's in Ynyswen. He won't leave her now. I think that piece in the spotty dress is from Porth. A right goer. Maggie they do say that some man once lost his horse and cart between her legs. Took him three weeks to find it, it did. Lennie. Tap Lennie. Well I think Biscuits is all right. He is the best dancer around 'ere isn't 'e?

But all such counsel did not work and the pain was still playing Maggie up like a renegade ulcer. She returned with the girls to their table. All the conflicting advice had made her brain go funny and Glynmor was still with the same old slag. Now he was even buying her *another* drink. He was going to lose more than his horse and cart the way he was going. She fished a lump of ice out of her drink and flung it at him. But he was so engrossed, leering down the slag's cleavage, he didn't hear the sharp crack of the ice cube against the wall by his head.

He was asking Ocelot Dress where she lived. She shared a flat in Porth with her friend? Well, that was promising enough. Got two bedrooms have you in this flat? Three actually. Oh aye?

Glynmor had heard stories about this one; this was the legendary Phantom Gobbler of Porth who liked to be tied up, then she'd suck you in and blow you out in bubbles. He had always fancied being a bubble, and those were a mighty pair of knockers and no mistake. He would have an awful lot of fun getting lost in them. The sap was rising in him – right up from his toe nails it was rising.

'You come up here this way much, do you?' he asked.

'I've been here a couple of times. I've seen you before too. I remember asking myself what you had between your legs. I'm like that you see. What I want I ask for.'

Uncharacteristically stuck for a few words Glynmor shifted his weight from one foot to another. Something explosive attempted to break out from between the buttons of his tloshes. He had struck gold. He took a swift glance over at Maggie who seemed happy enough with the rest of the girls. It didn't look as if he was going to be with her for the last few dances. He was fond enough of Maggie. He wasn't crazy about her or anything like that but he was fond of her, that figure and all. The boys agreed that Maggie was a good laugh but you couldn't screw a good laugh could you? All he ever got from

16

Maggie was a knee trembler; a dry run which, apart from messing up his underpants, gave him lover's nuts, an ache so fierce that, the next morning, he had to walk bow-legged to the pit, like some old cowboy.

But tonight, as long as he played his cards right, he had a real goer. He was not going to give it up either. After all – as he had always told Jampots in that merry, poetic way of his – a fuck's a fuck.

It was turning half past ten and the Shirelles were singing of the unutterable pain of being stood up on your first date. Smokey was presiding over a crowded, largely drunk, dance floor, all swaying around with groin pressed to crotch, lips locking against others and fingers feeling bra straps. It was all like a great bed of flowers in a tropical storm.

Glynmor sniffed Ocelot's perfume as he brought his mouth close to her ear. 'Shall I see you home? I've got a car,' he whispered.

'There's a problem,' she said. 'I've come with my friend.'

He studied the inside of his half-empty pint. Whenever you were ever getting anywhere with some piece around here there was always this bastard friend; usually some cock-eyed bint with a stammer and a brain the size of a maggot's.

'Where's she to?'

He looked up and followed the direction of her pointed finger. The friend, slumped unhappily over a glass of orange squash, looked even more slummocky than he had feared. She had pebble glasses and her name was Thelma.

'Well I've got just the boy for Thelma and that's a fact,' Glynmor declared. 'My best butty Jampots will look after her. I won't be a minute. Here. Hang onto my glass.'

'One thing. Thelma's got a thing about bad language. Tell him he'll have a lot of fun as long as he doesn't use bad language.'

Glynmor went over to the other side of the bar and cornered Jampots. 'You fancy a nice bit of snatch tonight, do you Jampots? That one's mine. The other's the friend. You've got the friend. She's weeping for it she is. She was saying she doubts she can last another minute without it.'

Jampots snorted into his beer; his reply was drowned by the shattering, erupting noises of tumbling tables and breaking glasses from up the balcony. The Treorchy boys were fighting

17

again. Committee men, whose job it was to keep law 'n' order in the club, came running in from all directions to smoke them out. *I'm gonna loooooooove you foreeeeeeeever …*

'You're well in there, Jampots,' Glynmor went on, oblivious. 'I know she doesn't look much but she's desperate for it. Desperate mun. Don't take any notice of her specs. You don't fuck her specs do you? She's been saying she doubts she can wait a second longer.'

'She's got crabs, mun,' said Jampots noncommittally.

Glynmor wasn't listening. 'The piece I've got says you'll do all right as long as you don't use any bad language. Thelma's her name.'

'You hear me did you Glynmor? Watch my lips now. She's got crabs.'

'Who's got crabs?'

'That piece in the spotted dress. She gave them to Punchy last month. Had to shave himself all over he did.'

'Crabs eh? Crabs.'

'Aye mun. Bastard millions of the little fuckers there were. Fred Dwarf got them off her as well. 'Orrible those crabs are too. 'Orrible. And there's this husband of hers. Plays prop forward; built like a brick shithouse. He comes down her flat in Porth now and then – usually in the middle of the night – to beat her up. Never got over her leaving him. And what he does to her is nothing to what he does to any man he catches with her.'

Glynmor looked sadly over to Ocelot Dress, still holding his pint. Tough. A fuck's a fuck but a dose is a dose and he didn't fancy the husband much either. Oh well, win a few, lose a few.

He decided against going back to retrieve his pint and went straight over to Maggie instead with one of those silly bloodshot smiles on his chops. All the girls looked at one another and shook their heads in genuine despair but Maggie stood up to dance with him immediately. The soft cow deserved all she got. Maggie knew all this, of course. She knew that she was little better than a bit of putty but there was nothing she could do about it. If you were crazy about a boy you were crazy about him and that was that.

Not that any of that mattered now. When you were dancing with Glynmor nothing else mattered. Fires of joy lit up

18

inside her as she jived to the voice of Marvin Gaye who had just heard it on the grapevine. Coloured shivers of light went flashing through the brilliantined darkness with her Glynmor smiling at her as they danced through the jammed bodies and ricocheting elbows. Just now he was hers and that was all that mattered.

And all this was as nothing compared with the final few smooches when Glynmor held her tight and the Righteous Brothers told how she'd lost that loving feeling. Not her. She could feel the electric warmth of his touch on her arms, the warm and vital jointing of his groin pressed into hers, his face nuzzling into the side of her neck. She thought she might even swoon in the ecstasy of it all. She felt warm, complete, alive.

A full moon gazed down on the Valley as fat, washing-day clouds went sailing fast overhead. Police Constable Watkins patrolled the gullies, his torch slicing up the darkness as he looked for the trouble that never came. Down on the dark, twisting floor of the Valley the river gushed and sang, the brown trout darting past the moonbeamed pebbles and waving weeds. Occasionally the fat black shadows of sheep crunched around in the ferns and their sorrowing bleats slipped out into the darkness.

In his Ford Consul in a lay-by next to the top of the tump Glynmor was laying siege to Maggie's body. Except that the ecstasy of the dance floor had long since deserted her and she was now making a firm defence of her virginity against his octopus advances. Oh, she fancied it well enough but, when she succumbed, it was going to be on her wedding night with crisp, white linen sheets and an orchestra playing on the wireless. There would be flowers in the room and a maid bringing them breakfast in bed in the morning. It was all going to be like in one of those Mills and Boon books that she loved to read so much. That's how she wanted it, not in the front seat of Glynmor Jones' Ford Consul. That's not how she pictured it at all.

She allowed him to play with her breasts. But now that he had got her bra off, he had tired of fondling them. Now he was trying to get his hand up her knickers as usual. But, at the top of her stockings, she had firmly clamped her hand on his wrist as usual. He could go back but definitely no further. The very windows of the car were misting up with the frustrated passion of the encounter.

After a bit more huffing and puffing he finally sat up

straight, putting both hands on the steering wheel. 'Anybody'd think your body was the crown jewels,' he complained angry.

'Well they are. They're my crown jewels, aren't they?'

'It's a wonder you haven't got a headache all day with that bastard halo of yours being so tight an' all.'

'Did anyone ever tell you what a lovely talker you were, Glynmor? You should write love stories with that lovely way you do talk.'

'Bollocks to love stories.'

'But you're so charming Glynmor. That's what they all say about you don't they? Glynmor Jones could charm the very ducks off the lake.'

'Bollocks to the ducks.'

She bit her lip, noticing by the whiteness of his knuckles on the steering wheel that he was very angry indeed. Men were such babies when it came to sex. And her Glynmor was the biggest baby of them all.

'I'm sorry Glynmor,' she said, more placatory now. 'But you can't put your hand up there anyway.'

'Why not? What's so special about up there?'

'It's my period. I'm on.'

Rather than calm him down, as she had hoped, this bit of news made him explode with rage. 'You're on. You're *on*. That's nice init? That's bloody nice that is. Why didn't you tell me you daft twat? Saved a lot of trouble, that would've.'

'What did you expect me to say?' She was getting her hair off as well. 'Did you expect me to say "Oh hello Glynmor. It's so nice to see you tonight but you can't go putting your hand up my skirt because I'm having a period." That would be lovely wouldn't it?'

'It might not be nice. But it would have saved a lot of trouble.'

'Perhaps I should have put an advertisement in the *South Wales Echo*? Maggie Evans of Bont Terrace hereby announces that she is having her period so any person intending to put his hand up her skirt had better wait a few days. Or we could have got Smokey to announce it at the disco? Is that what you wanted?'

'Oh shut your gob. You're getting so that your mouth is getting bigger than the Severn Tunnel.'

'Is that so now? That's rich coming from the biggest

mouth in the land. They do say that you're the only man around here who eats bananas sideways.'

Glynmor blew out a stream of exasperated air. It was a considerable thorn in his side that she could always give as good as she got. There was a part of him that quite liked and even respected that but, for most of the time, he found it a right old pain in the arse.

'What about that bit in the ocelot dress?'

There it was. She was winding him up again. Pains in the arse just didn't come any more painful than her when she got going.

'What about her?'

'They do call her the Boat down in Porth 'cos everyone has sailed in her.'

'Don't be so crude.'

'Me! Crude! Glynmor they do say that you're going to get a special coal board pension for crudity.'

He flicked on the ignition and started the car first time. 'I'm taking you home,' he said flat.

'Oh let's have a wank,' she said, changing her tone.

He turned the ignition off again, hardly able to believe his ears. 'What did you say girl?'

'Let's have a wank. I'm starving. Lee Hoo Wonk. Let's have a wank. That's what my sister calls the Chinese takeaway. Haven't you heard that one?'

He laughed softly and started the engine again. Some, but not all, of his good humour had returned. It was true what the boys said. Maggie was a good laugh well enough. But it was also true that you couldn't screw a good laugh. That was the trouble with going out with Maggie. Perhaps he should have run the risk of catching crabs from the piece from Porth. Even as he drove past the tump he could feel that his balls were already aching from a savage case of lover's nuts. That was the other trouble with courting Maggie Evans.

Chapter Two

Then the month of May came and took up lodgings in the Valley and, with her, she brought the rain. Lots and lots of rain.

On some mornings you could actually see pillars of rain building up over the reservoir and then walking down the Valley in giant strides, washing against the patches of green fern and grey granite of the steep slopes, hissing softly on the dry stone walls of the farm which curled over the grass foothills, sheeting down on the piled pit props and rusty iron drams dotted around the pithead, soaking the wandering sheep and pit ponies alike as well as pattering down on the grey slate roofs of the terraces.

The rain filled up the cattle grids, making the rubbish trapped inside them rise up and float against the thick round iron bars. It made black rivulets pour out of the piles of concessionary coal dumped on the roads. It made even bigger rivulets come pouring out of the sides of the tips to dance and leap down the slopes to swell the already swollen river in the Valley bottom. Nothing escaped the rain; even the sodden blackbirds took shelter in the hissing eaves where their dirty white droppings gave a little splash of colour to the wet grey walls of the houses.

Such persistent dampness invaded Bomber Jones' lungs as he lay in the suffocating warmth of his bedroom. Every part of his body was fighting for breath. Any day now the Grim Reaper would be calling out his number for him to row his boat in and it would not be an hour too soon. His face had gone as old and withered as a blind cobbler's thumb. His nails had blackened and his eyes had sunk into dark sockets. His whole body had gone as thin as a sprat on a hunger strike. Much of the time he

22

just sat propped up by a couple of pillows as his mouth searched around in the air for some relieving oxygen. He was, as they say around here, dying by inches. His tools were on the bar.

He did have oxygen bottles next to his bed, which sometimes gave his squealing lungs some relief but he did not like having the mask on for long. And blindly, madly – or so the family kept telling the silly old bugger – he refused to give up smoking his beloved Woodbines.

Even when he had a terrible bout of coughing and it looked as if his frail body was going to break in two under the jolting strain; even when his guts were bringing up great globs of blood-stained sputum, one of his hands would soon be reaching out for a fag. 'Health be buggered,' he would say, his pink eyes watering and mouth dribbling as he began to cough his guts up again. 'My health went the day I went down the hole. I can't get out for a drink so my fags are the only pleasure I've got left.'

He shared No. 9 Bont Terrace with his nephew Glynmor who never lost an opportunity to insult the dying old miner. 'You're a silly old wit-wat and no mistake,' Glynmor would say, fag in his own hand. 'You know we're going to bury you with two hundred Woodbines in your coffin. But we're not going to put any matches in there. Think of it you old goat. Lying there for all eternity with two hundred fags next to you which you can't light. Now that would be a real hell for you wouldn't it? Worse than any of those chapel flames an' all that.'

'I'd find a way to light them,' Bomber would declare between coughs.

'I – I – I – That's all you think of is your bastard self.'

Glynmor was peeved because he was the one who had to share their three up, two down house. While the family took it in turns to come from far and near to look after Bomber and then go home again, he was the one who had to listen to all that terrible coughing day and night. On and on it went. The night was the worst, the honks and heaves amplified by the big enamel bucket into which Bomber was for ever coughing his guts. This had gone on for nearly three years now. On some nights – particularly when he could hear the rustle of a cigarette packet and the dry flare of a lighting match – Glynmor really felt like going in there and holding a pillow over the old miner's head. And he would have done so if it wasn't that he could almost hear Bomber laughing in his coffin as Glynmor stood in Cardiff Crown Court on a life sentence for murder.

'Still hanging on then, are you?' Pauline, Glynmor's younger sister now in Taffs Well, would say to Bomber, again almost as if it was a matter of the utmost regret. 'You're like some bloody weed you are. Every time you get chopped down you spring back to life again. Isn't it time you gave us all a bit of a rest?'

'Well he's going to give us a very long rest quite soon and that's a fact,' Glynmor would add with some venom. 'The only time I can get some sleep now is around the back of the washery in the pit. It's noisy there but not half as noisy as being in 'ere with that old swine coughing his boots up all the time. It's not that pit that's done this to his lungs either. It's those bastard Woodbines of his. Coffin nails that's all they are. Why don't you give them up, you dopey twat?'

'Aw, why don't you go and boil your head?' Bomber would say. 'Talk, talk. All your talk just gives me a headache it do. I'm really looking forward to getting planted if you must know. Then I won't have to listen to you lot all the time.'

There was still a bit of fight left in Bomber and that was another source of aggravation. Even though his body might have been all washed up, the old reprobate had never lost the great sexual urges he had known all his life. Like his Woodbines they gave him his last tenuous hold on the world and he would grab hold of the district nurse when she tried to take his pulse or else whip his hand up the skirt of the Meals on Wheels woman as she handed over his roast beef and two veg.

'We're going to be tying boxing gloves on those dirty paws of yours the way you're going,' Glynmor scolded him again. 'Leave the poor woman alone, can't you?'

'It's only a bit of fun, mun.'

'Bit of fun! Who'd want a bit of fun with some randy old swine who dribbled all the time? Tell me. Do you get a hard on, do you?'

'There's still a bit of life down there.'

'Bit of life! When are you going to die and give us some peace?'

'I'll die when I'm ready.'

'I – I – I – Just thinking of yourself again.'

24

These days the Meals on Wheels woman had now taken to putting his meals just inside the bedroom door rather than risk a mauling at Bomber's hands. And it had been ages since the district nurse had taken his pulse.

But it was that rainy day in May, when Pauline was cleaning the front room, that, hidden down the side of the sofa, she discovered all Bomber's pension books.

Now it was always assumed that Bomber lived on CID – compensation, invalidity and dole – but the truth of the matter was that no one had ever thought much about it. Yet these slim books in their different coloured covers, tied together with elastic bands, told another story. He had got a hardship pension from the N.U.M.; an old age pension from the Post Office; two private endowments with the Prudential and Hearts of Oak *and* an invalidity pension from the N.H.S.S.

It took Pauline ten minutes of scribbling on the back of an envelope to work out that Bomber's total income was well over a hundred pounds a week. But Bomber's stinginess was a legend, even in the pubs of Cardiff. He was far, far tighter than a crab's arse was Bomber. He sold his concessionary coal, he split his matches into threes with a razor. He had learned that trick in prison, locked up for thirty days he was for, appropriately enough, refusing to pay an alleged debt. He was always rummaging around for empty pop bottles to take back to the shop and he would walk a mile to avoid facing a flag seller. From all this miserly behaviour everyone – chiefly Glynmor – had always assumed that Bomber did not have a pot to piddle in. For almost all Bomber's retirement Glynmor had forever been bunging him a few bob for beer or a flutter on the horses.

And now this.

Pauline's sums caused something close to a nuclear explosion when she presented them to the rest of the family. Glynmor had to go to bed for a few hours to recover. So what had the mean swine gone and done with all that money? Where had he stashed it? What if he snuffed it and they still did not know where all the money had gone? What if he had buried it in a biscuit tin somewhere in the tip? Come to think of it he had often been seen walking down there, hadn't he? What if ...

So, ever since the Great Discovery, the family had flocked around Bomber's bed. Just like vultures wheeling around carrion they were. They chivvied him, flattered him, cajoled him, even threatened the stubborn old bastard with eviction.

'We could always send you into that home in Bridgend,' Pauline offered. 'There'd be no smoking your Woodbines in there.'

'We'd even get you a nice new bed-cover,' said Aunty Phyllis, trying a softer tack. 'Look, there's cigarette holes all over this one.'

'Tell us where the money is or I'll bloody throttle you,' said Glynmor – as subtle as a car crash as usual – his cheeks streaking white with fury.

Bomber neither denied nor confirmed their suspicions. In the face of this hurricane of threats and abuse he chose to lie there and say nothing whatsoever.

Finally, in despair, the Jones family sent for Aunty Maude down in Treforest. Notorious for her war-like manner it was assumed that even poltergeists would abandon their ways and go find another calling rather than face Aunty Maude. She came on the next bus, the plastic fruit piled up high on her hat.

She sat and listened gravely to the problem – as outlined by Pauline – and then marched straight into the bedroom and delivered a great Churchillian speech to Bomber. She told him about the need for him to show a moral responsibility to his family; she underlined his Christian duty to provide for those who had the greatest difficulty in providing for themselves; she reminded him of the great strain he had put them all under for the past three years; she implored him to think of those who had nursed him through his dust an' all.

Warming to her theme, she recalled all those nights that Pauline had sat next to his bed mopping his brow when he was with a fever; the way that Glynmor had ferried the family back and fore – without asking for a penny for the petrol – when he had first been taken to Church Village Hospital. She recalled the way that Aunty Phyllis had cooked all those meals without receiving so much as a word of thanks. She even, towards the end of her address, spelled out the awful details of the pauper's funeral he was certainly going to get unless he spilled the beans about where he had hidden all his money.

The canny old sod allowed himself a bit of a smile at that. He was a member of the Royal Antedeluvian Order of the Buffaloes and, if nothing else, you were always sure of a good funeral from the Buffs. Pauper's funeral indeed. But he didn't let on.

When Aunty Maude finally finished her address she went off downstairs for a cup of tea. Bomber needed time for her words to sink in. When she returned he indicated to her to draw near. She lowered her head and he softly wheezed a sentence into her ear which almost made the plastic fruit in her hat melt. 'Go and have a flying fuck on your broomstick you old bag,' he whispered. By way of an exclamation mark he whipped his hand out from under the quilt and sent it up her tweed skirt, giving her crotch a quick squeeze.

This was the first time any man had ever got his hand up Aunty Maude's skirt – let alone given her crotch a good squeeze – and, after they had revived her with smelling salts Glynmor had to drive her back to Treforest. 'There's the thanks for you,' she moaned piteously, all the way home. 'And after all we've done for him.'

In No. 41 Roberts Street, which ran off Bont Terrace and joined School Street down by the river, Maggie was sitting in the kitchen, eating a boiled egg and reading a Mills and Boon romance.

She had inherited her love of reading from her father, William, a primary school teacher who had enjoyed respectability and respect in the community until he had died of a pull while walking up the hill some five years earlier. It was he who had encouraged her to carry on in school and pick up a few 'O' levels but, try as she might, she had never liked studying which always gave her a stiff neck and, after her father's death, she lost what little enthusiasm she had for it.

Her Mam, however, a pushy type with far too many airs and graces for somewhere as gritty as Bont, was desperate to get Maggie into night classes, still hoping that she would go on to uni., but Maggie had firmly resisted this, taking a job as a receptionist in an upholstery factory down the Valley and insisting to her Mam that it was just a temporary job while she got herself worked out.

Maggie's real problem was that she was an incurable dreamboat, which was why she had come to love her Mills and Boon novels so much: this breathless world of eternal fidelity and dreams that always came true. Even as his soft lips were

27

closing in on hers and he was telling her that he would love her forever the yellow yolk was dribbling and hardening unnoticed at one side of her mouth as a new record was playing unheard on her Dansette. A powerful romantic song it was too, bought out of the bargain bucket in Woolworth's over in Aberdare.

Out in the front parlour her Mam was busy dusting the delicate porcelain statuettes in the china cabinet. Everything was polished and dusted once a day in the front parlour – the souvenirs of day trips to Weston-super-Mare and Barry Island; the neat piles of crockery brought out with the tin of salmon only for the annual visits by distant and largely forgotten members of the Evans tribe; the music boxes and gaudy spray of artificial flowers. The red roses, in particular, were the very devils for picking up dust.

There was never a speck of food on the carpet of the front parlour because no one was ever allowed to eat in there. The antimacassars on the armchairs were never an inch out of place either because no one was ever allowed to rest their heads on them. You might, if you were lucky, get to lie down in the front parlour – when you were dead and waiting for the undertaker perhaps – though Mrs Evans did allow the family in there once a year, on the afternoon of Christmas Day, to play Monopoly.

The front parlour had always enjoyed a mystical function in the life of the valleys because no one was ever quite sure what it was for. 'After all, if you only ever got in there either when you were dead, or for a few hours to play Monopoly on Christmas afternoon, it's hardly what you would call an efficient use of space is it?' Glynmor had once complained to Maggie.

Space was the one thing the Valleys did not have. The houses were so small they only made sense for pygmies or storing cabbages. There were no gardens to speak of and the front door was set almost on the road. Even the rooms themselves had barely enough space to swing a dead cat around.

So why was the front parlour, the largest room in the house, kept as inviolable as the most sacred shrine? It was a Valley secret; a cultural hiccup, as devious and unfathomable as the short, insecure people jammed into the crowded villages along its length.

Not that such metaphysical reflections had ever bothered

28

Maggie's mother. Her front parlour was her front parlour and that was that. It was only young tearaways like that Glynmor Jones who spoke of knocking down the middle wall and making one big living-room. That was just the kind of left-wing twaddle you only ever got out of someone like him. She could never stand the sight of him and hoped that her Margaret would get rid of him as soon as possible. As far as she was concerned that Glynmor was about as welcome as an outbreak of anthrax.

Maggie stood up and changed the record on the Dansette, pausing briefly to look out through the window at the rain washing against the coal shed out the back. Then she picked up her book again. Now the hero, an architect taken by his job to Peking, had sent his love a gorgeous set of Chinese pyjamas along with a note saying how his love for her came up every morning with the sun. Lovely she called that. Just lovely.

All she ever got from Glynmor was the job of doing his Spot the Ball competition each week in the *South Wales Echo*. She was on half shares if *she* won. That was about the extent of Glynmor's love. *Duw*, there was more feeling in a snooker ball.

The front door opened and closed letting in a youngish woman, cussing softly as she took off her overcoat. Yet to lift the latch on thirty she was attractive with a vivid shock of peroxide blonde hair and lots of expensive rings on her hands which had long, intensely maintained fingernails. It was Maggie's eldest sister, Daisy.

'Hiya love,' said Maggie barely looking up from her book. 'How's tricks?'

'Tricks are terrible,' said Daisy, going over and giving the kettle a soft knock with her knuckle. 'I thought that Ivor Llewelyn was going to give me a lift down here but these days he's getting too lazy to get out of his own way. Just wants to stay in the bar of the Hall, boozing all the time. That's the trouble with men these days isn't it? Beer. That's all they think of. Most of them have only got one good one in them and that's holding them together.'

Maggie continued reading her book as Daisy prattled on above the music from the Dansette. You never had to make any conversation when Daisy was around. She just jawed non-stop – about clothes and money but mostly about men. In many ways they resembled one another both facially and physically though their ideas could not have been more different. Maggie still retained a lot of her Girl Guide ideals such as helping others, while Daisy was drummed out of the Brownies before even getting to the Girl Guides. The sole star in Daisy's firmament was Daisy.

When the record had finished Daisy sat down with her cup of tea. She looked a bit lost for words, for once. 'Maggie I'm that worried,' she said finally.

Maggie turned over the page of her book. The sun was rising over Peking and he was writing to her making a solemn promise that he would get back to her arms soon. The oceans between them would be as a stream.

'Did you hear me Maggie?' said Daisy. There was concern in her voice. 'I'm that worried I don't know which way to turn. I need advice.'

'What about?' His head office was now forcing him to decide between his architectural career in China or going home to his wife in Surrey. The problem was he wanted to go and see his love in Paris. He decided to go and see an old Chinese fortune teller.

'Maggie. Don't tell Mam will you? But I'm having a bit of a rub with the man from the Prudential.'

Maggie swallowed and put down her book as she digested this sorry bit of news. They didn't put lines like that in Mills and Boon, she was glad to say. 'So how long has this been going on then?' she asked disapprovingly.

'A month? No, two at least. You won't tell Mam will you? I don't know how it started. I paid him a month's subs in the passageway and he just started kissing me. Just like that. He started kissing me so I started kissing him. Next thing we're in bed. Now he's collecting his subs every week.'

'But you've got a husband and a son,' Maggie pointed out.

'I know all that. Don't preach at me Maggie. Just advise me.'

'Well stop it. That's the only advice I can give.'

'I just can't help myself. It's so fantastic. Fan-bloody-tastic it is. Talk about the heavens moving. After he's gone I'm shaking for hours. I've never known anything like it.'

'You've got to stop it and that's the end of it.'

'Maggie, I can't! That's the trouble. It's got that he's all I ever think about. He's in my head all day long. And he's nothing to look at either. Denzil knows that there's something up but naturally he doesn't know what. I'm so ashamed of myself. I don't know which way to turn.'

Maggie had seen this happen often enough before, of course: the way her big sister had always grabbed, greedy and regardless of the consequences. What Maggie had never quite understood was why she then always came and told her all about it. It was their Dad Maggie had always blamed. He had always spoiled Daisy rotten, giving in to her every whim largely because she could always twist him around her little finger. He had never acted quite the same with Maggie.

Maggie looked down at the cover of her book; at the sunset where the silhouettes of two lovers were drawing close for a kiss. The wife would be hurt there too, if she ever found out about what was going on in Paris. Meanwhile, here in Bont, Daisy was clearly poised to break the heart of her husband Denzil since he was bound to find out sooner or later. There were no secret affairs around here. It was such a shame, Maggie thought. Denzil was such a wonderful man who had always given Daisy everything she had never wanted while their son Bobby – known to all as Gnasher – was one of the great characters of Bont.

But who to turn to, Maggie wondered. They didn't have Marriage Guidance Counsellors in Bont. 'Daisy, go and see that Baptist minister up in the Libanus and tell him all about it.'

'What good'll that be?' Daisy asked with her eyebrows rising into her hairline at the absurdity of the suggestion. 'He'll just tell me to stop it. They don't even like sex *after* marriage in the chapel. I told you. I can't stop it. I'm telling you Maggie that when …'

'No. Not necessarily,' Maggie interrupted. 'He might tell you how to come to terms with it. These chapel people know about these things. They do look a bit starchy but they know it all.'

'All they know about in the chapel is money in the collection plate.'

'But try him Daisy. He's sure to tell you what to do about it. He's been friendly with Mam over the years and she's always sworn by him.'

'He wouldn't tell her anything would he?'

'Of course not. I've spoken to him lots of times. He gets a bit craxy from time to time but he's got a good heart. I'm sure it's worth at least trying.'

Daisy screwed up her nose in mock disgust. '*Ach y fi*. You've got egg all over your face you have.'

Later that afternoon the sunshine staged a comeback, forcing its way back into the Valley and driving out the rain. So strong and brilliant was it that it quickly dried up the huge damp patches, making steam drift up from the roofs of the garden sheds and grey slates of the terraces, creating the illusion that the whole village had been set on fire. The marching ferns out on the Valley walls shimmered a bright, rich green. The hurrying river glinted ferociously. A few optimistic housewives were pegging out their washing which was soon flapping soft in the lazy summer breeze.

In the midst of this brightness came a cacophony of whistling and then three, four, five, seven, eight, nine sheep came running down the pavement of Bont Terrace. They were dirty, scabby scavengers who normally butted down gates to get into allotments or curled up into balls to roll over cattle grids. But this now-glorious afternoon they were on the run as they were being sheepdogged along the terrace by Gnasher and his gang – Cocoa, Iffy, Nipper, Dick and Gaffer – running around and waving their arms around like demented scarecrows.

The sheep dodged this way and that but Iffy and Nipper managed to get in front of them. Just as the flock threatened to break loose outside The Bug there was a renewed flurry of whistling and shouting and the boys drove the sheep smartly through into the cinema foyer.

The cashier leaped around inside her kiosk like a startled goldfish as the sheep streamed past her and into the auditorium where some forty people were fanning themselves in the suffocating heat. They were perched nervously on their rackety, broken-springed seats as, on the screen, Janet Leigh was taking a shower in the film *Psycho*. Then, just as Anthony Perkins began going berserk and chopping her up with his knife, the whole cinema erupted with the alarmed bleats of sheep and customers alike. The usherette, chasing around and around with her torch, was hard pressed to say which was which.

'I've got all your names,' the cashier screamed as Gnasher

and the boys scarpered down the road. 'I'll be up seeing your mothers and fathers about all this.' That Daisy Bland especially, she reflected bitterly.

Once down by the waste-paper factory the boys flung themselves down into the long grass laughing rapturously. They had timed it to perfection and it had worked out just great even if nothing like the time when they had flung four of Dai Morris' chickens off the balcony during the climactic moments of Alfred Hitchcock's *The Birds*. That had even got into the *South Wales Echo* that had.

Nipper handed out some Woodbines to celebrate their coup. They lay around still laughing and coughing; now they were a force to be reckoned with in the Valley. Much of their success was down to the imaginative powers of Gnasher, who had a natural talent for devilry. Just a few weeks earlier they had unscrewed a belisha beacon and been chased by the local copper. Then there were all those cats who kept being mysteriously tied together and the tin tacks which kept finding their way onto teacher's seat in the Clay Class.

It wasn't that Gnasher was a bad lad as such. He was just a wild Bont boy like the other wild Bont boys, always running around harum scarum with the terror of the boogie man in his sails. He was just another Bont Boy with scuffed, blackened daps and the sleeve of his shirt shiny and stiff from using it as a handkerchief; just another boy who, if he saw anything marked WET PAINT immediately went over and put his hand on it; just another who, if the putty around the window was still soft, went and stuck his thumbprints all around it; just another lad in the Clay Class (where you were put if you were thought to be beyond hope and therefore given a lump of clay to play with all day long) who, like his other pals, just wanted to get out of school and into a job which would give him money to drink beer, drive a car and chase a bit of skirt.

But the terrorist was sometimes terrorised too. The night he saw *The Beast with Five Fingers* in which Peter Lorre's severed hand played the piano and went about the place strangling people, Gnasher sat outside his mother Daisy's bedroom door and whimpered for her to let him into her bed. She was having none of that, though his father, Denzil, did take him down to the kitchen to give him a cup of soothing Ovaltine and a talk about how films were nothing like real life.

Gnasher put a lot of store by his Dad and hoped he would grow up like him.

One of the boys produced a grubby, well-creased magazine. Flimsily-clad housewives hovered in unlikely poses with vacuum cleaners and washing machines. The sights and smells of sex enthralled the Clay Class. It had taken them an awfully long time to recover from their first sight of pubic hair. Indeed it had taken them ages to even understand that such things existed until one momentous afternoon down near the tump when a certain Tinker Harry had pulled his trousers down and shown them a bush of short and curly hairs far bigger and uglier than anything their mothers ever used as a lavatory brush.

On the strict understanding that they told no one Tinker said that you could get such hairs by rubbing certain ointments over the bald bits. After that the Clay Class was forever rubbing ointments over their bald bits – any ointments they could lay their hands on – and all to no avail. The bald bits stayed distressingly bald.

The boys' favourite activity, though, was watching the gropings of the lovers on the river bank up towards the reservoir. There were times when, depending on what was going on, they all but fainted away in the heavy excitement of it all. As summer spun warm evenings on the river bank and midges danced in the shadows of the bushes the Clay Class stood enthralled by the goings-on of the local lovers, sometimes, asking for a tanner to go away.

Such games could be very hazardous though. One day Gnasher had spotted a pair of crutches lying next to an unfamiliar pair of lovers on the river bank. He crept up through the long grass and stole the crutches. Then, from a distance, he stood up and began shouting, waving the crutches around in air before flinging them into the river. Now the man may have been crippled but the woman could run like the very wind and very soon she had caught Gnasher by the scruff of his neck and flung him into the river as well.

There were no lovers around this hot weekday afternoon, though. The Class was bored. Trying to put a spark of life into the day, Dick jumped on Nipper and wrestled him to the ground. The pair of them rolled over and over, hands grabbing at ears and hair until, all of a sudden, they tired of the horseplay. Gaffer blew a quick series of smoke rings, a skill which was the source of some envy with the others. Gnasher, bored too, took little notice. He sat on a rock slightly apart from them, one hand dangling between his knees as he gazed down the Valley.

'I'm getting a hundred Players on the weekend,' Iffy announced brightly. He was always getting something from somewhere was Iffy.

'Where're you getting them from?' asked Nipper.

'Think of it. One hundred Players.'

'Where's Cocoa to?'

'A hundred players,' Iffy went on. 'I can smoke one an hour for the next six months.'

'Where's Cocoa to?' Nipper was now getting highly agitated. 'Where's he to? Where's he to, mun?'

'I've got cigars coming as well I have. Hundreds of them. Anyone want any cigars? Put your order in now.'

'Cocoa. Where's he to?'

'Let's go up to the res.,' said Gnasher, standing up. 'There's a naked woman up the res.'

All the boys stood up and dutifully followed their leader up the path towards the reservoir. They all knew there was no naked woman up there but moved along eagerly enough. The promise of a blimp of a naked woman was just Clay Class language it was.

The sun sent a great golden kiss thwacking against the brown walls of the Valley, dipping out of the sky with such speed you could actually see the shadow of the north east wall rising like a fast-moving eclipse. The disappearance of light and the appearance of shadow was always at its most dramatic in the Valley. Here, in the bottom of the volcano, the sun stayed shortest and the snow the longest.

Not that there was any snow around this warm summer evening, just darting swallows yawing above the twisting gurgling course of the river as huge patches of light and shadow built up over the ancient hills of coal.

'You know girl I was up and down all shift like a shithouse seat. Whenever we chocked up the Dosco the face just kept crumbling and falling and we had to jump out of the way all

35

the time. We shored it up. We put in new rings. But then there was another of those bastard squeezes and it all came down on us again like a shower of black shit.'

Glynmor and Maggie, love's young dream, were walking together along the river bank with Glynmor giving one of his poetic lectures about his early shift down the hole. Following a hundred or so yards behind them, Jampots, hands in disconsolate pockets, was kicking around a tin can.

'It's these bastard surveyors it is. They don't know shit from clay those boys don't. I can smell coal, you know, Maggie. But those surveyors are forever setting up their fancy instruments and getting it wrong every time.'

Maggie made interested noises as he spoke about his work. But in truth she would have found slowly dipping her left elbow into a bowl of cold porridge marginally more interesting. But it was nice of him to call and offer to take her for a walk. What she had long found in Glynmor was a whole mountain of vices and virtues. One minute he was generous and the next he was mean; one day he was being cruel to Bomber then he was being as soft as putty with that Jampots who, come to think of it, was getting her down at the minute.

'I don't mind it so much when we hit stone 'cos we can scaffold the face an' rip it out. After the shot-firing I do love to be there with Jampots next to me and just crack it apart with pinch-bars. Plucking the lip we call that.'

'Talking of Jampots, it's lovely us having a walk together an' all but do we always have to take him along with us?'

'He's all right. There's no harm in him.'

'I'm not saying there's any harm in him. I'd just be happy if he wasn't tailing us all the time. He's like some second shadow he is.'

They both stopped and turned around to look at Jampots who was still shuffling along, kicking his tin can, now stopping himself, shoulders hunched and head lowered sheepishly as he watched them looking at him.

The way men buttied with one another and watched out for one another was a strong feature of Valley mining communities, perhaps inherited from hours of fire and flood in the pits when men needed to look after one another to survive. Glynmor and Jampots, like so many other butties, worked together, dressed together and drank together. Sometimes, when they had drunk a drop too much, they even slept together. It was this kind of kinship which made the Valleys so warm, so much like being part of an extended family.

'It's just that he makes me a bit nervous,' said Maggie.

'Oh I'll tell him to push off for a bit then,' said Glynmor walking back down the path towards Jampots. 'He won't mind. I'll be seeing him later anyway.'

With Jampots given his marching orders they sat down on the river bank near the waste-paper factory where, abandoning his lecture on coal mining, Glynmor climbed on top of Maggie for a smooch. At least that was how it started but she could feel that he was getting unusually excited. It must be something to do with the warm weather. She didn't mind all that much either. Just as long as that Jampots was not still around somewhere watching them.

They remained in the grass for some half an hour, their lips sliding wet and warm across one another punctuated by huge sighs and long snorts of breath. She could feel his heart pounding as if trying to break out of his chest. Satisfied now that Jampots was nowhere around, her heart soon began pounding as well. Like some great sledgehammer it was and, with every bash, her resolve to keep her virginity intact for her wedding night was falling away into the carnal quicksands.

She could not keep saying no forever, she reasoned. There were plenty of old slags who had their big cowing eyes on him and were only too happy to drop their drawers. She had to give him something didn't she? He might find it so good he would never then leave her. Might. She wasn't at all sure about our Glynmor. That was the big snag with him.

His hand went edging up her fleshy leg slow and tentative like a spider moving out onto some luckless fly trapped in its web. He waited for the halt sign that never came. Then he pounced. To his astonishment there was no resistance at all – no clamping hands, no angry cries, nothing at all. He worked his fingers around the elastic of her knickers and began trying to disentangle them from her roll-on.

'Tell me it's more than a quick bang, Glynmor.'

'It's more than a quick bang.'

'Sound as if you mean it, Glynmor. Go on. Try to show me you mean it.'

'It is more than a quick bang.'

'Say you love me Glynmor. You don't have to mean it. Just say it.'

'*It is* more than a quick bang.'

'Love Glynmor. Say you'll love me for ever Glynmor. Just be a little romantic init? Just say it once and I'll take my things off. Here. Now.'

'I love you Maggie. I'll love you for ever I will.'

'You're not just saying it are you Glynmor?'

'No lovely. I'll love you for ever.'

'And you do mean it don't you Glynmor?'

'For God's sake girl. You want me to go down on my knees with a fiver in my teeth?'

She moaned soft and wriggled out of her corset with what Glynmor could only describe as unbelievable skill. Left to his own devices he would have been there all month trying to get that thing off. Next her knickers had gone sailing somewhere too and he was fumbling inside his unzipped fly.

She moaned again and sent her pelvis crushing up into his, even actually beginning to enjoy it, she was surprised to feel. One second her emotions were running boiling hot and the next freezing cold. Her brain was waltzing in a fever. Fantastic streams of passion shivered right down her body making her toes curl up in throbbing tension. Oh well … this was it all right … this was it …

Then she watched, aghast, as a row of heads appeared over the top of the grass bank. 'Give us a tanner Glynmor. Give us a tanner and we'll go away.'

It was Gnasher and the Clay Class back from the reservoir. What was infinitely worse was that Gnasher was wearing her knickers on the top of his head like a party hat.

'Bugger off,' groaned Glynmor. 'Bugger off, go on. Bugger off or I'll be hitting you sick. The lot of you.'

'Just a tanner Glynmor. Just a tanner and we'll go away we will.'

'You lot will get the mother and father of a hammering if you don't shift.'

'It's only sixpence,' Iffy interupted. 'Give us sixpence and we'll go away.'

As the argument continued Maggie began giggling, putting Glynmor in an even blacker mood. He rolled off her knowing that once she started laughing she'd be at it for hours.

There would be no fun and games with her that night. He was going to fix that bastard Gnasher for this he was — no matter if he was the son of Maggie's sister. He was going to fix him good.

Glynmor's aggravation turned to fury when he recognised Maggie's knickers on the top of Gnasher's head. He jumped up and gave chase, letting the others go and concentrating on Gnasher. But Daisy's lad had long legs for a boy of his age and Glynmor, struggling into his trousers, had a lot of ground to make up.

He was just about to give up the chase when Jampots flew out from behind an abandoned coal wagon and rugby-tackled Gnasher onto the railway line.

'Right, you little bastard.' Glynmor's joy was unconfined as he ran towards the panting, struggling heap. 'Right, you little bastard. I'll give you a tanner I will. A tanned arse for you.'

Jampots took one arm and Glynmor the other as they marched Gnasher, still with Maggie's knickers on his head, down to the river bank. Savouring his terror for a few seconds, Glynmor then gave him a good cuffing and kicked him into the water.

'I'll get my father on you for this,' Gnasher wailed, alternately standing up and slipping over in the rushing torrents. 'You see if I don't.'

'Go get your father. See if I care. Bring your mother too.'

'He'll get you for this. You just wait,' Gnasher went on, taking Maggie's knickers off his head and flinging them down onto the water. 'Just a joke it was. Can't you take a joke?'

'Some jokes just aren't very funny, are they?'

A knickerless Maggie had left the river bank when Glynmor returned to look for her. Not that he cared now. He went back to the Welfare Hall with Jampots, arms around one another as they walked up past the tump, quarrelling about whose turn it was to buy the next round in the bar.

Just been to that Dr Teifi Edwards with a bad back looking for a note, said one of the boys in the bar as Glynmor and Jampots sat down at the table with them. Oh aye. What did 'e say then? 'E knows bugger all. Always on the piss in 'e? This back, he said. I'll have to have some heat treatment for it, he said. Where's that then? In a bloody crematorium, he said. Aye. In a bloody crematorium.

Chapter Three

From out of the darkness a gunmetal dawn was coming up in a silvery haze to sit on the far rim of the Valley.

The terraces of Bont sat silent and still. Away down by the Co-op came the faint musical rattle of milk bottles. But, even at this grey hour, groups of men were following the road leading up to the pit for the morning shift, their eyes still puffy from lack of sleep, their bellies churning from too much beer. They talked little as they trudged along with their tea jacks and tommy tins.

The growing light sought out the harsh, ugly contours of the pithead; the long, rising oblong of the conveyor leading from the washery to the rail track; the squat Nissen-hut shapes of the canteen and changing rooms; the coal-grimed grease and rust which caked every inch of the wheel-house. The light touched the untidy piles of pit props and the huge spokes of an iron, winding wheel which rested, knackered, against the side of the welding shop. Down in the chocolate brown puddles of water in the yard the light played on the rainbow splashes of industrial oil, making unlikely swirls of colour.

Most dramatically highlighted, perhaps, on that grey still morning, were the moving black lines of the slag buckets being carried up to the top of the tip by the overhead conveyor. Day and night these buckets went tirelessly up the slopes, as if pegged out on a giant iron washing line, always on the move, always rising and rising like a ski lift carrying passengers up to the top of the glacier, until there was the dull click of the bucket hitting the trip mechanism followed by the soft swoosh as the bucket emptied its black slurry out onto the top of the tip. *Click, swoosh. Click, swoosh.* Such were the sounds of the hours and minutes in this Valley of coal.

The men were undressing in the changing room, many already coming to life in the company of their butties. Some stood around belching and farting, a few aimlessly scratched their balls and stared out of the grimy windows. Others began their loud banter which would continue throughout the shift like some endless tennis game with words. Nothing was ever spoken in a speaking voice; everything was shouted in a shouting voice, even between those who were standing next to one another.

' 'Aven't 'eard from 'im f'r ages. Did 'e phone you last Tuesday did 'e?'

'Who was that?'

'The one who said 'e was going to phone you on Tuesday.'

'About what was that?'

' 'E was going to tell you on the phone.'

'What? Last Tuesday you mean?'

'Well aye, mun.'

Glynmor was standing with Jampots, Ponty Williams and Crow Parcel. 'That Maggie Evans is going to wear my cock down to a little stump and that's a fact that is,' Glynmor was telling them. 'The way she's going on I'm going to wake up one morning and find it just sitting on the pillow next to my head. On my mother's life she's after it all the time she is.'

'Isn't she a bit fat to be good at it?' Ponty Williams asked with genuine curiosity. 'I mean I used to go out with that piece – what's 'er name now, oh, what did they call 'er? Big Tit Lu from Taffs Well, that's it. I did used to screw 'er an' it just kept popping out all·the time.'

'Maggie's not that fat,' Glynmor objected. 'Nor her sister Daisy – Fatty Arbuckle they do call her but she's just got big ones, is all. They say fucking her is just like throwing a carton of cream down the mine shaft. Or waving a chipolata in the Cheddar Gorge. But she knows a trick or two does our Daisy.'

Glynmor returned to his epic sexual encounters with Maggie as they moved on into the lamp room and the grease room. PLEASE USE GREASE SPARINGLY implored the notice as they scooped up great gobbets of the stuff with a stick and plastered it all over their boots. Almost all the shift had now gathered around Glynmor, like tourists around a cathedral guide.

'The other night we'd got this big pile of cushions on the

floor of her mother's front parlour an' she'd got hold of this tin of vaseline and, jonic now, she ...'

'*Duw* mun! Not on the floor of the mother's front parlour?'

'Well aye. We even had her budgie watching us. An' I'm telling you now, boys, it's fucking good job that budgie has trouble talking 'cos when she got this vaseline – no word of a lie now – she plastered it all over an' there was this cucumber an' she ...'

And so it continued all the way to the wheelhouse with Glynmor's fertile sexual imagination firing and sparking every step of the way. The vividness of his accounts suggested that he had lost his true vocation as a writer of dirty books. Not that anyone doubted that his stories were anything but true. They were just too enjoyable for anyone to go casting doubt on them. A morning shift wouldn't be a morning shift without Glynmor Jones giving them all an uplifting talk about sex.

But Glynmor did stop talking – as did the others – when they all crowded together into the tiny iron box of the cage. Even after a lifetime in the pit, men fell silent at that awful moment when the banksman flung his lever lifting the cage off its keps and sending it freefalling down into the very bowels of the earth. That moment when your belly was suddenly sucked up into your throat was a religious moment; a time, perhaps, when you wondered if you would see daylight or taste fresh air ever again; if you would ever hear the *click* and *swoosh* of the aerial ropeway; if you would ever hold a woman in your arms and know how loving made you alive. The Bont miners had something else to think about: the accident seven years ago when the wire snapped and the brakes failed, sending the cage smashing down against the floor below, killing all eight occupants with the shock of an executioner's axe. Three had died of castration.

Not that the silence lasted long on that particular shift. They could scarcely have dropped a hundred yards when, without a word of warning, Dibber Jones began puking his heart up. You dirty bastard, the boys shouted, clinging to one another and moving away from him in mock horror. You filthy cunt, they shouted as he heaved his guts up again, spraying their boots with a shower of stale beer and bits of carrots. Must be that beer in the Hall again, Glynmor cried as they plunged

42

on downwards. They say the steward's got his barrels piped straight into the piss-house.

Down and down they hurtled into the dark hidden kingdom of the South Wales coalfield. Below them lay the No. 4 Glamorgan, a rich fat seam of antediluvian sunlight and compacted forest stretching the length of the Valley and crossing over from the No. 2 Glamorgan which began at Porth and stretched up to the No. 5, a dark still river which opened out at Nantgarw. Each part of the No. 4 was known by its own name: Red Vein, the Four Feet, the Six Feet, Trelewis, Pentre, Meadow and so on. The Bont mine was working the Meadow B2 where, for close on a hundred years now, men had worked and died ripping out a dry and fiery anthracite as their contribution to keeping the world comfortable and warm.

The cage landed with the softest of bumps. Once out of it and on to the main roadway, the shift leaped onto the conveyor belt, turning on the lights of their headlamps as they travelled along, on the singing wheels and sprockets, down towards the B2 face. The bright yellow funnels of their lamps flashed around them, making the girders and rings sparkle as if in a Christmas bazaar, sweeping into the great dark webs of the ventilation tunnels where you could still see the remains of the old oak trees which had once so thickly graced the Valley. Occasionally there was the sudden furious bellowing of the ventilation pumps but, for most of the time, there was just the agitated squeaking of all the tireless wheels and sprockets of the conveyor belt.

The belt took them down to the locking station where a deputy took their registration number as the black, tired faces of the night shift came trudging up the puddled roadway. Everywhere there were the bright cheery greetings of 'All right' and 'How be?'

Now it was their turn to wade through the great sloshing puddles, the constant dripping echoing in the warm, still air. Jampots, as usual, was right behind Glynmor, both of them even going over to the gob for their ritual piss at the beginning of each shift. 'You know this dick of mine is so sore it's a pain to hold it,' Glynmor told Jampots as they both pissed into the big black hole of the gob. 'I'm going to 'ave to start taking iron pills or something if this keeps going on.'

They turned the next bend and came out behind the

Queen Bee of the hole, the Dosco cutting machine which was the size of a small room and whose functions they were all paid to service ... the chargemen, the machine operator, three on the tail gate and seven ramming, chocking and grading. The rest of the shift worked shovelling the coal onto the armoured conveyors of the Panzers and, when the Dosco erupted into noisy life with its chains cracking and dust billowing everywhere, the men all fell to their tasks with a will as the great blades scored and slashed into the coal face.

It was a scene straight from Dante's Inferno when the Dosco was at full bite, everything all around shaking like a jelly in a storm ... the ground, the walls, your feet, your legs, your very teeth ... Added to this was the shocking, earth-shattering noise and the choking dust which kept your mouth permanently thirsty. Then there was the warm smell of stale piss and the way the bits of coal shot straight into your eye. Worse still was the foul brown water which kept seeping in from everywhere, always keeping your feet freezing cold no matter how hard you worked.

Glynmor and Crow Parcel went up a small tunnel on the side of the face where they had been firing and digging an advance heading. 'Better shovel out this duff before we can fire again,' Crow Parcel shouted over the roar of the Dosco.

Glynmor liked to work here on the advance headings. If he was to work down a mine at all he liked to be close to the coal rather than just servicing the Dosco with the others. Here on the advance heading he was right at the sharp end of the industry, intimate with the black gold of the centuries, face to face with what had provided his family with a living for as far back as he could trace his family. A sense of continuity was important to all miners; that sense of shared experience which anchored them in the past and made them confident with the future.

But the problem today was that they had been cutting a heading into a seam which only seemed to want to fall in on them. They'd discussed it many a time: the problem was that this coal was just too loosely jointed and, no matter how many times they shored the roof up, *bang*, down it all seemed to come again. But, so far, it seemed stable enough as Glynmor and Jampots shovelled out the duff. Occasionally the light of their lamps caught in the stampeding coal dust in the air, making it glitter like hovering fairies.

Some hundred yards behind them the pump man, Tom

Laws, tapped the methane gauge which measured an escape of 2 per cent. Slightly higher than normal but nothing at all to worry about.

The Rev. Mordecai Hughes, resident minister at the Libanus Chapel, was in his dog collar and shirt sleeves as he fussed around in his pigeon loft, one minute sweeping down the shelves and the next picking up one of his most treasured birds, turning it over to examine the texture of its white belly before gazing into the veined magical rings around the bird's eyes.

He had eight birds in all. Now he was getting them ready for the Welsh Open, when truckloads of birds would be taken up to Lerwick in the Shetlands, there to be released and race the 580 miles back down to Bont. The Welsh Open, held at the end of every summer, was the most coveted jewel in the pigeon fanciers' crown and this year Rev. Mordecai had the bird he just knew was going to win the title, by a good few minutes as well. Even now he was hoping to be elected onto the committee of the Bont Pigeon Fanciers who met each Sunday in the Starlight Lounge of the Welfare Hall.

Nothing was too much trouble for his pigeons. Each day he fed them twice and cleaned them out once. He would even rush a funeral if the birds' feeding time was approaching; as any fancier would tell you, regular eating is the key to fast flying.

Sometimes he drove them over to a neighbouring Valley in his Morris Minor, releasing them and thrilling to the sight of them whirling around and around the green hills before flying off home. How they found their way home – particularly from long distances – was, he readily admitted, one of God's mysteries. Some sort of radar in the brain, the scientists said, but God alone knew the full story. Being with his birds made Rev. Mordecai feel close to God and the mystery of His ways.

He heard his letter box click and left his pigeons, walking back into the manse and picking up the pile of letters which had spilled over the hall carpet. They looked the usual clutch of bills and advertising leaflets so he didn't even bother to open them, just carrying them into his study and placing them on his desk next to a very old typewriter.

He pulled a sheet out of the typewriter and read what he had typed the previous evening, the great beak of his nose almost touching the paper which, together with his longish silvery hair and small beady eyes, always reminded his parishioners of some great bird of prey. On some Sunday mornings, when he was in full oratorical flight in one of his sermons with a splash of sunshine glazing the great dome of his forehead, some of his flock half expected him to sprout wings and fly off into the very rafters of the chapel.

Not that he had much of a flock these days; about three dozen regulars, mostly women, who still enjoyed such as the knitting circle or the coffee mornings. The writing was on the wall for the chapel, he could see, with more and more of them being abandoned and left derelict throughout the Valleys. He saw nothing he could do about this except to hold fast onto his own flock and wait on the Lord's pleasure. Meanwhile he husbanded his other passions for privacy and silence.

The sheet of paper contained a description of a long service in the Swansea Valley at the turn of the century since, apart from his pigeons, Rev. Mordecai was working on a long evangelical tome – *Reflections On The 1904–5 Chapel Revival : An Informal History* – in which he was charting the great Evan Roberts chapel revival which had so briefly and dramatically shaken the Welsh nation.

Like every other non-conformist man of the cloth he longed to see another revival, of course, but, with the advent of bingo and television, he did not really see how it would ever become possible. The chapel movement had lost its way. He accepted that proposition calmly enough but was nonetheless more than happy to write about it when it was at its full power and height; when the charismatic Evan Roberts had held the whole of Wales in the mesmerising palm of his hand.

Evan Roberts had even once spoken in the Libanus Chapel too, Mordecai had excitedly discovered; a long and tumultuous service which had converted almost everyone in the building.

Just now, surrounded by piles of damp and dusty books borrowed from the Evangelical Library in Cardiff, he had reached the Christmas period of the Revival when half of Wales had succumbed to the magic of Evan's oratory. They were thrilling times for the austere non-conformist soul were those services. Mordecai never tired of reading about them, sometimes actually able to feel the rapture of an era when the

Welsh were renewing themselves in their love of God.

The silence hung heavy in the manse and the sounds of those Revival services were again hovering on the edge of his consciousness when the front door bell rang. He sighed but simply picked up another of his typed pages. Someone was either dying or wanting to get married. There was always something wasn't there? Sometimes he just wished they would all leave him alone. Why didn't they take their burials and weddings to that Methodist upstart down in Ferndale. He could do with the money and anyway he, Mordecai, had a small inheritance on top of his meagre stipend which meant that, in coldly cash terms, he never had to marry or bury anyone ever again.

When the bell rang again he answered it to find the most familiar figure of Daisy Bland standing there with her hands in coat pockets. 'Yes, my child,' he said soft.

'I've got a problem and I was wondering if I could have a chat with you about it, vicar.'

'Certainly, my child. Come into my study.'

He escorted her inside, sitting her in the armchair next to the fire-grate and sitting himself down at his desk before inviting her to tell him about her problem. There was barely an expression on the tired archaeology of his face as she told the story of how she was having a bit of a rub with the man from the Prudential. Only occasionally did the tip of his fingernail scratch the tip of his nose or toy with the ends of his hair.

As she went on his attention wandered onto a familiar moral path. This was all of a piece with the way the village was going, of course. When he had taken up his incumbency he had met warm, honest people full of decency but not any more. Just look what they got up to nowadays! Almost to a man they were gambling mad, forever buying raffle tickets, filling in betting slips, doing the tote in the Welfare Hall, fretting over the Pools or pouring money into the aptly-named one-armed bandits. Crime was even breaking out in the village too where, only a few years ago, the Yale lock was unknown. Every door had been left on the latch then with such as the rent man coming in and helping himself to the rent money, left with the book, on top of the china cabinet in the front parlour.

Now, as if all this wasn't enough for them, they were practising adultery like it had just been invented. It was shameful and what made it worse was that they had the gall to come and tell him about it. Now this brazen hussy was sitting in *his* chair, in *his* study telling him how she could not keep her hands off the man from the Prudential.

'But why have you come to me my child?' the habitual softness of his voice disguised the weary antipathy in his chest. He just didn't understand why they always walked all the way up that hill to tell him about their sins, as if they hoped he would somehow make them feel better about.

'I was told you understand these things. I was told you might be some sort of help.'

'But you used to come to this chapel, my child?'

'When I was a little *dwt*, yes. But those days are a long time ago now. We seemed to understand things in those days but we don't any more. It was easy to understand the rules then. But times have changed.'

Not the times, he thought sharp, getting up out of his chair and walking across the study to stare down at the village. The people; it's the people who have changed.

'I don't really know why I've come up here to see you. It's just … oh I don't know … I really don't know.'

'But why come to me, Daisy?' Mordecai asked, unwillingly to make it easier for her. He really didn't want to talk about it. She knew that it was wrong just as well as he did.

'It's difficult to put into so many words so I was hoping you, with all your experience with such matters, could give me some good advice.'

'Well I haven't any better advice than St Paul. He said much about the mind of the flesh and how it was death. When you keep your mind pure and concerned with spiritual matters then you have life.'

'I don't understand, vicar.'

No you wouldn't would you? he thought. Sex-crazed reptiles like you wouldn't. It made him so angry. He wondered idly if she left a patch of slime on the bed after she'd had a bit of a rub with the man from the Pru? Did the sheets rot and fall to bits? Did they fumigate the bed?

'This course you have taken,' Mordecai continued still staring out of the window. 'These rubs, as you so fetchingly call them, will bring you nothing but pain. You will feel the pain, so will your husband and so will young Gnasher. There's just nothing more I can tell you. These rubs will bring you nothing. They are of the mind of the flesh. Which is death.'

'I was hoping you might tell me how to stop them.'

'You stop them by stopping doing it.' His impatience was showing now and he was making no attempt to conceal it.

'Well, that's not much use is it? But how do I stop them when they make me so happy? That's what I want to know vicar.'

He shook his head and took a long intake of air. He clearly knew nothing that she wanted to hear and life was too short to sit here listening to such silliness. 'Right, my child, if you'll excuse me, it's time for me to feed my pigeons. You can find your own way out can you?'

'Oh well we know why your chapel is so empty, don't we?'

'Please leave me now. If you really want my advice, which you don't, then just try reading the Bible – and particularly Paul who will tell you all you need to know. But thank you *very* much for coming up here to see me.'

There were two sharp raps on the door in the basement room of the Miners' Welfare Hall. The City Tyler opened the peep-hole and asked for the three secret passwords of the year. The reply was soft and insistent. GOLD. BRAINS. MARLOWE. The door was then opened and a blindfold man was lead inside with his hands resting on the shoulders of two men.

Cigarette smoke curled around the thin bright strips of neon light. Here and there tiny blue pancakes of chewing gum were caked into the wooden parquet floor. The crowds of men already inside the room parted ranks as the blindfold figure was taken up to a plinth at the far end of the room where, beneath a huge pair of Buffalo horns suspended off yellow flock wallpaper, Worthy Primo sat on a wooden throne with gavel in hand. He gave three sharp bangs of the gavel – *bang, bang, bang* – stood up, adjusted his elaborately tapestried and tasselled apron and duly began the initiation into the great and sacred mysteries of the Royal Antediluvian Order of the Buffaloes.

Much of the business and secret life of the valleys was controlled by these Buffs; a sort of working class freemasonry, drawn from everywhere from skilled tradesmen to shopkeepers and middle managers of the pits, who met here each Tuesday evening to swop jokes and insults as well as making contacts useful to their work. Largely shunned by the miners themselves, the Buffs wore so many medals and chains of office they might have been the veterans and heroes of every campaign since the Zulu War. It was said that even Field Marshall Goering gasped in envy when he saw how many medals the Buffs had.

This group was the Captain Laggard Lodge of Bont; some forty solemn, bemedalled men whose organisation had so many rules and secrets it might have been hatched up by the Department of Health and Social Security in collaboration with the K.G.B. In this strange world the rule book was both the king and queen. Every brother was expected to know its eighty-six pages inside out; to learn everything from how many trustees the Grand Lodge of England had, right through to how the balance sheet should be forwarded in accordance with rule 31(b).

The brothers crowded around the initiate in a tight circle, their right hands over their hearts. The initiate held a clay pipe to his own heart, promising to keep all Buffalo secrets and passwords. He was then called on to break his pipe, the act by which he was duly initiated into the mysteries of Buffaloism with all the ancient rites and ceremonies, under the authority of the Grand Lodge of England.

Worthy Primo then handed him his membership scroll, making him read out the solemn promise. Hands were raised twice with the tray of juniper held forwards.

Down at the table at the opposite end of the room sat the City Marshall whose function was to keep order. There, behind the bar – known as the royal foundation – was the City Waiter who would soon serve the brothers with their pints of cloudy, flat All-Bright beer. Waiting with lolling tongues, each with his individual chain of office, were the City Chamberlain, the City Registrar, the Alderman of Benevolence and the City Constable who – collection tray in one hand and a small wooden truncheon in the other – had to collect the monetary fines imposed by Worthy Primo on the brothers for such grave un-Buffalo offences as using obscene language, belching, picking noses or being unfriendly to a fellow Buff in the street.

The initiation ceremony concluded with the newcomer, Ray Pryce, a local electrician, having his blindfold taken off and everyone congratulating him. Then the normal Buff session – an uproarious banging of gavels, screaming shouts and instantaneous charges – began.

I want to lay a charge Worthy Primo. Against Brother Wayne. Be upstood Brother Wayne. *Bang, bang, bang.* What's the charge Brother Jeffrey? Brother Wayne did swear at me in the Starlight Lounge. No, I fucking never Worthy Primo. He fucking did Worthy Primo. Aye, he did. An' I heard you. *Bang, bang, bang.* A twopenny fine on Brother Wayne. That's not bastard fair Worthy Primo. Another charge Worthy Primo. Brother Howard is not wearing his jewels. What do you have to say in your defence Brother Howard? Well, when I moved Worthy Primo, I did leave them in the coal shed an' I've not been able to find them Worthy Primo. *Bang, bang, bang.* A penny fine on Brother Howard. Well that's a load of Buffalo bullshit that is Worthy Primo. *Bang, bang, bang.* A penny fine on all those on that side. Why do we always have to drink this beer Worthy Primo? It's gnat's piss that's all it is. *Bang, bang, bang.* Best of order now brothers. You brother Emlyn. No, you Fred. Right, the whole bastard lot of you. City Constable collect a fine off the whole bastard lot of them. Are we going to get any graze tonight, Worthy Primo?

Just then, for no apparent reason or sign, this noisy period of bawling and shouting suddenly stopped. They all stood up in an impromptu choir and proceeded to sing the Buffalo song to all their absent brethren.

Spirit of Truth, before we homeward wend,
   On Thee we call:
Assist us each to succour and defend Good Brethren all.
From all cares and sorrows, ABSENT BRETHREN free,
Where'er they roam, in air, on land or sea.
Let thy kind spirit hover round them now,
   And so enthrall:
That they will keep their Obligation Vow.
   So say we all.
And when on us the ivy leaves descend,
Grant we may join Thy link, our Brother's Friend.

When the song had finished, Worthy Primo announced that, as the brothers already knew, passenger services on the Bont railway line were about to be withdrawn. What was the brothers' pleasure? Should they draw up a petition or what? The brothers looked at one another. Do! A petition! More light Worthy Primo.

'Well what does the loss of the rail line mean?' Worthy Primo continued. 'Does it mean anything to us at all or what?'

'We don't want to get mixed up in all that Worthy Primo. Most of the brothers have got cars anyway. And, anyway, we've got enough to do with all the risings in the next month or two without getting involved in petitions.'

'So we take no action on the rail line then?'

An instantaneous charge, Worthy Primo. Against Brother Fred. He did fart while you were talking, Worthy Primo. A big deadly fart it was. One of his silent killers. No, I never did, Worthy Primo. They always say that a fox do smell his own hole first don't they, Worthy Primo? Brother Fred be upstood. *Bang, bang, bang.* A penny fine for farting while I was speaking. *Bang, bang, bang.*

And so the session prattled on. At 10 o'clock Worthy Primo formally suspended the meeting and the brothers all trooped upstairs to the Rainbow Room saying what a wonderful meeting it had been that week and how lucky they were in getting someone like Ray Pryce joining the order. 'I've got a few 'lectric jobs I can put 'is way, aye.'

Even upstairs the Buffs stuck together, as far away from the miners as they could get. There was little love lost between them.

Chapter Four

Two days later, a Thursday, the morning shift were working the B2 face. Unseen, the pointer on the methane gauge rose to 12. As Glynmor walked along the roadway to pick up some cartridges from the stores, the gauge rose higher. But no one was watching it. Just nearby, two pump men were quarrelling. The argument claimed everyone's attention.

'I gave you the message when the van was coming didn't I?'

'Aye. You did. But I didn't 'ave my teeth in.'

'What's that got to do with it? Are your teeth fixed to your brains or what?'

'I told you often enough. I can never remember anything if I 'aven't got my teeth in.'

Coal dust and noise was erupting out of the Dosco as Sam Swambo stood in the advance heading, stripped to the waist. As he clung to his chattering drill the coal face all around his head began spalling and crumbling. He took one step backwards and something fearful turned over inside him like a pregnancy of snakes.

From deep within the coal there were great ripping sounds as if a giant was tearing up calico sheets.

Immediately behind Sam Swambo, Jampots was shovelling away the duff. Ponty Williams, Crow Parcel and Dibber Jones were working on the chocks under the conveyor belts. They worked in torn vests with their trousers hanging low on their massive hips. Respirators were available but always scorned. Only pansies used respirators. Just visible beneath the grime on Crow Parcel's back was the tattoo of a pair of dogs chasing down through his shoulder blades to his waist-line. The brush of the escaping fox was just poking up out of his arse.

'Hey Sam. What's yellow and stupid?'

The heading screamed hard with the promise of murder again. Sam swallowed and dropped his drill, taking three steps back from the dissembling coal and bumping into Jampots.

'Watch where you're going *mun*!'

Now it was as if a whole army of demons was baying and screaming in the coal face. Angry jets were whistling out of tiny holes. Loud cracks ripped through the screams of the demons. The methane gauge shot up to 28 and the pump man banged it with his hand in disbelief. Five to 15 per cent was an explosion but, if this was registering right, the whole mine was about to be blown sky-high.

In the store room, Glynmor was signing for the cartridges when he felt a cold shiver. It was as if someone had just stepped on his grave.

'Run boys,' Sam shouted, his mouth parched and dry something dreadful. 'It's a bastard blower.'

Jampots dropped his shovel and was off faster than a whippet with its back on fire. Sam was quickly after him too but cursing and swearing all the while since his legs were almost paralysed with fright. The screaming became more intense, filling up the brains with pain, slashing against the ear drums with acid. Ponty Williams, Crow Parcel and Dibber Jones were racing down the roadway as well – their huge boots dragging them down as they pulled at one another's arms urging them to go faster. They knew that, at the most, they had ten seconds to reach some sort of safety. 'It's a blower,' another called out in the screaming darkness. 'It's a bastard blower.'

Sam was still struggling with the effort of getting his legs to move at all. His head turned back to look at the screaming hole. A whole gale of hell erupted out of the wall like a great black breaker in the sea. Huge milky balls of fire rolled towards Sam with lumps of coal flying out of it. He could never remember seeing something so colourful or ferocious and was transfixed by its brilliance. Then a huge rock shot out of its very heart, breaking both his legs with the quiet ease that a child might break a lollipop stick. The very last thing he saw in his life was the tattoo of the fox being chased by the dogs down Crow Parcel's back. Those dogs will never catch that pissing fox now, he thought grimly as a romping tongue of green and white fire completely incinerated his body.

By now the whole morning shift was running down the roadway as the gale of fiery methane – suddenly released after centuries trapped in the coal – went sweeping all around them. Some clutched at their throats and fell to their knees coughing. Others pulled their blackened vests up to their mouths to use as a sort of makeshift gas mask. A flying cob of coal split open a man's head but still he kept running the blood running, red on black, down his neck. The metal rings were buckling in the heat; even the dry lagging above the rings bursting into flame.

Jampots was brought down by another cannoning rock. With a soft sob, he fell forwards with his cheek resting on the cold metal railway line. He lay there unable to move as he watched one of the rusty nuts on the sleepers dance about in the flashing colours. His back felt red raw with the heat and he wondered how much he would be able to claim for this. He'd go all the way this time as well. Get some real compensation out of those bastards in the coal board. He thought of his best mate Glynmor and how, only that morning, he had loaned him a fiver. He wanted that fiver back, he thought. Then, in another burst of heat, he died.

Meanwhile Crow Parcel had plunged into a growing pile of dirt and rings, his big arms and body thrashing around, almost as if he was trying to swim in the stuff. More red-hot coal piled up on top of him and now he could not move at all with just the distant cries of his work-mates echoing dimly on the far edges of his mind. Oddly enough in the circumstances, Crow Parcel relaxed and even felt happy. He wondered what his wife had put in his tea jack. He hoped that she had not given him that bloody India tea again. He liked the tea from the Co-op but she was always giving him India tea – almost as if she wanted to show him up in front of his mates. Only pansies with poodles drank India tea. Everyone knew that. He sighed in exasperation as he thought of all her airs and graces. Twenty-nine years he had been married to all those airs and graces. He had only gone and got that giant tattoo of the dogs chasing the fox just to get up her nose. It had worked too. He sniffed a sort of smile as he remembered how she didn't speak to him for ten months after that. Ten months of bliss that was. Just what, he wondered, would she make of all this? Then, with the broadest of smiles on his lips, he, too, died.

Ponty Williams lay, on his side, on the roadway

half-covered in coal, with great swords of flame slashing the air above his head. He moaned soft and tried to turn over. All this running and screaming had given him a right old headache too. At least he'd have no trouble getting a week off with a doctor's note, he supposed. The doctor surely wouldn't quibble about a sick note after all this. The boys would get him out all right. That was a racing certainty that was.

With that the roof fell in on Ponty Williams. In the crushing darkness he thought of his small boy who he loved more than his own life. He prayed to God that his small boy would never have to go down the hole. He prayed that his small boy would never, *ever* have to go through all this. Not this. He groaned quiet and tried not to move as he thought of their walks together around the *cwm* with the sun shining down on their heads. He could hear the boy's voice, his very laughter. *Dada where do baby lambs come from?* His hand reached out to hold onto the boy's shoulder. How he loved to have someone to instruct; someone not yet wise in the ways of the world. *Baby lambs do come from their mother boy. They do come in the spring.*

Why just in the spring Dada?

Because the spring is the time when all things in nature come to life, he replied. A hysterical choking caught in his throat and a terrible claustrophobia swept over the dying miner. *And tell your mother I've always hated India tea,* he added before he, too, stiffened and died in all that black sunlight of an antediluvian forest.

Glynmor shot off down the roadway as soon as he heard the alarm sounding. Only when he had reached the locking station did he stop running. Horror-stricken, he watched them sealing off the B2. 'Oh shit me, oh fuck it, oh …' he cried incoherently and uselessly as he gazed at the rumbling ball of fire which was holding steady about two hundred yards away.

Even so far away he could feel the ferocious, scorching heat of the blazing fire damp. He ran towards it and was pushed back, his eyebrows and cheeks seeming to burst into flames. He glanced away and began running at the fire again – almost like a moth bent on its own destruction.

Now he was crying and so close to the flames that his tears were drying up before they had fallen the length of his cheeks.

All he could see behind that wall of flame were all his butties in general and Jampots in particular. Amazingly, recklessly he began running towards the terrible colours of the fire again, almost as if he was hoping to run right through it. Others were gathering around the locking station calling out for him to come back.

'We'll get you out Jampots,' Glynmor shouted as the hooters blared havoc. 'We'll get you out if I have to do it myself.'

And the tongues of fire came romping and flashing down the roadway, all but incinerating his trousers as he continued standing there as if looking for some alleyway in the flames through which he could run. It was, they said later in the Hall, the most stupidly courageous act they had ever seen.

But they did not manage to rescue Jampots, nor Sam Swambo, Crow Parcel, Dibber Jones or Ponty Williams. It was hours before the rescue team managed to get in there at all, digging out the charred remains of what they could only guess were bodies.

'The price of coal they say, don't they?' cursed Glynmor, the tears still running down his face in the changing room. 'The price of that bastard coal.'

He could not face hanging about the pithead. A small crowd had already begun to build up around the main gate so he went, instead, out through the rear of the welding shop and up past the washery. Even as he walked along the river path leading up to the reservoir, his face still black with coal and stained with the streams of his tears, he was surprised how bad he felt at the loss of his butty Jampots. It was almost as if someone had gone and tied a reef knot in his guts. He had not felt as bad as this since his Mam had died some seven years earlier though, oddly enough, he had felt nothing at all when, a year later, his Dad had died.

They had come through a lot, he and Jampots. It had begun in the nursery school and, even to this day, they had shared any winnings on the horses, raffles or one-armed bandits. Even if they weren't together at the time of the winnings they always, religiously, shared out the loot as soon as they met. And how, now, was he going to pay him back the fiver he had borrowed off him? They had always repaid each other's debts as well.

A soft wind ruffled the waters of the reservoir, a few brown ducks huddled together near the waterfall. At least the air was fresh and clean up here. He wiped his nose with the back of his hand. Stan Hughes had killed himself near here, he remembered. He was a local baker and the police had been after him for interfering with children. He came up here by the reservoir, filled his pockets with stones and jumped in. They didn't find him then, but only last summer, with the water levels low with drought, they reckoned a dead sheep was blocking one of the pipes. A diver went down to haul the carcass up. But it was no sheep. It was the skeleton of one sad and frightened baker, whose knee-cap actually fell off as it was hauled up out of the water. He and Jampots watched it all from the very bridge on which he was now standing.

Duw, they had even thrown a bag of lime into the water here and picked up seventeen trout one afternoon and Jampots' Mam had made them throw away in case they were poisonous.

The tight knot in his guts grew tighter as he climbed on up through the ferns to walk along the top of the Valley where there was a forest of Christmas trees, all now dead after a fire. Dotted around on the paths were the black polished olives of sheep dung. You could see the pit from up here, watch the crowds and ambulances thronging outside. But, strangely, you could hear none of the noise. He pressed his fingertips into his belly and was sick, again and again.

He continued along the thick promonotory between the two valleys, the dusty sheep lifting their heads from their endless munching and looking at him curiously. He and Jampots had actually nobbled one of those sheep once – luring it into a shed with a trail of bits of bread before jumping on it and trying to stab it to death with a carving knife. All that got stabbed though was Jampots' leg. The sheep escaped and they went down to the hospital in Aberdare claiming that Jampots had fallen on a bottle.

Even as he stood there looking down on the village, with the thin blue wisps of smoke drifting up out of the chimneys, he could see him and Jampots racing down the gullies up to no good. He could see them together sliding down the tump on dustbin lids. He remembered the way they hung around together after school down the gully hoping for a quick feel off one of the girls. Just how was he going to live without Jampots? Everywhere he went the dopey bugger would be somewhere around wouldn't he? Perhaps he would have to leave the Valley and start again?

There was only Maggie now – but he was hardly in love with her. There didn't seem any point in going out with her any longer. He would put a stop to all that before it got out of hand. Everything was so serious with the girl. And she didn't drop them either. Why did she think she was so bastard special? Whatever Jampots had was yours but not with Maggie. Oh no. What was yours was hers and what was hers was hers.

The sun was dipping out of the Valley and he was getting cold. He followed the twisting, rutted track down the side of the Valley and back to the village. A group of clacking blackbirds were swooping down on the bread that someone had thrown out in one of the back gardens. The 5.35 passenger train to Cardiff went burbling around the bend. There were only three trains a day and they would be stopping soon, he had heard.

A lot of the boys were already sitting around in one of the bars of the Welfare Hall when he got there. Almost all their families had been touched in some way by the accident. The steward had served each of them with free pints but there was not much being drunk or said as they sat around their tables together in their communal grief. Glynmor took his pint and went to sit next to the television. It was switched off for a change. He sipped his All-Bright; it tasted of coal. He wiped his mouth with the back of his hand but still that was the tang of anthracite. He had not so much as looked at a bar of soap since he had come up. That was the thing about coal wasn't it? It got into everything. Your beer. Your sandwiches. Your lungs. Your blood. Aye. Your very bastard blood.

He spat beer between his knees then finished his pint in two gulps. 'Are we going to drink or what?' he asked no one in particular. 'C'mon boys let's 'ave a fucking drink is it?'

'You're right there Glynmor. Let's 'ave a drink.'

The steward began lining up more pints on the counter. Stan Swansea was passing them back when the swing doors to the bar burst open with a whinnying bang and Maggie came rushing in, her big black eyes wide with panic, her face as white as a sheet.

The boys in the bar were to talk of that entrance for some time – '*Duw* mun she did come in like a clap of thunder' – since, no sooner had she spotted Glynmor, than she stood stock still, lowered her head and began blubbering into her two cupped palms. She did not move at all, just stood there with her whole body convulsed with shivering, pitiful sobs. Tears and cries just poured through her fingers as the boys gathered around her, unsure of what to do. One of them patted her on the back when Glynmor stepped up and took her by the wrist. 'Come and sit you down,' he said. 'Have one of those port and brandies.'

Even an hour — and several port and brandies later — she was still shivering and crying, holding his hand tight unable to believe that he was still there. 'I'm sorry,' she sobbed. 'They told me you'd got it and I couldn't find you anywhere. They said they'd all got it.'

'Cool head now. Do you want another?'

'I'm getting a bit drunk, I am. How are you feeling?'

'I'm feeling like another pint.'

'Well I'll have another port and brandy then. You don't mind do you?'

'Why should I mind?'

'The money. Those port and brandies are half a crown aren't they? Here I've got a few quid. Take them.'

The girl had a big heart, he decided, taking the money off her. He had to grant that. She would give him her last penny if he had wanted it. Probably make a good mother as well. It was funny how he always felt that much fonder of her after he'd had a few drinks. He patted her hand reassuringly and stood up to go to the bar.

'Tell me Glynmor, do you think I'm too fat?' she asked him when he returned.

'I wouldn't say fat exactly,' he said hesitatingly.

'What would you say then?'

'Well, sort of ... round ... kind of ample like.'

'I've decided I'm far too fat. I'm going on a diet soon. I'm going to stop eating all those chips and pasties, make myself beautiful for you.'

'But you do look beautiful already girl.'

'You're not just saying that are you? I do want to look beautiful for you Glynmor.'

'But you are beautiful to me.'

'I'm not beautiful. I'm fat I am.'

'But you're not fat.'

'I am. You're the one who's always telling everyone about how I got stuck on that slide.'

'Never.'

Most of the boys were sitting around morosely listening to this low grumbling argument which, like most low grumbling arguments in Bont, seemed to be getting nowhere at all. Stan Swansea stepped up to the bar and turned on the television. A chorus of cries told him to turn it off again.

'It's time for *Peyton Place*,' Stan explained.

'Bugger *Peyton Place*. There's been an accident mun.'

'Well, anything's better than listening to those two arguing,' Stan persisted pointing to Glynmor and Maggie.

'You've got an awful big mouth,' Glynmor warned him.

'If you two want to argue why don't you go somewhere else and do it?' Stan went on dangerously.

'Who's arguing?'

'You are. And, anyway, everyone knows she's too fat.'

It was not the moment to get controversial, as Stan Swansea soon found out, since Maggie let out a wail of agony as Glynmor went hurtling up out of his chair running towards Stan with his forehead flying into the startled miner like an avenging cannonball. The way that Glynmor put the head in was famous in the valleys. And it didn't matter how big they were either since Stan Swansea might even have been twice his size. If anyone upset Glynmor he all but turned into a human rocket and – wham! – it was usually a broken nose.

Except that this time he missed.

Clearly all the aggravation of the day had done something to his normally immaculate timing since he didn't even come close to connecting with Stan Swansea's nose and, the next thing, a man in a baseball hat and a woman in a bathing suit were swearing undying love to one another in *Peyton Place* as the two men were both locked together and rolling around the floor of the bar, punching and kicking like a pair of wild cats.

Glynmor managed to work his knee into Stan's groin a few sharp and painful times while Stan retaliated with a few punches into his eye and ear. It was just then that a few of the boys managed to pull off Stan while Maggie grabbed hold of Glynmor in a Double Nelson. She could feel the tremendous rage of his fury as she held him tight. He had a terrible temper to be sure. The boys in the bar swore that Glynmor would fight a brick wall if it upset him. She was even half worried that he might inflict a serious injury on Stan and was still holding on for all she was worth when his feet just leaped forward and, using Maggie's tight hold as a launching pad, he managed to give Stan a fair old kick in the balls.

Next thing Stan had broken loose and they were all rolling around the floor again until more committee men came running in, finally managing to break up the fight through sheer force of numbers.

'Right, your beer is stopped and both of you are up before the committee,' said the committee chairman, Max Million, a man of military bearing as befits someone who lives his life in accordance to the 151 rules of clubland. 'I know there's been accident in the pit but that's no excuse for fighting in here.'

'What a bastard of a day this has been,' sighed Glynmor as he and Maggie were walking arm in arm down by the river which hurried and twisted and dawdled in the starlight.

'Poor Glynmor,' she commiserated. 'Well, you've still got me and I'll make you feel better.'

And she would too, as he found out that night on the river bank. She wanted to take some of that pain out of him, and letting him have all her body was the only way she could think of doing it. She had even foreseen it by leaving her panties and corset behind in the Hall's ladies toilet. They lay down together in their usual spot in the long grass and, without any preliminaries at all, she took his hand and placed it squarely on her soft pubic mound.

He just lay there for a few moments, listening to the laughing trickle of the river. She undid the buttons of his dungarees and began playing with him, quietly kissing the coal streaks off his face and nuzzling her face into the sides of his neck as she opened her legs wider, wanting him to sink right inside her where he could get warm and comfortable and lose some of that hurt.

She began handling him with quite ferocious tenderness, moving him around one way and another, kissing the coal off his cheeks and circling her hand round and round his confused member until she lowered him into her, feeling it ease into her with a surprising lack of pain, gritting her teeth a bit as she moved her body around again trying to get settled.

She gazed up at the stars and even felt happy as he just lay there deep within her. She was glad that she had finally given in. She wasn't going to have any regrets now. She did, after all, love him dearly. There was no doubt about that.

He continued just to lie there in her arms, doing nothing. His real problem was that he did not want to pick up the ball and make a dash for the line. He was convinced that, any minute, she was going to blow the final whistle. Just how had he made so much progress with so little effort? After all, the boys were supposed to do all the running weren't they? It was up to the boys to fight to get their knickers down wasn't it? But it felt pretty good. There was no denying that. He pressed his pelvis into her and, when she did not cry out or push him away, he pressed down again.

Oooh that was very nice indeed, she thought. They didn't get up to this in her Mills and Boon books, but there were plenty of suggestions of it. She could almost feel the way she was draining the pain out of him; somehow she was taking his burden on herself and that was such a great joy to do. She could really get into this.

'Oh yes my lovely,' she whispered and he knew that she was not going to blow the whistle. He scooped up that ball and flew for the line, humping away like mad, almost as if he had just been given the word that all sexual activity was going to be banished from the valleys in ten seconds' time.

'There's plenty of time,' she soothed as he bucked and swerved. 'Take it slow. We've got the rest of our life.'

He came to a sudden cold halt. We've got the rest of our life? Oh so that was it? And what else had she called him? My love? Distant wedding bells began ringing in the far corners of his mind. So she was going to get herself a bun in the oven and get him up the altar with a shotgun at his elbow and a ring in his nose. His head lay on her heaving bosom and he looked out into the dark tangled grass like a hunted fox settling down beneath deep cover.

So what was the matter with him now? She wondered. Men were funny things and this one was the funniest of the lot. You could never quite make up your mind if he was a boy or a man. You could never really decide if he was generous or mean. One minute he was the loving soul grieving about his lost mate and the next he was shouting at you and treating you like rubbish. Just what did he want from her? Was he looking for a mother or a spot of target practice. Who could tell? She couldn't that was for sure.

Paranoid about churches and weddings, Glynmor took a few slow stabs deciding that he would pull it out before he came. That was the way the Catholics did it, he reflected. He really should have got some johnnies from the machine in the gents, even though that was a bit like sucking a sweet with the wrapper still on. Besides he didn't know this was going to happen. It was his Uncle Bomber who had always advised him never to leave it in to soak. Bomber had always told him that it only ever needed one tiny tadpole to start a baby and those little bastards could do an awful lot of swimming when they got moving. There were millions of them as well but it only took one to swim the length of the fanny, Bomber had always said. The old bastard. It was a pity that tadpole swam all the way to make Bomber.

He thought of that old bastard lying in his bed coughing his guts up. He thought of his butties who died down on the B2 face ... of Crow Parcel and Sam Swambo and his great pal Jampots ... the untidy hair and patches of freckles ...

Then Glynmor cried out as if in pain and he was off on a gallop again, wild, oblivious, driving into Maggie like he was trying to find a way inside her; pushing hard and yet harder like he wanted to disappear within her and leave this valley of pain altogether; whimpering in the running stream of his sorrow when he felt the base of his belly about to explode ... and he pulled it out hurriedly, his whole body leaping upwards as if he had just been electrocuted and − zoom, zoom, zoom − millions of tadpoles went spurting and slithering all over Maggie's bosom.

Chapter Five

On the day of the funeral high winds whipped fat washing-day clouds over the roof of the Valley. They dashed along the backs of Bont Terrace, rattling on the windows and shaking the doors, blowing gasps of soot and coal smoke down the chimneys into the living-rooms, sometimes catching in the heart of the flues and moaning piteously. If it caught a door open, or a window, the wind would dash through the hallway and up the stairs, whirling and slamming about the place like a demented witch looking for her broomstick. The winds made the sheets flap on the washing lines with the flat boom of guns. Everything was noise and drama with those valley winds.

In the street outside the Libanus Chapel, Emlyn Kremlin stood to attention among a group of some twenty best-suited miners. Sung by the colliery choir, *Abide With Me*, came drifting out of the open vestry doors. Even Emlyn, who had no truck with the chapel, thought that it was a fine hymn, perfect in its way for expressing the sorrows of his battered collier tribe.

He took off his bowler hat and almost made a military click with his finely-polished shoes as the coffins of the men were brought out of the chapel. Undertakers in shiny top hats and black tails circled around, quietly forming the pallbearers and mourners into the procession down to the cemetery. Those undertakers all had the fat, bloated bellies of Tories, Emlyn noted. Only some capitalist Tory would choose to make a living out of the business of death.

Emlyn and his group moved across the road to join in the cortége, just behind the members of the choir. As befitted the top official of the National Union of Mineworkers' local lodge, he was wearing an immaculately pressed black suit with a high

65

starched collar, a grey-striped waistcoat and a gold fob watch. He always dressed with fastidious care for such funerals. It was, after all, the last thing you ever did for them. Turning out at your very best was the mark of your political respect for those who had died in the long struggle to win that bastard coal from the bowels of the earth. Weren't all those hundreds of thousands of others enough for them?

He had huge, gnarled hands, ripped and torn by a life of hard work as a pick and shovel man on the face. His face was beefy and ruddy with the vitality of tremendous power. His back was ramrod straight though he did walk with a slight limp where once, as a boy, he had been dragged by a horse in traces some two hundred yards along a roadway. Four pounds the pit owners had paid him in compensation for that, he would tell you readily. Four pounds was the price of a crippled leg.

Rev. Mordecai walked alone with the Prayer Book in both hands, looking even more like a great vulture searching for carrion in his flowing black hassock which contrasted vividly with the pastiness of his complexion. The daylight showed up the thin blue veins on his cheeks and face while he kept his lidded eyes lowered in suitable piety. Such times were always difficult and frustrating for him since everyone always asked him the same question. Why? To which he always gave the same, slightly unsatisfactory, answer. He didn't know.

The winds dropped as the cortège moved off, making the Valley strangely hushed, as if even the walls were standing stiff and silent out of respect. Crow Parcel's family had chosen cremation so there were just four coffins, piled high with flowers and wreaths, six pallbearers to each. Behind came a drift of black-veiled widows and daughters, the rest of the shattered families behind. What with friends and the colliery choir just about everyone in the village was there. It was the biggest funeral in the Valleys for twenty years, it said in the afternoon Valleys edition of the *South Wales Echo*. Some 800 had joined the cortège; relatives of two of the families had flown in from Canada and Australia.

A few tiny groups of housewives stood around on corners, their faces grim, their arms folded tight. The shops were closed and every curtain was drawn. Even the normally boisterous children stood around in still groups near the clock tower, staring at coffins which seemed to be telling them something about their lives stretching out before them, and the manner of the deaths which might await them too.

Emlyn, a true melancholy Marxist, had a strong and despondent feeling for the lessons of history. And this accident had considerably thickened his melancholia; it had given him a sudden glimpse of that old hated Hades full of lock-outs, explosions and Tory coal barons, long thought dead but clearly still very much kicking. Such deaths diminished them all; they took away a part of everyone. Every family in the village had been affected one way or another by the accident.

He took out his fob watch and checked the time, put it back into his waistcoat pocket and blew his nose. To him it seemed incredible that old Lord Firedamp had come riding his chariot into the Valley again. Emlyn had long thought that they had got the problem of blowers under control. *Duw*, they had even accepted a report at their last regional conference, two years in the making, that had concluded that there were now sufficient controls to detect any build-up of gas. But Lord Firedamp was not going to be beaten so easily. It clearly took more than a report to control that old swine.

Keir Hardie must be turning in his grave. On the day that the Duchess of York had given birth to the boy who later became Edward VIII, 260 men and boys had died in an explosion in the newly-dug Bont pit. And everyone knew what the front pages had been full of that day. Now, a hundred years later, they seemed to have learned nothing and progressed nowhere. Emlyn almost spat at the road in the bitterness of his thoughts.

Emlyn Thomas – dubbed Emlyn Kremlin because of his lifelong connection with the Communist Party – was a man of the most perfect rectitude; an assembler of political ideas and a master of rhetoric. He was committed enough to the cause of the working class to hang the red flag of the hammer and sickle in his window on the occasion of royal weddings and coronation days.

A pick and shovel man, long before the soft days of the totally mechanised face, Emlyn was also a man of memories. Mostly he remembered the colour and detail of that old world of zinc baths and wooden lavatory sheds at the end of the garden; those bad old days of black pats in a collier's sandwiches and rats swarming in the dung of the ponies' stables. He still felt twinges of bile when he remembered the way they stopped money for candles, the oil for the lamps and even the chalk for marking the drams. Tell him any story of hardship and he always knew a worse one. He knew horrifying stories of miners covered in boils from head to toe; of men spending long hours on their sides in half a foot of water trying to dig out the coal. He would tell you about when the women used Robin starch on their babies' bottoms because they could not afford talcum powder. Emlyn Kremlin knew everything about this coal game; this the hardest work under heaven.

But the acid bath of his memories were those dread times when the pit hooter sounded after an accident. Then there came the terrible cleats of the hobnail boots in the streets when the bits of the dead men were taken back to the widow in a sack. At least they had stopped that obscene practice now.

Emlyn trudged along with the cortège, past the Welfare Hall where a woman, with a baby in a shawl, was standing outside the door weeping silently. The Hall looked extremely shabby in the sunshine, Emlyn thought: a real broken-jawed hulk of shattered windows and rotten splintered window frames. Every part of it cried out for a coat of paint. It was, he supposed, a definitive symbol of how low everything had fallen. The committee was even now on the point of selling off the library, one of the finest collections of Marxist literature ever assembled in the country. The University of Wales desperately wanted to buy the books and pamphlets and Emlyn had fought hard against the sale. No deal had yet been struck with the university but, in the end, even he had to accept that the men did not want to read the great texts of Marx and Engels any more. They were not interested in the philosophic heroism of those first early prophets of socialism. They did not want to understand the historic inevitability of the class war. Only professors and students were interested these days, sitting there polishing their library seats as they waited for someone else to start the revolution.

The modern miner, he saw, was no longer a man of culture who wanted to learn how to play a musical instrument, sing Haydn or make furniture. All the modern miner wanted was to rot in front of his television, or play bingo, or drive fancy cars. And now here they all were united again, burying the dead who had not lived long enough; burying the poor who had perished so that the rich might stay warm.

A dog was barking at one of the undertakers as the cortège moved in through the green wrought-iron gate of the cemetery. By now the sun was smashing against one side of the Valley with the shunting clouds sending speeding shadows racing along its length. The opposite wall of high brown rock was already darkening fast. Sunlight and shadow moved in fast and endless interplay in this valley of coal. So did the lives of the people who lived here.

Now the mourners were threading their way past the massed ranks of the tombstones and up to the newly-opened graves at the top of the cemetery. The sunshine caught in the gilt handles as the pallbearers prepared the ropes to lower the coffins into the ground. Rev. Mordecai read from the Order of the Burial of the Dead, the wind blowing his words away.

As Mordecai continued reading, Maggie stood next to her sister Daisy, her arm linked with her mother's. Her beloved Glynmor was standing with an old friend of his, Dai Waterboard, and the pair of them were standing so near Jampots' grave there seemed a danger Glynmor might even fall in. She could tell from the greyness of his face and black bags under his eyes that he had not been sleeping properly again. Even so far away she could see that his body was shaking slightly. She so wished that she could take away some of his pain.

But, since the night of surrender on the river bank, Glynmor had stopped speaking to her. He had developed this alarming sense that he was going to be well and truly trapped if he didn't watch it and, as there were many acres of wild oats that he had yet to sow, he was now avoiding Maggie assiduously. She had even sent notes over to his house asking if they could talk but he had replied in kind saying he had a bad back and didn't want to talk about anything. She had long suspected that this would happen and her suspicions proved correct. In that schoolboyish way of his, she reckoned, he had concluded that she was just some tart who would drop her knickers for anyone. She hardly knew what to make of it.

'Forasmuch as it hath pleased Almighty God of His great mercy to take unto himself the soul of our dear brothers here departed, we therefore commit their bodies to the ground; earth to earth, ashes to ashes, dust to dust ...'

The whole of Glynmor's insides were shaking like branches in the wind as he lined up behind Jampots' mother to throw a handful of earth onto the coffin. For a second, fearing that she was going to throw herself down the hole, he steadied her with a grip on the elbow. For what seemed an age she stood there, what was going on in her mind he could not imagine. And when she had moved away Glynmor too took his time over the coffin sitting down there in the tiered layers of clay.

'... Our Lord Jesus Christ who shall change our vile body that it might be like unto his glorious body, according to the mighty working, whereby he is able to subdue all things to himself ...'

Glynmor picked up a handful of earth and flung it down on the coffin. Even as the fine lumps of earth bounced off the polished wood, the mourners could see the rolled up bank-note he had thrown down too. It was the fiver that he had borrowed off Jampots just before he died, given back now, the debt repaid in full for all time.

He then moved on, looking up into Maggie's quizzical stare and nodding at her before walking away with Dai Waterboard. He did hope that she wasn't going to dog him all the time. Everywhere he turned she seemed to lock her big black eyes on him. It was that hurt look that got right to him. Even when she wasn't doing anything she seemed to upset him – as if he wasn't upset enough. Women were always pains in the arse weren't they? They didn't even have to work at it.

Once back in the Starlight Suite of the Hall the mourners gathered around the trestle tables piled high with ham sandwiches, sausage rolls and pickles. At the far end of the table Stan Swansea was already eating a sausage roll, poking the air with it as he spoke. 'Crow Parcel always told me that there was gas down there.'

'Well why didn't you report it mun?'

'I never did speak to him did I?'

'But you said he was talking to you.'

'Aye mun. He was talking to me but I never did talk to him. 'Aven't talked with Crow f'r ages.'

Emlyn Kremlin sat at his usual table near the bar among his cronies. Already he was sounding off again about the terrible cost of that bastard coal. 'Heard did you? The Queen has sent another message of sympathy. Why doesn't she come down here and dig the cowing stuff herself? Eh? Could you just see Queenie sitting down there eating coal dust sandwiches with black pats running around her velvet feet? Could you just?'

'These cowing tips are none too stable either,' he went on. 'That's what's going to happen next. Some of us are going to get killed by one of them one day. There'll be a fuss if it kills someone high and mighty from the N.C.B. but, as long as it only kills miners, we'll just get another message of sympathy from Queenie in Buck House. And sod all else.'

'The pit manager sent some flowers I 'eard.'

'He's a bloody flower himself in 'e? It was his job to check the machinery but, what with that woman he calls a wife and that fancy piece he calls his mistress I can't see that he's got any time for anything. Every time I go into his office he just seems to be kipping like some cat. We go and see him about conditions and he just refers us to the board. Mines were always the responsibility of the managers not the board.'

The sombre mood was lifting slightly with the beer. Cigarette smoke curled sluggishly around the neon lights. People began to talk of other things.

'Hah it's the gentlemen from the N.U.M.'

Emlyn looked up at Mordecai, glass of orange juice in hand looking down at him. Emlyn had little time for old Mordecai but, for some reason, the minister seemed to enjoy coming over and needling him. Not that Emlyn took any of it lying down. He had long learned that it was best to get in the first punch.

'Another act of love by your wonderful God then,' Emlyn told Mordecai. 'A fine father I do call him.'

'Accidents and tragedy are not the work of the holy father,' Mordecai replied evenly and without rancour. 'Everything we receive from the Father is a blessing. Accidents like this come from the opposition, I fear.'

'Accidents like this come from human negligence, minister. That's how men have always died in the pits. Through the negligence of men who put profit before everything. Why does your God allow that then?'

'I can't speak for God Emlyn. You must look on God as a great gardener trying to make sense of a wilderness. He has submitted himself to a long and difficult work. He works in ways none of us will ever understand.'

Emlyn took in this bit of theology with a soft derisive snort before sipping his beer with a slow exaggerated care. 'This God who created us all can't think too much of his children if he allows them to be snuffed out like that. He did create us all didn't he? That's what you do say isn't it?'

'He did indeed Emlyn. He did indeed. But there are many in this Valley who have turned their backs on God and, when they did that, He gave them up. That's the real reason for our sorrows these days.

That Saturday the passenger rail line service in the Valley was finally axed. Falling revenue from passengers, British Rail announced. A circular from the South Glamorgan Education Authority was also posted through the door of every home in Bont. It said that due to the rationalisation of the health service, the village primary school would close at the end of term. Each day, in future, all children would be taken by bus, free of charge, to a new school in the next Valley. It was earnestly hoped that this rationalisation would not cause the parents too much inconvenience.

Chapter Six

After the interruption caused by the funeral, the little rituals of life quickly re-asserted themselves on the streets of Bont. Evans the Milk began his rounds at six in the morning and the shops opened at eight thirty, closing for an hour between one and two when the fish and chip shop was frying. At two thirty-five the first edition of the *South Wales Echo* was heaved off the van onto the pavement and, at four o'clock in the afternoon, the Welfare Hall was closed for an hour for the cleaners to sort it out after the afternoon session. The film programme in The Bug began at seven in order to finish at ten and give the manager and patrons time for the final hour for a drink in the Hall. At eleven Lee Hoo Wonk was at his busiest, frying up noodles and chop suey in his vast steaming woks and, unfailingly at eleven fifteen, Ivor Massey stopped behind the Post Office to relieve the strain of many pints of All-Bright bitter on his bladder before getting on his way home. At midnight Police Constable Watkins began the first of his hourly rounds on a bicycle, patrolling the dark gardens and slumbering houses until dawn when Evans the Milk began his rounds again.

In this way the life of a Welsh pit village moved from one day to the next; softly, irrevocably, almost without a join, a little like a snake bent on eating its own tail.

The patterns of life behind those frothy lace curtains were much the same as well. In his lonely, painful bed Bomber's coughing had, if anything, got worse. His neck had shrunk, his chest had become increasingly swollen from his gasping fight for air. He was also getting a terrible stitch in his side and bringing up whole lumps of black spit. Even as they slid out from between his teeth like slimy black sweets they told him that the end would be very soon.

But still the stubborn old bastard refused to give up his beloved Woodbines. Even as his eyes were bulging and watering with the strain of coughing up his insides into his bucket, his fingers, as black as his lungs, still clutched a smoking cigarette.

Even more embarrassingly, the irascible old bugger was still trying to maul the district nurse and work his hand up the skirt of the Meals on Wheels woman. Glynmor had never wanted anyone to die so much. He knew that it was wrong but he really was going to dance on Bomber's grave. A mad dance of the greatest joy it was going to be as well. Except that there was one big bastard of a nigger in the woodpile.

Bomber still hadn't told anyone where he had hidden his money.

And that small fact – or, to be precise, that lack of a small fact – stuck in Glynmor's throat even more painfully than Bomber's continued existence on this earth. He could hardly bear to speak to him any more. There was still no communication between Glynmor and Maggie either. Every day she took the early bus down to the factory just down the Valley. And when she returned she sat in her bedroom where she continued reading her Mills and Boon books and playing Hollies records on her Dansette. She also continued to moon about her Glynmor, but he showed no sign at all that he was mooning about her.

After years of worrying about her weight – probably without reason – she had also decided to do something about it. She'd start on a crash diet which involved stopping eating just about everything she loved – like Walls pasties – and starting on just about everything she hated; a meal of crisp bread, cottage cheese and carrot juice. She weighed herself unfailingly first thing in the morning on the bathroom scales – as advised in the slimmers' book – and religiously wrote down the dates and weights in her little red notebook.

The snag was that, far from losing weight, her little notebook was telling her that she was putting it on. And at an alarming rate as well. She was feeling very tired and weak too, which she put down to her horrible new diet.

She had also missed her period. Twice.

In many other ways the rest of the village was continuing much the same. Aunty Phyllis was still gossiping ferociously with her next door neighbour. The clock in the square was still ticking away the hours and minutes. The coal conveyor still went *click*, *swoosh*, *click*, *swoosh* and the sheep still kept knocking over the dustbins to forage in the rubbish. Daisy Bland was still having a bit of a rub with the man from the Prudential.

This peaceful cycle of work, play and sleep was interrupted on a glorious day in June. The musical cheeps of the blackbirds hung in bright clumps over the roofs of Bont as the twisting spine of the Valley basked beneath a bright golden carpet of warmth. Denzil Bland was driving his huge yellow concrete mixer over to Mountain Ash when he remembered that he had left his sandwiches and flask of tea back home. He drove back to Bont Terrace, noticing a dog piddling over the front wheel of a new convertible car that was parked, with the hood down, outside his own front door. He pushed the door open and walked into the house, calling out Daisy's name. Finding no sandwiches in the kitchen, he went up the stairs. Half-way up the stairs he heard, coming from his bedroom, the unmistakable noises of his wife, Daisy, having a bit of a rub with the man from the Pru.

Cool head now, Denzil.

Without a word he tiptoed back down the stairs, went out into the street, backed his concrete mixer up against the new car outside the door and tipped some ten tons of ready mixed concrete into it. With grey sludge brimming over the car doors Denzil went back into the house and screamed blue murder at the insurance agent who, forewarned by all the noise, had already got all his clothes on before running down the stairs, jumping on the bicycle he'd thoughtfully left a couple of doors down the street and pedalling off into the sunshine.

So who owned the car with the new concrete lining?

Three weeks later Denzil Melvyn Bland of 31 Bont Terrace appeared before the Stipendiary Magistrate in Pontypridd and received three months imprisonment suspended for two years, for malicious and unlawful damage to property, to wit his neighbour Clay Evans' new car which had only been delivered the very morning of The Great Concrete Downpour as it became known in the Hall. Clay Evans had not wanted to take Denzil to court – particularly under the sorry circumstances of his wife's adultery – but the insurance people

– by some sick irony, the Prudential – had insisted on it.

'I just don't know what came over me,' Denzil told the Stip. as it was reported in the *South Wales Echo*. 'They say you see red when you get upset but all I saw was black.' On top of his suspended sentence Denzil was also bound over for a year to a sum of £50 to keep the peace.

Denzil said he'd had enough of Daisy after the court case, said Aunty Phyllis to her neighbour over the garden fence. He said all he wanted was the portable Teas-maid out of the bedroom. He'd told her she could keep all the rest, she said. He'd said that he'd never loved her anyway an' he cried when he said goodbye to Gnasher. I heard he went off to live with his mother down in Tonypandy said the neighbour. I don't know if it's true like. That's just what I've heard.

It was but a few weeks after Denzil went off to live with his sister in Upper Boat that certain things began to go missing in the night. Maggie's Dansette record player upped and walked out of the back door, then one of the Pandy boys lost his bicycle, later found in the river.

A few thefts do not a crime wave make but in a village where no door had ever been locked and crime was virtually unknown such disappearances were particularly upsetting. Maggie did so love her Dansette and the Pandy boy had got his bicycle for Christmas and was on it virtually every hour of the day. The wild finger of suspicion went pointing in all directions, of course, and none more frequently than in the direction of Gnasher and the boys of the Clay Class. Could it be that after years of mindless vandalism the Clay Class had now finally graduated to mindless crime? No one could be absolutely sure but, as is usual when there is an absence of fact, there was plenty of inaccurate and malicious gossip.

That very week a new branch of Lipton's opened in the premises of the old cobbler's in the square and immediately plunged into a bitter price war with the Co-op. Huge posters went up in Lipton's windows detailing what was being cut off staples like bread, butter and fags. The Co-op had the advantage of trading stamps, of course, and when they began announcing treble stamps with everything, Liptons hit back with a vengeance slashing all prices down to the knuckle. With every five pounds of potatoes there was a free small packet of Persil.

These days the Clay Class was roaming about with a restlessness no one could quite understand, absorbing the edginess of the leader, Gnasher, who was becoming more moody, ferocious and watchful with every day that passed. No one ever really knew how much the loss of his father had affected him because he had never told anyone. Only girls ever spoke of emotional hurts deep inside, but a right old hurt Gnasher had now – and no mistake.

Sometimes, after breakfast, he had to run out to the lavatory shed at the end of the garden and bring it all back up again. His voice had broken too and he would stand around moodily, never speaking when spoken to. Stubble began growing on his chin and strange stains appeared on his sheets.

Daisy could watch all these changes in her son but did nothing. In truth, she did not see what she could do. When anyone got grumpy in her view they were best left alone. Sometimes she would shout at him to brighten up his ideas and stop being so shandyvan about the place but he just stared back at her, sullen like a whipped dog. Anyway Daisy had enough problems of her own. On top of the fuss about the concrete mixer and seeing her name in the papers, the man from the Prudential was quietly relocated to West Wales which left her temporarily without a man. But things were always very temporary with Daisy. It was only a matter of a few days before she began having a bit of a rub with Walford Evans, the bingo caller in the Hall.

She had long heard it rumoured that his was a whopper. He also allegedly gave away free strips of bingo cards to the favoured few. It would have been more than Walford's job was worth to have actually fixed the numbers in Daisy's favour – it would have been more than his life was worth come to that – but Daisy was delighted to learn that all those other rumours were absolutely true and so, after each bingo session (when he had finished counting the bingo takings and filling in the forms) they would have a bit of a rub on the polished circular table behind the locked doors of the committee room.

With his bald head and different coloured eyes – one pink and the other a forget-me-not blue – there was something about having it off on the sacred committee table that appealed to the

77

primal part of Walford's chemistry. He found something emblematic, almost sacrificial, about the act. It was a form of religious desecration, a way of sexual protest against the dark influence of the chapel which, he believed, had brought about the closure of the railway line. He was a very strange man with elliptical thought patterns was Walford Evans – even his wife went around the shops saying that he would be best off consigned to a loony bin.

For her part, Daisy found the twice-weekly tryst on the committee table considerably more exotic and pleasurable than the normal communion between the sheets. With her eyes closed and a broad smile on her lips, she imagined the faces of those solemn stuffed shirts of the committee as they sat around this very table on Sunday afternoons, trying to decide who they were going to fine or box for such grave offences as fighting, gambling, using bad language, drunkenness or standing at the bar during bingo sessions. Occasionally, as Walford went galloping away into the distant blue yonder, she would actually burst out laughing at the very thought of them deliberating over what the two of them were up to at the moment.

That night, after the bingo had ended, Daisy had been serviced and the last drunk had stumbled down the last slope, Gnasher, Nipper and Gaffer, made their entry into big-time crime. Carefully they levered open the back door of the Co-op with a crow-bar. The problem then was they were not quite sure what to do next. It was Nipper who decided that the bell would ring if they opened the till looking for money. Then Gnasher almost expired when he noticed that Gaffer had knocked over a rack of birthday cards and was even now down on his knees carefully picking them all up. Nipper made this, the crime of the century, complete when he announced that he had shat his pants and did any of the boys know where, in the shop, they kept the lavatory paper?

Dr Teifi Edwards took his pince-nez off his nose and put it down on his desk with a sigh. He looked at his consulting couch and up at the cornices on the ceiling. He so wished someone would come to him one day with an original complaint. 'When was the last time you had a period, Maggie?' he asked finally.

'Dr Edwards?'

'Your period. When was the last time you were on?'

78

'I'm not sure. Three. Four months.' Her lips were going dry and panic was decanting in her belly. She could see the writing on the wall. 'But they've never been reg'lar at best though. I went six months without a period once.'

'Well I'm afraid that you're up the spout. Welcome to the pudding club. About five months I'd guess. We'll have to do some more tests to work it out proper.'

'Are you sure it couldn't be something else?' Maggie swallowed. 'A bug? They do say there's something in the air at the moment.'

'The only thing that's been in the air, my girl, is your legs.'

Dr Edwards was something of a specialist in blunt remarks and small savage jokes. Even those who came to him in good humour and fine health would leave his surgery with bruised feelings and a flood of tears. The wonder was how anyone ever went to him in the first place.

'I've suffered a lot with indigestion lately. I thought it might just have been too much air.'

'So who's the lucky father then?'

She shook her head and began crying again.

'You mean you don't know? How many have there been then?'

She kept shaking her head and examining her handkerchief looking for a dry bit. 'It can only be that Glynmor Jones. He's been the only one.'

'Glynmor Jones. I might have guessed. They do say he'd rape a hedgehog that one but, between you and me, I'd say that he's all jaw. Did he do it bareback do you remember? You know ... when he did this to you.'

'He had some clothes on as I remember. His working clothes they were. We were down on the river bank.'

'A contraceptive girl. Did he have a johnny on at the time?'

'No. But he did say he'd pull it out first. He said that his Uncle Bomber had always warned him not to leave it in to soak. Then he sort of went crazy.'

Gnasher's big-time career lasted but a short while. One night, his pockets bulging with stolen tins of salmon, he ran straight into the arms of P.C. Watkins as he darted away from the back of Lipton's which he had just done over.

He ended up with three years' probation, I heard, Aunty Phyllis told her neighbour over the garden fence. Daisy was afraid it was all going to get into the *Echo* so soon after her divorce case an' all. Emlyn Kremlin went down to the juvenile courts with Gnasher. He spoke for the boy and said he was his guardian, being Daisy's uncle an' all. Now they say that Emlyn is going to look after him till he leaves school. Some hope. A proper handful he's become hasn't he?

You can say that again Phyllis.

This is all because his father went away you know. Gnasher looks a hard case but he did love his Dad. That was for sure. Most Sundays they did go riding in that concrete mixer of his down to Porthcawl. Denzil even used to buy the boy beer.

Never.

Now I'm not saying anything but I hear that Maggie Evans has gone and got herself pregnant.

Never.

That's what I heard. I was in the Co-op this morning and Jean from over in the bakery was telling Cynthia that she had seen that Maggie coming out of the doctor's in tears. Now I don't know if it's true but I heard that she's been carrying on with that Walford in the Hall.

Never. Him a married man an' all.

It's only what I've heard but Walford's been going home late and Maggie has been seen out on her own late too. Of course she won't have anything to do with our Glynmor now. He's been carrying on with some piece from Cymmer I heard. He can be as common as muck when he wants can't he?

As muck.

But, funny thing, I heard years ago that Maggie had the hots for that Walford. I don't understand the young any more. How can you carry a torch for someone as daft as him an' he's as bald as a billiard ball too? I don't know. It must be the age we live in.

Chapter Seven

The morning the Juvenile Court first entered Gnasher's name in their records was also the day that the Grim Reaper finally began calling out Bomber's number.

Bomber hardly had the energy to breathe at all. He just lay there with the thin sound of his lungs squeaking so thinly and distantly it might have been coming from another body altogether. His alabaster cheeks were but thin, hollowed-out scollop shells. His gnarled hands were useless claws. His whole chest swelled grotesquely through the final days of fighting for air. He discovered that it was best not to try and move at all; he just lay there motionless, as if already dead, looking out through the lace curtains and down onto the small gardens with their ash paths and rackety make-shift sheds. He had always loved looking out of the window into his Valley volcano home had Bomber; loved just lying there counting the clouds as they moved in fast procession high over the roofs of Bont.

Sometimes, he fancied, the clouds came together and formed the great shape of a man with a scythe on his shoulder. 'It's time to come in Bomber,' he could hear in a voice as soft and loud as the summer breeze. 'Your time is up Bomber and we want you home.'

He was so inert these days that even the Meals on Wheels woman felt safe going near his bed again. He never touched the food, of course, but they decided to keep bringing it regularly in case he rallied and felt like a bite.

'Still with us then are you?' It was Glynmor come up the stairs to rub salt into his wounds. 'Still hanging about keeping the sheets dirty then?'

One of Bomber's tired old eyes ratcheted towards Glynmor – a little like a chameleon's keeping watch on a fly.

He also straightened a finger and beckoned his nephew to come near. After much effort and sighing and licking of the lips he managed to get a few words out: 'Glynmor. I've got to see Guto. Guto. Get Guto.'

'What do you want to see that smelly old bastard for?'

'Guto. Send Guto here.'

Glynmor shook his head in wonder. Guto had been around almost as long as the Valley, a truly horrible man who spent his days and nights scavenging. By night he was worse than the sheep, forever sifting through the dustbins in the gullies for any useful items that he could take home. By day he would journey to all the tips in the Valley towns and spend endless hours poking about in the foul maggot-ridden walls for booty as he called it. Beautiful booty. Anything was beautiful booty to Guto and on almost any sort of day you might spot an old mattress or a couple of old armchairs walking down the path along the side of the Valley. Somewhere underneath would be Guto's legs.

But why now did Bomber want to see Guto?

Glynmor had long suspected that Guto had something over Bomber but had never quite been able to work out what it was. About the same age, the two men had certainly once been butties for a while together in school but then something dark and difficult had happened. Something dark and difficult which no one had ever spoken about.

But even when they had stopped being drinking pals, and Guto had begun looking for the meaning of life down the bottom of every dustbin, Bomber had continued watching out for him. Bomber had once even bailed him out of the nick after he had been caught hurling a brick through the window of a shoe shop in Porth. The police had caught him merely by following a trail of left shoes dotted around the town.

Such acts of friendship and charity were totally alien to Bomber's nature so what had happened between them? Why did Bomber want to see him now? These were questions to which Glynmor would clearly get no answers since, after he had sent over a message to Guto, the old scavenger came and smelt so foul that not only did Glynmor have to leave the bedroom but also had to leave the house as well.

He stank even worse than a rubbish tip on a sunny day did Guto. His raincoat, which he wore in all weathers, was thick and shiny with oil and held together with a length of rope. The bottoms of his trousers were tucked in with bicycle clips and the only thing that quite matched the skinniness of his dirty ankles – since he wore no socks – was the dirty scrawniness of his neck. With his torn flat ratting cap, long bony face and stubbly grey beard he had the strange twisted look of a murderer standing before one of those crazy mirrors in a fun-fair. Neither was strangeness much helped by his lack of teeth. He did not possess a single one and the boys in the bar reckoned Guto only searched the Valley tips and dustbins, with such care all the time, because he was looking for a set of false teeth which actually fitted him.

Guto even examined the skulls of dead sheep, the boys in the bar reckoned, to see if the dead animal might have anything by the way of dentures he could recycle.

'You wanted to see me Bomber?' Guto muttered.

Bomber's beady eyes flickered open again as Guto came near the bed and sat on a chair. 'The money,' Bomber croaked, suddenly becoming lucid and almost animated. 'You looked after the girl. I want you to have the money.'

'What money *mun*?'

Bomber closed his eyes almost as if he was having second thoughts about revealing his great secret.

'Bomber. What money?'

'My money, Guto. All my money. My tools are on the bar. I want you to have the money.'

Guto looked behind him at the bedroom door and then moved his chair closer to the bed. 'So where is this money, butty?'

Bomber's eyes opened sharp at this term of endearment. Just about the last thing he wanted to be remembered as was being Guto's butty but, nevertheless, this old sledgehammer had once done something for which he would be eternally grateful.

A piece of folded up paper slid out from beneath the top of the blanket. 'It's all here Guto. Put it away safe. Don't tell Glynmor. Don't tell anyone. You hear me? No bugger at all.'

'You can count on me Bomber.'

Guto looked behind him again and slipped the paper into his pocket.

'There's one more thing you can do,' Bomber continued.

'There's a packet of Woodbines in that drawer. Light one and put it in my mouth.'

Bomber moved his body and lay face-up as Guto lit a cigarette, putting the packet into his own pocket before placing the cigarette between his lips. A look of the most heavenly pleasure crossed Bomber's eyes as the smoke drifted around his lips and poked up his nostrils. His lips tightened and he took the gentlest drag on the cigarette, taking it down a little before letting tiny wisps drift lazy up towards the ceiling.

If heaven had no Woodbines, then he wanted no part of the place, he decided; when the cigarette tumbled out of his lips and, with a soft wheeze, he died.

Guto picked up the smouldering cigarette and sat smoking it as he stayed with Bomber. Even as he tapped the cigarette half-way through, blowing on the butt-end and putting it away in his pocket, he said nothing as he wondered why Bomber had given him all his money just because of that girl? He hadn't done all that much for her.

The minutes passed. Guto was no nearer fathoming the mystery, not even when he looked at the piece of paper which Bomber had passed to him. He looked at the dead eyes, at the hands on the counterpane.

'Time to go Guto,' came Glynmor's voice from the bottom of the stairs.

'He's dead, mun,' he called back.

Glynmor came scrambling up the stairs.

'He's dead,' Guto repeated.

'Did he say anything before he died,' Glynmor asked, breathless.

'He asked me to light a fag for him.'

'Did he say anything at all about money?'

'No. All he wanted was a fag.'

'You black enamelled bastard,' Glynmor spat at Bomber, still lying there with his eyes open, still with a bit of a smile stitched to his lips and that same look of heavenly pleasure in his eyes. 'Where's the thanks, eh? And after all we've done for you. Well it's no fancy fucking funeral for you, mate. You get the cheapest cremation on offer and that's a fact.'

'Wasn't he a Buff?' asked Guto. 'The Buffs will pay for a proper funeral.'

'No fancy fucking funerals for you,' Glynmor continued,

addressing Bomber's dead body. 'You're going to get a bargain-bucket cremation and then I'm going to turn you into an egg-timer.'

'I'll get you an egg-timer if you want one that bad,' Guto offered.

'No. I want *him* as an egg-timer. Just that old goat's ashes. In fact I'll ask them to put him through the oven twice so that he'll make a good egg-timer. Perhaps he'll be of some use now he's dead. He was no use while he was alive.'

Seems a lot of trouble just to get an egg-timer, Guto thought.

When the Buffs examined their subscription book they found that Bomber had been out of compliance for seven years so they decided not to pay for his funeral after all and Bomber ended up with the cheapest cremation on offer.

Not many attended the old miner's funeral service at Glyntaff crematorium. But there was Maggie circling around the forecourt, watching Glynmor talking to the other members of the family. He didn't know, of course. Technically they still weren't speaking.

Since she had been to the doctor she had sent Glynmor no less than three letters asking for them to meet somewhere. He had ignored all of them. She had even hung around outside the pit at the end of the shift, waiting for him to come out. But he still evaded her and there she was getting heavier and heavier – and more and more frightened – by the hour.

She had not actually been invited to the cremation, though he could hardly have stopped her coming. Now she had finally caught up with him and she was determined to break the news to him while she still had him in her sights. It was hardly the right time but she wasn't feeling in the mood for niceties any more. She paused beneath the spiky curving branches of the monkey puzzle tree, standing stock still, watching and waiting. Glynmor knew, without having to be told, that she was there. He was careful not to go near her. He had seen her waiting for him outside the pit; that was why he'd been smuggled out on the back seat of a car. It was all over now, as far as he was concerned. He had other fish to fry.

Another funeral cortège came filing up the path of the crematorium. The sight of the veiled weeping women made

Maggie's pain worse. But there had been no tears shed for Bomber. Even as Glynmor continued moving from group to group she could see the way they were all laughing when he spoke to them. That was the trouble wasn't it? He was always such a laugh to have around. You could never get bored with a man like Glynmor. He had that lovely way about him with his bright laugh and big joke for everything. She knew now that she was too mad about him for her own good.

And then, as if by a trick of mirrors, Glynmor had vanished. The others were climbing into their cars and returning to Bont but Glynmor was not one of them. Panic mounted inside her as she hurried back to the monkey puzzle tree and looked down the newly-arrived cortège. She peered out over the lawns and distant grey headstones but still the lucky father-to-be was nowhere to be seen.

But he had only gone back to the office to pay for the cremation and to pick up Bomber's ashes. 'We could always scatter them around the grounds if you'd prefer,' said the caretaker. 'The grounds could then become his memorial and you could come here whenever you liked to pay your respects.'

'We've got somewhere special to put him and pay our respects,' Glynmor said, taking the vial and putting it in a Co-op bag. 'He had a favourite spot so we're going to put him there.'

Bravura made him careless. He came striding down the side of the crematorium swinging the carrier bag around and whistling when Maggie came sailing around the corner and buttoned him.

'Glynmor. I want a word with you,' she snapped.

'Mag, it's over,' he said. 'Can't you see? It's finished between us.'

'No it's not. It's anything but finished, Glynmor.'

He didn't see how he could take the argument much further than that. They had stated their positions and that seemed to be the end of it. There was a long silence. 'I've got Bomber's ashes in here,' he said, trying to break the deadlock.

'How interesting.'

'I thought we might scatter them over the floor of the bar of the club.'

'I see.'

'I had this other plan to turn him into an egg-timer. Did I tell you?'

'Glynmor, I'm pregnant.'

'He was no use when he was alive so ...'

'Glynmor, I'm pregnant.'

He looked quickly behind him as if she was talking to someone else. 'Are you saying ...'

'It's you, Glynmor.'

'Me?' he mimed silently.

'You.'

'It can't be.'

'It's you. There's been no one else.'

'Fair's fair girl, I pulled it out.'

'Fair's fair be buggered. You can't have pulled it out fast enough then, can you?'

'I pulled it out, didn't I?'

'Not fast enough.'

'Bloody hell.' He looked down into the carrier bag at Bomber's ashes. For one terrifying moment he thought that he was going to be sick all over them.

'Yes, bloody hell. So what are you going to do, Glynmor?'

'I'm not going to do anything. What are *you* going to do?'

'You're the father.'

'You're the mother. Can't you get rid of it?'

'No. We'll just have to get married.'

'Married?'

'Yes. Married.'

'Oh no, Maggie. Not me. You're not getting me like that. Not Glynmor Jones. I've got a lot of fish to fry before I get married. You have the kid if you want it. But you're not having me. This is just one of your bastard tricks isn't it? That's what Daisy did didn't she? Well it's not going to work. Not this time it's not. I'm not marrying you and that's bastard that.'

Guto came running down the side of the neighbouring Valley so fast his legs almost ran away with him. It was a fiercely hot day, full of midges and drifting dandelion seeds, making breathing as difficult as swallowing lumps of toffee.

Sweat poured off Guto's brow as he stood still near a refuse tip and studied Bomber's piece of paper again. It was the simple child-like diagram of a mound with the rough sketch of something like a tree next to it. At the base of the lump was a big arrow pointing to a spot marked X with MONEY written next to it.

The more he studied the map the more he had come to believe that it had the same outline as the Tonypandy tip. He now took a trowel out of his oil-stained pocket and began digging a hold at the spot marked X.

The sun scorched down into the refuse hatching thousands of wriggling white maggots and a smell as striking as a punch on the nose. But Guto, hardened by a life of scavenging, hardly noticed anything. For the first time in his life he had the smell of some real money in his nostrils – money with which he could get a fitted set of false teeth – and just for those teeth alone he would have dug right through a hundred tips.

He had been toiling for about half an hour when his trowel bumped into the side of a carboard box. His excitement mounting, he excavated all around it, finally managing to work it free. It had not even been opened. He ripped open the lid to find, inside it, not Bomber's money but a brand-new tumble drier.

Perhaps the money was in another tip altogether, he thought as he hoisted the tumble drier on his shoulder and began the epic walk up one side of the valley and down into Bont. It was so heavy he could only walk very slowly, the sweat pouring out of him in great fists as he struggled up the stony path. Sometimes he had to put the tumble drier down and sit on it to catch his breath before staggering on again. It was terribly heavy. *Duw* he could actually feel his balls cracking up. The thought of what he might do with it had never occurred to him.

Chapter Eight

The white cards, inviting family and friends to the wedding of Glynmor Jones and Margaret Evans, had gold edging and fancy silver letters. The service would be at 11 a.m. at the Libanus Chapel. The reception would be at 12.30 in the Miners' Welfare Hall. R.S.V.P.

When the great day arrived there were such savage summer showers the sheep huddled together under the dry stone walls and even the retired pit ponies went back into the colliery looking for shelter. They stopped, they started, they stopped again did these showers. You just never knew where you were with them. One minute it was sunny then it was some bastard monsoon. You poked your hand out of the door and it had stopped. You stepped out with your shopping bag and it had stopped. You made your way to the Co-op and – *wham!* – a shower started out of nothing with those raindrops smacking against your cheeks and getting right inside your collar to dribble the length of your fed-up backbone.

Stop – start – stop. Cloud – sun – cloud again. Wet – dry – wet again. It was pure valley weather this. Bont weather. In such weather it was best not to take a chance. In such weather it was always best to stay indoors.

But the trouble was that, this day, Glynmor Jones was marrying Margaret Evans so everyone would have to come out sooner or later.

In Maggie's home her mother and sister Daisy were anxiously pinning and repinning the bride's white wedding dress in some vain effort to soften the romping contours of the pregnant bulge which told its own sorry story of sex before the altar. Everyone knew the naughty news, of course. Getting to the altar without actually being banged up was only something the posh from somewhere like Cardiff did. The villagers even knew the date the baby was due.

For his part Glynmor had finally given in under pressure from Maggie's family and accepted that he couldn't have pulled it out soon enough after all. The previous Saturday morning he had gone off to the Dak's suit factory in Caerphilly where, once a month, they sold off their rejects. For three pounds ten shillings he had got a smashing blue mohair suit even if one trouser leg was slightly shorter than the other. He had also acquired a pair of black winkle-picker shoes, a bright green tie and a pair of pink socks which had all but made his Aunty Maude faint when she beheld their luminous splendour.

'You can't get married in them,' she exlaimed aghast.

'Why not?'

'It's a good job your mother's not still alive. She wouldn't have let you get married in pink socks.'

'They're better than no socks at all.'

'Not that much better, they're not.'

Glynmor's best man, Dai Waterboard, had also gone and bought himself a second. He might even have looked as splendid as Glynmor but for the fault in the suit which he had only spotted too late. Dai did not somehow look quite right with his white carnation, Brylcreemed hair and his fly held together with a large safety pin.

The rain eased off for a second and, at that appointed hour, half the village sprinted up the slope. Most got inside the chapel before yet another shower started. It pounded down that rain did, hammering on the grey slate roof and banging on the wooden door of the vestry like a gang of bailiffs come to take possession.

Maggie exercised her womanly right in getting to the altar five minutes late. However, because of some even obscurer custom, Glynmor and his best man arrived later still. It was going to be one of those weddings, Rev. Mordecai decided, as he watched the two of them dash up the aisle and stand before him, soaking wet and stinking of beer.

After the first hymn Rev. Mordecai said his bit about the dearly beloved being all gathered here in the sight of God but then it all began going wrong when he asked the pair to take their marriage vows.

Glynmor managed to make his reply, but, when Rev. Mordecai asked Maggie if she would have this man to be her wedded husband, she broke down in helpless laughter. It wasn't that she wanted to be disrespectful to the vicar. It was just that she was so overwhelmingly happy that she had actually finally got Glynmor to be her wedded husband she just felt like laughing. And laugh she did. Like a drain she laughed, with her head bent forward under her veil and her shoulders shaking up and down like a pair of see-sawing jelly fish.

This outbreak of mirth confirmed Glynmor's doubts about the whole venture. Even when she did finally get her 'I will' out and he took the ring off Dai Waterboard to slip on her fat finger he wished he was back in the Welfare Hall drinking beer with the boys. He had slipped up badly here and no mistake.

And why hadn't this giggling moron taken any precautions either? That was the woman's job wasn't it? It wasn't the man's job to have to mess about with things like that. It spoiled his enjoyment. She had just wanted to trap him she had.

After the Lord's Prayer the Rev. Mordecai, clearly disgusted by all this levity in a house of God, then chimed in with a few words of his own: 'The Bible teaches us many things about our Lord Jesus but nowhere in the Bible do we read of Him actually laughing.' At this point he stopped and waited for Maggie to take control of herself again.

'This absence of laughter is not surprising when you think about it,' the Rev. went on. 'Laughter makes fun of our most precious things. Laughter is what dirty little boys do in lavatories. Laughter is all jests and dirty jokes. There was no laughter with the holy men of old. As soon as laughter enters a marriage it is finished.'

Maggie had now stopped laughing and just stood there taking hold of Glynmor's wrist and keeping her head bowed. She had just never realised that laughter rated with adultery as a mortal sin.

Glynmor, however, was quite positive in his own mind that laughter and adultery – together with the drink – rated the absolute top of the pops and just stood there glaring at the vicar wondering whether to stick the head into him.

'It is not really surprising that it is raining today,' the Rev. went on in that soft merry way of his. 'All this rain is but a sign of the way God is feeling about a marriage like this. It's His way of showing His sadness at the way young people are not keeping one another for the altar.'

Isolated snorts of suppressed laughter burst out of various parts of the congregation at this point while Glynmor turned around to them waving his hand around and around as if turning a starting handle while giving one of his best dirty shark's teeth smiles. Dai Waterboard had to smother his mouth with a handkerchief.

'The reason why marriage is everywhere failing is because the young now insist on regarding it as purely a laughing matter,' the Rev. continued. 'They think it is all a bit of a laugh for the woman to get pregnant before holy matrimony ...'

Apart from Aunty Maude, whose hat was nodding in agreement with the Rev.'s every pained word, the laughter in the congregation was now becoming louder and more widespread. Many of the men had their heads down behind the pews with the women biting hard on their fingers as their eyes watered and they tried to keep a straight face. Glynmor was now back on his starting handle while Dai Waterboard's handkerchief was fluttering out in front of his face like washing in a high wind.

'They think it is all a bit of a laugh to come to the altar late and smelling of alcohol,' the Rev. began shouting above the increasing laughter. 'They think it is all a bit of a laugh to roll around in the slime of their carnal lusts. And when the woman becomes pregnant they think it is all a bit of a laugh to claim it's something to do with the wind.'

That was it. The vicar's seriousness was all too much for them at that point and, as one, the whole congregation collapsed into helpless, terminal laughter.

'Is this wedding finished or are you going to keep us here all day?' Glynmor asked out straight when most of the laughter had subsided.

'The minister is supposed to say a few words but ...'

'Are we married or not?' Glynmor interrupted him again.

'You are indeed. But God ...'

'Right. Come on Mag.' He took her by the elbow and led her firmly down the aisle as he lectured her. 'You be sure, in the future, to laugh any time you want do you hear? Any time you want.' The further away he walked the louder he made his voice so that the vicar could hear his every word. 'At any time you feel like laughing then you get laughing. When you feel a

92

laugh coming then it's just like a fart. You've got to let it rip. You've got to get it out. And if anyone tells you otherwise then you tell them "Bollocks" from Glynmor.'

As the newly-married couple left the vestry, followed by all the highly-entertained friends and guests, God must have changed His mind about the marriage since bright hard sunshine was bouncing everywhere, glittering on the grey slate roofs, glowing ferocious on the windows and drying up the asphalt on the road in huge steaming patches.

Maggie could never remember feeling happier as they both walked hand in hand down the hill to the reception in the Welfare Hall. Glynmor walking out of the chapel like that had confirmed what she had always felt – that our Glynmor was thrillingly unique.

As they walked ahead of the procession of guests other people came out of their homes, smiling and waving at the happy couple. Blackbirds flew in cheeping bunches overhead. Car horns were sounded. Maggie's eyes misted up and she waved regally when she again began laughing uncontrollably.

The Jones family had always been popular in the Valleys but even Glynmor was surprised at all the local characters who had come flocking from all parts of South Wales for the reception. As they filed into the Welfare Hall they put their presents on a display table in the Rainbow Room and, to date, there were blankets, two bedspreads, four sets of glasses, a tea set, cushions and, unbelievably, a tumble drier given by Guto. It even had a receipt suspiciously attached to it. So what were all those scratches doing on its side then?

Some fool even gave some baby clothes which, fortunately, were spotted before Maggie's mother inspected the presents and quietly removed them.

Dai the Rat had walked over from Porth and it was the first time many in Bont had seen him since he had officially retired as the chief rat-catcher in all the pits in the Valley. He could track down those rats in the pitch dark could Dai the Rat. No rat ever slept sound when Dai was around.

Three Teddy boys from Treorchy, distant cousins of Maggie's side, coming over looking simply wonderful in their multi-coloured Edwardian suits as they stood together combing their hair. Then there was poor Danny Bits and Pieces, his pockets full of all manner of odds and ends with the fork of his trousers hanging so low it was if he was joined at the knees. Even his jacket was so bulky he might have had a few dozen ferrets secreted in the lining.

No one quite knew who had invited Danny Bits and Pieces since he was not quite sixteen ounces to the pound and might at any moment go pot-holing under the chairs while the guests were eating. His latest stunt was to keep his wrist watch in his pint of beer as he drank it – just to show that it was water-proof. 'See, boys, I can drink and tell the time as well.'

Then there was Dan Bag O'Shit who once used to be the drinking butty of the singer Tom Jones' bodyguard down in Pontypridd. Ted John North, a wiry Anglesey man who had been the veteran of many sheep and dog rescues down the steep narrow gullies of the Valley, was there. So was Exactly Jones, a money-lender with crocodile shoes from Church Village, who came with the fancy woman he was living tally with – and their dog.

Everyone was surprised and delighted to see Donny Hughes – Donny the Ding, the young banjo player from Sunny Hill, whose playing had once delighted the whole of Bont. Donny had taken lodgings down in Cardiff as his launching pad for crashing into the big time. No one ever quite knew what had happened to him since he had gone to that infernal city but he had clearly gone as daft as trimmings. Where once he had been a tidy boy, swilling behind his ears every morning and going around delivering *Echos* on his bicycle, he now had long black dandruffed hair with huge sun glasses, and had turned into a self-styled Prince of Darkness in his black velvet cape. His ideas about orgies, drugs and Satan worship all but made the elderly women swoon in terror when he spoke of them over a bag of crisps and a pint of All-Bright.

Donny the Ding's girl friend, Splodge, was very strange too. Not only did she seem to be unable to use the English language, as they do speak it around 'ere, but she also seemed to favour baking flour for her make-up with dartboards of mascara around her eyes and black lipstick, for goodness sake! Black? I ask you. There's no shape on 'er at all. And even so early in the morning she looks out of it don't she? Drugs she's on. Smoking that LSE.

Everyone, of course, was still talking about the Rev. Mordecai's outburst against the sin of enjoying yourself in the chapel. It was further evidence – if any were needed – that he was beginning to crack up. 'And don't you come in here claiming the boy's wind,' they would mimic out loud. 'Next thing you'll be saying that Glynmor's dick is a bicycle pump.'

Maggie moved through all the people and laughter, glass of Pomagne in hand, with all the quiet pride of a gardener inspecting his prize allotment. Sometimes she stopped for a chat or a quick kiss. But most of the time she was keeping her eye on Glynmor, who had barely moved from the bar since they had all come in. 'You'd think he would at least go around and welcome the guests wouldn't you?' she whispered to her mother.

Glynmor was on his fourth pint of the morning and telling his favourite dirty story about the queer who got raped by a gorilla in the African bush when the call went out for everyone to take their places for the meal.

He finished his pint in one gulp and Dai Waterboard bought him a fresh one before going to the place of honour next to the bride on the trestle tables in the Starlight Suite. Some wine was then served and Maggie was alarmed when she noticed that Glynmor was now mixing up the wine with his beer. 'Cool head now, Glynmor,' she said touching him lightly on the wrist. 'We've got all day you know.'

The soup was served and Glynmor gave his first indication that all that wine and beer had gone straight to his head since he soon managed to get his new green tie floating in the Brown Windsor. She shook the drops off it and tucked it inside his shirt, next opening the napkin and placing it on his lap. 'Did I tell you how much I liked your new suit today?' she asked.

'Three quid in Dak's,' he said cryptically.

'Three quid in what?'

'Three quid in a sale over in Caerphilly. It's a reject see. One leg is shorter than the other.'

'Oh I see. Did you get those fabulous socks in that sale as well?'

'Oh no,' he said missing the edge of her sarcasm and picking up his soup spoon. 'I got those new in Woolworth's in Ponty. Five bob they cost. Like them do you?'

'They're lovely,' she said deadpan. 'Just lovely I do call them.'

'I'm glad you like them,' he said, whereupon he started slurping his soup like he had just got his snout into the trough.

He had another swig on his wine followed by another on his soup when he turned to her with a wink. 'I'm telling you now and this is a fact,' he said. 'This soup here is thirty farts to the ounce.'

'Oh that's a fact, is it?' she asked.

'It is. So hang onto your bedclothes when the thunder starts in bed tonight.'

It's a funny thing, Maggie thought, how one second you think you are madly in love with a man and the next second you would quite cheerfully drown him in his own soup. She finished her own soup and wiped the corners of her mouth carefully and theatrically before putting the big question to her new husband. 'Tell me Glynmor. Why is everything some sort of dirty joke with you?'

'You're beginning to sound like that daft old vicar.'

'You just can't say anything unless it's filthy, can you?'

'Bollocks.'

'If you do have a clean thought ... *if* ... do you throw dirt over it before it gets out?'

'I'll be throwing some dirt over you if you don't watch it.'

'Did your mother ever wash your mouth out as a child did she?'

'Leave my mother out of this.'

Even though they were arguing out of the sides of their mouths in low grumbling tones everyone was now watching them intently as they had their very first married quarrel.

One man who was taking particular interest was Emlyn Kremlin who took out his fob watch and checked the time. Somehow he did not see this marriage lasting long. He liked Glynmor well enough – let's face it *everyone* liked Glynmor well enough – but feared that he was too much of a Valley boyo to make any marriage work. Valley boyos liked the beer too much and loved nothing more than chasing new bits of skirt. The most complicated things they did was to fill in a betting slip. Their greatest exercise was leaning against the wall outside the Labour Exchange. They had no fidelity to people and issues like Emlyn's generation. His generation had always been faithful in their politics, work and marriages. His generation of men had always gone home on Friday afternoons and put their unopened pay packets on the table. He doubted if Glynmor would get home on a Friday afternoon let alone hand over his pay packet unopened.

It was a great shame really, Emlyn thought. His niece

Maggie was a fine girl with fine ideals. She would have made someone a fine and faithful wife as well. But not for Glynmor. He was a firebrand, a leader in odd sort of way what with his fluency with words and ability to make men laugh. When he stopped messing about he might even be able to do something very well indeed. He did have bottle and a certain recklessness. But what he would never be was a husband. Not as long as he had a hole in his arse he wouldn't.

As the chicken salad was being served there came a scream from one of the other tables. Danny Bits and Pieces was yet again demonstrating the ancient custom of pot-holing between people's legs and yet again everyone was asking who had invited the dopey sod. The Evans tribe blamed the Jones tribe and the Jones tribe blamed the Evans tribe.

When the ice cream and strawberries were finished Dai Waterboard, none too sober, read out the usual crop of vulgar messages. 'Today's the day, tonight's the night, we've shot the stork so you're all right,' he sniggered. 'From Aunty Mae and Uncle Ernie in Rhyl.' He also thanked the guests for their presents but wondered aloud who had the nerve to give the happy couple baby clothes. What kind of present was that? What were they trying to say? Nudge, nudge. More lewd telegrams.

Later still the drink flowed more freely and tables were cleared away. The celebrations moved into overdrive. Donny the Ding forsook his banjo for the piano and quite soon everyone was giving a spirited rendering of *Toot, Toot, Tootsie*; *Old Man River* and *Begin the Beguine*. They all danced the *Breakaway Blues* and the *Royal Rhumba*.

The first real solo was performed by Peter Star – a Bont collier who usually spent an unhealthy amount of time patting and combing his hair – who did *Old Macdonald's Farm*. He took off the likes of Harold Wilson, James Stewart and John Wayne in each verse but, by the time he got near the end, he was so drunk he kept mixing them up with one another.

Biscuits tried to do Elvis Presley's *O Sole Mio* but the sound was so unutterably awful a group carried him off to the lavatory where he was locked in and left to get on with it alone. Dan Bag O'Shit played a rapturous tango on the spoons.

Away with the fairies though he clearly was even Glynmor got up when it was nearly time to go and sang that deathless, tear-stained legend of the man who, when mashed up in a motor bike accident, lifted up his broken neck and warbled *Tell Laura I Love Her*. The applause was rapturous and, by now, Glynmor was enjoying himself so much he did not want to go on honeymoon at all. 'We'll go tomorrow,' he kept shouting as Maggie dragged him out of the hall. 'Who wants to go to bastard Barry Island anyway?'

He was bundled into the back of Penguin's Mercedes hire car and was still trying to get out, with Maggie hauling him in by one arm, when, beneath a hail of rice and confetti, the car took off with a row of tin cans and old boots tied to the rear bumper.

The reception was far from over, however. Now the serious drinking began when Aunty Phyllis passed out Lucozade bottles full of her lethal, smoking, home-made punch. No one ever knew what went into this alcoholic Molotov cocktail. It blew your brains away with a wallop which separated you from the world just as convincingly as death. The very smell of it drove you bananas. All that you really knew about it for sure was that it was best drunk already lying down, preferably in a bed.

It appeared that she had made a special dozen bottles for the occasion and, in no time at all, everyone was as pissed as parrots with the various tribes half-clinging to one another and half-falling about like the dazed survivors of a nuclear holocaust. Donny the Ding pounded those ivories and the women hitched up their dresses to do the can-can. The men, many with the tails of their shirts hanging out, formed impromptu choirs. Even Dai the Rat did a small tap dance until he too fell over.

A large group was shuffling around together in one corner of the dance floor doing some strange tribal dance revealed, on closer inspection, to be the beginnings of a brawl. Biscuits was still in the lavatory doing his terrible imitation of Elvis Presley. Some dirty bastard was being sick over Aunty Maude's new hat.

Unnoticed by the revellers the day bowed out of the Valley. As the blotto throng continued with their celebrations, Walford and Daisy were even now downstairs in the committee room having a bit of a rub on the committee's sacred, circular, polished table. Daisy, very badly affected by Aunty Phyllis' punch, was hanging onto Walford's neck so tight it was as if she was up to her neck in a swamp and about to go under at any second.

The committee chairman's wife, Maisy Million, was on her way to the lavatory when she first heard those suspicious grunts and sighs coming out of the locked committee room. She immediately abandoned the mission at hand and went upstairs to the bar. There she told her husband Max that she suspected that some couple were having it away in the committee room. As chairman, Max took a very strong line on people having such fun in his club. A man of striking, dark features, his brow was always furrowed in a permanent frown. Now it hardened as if encased in cement at this disturbing information.

He called over his sidekick, Stan Prees, another committee man, and they both went below to investigate the matter.

Walford was in full thrust with his hips exploding against Daisy, whose nose was only just poking up out of the swamp, when the committee room door flew open and the unamused faces of Max Million and Stan Rees were revealed.

'Well, well,' said Stan. 'This looks like one for the committee, Max.'

'You can say that again Stan,' said Max.

'Oh blimey,' was about all Walford could manage.

'Oh shit,' said Daisy, strangely sober and sinking into her swamp.

'But on the committee table,' Max said, pained. 'The committee table, mun.'

Maggie sat upright in her hotel bed, her arms folded, and the corners of her mouth turned down. Wearing her new négligée she looked very fetching as the bright lights of Barry Island funfair flashed across the darkened room. It was little after ten.

But where was her Glynmor? Her new husband had somehow gone missing. He had gone into the bathroom but did not seem at all keen on coming out again. She heard the shower going and decided that he had just gone in there to sober up. But now he had been taking a shower for over an hour which seemed excessive even by Glynmor's excessive standards. A sudden thought came to her. That Hitchcock film – *North by Northwest* – when Cary Grant pretended to be taking a shower so that he could listen in on something while out of the room.

Maybe Glynmor's up to something, she thought with a twinge of alarm.

She slipped quickly out of the bed and opened the bathroom door. But there he was, still taking that shower, still fully clothed in his new Dak's mohair suit and horrid pink socks. Even more alarmingly he had somehow managed to get hold of a Lucozade bottle full of Aunty Phyllis' punch. Standing under the running water with his head bowed, he would occasionally lift his head and take another swig of that lethal punch. She had never seen anyone so ratted. And this was her new husband! Cary Grant he wasn't, that was for sure.

'Glynmor! Get in this bed!' she cried.

He looked up at her with eyes which were but tiny dead spots. 'As of tonight,' he shouted as if he was trying to be heard in the Butlin's Holiday Camp on the other side of the island. 'Asoftonight,' he repeated. 'I am never going to drink again. Neverdrinkagain.'

He was about to take another swig when she grabbed him by the wrist and yanked him out of the shower so sharply she sent him whirling across the bedroom like a spinning top. He collapsed on the floor by the side of the bed with the bottle still miraculously glued to his hand. Then he began to weep inconsolably.

Maggie stood over him with her hands whirling around uselessly. Just what was she going to do now? 'Come on Glynmor. Let's get you undressed.'

With that he began to wail so loudly she began to worry that he was in real pain, sitting down next to him and putting a comforting arm over his shoulders.

'Just promise me one thing,' he blubbered. 'Promise me one thing.'

'Anything my lovely.'

'If the baby's a boy ...'

'Yes, if it's a boy.'

'If the boy's a baby ... we'll call it Jampots.'

'Jampots. Yes.'

'If the baby's a baby. Jampots. Not if it's a girl mind. If the girl's a boy. Jampots. Right?'

'Anything you want my lovely. You are the father after all.'

'I'm not the fucking father. Not me.' He scrambled to his

100

feet like someone had lit a fire under his bum. 'Not me. No sir. Not this boy.' He took another swig from his bottle and, for a moment, Maggie feared he was going to brain her with it. Indeed he looked just like a murderer in a Hammer horror film as he swayed dangerously, bottle in hand with the multi-coloured fairground lights flashing all over him. She was going to get that Aunty Phyllis for this.

'Me! The father? Huh. Do I look like the father? Are you a father? Look at you. A fat father. Fucking fat. There's nothing left for me any more now. You trapped me in pain you did. Yes you. Just pain and that's a fact. That's what I've got. My pain. Here. See? See this belly button? That belly button is all pain.'

Maggie was now crying softly into her palms. He was not making a lot of sense but it was sense enough to her. He would never believe that he was the father. He would always be accusing her of trapping him in marriage – no matter if he was drunk or sober. He would always be going on about it for the rest of her life. She knew our Glynmor.

Glynmor pushed her to one side and hurled himself into the bathroom. He vomited loudly and abundantly. The honkings were amplified by the porcelain pan and Maggie sat listening to him talking to the Lord on the great white telephone with a great strange sense of emptiness inside her.

Something had gone wrong somewhere and that was a fact, as Glynmor himself might have said. He gave another long whinnying heave. They didn't have men like Glynmor in Mills and Boon – thank heavens. There was no puking up and foul language with them. They said nice things, all romantic, in Mills and Boon.

On the drive down here in Penguin's Mercedes Glynmor had stopped belching long enough to pick up her hand and ask her if he had ever told her what his Uncle Ianto had always said.

'No. What does your Uncle Ianto always say?'

'He always told me never to go out with a girl with big hands 'cos it makes your dick look small.'

'Oh that's a fact, is it?'

'Aye girl that is a fact.'

She was stuck with him now, him and his elegant wit, the wonder lover of the valleys, here on his wedding night, soaked to the skin and throwing his guts up into the toilet. She sighed and looked down at her hands. They weren't all that big.

Suddenly tiring of all this she stood up and got dressed, walking out of the hotel and down to the sea-front where the promenade lights were strung out all around her like a giant gaudy necklace. Just behind her was the funfair and over on the prow of the distant hill the giant neon castle of Billy Butlin's, a place she had hoped never to visit on a holiday or any other day come to that. Far away across the Bristol Channel were the distant promenade lights of Weston-super-Mare. A warm wind whipped in over the sand buffeting the sea-front walls with the numbers painted on them. When they had come to Barry they had always gone in front of the Number Three wall. That had always been the Evans spot, that had.

She leaned against the Number Three wall, looking down at the self-same spot where they had spent all those blessed sunshine days. A patch of smooth sand it was with a derelict sand castle in it now, all lit up by the brilliance of the moon. The Evans family would come here three or four times during the summer – or else for the Whitsun treat, with the chapel, when trains from all over the valleys queued up for hours to get into the station and again to get out again in the evening.

As soon as they got off the train she remembered that they would run as fast as they could to bag a place just here in front of the Number Three wall. Here they'd sit together making sandcastles, drinking tea out of a Thermos and eating tomato sandwiches which always seemed to have sand in them. Funny thing but she had always hated tomato sandwiches unless they were out on Barry sands.

She gulped the fresh sea air, feeling a little better now as her mind wandered in the corridors of her most pleasant memories. She could even see her father with a knotted handkerchief on his head and trousers rolled up to just below the knees as he paddled around in the dirty, brown waves. And there was Mam sitting next to her buttering yet more bread for yet more tomato sandwiches.

But Mam had never wanted to come to Barry any more after Dad had died. A lot went out of their lives when he left them. Some nights she could hear her Mam lying in bed still talking to him in her sleep, still asking him to do things about the house.

Maggie swallowed hard, remembering how she and Daisy used to make buckets out of old baked bean tins, how they'd spend hours building sandcastles which were then swept away by the tide. Then there were the donkeys which took you down into the water, and the Salvation Army band which played to try and save your soul.

They'd been wonderful hours out on these sands, aye they had. They had been gurgling days which had gone in and out as regular as the tides; the world outside was gigantic and hostile but that did not matter because, for the moment, you were safe and protected. And urgently happy.

That was why she had wanted to come back here for her honeymoon. She had wanted to reap a few of those golden hours again. She wanted to savour those great days once more. But you could never do that, could you? Those you loved went and left you. Those you didn't love came right into your life and made you unhappy. Sometimes those you loved didn't love you and that was worse than anything. That was her big problem wasn't it? Her Glynmor was just too selfish to know anything about love. That Glynmor who she still loved more than life itself.

She walked up through the terraced gardens and over the road to the funfair. The smell of frying hot dogs mingled with and dominated that of chips and candy floss. A woman in a stall offered her some hoop-la rings. 'A nice prize for everyone, dearie,' she called, but Maggie had already won one prize too many that day. The dodgem cars went banging and swerving around her, the people on the scenic railway screamed out their delicious fear at her. She stopped and looked up at the lights of the giant big wheel as it bore down on her from high above.

But, instead of hauling her out of the dumps, all this noise and laughter made her whole body ache with sadness. She began crying again; from a nearby loudspeaker the voice of Otis Redding sang of how they called him Mr Pitiful.

She stood outside the Haunted House with the noise filling up her mind, and the coloured lights glittering in her tears. Just over there she had once caught her Dada watching What The Butler Saw in a peep-show. Him a teacher and doing that! Just here Mama had held her when she was crying her eyes out after bumping her nose while driving the dodgem cars. She wanted her Dada to come and hold her again. She wanted her Mama to

103

come over and kiss away the pain. She wanted simple love, that's all she wanted. She knew that well enough. What she didn't want was to be married to a man who hated her. She just wanted a few of those golden Barry hours back again. Dear God, that wasn't too much to ask for. Well was it?

Back in Bont the wedding reception was winding down. Groups of guests had broken up into a dozen competing choirs. Ragged versions of *Sospan Fach* fought with off-key renditions of *Bread of Heaven*. Hymns grappled with drunken arias. Everyone, just everyone, was as drunk as skunks. They fell over one another, they held one another up. Dai Waterboard's feet could just be seen poking out from beneath one of the tables. Biscuits was still locked in the lavatory, singing his Elvis Presley numbers. Emlyn Kremlin was done for too, sitting there in his shirt and braces conducting one of the choirs with a bread roll. Even Exactly Jones' dog had got into Aunty Phyllis' punch. He was a depraved pisshead at the best of times, with a perverse taste for goosing cats. People swore that they saw him stagger out of the Hall, lift a leg up against the lamp post and collapse flat on his back, pissing himself.

As they came out of the Hall, stepping over the comatose dog, it was Dan Bag O'Shit who opened the traditional assault on the village clock by hurling an empty flagon of cider at it. Next to step up was Donny the Ding who flung a rock. His girl friend, Splodge, threw a milk bottle. Others stepped forward to take a shy at the luckless clock; but, it being late and their eyesight blurred, most missed by a mile. Rocks, bottles, plates, shoes ... anything that could be thrown at the brightly-lit Roman numerals.

No one had ever worked out where this strange custom had come from and what, if anything, it signified. It was never planned either; it simply happened about three or four times a year when the whole village expressed its communal happiness by flinging things at the clock. It was a time when even the ubiquitous sheep stayed well clear of the area.

Fortunately the flat-bed clock had been built in an age when they built clocks to withstand a siege. No matter what hit it, the hands kept going around and around, marking out the hours and minutes in the life of this Valley of coal.

Chapter Nine

It was one of those days in the Valley which was neither sunny nor rainy, neither hot nor cold. It was just a nothing day, reflected P.C. Watkins as he stood in his living-room ironing his uniform. As befitted the long arm of the law in the village, his flat was immaculately polished and tidy. Police school certificates had been framed and hung on the wall, silver soccer trophies bedecked the mantelpiece. P.C. Watkins, forty-six years old and a confirmed bachelor, took an intense pride in order and tidiness. The way a man lived on the outside, he believed, was a sure sign of how he was inside.

The actual police station downstairs was a model of polished cleanliness as well. P.C. Watkins was not too proud to go down on his knees and scrub the floor himself. He was given an allowance to hire a cleaner but none of them ever seemed to do the job to his exacting satisfaction. No one seemed to take a pride in their work any longer, he reckoned. So he did it himself.

Just behind the reception area was the cell, so warm and sunny he kept his tomato plants in it. There never was much of a call on his cell unless Curly had been thrown out by his wife again and wanted somewhere to get his head down for the night until she had cooled down. Such crime as there was had, by and large, been trivial and easily detected. It was difficult to have a quiet fart in Bont without half the street knowing about it and, sooner or later, P.C. Watkins, who had been blessed with a fine and ferocious sense of gossip, would get to know about it too.

For a long, long time the only incident that had stayed in his memory was when a whole rack of sunglasses had disappeared from the chemist's. P.C. Watkins had soon tracked them down, since the culprit, Danny Bits and Pieces, who was never sixteen ounces to the pound, had been selling them for a penny each in the Hall. P.C. Watkins just walked into the bar and found virtually everyone sitting there wearing sunglasses with tiny gold stickers on them.

For the rest of the time it was the not unpleasant routine of old pit ponies dropping dead in the street, the odd domestic argument that had got out of control or a spot of after-hours drinking that had gone on long enough even by the boozy standards of the Valley.

Things changed when Gnasher and the Clay Class began performing in earnest.

When P.C. Watkins saw them coming out of the shop weighed down by salmon, the shock of actually apprehending someone in the act of burglary and the prospect of locking Gnasher up with his tomato plants had been so great that the constable had begun to wonder if the Mafia had finally decided to set up their headquarters in Bont – or worse. This was real breaking and entering, he told the old-timers on the bench near the clock. Imagine Bont lads making off with loot in the middle of the night. Kids whose parents you grew up with. And then all they got was a bit of probation. They didn't seem at all ashamed either. It was the parents he blamed. It's the telly, said the old-timers.

The bell on the station desk rang and he went down to find Mrs Muriel Davies there with a query. If a dog did his jobs outside her door was it illegal to scoop it up and take it to the dog owner's home and post it through his letter box?

P.C. Watkins shook his head from side to side. 'The long and short of it Mrs Davies, is that I just don't know.'

'You're the policeman here, aren't you?'

'That is correct.'

'Well why don't you know then?'

'It's a problem I've never come across before.'

'Well I done it. I posted the dog's jobs and he's coming to see you. I'm turning myself in first. I done it.'

'Who's coming to see me?' P.C. Watkins asked trying to keep a straight face. Mrs Davies took herself awful serious when she got going.

'Percy Pugh. He says he's going to have me locked up so I'm turning myself in. I done it.'

'Well I'd better check what law you've broken first Mrs Davies. Will you come and turn yourself in again after I've checked with headquarters?'

'What time would that be?'

'Come about five and I'll know by then.'

Mrs Davies left and P.C. Watkins was about to close the station door when he spotted the Clay Class all heading down to the railway sidings. He watched them intently as something sickly turned over inside his belly. They were up to something that lot. That was a racing certainty that was.

He was fairly sure that they were not up to anything criminal but was highly suspicious at the way they seemed to be so happy all the time. He saw them at odd times of the day, gathered on the swings in the playground or down on the river bank, all forever laughing their socks off. He had never known anything like it and wished it would stop. He far preferred them when they were moody and scowling. That was the way he preferred the Clay Class.

Not that they laughed much when he was around. Their smiles froze at the very sight of his uniform and they stared cold at him and ran away. Come to think of it there'd been reports that a load of hospital ether had been stolen from Tonypandy hospital. He had read that funny things happened to people when they sniffed on that. He wondered if a bottle of that might be accounting for all this riotous laughter.

He closed the station door and picked up the telephone, dialling headquarters in Pontypridd. 'Hello sarge. It's Trevor Watkins in Bont here. Tell me now. What do you know about the law relating to dog shit?'

That same afternoon, in the basement of the Welfare Hall, the committee was also worrying about matters of crime and punishment as they prepared to consider the latest crop of infringements of the sacred rules of clubland. You name it and they had a rule about it. If any misbehaviour was not quite covered by one rule they could usually get you with a sub-section of another. Every smallest corner and cupboard of the club was penetrated and fully covered by some clause or another and, as befits the chairman, Max Million knew every one of them. He wielded the rule book with the ferocity of a tomahawk; those neatly numbered lines of fine print even staked out the parameters of his thoughts and he might even, right in the middle of the night, wake up and begin reciting out loud, say, rule 16 sub-section II; *No payment shall be made from the Welfare Hall's banking account except by a cheque signed by the chairman and treasurer.*

'So what if the chairman and treasurer are sick?' his wife might ask, merely trying to wind him up.

'Then the cheque will not be paid until chairman and treasurer are fully recovered.'

The committee took their duties seriously. Even as they sat around their great polished table, some scratching their balls or clearing out their ears with a matchstick, you could tell from the starched immobility of their features, that these were men come together to do serious business. There was no laughter in committee meetings under Max Million's chairmanship. When he was in the chair it might have been the annual general meeting of some secret police controlling a Caribbean banana republic for all the laughs he allowed.

These chapel-solemn men were the very fabric of the Welfare Hall. All posters were signed by order of the committee. The committee patrolled every room during opening hours. The committee could elect honorary members. A committee man could refuse admission to anyone at such times as they deemed it to be of interest to the club. They could expel, suspend or issue a lengthy reprimand. They could issue beer cheques for favours done to the club or, conversely, stop someone drinking there for any offence, like being caught pinching a lavatory roll. The committee had the right to call any member to appear before them to explain themselves at their disciplinary meetings on Sunday afternoons. If a member chose not to turn up then so much the worse for them. Under CIU rules the minimum was a one-year ban from using the Hall which, since it was the social centre of the village and only provider of strong drink, was death.

Most of their disciplinary sessions were spent adjudicating on and punishing matters relating to fighting, swearing or the bingo sessions. Today, however, it was all far worse. Today they had to deal with the sad and sorry case of Walford Evans and the incident with Daisy Bland.

Even to think about that horrific sight made Max Million sick to the very core. Was nothing at all sacred? The limit of the committee's sanctions was to expel a member for life but he wished that there was something far worse that he could impose. Fornication was bad enough but when it was right here on the committee table? He lifted his elbows up off the polished mahogany at the very thought of it.

Neither was Daisy at all repentant, he was mortified to see, when she was called to explain herself. She just sat down in front of them with a cigarette in her hand and smiled.

'Have you anything to say about this alleged incident?' Chairman Max asked. Even when cases like this touched his bare nerve so deeply he always tried to be fair. What you had to say about Max was that he was always fair.

'Well there's nothing alleged about the incident, is there Max?' said Daisy taking another puff of her cigarette. 'I mean you caught us bang to rights, didn't you?'

'In committee we call Max, Mr Chairman,' said Max's lieutenant, Stan Rees.

'Oh do we?' asked Daisy all sarcastic. 'That's nice for you then init?'

'Would you mind telling us how long this has been going on?' asked Max.

'No.'

'No what?'

'No Max.'

The men sat glaring at Daisy who crossed and uncrossed her legs in great shiverings of rustling nylons. She had deliberately not put on her brassière and her nipples stuck out like walnuts. She enjoyed the hold that she had over men and even now knew which of them would be mentally pulling down her knickers and getting twinges in their sad little worms. Daisy wasn't like the rest of the women around the Valleys. She wasn't scared of these oafs who saw the wife as little more than a doormat who cleaned the house, cooked the food and got fucked, if she was lucky, late and badly on a Saturday night. Daisy was only like Daisy and that was the way she was going to stay.

'You see Daisy,' said Max holding up his hand carefully and theatrically while examining the surface of the table, presumably for any signs of scuff or stains. 'This is a most serious matter. Most serious indeed. If you must have affairs with men it is not normally our business. But this was with the bingo caller, who is in our employ, and on the committee table, which is our property.'

'Damaged then, is it?' asked Daisy, leaning forward and

studying the table along with the rest of the committee.

'There's a long scratch up here,' said Geraint James.

'There's a burn mark down here,' said Brian Thomas.

'Now hold it just there,' said Daisy. 'Now I don't know what the committee does when *they* have a fuck ...'

'Your language,' they protested almost as one.

'Listen. I've heard you lot talking so don't tell me anything about *my* language. As I said, I don't know what *you* do when *you* have a fuck but my bum doesn't make scratches and neither am I so hot I scald holes in the polish. Just tell me what's going to happen to me, will you? I've got a date soon. There's these three black seamen coming up from Cardiff and we're having a party.'

A sagging silence enveloped the committee as they stared down at the surface of the table. So much activity on so little polish. Max caught Stan Prees' eye. We're not going to get anywhere here, are we? he pantomimed.

'Well that just about sums it up I suppose,' the chairman said finally. 'Unless any committee man has any further questions I shall ask Daisy to step outside while we consider our verdict. Any questions are there?'

'One thing though,' Daisy added half-rising from her chair. 'I would be grateful if you would go easy on poor old Walford. You can ban me for however long you like but poor Walford's dead upset he's going to lose his bingo job over all this. It's that Aunty Phyllis' punch that I blame.'

'Just leave it with us Daisy,' said the chairman. 'You can always rely on this committee for its sense of justice.'

'Aunty Phyllis shouldn't have handed out her punch in this club,' said Stan Prees. 'These are proper licensed premises. How can we run a club proper with her handing out all that jungle juice all the time? It's enough to drive any man crazy that stuff.'

After Daisy had withdrawn, Shonny Roberts began one of his wandering perorations before the chairman gavelled him into silence. 'In my view,' the chairman continued, straightening his back as he imagined a judge might when handing down the death sentence. 'Daisy Bland in is breach of most of the rules concerning good behaviour in the Hall and should accordingly ...'

'But what rule has she broken, Mr Chairman?' It was

Vinny Price, a fierce dialectician when he got going, who was clearly signalling the start of an argument.

'You name it and she's in breach of it,' the chairman blustered.

'In breach of what though precisely?'

'"Offensive behaviour shall not be permitted in the Hall." Rule 9 – sub-section 1.'

'But, with all due respect Mr Chairman, fucking behind locked doors is not offensive behaviour.'

'Well the doors weren't locked were they? I opened them didn't I?'

'You opened them with your own key. As far as the rest of the members were concerned they were locked.'

'There's others with a key to this room.'

'The key went with the man who came to service the one-armed bandits,' Shonny Roberts chimed in with his uncanny sense of the irrelevant. 'You couldn't even get a cherry after he fixed those bandits. Not a bastard cherry you couldn't.'

'Look, Vinny, fucking is offensive behaviour,' the chairman insisted. 'What is it you want, Vinny? You want people fucking all over the Hall. Is that what you want?'

'Well it's better than people fighting all over the Hall isn't it? Perhaps if we had a bit more fucking around here there'd be a lot less fighting.'

'Now you're really mixing your drinks.'

'Who's mixing his drinks, Mr Chairman? I'm talking about fucking. You're talking about fighting. Two entirely different things. Anyway I seem to remember that you used to enjoy a bit of fun fucking down in the cellar when the bar was locked. Rachel Bennett. Now we all remember her don't we?'

'That was a long time ago. And before I married Maisy let's not forget. At least it wasn't on the committee table.'

'Ah so that's what's getting up your nose is it Mr Chairman? But the table's all right. There's nothing wrong with it is there? I'm tired of all this bastard hypocrisy on this committee. It's getting worse than the chapel in here. The Hall can't afford to lose a girl like Daisy. We can't sit in judgement on women like her. We need characters in this place. The Valleys were built by characters – not moralising committees.

'It's Aunty Phyllis who should be up here for dishing out all that punch.'

'Leave Aunty Phyllis out of this.'

'Why don't we get another contractor for the one-armed bandit?'

'Why don't you shut your face?'

In the end it was decided to let Daisy off with a reprimand; that Aunty Phyllis should be sent a written warning not to dispense her punch on the premises in the future and that Walford be duly given his cards and sacked like a dog. He was always getting his numbers mixed up anyway.

'Spunky girl that,' observed Vinny Price. 'A shame about her sister, though, being married to that Glynmor Jones.'

'What's that?' asked Max Million, all ears. 'They're still on honeymoon aren't they?'

'They went on honeymoon Mr Chairman, then they went straight to the divorce court.'

'Can we have a little less of the jokes and get on with it?' said the chairman gavelling the laughter into the table. 'So then? Where is Glynmor? Is he in Bont or what?'

'He's home Mr Chairman. He's been home f'r ages. They had a big fight on the first night of the honeymoon, I heard, and came home. He came home by bus and she came back by taxi. It's awful terrible it is. Her so far gone in the pudding club an' all.'

'What happened then?'

'It was murder all the way, I heard, Mr Chairman. It seems he got hold of a bottle of Aunty Phyllis' punch ...'

Committee rumbles and erupts with cries of 'Not that bloody punch again.'

' ... and on their first night together he went and took a shower with all his clothes on. Then he started crying about losing his best friend Jampots and telling Maggie they had to call the baby Jampots – no matter what sex it was. Then, the next thing, she goes out for a walk and he's down in the bar in the hotel, still in his wet clothes an' all, trying to pick up some horrible piece who turns out, Mr Chairman, to be one of those sailors dressed up as a woman. But Glynmor is so pissed he takes this queer up to his room, shoves his hand up her skirt like and, the next thing, he's grabbed a big handful of knackers ...'

Horrified cries of 'Oh no' from the committee.

'Whereupon Glynmor goes absolutely potty and starts kicking the shit out of this sailor who's screaming blue murder.

At one stage he's trying to shove him out of the window, then he breaks one of those big bedroom mirrors over his head ...'

Committee clucks with choruses of approval at this.

' ... an' then the police come who arrest Glynmor and the sailor and take them away in one of those sit-up-and-beg police vans in which Glynmor starts hitting the sailor again. Then they're both flung into separate cells and Maggie goes down there in the middle of the night with some fags for Glynmor an' saying that it's their wedding night so can she sleep in the cell with her new husband.'

'Had she been drinking that bastard punch as well?'

'Well, they won't let her sleep with him so the next morning he's done three pounds with two pounds costs in Barry Magistrates for being drunk and disorderly and gets back to the hotel where they're wanting him to pay for the mirror he broke over the head of the queer boy. He refuses natural and next thing they're trying to get Maggie to pay for the mirror.'

'Bloody great honeymoon this is init? Made in heaven they said that marriage was an' all.'

'Well you haven't heard the best part yet. Maggie says she's not paying either and only then does it come out how the mirror got broke in the first place. She just thought it was one of Glynmor's fights 'cos she hadn't, in fact, known that the man was dressed up as a woman. So after they scrape her off the ceiling she's throwing things around in the hotel foyer – everything she can lay her hands on and the manager rushes off to call the police again. Anyway, by now Glynmor has got his hair off so much, blaming the hotel for all his troubles, he picks up a great bunch of the hotel's keys, walks over the road and flings them over the cliff and down into the sea.'

'What did he do that for?'

'Well, you know Glynmor. Always does the first thing that comes into his head.'

'When the police arrive they chase him through Barry funfair but he's too fast for them and, after hiding under the scenic railway, he finally gets a bus home. They detain Maggie in the lock-up for a bit but don't charge her for anything 'cos she's so upset by the early collapse of her marriage and is saying that all she wants now is a divorce. They've still got Glynmor's suitcase at the hotel. They say he can have it when he pays for the keys.'

113

'Do you know boys,' said Alec Central Heating after hearing this story of thwarted love and passion, 'that must be the most romantic story I have every heard. The wife was down in Cardiff again last week to see *The Sound of Music* but Glynmor's story licks Julie Andrews' by a mile.'

Everyone agreed that it was one hell of a story. They just didn't write scripts like that any more. Even the chairman had put his gavel on hold as the sorry saga unfolded.

'So where is Glynmor now?'

'Maggie went back to live with her mother, Mr Chairman, and Glynmor is living where he's always lived, in Bomber's house. He's not been seen out at all – except late some nights in the Chinese takeaway. They do say there's been a lot of knocking and hammering coming from the house, so he's probably knocking the wall down to make a bigger living room.'

'Doing away with the front parlour is he? Always the rebel eh? You know I've been thinking of doing that fr ages. Can you just knock the wall down?'

'You need an R.S.J. Twenty quid that's all. They do them in the new Do-It-Yourself shop in Porth.'

'Deliver them do they?'

The gavel came down with a resounding crack and the committee moved onto the next case: that of Danny Bits and Pieces.

'I really don't know how to approach this one,' said the chairman. 'But approach it we must since Danny is going around upsetting everyone with his daft behaviour. He was never sixteen ounces to the pound, what with his pot-holing under the seats during the dances, but, after his brother, Sam Swambo, died in that pit explosion, Danny has gone right round the twist. Speaking for myself I would just like to ignore it. As you know he has always been putting his watch in his beer and leaving to show that it's waterproof ...'

'Harmless enough Mr Chairman.'

'Yes that is harmless enough but now he's actually started washing his socks in the beer in the Starlight Lounge and upsetting the ladies no end.'

'He says it's because his feet do smell something terrible.'

'You know, boys, it might be something to do with the beer as well. It's not been too good of late Mr Chairman.'

'But what can we do? His brain can't be any bigger than a canary's.'

'That might be insulting to a canary Mr Chairman.'

'Well we've got to do something or else we'll be having everyone doing their laundry in the beer,' the chairman insisted. 'I suggest we stop his beer for three months and give him a stiff warning. Any disagreements? Right.'

The gavel came down twice signifying the end of the committee meeting.

Later that night, with the Welfare Hall closed and just Curly there in the queue waiting for Lee Hoo Wonk to make him some chicken fried rice, the sky over the Valley was a light blue canopy with the odd dark smudges of frothy clouds. Here and there the street lamps shone like matchless diamonds in the drifting mists. In such deep darkness even the pit looked like a gorgeous Indian temple, with shafts of light breaking out of its canteen and the white mists wrapped around the black girders like a ghostly ivy.

In the wheelhouse the banksman was reading the *South Wales Echo*. The news of the day was that there had been another night of violence in Ulster.

Down in the gulley behind the Hall a couple of sheep were trying to knock over a dustbin, the one with his shoulder on the one side of the bin and the other with his shoulder on the other, rather like a pair of Pontypool front row forwards packing down for the big push.

These Valley sheep were nothing like the fluffy balls of loveliness found in the nursery books. They were temperamental and not above biting you. Their coats, more grey than white, were criss-crossed with scabby scratches where they had been rubbing themselves on barbed wire or picking a fight with some local mongrel. In their eternal quest for food they would even climb up on one another's backs to scale a garden fence. Some desperate gardeners had even taken to putting the sharp end of nails through their garden doors to stop the sheep butting them down and getting at the cabbages. But the sheep's bony black heads were so hard that all that happened was that the nails were bent in half and the door opened anyway. When there was a funeral, sheep came from miles off for a good scoff of the flowers after the mourners had left. One animal-hating

115

florist in Aberdare had recently taken steps to forestall such graveside banquets by offering to supply plastic flowers to all funerals. Like empty pop bottles, they would be returnable after the burial. But, most of the time, the sound of the sheep's munching gnashers was one of the authentic sounds of Bont.

That night Bont found itself a few more night sounds too. Danny Bits and Pieces, in despair at being boxed from the Welfare Hall, began potching about the gullies, singing hymns on the top of his voice. Like some bloody coyote in the middle of a vasectomy he sounded, said the boys in the bar, the shrieking off-key wails drifting up over the slate roofs of the terraces and down the walls of the Valley. Windows were opened and boots flung and oaths unleashed but still Danny wandered on in an unmelodious cloud of hymns and arias.

Meanwhile there were unfamiliar bangings coming from No. 9 Bont Terrace. Hammer in hand, Glynmor was busy knocking down the partition wall between the living-room and the parlour. Glynmor had always hated the idea of parlour but Bomber wanted the wall left intact. This bit of renovation was another way of dancing on the old bastard's grave. The house had been turned upside down and inside out but still they hadn't found the money.

Just over the road, in the doorway of the Co-op, Maggie was standing in the darkness watching Glynmor work. She was worried about his behaviour. People just didn't go knocking down walls in the middle of the night. Just what was she going to do with him? He made her heart ache when he was around and it was even worse when he wasn't. She was sorry now that she had left him in that hotel in Barry. After all, if she couldn't put up with a bit of drunkenness from a man she couldn't put up with much, could she? She hadn't been much of a wife, had she? She had just walked across the funfair, hopped on a bus to Cardiff and spent the night in the bus station there before coming home to Bont the next morning. The gossip, she'd heard, had somehow created some monstrous story of Glynmor fighting and wrecking everything. How she hated all this gossip with everyone forever gunning one another down with their lying sentences. This gossip was never correct, always cruel and spiteful. How she wished she could get away from it all and live with some dignity and privacy with her Glynmor again. Somewhere away from all those gossiping, lying tongues.

And there was another problem which was weighing on her mind and was going to hurl her right into the middle of a storm of gossip if she didn't watch it. After further examinations by Dr Edwards her pregnancy, it seemed, was much further advanced than she had thought. According to the doctor she was now well over seven months pregnant which hardly tallied with the time when she had lain with Glynmor on the river bank. Perhaps he really had pulled it out as he had claimed all along but then, if so, how had she got so far gone? That nasty doctor had even been asking her if she had been seeing any other men before Glynmor. As if she'd do such a thing. Well, she wasn't going to be seeing that doctor again. That was a fact that was. Oh Lord, she was even beginning to think like Glynmor.

P.C. Watkins rode past on his bicycle, glancing over at Maggie in the doorway, but not stopping to talk to her. He knew the troubles she had with her new husband. *Duw* everyone in the Valley had heard what had happened on that honeymoon. Handful of knackers indeed.

Maggie crossed the road and tapped on Glynmor's window. He came over and lifted the lace curtain. His face was dusted with white plaster from his labours but she could see straight that he was happy enough to see her. He wasn't exactly smiling but there was a sort of amused twinkle in his eyes. 'Hello lovely,' she said through the window, her lips almost miming the words. 'Having trouble sleeping are you?'

He shrugged and looked down at his hammer.

'What are you doing, then?' she asked.

He looked behind him. 'I lost the key to the front door.'

'Oh I get it. You lost the key to the front door so you knocked down the wall. Typical.'

He was back studying his hammer again.

She tapped the window. 'Have you been eating at all?' she asked. 'I've been worrying about you. Look, can I come in, can I?'

'Why should I let you in? Eh? Why should I? I have a few drinks and you leave me on my honeymoon. Who wants a wife like that? There's some gossip I went off with some queer in Barry as well. You know anything about that do you?'

She shook her head. She didn't. 'Glynmor. Just let me in. We can't talk through the window.'

'The door's not locked. It's your house as well, remember?'

She walked in through the hall and they stood facing one another over the pile of rubble. 'I've always liked one big room,' she said.

'Well, that's as well. I wouldn't know how to start building it up again.'

'Safe is it?'

'I suppose so. We'll soon find out won't we?'

She eyed the ceiling and took one step backwards. 'Are you going to put some sort of arch in here, are you?' she asked.

'Haven't thought really. What do you think?'

'Some sort of glass doors perhaps?'

'Perhaps. Are you staying with me tonight or what?'

'I could.'

'What do you mean "I could"?'

She smiled at him and he fell on her like the ton of rubble that came crashing down from the ceiling.

Chapter Ten

Autumn came stomping into the Valley like some harridan
queen with a hangover. Screeching with cold showers of rain
and belches of freezing wind she was, opening wider fissures in
the high Valley walls, spitting hard on the terraces 'and even
making the river break its banks, flooding the allotments and
chicken runs and making Mrs Pryce's cockerel climb onto the
roof of its shed where it strutted about angrily snorting at the
effrontery of it all.

Occasionally the rain would stop and allow a brilliant
column of sunshine to go marching the length of the Valley,
infusing everything with a warming buttercup gold, making the
asphalt in the streets steam. But then the dark clouds would
gather again and disgorge yet more freezing rain. It was
something and nothing weather, aye; fine and wet at the same
time. Real Valley weather this was. Bont weather.

It was on just such a day that Rev. Mordecai was standing
in the backyard of his manse with his binoculars, anxiously
scanning the leaden, windy skies for the return of his pigeons in
the Welsh Open. The birds had been released the day before in
the Shetlands but where they had got to now was anyone's
guess.

On fine days they always flew in up the Valley. On bad
days they came in down the Valley. But, on such days as this,
he just couldn't make out which way they would come. And
they were very late. He checked his watch for the umpteenth
time. They had to get back before dark or else the clock would
be stopped at 4.30 p.m. and he would have to get up at dawn
again. Pigeons did not fly in the dark.

Such days were a terrible strain on the other pigeon
fanciers as well. Despite doctor's warnings, John Abdabs kept

racing his birds; and he frequently ended up in hospital during the racing season since all the excitement aggravated his angina. Even the pigeons would get tense too, sometimes flying around and around their lofts and refusing to come in. At such moments Mordecai would dance around below, frantically rattling a tin of corn.

His binoculars scanned the rim of the Valley again and again. Then his heart leaped when he spotted a whole group of them coming in fast and low over the outcrop on the south east wall of the Valley. Any second now he would feel the familiar, throbbing excitement as his birds peeled off from the group and headed home, flying at 1200 yards a minute, to have their rubber rings plunged into the timer.

But instead of unutterable excitement he felt unutterable dismay.

The pigeons headed straight to John Abdabs' loft built against the side of the cinema. If a man could have foamed at the mouth then old Mordecai would have done just that. So it was true then, the rumour that Abdabs was experimenting with the new Belgian method. All based on sex it was. The cock was kept in the next cage to his favourite hen and was thus encouraged to fly home fast so that he would be allowed to mate with her. If he flew home very fast indeed he was allowed to mate with a few more hens as well – as many as he could really. As a man of God the good Rev. could not condone the idea of offering to set up sex orgies for his pigeons in return for flying home first. Just the very thought of what was now going on in Abdabs' loft made him feel very ill indeed. Uncharitably, for a man of the cloth, he hoped that Abdabs' angina would play him up again.

It began pouring with rain.

I'm not saying a word but I heard that Glynmor and Maggie are getting a divorce after all.

Never. I thought they'd patched it up.

They do say he's cracking up with it all. He's always got his rag out about something and she's been going up to the cemetery late at night to talk to her father.

Her father's dead isn't he?

'Course he's dead. He's been dead for years but she always got on with him and goes there when she's upset. Sometimes her sister has had to go up there and get her to go home.

What's the matter with Glynmor then?

It's his nerves, they do say. He's been getting pills from the doctor and they're making him worse. Eats them like sweets he does.

When's the baby due then?

Well I'm not saying anything but it's due any day now. Two months three days before time an' all.

That baby's never his.

That's what he says as well. But a boy like Glynmor would wouldn't he? Common as muck.

That morning it was market day down in Pontypridd, the rain beating down on the tented stalls strung out along the twisted cobbled streets, all so tightly crowded together around the market hall it only needed a couple of prams and a wheelbarrow to start a traffic jam which would take an hour to unravel.

Maggie, heavily pregnant and loaded with shopping, had eaten some faggots and peas in the market before struggling to the exit. Smells jostled one another: mountains of fruit and china were piled high in the multi-coloured stalls and indefatigable traders were offering their never-to-be-repeated bargain. 'Today, 'cos it's Wednesday,' shouted one. 'I'm giving the stuff away, asking not ten pounds or five pounds but, look, three pounds – no, 'cos I'm feeling barmy today and it's raining, one pound four shillings for this, that and that over there …'

Maggie hesitated, but only briefly, before forcing herself to walk on. Those traders had the gift of the gab all right. The last time she had stopped in front of one of them she had ended up with enough black shoe polish to last a lifetime. And she didn't own any black shoes.

Outside the market it was still raining heavily. Cigarette packets and bus tickets were swirling down the overflowing gutters in disorganised armadas, making their way to distant battles at sea. Even such torrential rain, however, did nothing to wash away the stink of rancid beer which hung around the doorways of the pubs. A jukebox inside the club was playing Martha and the Vandellas' *Rescue Me*. Oh yes, Maggie thought. Come on baby and rescue me.

When she got to the bus station the driver had no change for her pound, again, so she had to go to the newsagent's shop, change it there and wait for the next bus.

The engine of the Bont bus chattered and groaned and whined its way up the great winding gulch of the Valley, past the aerial ropeways and spinning wheels of the mines, past the rows of pigeon lofts and the colossal black pyramids of the tips. The air in the bus was as warm as the inside of a baker's oven and, when a man in the seat in front of her lit a pipe, Maggie thought, for a second or two, that she was going to faint. The mist on the windows was so thick you could barely see out. She rubbed a small hole with the ham of her fist and saw a dog sniffing at the base of a lamp post.

The bus stopped and started through the townships scattered around their closed mines. The lines of the terraces were as formal as drilling guardsmen, their dripping greyness relieved only by the odd dirty-white smudges of the starling shit nesting in the hissing gutterings. The Valley had long been shorn of all its trees; they had been used as pit props when foreign supplies of wood stopped in the Second World War. Here and there on the roadsides at the end of the terraces were gaudy coloured advertisements for Hovis bread and Guinness Stout. Water tanks stood on small plateaus of the Valley walls just above the towns like giant fawn mushrooms. A poster on a chapel noticeboard announced: JESUS HEALS ALL BROKEN HEARTS.

The journey wouldn't have been nearly so uncomfortable if she didn't have this huge bump to contend with. It was as if there were now two of her. Where once she had felt fat, she now felt positively elephantine. Glynmor was no help, of course, forever calling her Michelin Man and now refusing to so much as touch her. It was as if she had become defiled. It was a shame really, for in those all-too-brief weeks after they had got together again, she had found their love sessions a great source of pleasure and relief.

Even Glynmor seemed to enjoy them for a short period, until he was overtaken by the glooms again. No more jokes or dirty stories either, none of his bragging lies followed by the inevitable 'That's a fact'. He just went to work down the pit as usual before coming home to eat. Sometimes he'd go straight to the Welfare Hall and miss the meal, which Maggie then flung straight in the ash-can. She thought it a great pity that the committee hadn't boxed him instead of Danny Bits and Pieces who was driving everyone daft about the place as he potched about singing his head off. At least Glynmor would have stayed home more if he had been boxed. As it was they had barely got to know one another and he was forever prowling about the place like a bear with a sore arse. Oh how she hated him when he got like that.

The bus laboured past the clock in Bont Square and Maggie got off outside the chip shop, the misery loaming thick inside her as she lugged her shopping over the road. All her life she had dreamed so fervently of breaking free of this vulgar place with all its nasty gossip but now, married and pregnant, she was stuck in this hole forever. Perhaps Daisy had the right idea after all. Fun. That was all Daisy had ever cared about.

She pushed open the front door to find Glynmor stretched out on the settee, snoring with his mouth open, next to the electric fire. She shook her head and took in a long breath. There he was, a miner with free coal, and he was too lazy to make a proper fire. She had got in the sticks too, which is probably why he hadn't touched them. *He* liked to get in the coal and sticks. That was the man's job and everything else in the house was hers. Huh! Judging by his snores he's been having a long session in the club – the more beer he had, the louder were the snores. What was even worse was when he got his nose stuck into the whisky and those snores sounded like the first rumbles of an earthquake.

She took off her coat, sitting down in the armchair and turning the electric fire towards her, warming her damp hands as he turned over on his side whimpering and chomping his lips. She sniffed a soft snort. Although so young he already had a few of those small tell-tale scars of the miner on his face and there were still coal rings around the inside of his eyes. That was pure Glynmor that was. He did not like to soap his eyes in the pithead showers since too many uncomfortable things happened when you were temporarily blinded. They pinched your soap for one or else someone grabbed your big toe and began yelling 'Rat, rat'.

But, even with all his present moodiness, he was still handsome. That was undeniable enough. His looks had been her downfall hadn't they? In the fight of love she had fallen for

123

the real sucker punch. Like an idiot she had gone and fallen for his dark Welsh good looks. Just like an idiot. She had liked his impulsiveness too; the way he went straight into a fight when he got his rag out. He was said to be the fastest and deadliest head-butter in the valleys. A Glasgow kiss, Glynmor called it.

There was always something attractive about being a bit of a lad but these days he was far from being the star of the party. He had got unusually withdrawn and seemed scared of something. To make matters worse he didn't want to seem to talk about it either. Sometimes she worried that he might be in some sort of trouble with the police. But, whatever it was, he was keeping his mouth well and truly shut. He had been getting such a pain to live with she'd been on at him to go and see a doctor but he wouldn't.

She got up and went into the kitchen to make a cup of tea. On the window sill next to the pantry was the egg-timer that Glynmor had made out of Bomber's ashes. They had never found his money so Glynmor had insisted on him becoming an egg-timer. 'He'd never been any use while he was alive so let him be some use now he's dead,' was his cryptic explanation.

Every time she looked at the egg-timer she let out a soft sigh. What a sense of humour.

She brought the tea back to her armchair stirring it thoroughly as she let the cup and saucer sit, steaming, on her pregnant bump. Her thoughts about him got blacker. Looking around she noted that he had not even finished knocking down the partition wall properly and there were jagged lumps of bricks poking out from the broken plaster. It was strange being married to a man who had given up on all the normal activities of marriage even before it had begun. It wasn't so much that the romance had gone out of their lives so much as it had never come in. There was more romance in a dartboard. She sighed and sipped her tea again. But she was stuck with this snoring bastard and, to make matters worse, she had his child inside her. She would not mind if the child had his looks but prayed that was all it had. Living with two like Glynmor really would be a fate worse than death.

'Any chance of a cup of tea is there?' he said waking up.

'There's one in the pot.'

'On bloody strike again, are we?'

'Glynmor. I've had a long day shopping in Ponty. Now

I'm having a rest. If you want a cup of tea there's one in the pot.'

'There's one in the pot,' he mimicked. 'There's one in the pot. Can't you do anything at all woman?'

'I'm not your slave you know,' she said, half-rising and spilling her tea which splashed in small venomous hisses on the bars of the electric fire. 'I didn't marry you to be your slave.'

'Slave! Slave! That's a laugh that is. A great bloody slave you'd make and that's a fact. The other boys get sandwiches in their tins. All I had yesterday was a poxy Mars bar. Then I got some cream crackers and you didn't even bother to take them out of the packet. Some bloody slave you are.'

'You were lucky to get them.'

'Lucky!'

'Yes. Lucky. Pregnant women are supposed to rest. A normal man would make his wife stay in bed at times like this. Not send her shopping and asking her to make him sandwiches.'

'How did you get pregnant? That's what I'd like to know.'

'We're not back on that one again are we?'

'Yes. We are. That bastard bump of yours has got nothing to do with me.'

'I'm not listening to any more of this,' Maggie shouted, standing up and flinging her cup and saucer against the wall. 'I just can't take it any more.'

'Well go then.'

'I will,' she stormed picking up her coat. 'I'm off for good.'

'Goodbye.'

'Goodbye.'

The front door slammed and Maggie, half-ran, half-walked down through the rain which was gurgling out through the drainpipes and washing across the pavement in hurrying rivulets. She was so angry she could have screamed out loud; at the sheep, at the houses, at the Welfare Hall ... Screamed abuse at anything, all because of the sheer unfairness of being stuck in this dump and being married to someone like Glynmor.

She turned past the Welfare Hall when she saw the Cardiff bus standing at the stop, blue puffs of exhaust chugging out into the sheeting rain. That was it, she thought exultantly. She would go and stay with her Uncle Jack down in Cardiff for a bit. Luckily she had her purse with her; she had just enough to buy a ticket and sat down next to a young girl reading a paperback.

Just the very movement of the bus, as it pulled out of the square, made her feel better; just the knowledge that she was putting some distance between her and Bont in general and Glynmor in particular had an amazingly soothing effect on her anger. Oh, she hated the place so much and, just seeing all those tiny houses and that ugly pit slip away from her view, into the tadpoling raindrops across the window, she decided that she would not care if she never saw it again.

Even as the bus was hurtling beneath the Pandy viaduct she was working out a plan. She would stay with her Uncle Jack in his council house out in Llanedeyrn estate until she had the baby. Then she would find a job with some sort of live-in accommodation so that she could work and keep an eye on the baby at the same time. She wouldn't work weekends though. She would set weekends aside for the baby and, if she made enough money, she would buy a car and the two of them would go off for day trips to places like Porthcawl and Barry. No, not Barry. She'd seen all she ever wanted to see of that place.

Rainy allotments chased past pit village and derelict chapels when they stopped in Upper Boat before moving on again, down past the billowing steam and spurting fires of Nantgarw pit, hurtling alongside the swollen black waters of the River Taff and the turrets of Castell Goch (sticking up out of the autumnal trees) and, soon, the very suburbs of Cardiff with its marching lines of semi-detached houses, wide straight streets, lived in by all those strange people. Immediately she began to feel very nervous. Cardiff was nothing like Bont. This was a strange, hostile city that she knew nothing about. This was the city that was always bottom of the league for donations to charity and always top for crime. Here, she had heard, they would rob you and rape you then leave you to die in the street. Nothing for nothing in Cardiff. She spotted the towering white Victorian architecture of the museum, city hall and law courts. Her nervousness began turning into blind panic.

She rang her Uncle Jack from the bus station but there was no reply. Oh well, she thought, I'll set off and walk. He never likes to be out for long. He'll be back by the time I get there.

The rain had stopped as she cut back behind the station and crossed a litter-blown car park where a Chinese man was sitting in a car, looking at her. From inside one building she could hear the shrieks of playing children and, following a high curving wall, she came across the even higher walls of Cardiff prison. Both hands smoothed her bump as her eyes rose up the wall in sheer amazement that anything could be built so high. She remembered that Glynmor had always told her stories about Cardiff prison; of how one of his uncles was once locked inside there for his part in the Tonypandy riots. They were always so hungry in there they had to scavenge for food in the dustbins, Glynmor had said. Just what was she going to do about Glynmor?

She walked back down past the prison and took shelter beneath a huge railway bridge. A deep pool of rain had gathered in the hollow at the bottom of the road and, when the cars raced through it, their wheels threw out huge chutes of water whose noise was curiously amplified by the high enclosure of the bridge. Just past the bridge, on the other side of the road, was a vast hoarding advertising Brains beer. A lorry thundered past, throwing out an even larger chute of water which caught her around the ankles. She turned and turned again, now slumping against the damp hard wall and crying piteously into her hands.

'I can be of help to you, lady.'

Even in her distress she liked the sound of his voice immediately. It had warmth and confidence. More to the point, it was an offer of help which was just what she needed at the moment. But, when she looked up, she began shaking her head and was about to make a run for it since this offer of help had come from some sort of tramp with a bushy brown beard, the large watery eyes of a Boxer dog and dirty clothes which were more like sack-cloth. 'I really could be of help to you,' he said repeating the offer. 'I live over the road. Come and join me for some warmth.'

But then the impulse to run subsided and she just stood there gazing into the stranger's eyes. Quite what it was that he had she was not sure, but he certainly had something which took away her uneasiness. It was something strong yet invisible like unshakeable faith; something which offered hope to the desolate. It was the promise of hope that kept her there and, after he had said a few more words, enabled her to have the courage to go off with a scruffy stranger like this. When there is a promise of hope to the hopeless you can do almost anything, she decided.

There also seemed to be something preordained about the meeting since, when he moved off, he did not even look around to check that she was following him.

The rain had returned, a drizzle with dim shafts of sunshine breaking through as the two of them crossed a main road and walked into the tiny terraced streets of Adamsdown where all the streets were named after precious metals. They came to Gold Street and the tramp pushed open the door to one of the houses which Maggie could tell immediately, by the musty smell, was derelict. He opened another door which led to a small kitchen, inviting her to sit down on a chair next to a small table covered by copies of the *Daily Mirror*. Great holes gaped in the plaster and a few of the floorboards were missing. 'I will make some tea,' he said. 'Make yourself comfortable.'

Maggie sat and watched gravely as the tramp filled up a billy can of water and put it on a primus stove. She just could not understand why she was so relaxed but relaxed she was – almost to the point of sleep. He took two cracked mugs out of a cupboard and just stood there waiting for the water to boil. His oddest feature, Maggie decided, was that he seemed to have no need to talk, even odder since she came from a village where they needed to talk all the time. But, when he did speak, it was in a voice so soft she had to strain to make out the words. 'Would you mind if I read your palm?' he asked.

'Not at all. I've never had my palm read.' She stuck out her hand immediately, like some small boy ready, and even willing, to be caned.

'I will finish making tea first,' he said. 'Put your hand down for the moment.'

On the wall, next to a shattered mirror, there was a calendar with 21 October 1966 marked with a cross. There was also no light, she noticed, wondering how he managed when it got dark.

'You are with baby,' he said bringing the steaming mugs of tea to the table. 'When do you expect birth?'

'I don't know. Soon though. I feel him moving around inside me a lot.'

'How does he feel?'

'Feel? He feels like any normal baby I suppose.'

'No. I mean is there pain with him? Or does it feel like, say, a smile?'

'A smile? Oh that's very nice,' said Maggie warming to him more. This was no Woolworth's tramp, that was for certain. Straight out of Marks and Spencer this one was. His brown eyes were fierce with intelligence and there was, somehow, a fragrance about him; not a soapy or perfumy fragrance either but something wilder and yet more subtle; something of rivers, trees and sunshine.

'Yes,' she went on, 'on some mornings, I do lie in bed and feel this lovely smile inside me. I don't tell Glynmor, that's my husband. He wouldn't understand anything like that. Tell me, what's your name?'

'John.'

'Been living here long have you, John?'

'Long? Yes, long. How often do you say your prayers?'

She smiled and blinked a lot but said nothing.

'You must say prayers Maggie. From now on there will be corners in your life only prayer will help you understand. Prayer will help you understand lots of things.'

'Would it help my marriage, would it?'

'Prayer helps everything and this baby of yours must be soaked in prayer right from the time of his birth. Let me look at your palm.'

He took her right hand with both of his hands and studied her palm with care, splaying out the fingers, shaking them and sometimes rubbing along her life lines with the tip of his forefinger. He seemed to take an age about it, and she began getting impatient asking if she could drink her tea. He nodded, letting her hand go.

'You must go home on the next bus and go to bed,' he said leaning forward slightly. 'You have the star at the beginning of the middle line. Lot of people have been waiting for the star. Baby is coming tomorrow. It will be a boy and you must always cherish boy because it will be a boy like no other boy.'

Her mouth went dry and she swallowed hard.

'Boy will be very different but never worry about that. He will also be under threat.'

'Threat?'

'Do not worry. There will be unseen eyes watching out for him. I will always be here too. Come down here if you need my help. Now, drink your tea. You must get home as soon as possible. Tomorrow will be our longest day. It will be long for everyone. When boy is born every eye will be weeping and every heart will be breaking. Every Valley will run with tears tomorrow.'

Maggie could feel a tremor in her hand as she drank her tea and looked into John's brown eyes. There were so many questions she wanted to ask but could sense that he wasn't going to explain anything even if she didn't have the slightest doubt that everything he said was true. 'Will you be around if ever I need you?' she asked.

'I will be here. But say nothing of this to anyone. Not even to your husband. The fewer that know about the boy the better.'

'John, I want to be a good wife. I want to love Glynmor more and I want him to love me more.'

He nodded and smoothed her cheek with his hand. 'You will find the love you want. After tomorrow there will be more love. But first there will be a great lament.'

Huge cartwheels of rain, whipped along by the winds, came rolling in over the rooftops of Cardiff. Milky, majestic thunderclouds belched over the castle and a shivering fork of lightning slashed down onto the twisted tubular shapes and squat furnaces of East Moors steel works. *Duw* there was wrath in the air that night. The rain was so ferocious they were going to talk about it for weeks and years to come. Another dazzling flash of lightning and, for a second, it seemed as if the very city had caught fire.

It was the second house of the Tuesday night bingo session in the Welfare Hall and the new bingo caller, Eggey Jones, was shouting out the numbers of the ricocheting table tennis balls. 'On its own number nine. Clickety click sixty six. Seven and six, was she worth it? Legs, eleven.' The silence on the tables was total, with some marking up to six cards, their Biros flashing up and down the pink sheets. Even the drinks were left untouched as those all-important numbers were read out. But the trouble was that Eggey's numbers were not very distinct, and there were occasional anguished pleas for him to put his teeth back in.

'You know, at that party, the greedy cow ate sixteen lamb chops,' the doorman was telling two women as they stood together feeding coins into the one-armed bandit.

'Sixteen! But she's no bigger than a whippet.'

'They do say she must have worms.'

'Worms! Snakes more like. Here. Got change of half a crown have you?'

'I didn't get invited to the party, mind. That's just what I heard.'

'Round here they do have a party for the death of a cat. I wouldn't go if they carried me there.'

'They'd need a dumper truck to carry you anywhere.'

'Watch your mouth now.'

From inside the concert hall there was a shout of 'House' followed by a widespread groan. That Madge Williams had called the flyer again. Just how did she do it?

The green baize of the snooker table was dotted with tiny white meteors of chalk. The white cue ball cracked into the black sending it shooting the whole length of the table where it caught in the jaws of the pocket. Bouncing heart-stoppingly from side to side, it finally stopped still just a hairsbreadth away from the all-important drop. 'Black be fucked,' Stan Swansea muttered to his cue. 'That's going to finish me that is.'

At the far corner of the bar Glynmor, his eyes already bloodshot with a few beers, was discoursing on the state of his marriage with his pals. 'You know I can only think it must be something to do with her being pregnant. I just never believed that anyone could be such a pain in the arse. Just everything she does gets right up my nose. Maybe that's what she wants. Who's to say? She gets in the coal and sticks – which is supposed to be my job init? – then she always leaves the coal door open, the rain gets on the wood and you can't get it to light. Then, when I come home, she's always sitting in my chair and, if there's one thing that drives me potty, it's the way she's always squeezing the toothpaste in the middle instead of rolling it up from the end. The silly cow can't even play the one-armed bandit properly. If she needs to hold a cherry you can bet your life she'll hold a pear. It's enough to turn a good man into a pansy.'

He picked up his drink, but put it down again as he thought of something else. 'If I'm not at home at the right time my dinner is straight in the ash-can. No messing about either. Whooosh. Straight in there. Not that it matters much 'cos she can't even boil an egg and that's a fact. Instead of putting sandwiches in my tin the other morning all I got was a Mars bar. Aye. One fucking Mars bar. Then she packed me some cream crackers and didn't even take them out of the bastard packet. Marrying her was the worse day's work I've ever done. She left me this morning, she said. I hope she's gone for good.'

'Well you're hoping in vain, Glynmor boy. I just saw her as I was coming in here. Soaking wet she was an' all. Better be careful. She's due any day now.'

'Shit!'

'You'd better get on home Glynmor boy.'

'I'll get on home when I'm ready. Who wants another pint?'

When he did finally get home he found Maggie sitting in her dressing gown with her hair tied up with a towel. And when she saw him come in through the door she smiled. Smiled! 'Hello lovely,' she said.

He just stood there smoothing the raindrops out of his hair as his eyes jerked around the room. She had lit the fire which was blazing in the grate. There was a pile of cheese sandwiches on a plate on the table and, just next to it, a jar of his favourite Branston chutney. There were a few bottles of beer on the television as well and, even more suspicious, she was not sitting in his favourite chair either.

A procession of emotions ... surprise, suspicion, guilt ... went marching through Glynmor's mind as he tried to absorb what she was up to now. Surprise at this upsurge of domesticity, suspicion about the motives behind it, guilt that he had been out in the Hall again while she had been trying to make it nice for him here. There was even some relief too that she had chosen to wave the white flag rather than push it deeper into some almighty row. It was this pregnancy that was making everything so difficult – without that they could probably just have knocked it all on the head and called it a day ages ago.

'I've just been having a drink with that Graham Pryce,' he said, picking a non-controversial subject as he took off his jacket and sat on his chair just next to the fire.

'I thought he'd given it up?'

'Well you know him. Nothing by halves. But he wasn't rotten drunk or anything.'

'I've made you some sandwiches,' she said. 'I've got some beer as well. But you can have tea if you'd prefer.'

'I'm not bothered about tea. But I'll have a bottle of that beer.'

She picked up one of the bottles and poured it into a glass before handing it over to him. 'Tell me, what happened to Graham's wife? I used to like her. A real tidy sort she was.'

'No one knows for certain. I don't like to ask Graham. Mmm. These sandwiches are nice. Cheddar is it?'

'Do you know I'm not all that sure. I just asked for a quarter of cheese.'

The coals on the fire fell in on themselves in a gentle series of creaks, the small blue flames spurting across the bright red fissures. 'I'm glad I bothered to light the fire,' she said. 'I could watch coal fires forever. They're so pretty the way they glow.'

'You look like some bastard sultan with your hair done up like that,' he said sipping on his beer with his right hand while taking one of those sandwiches in the other. Then he spread his legs apart with the warmth of the fire settling over his belly feeling, perhaps for the first time, that marriage might not be quite as bad as he had always thought. 'I do want this to work out between us,' he said. 'I know it often doesn't look like it but I do want us to stay married. I think it could be good if we made a bit of effort.'

Maggie gulped at this sudden outbreak of common sense. She couldn't have agreed more but said nothing.

'I know I get all these bad moods and I'm a pain to have around but I just can't seem to help myself,' he went on. 'The real problem is that there's things going on inside me but I can't seem to explain what they are and I do get frustrated and bad tempered.'

'Oh I wish you would Glynmor. If you could only tell me about those ... about those things of yours then perhaps I could do something about them. We could do almost anything if only we'd talk about it. I do get fed up with all this rowing the same as you.'

'But I've never been able to talk about anything inside

here.' He gestured vaguely towards his chest with his glass of beer. 'I'm sorry girl but I've just never been able to do it.'

'Well, at least try, my lovely. I'm sure we can do anything if we try. Both of us now. Both trying like mad to pull it together. Because that's what we want. That's all. 'Cos we want it.'

Chapter Eleven

Swirling mists and yet more rain crowded into the Valley the next morning – a morning so thick and dark it was as if the dawn had decided not to turn up. Even Mrs Pryce's cockerel failed to bugle in the day, preferring instead to hang around, warm and dry, inside his hutch.

Glynmor was downstairs in just his trousers and vest, building up the fire which had held well through the night. Outside he could hear the sounds of milk being delivered. He turned on the wireless and Stevie Winwood was singing about how he was so glad he'd made it. You and me both, kid, Glynmor thought.

He held some newspapers across the front of the grate to make the fire draw. When it roared with the sudden inrush of air he crumpled the newspapers into a ball and flung them into the fire. Now he lit one of his Capstan full-strengths and coughed his way into the kitchen where he filled the kettle to the brim and put it on the stove before emptying the tea leaves onto the ash path out the back. After rinsing the pot in the Typhoo. Then, his eyes still puffy with sleep, he just stood there looking blankly at the wall.

The front door opened with a bang and he knew straight that there was something up. It was Stan Swansea who had never, ever walked into his house before. 'Better get your clothes on mun,' he said looking anxious. 'The call's gone out for men. There's been some big mischief over in Aberfan. Better hurry now.'

Glynmor grabbed his jacket and shouted up the stairs. Outside his door was a car with Emlyn Kremlin and Ted John North in it. Glynmor could tell from the white seriousness of their faces that something very nasty indeed had happened.

'Some sort of accident is it?' he asked climbing into the back seat next to Ted John North.

'A problem with the school we've heard,' said Emlyn as he accelerated up the road. 'Something to do with the roof.'

'It'll probably be cleared up when we get there.'

'It was serious we've heard. The word went around the pit for everyone to take their shovels.'

'Anything on the radio?'

'I heard nothing.'

Sometimes on the winding, twisting Valley roads the car came out on the very roof of the drifting white banks of cloud and the air was surprisingly clear with views of forests and distant peaks. But then, as if on a roller-coaster, they plunged down into the rain mists again, moving past faint outlines of shop, pub and terrace. The four men drove on in silence and, apart from the eager scrape of the windscreen wipers, all that could be heard was the doleful sound of a distant chapel bell.

'There's some very bad mischief up here today,' said Emlyn. 'I can just feel it in my water.'

'I've been dreaming of something bad for weeks,' said Glynmor. 'I haven't had them for a few nights but I've been getting these terrible nightmares.'

'I've heard you've not been treating Maggie very well,' said Emlyn with some real edge.

'Well, we won't go into that now will we?' said Stan Swansea.

'No we bastard won't,' Glynmor added.

They drove through the village of Mount Pleasant and down into the scattered township of Aberfan, a gloomy gathering of grey buildings, flung around a main street and at the base of a long brambled slope. At the bottom of the hill, just before a level crossing, they stopped behind a line of other cars. Men were stepping out of them carrying picks and shovels and hydraulic jacks, running up into the thick mists shrouding the village.

When Emlyn drove over a level crossing a policeman waved them down. 'Park your car over there, boys, and get on up to the Pantglas school. You've got to dig the children out.' The policeman had difficulty speaking his words. His eyes were red with tears.

Emlyn did not even bother to park his car properly and

was out and running across the field with a surprising lightness for a man of his size and weight. The other three took the shovels out of the car boot and half-walked, half-ran past a row of shops and along the main road until they came to what seemed like a black wall built high across the road. Figures were running back and forth and Glynmor stopped, his heart pounding, his eyes narrowing with the shock of recognising something both strange and yet very familiar. But what was it exactly?

A tiny woman, with tight grey curls and hands thrust down into the pockets of her brown mackintosh, was standing on the garden wall to get a better view of all the activity. Holding his shovel on his shoulder like a rifle Glynmor asked her what was going on. She did not reply so he asked again.

'The children,' she said. 'They're all in there.'

'How many is that?'

'All of them. Would you believe it? 'Course you wouldn't. Every child in that school is under that slurry there.'

He walked closer to the school and indeed was almost on top of it when he saw that it was no longer there. It had been completely covered by a wave of black slag which stretched right across the road. His vision swam with the monstrous dark shape of the killer tip. His belly lurched and heaved again and again with acid. He was sick again and again. So it was back in their hands again; yet another bill to be paid in the terrible cost of that bastard coal.

A man came running down towards him. 'We need that shovel up there quick,' he shouted at Glynmor. 'We've got to have as many shovels as we can. There's still a chance that we can dig some of those children out. There's word they've been hearing crying coming from up out of the classrooms.'

Back in Bont Terrace yet another shower of rain was washing around the tea leaves that Glynmor had flung out only that morning. The black leaves swirled around, clinging together in tiny black mounds as they were washed deep into the ash path.

In the kitchen, the kettle which Glynmor had left untended was still boiling furiously, the steam chugging up out of the spout and against the lace curtains on the misted windows. The fire was blazing emptily in the living-room, which Maggie had been gradually trying to transform from the

137

dull male stronghold of silly posters and ash-trays. She had thrown rugs over the settee and the mahogany armchair that she had always hated. She had put the odd painting on the wall and a spray of flowers on the window ledge. What she really wanted, when they got some money together, was to furnish the room in G-plan. The carriage clock on the mantelpiece said that the time was 9.25 a.m.

Upstairs in the bedroom where Maggie was still half-asleep the wireless was playing her current favourite, the Hollies' *The Air That I Breathe*, when the voice of the news announcer broke into the music. 'This is a news flash. Early reports from Aberfan in the South Wales Valleys say that a coal tip has fallen on a school there burying up to 200 children. The Civil Defence has been contacted and told to come with all the equipment they can muster. All the miners in the nearby area have been called to help in the rescue operation.'

'Oh God, no,' Maggie cried out, her throat clogging up and eyes swimming with tears. 'Oh God no. Let it not be true. Please let it not be true.'

'The nature of the rescue operation precludes the use of heavy machinery,' the BBC announcer continued. 'So the miners are digging out the children by hand.'

'Oh God please let it not be true,' Maggie called out, instinctively holding onto her bump. Suddenly she was almost doubled up with a shivering spasm of pain. Then she began getting strange bursts of cramp in her loins. 'Glynmor,' she called out, but he was nowhere around, 'Glynmor, where are you?'

'One report says that the tip moved over a mile before engulfing the school just after the children had gone into their classrooms after the school assembly.'

It had stopped raining by now with just thin mists curling over the grey slate roofs of Bont. The shops were empty, the Post Office closed and even the milk cart had been left abandoned next to the clock. The time was 10.05 a.m. Further up the sides of the volcano the mists were thickening up again so that the Valley rims could not be seen from below. With a white sheet of mist bearing down on the village it was almost as if great hands were coming down to wrap up all this grief forever.

With every fresh item on the news Maggie cried out in

horrified disbelief, her contractions coming on more regular now as her hands gripped the brass bed knobs of the bedstead behind her head.

'Early reports say that the tip moved over a mile and was over thirty feet high before engulfing the school. Just in the last minute the bodies of three more children were discovered.'

Glynmor found himself but one of three hundred miners and soldiers frantically digging down into that evil slurry. Matters had been made worse by a broken culvert which sent streams of water coursing down past the uprooted trees, broken water mains and ruined cottages, turning the slurry into a shifting glue which maddeningly stuck to their shovels.

'They do say the poor dab can hear his girl crying in there.'

'*Duw* an' he loved that girl so much as well. Waited for her every day after school he did.'

More men came with offers of even more help. As the minutes turned into hours they might have been a defeated army stumbling and staggering across a Second World War battlefield unsure of what or who they were supposed to be fighting. Their warm breath plumed against the cold air. Wellington boots squelched across the black swamps. About a dozen were trying to pull a tree away while a dozen more were trudging across the black, pocked slopes carrying sheets of corrugated iron on their backs. Yet another helicopter bringing in yet more members of the media came chattering up the valley, its swirling rotor blades making the hair of the workers almost stand on end. Ambulances were roaring in and out, and there was an endless line of lorries turning up from all over South Wales to carry away the slurry which was being loaded into them by chains of buckets being passed from hand to hand. Men were sweating and crying at the same time, their features unrecognisable in their stained dirtiness.

The grind, clash and bustle of the work directly above the shattered school would last for thirty seconds and then everything would stop as a whistle was blown. Each of the pauses was part of standard mine rescue technique when, for just ten seconds, silence fell and every ear listened for any cries for help from beneath their silted-up boots and shoes.

These ten second silences were the longest anyone could

remember or would remember. They were like great prayers that there would still be life in the tomb of death. Even Glynmor had the overwhelming sense of all the Valleys down on their knees in these silences, all holding their breath and praying with bunched fists held aloft for just one shriek, just one howl of pain which would tell of life. In those silences he just stood there, listening to the frightened pumping of his own heart. Even in his short life he had seen blood on the coal often enough but, as he looked around him, he knew that nothing could have prepared him – or anyone else – for this. This!

He plunged his shovel down into that foul-smelling black glue again, his whole body shivering and teeth chattering as if he had just caught a dose of 'flu and just couldn't get warm. At one stage his hands were shaking so much he could not even hold his shovel properly, letting it slip out of his hands with the handle cracking against his shin. Jesus, miners always expected trouble but not their babies. Not their babies as they sat in their classrooms only to be buried in slurry and killed before their young lives had even begun. His shivering kept up unabated and he finally had to put down his shovel and hold himself tight. Fortunately the others around him were too busy digging to notice him just standing there. His skin was goose-pimpling with something very strange too.

It was now 10.45 a.m. and the reason for his strange sensation, perhaps, was because he had somehow become aware that, at that very moment, on 21 October 1966, his first son was being born in Bont.

On normal days her sister or mother were always calling round Maggie's house to borrow a cup of tea or to bring a bit of hot gossip. But today was far from normal and no one had called over at all. By eleven Maggie had given up shouting for help and could feel the bump beginning to work out from between her legs. *Duw*, it was as if someone was trying to split her apart. Her fingertips fluttered around and touched the hairy head of her pain. She lay back, trying to keep her legs as far apart as she could. But, with each agonised contraction, she could feel a little more of the baby inching its way forward. And each time it moved, her legs twitched as if being touched by live electric wires.

But still, amazingly in such pain, all her mind could think

about was all those children drowning in that sea of black slurry. All she could visualise were all those small bodies swimming around and crying out with silent drowning screams. She too was swimming around in a sea; she was moving around in an ocean of immense and inconsolable grief. The pain of the Valleys was being driven through her heart like some giant wooden stake.

Now the slime-covered head and bunched fingers of the baby were just poking out of her vagina. Her contractions had stopped. She just lay there, panting and crying softly, for almost twenty minutes, still torn apart with misery as the news continued to wash over her.

'The rescue operation has now been under way for nearly two hours but still no one has been brought out alive. Parents offering help have been told to go away and let the miners deal with the rescue.'

She just kept her legs apart and lay perfectly still. She was not at all sure what to do anyway. The tears ran hot down her cheeks.

A van piled high with jangling new buckets from a hardware wholesaler came slithering and sliding down the main road leading up to the destroyed school. As people came hurrying up Moy Road to help unload them and pass them out, no one noticed the Secretary of State for Wales, George Thomas, walking with an ashen-faced Lord Snowdon. Another body had been found, someone said and the word swept around the village.

'Did the girl say anything?'

'No mammy, she was sleeping.'

The whistle blew again and the policeman with a loud-hailer called for silence as everyone held their breath just listening to the creaking thumps of their breaking hearts. In one of the gardens in Moy Road an old miner stood in the garden looking down unseeing at his cabbages, his eyes wide and transfixed with sheer disbelief. A man of the chapel all his life he was asking himself if they finally were putting the children of the earth to the sword? Was this the start of the age of prophecy when the all the first-born must die first?

Glynmor was now working feverishly with his particular group when a cry went up nearby and they hurried over to

141

prise up a blackboard. As they eased it up children's drawings fluttered in the breeze like dead leaves. When the blackboard finally came clear they found one of their teachers lying on his side, holding two children in his arms. Another child had fallen just near the teacher's feet. He had clearly been using the blackboard to try and shield them from the black tide.

Glynmor averted his gaze, the bile rising in his throat. Even though the sun, with brittle irony, was now beating down on Aberfan his vision was darkening. Even though breathing on the sharp morning air he felt himself drowning in the suffocating blackness. Like Maggie he too could see all those small bodies swimming around. He too could hear all those silent cries as their lungs struggled for air in that terrible darkness.

Blankets were held high as the miners picked up the black and broken bodies before placing them on stretchers. Glynmor stepped forward ready to help but there were already enough willing hands. Miners had long learned how to do the most unpleasant things without flinching; it was only later in the privacy of darkness that they did most of their crying. After the teacher came the children. One of their small hands was holding an apple, still ripe, red and shiny in all that dripping slime.

The sun had now risen high in the sky and Glynmor looked up at it, holding up his dirty arm to create a shadow. Just then something huge and dark seemed to move inside the fiery heart of the sun, growing and growing more until the whole of the sun had gone quite black. In the thickening darkness he couldn't see anything at all, though he could hear the sounds of some singing. But there was no fear in him as there might have been with someone who had lost the use of his sight. He was quite calm and still holding up his arm when the light began growing again and a dark spot was still coming out of the sun except that, this time, he could see clearly that it was another helicopter clattering down from the top of the tip. He wiped his eyes with the back of his arm.

Maggie let out an agonised cry and the baby burst forward from her in a tumbling mass of flailing limbs. Its legs and arms opened like an unfolding flower.

Breathless and close to exhaustion, she sat up and looked

142

at it, unsure what to do now. Where was Glynmor? Where was Daisy? Where was her mother? Where were these people when you needed them? The thick umbilical cord dangled from the baby's belly like a fat tail. The little sausage between its legs told that it was a boy. She recalled the strange words of John the tramp: 'You will always cherish the boy because he will be a boy like no other boy. There will be unseen eyes watching out for him.'

But she did not pick him up. She knew what every mother knows at such times. This boy was like no other because this boy had been born dead.

'The body of one of the teachers, Mr David Beynon, has just been dug out of the tip which engulfed the school at Aberfan,' said the news announcer. 'He was holding two children in his arms and others were dug out near his feet. It seems he was trying to protect them with a blackboard when the tip burst through the classroom wall.'

Tears spurted from Maggie's eyes and, biting her lip, she reached forward to pick up the ruddy splodge of her dead son, holding him in her arms and bathing him in the salty tears of her total grief. The baby's death was right somehow. Who wanted to bring a child into a world where they poured tips over the schools? Well, you were the lucky boy then, weren't you? Out before you were in. That's the way it should be, isn't it my lovely?

She gazed down at her son with her tears still pouring over his beetroot, almost angry, face, smoothing his thick thatch of greasy hair with her palm and now recalling those words she had first heard in Sunday School. 'Our Father which art in heaven,' she recited softly beginning the Lord's Prayer, 'hallowed be thy name; thy kingdom come, thy will be done on earth as it is in heaven. Give us this day ... ' She smiled and ran her hand under his chin. 'Give us this day a son for us to love.'

She stopped speaking and blew soft on the baby's mouth, now washing his cheeks and lips with her tears. Just then the baby's body gave a sudden shiver and, with his fingers bunching tight, his eyes opened and gazed up into hers with a long mysterious look which made her shiver too.

'Was the girl crying at all?'

'No Mammy. I said – I said she was sleeping.'

Outside in the backyard there was a furious fluttering of wings, so loud they made Maggie jump. She looked over at the window and then down at her baby again, feeling no fear. Rather a great gladness had exploded in the midst of her grief and she felt released from all her pain. She was the warm woman now, replete and happy holding her new-born in her arms.

Sunshine breezes were now gusting down the Valley, bustling and vaulting over the backyards and small sheds built of odd planks and asbestos sheets. Maggie's backyard had a small lilac tree next to the broken fence and, just near it, was a cucumber frame which had long lost its glass. A pile of breeze blocks stood next to a zinc bath with the washing line nailed to the roof of the coal shed and stretching to a small metal pulley on the wall of the house. The breezes were making the washing line sway drunkenly when three pigeons came down to perch on it, their wings hovering in a blur around their pink chests as they tried to hold their balance like tightrope walkers. They stayed there for, perhaps, three minutes, then flew away again.

Even as night stole on Aberfan its soothing blackness was denied. The sights which the village had witnessed could not be so easily veiled. They had already erected giant sodium lamps over the ruined school. Moths were attracted to their ferocious glow and sent small shadows dancing over the broken ribs of the school which poked up out of the still, black tide. Men were still labouring on; every part of Glynmor was aching, not so much from a day of shovelling the black glue, as from struggling to move his feet around in the stuff.

But when he did take a break, other men moved quickly to take his place. Legs like rubber, he lurched down a slope where a W.V.S. woman with burly arms served him a buckshee mug of tea out of a silver urn. She gave him sandwiches too so he took the opportunity to walk away from the disaster area and find somewhere quiet to be alone.

The rescuers were still taking the bodies out of the slurry and carrying them down to Bethania, the chapel of death in Moy Road, which was now being used as a mortuary. Nearly a hundred children had been dug out. And some of the teachers too. Glynmor stopped briefly, watching the crowds of anxious parents standing outside the chapel, hoping against all the odds that it was not their little one who would be laid out on the pews; that, somehow, their child had decided not to go to school that morning and jumped on a bus to go somewhere else. In the gilded darkness, still throbbing with generators and ceaseless effort, Glynmor turned around the back of a terrace and climbed up the side of the mountain until he came to a grassy bank where he could sit and sip his tea. At this distance the school had the gaudy, almost raucous atmosphere of a circus or a funfair. At least it had stopped raining. The rescue work would have been hopeless if they'd had to contend with more rain. It had been hopeless enough as it was. None had so far been dug out alive. He bit into one of the sandwiches and spat it out. It was spam; he'd always hated spam. A quick look into the others showed that they were spam also. He flung them all to one side and drank his tea. He had not been hungry anyway.

Another whistle sounded and all activity stopped for another ten seconds of silence. Here and there white smoke was drifting up against the darkening sky and a dog was howling, distantly and incessantly, as if in pain. Further away yet there was the noise of distant traffic in some distant Valley going about its distant business. The whistle blew and the shovelling began again.

By now Glynmor was too tired for anger, too tired for bitterness, too tired to even think straight. He just felt like every other tired rescuer in Aberfan that day; damaged beyond words, overwhelmingly defeated, aye. He covered his eyes with one hand as if in prayer.

'I thought it was you sitting there mun.'

Glynmor looked up startled. It was Emlyn Kremlin.

'Just came up for some fresh air,' Glynmor said. 'You know I fancy you can smell death in the air everywhere down there. It's in the slurry. It's almost like you can taste it.'

'You're right there, boy,' said Emlyn sitting down next to him. 'You get to know death in this game. Death has no mystery for the miner. He lives with bastard death all his life. Some of those old miners could hear death in the way the pit props did creak.'

They both sat looking down at the school in silence for a while. That dog had stopped yelping but now a few men were shouting, their angry voices curiously amplified by the desolate Valley night. There was a rustling of fat shadows nearby.

Sheep had found the sandwiches.

'It's bloody marvellous init?' said Emlyn finally. 'We used to beat children for sleeping down the mines. Now we pour slurry over them in the classrooms. You should get more political Glynmor. You drink too much and have got plenty of filthy gab but you should get more political and fight this sort of thing.'

'How can you fight this, mun? How can you fight all those fucking bastards who've done this? There's a century of neglect lying on that school.'

'Yes, but neglect by who?' Emlyn wondered. 'Those champagne socialists in Westminster? Those twots around here they call M.P.s? What happened to the Labour Party? That party was born in these Valleys, Glynmor. That was the party everyone fought for but then it went and died on us. We need new leaders, mun. Men with fire and guts. I know you Glynmor. I see what you are. You should look at that school and think of doing something.'

'Think of doing what?'

'Of standing forward and doing something, that's what. I'm getting old now. I can't do much any more.'

'Old be buggered. You'll still be fighting the management when Maggie and me are pushing up the daisies.'

'I need to know there's some men coming after me, Glynmor. I want some disciples. Men like me need to think we've got someone to hand the torch on to. You're young and you haven't been shocked enough yet. Be shocked by that school mun. Be desperate and angry about it. Let your guts boil in rage 'cos I'm telling you now there'll be a lot of hot air but precious little else when all this dies down. Now the Labour Party has gone to sleep on us there'll be no one to orchestrate our rage; no one at all to stand up and scream about our pain. In my time there'd be a whole revolution pouring out of the Valley after something like this. But not any more. We've been made sick by all our handouts and lies from Westminster. We're confused and have lost our pride. We've lost our anger, Glynmor. Someone like you should step forward and lift the flag for us. You should become more political and give us lessons in anger and feeling. That's what we need most in the Valleys now.'

Glynmor said nothing for a change. Such words had come

as something of a shock. He had worked so hard at being Jack the Lad it had never once occurred to him that he could be anything else.

Yet another helicopter came in, chattering low over the valley; moving one way and another before taking off again without landing. 'That was the Queen's visit, I s'pose,' said Emlyn. 'A quick rattle of her diamonds and she's gone.'

On distant parts of the mountain, banks of sightseers, many with lamps and torches, were building up like long lines of glow-worms, yellow on black, in the darkness.

'We'd better get back down there,' said Emlyn. 'You know my old body has all but fallen to bits but I'd never be able to sleep if I lay my head down. Not with a ton of sleeping pills and twenty pints would I. All that's keeping me going now is a drip-feed of bitterness.'

Glynmor stood up and followed the old miner down the slope. 'Tell me, Emlyn,' he asked. 'Is it true that you sent a telegram of congratulation to Mao Tse-tung when he took over China.'

'I did.'

'What did he say? Did he ever write back or anything?'

'No but every Christmas I do get a Christmas card from the Chinese Consul down in Cardiff.'

'I didn't know the Chinese went in for Christmas.'

'Neither did I. But, you know, I do send him a card every Christmas too.'

'Well don't that beat all? Two bastard Commies sending Christmas cards to one another.'

When they had walked back up Moy Road there was still a large crowd of parents outside Bethania Chapel, waiting anxiously for their turn to go inside. Many would queue all night until that bitter dawn when the last of the children had been dug out. Emlyn had stopped to talk briefly with a woman he knew when there was a commotion. A photographer was being kicked across the road. Word had gone around that some Press men had broken a window at the back of the chapel to photograph the dead children laid out on the pews.

What they had seen was the broken heart of Aberfan. They had seen and photographed some twenty-eight adults and more than a hundred children lying there on the hard wooden pews; all those small broken bodies with their faces dirty with slurry, their hair blackened, their lungs never to draw on the fresh mountain air again ... those beautiful mouths ... jammed full with silt ... never to ... never to laugh again.

Somehow Emlyn and Glynmor managed to push their way inside. The aisles between the bare, shocking pews were black with muddy footprints. A lone figure was kneeling at the altar. Even in the smell of the polish and the dull tang of coal this sense of death hung in the very air, as real and as oppressive as the yoke it would forever become. Even just standing there with his hands trembling and looking at the small heaps on the pews, Glynmor's mind told him to refuse to believe what he was looking at. Until he saw a small hand sticking out from beneath a torn sheet, clutching at a sixpence; until he saw another still clutching a birth certificate; until he saw another hand with small lifeless fingers stretching out and clutching nothing at all. And his throat choked and his eyes misted over and yet his mind still refused to believe what he was looking at. Here on these pews was the ultimate obscenity: the murder of children who were young, beautiful and without sin.

'I need disciples Glynmor. Be shocked by what you're looking at. Let your guts boil in rage. We've lost our anger, Glynmor. Worst of all we've lost our pride. The Valleys have gone on a long walk and forgotten their deepest feelings, lost the love that always made them special, lost the politics of brotherhood that made them the finest. Just look at all these lovely dead flowers, Glynmor, and tell me what's happened to our self-respect. This is how every Valley child will end up unless we rediscover ourselves. Look at all these lovely, dead flowers, my brother, and never forget.'

Footsteps echoed in the chapel rafters as a mother almost marched up the aisle. She almost marched because she could not walk. Had she tried to walk she would not have been able to at all; she would have been like her husband who just lay down on the kitchen floor unable to get up again. So she marched this, the longest march of her life and, when she looked down at the body of her daughter, she knew that she would be broken for ever. All she could do was swallow hard and march straight out again, bumping into the pillars and bashing through the swing door of the vestry as if she was on some sort of automatic pilot where, with her sight swimming, her legs gave way and she fainted, to be caught by two pairs of strong hands before she slumped towards the tiled floor.

Glynmor could almost feel his own legs giving way now. A mother and father had come into the chapel and stood briefly, their arms round one another, before moving shakily up the aisle. They hardly dared to look from side to side. A policeman came and pointed at a pew near the baptismal font. When they looked down on that child their hearts seemed to stop beating too. For that broken scrap was their blood. What broke the children broke the parents too. None of them would ever recover.

There was not one mother or father who stepped into the Chapel of Death that night who would not have, happily and with the greatest gladness in their hearts, been inside that school on that morning of mass murder if, by some bleak transaction, it would have meant that their own children could have been alive and free.

It was speckling lightly with rain when Glynmor returned to the spot where he had been working just above the playground. They were still not using any heavy machinery and yet more men had turned up. He waited patiently, his shovel in both hands, for someone to tire and step aside. Even in such a crowd no one spoke; a constant flow of empty and full buckets circled around.

After more than twelve hours of digging the men had given up their ten second silences. They were just going like hell now. Even in all this noise there was a strange sound issuing from the earth, a car horn which continued blaring, maddeningly, for hours until the battery had run flat.

Two men in front of Glynmor stepped aside and he had only just plunged his shovel into the black glue when he felt someone gripping his arm. He turned his head to see Stan Swansea, out of breath.

'Glynmor, I've been looking all over for you,' he panted. 'It's Maggie. She's been taken to hospital, she has. She's had the baby, mun.'

Glynmor looked down at his shovel. This day was becoming far too much for him. 'She's all right, is she?'

'She's all right, yes. But there's been complications. You'd better get over to the hospital. Don't worry about here. It's the living that need you now.'

'Did you hear if it was a boy or a girl, did you?'

'I didn't but you'd better get over there fast.'

He handed his shovel to Stan Swansea and walked down to one of the ambulances, hoping to hitch a ride over to the hospital in Church Village. What a day this was turning out to be, he thought as he pushed his way roughly through a bank of sightseers standing near a glowing brazier. A day without end, aye. He heard something and looked up into the night. It was that singing he had heard earlier ... mellow, gusting ... the hymn of a sorrowing wind.

The following Sunday the Rev. Kenneth Hayes, who had lost a child in the slide, stood in the pulpit of his Baptist chapel in Aberfan. 'Let us thank God that things were not worse,' he began. 'We must not be bitter, but we must approach it with a spirit of love. Let us be thankful for miracles and thank God for those who survived.'

Chapter Twelve

Ever since that day, a century ago now, when Rupert
Posthumous Evans bought the mineral rights to Bont farm and
a gang of sinkers dug a shaft right in the middle of a wood alive
with nightingales and squirrels, there had been grief in the
Valley. No sooner had the sinkers brought up that first lump of
steam coal when old Posthumous himself fell down the stairs of
his house and died of a broken neck, leaving his widow and
three sons to develop the mine and an early taste for living in
bungalows.

Almost from the first month of its operation the pit had
been dotted with disasters. It was the grief these accidents
created which contributed in no small manner to the very spirit
and texture of the community.

For, in ways difficult to understand and even more
difficult to explain, they seemed to help strengthen the
community by bringing it closer together. Those who mourned
in the Valleys – and there were many – observed this
phenomenon at almost every funeral from that of Teddy
Davies, the cobbler, to that of Mrs Elme Thomas, the
chapel-cleaner: the way in which grieving hands of every
persuasion came together to heal the hurt. And strange and
wonderful things happened in this healing process. Men
became better husbands and women became better wives.
There was even a more loving, prayerful spirit in the chapel
with many going who had not been there for years. Branches of
the family came together with other branches of the family
with whom they had not spoken for years. In a positive way
grief – as much as joy – was the very mulch of the community:
it was as if all those tears sprang from the same wound; as if a
pain shared was a pain dealt with.

At such funerals it was as if, deep in their grief, they were being told by silent, if insistent, voices that there was but one life which was as short and as a straight as a bit of rope. And in this life there were no rehearsals. At such funerals, then, it was time to put a poultice over the boils of long-festering insults and reach out to one another – in love. There would always be days for fresh insults but, just for now, it was the moment for putting your arms around one another and enjoying love's capacity to heal.

Except that no such process happened in Bont after the diaster in Aberfan.

Everywhere, from the Welfare Hall to the Co-op; from the washery to the time office; from the back seat of The Bug to the counter of the Chinese takeaway, it was the same. The shock of the loss of those children had turned to numbing sterile grief and the bitterness of acid tears. On the first day they gathered in small groups on corners and outside shops … silent, stricken, full of pain. And on the second they were much the same and on the third, and the fourth. As time dragged by and the winter stripped the slopes of the Valley, the villagers of Bont recovered little of their old vitality and ebullience. Men simply hung around, hands thrust deep down into pockets and shoulders hunched, not even drinking or swearing much, their spirits broken just as surely as if they had been smashed by a hammer on the anvil. The women went about their business and gossiped less, always keeping a particularly watchful eye on their own children, making sure they always got home before dark and giving them a good clip across the ear if they didn't.

Each had to handle the shock as best they could; either taking to their beds, or to drink or, even as Madge Williams did, taking a long holiday over in Shrewsbury – where there were no coal tips – and from where she sent a letter to Cynthia saying that she would never return.

But the most visible and obvious effect on the village was to be seen in the attendances at the Libanus Chapel which almost immediately plummeted from a few dozen to around half a dozen. Never a great success story at the best of times the chapel had now hit rock bottom and even old Mordecai, who had long felt that it was coming anyway, could hardly believe it when he looked out on that sea of empty pews on Sunday mornings. He even lost three of his deacons who just stopped coming. If Evan Roberts had presided over this chapel when it was at its height and strength, then Mordecai was surely now presiding over it at the time of its death. But it was hard for his parishioners. He could see that. He just didn't know how to stand up in that pulpit and make any sense of Aberfan and God's reasons for allowing it. Wisely he never tried but, anyway, it was by now all too late. People had made their decisions and voted with their feet. At least it left him with a lot more time to work on his book about the Great Revival and, his principal passion, his racing pigeons.

Yes, something vital had got up and walked out of Bont after the Aberfan disaster. You could not be sure what it was exactly except that it had gone. Even The Bug, which had been struggling for years in a mortal fight that with upstart television, succumbed and was boarded up. In a desperate ploy to boost attendances they had even managed to get in *The Sound of Music*, which had been breaking all records in Cardiff that year, and Stan the Box confidently predicted that the film would do even better than *Cosh Boy* which still held the box office record. But it was not to be. With so many children dying under a black mountain of sludge no one was in the mood to watch Julie Andrews leading her laughing tribe over the sunny Alps of Austria.

Come bonfire night, and the last performance at The Bug was a melancholy affair. Two couples over from Porth grappled and steamed in the back row while the six other people in the audience tried to ignore them. Then, when it did look as if Julie Andrews was going to get away safely, Gnasher and the Clay Class – taking a break from a nearby bonfire party – dropped Jacky Jumpers off the balcony and for one awful moment it looked as if those Nazi bastards were actually gunning down poor Julie and all her singing brats. Even the grappling lovers stopped to look up as the usherette chased the Clay Class down the street.

The next day, rather than face bankruptcy proceedings, Stan the Box left Bont on the first bus. Although gossip had it that he'd been carrying on with Madge Williams no one was ever to see him around the village again.

With no one coming to him on N.U.M. matters – what was there to complain about after Aberfan? – Emlyn Kremlin spent a lot of time brooding in the Welfare Hall library which had still not yet been sold to the University of Wales. Emlyn found the presence of all those books on the inevitable breakdown of capitalism some sort of consolation and he was going to be very sorry indeed when they did go.

He was always first into the library in the morning too, waiting for Tudor to fit the newspapers into their wooden spines and then reading, with mordant interest, how each paper treated the story of Aberfan. He watched it over the weeks, going from the screaming headlines of page one to the small paragraphs on the bottom of inside pages and then out of mind. 'Well, out of the capitalist world's mind,' thought Emlyn, 'but not out of the Valleys.'

The Press turned its attention to other matters. 'Just listen to this,' said Emlyn to the dinner-time drinkers as he skimmed the mid-day edition of the *South Wales Echo*. 'A 45-year-old man was remanded in custody yesterday pending psychiatric reports. Despite persistent warnings, the man, John Tasbib of Adamsdown, Cardiff, continued immersing children and tramps in the river, the court heard. The man, who has a history of schizophrenic disorder, was remanded in custody for fourteen days. He was said to suffer from paranoid delusions of a religious nature, according to one doctor. He was very persuasive in getting the children and tramps into the water, being observed on four separate days dipping them into the waters.'

Emlyn flung the newspaper across the table. 'The biggest disaster in Welsh history and all they can write about is some fruitcake and his crackpot theories.'

There was always something in the news to make his bile rise. Now there was the royal appeal for toys and teddy bears which had all but engulfed the village again. Archbishops, who would be hard pushed to tell you the actual colour of coal, wrote angry letters to the Press. Then there was the appeal fund itself, which soon attracted a million pounds and was leading to endless internal rows in the village. Even then Emlyn could see it was going to turn out to be a disaster almost of the magnitude of the killer tip.

A tribunal was set up to discover the reasons for the disaster and, again, Emlyn was careful to read the Press reports each day. It turned out in the end to be the longest in history, lasting five months, hearing 136 witnesses and listening to 2,500,000 words recorded on 4500 pages of transcript. Sometimes, in his anger, Emlyn practically stabbed a hole in the newspaper with his forefinger. Here it was again, the endless, cultured braying of many people busy trying to shift the blame onto someone else; an ocean of words in search of a reason which could be swiftly dumped on someone else's doorstep.

The reason was simple enough: capitalist greed and socialist weakness. The rich, who had once plundered the Valleys, were strong and the poor, who had been abandoned after the plundering had finished, were weak. End of tribunal. Discovery of reason for accident. Q.E.D.

If it wasn't raining Emlyn might go to the bench near the clock in the square and sit chatting with the old-timers. They would all sit there together and watch the comings and goings of the villagers or nod a greeting to whoever. Maybe they would just try and work out what old Guto was trying to dig up. A day rarely went by when Guto wasn't wandering off to some distant corner of the Valley where, like some demented badger, he would proceed to dig a sodding great hole in the ground.

'That old Guto do work harder than any miner I've ever worked with,' Emlyn would say. 'What's he trying to find? Is there some gold around here that we haven't been told about or what?'

On some mornings the melancholy quiet of a Welsh mining village going about its lawful business would be suddenly interrupted by a red and white helicopter turning this way and that over the great black tips. The sound of the rotor blades would crack against the rock walls of the Valley and the old-timers on the bench would watch it, saying nothing. After Aberfan the cry had gone up to reclaim the Valleys. It was too expensive to remove the tips, they said, but grass was cheap. So they would grass them over instead. But everyone in the Valley knew that not even radishes would grow on those black slopes — and radishes will grow in pure arsenic. So some bright spark in the Welsh Office went back to the drawing board and discovered that grass grew well in chicken shit. A fleet of helicopters duly arrived and were even now streaming up and down the valleys spraying them with chicken shit.

The very sight of them made Emlyn's boots dance about

155

in rage. 'Look at it,' he would shout at the old-timers on the bench. 'They drown our children in coal slurry and now they're trying to gas us with chicken shit.'

As if the stink of chicken shit on every corner was not enough the same grey functionaries in the Welsh Office let loose a hurricane of empty rhetoric and documents about the way ahead for the Valleys. Learned papers examined the nature of the communities; orators spoke of the need for the provision of multi-purpose sports complexes. Experts argued new socio-economic strategies; the planners outlined how the infra-structure could be restored.

The result of all this urgent sociological bullshit, Emlyn raged, was that even now a third of the youth of the valleys were unemployed, another two mines, the Bwlch and the Ferndale No. 3, were due to be closed early next year and the valley communities were continuing to disintegrate on every level.

'And what are they doing about it?' Emlyn would go on at the old-timers as if, somehow, they might be able to set up a little parliament on their bench and legislate all the Valleys' problems away. 'I'll tell you. Not a thing. All my miners want is to drive a new car or lie on a fitted carpet or rot in front of a colour tele. Even the ones that *can* do it won't. Look at that Glynmor Jones. With what's happened to him and his family you'd think he'd do something but he won't. There's his baby still struggling for life in intensive care 'cos they couldn't get that doctor to come after he was born. And we all saw old Bomber dying by inches 'cos of the dust. But Glynmor won't do anything. None of them will. They just make jokes all the time and there they are with chicken shit running in over their wellies. *Duw*, boys, am I the only one who can see what's going on in these cursed valleys?'

Maggie brought her baby home from hospital two days before Christmas. Something quite remarkable had happened to her in hospital as well. She had shed all her excess weight and, with a large full bosom and legs like a greyhound's, Glynmor had the gravest difficulty in keeping his hands off her. 'I could barely wait till the nurse got out of the ward,' he told the boys in the bar. 'When I did get on her the nurse actually came back in as well. She just said, "Oh if that doesn't get her right then nothing will." '

To almost everyone's surprise – not the least to Glynmor's – he seemed even dafter over the baby than Maggie, actually taking him out for a walk in the pram on his first day back in Bont. He pushed the pram up the slopes with a cheerfulness that made some of the old-timers shiver with shame. In what he said and did he was almost acting like a man in love. From head-banging drunk he seemed to have changed into a doting, loving father who was a pleasure to know.

In the weeks that Maggie had been in hospital, even the dimmest observers in the village had seen a change come over him. When he had not been visiting Maggie or actually working down the pit he had not been going out at all, staying at home busily plastering and painting the new extended living-room, flinging out that old mahogany armchair that Maggie had always complained about so much and going down to Maskrey's in Cardiff where he shelled out for a new G-plan three-piece suite on the never-never. He also bought a plum-coloured fitted carpet which flooded every corner of the space-age room in a wine-dark tufted sea. He was even doing the shopping. All the gossip had it now that he was really cracking up.

It won't last long you know, Aunty Phyllis told Enid. I know our Glynmor, up one minute, down the next. His father was just like that you know. A devil for the horses he was. One week he'd be riding around on a new motor bike and the next he'd sold it and didn't have enough for the bus fare. Erratic. All that Jones family have been erratic. But where did he get the money from for that G-plan suite that's what I'd like to know? From Johnston's in Swansea he got that. Money like that doesn't grow on trees does it? Perhaps he found all those thousands that Bomber salted away. Yes. It's true that is. Thousands Bomber was worth when he popped his boots. Trefor, up in the garage, said it might have been a million.

December was the coldest anyone could remember. The thick night frosts lingered right up to the middle of the day when it would finally be melted by the thin cold sunshine. In some parts of the Valley the frost never melted at all and the huge boulders perched on the Valley walls seemed to have been dusted with finely crushed diamonds.

But that Christmas everyone had made an effort: ceilings were thick with gaudy trimmings, Christmas trees with coloured fairy lights stood guard behind the net windows of the front parlours. The sheep came wandering up the gullies looking for food and warmth. At this time of year they were fed too, instead of being driven back down the Valley slopes. The villagers even threw their scraps out to them and a few even obligingly turned over their own dustbins. Daisy – ever the soft sentimentalist – went so far as to put out a plate of mince pies for them. It was after all, Christmas; the time of the birth of the Lord of love.

The pit was closed down for three days over Christmas. On Christmas Eve the manager laid on a party for the boys on the afternoon shift. Even Emlyn Kremlin went along to the canteen for it and was actually civil to the manager. He could hardly have been otherwise since even a diehard Communist had to make an effort, standing, as he was, with a glass of N.C.B. whisky in one hand and an N.C.B. chicken sandwich in the other.

It was getting dark when the party broke up and some thirty of them, many still wearing their miners' safety helmets, walked along the mile-long road back to the village. The bleats of the sheep echoed out of the dark surrounding tips and, with their bellies glowing with a lot of fiery Scotch, they sang Christmas carols, their warm breath pluming in the shafts of their lamplights, their words somehow amplified by the cold stillness of the bright moonlight and transported high over the roof of the village where the quiet, blue smoke from the chimneys curled in the moon-varnished night.

In the square outside the Welfare Hall the singing miners were joined by yet more villagers, moving now onto some of the minor-key hymns of old. John Abdabs, one of the finest tenors in the Valley, led *Abide With Me* and more and more doors opened as that fatally beautiful hymn rose up to meet, warm and melt the stinging coldness of the night.

Glynmor, who had been sitting with Maggie roasting chestnuts, went out to stand at the door. He was just wearing trousers with a vest and braces dangling on either side but, strong and fit as he was, the cold did not bother him as it might have someone who had not spent all his life working in the damp and cold. Maggie came and stood next to him, holding

158

him around his waist, resting her cheek on his shoulder as the impromptu choir continued to swell. Now they moved into *All Hail the Power of Jesu's Name*.

Maggie just couldn't understand what had happened to Glynmor. He did not even seem to want to go to the Hall for a couple of pints of beer. What was even more puzzling, he wasn't complaining – or bragging – about it either. All he'd say was that he'd got fed up with the Hall and preferred to stay in with Maggie and the baby who, for the moment, they called The Boy since they were deep in an official dispute about his proper name. Glynmor wanted to call him Jampots but Maggie was having none of that and was holding out for Huw.

Glynmor also seemed to have abandoned all that old nonsense of him not being the father as well – even though the dates of the alleged dirty deed up on the river bank and the actual birth had never remotely matched up. In fact he just seemed to be hovering around the cot all the time waiting for The Boy to cry when he would be picked up and taken to Maggie's overflowing breast. He took immense pleasure in watching the baby being fed; in the small red fingers reaching out expectantly, the trickles of milk running down the side of his blotched hamster-like cheeks, the steady chomping of the tiny lips. And when he had been fed it was Glynmor who took him in his arms, as gentle as if he was about to fall to bits at any second, now patting his bum until that bright burp of wind erupted. Maggie always clapped theatrically when he managed that.

The hymn-singing continued, with yet more joining in. Never slow to miss a trick, the boys from the Clay Class were even now out knocking on the terrace doors demanding money. They served to bring out yet more poeple to join the choir and quite soon almost the whole of the village was crowding into the square.

Communities grow around their traditions but nothing like this had ever happened before while Emlyn, in particular, was pleased that they could still respond to one another; that they could still enjoy the carolling ease of good singing. The surging voice of a choir had always been the perfect expression of the Valleys at ease with themselves and happy with its future. There had been little singing lately and particularly after Aberfan. Wounds like that take years to heal. It takes a lot

159

of song and drink to heal up a wound like that, Emlyn thought.

And yet ... and yet he could sense that they were strangely happy about something. These sad minor-key hymns were always the way they expressed their happiness. Miners had always gloried in the glamour of sadness and, if a hymn wasn't sad, then it wasn't considered any good. If they didn't make you cry then they were no fun. Those songs of pain were their way of telling everyone that they were happy.

But were they? And, if so, why?

Emlyn was not sure. He felt something else in the night air; something which was not quite requiem but not exactly aria either. There was a trembling in pit props which was telling of something strange. A cloud passed over the face of the moon, briefly throwing the choir in the square into darkness before the light took over again, making everyone seem either black or white or even ghostly. He held his hand over his mouth tight.

John Abdabs led another hymn when the Boy began snuffling sending Glynmor and Maggie hurrying back indoors, she narrowly beating him to the pram when she picked him up and held him to her cheek. 'I'm so happy Glynmor,' she said. 'It's got that all I want to do is laugh all the time. You remember how I was when we got married. This morning I had to go out to the coal shed and have a quiet laugh. This is going to be the happiest Christmas of my life.'

'The happiest of all our lives and that's a fact,' he said holding out his hands, trying to take the baby off her. 'Here, shall we give him some beer or something shall we?'

'Certainly not.'

'Sherry then?'

'Certainly not. I don't want him growing up a drunk like his father. Speaking of which, why don't you go out for a few pints? I won't mind.'

'No. I told you. I said I'll stay here with you.'

That night they went to bed early and The Boy whiffled and snuffled in his cot as they made love, warm and slow.

'You know that bit when I come,' Glynmor said later in the darkness. 'I always think of a crowd of drunks barging in through a pub door at opening time.'

'Really?'

'The whole lot of them come charging in and then start

160

falling all over one another – bing, bong, bing – just like skittles.'

'You should have been a poet Glynmor. I bet Dylan Thomas never thought of anything like that.'

'What do *you* feel when you come?' he asked.

'Oh. I don't know.'

'Go on. How do you feel?'

'I feel … I don't know … I don't feel like anything really.'

'I'll tell you another thing as well. I can't decide whether your fanny smells of performing seals or fish fingers.'

'You're such a smooth-talking lovely. You should write all these gems down you know. Glynmor Jones. The great poet of the Valleys. Can't you just see all your collected poems on the shelves of the bookshops?'

'Do you think?'

'No, I don't think. Fish fingers indeed. And stop talking filth in front of The Boy. I don't want him growing up with a mind as filthy as yours.'

'Why can't we call him Jampots eh? Anything you want for his second name.'

'Never. Not ever. And take your hands off me Glynmor Jones. You've had your Christmas ration you have. It's like coming home to some over-sexed animal it is. I'm fagged out with it all.'

'What do you want to call him anyway?'

'I told you. Huw. And it's no sex for you till he is called Huw. So get your hands off me now do you hear? None. No drunks banging through doors. No smell of fish fingers. Nothing. Get off.'

'Stop shouting girl.'

'I'll shout if I want. You really make me mad sometimes.'

'If you don't stop shouting you'll wake Huw up.'

A long silence as she lay looking up at the dark outlines of his face. 'Glynmor,' she said. 'Why don't we have a few more drunks banging through a few more doors? And another thing. Don't compare me to the smell of fish fingers is it? If you must, compare me to a performing seal. I've always liked seals I have. Saw them in a circus in Cardiff once.'

'You're enough of a bastard circus on your own girl.'

Strong winter winds were now roaring off the high rocky screes of the Valley, sometimes dislodging a stone and making it bounce

161

and dance off the rocks until it fell onto the road. The winds rattled against all the windows too, shaking them endlessly in their putty surrounds or else pushing up and down on the gutterings of the terraces, like a plumber looking for weaknesses, or even sometimes managing to work free a slate and send it crashing down into concrete patios in the back gardens. The winds seemed to be busily at work in every single corner of the village, if not down in a gulley bumping around a few empty chop suey cartons then up at the Post Office whistling in the mouth of the red postbox or else simply dashing across the very heavens, shipping the dark clouds before them through the moonlight.

The winds were so cold they had even driven the impromptu choir into the Welfare Hall where even now they were carrying the sounds of the continuing hymn singing into every part of the night. But you could only ever pick up the odd phrases as they were blown across the roofs or blown sideways up the slopes. There was no continuity in the sorrowing melodies but there was sweetness in abundance and, as they drifted into Glynmor's bedroom, they even woke up baby Huw whose eyes opened and looked at the ceiling.

The colour of his eyes was not visible in the darkness but, on closer inspection, there was something else; something strange and even magical. There were faint shooting lights in those eyes; sparkly lights that changed colour from purple to orange and green. They were unbelievable colours, almost like a tiny firework display seen from a great distance away.

There was a soft puttering noise too – the racing beats of his heart and the occasional soft sigh which, when listened to closely, sounded like the sigh of an old man.

But then both the lights and the sounds disappeared and all that could be heard were the breathings of his mother and father with, on occasion, Glynmor lifting an elbow into the air and then letting it fall again. Outside the winds were still bustling the length and breadth of the Valley as if looking for a way out.

Christmas Day was a joy; muted, perhaps, but a joy nonetheless. The strong winter winds had wandered off to ransack another Valley while great spinning tops of sunshine came whirling down from the reservoir, dancing gold on the hurrying river, slipping through the gaunt, black shapes of the silent and abandoned mine and running amok around every corner of the village where almost all of the children were up and about the pavements, showing off their new toys, pedalling their new cars down the slopes or wobbling about the place on shining bicycles far too big for them.

Back indoors, the elders were staring into the grey painful dawn of mighty hangovers. The rich aroma of roasting turkeys and cooking vegetables seeped out into the backyards, making even the wandering sheep slaver at the mouth. Some had gone to Oboe Parry's house for a quiet sherry while others, looking for the hair of the dog, were even now waiting outside the Welfare Hall, ready to fall in the door when it opened for the midday session.

The service at the Libanus Chapel that morning was the oddest ever. Rev. Mordecai, as was his custom, waited in the vestry to welcome his parishioners except that, this morning of mornings, only six old ladies turned up – each wearing flowery hats and carrying huge handbags. At one point he was almost tempted not to continue with the service at all but, when he did, his sermon was something of a classic of defeated bitterness.

He began by explaining that the valleys were clearly going through a long dark night and that it seemed to him that the disaster at Aberfan was merely a prelude to all sorts of other troubles which were going to engulf the people and make them cry out for mercy. It was, he continued, clearly a just and fitting punishment for a people who had given up on God and taken to adultery, bingo and the drink. A just father could not allow such behaviour to go unpunished; a just father was a disciplinarian also and what we were seeing was merely the beginning of a long chastisement which was going to be unbelievable in its fury and intensity.

There were few real options open to us, he went on, except to wait on the Lord's infinite and tender mercy. There was no point in even behaving like Moses who prayed that God would change his mind. We now had to face what was due to us and, when it became too bad, the only possible way of salvation was for us to have another great revival when, with glad hearts, the whole nation would turn again to God.

In the absence of that, he said, we can only stay good and keep our faith as best we could. Anyone who read the Bible would know of God's marvellous sense of timing and so we had to believe that the right moves would indeed be made at the right time. Mordecai added that he would now be withdrawing though quite from what he did not explain.

Afterwards, in the vestry on the way out, Mrs Muriel Price told the Rev. that she did not think much of the sermon. She went further. She added that it was the worst sermon that she had ever heard.

'I'm sorry to hear that Mrs Price,' said Mordecai. 'It was a sermon about the complexities and mysteries of the ways of God. You clearly didn't understand what I was saying.'

'I understood well enough. You were telling us that God sent us Aberfan to punish us for all the adultery you say is going on everywhere. Well, let me tell you there's no adultery going on in my house. If you'll pardon the language, vicar, you were talking a load of old balls.'

'Well I don't pardon that language Mrs Price,' said Mordecai, a man of the most spectacular piety when he wanted to be. 'I don't use that kind of language in my father's house so I don't see why you should. But, if you'll excuse me, I want to lock up the chapel now.'

'The trouble with you vicar is that you've got sex on the brain and that's not a very good place to have it,' Mrs Price went on, undeterred. 'The only one to enjoy the sermon was Mrs Pandy and we all know she's as deaf as a post. Well, someone's got to tell you haven't they? This used to be a great chapel – all my family went here they did – but you're driving them away with your daft remarks. Well someone's got to tell you haven't they?'

The Rev. retreated into the chapel, unwilling to confront this outbreak of nastiness any further. He had never understood why there were so many idiots in Bont; even more puzzling was how Mrs Price, the biggest idiot of them all, kept coming to his chapel when everyone else had clearly decided to stay away.

'People don't want to hear about your cruel and unjust God,' Mrs Price shouted after him in the chapel. 'They want to hear about a God of love who forgives all.'

'Please don't talk like a turnip Mrs Price.'

'Who are you calling a turnip? That's a tidy language from a vicar, isn't it? That's bloody tidy that is. Vicars are supposed to speak proper and there you are calling me a turnip.'

'It's perfectly simply,' Mordecai rallied again. 'If you don't like what *I* say in *my* chapel then stay away. Do you think I would cry if you didn't turn up here again? Can you see that? Can you see me in my pulpit crying into my handkerchief because a bunch of turnips haven't turned up to hear a sermon they are too thick to understand.'

'You'd better watch who you're calling a turnip you had. If you weren't a vicar I'd hit you sick with this handbag I would. I've never liked you either. None of us have. Ever since you came here with your bloody pigeons you've been nothing but trouble.'

'Look, I want to lock up this chapel. There's things I have to do.'

Meanwhile the Hall had filled up quickly. It being Sunday opening hours on Christmas Day most of the men were trying to get down as many pints as possible before the bar closed at 2 o'clock sharp. There were a few women piking coins into the one-armed bandits but most of the wives were still back home putting the finishing touches to their turkeys or thickening up the gravy with the backs of spoons.

The crowd at the bar suddenly divided as Guto walked up to the counter asking for a bottle of Guinness. He only ever came in once a year, did Guto, as filthy as ever, and had one bottle of Guinness. The way all the other members moved away from him, as if he had some new African pox, did not bother Guto in the slightest. He got his Guinness and went to sit out in the library to drink it alone.

Here, Dai. Did you hear what happened to Gnasher this morning did you? He got this airgun off Daisy for Christmas he did. Went out this morning and Trevor the Copper took it off him in the street. If you're out on probation then you're not allowed to carry a gun, Trevor the Copper said. I'm not saying he's right. I'm just saying what he said. An' Gnasher is going mad over it. Daisy has gone to the police station asking for the gun back.

That old Snipe Wilson is going to need a police station

before he's through. Heard have you? Do you know what the daft bastard went and done? He went to Aberdare yesterday to get the Christmas meat like. He goes an' 'as a few beers in the pub and someone gives him a tip for the 3.30 at Newmarket. Absolute cert it is.

Never.

Anyway the dopey sod goes into the betting shop and bets his Christmas turkey on a horse that's got three legs and is still running around the track. Hang on now. This is the best bit. Snipe decides to confess all to Doris so she asks him what happened to the pork chops. You know what he did? He used the pork chops for the betting tax. I ask you. Pork chops for the fucking betting tax.

Dopey git.

Aye. He did. Doris flipped her lid an' he's gone off to live with his aunty the last I heard.

Well I'll tell you something else boys. We're going to have to do something about this bastard vicar of ours. He's got duck eggs in his duck eggs he has. There's practically no one going there and this morning he was calling the women a load of parsnips.

Go on with you.

He was. He kept on calling them a bunch of parsnips all the time. Muriel Price was real upset with it all she was. He threatened to hit them too. On my baby's life. I heard she said that the sermon was the stupidest sermon she had ever heard an' he threatened to beat the shit out of all of them.

He used those words? Him a vicar an' he used those words? You're pulling my leg mun.

On my baby's life. Mind you he'd have to grow a few feet before he started beating the shit out of our Muriel. Have you seen those arms of hers? But that's what he threatened right enough.

Why are you pinching my bastard fags all the time for? Buy a bastard packet will you?

What's the matter? Poor are you? I'll go out singing carols for you with a tin mug.

You don't have to go singing anywhere. Just buy a packet of fags. Where's Den anyway?

I don't know. How should I know? Last I heard he'd gone to a party at Sandra's and no one's heard of him since.

166

Tell me Dai. Just when is this school closing anyway? One minute it's the school, then it's the railway line.

Well it's both, I heard. But they haven't fixed any dates yet have they? They say they're going to keep the junior school and send the seniors to Tylorstown.

It was the other way around, I heard. They were doing away with both schools and sending all the kids to Treorchy.

Treorchy! How are my kids going to get all the way to Treorchy?

Well they can walk like every other kid can't they?

Not the ten miles to Treorchy they can't. They have enough trouble walking out the back garden for a piss. If our Billy goes to get something in the shop he's got to come home and have a lie down for an hour after. There's more life in a bottle of pop than my lot.

You know, boys, I really am very surprised that Glynmor hasn't come in for a few pints. Today of all days.

A chorus of ayes and sighs.

I really miss him when he's not around you know. He was such marvellous company too, a real bad bugger. And fight! You know, Dai, he'd fight a brick wall if it upset him. He was even banned from the Chinese takeaway once for fighting in there. An', as it's Christmas Day, I won't even start telling you what happened to that Pole's bollocks when they got down to it in the pit once. He reduced them to a tiny pile of jello he did.

The Pole still walks about the place like Hopalong Cassidy you know. He's so bow-legged you keep looking around for his bloody horse.

But he's really fond of that new baby of his mind you. Look at the way he went down to the hospital every day while she was in. An' he's been out taking it for walks. When did you ever think you'd see Glynmor wheeling a baby in a pram?

Well I'm not saying anything but I heard that Maggie has won some money on Spot the Ball in the *Echo*. Glynmor's just being nice to her till the money comes through.

Never.

It's true that is.

Never.

That's what I heard anyway. She's picked up about four grand from The *South Wales Echo* so he's not saying boo, bah, bob's your arse till the money comes in. He's been getting into trouble lately. I'm not saying anything but I heard he's put some piece up in Penrhos in the pudding club.

Get away.

Well you know what he's like. A leopard doesn't change its spots well does it? Glynmor always said that he'd fuck a frog if it stopped still long enough. So he'll be needing Maggie's money to pay the girl off won't he? It's only commonsense init? He doesn't want some bint standing outside the pit, at the end of the shift, holding a baby in a shawl an' shouting it's his. Well does he?

They do say Glynmor has had more nookey than Tom Jones. How many women do you think Glynmor has fucked in his life?

Well he always said he wanted to fuck a million before he dropped. I shouldn't think he's too far off that. Aye. A real bad bugger. I really miss him, you know. Him and his stories. You remember the one where he fucked that piece up in the big house on the corner. I still laughs when I think of that. Anything from eight to eighty he said he'd fuck. Him an' all his bastard stories. There was never any truth in any of 'em you know. He could never open his mouth without telling a lie.

Dead pigeons, all with their necks pulled, lay around the floorboards of Rev. Mordecai's loft. Already their eyes had filmed over with the milky blue gauze of death. Some of their beaks were slightly ajar as if about to pluck a worm out of the grass. Their wings were crumpled with the feathers sticking out untidily so that you could never have guessed that these were once great flying machines of the air, ready and willing to fly through thousands of miles of sky to return home. Home here. Home sweet home.

Now they were just lying there, a defeated army in the aftermath of a total rout, amidst the muddy white splashes of their droppings. Their wings were still, their eyes blank, their radar cut off. All dead now. Here in home sweet home.

Inside the chapel the Rev. Mordecai was standing on the altar all twirling elbows and wrists, polishing the communion silver with a white cloth, occasionally holding it up to the light to ensure that he had taken off all the fingerprints and wine stains. It was the fingerprints that worried him most. Those hands that had defiled the sacred silver. Satisfied, he then put them away in the corner cupboard beneath the board announcing the hymn numbers. He tidied the sheet music on the old harmonium before picking up the few hymnals dotted on the pews and placing them in a neat pile on the table next to the vestry door.

His movements had an exaggerated sense of slowness about them, all somehow as if he had to do everything at the right moment and in the right way. There were lots of tiny white feathers attached to the sleeves of his jacket, a dribble of bird droppings on the front of his trousers.

He stood on the backs of the pews near the walls and went around drawing each of the thick curtains, blocking out the thin light of Christmas afternoon. When he had finished and the dark shadows had huddled together in every corner of the chapel he took the large metal key out of his jacket pocket and locked the front door from the inside in a series of soft revolving clicks. Now he returned back down the aisle, stopping for a moment, as he held the key out in front of him, to look up at the pulpit where the Bible sat closed and shrouded by darkness. He had spoken many words from that pulpit.

But no more.

'Lord come back to us,' he prayed aloud, holding up the key towards the pulpit with both hands. 'We your servants are weak and everywhere your enemies are strong.'

He stayed still as if waiting for a reply and, when there was none, he shook his head in some secret sorrow before putting the key into his pocket and shuffling out of the chapel and back to the coal-fired warmth of his manse.

The body of one of the dead pigeons in the loft shivered suddenly as if being touched by a live electric wire and then it fell still again. A wing on another pigeon lifted slowly before collapsing down to the boards again. Even so early in the afternoon the light was breaking up fast with thick cold shadows stretching down the valley walls.

And so, that Christmas Day in 1966, the Libanus Chapel, set high up on the south east face of the Valley, just on the edge of the village, became a place of death and long winter shadows. The damp darkness inside the building became so musty you could practically eat it. Mould grew on the hymnals and cobwebs fanned out on the windows. Most of all the place missed the sun.

169

When it was sunny the sun glowered on the opposite face of the Valley all morning. Then, as the sun moved around on its high wide circle, it did briefly shine on the grey slate roof of the Libanus but never for longer than an hour since it quickly dipped behind the outlying pile of jagged brown rocks of the *cwm*, plunging the chapel into yet deeper shadows. The sun came late to Libanus and then left early.

And that was on sunny days. Most of the time it just rained.

Part Two

The Song of the Cave

Now the steelworks are silent
Cenotaphs, memorials to a nation's
Earnings but not its wealth,
And the dead pits, graves that
Echo with the ghosts of young
Men's laughter and flood
With widowed mothers' tears.
My grandsons will not inherit
My blue scars nor the coal that
Has filled my chest and chained me.

Gwaed, Bob Reeves

Chapter Thirteen

The hard yellow vein of sandstone just appeared in the black coal face, as welcome and inappropriate as a streaker at a funeral. The cutting blades of the Dosco sparked and stuttered; the engine sent out high-pitched squeals of frustration. There was just no way those blades were going to eat into that sandstone with the men having difficulty getting their handpicks to chop around it to loosen it a little.

It was the way it had been for days with this Meadow seam. The shift had been asked to make forty feet in a week and, indeed, got off to a flying start, getting out ten feet on the first Monday. After that everything that could go wrong with a heading went wrong. First the seam changed its gradient and began moving upwards turning the working floor into the texture of puddings. Then they had to use special hydraulic jacks to shore up the sloping roof which slowed them up yet again.

Now they were working a one-in-seven slope on a 200-yard seam and this thin yellow yawn in the face had come and dashed all hopes of meeting the shift target.

Such coal as they had been winning had not been up to much either. Some of it had even looked like ash, as if it had already been in the fire-grates and was about to be thrown out. By the time it had gone through the sieving process at the washery there would be very little left to burn.

The engine of the Dosco was cut off and the men changed the positions of the chocks to see if that would help. But it was no use. Again the blades began chattering into the sandstone, slashing on the vein again and again but barely making any impression at all as the engine howled and screamed dementedly.

This lack of progress was spelling out a lot of trouble for the already troubled shift. In their ceaseless search for higher quotas the N.C.B. was now asking for 1800 tons a shift a week out of the pit and, over the past two years, the Bont mine had developed three faces: this one, the Meadow B2; another face on the Six Feet and another running down to Trelewis. These faces had been productive enough at the beginning, maintaining high quotas and keeping the Bont mine open as the other mines in the Valley were all closed, one after another. (Danny Kettle from Porth reckoned that he went through three mines in 1969 while he was still on the same bar of soap.) But last year a squeeze had developed in the Trelewis face and, no matter how many rings they put into it, the roof seemed to insist on coming down, buckling everything in sight until the work there was finally halted and the face abandoned.

So now they were only working the Six Feet and the Meadow B2. Plenty of coal was coming up out of the Six Feet, but hardly enough to keep the pit viable, so a lot was riding on the Meadow, with Emlyn Kremlin, hardly an N.C.B. lackey, telling the men that they must make their quotas.

And now this.

The Dosco was pulled back again and the men stood around in a group with the lights of their helmets shining on the obdurate wall, revealing in the bright blackness the long yellow sliver running through it like a map of the Ganges, perhaps, or even a vein of gold. Except that there was nothing precious about sandstone.

'Why don't we drill it and blow it up,' suggested Tom the Nutter.

No one said anything because no one ever took any notice of anything that Tom the Nutter ever said. Indeed no one had ever figured out how Tom the Nutter had ever got a job down the mine in the first place. You didn't need a degree to work down here but even N.C.B. officials could see that the Nutter was very thick indeed. He had always been called Tom the Nutter because he was nuts and never showed any sign of improving either. He had, however, become Glynmor's new sidekick and they spent most all of their working time together, if not actually studying the topless model on Page Three of The Sun then sharing the contents of their snap tins. Glynmor had found long ago the Tom the Nutter's missus was marginally more creative with a snap tin than his Maggie.

'We'd better call up the manager,' said Glynmor.

'What do we want that silly bastard for?'

'Well we're going to have to see him sooner or later.'

'Perhaps we could pick it for a bit to see if it improves?'

'We could cut it out there,' said the shift foreman. 'But we're going to have to call the surveyor.'

'That won't improve it,' said Glynmor. 'Not that. This fucking rock is only going to lead to more fucking rock.'

His boot kicked out in a gesture of futile bitterness. How he had come to hate this bastard coal. He had been working down this mine for close on eighteen years and he could still remember the times when it had been like a family with its own customs and soft jobs for the disabled. They had been good days too, with men always covering up for the others and familiar with the routines of a friendly management. He could still remember those mornings when the men had been happy to go down the hole and work on a heading where all was jokes and laughter in that warm shawl of brotherhood.

But today nothing could be less likely. This was another Britain. This was the monetarist year of 1980; an era of high productivity quotas and economic efficiency. If it did not make a profit then it was to be butchered. If it was ailing it had to be booted hard like a dog. Everyone was feeling the chill monetarist winds – even that morning shift now staring at a sandstone-ruined face on the Meadow seam.

It wasn't just hostile economic and geological conditions that they had to work against either. A 1967 redundancy scheme allowed those over fifty-five and the disabled to make fast and profitable exits. These old miners had been the keepers of the culture but, as they retired and the other mines in the Valley were closed, younger miners came flocking in. These boys knew nothing of the mine's customs and cared even less to learn them. They would probably be driving their new cars somewhere else again next year. These were the young cowboys of the industry, mavericks who would never stop anywhere long enough to learn about the secret language of the pit props. All they were keenly interested in was the size of their wage packets.

But, even with such problems; even with every rotten mine in the area now closed and almost half the Valley youth unemployed, the pressure on the Bont pit to turn out high quotas was enormous. Men with stopwatches and clipboards would turn up suddenly on the face. There was a lot of talk about 'disturbance' allowances; redundancy in disguise, the old guard called it. They'd seen it all before too. This was nothing but the old hated piecework scheme, believed eliminated in the National Power Loading Agreement of 1966 but now back again and raring to go. Even more insidiously, junior managers with English accents kept making random checks on places like the stores looking for anyone trying to get their head down under a blanket.

Yet, happy or not, the boys did get down to their work, knowing that, if the new quotas were not met, it would be the dole queue and the end of their working lives. Most were unwilling to face the prospect of ending their working lives so soon – most, but not all. Some were forever calculating the likely amounts of their redundancy and wanted to get out any way they could. These were the ones who were often accused by the others of willingly and even happily putting the boot into the pit.

Where there was once brotherhood there were now multiple divisions in the family.

The young were pitted against the old. Sections of the face workers were pitted against the management. The pit deputies were at permanent loggerheads with the electricians. Glynmor had noticed of late that even the face workers had been quarrelling with one another, something unheard of only a few years ago. Somehow – and no one was quite sure how – a lot of laughter had seeped out of the old mine.

You could see the strain in a lot of their faces. You could see it in Glynmor's for certain. Where once there were bright laugh lines there were lines of middle-aged puffiness. The flesh had closed in around his eyes too and there were grey streaks in his hair. He had grown a bit of a beer paunch too and could not even remember the last time he had butted anyone. Somehow he had lost his puff. He made no secret of the fact that he would dearly have liked to have got out of the mine. But to do what? He was too old to be retrained for a job in one of those banjo or pop factories that were sprouting up here and there. He had become yet another slave of the lamp like his father and grandfather before him. He accepted that well enough. It didn't stop him from dreaming though.

'Why don't we blow it up?' the Nutter asked again.

'You'll get blown up if you're not bastard careful,' Glynmor replied.

Just as they were all still staring at the face, like a defeated family gazing out of a boarding house window on a holiday pouring with rain, there was a soft plop as a lump of coal worked loose and brown water came pouring out of a hole the size of a fist. Well I'll go to bastard Africa, Glynmor thought. A vein of sandstone that does not want to be cut and now a pocket of water that had to be pumped. All they needed now was a blower of gas to make the party complete.

'I think this face is knackered,' said Danny Kettle, the shift foreman as the water continued to gurgle out into every corner of the heading.

'Where's your crystal ball?' asked Glynmor.

'One thing's for sure. This shift is knackered till they get the pumps in. Knock off that conveyor Jim.'

The sudden gush of water introduced an unexpected taste of freshness into the turbid, coal-speckled air. It was the taste of a lollipop on a hot summer's day; a taut little reminder of the life that still bloomed above the earth and beneath the skies away from this troublesome seam of coal. Glynmor took a deep breath on it before turning and walking away through the sloshing puddles that were already building up everywhere. 'There's more coal in my shed than down here,' he muttered to Tom the Nutter. 'And, come to think of it, I've got sod all.'

'You can have some of mine if you like,' the Nutter offered brightly. 'I'll let you have it cheap as well.'

'That was always your trouble wasn't it? All heart and no brains you are. It's a wonder you haven't given away your house before now.'

But Glynmor's taunts were always lost on the smiling Nutter. He accepted such comments as gestures of friendship which was perhaps why they both got on so well. Most people misunderstood Glynmor's little ironies and sarcastic flights.

Up top it was a day of bright sunshine. The young heather was poking up out of the dead brown bracken and waving in the breeze as the boys from the morning shift walked back to Bont. Those in cars whizzed up the mountain road while, high up the side of the Valley, a farmer on his horse was rounding up his sheep with the help of three dogs. His whistles and angry shouts carried on the breeze as the sheep themselves tumbled over the rocked face of the *cwm* in fluffy white avalanches.

Glynmor walked along the pit road with Danny Kettle. 'Just look at that bloody mess down there,' he said. 'Sometimes I do feel ashamed when I do look at that dump and know that it's my home. We live in that shithouse mun. What's happened to us eh? A thousand pounds for the first bright bastard who explains what's happened to us.'

Even viewed from as far away as where they were both walking, just past the pit main gate, the buildings and terraces of Bont told their own story. It was the sad story of a village that had died before its time: the railway station long closed, the weeds shunting over the roof of the waiting room; the streets themselves but loose collections of holes held together by tarmac; the outlying fields scattered with litter or the odd abandoned car. A few of the shops had closed too, with planks nailed across the windows. Those still in business had wire grilles over theirs.

There had been other significant changes in detail. The roof of the derelict cinema, The Bug, had fallen in on itself and Lee Hoo Wonk had finally sold enough Chop Suey to save enough to return home to Hong Kong. Walford James, the former bingo caller in the Hall, had left the Valley to seek his fortune but had now returned somehow having got shot of his wife in the process. Walford also had a trail of fluttering affiliation orders in his wake, said the gossip. He seemed to have found a bit of money, however, since he opened one of those new video libraries in the premises of the old Chinese takeaway where, for £1 a night, you could rent all the latest video cassettes. You could also, if Walford knew and approved of you, rent videos of a very different kind; plain, discreet cassettes in which various people of several sexes tied themselves into various reef knots lasting an hour or so before they tied themselves into yet further knots for another hour. Such entertainments were very popular, particularly up in Giro City, the small, award-winning council estate which had sprung up just outside the village.

The school had also closed. There just weren't enough pupils to justify the cost of its upkeep, said the education authority. Now the children were bussed over to Aberdare and the old school had become a garage. There was a high wire fence where the playground used to be and alert Dobermans ran around the dumped cars, their bonnets agape and engines ripped out. Motor parts were now stored in the old school lavatory.

Even the police station had long been closed, with the windows boarded up and clumps of weeds growing out of the gutterings. Graffiti announcing nothing at all had been sprayed on its walls in huge aerosoled whorls of purple and yellow. The Glamorgan police had closed the station in a bid to improve crime detection, finally withdrawing the local man, P.C. Watkins, who was given a desk job in headquarters in Cardiff in favour of a wide network of Panda cars which would cover the five Valleys and enable them to speed to any incident within seconds of it being reported. Ho, ho, said the rude boys from Giro City.

These days, where once every door had been left open and every window unlocked, an unprecedented crime wave was sweeping up and down the Valley with things, large and small, walking out of the houses, day and night. If a housewife wanted to clean upstairs, she first had to lock the front door downstairs. If it was fine enough to peg the washing out to dry on the line it was also fine enough to sit out in the back and keep an eye on it to see that it was not pinched.

The Welfare Hall had not escaped this steady dive into dereliction either. Even as Glynmor and the boys went into the bar for a few pints to wash down the coal dust, you could see its decline in the broken window frames and unpainted doors; in the filthy lavatories and peeling wallpaper. In its whole dusty decay there was the same melancholy music as there was surrounding the rest of the village; the same sad tune of a building that had given up the ghost.

The loss of the library there – together with the closure of the reading room – had, to this day, been one of the bitterest blows in Emlyn's Kremlin's life. He had campaigned long and loud about the committee's decision to turn the library into yet another bar but, in the end, had to give way. So now, where once there were the sacred texts of Marx and Engels, there were now one-armed bandits, a colour television and a pool table – the inevitable notices signed by the committee warning against the doing of this or the forbidden doing of that.

The scale of betrayal was almost Tory in Emlyn's eyes. A group of committee Hitlers – many of whom had nothing to do with the mine anyway – had pulled the plug on a century of miners' learning and quest for self-improvement. They had come and pissed on the very altar of the working class, had deprived them of one of their few hopes of ever gaining political control.

Nevertheless Emlyn nowadays conducted most of his business in the Hall, sitting at his own little table in the corner of the bar, just next to the telephone. From this convenient seat of office he would make himself available to anyone who might want help or advice on the usual issues; claims for 'dust', widows' concessionary coal or some fight for injury compensation.

'So how's the red revolution coming on this morning?' asked Glynmor, going over to the table with two pints in his hands and putting them down next to a pile of papers.

'The red revolution has turned blue – just like everything else in this Valley,' Emlyn replied, straight-faced.

'I think the Meadow seam has turned blue too,' said Glynmor. 'We've hit sandstone and water there this morning.'

'Aw, that does it then.' Emlyn seemed genuinely dismayed by the news. 'They're going to come after the pit with the biggest axe you've ever seen if that face goes.'

'You almost sound as if you care, mun.'

'Care? 'Course I care. When that pit goes this Valley is finished. Dead.'

'It looks pretty dead to me already.'

'It's dead 'cos there's no economic muscle in it. No factories, no roads, no railway, no nothing. When are you going to do something, Glynmor? We need another man on the lodge committee. It's time you did something. Well, isn't it?'

'Not me Em. This place is dead 'cos the people in it are dead. You can't fight with death, mun. Not even the lodge committee can fight with death. Death is death and every bastard one of us has got one foot in the grave.'

'Well wake them up. Someone like you could do it. You could carry people with you if you only tried.'

It was the way the two of them had been with one another over the years. Emlyn Kremlin, the old N.U.M. warrior, forever trying to get someone young and talented to lift up the spear. But, fond though they clearly were of one another, it was no use. In almost every way they were in fundamental opposition to one another. When Emlyn looked at the floor all he saw were principles. When Glynmor looked at the same floor all he saw were fag ends. Emlyn was the defeated idealist looking to others to light the flame. Glynmor's ideals had never been defeated, because he had never espoused any. The pair of them did not even agree on why the Valley had slid into such ruin. Emlyn blamed the economic order and the continued butchery of the pits. Glynmor threw much of the blame on the people and pointed out that the Bont mine was still open.

As if that philosophic chasm was not enough there were many in Bont who did not believe that there was anything wrong with the place at all. It was, they told one another repeatedly, the finest village in the world.

'So how's my favourite niece keeping?' Emlyn asked after taking a long ruminative sip from his pint.

'She's great mun, and Huw is as daft as ever. What's the news on Daisy?'

'Don't ask.'

'Go on.'

'She's gone and run off to Greenham Common. Went last night.'

'You're pulling my pisser surely? That women's peace camp thing? And what about the boy? Who's looking after him?'

'She's asked me to keep an eye on him. Aye. Me! Came to see me before she left. But there's not much I can do with the skinhead bastard. He won't get out of bed all day and roams the Valley at night. I wrote to his father the other day but he doesn't want to know. He said anything to do with Daisy was bound to go rotten.'

'*Duw*, well what a turn up for the books that is.' Glynmor was almost stuck for words looking down into the foam-curled throat of his half-finished pint. 'What a turn up. Daisy can't control her own son so she runs off to Greenham Common to save the world instead. Maggie will go potty when I tell her.'

'Perhaps you'd better not tell her. She's got her own problems with young Huw after all.'

'She doesn't have any problems with him. She bastard

idolises him. Makes me sick sometimes it do. The way she slobbers and drools over him you'd think we had a fucking pop star in the house.'

'It's good that one of them looks after their kids proper.'

'What! If anyone laid a finger on Huw she'd kill him stone dead and that's a fact. I'm not even allowed to shout at him let alone give him a clip across the ear. Here. Do you want another pint of this piss or what? You do? Well get up there you mean bastard. It's your round.'

Several pints later, the afternoon sun was still singing in the rooftops of the terraces as Glynmor, in a cheerful alcoholic haze, walked home. But his good mood soon drained out of his very boots when he saw that his portable television had been put out on his doorstep again, along with the empty milk bottles. It was that cowing son of his again. Every time they took their eye off him he unplugged the television and put it out on the doorstep. Just what was the matter with the nutcracker?

Glynmor picked up the television and carried it back to its place in the living room before going out into the kitchen where Maggie was sitting next to the stove looking through into the bathroom where their son Huw Bungalow, now 14, was splashing about in the bath and shouting noisily.

'Do you think you could stop putting the television out in the street?' Glynmor shouted at Huw. 'He's been at it again,' he snapped at Maggie. 'Leave the thing just where it is,' he shouted again at Huw. 'You hear? Just leave the thing where it is.'

'There's no need to yell,' Maggie said, unconcerned. 'You should know by now he can't understand anything you say. And he still can't understand it if you shout either.'

'Well, why doesn't he leave the television alone?'

'Why? I don't know why. I think it gives him a bad belly.'

'How can television give you a bad belly?'

'I don't know. It certainly gives me a bad head sometimes. So why shouldn't it give him a bad belly?'

'Just watch your step you,' Glynmor shouted at Huw again. But the boy simply splashed him with a shower of soapy water and began laughing uproariously. With soap suds dripping down his face Glynmor just had to sit down on a kitchen chair and smile. It was, he had to grant, impossible to be serious with an idiot in his bath-tub.

He was lucky to be alive at all. Huw was seriously handicapped, his whole body twisted at the spine. His facial features were fine, even handsome though with huge black eyes and a Beatle haircut, a style which had long been abandoned by other boys in the Valley but which, somehow, seemed to suit him. Apart from making loud noises he could not speak either. But he could laugh like a drain and, for most of the day, just wandered the streets of the village in a continual gale of laughter which, in its turn, made everyone else laugh as well.

Loved by everyone, he was known throughout the Valley as Huw Bungalow – on account of he had nothing up top.

At first Glynmor found it difficult to come to terms with having a son who was as thick as a canteen mug. When the severity of the handicap became apparent he even stopped taking him out for a while, blaming the doctor for not coming promptly enough to the birth. In a way he had blamed Maggie too. She surely could have shouted out of the window and got someone to come in. Only Chinese coolies, as he had once seen on television, gave birth to babies on their own.

'Can't you shut the bathroom door when he's having a bath?' Glynmor asked irritably.

'Don't be silly. He might have an accident. Anyway, I like looking at him.'

But soon Glynmor came to accept his son. Right from the beginning, Huw Bungalow let it be known that he might not be able to talk so he was going to laugh his head off. Even when he was still in his pram the sounds of his laughter would drift to every corner of the Valley, be it the pit canteen or down by the river. Ah, the miners would look at one another and smile. It's Huw Bungalow it is.

All this laughter soon undermined Glynmor's hostility. With Maggie in one hand and Glynmor in the other, Huw Bungalow would take them on long walks up to the reservoir on afternoons when it was as if their childhoods had been handed back to them.

'Look at him now,' said Glynmor. 'He's farting like he's in some sort of bubble bath.'

'He does fart a lot,' said Maggie, taking a bath towel over to him. 'It's those Heinz baked beans he loves so much. And it's got to be Heinz as well or he won't touch them. He'd have them morning, noon and night if he had his way.'

'The beer can't help either. The boys are always slipping him a pint or two.'

'Yes and they do slip him a few too many as well sometimes,' Maggie said wrapping the bath towel around Huw and taking him over to sit on her lap in the armchair. 'You came home as pissed as a parrot yesterday didn't you my lovely? He even fell over and got his best suit dirty. *And* they've been teaching him dirty signs. I'll give them dirty signs if I catch them.'

Huw began stroking her hair as she continued rubbing down his body. They were always making physical displays of affection towards one another like this and Glynmor had to look away feeling slightly jealous. He did indeed love the both of them but the blunt truth was that, over recent years, he was coming to feel increasingly envious and excluded.

'Any tea in the pot, is there?'

'Well if you get up and have a look you'll find out, won't you?'

Very soon into their marriage they had discovered a terrific love for one another. They had been talking one night about a line in a popular song – 'the love you take is equal to the love you make' and then stumbled on one of love's sweet secrets: you only ever get out of it what you put into it.

From that night on, Maggie got down to the business of marriage with a clear resolution: cleaning and tidying the house (not so easy with smudges of coal everywhere); having a meal ready for him when he came home from the mine (which went straight into the ash-can if he was more than five minutes late) and, with the help of Spanish red wine and saucy French underwear – together with a sex book which they kept in a brown paper bag under the wardrobe – having some steamy joyous sexual sessions which gave a whole new meaning to the Valleys' expression of having a bit of a rub. Emancipated she wasn't, but happy she was.

For his part, Glynmor shook off many of the old valley habits of his work-mates, coming home sober (if he went to the Hall at all) bringing her a cup of tea in bed in the morning after he had lit the fire; handing over all his wage packet unopened on Friday afternoon and, as often as not, bringing her a bunch of flowers from the grocer's or a bottle of wine which, he had soon come to learn, meant that the sex book came out of that brown paper bag faster than a rabbit being chased by a ferret. He was a very quick learner was our Glynmor.

And, simple as it all was, it had worked beautifully.

'I thought we might all go to the disco tonight,' said Maggie as she pulled on Huw's blue drainpipe trousers. 'I heard they've got Smokey and his Sounds on there tonight.'

'He's still playing the same old rubbish is he?'

'That's not rubbish. They're great records. We fell in love when he was playing those records. The Supremes – You remember Babbeeeee loooooove …'

Huw began laughing out loud, putting his arms around her neck and hugging her.

'I'm not bothered about going,' Glynmor said moodily. 'It was a hard shift this morning an' I've got to be up early too.'

She looked at him curiously but said nothing. He had always said that he loved Smokey and his Sounds so she was sure he'd be very keen on going to the Hall. But she knew what the trouble was all right. He was getting more and more jealous of Huw and wanted just the two of them to go to the dance on their own. She could see that was why he was getting so edgy all the time but didn't see that there was much she could do about it. She wasn't like her sister Daisy after all. Huw *was* allowed out on his own but she always liked to know where he was. He never usually stayed with them in the dances, come to that, wandering off to sit in with the band or, if it was a lady singer, trying to get a look up her skirt. But Maggie always knew what he was doing every second of the evening. She was just that kind of mother.

Glynmor had no objection to this as such, he said. He just wanted more of her for himself. It was a position in which Maggie just could not win.

Huw Bungalow stood obediently as his mother dressed him in his favourite Teddy boy suit, one of three given to him by a retired rocker from Pontypridd whose girlfriend had nagged him into the somewhat cooler fashions of the early eighties. Huw loved the suit so much he just would not go out of the house unless he was togged up in his blue suede shoes, pink socks, blue drainpipe trousers, long pink, draped jacket with black velvet collar and bootlace tie.

'There you are my lovely,' said Maggie smoothing down the velvet collar with the palms of her hands. 'You're going to have *all* the girls chasing after you now. Just the same way they used to chase after your father.'

'What do you mean "used to"? I can still pull a bird or two you know. An' I don't have to dress up like a Piccadilly pimp to do it either. I'm not past it yet.'

'So why don't you come to the Hall with us tonight?'

'All right. I'll come then. An' I'll show you how a real master picks up women, don't worry about that.'

'Oh Huw boy, we're in for a real treat tonight. The master is going to show us all how to do it. You'd better tell him to get his dinner out of the oven and have a lie down first then. Old men need sleep before they go out dancing and picking up women.'

There was men in suits down at the chapel vicarage again this morning, Aunty Phyllis told Enid over the back fence. I don't know what they're after but they do say the vicar may have to leave after all.

Never.

That's what I heard anyway. He hasn't paid any rent for years either and he's never open is he? Therese in the bakery was saying she hears him singing hymns on his own in the chapel sometimes. Or he might give a Bible reading for all spiders in the cobwebs. As mad as a hatter he is. It's a wonder they've left him there that long if you ask me. I can still remember when it was full every Sunday. And that other chapel where the school was.

Bingo. That's all they worry about now. And that Tote thing. Got your tickets, have you?

Aye. What was the name of that other chapel?

Soar. It was Methodist as I remember.

Soar. That's it. He was such a good vicar too that one. Not at all like old Mordecai. They do say he drinks a lot you know. Whisky and gin mostly. That's right. He spoke to me the other day in the Co-op you know.

Never.

He did. He said that he just couldn't get over the price of butter, he said. He said he was giving up on butter and starting to buy Stork, he said. You could tell the difference no matter what the ads might say, he said. Stock was much cheaper, he said.

What did you say?

I didn't say nothing. What could I say?

Guto's new mine working, even by N.C.B. standards, was an impressive piece of work, let alone by Guto's. After years of trying to transform the Valley into a large-scale hunk of gorgonzola, Guto decided that he had not been digging his holes deep enough for Bomber's missing millions. He had, so to speak, just been scratching the surface. So, for this hole, he had gone back to the site of his very first excavation just near the tump, down by the waste-paper factory. He decided to make a proper job of it this time. He had cut into the earth with a hand drill and bow, using the old mining wall and box method, so that he would cut his own natural pit props as he tunnelled inwards, searching out the secrets of the darkness. He had been a miner as a lad had Guto but was kicked out of the Ferndale No. 3 for reasons he had never divulged and no one had ever found out about for sure. Wanking into the shift foreman's sandwiches, the boys in the bar reckoned.

He had been working on this particular heading for close on three months now, shovelling the earth, rock and shale into a wheelbarrow and carting it all out where it was dumped, in a growing mountain, next to the tump. Occasionally an N.C.B. inspector came wandering around to see if Guto had struck some unknown outcrop of coal. But he never had and it didn't bother the N.C.B. anyway since it was the best-known secret in the Valley that Guto was interested purely in the quest for Bomber's millions.

It was a rare day indeed when no one came to watch Guto at work in his new hole. It was as if they were hoping he might one day emerge triumphant, with all Bomber's loot in his hands. Then, the general idea was, someone would crack him on the head and run away with all the dosh, just as invariably happened to those nutty old gold prospectors in the final reel of those rotten cowboys films they always showed when stuck with an hour or so to fill on television.

Guto emerged all right. But usually waving a mandril around in the air threateningly, with sweat and snot flying in all directions and telling any nosey-parkers to 'Bugger off out of it.' He had seen all those films too.

Village gossip marvelled at how hard Guto worked. After all those years of tunnelling, the boys in the bar calculated, even if he found a million pounds, it could only at best work out at something like a shilling an hour. But, by and large, they just decided that Guto had simply forgotten what he was looking for; that the search had become such a rampant bee in his bonnet he had forgotten the purpose of the operation.

It didn't take an Einstein to work out that Bomber's millions, even if they existed, could not be buried very deep in the earth. Even when he had his cushy surface job as a labourer in the mine Bomber's lungs were so dicky he only to dig down into an inch of sand to go into a swoon and be rushing down to the doctor for a paper. Towards the end it got that Bomber could not even lift a heavy pint of beer in the Hall. Guto chose to ignore this irrefutable logic.

That fine Spring evening he was stripped to his waist and bringing out his final load. The sun dipped out of the Valley, suffusing its high dark edges with a buttercup gold. The first swallows of the year were already swooping and yawing through the twilight, black on yellow, as they chased insects. Up at the mine a huge flame of gas spurted and waved in the lengthening bars of darkness and, just by the breeze-ruffled reservoir, two foxes came down together to drink.

He upended his barrow and walked down to the river where he washed himself carefully before putting on his shirt and coat. The ribs on his long body rather resembled the keys of a xylophone but his muscles were clearly strong enough, lean and sinewy without an ounce of fat anywhere. Once he had dressed he flicked two handfuls of water onto his hair and slicked it back on both sides. In fact he was preparing himself for work since, needing money to buy capital equipment for all his excavations, he had now acquired himself a proper job with a proper wage packet. By night he was in charge of security in the new supermarket in Giro City. It was not much of a job but it was a job nevertheless.

Giro City – so-called because its economy depended on Giro cheques from the S.S. (Department of Social Security) and its days were worked out in Giro days or double Giro days – was a development of 142 council houses built under the aegis of the Welsh Office on the north edge of Bont in 1972. The next year it won a gold award from the RIBA and, early the following year, the main support walls of one of the houses collapsed, killing a young mother and her baby.

Investigations revealed that mining subsidence had made

many of the houses unsafe, so most of the tenants had been rehoused in other parts of the Valley. Such houses as had been left empty were soon squatted in, largely by families who had been evicted from elsewhere for non-payment of rent. Quite soon Giro City began winning further awards for dereliction and lawlessness. The council relied on the rain to clean the streets and the sheep to cut the grass verges. Exploded bags of rubbish lay in every corner, graffiti swirled around broken windows.

The supermarket itself – despite security which would have been the pride of Fort Knox, from the thick steel shutters to a grille over every orifice – had been done over repeatedly, with even a guard dog poisoned. Finally, in desperation, Evans the manager had hired Guto to sit in a deckchair guarding the long silent rows of soap powders, frozen meats and high piles of vegetables.

This, as it happened, had been the most inspired bit of casting ever, since the break-ins stopped immediately. The skinheads of Giro City – who had been responsible for most of the break-ins – had a healthy respect for old Guto and his strange tunnelling ways. Somehow they had learned that he had a black belt in Kung Fu and had done time in Dartmoor for murdering two little boys with knitting needles. No one quite knew where this nonsense came from, since Guto could not have fought his way out of a wet *Echo*, though the smart money was on Evans the manager who had discreetly mentioned it to one of the skins one afternoon near the biscuit counter, all in the *strictest* confidence, of course.

This reputation for Kung Fu carnage with knitting needles ensured that no one ever bothered Guto. Together with the fact that he never seemed to need any sleep, it made him an ideal guard for the besieged supermarket and, behind him in the manager's office, was the hot-line for making an appointment with the police.

Twilight was thickening as Guto locked himself into the grey, boarded-up supermarket. He peered out at a gathering gang of youths beneath a street lamp which coated everything with a sodium orange veneer. Yet more youths were coming now. At first there had been three then four ... six, seven eight ... all skinheads, all gabbling to one another in skinhead language – short uncompleted sentences seasoned with lots

189

'fuck this' and 'cunt that'. When they weren't talking to one another they liked to spit in long dribbles or rocket-like flobs.

Occasionally one would walk up to the other and kick him, wrestling him to the ground and trying to stuff some grass into his mouth. Another would walk over and kick out at the two of them as they rolled over and over on the ground. Then suddenly and for no apparent reason the fighting would stop as casually as it had begun, with the three of them brushing themselves off and walking back to their position under the lamp.

Their heads were as shaved and stubbly as sides of bacon. Their jackets were a variety of torn denim or camouflaged combat jackets with tight jeans shorn off just below the knees, showing bright luminous socks and high laced Doc Marten boots. All had rings in their ears, some had them in their noses. They had a weakness for safety pins too, dangling in long chains down to their shoulders. Crude tattoos had been pricked out with a needle and black lead, HATE was favoured on many fingers. SCUM was another. MAM got a look in while one hand MADE IN WALES tattooed right across his forehead.

Here was Iffy and over there was Nipper, Dick and Cocoa. The Clay Class had finally come of age. All now in their mid-twenties, they had never known a job. Just recently they had all gone as a gang one night and trashed the Job Centre in Treorchy, kicking over the notice boards and throwing the filing cabinets out through the window. Everyone in the Valley knew who had done it but, since the Job Centre had signally failed to come up with a job of any description in its two-year history, the police were not called in, nor was any kind of investigation ever launched.

Iffy began running down the road, kicking a tin can. The others chased after him. They kicked it around and around in circles, tackling one another hard until the can was lost in a pile of garbage. They trooped back, with their hands in their pockets, to take up their position under the street lamp outside the supermarket.

'Better get some fucking chips init?'

'Who's got the money? You twat. You borrowed it.'

'What money's that? Haven't got your money. Haven't got our fucking money, mun.'

'Who the fuck's got it then?'

There was a yell in the darkness and a lot of low whistling. Another skinhead came running up the road shouting that the Penrhos lot were coming. They began running helter-skelter down the road, dodging behind fences and hurdling over bags of rubbish. There was yet more frantic whistling, with a few doubling back around the supermarket and tearing down the gulley. A short silence followed and then all the whistling and shouting stopped.

It was a false alarm. There was no mob coming from anywhere.

Hands thrust back down into pockets, they came drifting back, now standing with their backs to one another and flobbing out into the orange darkness.

'Just let them fucking come here that's all.'

.'We'll have the cunts. Aye, we'll 'ave the bastards.'

'Just let 'em fucking try that's all.'

Guto watched all such comings and goings through the supermarket letter-box, but said nothing. The skins were aware of him well enough but they always stayed well clear. They were very impressed by all those stories of the knitting needles and, even if false, they were taking no chances.

Nipper produced a tube of glue which he duly squeezed into a plastic bag. They took it in impatient turns to grab the bag and sniff on the glue in deep draughts. Soon they were dancing and giggling and falling about drunkenly. Sometimes they snorted on Butane lighter fuel or they painted solvent on their upper lips. Then there might be sulphates or, if they were lucky, some whaccy baccy or magic mushrooms. Anything that damaged the brain was acceptable.

Another skin rolled up to join the gathering tribe. It was Bobby Bland alias Gnasher except that there was nothing bland about him now. He didn't so much walk as move in a slow-rolling swagger, with his long ape-like arms dangling at his side, his bull-neck squatting in the middle of his shoulders reaching straight up into his brawny shaven head. When he had reached puberty he had just started growing and growing. But no one detected much growth in his brain since he was almost always in trouble with the police.

'Gis that fucking stuff,' he said, snatching at the bag of glue from Iffy and taking a big sniff. 'Gis it 'ere,' he mumbled on before inhaling again, holding his breath as if he was underwater. 'Terrible this,' he exhaled in a long puncturing hiss before going over to the supermarket door and giving it a good kicking. Where once he was once the roaring young lad, afraid of the boogie man – the mythical nightmare figure of the Valleys who came and took naughty boys away in a sack – now he was Gnasher, chief of the skinhead tribe of Bont and gossip had it that the boogie man was even afraid of him. He began kicking the supermarket door again. He wasn't afraid of Guto and his fucking knitting needles.

'I'm going to call the police!' they could hear Guto call from within. 'You'd better stop that kicking, you had.'

But his words only served to animate Gnasher further, making him kick at the door again and again, rattling the bars of the grilles with stubby hands like a gorilla trying to get inside his cage.

A veteran of numerous remand homes – and two brief spells in Cardiff prison – Gnasher might have been reared in the company of Genghis Khan and Tugboat Annie. Whenever anything went wrong or missing, the CID always lifted Gnasher first. As far as he was concerned there was nothing that was too hot or heavy. One of the main reasons why his mother Daisy had finally run off to Greenham Common was that she was fed up with answering the door and making so many cups of tea for visiting policemen. Gnasher was so notorious there were usually at least four cars surrounding the house before the police, unannounced and always without knocking, came steaming in through the front and back doors simultaneously.

Since leaving school Gnasher had never known any form of employment. He burnt off his ferocious energy bustling around the village with the rest of the dole boys or perhaps occasionally organising a raiding party and steaming over to Penrhos, a huge new council estate over in the next Valley where they could usually get a good fight going with the skins over there.

Just anything Gnasher did was all right with the skins of Bont. He was their undisputed leader, the hard man, who, somehow, was going to lead them out of all this and into the promised land with plenty of naked women and whaccy baccy growing in every field.

Neither television nor bingo had ever come near to closing the dances in the Welfare Hall. Indeed the dance floor was jammed solid the night their old favourite, Smokey and his Sounds, was back.

Smokey had become something of a cult figure throughout the nightclubs of South Wales, even had his own late-night programme on a Saturday on Cardiff local radio. Neither was he cheap any more, as the committee discovered to their shock. Once it had been a tenner and a pint or two of All-Bright. Now it was two hundred pounds in cash and a bottle of Bell's whisky, plus ice cubes, in his dressing room. But even the most frugal members of the committee had to admit that Smokey was always well worth it; a queue had formed long before the doors had opened and no one could remember when that had happened last.

And sure enough Smokey was still fabulous, taking them all back through a time warp to those hot, luscious nights when their hearts were full of teenage longing for some boy or girl and they danced and danced till they could dance no more. The Shirelles, the Ronettes, the Supremes. The music was still the same. One part of Smokey's act had changed though: instead of a rackety system of stolen traffic signals and parking bollards he now had an incredible light show – one of the most advanced in Europe, it said in his advertising brochure – with laser effects which could explode starbursts over the heads of the dancers, light up any corner of the Hall in any colour or else make the very dance floor vibrate and shiver as if they were on some magic carpet ride through the distant cosmos. *Why won't you be my babeeeeeeeeee ...*

Even as they had come as teenagers they still came now. Biscuits, looking like a slightly overweight tarantula these days but still in the same all-black gear and shifting about the dance floor, all limp wrists and wobbling pelvis, as if he had just been given a lesson by the ghost of Elvis Presley. And Peter Star was still as mean and magnificent as ever, holding up that great haughty nose in the dancing lights like it was Concorde coming down into Bont to land next to the pit.

But it was the girls who had turned out in force, almost as if all those years had never gone away. The same groups were still friendly with one another, still danced with their handbags at their feet. They still all smiled at one another and snapped their fingers to the beat, still sang those golden words to one another, still did the same steps they had done together when the music had first come out and they were being torn apart by the unutterable pains of being young and in love. *I'm going to wait for you for ever ...*

Huw Bungalow, the Teddy boy peacock, strutted through this bright musical mayhem as if he owned the joint. The girls practically queued up to give him a hug. He danced with whoever he pleased, and whenever he went near the bar the boys bought him drinks. Then, as he stood around getting a bit tipsy, one of the boys might tickle him or one of the girls take a brush out of her handbag and give his hair a quick once over if looked slightly out of place. Strangers in particular almost cried when they saw the way the spirit of the community still worked through Huw Bungalow; the way they absorbed his handicap and cared for him; the way he, in his turn, went among them and brought them joy. It was as if he had become their talisman, the one bright focus of their dark lives which brought them together as one. Even though the chill winds of dereliction and lawlessness were blowing hard through the Valley, Huw Bungalow gave them warmth for all kinds of reasons. They rejoiced in his infectious laughter and the incredibly vivid colours of his gaudy suit. They warmed to his helplessness and uncluttered happiness. He told them something of their lives which had left the Valleys for ever; something warm, loving and innocent which had once made their communities vivacious and tremendous forces to be reckoned with.

As he jived, he was a shoulder-padded poem of coloured movement was our Huw, his hips swaying around, his head nodding along with the beat, his pink socks and blue suede shoes shuffling back and forth, his long drapes flying one way and another, his neat strong hands always there to catch his dancing partner's hand as she whirled breathless around and around like a beskirted spinning top. But then it was time for the raffle to be drawn, for Smokey to take a break and all the dancers to return to their seats. Huw went and sat with his mother, putting his arm around her shoulders as his big black eyes looked around the dance floor. Maggie felt inexpressible joy whenever Huw was near her and they were forever touching one another even when she was talking to someone else, as she was now, sitting at her usual table with the girls.

They were all having a good laugh about how old Jackie

Davies and her boy friend Ian had taken their sickly dog down
to the river to drown it. The trouble was the dog escaped out of
the sack and ran back to the house before they got home. Now
Ian didn't know what to do about the dog and just hadn't the
heart to take him down to the river again. Jackie said that it
was a sign that the dog was going to get better.

Then Thelma told them that Mrs Walsh was going at her
boy Peter again for playing rugby. All right go and play rugby
then, she had shouted after him as he walked down the street.
But, when you break both your legs, don't come running back
home here to me.

The girls roared with laughter at that one, brushing tears
out of the corners of their eyes with their finger-tips or else
holding a steadying side of a hand to their chest as if it was
going to burst. If you break both your legs ... Thelma laughed
louder than any of them.

The raffle was drawn and, no sooner had Smokey started
up his wondrous sounds again, than Huw went loping off,
looking for a new dancing partner. Maggie was looking
anxiously over at Glynmor who was sitting morosely with a few
of his mates on the next table. She could see that he was
sulking; jealous of Huw again probably and uptight about her
sitting chatting with the girls. He had never liked the girls;
never really liked anyone who took her attention away from
him.

Glynmor had a right cob on, he knew. And a large part of
this was because he was depressed with himself for the way he
behaved. He remembered well enough how he had been a free
soul when he had first got married but that had disappeared
quite soon and he was astonished at how soon he had come to
rely on – and need – Maggie's body. If they didn't make love
for three days he began feeling physically sick with large parts
of his insides wobbling about in frustration. When she wasn't
around he actually missed her – even sometimes when he was
working down in the pit. Of late he had even begun to resent
the way Huw was around all the time; the way she always
showered affection on the boy when she could have been
showering it on him. He would have quite liked a bit of the
attention that the rest of the village always gave Huw too.

He disliked finding all this in himself, of course; resented
this childish jealousy which flared up inside him. But his

jealousy was a fact and there wasn't much he could do about it. He knew the way jealousy destroyed all it touched. He knew all that but there was this bright green glow inside him; right in the very pit of his belly. It made him sick it did. But there you are. You can't help the way you're made can you?

He picked up his pint and went downstairs to play the new one-armed bandit in the foyer but that didn't improve his humour much either. He put about two pounds' worth of coins into the machine and hadn't seen so much as a cherry when, lo and behold, he got a line of grapes worth a lovely ten pounds. Then the heavens must have farted since, instead of pressing the COLLECT button, he pressed GAMBLE and, in so doing, lost the lot.

'It's a bastard electronics degree you need for these machines and that's a fact,' he complained to Dai Fat before giving the machine a kick.

'They must have fixed it because it paid out over a hundred pounds last week,' said Dai Fat. 'The chairman went mad and ordered the plug to be taken out.'

'What'd you mean taken out?'

'He had it taken out, mun. Took it home for the weekend and used it for his electric kettle.'

'What's the point of that?'

'Saving the club money. He said the club couldn't afford to pay out another hundred pounds on the bandit. It'd be finished, he said.'

'It's his brain that's finished.'

The colours of Smokey's light show were spurting and flashing over the tables when Glynmor walked back into the dance and Maggie grabbed him, hauling him back onto the dance floor. As though a decade and a half had never passed the Righteous Brothers were still going on about how you had lost that loving feeling and she pulled him close to her, nibbling at his ear and rubbing her crotch up and down against his leg in the glittering darkness. She knew what he liked and had been getting worried about him.

She knew that he was jealous of Huw but, as she repeatedly pointed out to the girls, she felt that there was nothing she could do about it. It wasn't her fault that Huw just loved to stroke her hair all the time and, despite Glynmor's suspicions, it wasn't her fault that Huw kept on putting the

196

portable television out with the milk bottles. Anyway, it was clear that Huw was totally dependent on her so that was that. It was a burden which she shouldered joyfully.

'So what chapter do you fancy doing tonight?' she asked in a low sexy whisper.

'Oh I'm not too fussed,' he replied, cheering up for the first time that night. 'We could try seven again.'

'You know I do sometimes get the stitch something terrible when we're doing seven.'

'Well, let's try eight then. I do most of the work with that.'

'You're on,' she said, giving his crotch another sexy rub. She knew her Glynmor. She knew exactly how to cheer him up.

The trouble was that Glynmor could see through Maggie's little ploys, sometimes feeling like a spinning plate on top of one of those wobbly bamboos in a circus act. When he looked like falling off she gave the bamboo a bit of a shake with her wrist and he went spinning on happily again. Mind you, it was worth it, he reflected, as he picked his way back to the bar. When Maggie was in the mood of an evening he was more than happy to play along.

'Hello Glynmor,' said a husky voice in the dark corner just next to the bar. 'I've got a nice little push-bike at home. What've you got?'

He turned a shade and saw that it was Xenia Prosser sitting alone in the shadows. She had always fancied herself as a bit of a Greta Garbo, had Xenia. As glamorous as a gladioli, she was married to Piper Prosser and the talk was that they were none too happy either. Piper was a pit electrician who was liked by no one. Glynmor wouldn't have pissed over Piper if the man had been on fire.

'I've got a nice little pump if you're short of one,' Glynmor replied, playing along.

He went over to her and offered a cigarette which she refused as she crossed and uncrossed her legs in a shiver of nylons and rustling petticoats. None of the girls could stand her since, at a time when baggy jeans and sweat shirts were enough for most of them, Xenia still insisted on wearing proper dresses with high-heeled shoes and stockings. She also had a full, bubble-blowing mouth and mammary mountains which could have cracked coconuts. She had long tickled Glynmor's fancy – and that of a lot of other boys as well – but even as she took hold of his hand with both of hers, as he held a match under her cigarette, he could feel, by the surges in the whereabouts of his flies, that temptation was the name of the game; that unless he watched it he was going to fall off his married perch. Oddly, in the light of his historic fecklessness, he had not strayed into another woman's bed – by design or accident – in the fourteen years of his marriage.

The dance began again with a multi-coloured explosion of lights over the floor and the very hall seemed to be moving about on great golden waves. The Hollies began singing *The Air That I Breathe* and, despite remembering that this was one of Maggie's favourite pop songs of all time, Glynmor asked Xenia to dance, surprised at how tightly she held his hand as they walked onto the dance floor. She pulled herself close to him and, never one to look a gifthorse up the arse, he decided to continue talking about his bicycle pump since about the only place it was ever safe to talk in Bont was on the dance floor.

'I could come around with my pump if your old man was on nights some time,' he offered.

'There's too many eyes around here. We'd better go up the mountain road one night.'

'Be a bit difficult on a bicycle.'

'A car mun. You've got a car, haven't you?'

'Aye. I've got a car but my car pump is much bigger than my bicycle pump.'

As the Hollies continued singing their golden oldie, Maggie actually began moving around the edge of the dance floor looking for Glynmor. In a way she regarded *The Air That I Breathe* as their record but, quite soon, she saw that Glynmor was indeed dancing to their record but with that fat cow Xenia Prosser. Now she was circling the dancers watching her Glynmor rubbing that cow's backside and her hand around the back of his neck. They were talking awful secretive too. Those bright green flames were exploding inside her. Now it was her turn to cry. She strode back to the girls, even ignoring her beloved Huw Bungalow.

He's only having one dance Maggie. It'll be all right. Even Glynmor will run away when the lights go on. They do say, the only way you could walk down the street with her was if you had a white stick and a Labrador. Who could look at that monster in the daylight? They do say that when she goes to a house all the mice commit suicide on the traps. Snipe was saying her tits are so big she has to put pit props inside her bra.

'But Glynmor's always going on about how he just loves big knockers,' she wailed. 'He's always saying how he preferred me when I was fat.'

'That's just Glynmor. He can never make up his mind about anything can he?'

The record – their record – finished and still Glynmor showed no sign of returning from the bopping scrum so Maggie went off in search of him again, wading past the arms and shoulders and catching him kissing her on the lips. On the lips!

Maggie didn't even think about it. She threw a punch, which might even have brought Rocky Marciano's career to a premature end, connecting on the back of Glynmor's head and, in the nasty collision between Glynmor's teeth and Xenia's teeth, he split his lip and the crown on her front tooth was knocked off. In all that tangled shifting darkness Glynmor was none too sure what had happened to him and was rubbing the back of his head vigorously as Xenia backed away shouting abuse which was not so much abuse as soft whistles through the big hole which had appeared in the middle of her most perfect set of gnashers.

Maggie lifted her fist to punch yet another big hole in her crowns when something very strange happened. It was as if her arm had suddenly frozen in the darkness and her aggression just drained out of her too. Someone might just have slipped her half a dozen sleeping pills, or she might have been bogged down in a slow-motion dream, when, for a split second, the whole of her body seemed immobilised too. It was only freed when all the lights came on to see what Xenia was shouting about. Now Glynmor was painfully touching his bloodied lip with his fingertips while Huw Bungalow was standing by his mother's side, laughing quietly.

'There was nothing in it,' Xenia shouted.

'Just leave him alone in the future,' Maggie told Xenia, surprised at the reasonableness of her voice. 'Come on Glynmor,' she added taking Huw's hand. 'I want the both of you home.'

The silent dancers parted as Maggie led Glynmor and Huw out of the hall. 'What've you been drinking tonight?' Glynmor asked as they went down the stairs. 'One sniff of vodka and it's got that you get fighting mad.'

'I'm not having anyone smooching with *my* husband.'

Glynmor was not entirely unhappy with this behaviour however – even rather approving of it. But what he really could not understand was why now she was being so sweet to him instead of continuing the row as she might have done in normal circumstances. When they got back to the house she made Huw his usual cup of cocoa and packed him off to bed before putting the new Crystal Gale record on their Ferguson stereo sound centre, turning off the lights and not even bothering to get out her saucy French underwear before all but eating him alive on the floor in front of the fire.

Afterwards, they lay back together on the sheepskin rug and she was all but purring with happiness, with a smile spread from ear to ear. But, even in her supreme contentment, her mind continued revisiting that moment when she was about to punch Xenia for the second time. She had just been unable to throw that punch when, at another time, Xenia would have got a few and then Glynmor would have been in for a wallop as well. But no. For no reason at all she was feeling very peaceful and ever since the incident had been throbbing with love.

'Don't go falling asleep now, Glynmor,' she went on. 'We haven't finished yet.'

He let out a mock groan of anguish but was, of course, secretly delighted, now understanding how a spot of jealousy was going to open up a whole new vista of pleasure.

For her part Crystal Gale was busy singing on the Ferguson stereo how it all made her brown eyes blue.

Chapter Fourteen

The village had long been accustomed to Rev. Mordecai's increasingly eccentric behaviour so few took any notice when, on some mornings, he was out and about the streets, shovel in one hand and bucket in the other, searching for animal shit – horse, dog, sheep, cat, it didn't matter – to dig into the earth of his allotment down next to the garage. The Holy Patch, the villagers called it.

With his pigeon-fancying days behind him when, in a fit of spiritual depression, he had pulled the necks of all his pigeons, he now had so much time on his hands after closing the Libanus, he had become an allotment fanatic. Each day he could be found – by those who cared to look for him – tending his vegetables with a loving care. They came up thick and fast did those vegetables, a tribute not so much to his agricultural skill as to his stunning ability to shovel up a pile of steaming shit almost as soon as it had plopped onto the road.

But it was not only the actual shit that got his parsnips so fat. Dead animals went in there too. Sheep, pigeons, goldfish: anything at all which had given up the ghost and fallen dead on the streets got a very swift burial. Talk was that the ground was so rich on the Holy Patch that no sooner had he planted anything in the soil than he had to stand straight back in case the growing plant caught him a fourpenny one in the eye. He was now hoping to exhibit with the Bont Allotment Society but they were being curiously evasive about his application for membership.

This morning he was planting new rows of radishes and onions, down on his knees pricking them out of their seed boxes and placing them in drills. Sunshine blasted down over the high walls of the Valley and sweat dropped off his brow as he worked. He took the quietest of thrills in bringing such life to this valley of death.

For dead he believed the Valley had become and there was no argument about it. Whenever he looked around him he too became increasingly horrified by the spreading dereliction of this poky, dying parish of Bont. Pit after pit had been closed the length of the Valley. More and more chapels had been abandoned and boarded up – even if it had been temporarily closed to the public except in the odd emergency, i.e. when the minister over in Ferndale was unable to marry or bury someone.

The exact position of the Libanus was slightly complicated by the fact that he had never told anyone – least of all the Baptist authorities in Cardiff – that he had actually closed the chapel doors. He told the authorities that the chapel was always opened – and cleaned twice a week – but no one chose to show up for the services. If there was so little call for his services, the authorities had then argued, he should perhaps be moved elsewhere. He wrote polite letters back to Head Office saying that God had, in fact, told him to stay put until further notice.

There was not a lot the Baptist authorities could do about such letters. They could hardly turf him out on his ear after all; that wouldn't look very good in the *South Wales Echo* and, anyway, perhaps God really had told him to stay put until further orders. If that was indeed the case then it was hardly up to them to quarrel with divine commands. There was clearly going to be no turning the Libanus into a bingo hall or a craft workshop while Mordecai was around. It wasn't as if the Libanus was unique after all. These days they had almost as many chapels on their books as members.

But the real reason for staying put with the chapel at the ready – even if the doors were locked – was that Mordecai believed that there was going to be another Revival in the Valley. The Welsh had, after all, had more revivals than any other nation in the world and his deep secret prayers and knowledge of the circumstances which surrounded the last great revival told him that such an outbreak of God's blessings was soon going to happen again. He was going to be ready for it and he saw his life now as one long period of intercessory prayer in preparation for it. It was only the Welsh who could do this and, he was convinced, it was only in the Valleys of South

Wales that such an event could happen again. He still hadn't finished his work on the Great Revival of 1904-5 and, in a sense, didn't see how he could finish it until they had seen in the Valleys the clear signs of yet another great outpouring of the Holy Spirit throughout the land.

And so, until such time as the Holy Spirit let his pleasure be known, Mordecai was going to continue with his allotment. He stood up to stretch his back after pricking out his radishes, looking over at Bont with its bingo halls and video shops, the decayed Welfare Hall and the loss of the train services: it was through just such a landscape, he guessed, that the Old Testament prophets had once moved announcing the coming of the Lord.

He had just resumed work when he heard the loud, almost blood-curdling laughter of Huw Bungalow going about his rounds. These days Huw's laughter had become almost as familiar in the Valley as the melancholy cries of the sheep. He sent his laughter cannoning down the lanes and ricocheting up the gullies. You could almost see the waves of laughter breaking over the very chimney tops as the villagers' own laughter rose up to join it.

Mordecai walked down to the end of his allotment and spotted the loping tea-pot shape of Huw Bungalow walking down the back lane towards the tump. Even the resolute seriousness of old Mordecai's mind saw that Huw was an epic creation of comic and loveable features which were not at all what they first appeared. Mordecai continued along the allotment path to keep Huw in view. Just as he neared the tump three seagulls were now circling over his head and seeming to call out to him. Mordecai was entranced. There was something deeply spiritual about the boy which stirred his old Baptist soul. Even though Huw could not communicate directly with people he generated love and laughter wherever he went. He seemed to have a Franciscan power over animals, too: even the usually nervous sheep came wandering up to him whenever he was around.

It was possibly the way that he radiated joy through the community that was his really unique quality. Mordecai had often noticed that he made everyone laugh in their turn. The shopkeepers, who had little to laugh about in these straitened times, laughed. Mothers, worried about making ends meet, stopped in their tracks and laughed. Children who maybe didn't get the kind of birthday presents they once had, laughed too. Even the old-timers forever moaning and groaning on the bench in the square lit up when he was around.

In the midst of the Valley of death Huw Bungalow had come to them with the gift of life. He had become for the village what the Rev. Mordecai, in his youth, had hoped and prayed the chapel would become; the loving and loved heart of the community.

It was at that moment, with his fingers still dirty from pricking out his radishes, that Mordecai began conceiving a plan which was both exciting and unfamiliar in its initial connections. Somehow – and he was not at all sure how – Huw Bungalow was the key to the new revival that Mordecai dreamed and prayed about so fervently. When the time was right he would use the boy for God's ends and bring an end to the weeping and death in the Valley. Yes, Huw was the key to the Valley's future and, when Mordecai had worked out a plan, Huw would undoubtedly be the one who would help him to restore God to his rightful place high on the Valley's throne.

I'm not saying anything but I heard that Glynmor and Maggie are not sleeping together any more, Aunty Phyllis told Enid over the fence. It seems she sleeps upstairs and he's down on the couch. They do say there might be a divorce too.

Never.

It's Huw Bungalow it is. Glynmor's just jealous of all the attention he keeps getting. I heard that Maggie just follows him around all day like a lapdog. Doesn't cook for Glynmor, wash his clothes nor nothing. I heard in the Post Office that he's been carrying on with that Xenia Prosser.

Never.

That's what I heard. I'm not saying there's any truth in it mind. You know that Glynmor. They said he was carrying on with a hundred women before he got married but no one has ever seen him go near another woman since. He was always saying that Maggie was the only girl for him. I don't think Xenia's husband knows what's going on, mind you. Perhaps he doesn't want to hear nothing 'cos they do say he's carrying on with that piece up in Giro City. But even if he is he wouldn't be very happy with Xenia would he? There's a lot of pride with that Prosser family.

A lot of pride.

An awful lot of pride. You remember the time he caught the milk man with her. They do say that he wasn't man ever again after Piper kicked him. And his milk money bag was thrown over the houses as well. Gnasher and the Clay Class made off with that. There was forty pounds in that bag and he never got a penny of it back.

Never. You know when I look at Gnasher these days I just can't believe it. There's no shape to him at all is there?

He's like something from out of a swamp in'e? I'm not saying that he sets fire to cats or eats babies but the talk is he's gone beyond with everything. Daisy has gone off to somewhere on Clapham Common so he's out all night breaking into places and pinching. The latest I heard was that those skinheads have got hold of some carbide from the pit stores. They do chop it into small lumps and feed it to the birds inside bits of bread. The birds fly off and, the next thing, there's this big bang.

Never to God.

It's true that is. On my mother's life. A big bang, lots of feathers and no more bird.

Even as Emlyn Kremlin held the telephone receiver in the Welfare Hall and listened to the voice of the union official speaking from London he understood that this could be one of the most important calls that he had ever received.

The N.U.M. had got its hands on a confidential list of proposed pit closures, the official had explained. In times of rising unemployment the board couldn't risk making such a list public. So while the officially declared policy was to keep every economic pit going for as long as possible, the truth of the matter was that they were trying to run down the pits on the hit list by a steady process of stealth and attrition.

Bont was near the top of the hit list in South Wales. At the most it had three years to go.

'What we want, Emlyn, is for you and the boys to get yourselves organised now,' the official went on. 'Get the lodge to start a local campaign, organise marches and call in the local media – we'll handle the nationals. What we are doing is asking all the pits on the hit list to organise a fuss and the N.U.M. will do what it can up here.'

'Well you've come to the right lot in Bont to start a fuss,'

Emlyn replied. 'We may not be able to do much but we're marvellous at making a row.'

He put down the phone. He had long expected such a call but he wondered if he really could mobilise the boys now. To a degree what he'd said was true. The Bont boys had once been known as the wildest in the South Wales coalfield but, to be honest, he didn't detect much militancy about them now. All they seemed interested in was the fool's gold of fat redundancy payments.

He picked up the receiver again and called Dan O'Neill, a feature writer on the *South Wales Echo* and an old friend. 'Can you get up to Bont this afternoon Dan?' he asked. 'I've got a good story for you.'

O'Neill, a small cheerful Irishman with an explosively red complexion that told its own story, turned up at the Hall an hour later and they talked together over a stream of pints on the N.U.M. account.

Emlyn had a quiet mastery of the figures and obscure economic forces which were already throttling the life out of the Valley. Patiently he explained that Bont was now the last pit in the Valley. Everyone – even the N.C.B. – agreed that there was still plenty of coal there, some 80 million tons in fact, the finest anthracite in the world which even today was coming up 95 per cent pure. Despite all this the board was claiming that the pit was uneconomic, losing some £140,000 a week. He had just learned that they planned to close it in the next few years.

'Much depends on whether the accountants who are doing the sums are right or left wing,' said O'Neill. 'I've long learned that when you do your business sums you can do them almost any way to suit your purpose or what you want out of the place.'

'Exactly.' Emlyn had found the right man to talk to.

The old miner took out his fob watch, checking the time before continuing his argument for keeping the pit going. Some 750 jobs would be lost in the event of a closure, he said; while there was a ready market available for their coal, there was no capital investment in the pit. Nor, for that matter, was there any in South Wales as a whole. This district was right at the bottom of the board's investment league. Yet it was precisely in a valley like this that work was needed since unemployment for

206

men was now running at 35 per cent with 20 per cent of those between the ages of 18 and 24.

Even as he was relating these figures the image of Gnasher and his skinhead tribe whirled through Emlyn's consciousness. They were enough trouble to the community now but he dreaded to think what they would be getting up to in the future.

'But you see Dan,' he said, dragging himself away from such thoughts, 'we've now got that Maggie Thatcher in No. 10 and a Tory government that argues everything on the basis of profit and loss. This Valley has kept the world warm for close on a hundred years now. Thousands of men have died down the pits. Damn it man, they *owe* us something now. Not only the dignity of work but something better than those new factories as well. We've got to fight to keep our industry here. This coal is our blood, you see. And there are still men prepared to lay down their lives to keep digging it out.'

Whether the men would make such a sacrifice was not at all clear to the old communist. But Dan O'Neill seemed to like it all well enough. In the next day's edition of the *South Wales Echo*, the headlines declared that the Bont miners were drawing up battle lines for a fight to the death. All the figures that Emlyn had related were there as he had given them; there were plenty of quotes from the men and their wives on how they were looking forward to a tussle with the board and the Tory government.

Emlyn folded up his *Echo* with quiet satisfaction, remembering those great days of 1926 when everyone flung themselves into an epic fight which, as he chose to ignore, the miners had lost.

The Valley had been bustling and bursting with small storms all morning. Great black tides of cloud and rain kept bursting over the village in angry formless waves. Spouts of rain sprinted off the slate roofs in blind, mad rushes going nowhere. In the streets themselves nothing moved as the winds drove all before them, sending the sheep looking for shelter, keeping even the bumptious starlings quiet under the sodden eaves.

Maggie was washing up the dishes in the kitchen while Glynmor, dressed only in his trousers and vest, was on the sofa next to the fire doing the Spot the Ball competition in the *Echo*. This week, if he managed to locate the football which had been erased from the picture, the jackpot prize was £30,000 in cash with a holiday for two in the Caribbean plus a new Ford Escort. The second prize was £500 or a Kawai organ. At 20p for thirty attempts the whole picture was now festooned with tiny crosses.

The living-room again reflected a story of growing affluence and changing tastes. The G-plan furniture was still there, even if looking a bit frayed around the edges, but the plum-coloured fitted carpet had been cut up and used for the upstairs bedrooms. Now the floorboards had been stripped down and varnished with thick creamy rugs dotted everywhere. There was a smoked glass table and, on the windows, the patterned curtains of Laura Ashley. When Maggie could give the G-plan the heave-ho it would begin looking like the castle that she had always dreamed of.

Glynmor, still engrossed in his competition, groaned and Maggie looked over at him. She had noticed how he seemed to have lost interest in the pit and was gambling with increasing intensity. He was presumably hoping to win enough money to get out of the pit – even if he never said as much. He was doing two Pools coupons – Zetters and Littlewoods – the spastics draw and the weekly Tote in the Hall. Neither did he seem to be able to walk past a one-armed bandit without piking in any spare coins. She hated all this and said as much.

'Keep your hat on girl,' he would reply, unconcerned. 'There's a woodpecker about.'

The real aspect of Glynmor's gambling habits that hurt Maggie so much was not the inevitable loss of money but the way he had become just like everyone else in the Valleys. They all gambled on something or other around here. The pools, they had come to believe, offered the only possibility of a way out. They had traded in their commonsense for an empty packet of dreams, in Maggie's view, though the real sin of such gambling was that it took away the will to better themselves. That was the way Glynmor seemed to be heading too. And she hadn't married Glynmor because he was like the rest of them.

She walked into the living-room wiping her hands in her pinafore. 'They tell me that if you take a pin and keep prodding the picture you'll find the ball because it'll start hissing,' she jibed.

'That is a very old joke,' he said, without looking up.

'That's no joke. They do say that half of Bont does that. I'm told that your butty Tom the Nutter does it that way, anway.'

'He's no butty of mine any more,' Glynmor exclaimed with real feeling. 'I can't stand being near the sledge. The other day he was around the back of the washery trying to boil a pork chop in an electric kettle.'

'And what happened?'

'The kettle went on fire an' the next thing he's trying to boil a kipper in it and that's a fact. Why there are so many sledges down that pit I'll never work out.'

'Well, you're no different are you? There's nothing very sane about sitting around looking for an invisible ball in the *Echo*, well is there? How old are you anyway?'

'Listen woman. If I find this bastard ball ... '

'If, if ... '

'If I find this bastard ball we're on to £30,000 in cash and a holiday for two in the Caribbean. Not in Barry Island but the Caribbean. You wouldn't say no to that, well would you?'

She walked the length of the room and lifted one of the Laura Ashley curtains to one side so that she could look out into the rain.

'Well would you?' he asked again glaring at her.

'I would. If the holiday was for two I would. We're three remember? I wouldn't go anywhere without Huw.'

'No, I don't suppose you would.' Glynmor got up, suddenly all irritable and flung down his newspaper. 'Being alone with your husband wouldn't do at all, would it?'

She bit the side of her lip but said nothing as she continued staring out into the rain. She knew that Huw would be upstairs in his bedroom watching and waiting for the rain to stop as well. There was nothing quite like the rain for making you feel trapped with nowhere to run or hide. Even breathing became a struggle on rainy days. And that was the way you were in marriage wasn't it? Trapped as surely as if you had a ball and chain clamped on your ankle, just standing around day after day, waiting for the rain to stop.

Glynmor left the room and she picked up the newspaper that he had angrily flung down. Holiday for two in the Caribbean indeed! What next? Who wanted to go to the

Caribbean anyway? She'd far prefer for the three of them to go somewhere tidy, somewhere very smart like the Algarve in Portugal. Now that's what she called a real holiday.

She turned to the front page and read the headlines. A Welsh Nationalist Member of Parliament, Gwynfor Evans, had announced that he was going to fast to death unless the Welsh language got its own television channel. Now who, in his right mind, would do something like that just for a television channel, she wondered. She hated television just as much as her Huw. He was still putting the portable out with the milk bottles and she prayed that one day someone would come and pinch the thing and be done with it. Perhaps Glynmor would talk to her again in the evenings since, these days, what with *Coronation Street* and *The Incredible Hulk*, she couldn't remember the last decent chat they'd had together.

Outside, the winds and rain were shaking the telephone lines up and down. The flowers in the gardens were getting shaken worst of all, their heads battering against the dry stone walls again and again. Apart from the hissing rain all you could hear were the hollow clangs of the huge aluminium beer barrels being unloaded off a lorry by the side of the Welfare Hall. A brown polythene cup was being blown around the doorway of the chip shop, making brittle dull noises a little like a baby's rattle that had gone on the blink.

But then, early in the afternoon, the rain cleared up as suddenly as it had arrived. The smoke from a fire inside the tump drifted down the Valley turning from white to brown to drifting black. One side of the Valley was covered and safe under a dark blanket of shadow, the other side glittering and vulnerable as the sunshine danced in the soft banks of rain mists.

It was the damp from all the rain which made the sun glitter so ferociously. The puddles and rocks and railway sidings all shone brightly, as if they were coated with lacquer. Sunshine burnished the windscreens of the cars coming down the mountain road, almost making them look like celestial objects. Splashes of sunshine hung bright in the clothes pegged out on the lines.

Everywhere you looked on the one side of the Valley this glitter was so hard, so bright like, you had to squint or shade your eyes as you looked around you.

It was into this great swirling symphony of sunshine and shadow that Huw Bungalow descended, soon after the rain had stopped, making his way towards the pit, which stood like a gaunt black fist just next to the river. This afternoon he was being followed by a couple of inquisitive pit ponies, retired long ago but still taking exercise wandering around their makeshift Valley paddock.

No one – least of all his father Glynmor – had even so much as guessed what it was that made Huw so happy all the time. After all, said the boys in the bar, your only real option when looking around Bont, would be to burst into tears. There was nothing funny about the place, mun. It was a rundown village with a rundown pit populated by rundown people who drank and gambled too much. So what did Huw Bungalow find to laugh about?

They would never have guessed the truth. Far from being empty up top, as his name suggested, fiery and miraculous visions were forever sweeping through his mind, making his whole body shiver with rapture. Sometimes, if she caught his eyes at a certain angle, his mother did spot an odd evanescent flash or a tiny eruption of brilliant colours. But this was nothing compared to some of the performances that were being regularly staged in the mystical amphitheatre of Huw Bungalow's mind.

Nothing about these visions made any sense, the colours and themes jumbling and crashing against one another like some old Celtic story that was just impossible to understand. On some days his eyes might settle on something like the streams of smoke coming out of the chimney tops, drifting and tangling with one another until they made a great silver cloud. The coats of the blackened scrawny sheep might begin glowing as if on fire, or the walls of the Valley might become veined with gold. Even the winds that whistled around his laughing head might become soft, warm and caressing like a shawl of the most marvellous silk.

Just near the pit he turned and looked down to where a group of white sheep were coming through the dark shadows on one side of the Valley. But, when they crossed over into the bright sunlight, they turned to black. Then other black sheep were coming down through the sunshine on the opposite wall and, as they moved over into the dark shadows, they changed to white. It was all a bit like gazing at a huge canvas in which the artist kept on changing his mind about how to colour his animals. Look and look again and nothing was as it appeared and the colours kept changing at the precise point where the jagged line of shadow interlocked precisely into the jagged line of sunlight.

Not that Huw ever worried about making any sense. He beheld such moments of tribal magic with sheer joy. His mind was very much the repository of what was true, pure and lovely in the ancient Celtic culture.

He stood watching the changing colours of the sheep for perhaps five minutes until his blue suede shoes began taking him down towards the river itself, jerking along the bank past waters hurrying over the rocks and around old prams and dumped armchairs which littered its length. Just near the railway bridge an old mattress was being buffeted around, the rusty springs breaking out of its worn sodden covering like mortal wounds. Then, just above the chuckling sounds of the river, he heard a thin cry of anguish.

A bird was lying forlorn on the river bank. Its body was half in and half out of the water as if its back had been broken. Occasionally it would raise its beak out of the mud and take in a desperate breath of air before its head fell forwards again.

Huw reached down and picked up the bird, laughing softly as he rubbed his cheek up against its head, smoothing down its ruffled dripping wings, now blowing the bird warm and dry all over. Its small blue eyes looked up at Huw's and a small song trembled deep within its throat. He blew on the bird again, smoothing its wings before, suddenly, flinging it up into the air with both hands. He let out a great gale of golden laughter as the bird circled his head three times before flying off over the tip, soaring on up into the sky, high and proud, way above the Valley.

Guto brought another barrowload of rock and shale out of his new working around the back of the waste-paper factory. The late afternoon had become terrible cold and a thin fog was rolling down the Valley. The lights on the terraces flicked on, making the village look like gaudy necklaces scattered about irregularly beneath the mounting bands of grey mist.

But despite this damp cold Guto was sweating profusely. His lamp, tied around his belt, made his whole body glisten. There was no time to rest with Guto. Even with this fog thickening fast he barely stopped for as much as a few seconds before unloading his barrow and trundling back inside his working again. *Duw* his every move suggested that there was simply not a second to lose; that tomorrow all Bomber's money would dissolve, and be no more, unless he found it all now.

He threaded past the natural pillars he had fashioned in the earth for some fifty yards before coming to a face studded with rock and red crumbling shale. It came away easily enough under the continued onslaught of Guto's pick; indeed it was so soft and loosely jointed he was now certain that Bomber must have buried his fortune here. Bomber was never very strong so he must have buried it in soft ground and he had never come across any earth which was quite so soft and damp as this seam.

He whacked the pick into the face and tried to work it loose. Then he felt his boots sinking into the ground. He tried to loosen the pick; his legs sank up to his knees. He still clung onto his pick as fissures began cracking and loosening up all around him. There was a great explosion of air, which sounded more like a tired yawn of a giant, and he could see, in the flickering light of his lamp, that he was hanging above an old and long forgotten mineshaft. So this was where Bomber had stashed all his money, he thought, with an internal shout of triumph, as his pick came loose and he fell and fell and fell.

There is a whole body of mythology of what happens to men when they fall down mineshafts; of the way their hair turns white and they hear the music of their lives. But nothing remotely like that happened to old Guto as he fell, since his only concern was whether at last he had finally, and after all those holes, fallen into the very hole which hid Bomber's missing millions. For maybe ten seconds or so he bumped around before hitting a soft ledge, bouncing off it and tumbling onto his side, gashing his head and smashing one of his knee-caps. Even though in the greatest pain he struggled to get his torch out of his pocket and shone it around him. But there was no big, golden cask with the name BOMBER written on it – just a lot of damp limestone walls and an awful lot of drips.

Unable to move his left leg he had begun dragging himself along by his elbows when there was another loud splintering of opening cracks. He pitched forward through yet another opening in the ground, falling through dark spaces until his body smacked into yet another level. He groaned in pain, rolling over just long enough to see the falling shadow of yet more rock as it rolled onto his legs, pinioning him to the floor as efficiently as a maggot impaled on the end of a fishing hook.

Just after three in the morning, with nothing moving in the village streets except the dark and the cool, you could see, by the number of doors broken off their hinges, that the boys had decided to have themselves a party.

The back door of Walford's video parlour had been smashed in and there was a big space in the top shelf of the back room where Walford normally kept all his extra-blue pornographic films. The side door of the Co-op had been jemmied, yet again, with five bottles of Southern Comfort and a carton of pre-cooked chicken legs having upped off the shelves and walked off into the night.

Meanwhile a window had also just happened to fall off its fixture at the side of the Welfare Hall while, inside, in the Starlight Suite, Gnasher and the skins were sitting around on the floor, eating chicken legs, watching a blue film on the committee's video recorder and getting ripped to the tits on Southern Comfort.

They were barracking some rotten sod for abusing a young woman when there was a long lingering shot of her naked body.

'Tell me one thing,' said Nipper. 'Can someone tell me what your belly button is for?'

A long, stupefied silence.

'Go on. Can't one of you clever bastards tell me what a belly button is for?'

'It's to keep your belly in one piece,' said Gnasher, spitting out a bit of chicken bone. 'It sort of ties your belly together an', if you didn't 'ave one, your belly would sort of fall to bits, like. You couldn't keep any food in it could you? Well, it stands to reason don't it?'

'Isn't it something to do with your Mam?' asked Iffy. 'Isn't it where you were connected with your Mam?'

Gnasher hauled himself up with a sigh and, none too steadily, went over to Iffy and kicked his leg a couple of times.

214

'I fucking tole yer didn't I? It's to keep your belly together. Anyway you didn't 'ave a Mam.'

'Well I think it's where you were connected to your Mam,' Iffy repeated bravely. 'I think it's where you were joined up to her heart.'

'Who wants to know what you think?' Gnasher asked, kicking him again. 'When we want to know what you think we'll fucking ask you, all right?'

'All right.'

'My belly button has got a bubble in it,' Dick announced.

All bloodshot eyes turned to Dick.

'You wanna look see. It'll cost you a quid.'

They all hauled themselves up, swigging on their bottles and examining Dick's belly button minutely. And sure enough it didn't go inwards like ordinary belly buttons but stuck out in a small bubble of white skin.

'That's the most disgusting thing I've ever seen,' said Gnasher, his back to the orgy that was raging on the video. 'Really disgusting I do call that.'

Just then all the lights came on in the Starlight Suite and everyone looked up from Dick's belly button.

'All right now boys,' said a huge Alsatian dog coming through the swing doors attached to a policeman on a lead. 'There's ten of us so stay right where you are.'

Gnasher dropped his bottle, his eyes darting about him like a cornered panther working out which way to leap. He was the first to stand up and the others followed looking at him for a lead as yet more policemen slowly filed in through the door. There must have been a dozen of them. Gnasher had never realised that there were so many policemen working in the Valley so late. He looked down at the floor and spat defiantly. The others spat too.

All the policemen's eyes were on Gnasher since they knew that, if they got him, the rest would give in quietly. If Gnasher decided to make a stand of it then all hell would break loose. The dog was snarling ferociously as he strained on his lead to try and get at Gnasher except that the brawny skinhead did not seem at all frightened, just standing his ground and spitting on the floor again, clenching and unclenching his fists as he had once seen Sylvester Stallone do when he was in a similar tight corner.

215

'Are you coming quite then?'

Gnasher shook his head and spat on the floor again so, without further ado, the policeman unleashed his dog and it leaped straight at Gnasher's throat.

Gnasher then executed a move which would even have made Sylvester Stallone gasp with pride since he went down on one knee and caught the dog's forelegs with both hands, whirling the squealing animal around and around. Then he ripped the dog's legs apart, tearing its chest and flinging it back at the police who had watched all this aghast. 'So then. Who's next?'

Then all hell broke loose.

The police stepped forward with all the precision of a Roman phalanx. Truncheons went scything through the air in all directions with Dick going down on the first blow. Iffy was also whacked straight to his knees while Cocoa merely held up his hands in surrender.

There were no thoughts of surrender on Gnasher's mind and it was around his defiant frame that the police largely massed, cracking him on the head and shoulders or working in a kick whenever they could. He sidestepped some of the kicks and indeed managed to get in a few punches of his own, fending off the truncheon blows with his thick forearms and now getting in a head butt before he too finally succumbed after receiving three separate blows on the same spot just above his left ear.

His shaved head was but a battered, bloodied beetroot as he sank to his knees with all those truncheons belabouring him again and again.

'You're killing him, you bastards,' Iffy shouted as a policeman tightened a grip around his throat. 'You're fucking killing him.'

'I wish I could sonny. I wish I could.'

With that Dick gave a terrific shove and small mountain of flailing skinheads and kicking policemen went rolling over and over the floor fighting with one another.

Now yet more policemen were streaming in through the door when there was terrifying scream and one of the policemen stood up with a hand running with blood. One of the skinheads had bitten his little finger off.

'It wasn't me,' Cocoa was protesting through a mouthful of blood. 'I didn't do it.'

Chapter Fifteen

Glynmor was on the early shift. Even as he walked down the pit road, in a misty dawn which was neither day nor night, he knew that it was going to be one of those days. Somehow he couldn't seem to get himself awake. He wouldn't talk to the rest of the boys either. Bleats of sheep slipped around in the air as they tramped along.

'Curly got stopped in the bar again last night, I heard,' one of the boys said in front of him.

'Oh aye.'

'They do say he was eating the glasses again. He's a crazy bugger when he's had a few. It's no wonder he's always getting his beer stopped. I saw him eat a whole pint glass in there one night.'

'Must be better than my old lady's sandwiches though. Jam I've got again.'

'I prefer jam to cheese. Cheese is all I ever get. You'd think she married a bastard mouse.'

'Tuna I really like. But she's always saying she can't get tuna.'

'The trouble with tuna is not that it's difficult to get. It just costs so much.'

Glynmor paused briefly to read the notice on the door of the canteen. There would be a full meeting of the lodge the next night to discuss the impending closure of the pit. There was going to be trouble in that meeting and that was a fact. Some of the boys were saying that they were going to give Emlyn Kremlin's bollocks a right roasting for telling the *South Wales Echo* all about it first. The boys could get very self-righteous when they got going on things like that.

But who gives a toss anyway, he muttered to himself. In

an even fouler mood he changed and went down to the Deployment Centre. There he put his plastic check into his pigeon hole before going into the lamp room, where he put in another, brass, check for the lamp. All this palaver was to monitor their time and safety. But it didn't end there. After a brisk frisk for fags, they had to hand in yet another tally to the banksman before going into the cage. Yet they had been going through these little rituals and tally checks for so long they never thought about it at all.

They were, as usual, silent the moment the cage fell but soon Oboe Parry was passing on the hot gossip that he had picked up. 'There were a dozen cops down the Hall last night,' he reported. 'They picked up Gnasher and all those skinhead bastards.'

'Never to God.'

'Everyone got injured I heard. Gnasher thought he was General Custer on his last stand. A terrible fight it was with ten coppers injured and three dogs killed.'

'Three dogs killed! How could three dogs get killed?'

'They even got reinforcements in from Cardiff in the end they did. I heard it from Ted the Milk. Fucking millions of them, I 'eard. Emlyn Kremlin had to go over the police station this morning to bail Gnasher out.'

'They won't bail him out mun. He's already been in the nick a couple of times. They'll throw away the key they will. He won't be sniffing glue for a long, long time.'

Glynmor kept out of the gossip for a change. He had enough problems of his own without worrying about Gnasher's. There was something going very badly wrong with his marriage and it was preying on his mind. There wasn't really anyone he was close enough to to talk about it all but, even if there was, he would have had grave trouble articulating the real nature of the problem. It was not so much one problem as an ugly knot of several. That Xenia Prosser had been coming on a bit strong again and he was getting more and more tempted to try and give her one even if he hadn't actually done anything yet. But then, with his relationship with Maggie at an all-time low, their marital rites were getting worse and worse which, in its turn, was making a tumble with Xenia more and more attractive. The other main problem, of course, was that his nutcracker of a son was standing in the middle of everything.

He genuinely didn't mind that his son was a nutcracker,

mind you. He didn't even mind when he began dribbling and making weird noises to himself. The boys in the bar had even taught him rude two-fingered signs which he now used on everyone he met. He didn't mind that either, or even the way Huw would always ostentatiously sit with his back to the television when Glynmor was trying to watch it.

In fact there was nothing he minded Huw doing except that he so wished that he would go and do it all somewhere else.

They crowded out of the cage and onto the little underground train which took them as far as the locking station, where they were again clocked in and the firemen checked their lamps. Then it was the long hard walk to the new face, a two-mile trudge up slopes which had been squeezed and down slopes which had been hollowed out, through puddles which were shallow and others which were knee-deep, with just the beams from their lamps shining everywhere, swirling like lighthouses when the men turned their heads to talk, lancing the darkness like bobbing beacons as they walked along the roadway, dancing in the puddles which were broken up by marching boots, slicing into dark holes where old pit props lay abandoned and forgotten, catching in the millions of drips which fell all around them, perfect, like jewels full of light.

The walk to the face was no place to be walking when you were down or feeling blue. The damp still air gave off no encouragement to cheerfulness. It was muggy like a hangover; depressing like an old-time Valley Sunday. This walk, deep down in the earth, even gave off its own little whisperings of the death that was certain to come one day. It was the silence that got to you most: this eternal silence, shorn of the street, the Valley, life itself – all locked away down a hole and in a seam that had been around long before the dinosaurs.

The men even gave up talking to save energy for the long march, though the silence was soon shattered by the roarings of the Dosco and the clanking spiked teeth of the armoured belts of the Panzer. This was rip-roaring life in the middle of silent death; this was the fury and greediness of man come with his grasping hands and great machines to plunder the deep secret kingdom of the earth ... *Varoom ... clug, clug ... varoom ... clug, clug ... varoom ...*

Thankfully this seam had not thrown up any geological faults lately. The giant teeth of the Dosco were eating into the face as effortlessly as a child eating ice cream. Sparkling clouds of black dust erupted and belched as the men got to work, silently and efficiently servicing the queen of the hole. Some were bashing in a few more chocks to stabilise its level, others were keeping the sides of the roadway clear by shovelling any stray coal into the Panzers which dragged it along on it spiky chains to the waiting drams.

Everything was directed towards the Dosco. When it was eating well the whole future and health of the pit was assured.

Glynmor had been shovelling coal into a panzer when Dai Blades, the shift foreman, told him that they needed some more chocks. Would he wander down towards Trelewis to see if he could find a few spare lying around? It was a job Glynmor was happy doing, wasting a few hours wandering about looking for chocks. If he located them quickly enough he could easily slip into some dark corner and get his head down for a few hours.

He was walking in the direction of the old Trelewis seam when his helmet lamp lit upon a couple of chocks lodged under a pipe. As he pulled them free he dislodged a small, sharp stone. He stepped back to avoid any other falling stones and the light from his helmet caught on his hand. He just held it there and looked at it with all the objective curiosity of someone studying something in a museum case.

Other than a slight burning feeling he had felt no pain, yet his left thumb had been sheared clean off. There on the side of his hand, where once his thumb had been, a white nerve end was moving around slow, like a tiny ballerina dancing under a spotlight. He couldn't believe it. There wasn't even any blood.

He swallowed and continued staring at the space where his thumb had been, wondering at first why had felt no pain. He looked around the ground for his thumb and, unable to find it, stared back at the dancing ballerina again.

This here, Glynmor, a small voice told him, is your long-awaited ticket out of this pit, butty. This here is £35,000 and a pension for life. If that Harry Bando could get £25,000 for his little toe then your thumb has got to be worth a good £35,000 and stuff Spot the Ball. This here is a caravan in Porthcawl and long holidays in Spain. This here, butty, is what you've been long waiting for.

But watch out for those bastard surgeons, the voice added. They can sew anything back on.

He took off his helmet and placed it on a pipe so that he could get a lower angle with his light and locate his missing thumb which he found after a while, about four feet away, lying on its own in the coal dust near some loose rock. It was an eerie feeling looking down at this thumb which he had sucked and bitten and played with all his life, lying there in the coal like a dusty turd, not his own thumb any more. Could have been anyone's really, he decided as he stood up and scrunched the steel-tipped heel of his boot around and around on it. Those bastard surgeons would have to be pretty clever indeed to have been able to sew that on by the time he had finished with it.

Then, quietly and even happily, he walked back to the working face and up to Dai Blades. 'I've had a bit of a bump Dai,' he announced holding up his thumbless hand.

'Gis a closer look,' said Dai holding Glynmor by the wrist, the lights from both their helmets flooding down around the ballerina. 'Does it hurt?'

They both just stood there looking down as the ballerina did a few more pirouettes. 'Hurt, does it?' Dai asked again.

'No mun. I don't feel a thing.'

'Where's the thumb? Did you find it did you?'

'I looked but couldn't find it anywhere. It's up towards the Trelewis.'

Jones the First Aid was sent for and the Dosco was shut off as others came over to examine the space where once sat Glynmor's thumb, each offering bits of advice or consolation.

'Could have been your dick, couldn't it?' asked Oboe Parry.

'Should get a fair bit of compo for that,' said Tom the Nutter.

'It's going to be murder playing snooker with no thumb,' decided Dan Box. 'It's not going to be much help to your love life either is it?'

'You don't fuck with your thumb do you?' Oboe asked.

'I do.'

'Oh that's why you've never had any kids.'

All this talk about what you could and couldn't do without a thumb was making Glynmor as sad as rain. Come to think of it he had often used his thumb when in bed with Maggie and he had always loved playing snooker in the Hall. Perhaps it hadn't been such a good idea doing a tap dance on it. 'Someone go and find my thumb will you?' he asked, miserably.

'Where's it to?'

'It's down towards Trelewis.'

'Where to down towards Trelewis?'

'Just before the locking station,' said Glynmor. 'Just whistle for it.'

'Now what are we looking for? A thumb or a dog?'

'My thumb mun. It always used to twitch when I heard someone whistling.'

'Whoever heard of a thumb that twitched when it heard whistling? No wonder the bloody thing fell off.'

'It's a pity your bloody tongue doesn't fall off. Go and look for it will you?'

But no sooner had Jones the First Aid given Glynmor a shot of Pentathol than he was happier than a small baby, laughing and cracking jokes like he had just won Spot the Ball rather than lost his thumb as they prepared to stretcher him out of the mine. '*Duw* that's some good stuff you've got in that needle Jonesey. I'll have another shot of that any time you like. I'm telling you, boys, that Whaccy Baccy has got nothing on this stuff.'

There was, as usual, a stampede to be in the stretcher party since, as soon as you got the injured man up, you could go straight home as if you had finished the full shift. You were also unofficially free to rifle the injured man's pockets for things like snuff or sweets that he wouldn't be needing for some time. By contrast an injured man would have his pay cropped exactly from the moment of the accident. No free time, no free sweets, no snuff, no nothing. Not that Glynmor was feeling terribly deprived at that time since he was on cloud number nine.

'Hey boys have I ever told you that story about the queer who got raped by a gorilla?' he asked as he bounced along the roadway.

'Did he use his thumb for this rape, this gorilla of yours?'

'No mun. Gorillas have got huge dicks they have. Didn't you know that? They can screw female gorillas six at a time, just like a string of conkers. They've got enormous dicks they have. Like bastard pythons they are.'

'Glynmor. Give your mouth a rest and your thumb a chance will you?'

'Gorillas' dicks are so big they do wash their backs with them. They're so big they do lasso their girls with them and drag them into their caves and that's a fact. You know, boys, they're so long their wives do use them for washing lines when they're sleeping. You could hang a pit cage on a gorilla's dick you could.'

'Shurrup Glynmor. Hey Jonesey. Give him another shot will you? The man's gone mental.'

By the time they got him out of the cage and into the waiting ambulance he had calmed down and was whiffling quietly to himself. When next he opened his eyes the heads of the stretcher party were around him with a hand holding up a black dog turd in an empty crisp packet. Except that this was no dog turd. This was Glynmor's missing thumb.

'Don't worry butty, we found it,' said Tom the Nutter.

Glynmor's brow furrowed into a question mark.

'Your thumb mun. We just all stood there whistling and it came running down the roadway, wagging its tail and barking its head off.'

Glynmor sat up on the stretcher and took the crisp packet with his left hand, laying it on his lap and flicking it around until he could see down inside the packet's mouth. He might have been looking down into it for a full minute when he asked 'Which one of you thieving bastards stole the blue packet with the salt in it? Some mates you are. You'd steal a man's wooden leg you would. I hope I don't get a wooden thumb or I can see you lot will be pinching it all the time.'

'Give your mouth a rest Glynmor.'

'Look here,' said Jones the First Aid as he proceeded to give Glynmor another shot of Pentathol. 'They want you to keep hold of your thumb until they get you to Chepstow where they'll sew it back on.'

'But I don't want them to sew it back on,' said Glynmor throwing his thumb onto the floor. 'They'll only sew it on backwards or something.'

'They might sew it into your mouth Glynmor. You might talk some sense then.'

'Well you never know with that lot do you. They took two legs off one man who went into Chepstow and he only went in for a check-up.'

'Oh shut up mun. It'll be better than new when they've finished.'

'But I don't want it better than new.'

'You don't want your thumb?'

'No. I want the blue packet with the salt in it.'

Now no one said anything as they looked down at him. Glynmor so resolutely mixed his jokes with his seriousness you just couldn't be sure what he was trying to say half the time. And anyway they had shot the poor dab full of drugs.

Now one of the ambulance men took charge of the thumb, transferring it out of the crisp packet and into a polythene bag full of ice which he put on a small table before sitting down next to Glynmor as the vehicle sped off, with flashing blue lights and blaring sirens, down the twists and turns of the Valley.

'We had a miner with us yesterday who had lost an arm,' the ambulance man said brightly as if talking about the weather.

'Did they get it back on did they?'

'No. We never found the arm. It got lost down some shaft full of water.'

Glynmor groaned and turned over on his side facing the side of the ambulance. His Pentathol haze was thickening up again though he felt curiously alert. His mind wandered around from Maggie to Huw Bungalow and then to all those years he had spent down the hole.

They came to him, those years, in strange bursts of disconnected music; the sounds and pictures mingling together with no logic or order. He saw Jampots' face laughing at all his dirty jokes. He saw the boys all holding down Danny Rees in the baths and giving him a love bite to go home and explain to his new wife. There were the roars of noisy laughter as the boys played cards next to the Dosco and panzers. There was everyone jumping out of the way in the cage when Dibber Williams began puking up the previous night's beer.

But gradually and again in no particular order, other, darker pictures came winging into his mind too. That coloured fireball just hanging there in the roadway after that blower that killed Jampots. The way you would be eating your sandwiches and have to spit the coal dust out of them. His Uncle Bomber just lying there in his bed fighting for more air after his lungs had been eaten away by the coal dust. Jampots' incinerated remains piled up on a stretcher. *You got that fiver I owed you*

Jampots boy. You remember I paid it back now.

He rolled onto his back and stared up at the ceiling of the ambulance. And after Jampots there had been Aberfan. Who could ever forget Aberfan? Even all these years later he still had black nightmares about that. They had been coming more regularly of late too; the dreams of another killer black tide that was going to sweep them all away to their death. He never even told Maggie about these dreams of course. Just woke up grumpy and blamed the beer.

But he'd had enough of this dark bitter struggle with the coal. Oh aye. Even in his Pentathol haze he was very sure of that now.

'We've got to stop for a bit here to get petrol,' said the ambulance attendant. 'I won't be a minute either. Got to have a piss.'

Glynmor closed his eyes and took in a sharp intake of air through his nose. Typical. They're taking a man in for a serious operation and they'd got to get petrol. It's a wonder there was anyone left alive in the Valley at all, he thought as he sat up and stared gloomily out at the petrol forecourt.

It was then, barely without thinking, that he decided to settle his job as a miner once and for all since he stood up and took his thumb out of the polythene bag and placed it on the ambulance floor. He then took one of his boots and, with the gusto of a cobbler who had not done a shoe repair for a year, proceeded to smash the thumb again and again. When it had been all but flattened he put it on its side and flattened it again, now placing it back inside the bag and shaking it about.

Well, they really would be very clever bastards indeed if they could sew that back on.

'Sorry about the delay,' said the attendant hurrying back and still zipping his fly. 'We didn't get a chance to fill up after the last job.'

'It doesn't matter mun,' said Glynmor po-faced, sitting on the side of his stretcher with his legs dangling down. 'I've got all day.'

The ambulance accelerated up the motorway and, on Radio One, Kim Carnes was singing about Bette Davis' Eyes.

Wood smoke drifted lazily in the clear, cold sky as Emlyn Kremlin stepped off the path to allow a small child to walk past. A tall tepee stood in a clearing surrounded by low bushes. Nearby was a crude encampment of tents, old cars and tarpaulins tied to tree branches. There was a large grey and white caravan with slogans daubed on it. The smell of brewing tea drifted past. He walked on, stepping on the broken cardboard boxes which served as makeshift paving stones in the squelching mud.

In his formal pin-striped suit with waistcoat, fob watch and bowler he looked like a VAT official or a bailiff sent in by the rent man. No one would have taken him for a tired and increasingly bitter lodge official of the National Union of Mineworkers, come looking for his niece, Daisy. Certainly some of the women of Greenham Common, wrapped in Mexican ponchos or embroidered kaftans regarded him with suspicion.

It was a case of hate at first sight for Emlyn Kremlin. Their hostile questions merely added to the antagonism which was now bursting out of him like a bad bout of 'flu. All this muddy adventurism offended his Marxist version of history. What could ever be achieved by a few women squatting in a patch of mud? Revolutionaries had to get inside the working class and *organise*. Only such class organisation would provide the real springs for revolution and change. Even being close to this lot irritated Emlyn.

He hated the unmistakable whiff of these women's piety. He hated the heady air of self-congratulation in these women's hugs; the way they smiled at one another in the clear understanding that they had become modern martyrs out this morning to save the world. What Emlyn saw when he looked around him was a world abandoned; a world where militants had no clear perceptions of their first duty to radicalise the working class. On the contrary, this lot were actually alienating them by sitting in the mud and parroting slogans at the American servicemen. The working class reject all this as the ravings of hippies high on magic mushrooms. But the really loathsome smell for Emlyn was that of academe. He could see that a lot of these peace campers were well-educated and this added, in his eyes, to the unreality of the venture. In his book, academics knew nothing about anything that was important.

The sunshine had become acid-fierce and Emlyn was grateful for the shade of his bowler. Realising that he could be here all day he approached a woman sitting on a log, quietly plucking a guitar. 'I'm looking for Daisy Bland,' he said. 'She's from South Wales.'

'There's lot here from Wales,' said the guitarist without looking up from her strings. 'The Welsh women started this camp. Did you know that?'

'I did. Do you know her? This Daisy Bland.'

'I know her. They call her Daisy Three Balls because she's got more balls than any man we've ever met. Quite a girl isn't she?'

'She is.' He could sense her reluctance to give him any specific information about Daisy Three Balls. 'I'm her uncle,' he went on. 'Chairman of the Bont lodge of the National Union of Mineworkers.'

At the mere mention of the miners – always a favourite with the Greenham women – the guitarist smiled and jumped off her log. 'Follow me. Daisy's in a tent on the other side of that hedge.'

Daisy was down on her knees blowing into the flickering embers of a dying fire when Emlyn, bowler in hand, stooped into her large tent. Even in the half light he could see that she had not quite lost the bloom of her famous beauty. But she was ageing and no mistake. The fireglow caught in the crow's feet around her eyes. The thick rim just above her upper lip had got thicker and there was little softness about her curls either. She was wearing frayed scrubbed jeans and a floral silk shirt busy trying to come apart at every seam. It was her complete lack of provincialism that Emlyn had always admired; she had never allowed herself to be enclosed by the Valleys and its conventional ideas.

'There's no bottle left in that fire Daisy Three Balls,' he said. 'You need some good anthracite coal from Bont to get that going.'

She looked up at the tall shadow framed in the V of the tent entrance. 'Well kiss my aunty's cat's arse,' she said. 'If it isn't Emlyn Kremlin. Funny but I was talking about you only last night. Do you still hang out the hammer and sickle on royal birthdays?'

He smiled and stepped forward for her to kiss him on the cheek.

'Welcome to Greenham Common,' she said.

'What's all this about Daisy Three Balls then?'

'Oh it's just a nickname. I've been pinched by the police so many times all the girls do say I've got far more balls than men. Then one of them started calling me Daisy Three Balls and it stuck. I thought it was just the Valleys where they had a nickname for everything.'

Daisy knew immediately why Emlyn had come so far but decided to let him get there in his own time as they sat outside the tent and he gave her all the news on the latest comings and goings in Bont. Glynmor had lost his thumb down the mine, he reported, but seemed unusually cheerful about it with Maggie and Huw visiting him daily in Chepstow Hospital. The pit was under an unofficial axe and the men were already getting themselves organised for a long fight. There had been two meetings so far and he couldn't remember them being so united.

She decided not to let him wander about any longer and asked out straight how her Bobby was keeping.

'He's ... er ... he's keeping very bad, Daisy. It's him I've come to see you about.'

'What's he done now?'

'It's serious this time. Breaking and entering. Burglary. Assault on three policemen. And that's just about half of it.'

'That's serious all right. That's serious.'

There was a muted yelp of pain inside her and her shoulders slumped forward. Emlyn could see that she was very upset indeed. The girl's heart was in the right place even if her ideas were all over the shop. 'I could never do anything with him Em,' she said finally. 'He had more spirit than six stallions that one. The very first time they sent him to an open prison he broke into the canteen. What could *I* ever do with him?'

A woman walked past them carrying a kettle and calling out someone's name. She then stood still holding the kettle up in the air, calling out the name again. No one came so, letting the kettle drop to her side again, she turned on her heels and walked back to where she had come from.

'I've come because I want you to come back for his trial Daisy. He needs all the support he can find for this one otherwise he's going inside for a very long time indeed. It's a real shame with the boy. He's got the brains you know.'

'I can't come Em. I know he's my son but this is my home now. I could never do anything for Bobby. Even when he was a kid he was always his own man, always getting into trouble. I always thought he he was born old. I never had any control over him. His father did while he was with us but, after he went, that was it. Let's walk for a bit shall we?' she added, suddenly growing restless.

They followed a path through the tents and clearings while Daisy explained a little of their fight against Cruise missiles, telling him of the beautiful moments, particularly at nights when they all sat around the fires, happy with the righteousness of their cause. She explained how the whole process had turned her into a feminist and how she had now come to realise that her own personal problems were as nothing compared with the larger struggle to save mankind from its own stupidity. The women were fighting for the right of the whole world to survive.

'So that's what you're all doing here,' Emlyn said finally taking out his fob watch and checking the time. All at once he felt very weary. He was very sorry that he had come. Amateur politicians had always depressed him.

'I'll have to be going now but let me tell you something, Daisy Three Balls.'

She looked away from him, not at all liking the sarcasm that he had invested in her new name.

'You say that you're here so that the whole world can survive but the Valleys of South Wales; your home, Daisy Three Balls, have already died. While you are here having your beautiful moments' – he spat out the two words as if they had been freshly lacquered in syphilis – 'there's fear come to every home. The communities are crime-ravaged. Our leaders have gone away because there's nothing to lead. We are the most depressed area in Britain with just one pit left as our children are standing around on corners. Soon we are going to be taking them home in coffins and your son is one of them Daisy Three Balls. So don't tell me about your beautiful moments at the camp fire girl. Come home to the Valleys. I'm sure you do care but come home and care about what's important. We need everyone we can get just now.'

'No one wants me in the Valleys, Em.' She made it sound like the silliest proposal she had ever been made. 'They never forgave me for finding out that I liked sex. They've always hated that in those preacher-ridden Valleys. All they've been good at is malice.'

'The preachers have all gone, girl. The chapels are closed just like everything else. The chapel is not even an issue anymore.'

'They're still around. Wherever the Welsh are, those moralising maggots will always be around. It was them that drove me out.'

'But your son, Daisy. Surely you care something for him?'

'I care. Of course I care, but I told you. I've never been able to control him. Never.'

The argument continued, attracting the attention of some women who, sensing danger, gathered around. 'Your place is in your home,' Emlyn shouted at Daisy provoking a chorus of whistles and ironic cheers. 'My place is in my home,' they mimicked in his strong Welsh accent. 'Peeling potatoes and changing nappies. That's my place.'

Emlyn glared around at them, backing away like a stag at bay, barely able to understand these absurd politics of self-indulgence that had gripped the women in modern times. 'You're just amateur politicians the lot of you,' he barked at them. 'It's people like you the Tories welcome just as the mincer welcomes the meat. You divide the working class. You make decent people hate you. You abandon your homes to sit out here but your homes are the world. Can't you see that? If you let your homes go rotten then the world will go rotten with them. Every revolution has gone wrong when it left the home for the street corner. You don't win anything on the street corner. You win by organisation, argument, through the ballot box.'

Even as he voiced the tenets of his old-fashioned Valley politics he could see that his words meant nothing to them. Women like these were going to stage a revolution and to hell with the practicalities of power. They were all just dreaming in their mud patches.

'Go and jump on your bike old man,' said one. 'Go find another soap box.'

'Fling him out,' advised another.

'Don't you lay a finger on me,' Emlyn warned in tones which left no doubt that there might be big trouble if they tried. 'I'm going to walk out of here on my own now. You just continue saving the world, since me, I'm going for a quiet pint.'

Guto groaned softly and dragged himself a further few yards

along the narrowing pot-hole. By the date on his wristwatch he could tell that he had been trapped underground for ten days now, and had taken five of them to scratch and wriggle himself out from beneath a rock which had fallen on and crushed his legs. Sometimes he blacked out for a few hours while trying to release himself. When consciousness returned he would scratch around his legs some more. At times he clawed so hard at the coal and shale his nails had been torn and his hands were ripped and bloodied.

He was so ravenous he had sometimes in desperation sucked on his bloodied fingers. Fortunately he had later located some dripping water which had slaked his thirst. Just occasionally – to conserve his batteries – he would turn on his torch to look around him and it was this single-minded obsessiveness that was keeping him going even now. He only ever used his torch battery just long enough to get his bearings then he switched it off again. From time to time he stopped crawling, listening to the sound of his breathing lungs, powerfully amplified by the dank stillness of the air. But he was going to survive this small setback just as surely as he was still going to find Bomber's missing millions.

When Maggie and Huw turned up, Glynmor was lying in his hospital bed with his hand bandaged up and smiling like he had been given a permanent lease on the sun. His smile dimmed considerably, however, at the sight of Huw's splendid Edwardian suit.

'Does he have to wear that suit in here?'

'He likes his suit.'

'Looks like he's going to some bastard carnival and that's a fact. This is a hospital mun.'

'So how's your thumb today then?' Maggie asked seeking to change the subject.

'It's a Piccadilly pimp he should be in that suit,' Glynmor went on. 'This is a place for the ill. Next thing he'll be making all those disgusting signs again.'

'Well we all know where he got them from don't we? I must say I never thought I'd live to meet the day when *you* would be complaining about disgusting signs. Glynmor have you heard the news? Everything you say is disgusting. So then. Let's start again shall we? How's your thumb?'

'Well it's not anything is it? It's not there any more

remember? I'm thumbless, woman.'

Even Huw could see that his father was in a foul mood so he wandered off up the ward, standing briefly at the end of each patient's bed, making two-fingered signs at them and roaring his head off with laughter. Even the most haggard; even those who looked as if they were about to snuff it any second lit up with his performance, some giving him the V sign back and all joining in the laughter. It was the sheer infectious quality of Huw's laughter that overcame them since it attracted yet more laughter to itself and yet more until the whole ward had become a sort of eisteddfod of giggles with barely anyone knowing what they were laughing about. Maggie shook her head and smiled after him while even the grumpy Glynmor was forced to concede a bit of a smile.

But Maggie was just dotty about her son. The whole village knew it and she openly admitted it. When the women gossiped together in Lipton's they would call her a saint for looking after Huw so well but they didn't understand half of it. Maggie had never ever seen Huw as a burden; had never known a moment when she resented having to do as much for him as she did. There had never been a second when she had regretted having him. He was the joy and justification of her life.

Which is a lot more than she could say about her Glynmor. When Huw woke up in the morning it was always with a whoop and a smile while Glynmor was invariably moaning and bad-tempered in a hangover. Huw always did as he was told as well, always ate his meals tidy and spent a lot of time outdoors, always coming back just before dark, when she would be out on the doorstep waiting for him.

On the other hand there was her moody sod of a husband forever pushing his meals to one side and complaining that there was too much water in the sprouts or that the gravy had dried up. He had also become a devil for staying out late with the boys in the Hall then coming home drunk and banging about the passageway like a deranged snooker ball. At least now that he was in hospital she was having some peace and quiet with her Huw. It's odd, she thought, how, not so long ago, the marriage was doing well when, suddenly, and for no reason at all, it turned sour and just getting from one day to the next became an exhausting and frustrating struggle.

'Emlyn called over the house last night,' she said sitting

down on the armchair next to his bed. 'He'd been up to Greenham Common to see Daisy. She won't come home for Bobby's court case though.'

'She wouldn't would she? Not her. Daisy only ever did anything to suit herself. Did Emlyn say anything about the compo for my thumb?'

'Well he said it depended on the reports of a few inspectors. He said there'll be an N.C.B. report on liability and a doctor's one on disability. The inspectors have already been to where you lost your thumb. It seems the lagging was all hanging off where the stone fell so there'll be no trouble about liability, Emlyn said.'

'What did he say about money? Did he mention a figure did he?'

'He reckons about £34,000. More if it had been a right thumb.'

Glynmor smiled broadly and looked up at the ward ceiling. 'Well I'll go to Swansea. Thirty-four thousand smackers. We can do a lot with that Maggie my girl. We'll get a new car for a start then a fortnight's holiday in Butlin's or somewhere nice in the sun.'

'I'd prefer it if you still had your thumb though.'

'Nonsense. The left thumb's nothing. What did you ever need a left thumb for? It's as useless as a foreskin a thumb is.'

'I would though. I wish you still had it. I never understood why they didn't sew it back on.'

'There was too much coal dust in it, they said. Miners are always difficult to deal with because of all the dust. They can't get it clean.'

'But I heard they said it was broken in too many places as well. I don't understand that. How could that be?'

They both sat staring at his bandaged hand like two workmen staring down a newly-completed hole. Just then there was a huge eruption of laughter down the end of the ward and they looked around to see that Huw was entertaining a large crowd with his laughter and crazy whistles.

'Did Emlyn have any idea when I might get the money through?' Glynmor asked finally.

'Money, money, money. Is that all you think of these days? What's the matter with you? You used to like the pit you did but now all you want to do is take the money and run away from it.'

'Used to Maggie. I *used* to like the pit. I used to like a lot of things but not any more.'

'Why're you looking at me like that?'

'Like what? I'm not looking at you like anything.'

'I married you because you were always full of fight. That Glynmor Jones, the girls would say. That boy would fight a brick wall if it upset him. Everywhere you were fighting – even got banned from the cockle stall in Cardiff once didn't you?'

'It was just a misunderstanding about some whelks.'

'But you fought quick enough. Now look at you. All you seem to want to do is run away. That's not what I married.'

They were arguing in low-toned whispers. The visitors and patients on the other beds were trying hard not to look over at them.

'Look. I'm lying here because I've just gone and lost my thumb. You've come here and are having a go at me. Why?'

She looked at him with her fingers playing and pulling on the strap of her handbag. Her eyes were bubbling with tears too. Just what was going on, he asked himself with alarm decanting inside. Had they found out that he had deliberately jumped on his own thumb?

'Emlyn told me something else too.'

'Oh aye.' His eyes darted around shiftily.

'They've put a date on closing the pit. It came through yesterday. A year next October. And they're going to fight like hell to keep it open.'

'We all knew it was closing. So what're you raving about?'

'What it means Glynmor is that all the boys are going to have a big, long fight on their hands and you're just taking the money and running away.'

'I don't understand any of this. What're you trying to say? That I took a pair of scissors and just cut off my thumb like that?'

'I think you smashed up your own thumb after it had been cut off.'

'Rubbish.'

'They're good at surgery here, the best. I was talking to one of the surgeons. He said it was a straight slice but you probably smashed it yourself afterwards. Don't worry. They've had cases like this in here before. They sympathise with men so desperate to get out of the mines. But you did smash it didn't you?'

'What a load of old cock you do talk sometimes.'

'Glynmor, you can lie to the N.C.B. You can even lie to the N.U.M. if you want. But I'm your wife. Don't ever lie to me, your wife, now will you? I've got to know the truth about this.'

He brought his face close to hers and wiped away her tears with his bandaged hand. 'I do and say a lot of things but I've never lied to you,' he said softly. 'All I've ever wanted is the best for you so please believe me when I tell you that some of the boys may have trodden on it accidentally when they were looking for it. But I would never do anything so daft as to smash my own thumb myself.'

Glynmor's coming home in a few days, I heard in the Post Office, Aunty Phyllis told Enid over the fence. They're asking a few questions about his thumb down the pit as well, I hear. I'm not saying anything but the talk is that he put his thumb on the railway line and let a dram run over it. He wouldn't have cut off his right thumb now would he? Stands to reason donit? It's that Maggie I blame. She doesn't seem to have any time for Glynmor. It's all Huw this or Huw that. Maybe Glynmor did it just to get some attention from her. Men always need to be looked after doon' they? If you can't mother 'em, smother 'em I've always said.

Chapter Sixteen

Sunshine burnished the cars parked along Bont Terrace and there was a stiff smell of frying chips in the breeze as Curly, Idris and Snipe sat on the bench in front of the village clock with empty cider bottles beside them, their arms folded in readiness for a lunchtime of amateur philosophy. All three of them were now working out committee suspensions from the Hall – Curly for fighting with one of the barmen, Idris for standing at the bar during bingo and Snipe for using obscene language in front of the committee chairman's wife.

They accepted their punishment without qualm or protest though, content to sit out their time on the bench in front of the clock if it was fine, as today, or in the bus shelter when it was raining. From this vantage point they could kick their heels and watch the comings and goings in the village; the white Sidoli's ice cream van rattling up the Valley in a cloud of golden chimes; the burly men on the Welsh Brewers' delivery truck sweating as they rolled the aluminium beer casks down the wooden ramps of the Hall; the Meals on Wheels van which always chugged past the boys on the bench just before lunchtime leaving a cape of boiling custard trailing in its wake.

'What've you got to do to qualify for that Meals on Wheels then?' Idris wanted to know.

'You've got to be sick mun,' replied Curly.

'Well I'm sick,' Idris boomed, retaliating as if a doctor had just told him that he was going to live forever. 'I'm bloody sick all right. Every morning I get up I'm honking into that bed pan for a good half an hour. That's bloody sick isn't it?'

'That's not sick mun. That's all the rough cider you do drink. That's not sick.'

'Well what's sick then?'

Curly paused, rubbing his tongue around inside his cheek and making it bulge out as if it was filled with air. 'Sick is being really bad like. Sick is when your legs won't take you anywhere and you can't have a pooh without three men carrying you down the back. That's sick. Sick is when you can't tell the difference between a knife and a fork and you have to suck up your gravy through a straw. Sick is when your arms won't move and you even haven't got the strength to lift a pint because it's so heavy.'

'Oooh that's sick all right,' Idris agreed.

'Sick, as far as the Meals on Wheels people are concerned,' Curly continued with his lecture, 'is when you are no bigger than a shoe box and they've got you in a coffin and are about to hammer in the nails.'

Idris pushed his cap up with his finger, marvelling at the awesome extent of Curly's knowledge. 'But Curly, tell me one thing now,' he said, pulling his cap down again. 'What's the point of feeding you, if you're inside a coffin? There's no point is there?'

Curly sighed and clamped his hands on his knees. 'It's a contract between Meals on Wheels and the council,' he explained patiently, as if talking to an idiot which, in a sense, he was. 'It's the law see. Don't ask me why but Meals on Wheels are obliged, by the law of the council, to feed you until you are dead.'

'Right up to the last minute? In the coffin?'

'Right up to the last minute. In the coffin. Even when the death rattle has set in, those women from Meals on Wheels have got to be forking in the food as fast as they can go. By order of the council.'

'But why's that then? It doesn't make sense does it?'

'I don't know. It's the fucking law. I didn't make them up did I? Go and ask down the council offices if you don't believe me.'

Idris looked under the bench to see if there was any cider left in the brown bottles. 'You'll never catch those Meals on Wheels in my house,' he announced after some thought. 'I'm told the food is shit anyway.'

Sunshine continued hosing the roofs of the village and there were isolated cheeps from the blackbirds breaking ambush from around the chimneys, always as if they were

237

about to start a song but never getting around to finishing it. Sometimes a whole group of them started their cheeping calls and then they just all cut them off abruptly, all as if belonging to the same well-drilled choir.

The next vehicle to attract the consuming attention of the boys on the bench was a police car which pulled up outside Lipton's. 'Oh finally made it have we?' the manageress, Mrs P.J. Jones, asked, all sarcastic, as three policemen got out of the car to examine the big hole in her window. 'Tell me, should we make an appointment when a crime's being committed next? Perhaps, when there's a burglar downstairs, you'd like us to send you a registered postcard or something?'

'We're very busy these days Mrs Jones,' the sergeant explained. 'You know there's so many burglars working the Valley at night they now do it in shifts to avoid traffic jams.' He could be very satirical too.

'Well it shouldn't be too difficult for you to catch them then, should it?'

'We do what we can Mrs Jones.'

'You lot couldn't catch a cold,' she sneered. 'This shop has been done six times since Christmas. When we had that Trevor Watkins stationed here he always knew who'd done it before it'd even been done. He was on his bike and picking them up even before they got home. Everyone knew him but you lot don't know anyone now do you? You just want to live in your new fancy bungalows down in Pontypridd.'

'Have you made a list of what's missing Mrs Jones?'

'But what I don't understand,' she went on, ignoring him, 'is that when you came for all those skinheads in the Hall you practically brought a whole army with you. When there's been a simple break-in you can't get a single one of you to come for hours. I was told all the break-ins were going to stop now you rounded up all those skinheads.'

'We thought they were too. But there's a storm of crime in the Valleys these days, I'm afraid.'

'They're not out again, are they? Those skinheads.'

'No. Mrs Jones. They're going away for a very long time indeed. This broken window is the handiwork of someone else. Now what, exactly, is missing?'

That same morning Gnasher, the still small centre of the storm

238

of crime in the Valleys, had been temporarily becalmed in the dock of Treorchy Assizes. In his ill-fitting, torn denims and scuffed Doc Marten boots, the swastikaed fingers of his hands clasping the dock bar in front of him, he stood to attention as the judge addressed him and his assembled co-defendants.

'It has been represented on your behalf that there can be some mitigation for these appalling crimes,' the judge droned on. 'But the law of the land has many attractive features and ...'

Gnasher stood a good head and shoulders above the rest of his pals who crowded around him, looking, with their ear-rings, black eyes and cuts, much like a defeated tribe of Red Indians who had missed the last bus back to the reservation. Practically every one of them had sustained some sort of injury or another, what with bandaged fingers and arms in slings. But it was clearly Gnasher who had taken the worst hiding from the police. There was so much sticking plaster over all parts of his head it was as if he was wearing a turban. His nose had been so flattened and broken in parts he might have been French kissing a dumper truck. Even in such discomfort he still had that special air of unremitting hostility that was pure Gnasher, glaring at the judge with his beady green eyes and occasionally squeezing the bar of the dock until his knuckles showed white.

'The attack on that poor dog was one of the most heinous that has ever been brought to my attention,' the judge went on. 'Then to argue, as your barristers have argued, that this was a clear case of self-defence is also inadmissable in my view. Police officers need the protection of such dogs against the growing viciousness of youths such as you and I want to be very clear ...'

Down in the well of the court the clerk was turning over the pages of a fat law book while a blind stenographer, with hands the size of small shovels, was taking a transcript of the proceedings. Just above him, on the Press bench, a reporter from the *South Wales Echo* was playing noughts and crosses with a reporter from *The Western Mail*. Fronting the well of the court were fourteen of the arresting police officers, sitting in a long blue line facing the judge and occasionally looking up at the defendants who, every so often, would giggle or pick their noses ostentatiously.

One of the policemen had lost his little finger in the mass

arrest but they had never got near to finding out who had bitten it off. Cocoa had been duly charged but they had to drop that one in the end since Cocoa pleaded successfully that he hadn't had his teeth on the night of the arrest and had difficulty eating biscuits let alone a policeman's little finger. He had got all the blood in his mouth from being punched there.

'The crimes committed on that night were serious enough but the far more serious charges concern the repeated assaults on the police officers and the death of that luckless dog. Now the jury have rightly found you guilty on all charges and it is something to your credit that you have not contested that guilt but ...'

In the crowded public benches at the rear of the court Emlyn Kremlin sat with his head in his hands. Next to him were Maggie and Huw Bungalow. The rest of the seats were filled with worried parents, relatives and friends who had come over every day since the trial began.

Bont villagers had always turned out in force when one of their number had fallen foul of the law. For this trial there had been so many of their own in the dock, not everyone had been able to get into the public benches. Those in the dock were, after all, their children – not sensationally good examples of children, admittedly, but their children nonetheless. This, after all, was the Clay Class, with whom they had grown up man and boy and of whom they all had some funny stories to narrate. Time and the calls of the pit a'willing as many came over in Trevor's mini-bus as possible, following the proceedings with the greatest care.

With most of her time taken up visiting Glynmor in hospital, this was the first time that Maggie had been able to come to the trial. She could feel Emlyn's terrible anxieties about the outcome. Huw Bungalow, on the other hand, seemed content just to sit there twiddling his thumbs. He was keeping quiet too but, at such times, Maggie could feel the laughter simmering away inside him. She did so wonder what it was that made him so happy. When Huw did catch her staring at him quizzically he would just give her arm a soft squeeze as if to say, 'It's all right Mammy. I'm just enjoying myself.'

'*Duw*, this judge is so boring he'd put a glass eye to sleep,' Emlyn whispered to Maggie. 'When's he going to get to the point?'

Maggie bit her lip but said nothing. There were many times when she had been grateful that Huw was as he was since she was sure he might even have ended up with the Clay Class in that dock if he'd been normal. It was so sad seeing those young boys, who really hadn't done anything really terrible, get into all this trouble. She always liked Gnasher as well, and was furious that her sister had not come home to be with him in the time of his trouble. She held Huw's hand. She would have travelled the world if she thought Huw had so much as cut himself shaving she would. She had that mother's love within which she was helpless and just couldn't understand why Daisy was being so hard about it. Mothers who didn't love their children – no matter what they'd done – weren't normal in her view.

'Of course the predictable defence is that you have all been unemployed since leaving school. The argument runs that these frightful assaults are not your fault at all but crimes that are somehow commissioned by the government of Mrs Margaret Thatcher. We have even had some less than notable members of the local miners' lodge coming here to this court and declaiming such specious nonsense.'

At this point Emlyn, who had stood in the dock and given a character reference on Gnasher's behalf, leapt to his feet. 'What does he mean by "less than notable" then?' he stormed. 'I'll give him less than notable.'

'Shush,' the court usher shouted at him. 'Shush up there.'

Emlyn reluctantly sat down again.

'So, before I deliver sentence, I'm going to ask you if you have anything to say in mitigation. Is there anything any of you want to say?'

'I've got something to say,' Gnasher announced evenly, in a voice which carried through the court with surprising authority.

'Very well, Bland.'

'You've locked me up before an' now you're going to lock me up again. I just want you to know something. When I come out you're going to have to lock me up again as well. From the day I left school all I ever wanted to do was to work, to set myself up with a car and a bit of money. But there was never any work an' we was left to the street corners where we learned 'ow to pass the time. That became our work; that's where we

241

learned to be like what we are. It's too late for you and yours now.'

'Get to the point, Bland. The point lad.'

'Well the point is – your honour – you might as well hang us all now since we're going to continue tearing this place apart till we get work. Do you hear me – your honour – send us all to the fucking gallows now 'cos we're going to tear this fucking place down if you don't give us more than the dole to keep us going. You hear me? Tear this fucking place ...'

The rest of Gnasher's speech, which was getting on for the first coherent – and certainly the longest – statement that he had ever made was drowned in a terrific uproar as uniformed arms went around skinhead throats, tattooed arms tried wrench other hands free, balding foreheads went butting blindly in all directions as yet more uniforms went vaulting over the dock rail and flung themselves into the ruckus with the whole struggling pile surging one way and another until, miraculously, Gnasher's whole body emerged from the fighting pack with his arms raised like an international line-out forward and the whole court looked up, with their eyebrows raised, half-expecting to see a rugby ball in his hands.

Emlyn's shoulders slumped downwards. 'There's another year on his sentence. But I'll tell you something Maggie. That was the finest speech I've heard many a man make. It had fight, spunk. I only wish I had someone like that in the union. "When I come out you're going to have to lock me up again as well." Fire, Maggie. If only we could get some fire around here.'

After the dock had been cleared and each of the defendants handcuffed to a policeman – two for Gnasher with one standing at his rear – they were brought back into the court to hear their sentences.

'Robert Emlyn Bland, you are clearly the ring-leader of this unhappy gang of thugs and I hereby sentence you to a total of seven years imprisonment.'

Seven years! Emlyn's blood ran cold and he sprang to his feet as some of the women groaned aloud. 'Shush!' the usher kept shouting. 'Shush! or he'll be clearing the court.' Gnasher began struggling with the policemen again before being led downstairs.

'Richard Michael Williams, I sentence you to four years imprisonment ...'

Others on the public benches jumped to their feet as the sentences were being read out, one of the mothers screaming and shouting hysterically. They may have been bad boys but they were Bont boys.

And so, one by one, the Clay Class, who had been schooled and come of age only to be given a handful of glass and a bucket of spit, were led down the stairs to their cells and the start of very long sentences. The villagers were still numb in their disbelief, some crying out in their anguish and shame at such young lives being chopped down at the knees. Finished before they had begun.

'Well he was right on one thing. This fucking place will be torn down. That's for sure.'

Emlyn was shaking with rage and Maggie had to hold on to his arm to try and calm him down. This capitalist system had nothing to offer its children so it just destroyed them instead, he now saw all too clearly. This was Aberfan all over again, this was. Why didn't they just shove slurry into their mouths at birth and be done with?

'Hey, Judge Jeffries, why don't you just do as he said an' hang them an' save the taxpayer some money,' Emlyn shouted, his cheeks streaked white with anger. Maggie had never seen him so livid. 'Seven years for killing a dog. What do you give someone who kills a man then? Do you kill his whole family do you? You would, that's for sure. *You* would. Well, wouldn't you?'

The judge stood up and stared down at Emlyn. 'Clear the court,' he said and walked out.

It was just after eight o'clock and the sun was sinking in a fiery red ball over the west side of the Valley when Glynmor was brought home in an ambulance from hospital.

It was an extraordinary sight as the ambulance followed the winding road up the Valley. The floating, still clouds turned from ice-cream white to candy-floss pink, throwing a brilliant red gloss over the grey and green slopes of the east Valley wall and actually changing the still surface of the reservoir, just above the pit, into a skating pool of fire. A few trout jumped, black on red, near the still, pointed reeds.

Next to the pit, a diesel locomotive, striped black and yellow like a hornet, was shunting some wagons down the line.

243

John Abdabs was driving a huge ten-wheeled Arctic truck down from its delivery of slurry up at the top of the tip. The old, overhead conveyor had gone now, with the sounds of the labouring Arctic replacing the trickles and swooshes of the old iron washing line. Down below, the river was laughing and hurrying around the abandoned hulk of a burned-out car. But it was the pit itself which looked the most emaciated, particularly at this time in the half-red night; not so much a pit as a giant modernistic cathedral which had fallen on hard times, its windows all broken, brilliant splashes of sapphire light inside rooms without walls and floors on hapazard levels, all just flung together without any shape or symmetry; an industrial ruin sorrowing against a red backloth for the boundless energy of its lost youth.

But this sense of death was belied by the sudden roar of machinery in the washery and the hollow clatter of coal falling down a chute into a waiting wagon. Then silence reigned again in this jagged-toothed cathedral. If you listened very hard you could hear the distant bark of a dog. Even then you could see that the pit, like the village, was already gathering around itself the dark shadows of ruin and decay. In this broken-jawed cathedral the Mass had gone silent and soon the very altar would be carried off to the knacker's yard. In this down-at-heel cathedral the soaring organ notes had finished and the air was alive with the dead music of dripping water and the persistent whine of electric generators.

The red sun sneaked away over the high, rock walls of the Valley and the bluish night thickened as the ambulance finally turned into Bont Terrace. Maggie was quickly off with her pinafore and out onto the doorstep to welcome her husband home. She had got her hair done in Sandra's that afternoon and even put on some lipstick, determined to make a fuss of him since she knew that he would be down in the dumps. Even in the unflattering glow of the sodium street lamp she did look a picture, Glynmor had to admit, after he had stepped out of the ambulance, waving his bandaged hand around at the neighbours who, as usual at the sight of an ambulance or fire brigade, had all come flocking out onto the pavement to have a good gawp.

'Hello there, lovely,' Maggie said, going over and taking him by the arm.

'It's all right. I can walk. It's my thumb not my legs. How are you girl?'

'Oh I'm as nice as ninepence.'

'You do look as nice as ninepence too.'

'Thank you Glynmor. You can come to this house again.'

There was a bunch of fresh flowers on the television in the living-room and he could smell stew cooking as he settled himself down into his favourite armchair. He could see that she had already put Huw to bed, since his clothes were on the back of one of the dining chairs, and this made him almost as happy as the glass of beer she put in his hand.

The truth of the matter was that Maggie still felt guilty about accusing him of crushing his own thumb. So much of this cossetting was penance, even putting his slippers on for him and lifting his feet up onto the pouffe. He accepted this treatment with faint agreeable murmurs since he loved nothing more than being pampered. Beneath all his vulgar excesses was just another Valley kid out looking for his mother.

'I went over to the court for Gnasher's case this morning,' she called out from the kitchen where she was plating up the stew.

'Oh aye. Did they hang him after all?'

'No but there was blue murder there was. Gnasher made this terrific fighting speech about the kids in the Valley being out of work and, at one stage, there was such a fuss I thought the judge *was* going to hang him. But then he got seven years. Seven years! Emlyn practically had a fit and I thought from all the shouting he was doing he was going to end up in the clink as well.'

'Oddly enough, I've been thinking a lot about Gnasher and the boys since I've been in hospital. You do get a lot of time to think when you're in there. If you're not going to give them work then prison becomes inevitable when you think about it. If I'd been a lad with nothing to do and no money there'd be nothing else but trouble for me to do, when you think about it. Still seven years is an awful long time and that's a fact. You can eat an awful lot of skelly in seven years. At least the shops around here are going to have some peace and quiet for a bit.'

'No. I heard Lipton's was broken into again last night,' she said handing him his meal on a tray. 'They got off with four boxes of meat.'

'Was it heavy carrying all those boxes back home then?' he asked, looking up from his plate.

'Oh shut up. I wouldn't have the strength to break the window let alone cart off all those boxes.'

'Mmm. Great smash 'n' grab team you and Huw would make. The Bonnie and Clyde of the Valleys. How is he, anyway?'

'He's all right. The boy's all right. They do still get him drunk in the Hall sometimes in the afternoons which makes me get my hair off 'cos it makes him dribble. Otherwise he's all right.'

'Can we have the television on?'

'If you want, my lovely, anything you want at all. I'll get you another beer if you want.'

'Why are you being so nice to me?'

'Because you're my husband,' she said all wide-eyed. 'And I'm glad to have you home.'

She sat at his feet on the carpet as they watched *It Ain't Half Hot Mum* which was interrupted, much to Glynmor's considerable irritation, by Mrs Pritchard from next door who called to see how he was. When Maggie managed to get rid of Mrs Pritchard they both sat watching *The Des O'Connor Show* and it was then that everything seemed to break inside Glynmor and he began crying. She could not remember when he had cried last and stood up with her hands flapping around in alarm. 'What's the matter lovely? We can always switch the tele off if he has that effect on you.'

'It's not that, daft twat,' he said, still sniffling and crying like a leaky tap. 'It's my hand. How am I going to manage without my thumb?'

'It'll be all right Glynmor. There's a lot of things you can do without a thumb.'

'I won't be able to go fishing, will I?'

'When did you ever go fishing? Glynmor, you've never liked fishing.'

'I was going to go halves with Tom the Nutter on a rod. We were going to join the fishing club, we were.'

'Well you can still do that, can't you? Since when did you need a thumb to go fishing? It's maggots you need for fishing, not thumbs mun.'

Des O'Connor was busy singing on the television as the

coal fire fell in on itself and glowed in the reflection in the china cabinet. Now Glynmor, still crying, was holding up his bandaged hand like that gravedigger examining poor Yorick's skull. 'Did you know I always used to suck that thumb when I was a kid,' he wittered on. 'My Mam was always complaining because I sucked that thumb and, in the end, it got slightly smaller than the other one. But there's not much to suck now is there? There's not much there now.'

Maggie sighed and stood up, switching off the television and shaking her head. And to think that she had once married the greatest fighter in the pit, the man who knew every dirty story in the world and had been banned from half the pubs in the Valleys for fighting. And here he was crying because he didn't have a left thumb to suck any more. She had never been able to make out if she had married a man or a baby though that, she freely admitted, was a great part of his charm – if ever you could use such a word about Glynmor. Come to think of it, she had long stopped reading all those Mills and Boon novels too. It was just too ridiculous reading about all those flash architects flying in with rare orchids from the continent and then having to face Glynmor covered in coal dust, smelling of the beer and bragging about the size of his dick.

'And how am I going to play snooker? I used to love snooker I did.'

'Glynmor, you're being pathetic now. Do you want another beer or what?'

He started wailing again. 'I just want my thumb back. That's all I want.'

'I know what you want,' she said taking hold of his right wrist and leading him up the stairs. 'And I've got just the thing for this little ailment.'

She had already made a few preparations for his return to the married bed. She sat him down on a chair and poured him a glass of red wine. Now she stepped out of her skirt and blouse, taking her time about hanging them up in the wardrobe. Next off were her stockings and suspender belt, leaving on just the tiny white bra which supported and displayed her lovely firm bosom and the tiny frilly panties of red silk with the black embroidered split in the crotch that always drove him daft with lust.

'So what have we got down here then?' she asked shoving

247

her hands down inside his pants. 'What's this then? Well, I do believe, it's my favourite big lollipop.'

Missing thumb or not he was on her in a flash, driving into her without taking his or her pants off: no foreplay, no kissing, no nothing but, although a bit dry, she let him get on with it, reasoning that he probably needed it now more than she did and, with a little bit more wine, she might get a decent one out of him later.

It all seemed to do the trick as well since, almost the second he had come, he had rolled off her and was talking something like the Glynmor of old. He discoursed for a while about the size of his dick and then asked her, in all seriousness, if perhaps it was just too big for her.

She rolled over on top of him kissing him on the nose, the mouth and licking him on both cheeks. 'Well I do have some trouble,' she mock-crooned. 'But there again you always said that I had a fanny like a council skip so I do manage it somehow. It's a lovely big dick, fair play. It's got to be the biggest dick in the Valleys.'

Now he was like putty in her hands and she smiled to herself. He could be such a boy sometimes. A drop of wine, a bout of slap and tickle and a few compliments about the python-like qualities of his dick and she had him purring with happiness for hours. They had not been getting on too well of late and she now saw that she had better work a bit harder since she could clearly make him very happy indeed when she tried. Over the years she had come to understand him quite well though she had also noticed of late that he was even showing signs of becoming serious about a few issues. He had been talking a lot about the health service while he had been in hospital and hearing him say what he had just said about Gnasher had been very surprising indeed. He normally had nothing but scorn for his wayward nephew.

They drank more wine and then they made love again, softer this time, more considerate, with her even rubbing his bandaged hand around inside her legs, moaning in comic ecstasy just to show him that, thumbless or not, his left hand was still a vital element in the truly fabulous sex machine that was her husband, Glynmor Jones.

'Doesn't hurt, does it?' she asked him. 'Your thumb, I mean.'

'Hurt? No, it's fine. Just itches sometimes but it's fine at the moment. Plenty of sex is clearly going to be good for it.'

'Oh so that's going to be your line now is it?'

Later in the contented darkness of the bedroom they both lay looking up at the shadows and sharing a cigarette. 'If it could only always be like this,' he said.

'But it could Glynmor,' she said, draping her leg over his. 'It's always down to us. We could always make it like this if we tried.'

'You know with all the compensation I'll be getting for my thumb we could afford to put Huw into a home. It would be good for the boy too.'

Even as he said this she slid her leg off his, took away her hand and moved over to the other side of the bed with her back to him. The warmth had gone and the frost was as certain as a winter's morning. Why did he always have to go and ruin everything? And after all the effort she had made to make him happy tonight as well.

'My compo should come through quite fast after the doctors have settled it,' he went on, oblivious to her hurt. 'Thirty-five thousand, Maggie. That's an awful lot of bananas and it would be good for Huw to get the benefits of a home. It's marvellous what they can do with handicapped kids, I heard. Only the other day in hospital I was reading about Remploy and the great work they were doing.'

She said nothing for a while, just stared into her hands which she could cheerfully have wrapped around Glynmor's neck and squeezed very hard indeed. Her belly was a taut knot of fury.

'They could teach him a trade if he went into a home. He'd be able to get a proper job.'

'He's not going anywhere,' she grumbled finally and incoherently.

'What did you say?'

'I said the boy's not going anywhere.'

'It would be good for the boy. Thinking of the boy I am.'

'No you're not. You're thinking of yourself as usual. That boy is not going anywhere. He's not going to any home. He's not going to learn any trade. He's stopping here with me.'

'Don't you want him to learn anything at all then? Is that it? Do you just want him tied to your apron strings all your life?'

'Yes. Yes, I do. You think he's daft but that boy knows more than you'll ever know. Just watch him one day and you'll see. There's things about him that would amaze you if you'd only look. But you don't, do you? You resent your own son and you've never even bothered to look at him proper.'

'All I see is a nutcracker who should learn a trade or something.'

'You would, wouldn't you? You would.' She was practically speechless with rage. 'Well let me tell you something now. He stays here with me. You go before he does. Got it? *You* go.'

Guto had been crawling along underground tunnels for a staggering thirteen days now and only the naked urge to survive kept him going at all. With just dripping water to sustain him he was barely strong enough to move. It might take him an hour to struggle a foot. Where he was going he had no idea. His body was really exhausted and he was subject to hallucinations.

These hallucinations, brought on by his deranged senses and lack of food, had begun as strange lights, some bright and some faint, like a distant firework party. But the more they came, the more elaborate they were. On occasion they were accompanied by their own sounds and smells. The first one was so real he jerked his head up sharp, giving himself a crack on the tunnel roof a few inches above him.

And still the hallucinations kept coming – stammering, vivid and as fleeting as waking dreams. A pack of white dogs with red ears went dashing and barking all around him. Even in his discomfort he struck out at the dogs with a fist, yelling at them to go away when, as if by a series of mirror changes, they all disappeared.

He dragged himself onwards and there was a faint whinny and a lady with gold brocade on her white silk dress went cantering past him on a big white horse. She was being followed by men with rag boots on their feet. Guto called out to them for help but his cries died away in echoes in the empty darkness.

Somehow, the hallucinations galvanised the remainder of his strength and he wriggled forward again still clutching his torch in his hand. The iron discipline, which had made him switch it off almost as soon as he had switched it on, had served him well since it still worked, albeit faintly, throwing a pale yellow stammer of light all around him. In some odd way the very constriction of his underground prison kept him moving along too. If he had been at all comfortable in that suffocating darkness he might even have stopped all his painful movement and just given up the ghost. As it was, he just kept moving, every last fibre of his being anxious to get out of this hellish tomb in the hope of finding some warm, well-lit place in which to end his days.

He crawled blindly on, squeezing past hidden obstacles in his path, inching uncomfortably through black muddy pools. Sometimes his movements disturbed stones that might never have been disturbed before. Then he found some space and he tumbled downwards hitting one side of a tunnel and then the other, feet high above him and arms floating around as if in water, crashing into another jutting rock again before falling with the softest of thuds on to a pile of coal dust and sliding down it, legs and arms akimbo, as easily and gently as a child coming down a playground slide.

Finally, exhausted by the effort, he lay quite still, not even sure if he was dead or not. He did not even try to open his eyes in case he found that he could not. Neither did he move any part of his body lest he could not. His smashed knee-cap was now so painful he could not feel his leg at all. In the dripping darkness all he was aware of was a faint quivering in his belly. This alone told him that he was still alive.

Had Guto not been past caring he might have realised that he had fallen into the Ynysybwl No. 2 shaft, sunk in 1886 and sealed off and abandoned after being swamped by firedamp in March 1889.

Everything around him was as still as it had been a hundred years ago. The gas had long seeped away but there were the wooden wedges and pinch-bars lying around next to splintered pit props. There were the old wooden tubs used to carry the coal out of the pit; even the iron man-rider trolley was still there on the rails. More ominously, there were the perfectly preserved skeletons of eight miners lying where they had fallen after the pit had been sealed off all those years ago. Their jaw-bones seemed to be sagging in frozen laughter at the cruel fate which had befallen them.

One of his old eyes opened and he switched on his torch. The pale yellow light stammered briefly onto the skeleton of a pit pony which lay on its side, its legs sprawled out grotesquely on the floor of the heading. 'Well I'll be buggered,' he said, believing that he was hallucinating again. 'Well bugger me.'

The yellow funnel of light swept around this deserted charnel house, picking out the white skeletons of the miners which glinted, white on black, against the seven-feet-high coal face and rickety structures of the pit props. This really was the eternal silence of the tomb, amplifying Guto's startled breathings and turning them into great shuddering gasps.

Realising that all this could be far worse than a hallucination he turned around suddenly and tried to scrabble back up the small mountain of coal dust down which had first slid. But, instead of taking him anywhere, this flurry of movement merely served to tumble him forward down against one of the wooden coal tubs on which he cracked the side of his head. He swore savagely again and, looking around, his torch beam picked up another skeleton, its skull lying incongruously next to its leg, the wooden handle of a pick lying across its rib cage.

By now Guto had no feeling in his broken body at all. He could sense the remainder of his life draining slowly out of his very legs and yet he felt strangely peaceable about it, his spirit already surrendering itself to the tomb. At least he had a sort of company with the other miners lying around him. Not much company, he thought blackly, but better than bugger all. Anything's better than bugger all init? Moving his arms around a bit to try and get comfortable he lay down next to the man-rider trolley and closed his eyes. He just wished that he could have had one last glass of Guinness.

But there would be no more Guinness for old Guto now. The all-time champion tunneller of the Valleys had sunk his last shaft and it was fitting somehow that he had finally come to rest here, miles below the sun. His forehead crunched down into the coal dust which billowed up in small choking storms all around him. 'Bomber, you bastard,' he cursed into the dust. 'Bomber you great bastard I'll get you for doing this I will.'

Even as he lay there he knew that he was but a heartbeat away from death. In all that perfect silence of the tomb, with smiling skeletons sitting all around him, he could hear his heart

252

puttering faintly — *pa, baam* — *pa, baam* — *pa, baam* — but so faint they were, so lacking in any conviction he knew now that this was going to be the very last beat of his heart. *Pa, baam* ...

Right from the day after Glynmor had come from the hospital the marriage went as sour as a crab apple. There was no wine, no saucy underwear, no slap and tickle, no nothing except a thick sulking silence and Glynmor sitting around watching television all day. He watched any old rubbish from *Blue Peter* to the old cowboy films and he liked the volume up so loud it made his son whimper with pain.

Huw would sit on his favourite chair in the kitchen waving his hands around his ears as if someone was pouring acid into them. He would stroke his belly as if he had a couple of dozen ulcers. Most of the time he tried to avoid the sound of the infernal television by going outdoors.

The sight of all that anguish in those big, black eyes was more than Maggie could bear. It usually led to another loud quarrel for the neighbours to cluck over.

'What do you want me to do?' Glynmor would shout. 'Take the bastard television up to the top of the tip?'

'Take it anywhere you like. We don't want it here.'

'What about me? Don't I live here? Don't I have any rights?'

'You don't have the right to upset us.'

'I thought it was his nibs that was getting upset.'

'It is him that's getting upset. But, when you upset him, you upset me too. At the very least, turn the sound down, will you? You could hear that down in Cardiff.'

Huw found the sounds of such arguments even more hateful than the sounds of television. That day, even though it was still raining hard, he loped out through the back yard and took to the slopes of his beloved Valley.

'See what you've done now?' screamed Maggie. 'You've driven him out into the rain.'

'I never done nothing. I was just sitting here watching the box. If he wants to walk around in the rain that's his look-out.'

Huw really cheered up, however, when he took to the rainy slopes, exulting in the thrilling fragrances of the damp heather and ripening blackberries, enjoying the company of the sodden sheep and the rich, green moss squelching beneath his shoes, wandering through the drilled lines of pine trees of the Forestry Commission where squirrels came bounding out of the hissing mists to look up at him.

Sometimes he climbed into the steep crevices of the Valley walls even in the rain; a familiar, if odd, sight in his Edwardian suits and yellow socks crossing crab-wise from fissure to fissure or else climbing yet higher up the steep volcanic slopes with the sure-footedness of a mountain goat. The gaudiness of his clothes ensured that he could be spotted for miles around and children in the village streets would stop and shout out: *Look there goes Huw Bungalow again*.

But today the streets were deserted and the windows misted up with the rain. No one was watching as Huw walked across the sewage pipe over the river and climbed the dry stone walls of the farm as he made his way down towards the Banana Tip. No one, that is, except Rev. Mordecai, who was standing in the opened window of his bedroom following Huw's footsteps with the same binoculars that he had once used to spot and track his returning racing pigeons.

The reclusive minister had developed a bigger obsession with Huw than he had ever had with his pigeons. When possible he charted Huw's every move, noting the times he left his home and the times he returned. When possible he logged the places Huw visited as well, trying to work out some sort of pattern to his movements. The boy was the key to something very important indeed, in the Rev.'s view, and neither could it have been an accident that he had been born on the morning of the Aberfan disaster. Through Huw's life God was clearly trying to tell his people something and it was up to Mordecai to help deliver the message even if he was not yet quite clear what it was.

As Huw walked on, the stiff winds punched hard into the rain, spinning it around and around into small frenzied whirlpools or else fashioning it into huge white toboggans of mist which were driven along the length of the high walls of the Valley as if in some great and endless race.

The winds were driving so hard and the rain coming down so ferociously Huw was forced to take shelter down the side of a deep gulley, an exploded slash of stone from whence a stream, swollen by the rain, was sprinting out beneath some rocks to dive over a high ledge to join the river below. He followed the stream right up into the mouth of the gulley until he came to a small opening through which he could just squeeze.

Inside he came out into a wide cavern, new to him, with small piles of rusty stones strewn over the floor. In the gloomy light he could just see some rusty old mining drams lying next to one of the walls and a neat pile of wooden pit props. There was an old wooden hut without a door and, moving further down into the mouth of the cavern, Huw came across a huge boulder which, in its enormity and presence, transfixed his eyes and made his spirits soar as if set on fire.

He had seen something like this somewhere before. It was on a postcard from a foreign land and something very dear to him which he had pinned on his bedroom wall. In its size and shape it was exactly like the rock in The Garden.

His jaw open in wonder he took a few steps closer to it, holding out his damp hands and touching the stone with the backs of his knuckles. Despite its size it was the softest rock that he had ever touched. He looked very closely at it and, from somewhere out in the storming rain, there was the sound of fluttering wings.

He touched the stone again, laughing this time and smoothing its contours with his palms when he could hear a strange music of organs and women's voices coming out of it. The music surged and faded away again. He saw the very veins of the stone light up with parts of the rock glinting as if they had become diamonds. He stamped his foot and laughed in delight at the beauty of his wonderful new vision. He stepped forward and laid his cold cheek flush against the warm rock, relishing its silk softness. There were those women's voices again, deadly in their pitch, heart-breaking in their sorrow.

Now he took the rock with both his hands and there was the sound of those wings beating again as he moved it one way and the other as effortlessly as if he was handling a fairground balloon. Now he moved the rock to one side and that sorrowing music came surging out again; the pure, crystal music of the tribe. He lifted his face and smiled into the rapture, turning his cheek from side to side as if warming himself in a gusting summer breeze. Now he joined in the sweet song of the cave as well, whistling along with the powerful many-layered sound of the resurrection morning.

Outside the cave, milky thunder rolled over the roof of the

Valley and joined in the music. The rains and the odd slash of lightning added their own voices to that of the women's. Even the sounds of the angry winds came to add texture to this universal song until it seemed that all the elements in the world were at it; joining together in the glorying passion of a wonderful music which penetrated and exposed the darkest secrets of life itself.

Something stirred in the sepulchral darkness. Unsure of its provenance, Guto turned on his torch and, without lifting his head, gazed at a group of black pats scurrying away from this sudden and unwelcome spotlight. The faint noise drifted through the air again and he knocked a couple of times on the iron rail with his torch.

Silence.

He knocked again and had closed his eyes when the sound drifted back through the darkness, clearer now, more assertive, a soft reviving whistle which told even old Guto something of the preciousness of life and made his failing heart quicken. He tapped on the rail again.

The whistle faded away but then became even stronger and, as the sweet notes sailed around him, his smashed body seemed to acquire a new strength. There was a new power in his broken knee and his very fingertips seemed to glow with a new purpose. He rolled over onto his back and could actually feel the blood moving through his ears. Every fibre of his being was humming as he painfully hauled himself to his feet and set off along the track.

As he staggered away from the face and down the tunnel the gradient of the track became quite fierce. Being dragged along on the tightening elastic of gravity, he soon found that he was stumbling along at a fair lick, his mind whirling around and around with that strange whistle still calling him home. Now he was lurching through the shifting darkness almost as fast as if he was on a train, scything through large puddles with enough water to dream of drowning, sweeping into a long curve, now chasing out into a pit-propped roadway where Davy lamps flickered like pale isolated fireflies.

Now Guto was running like a man possessed, barrelling out into an even larger cavern where he plunged straight into a blazing hallucination which made him cry out and keep running faster than ever before.

Skinny children were working the wooden handles of rag and chain pumps. Bilious jets of steam were exploding out of spluttering tappets. Grieving women were carrying wicker baskets full of coal, some in their arms and others with hemp ropes tied around their foreheads. The air was thick with shrieks and obscenities as men in moleskin clothes and trousers yorked with twine below their knees were wheeling barrows or whipping the mange-ridden rumps of the pit ponies ... everywhere, just everywhere, there was noise, pain and frenzied movements as these people, these slaves of the lamp, toiled in their bitterness and pain, mauling and scrawling to win the black gold from the earth.

Some of the moleskin miners shouted out at Guto in a strange language and others waved their Davy lamps as he staggered past, still so terrified he could only cry out loud as he hauled his screaming body through the flame and flood of an old working mine; too terrified even to dare to believe that he was still alive as he chased his own hallucinations down through the fires of hell; too terrified even to notice the great boulder which he had stumbled against.

Guto put down his head and cursed his fate piteously. He just did not understand it all and had no words to even try and explain it. For someone who was expecting and even hoping to die he just seemed to be moving on to fresh forms of torture. Now his escape was blocked by a great boulder. He sank to his knees in a frenzy of despair. 'Bomber, I'm going to have you for this,' he cried out, shaking his fist uselessly in the darkness. 'I'm going to have you, you great bastard you.'

But even in his darkest despair he was released from it yet again by that strange whistle. And yet again his bloodied and battered body sang along to its mesmerising lilt. He cocked his head to one side and spotted a grey shaft of light, thick with drifting mist. A black bent figure, with Edwardian drapes, a bootlace tie, drainpipe trousers was silhouetted in it. Huw Bungalow lifted one of his hands and waved at Guto.

'Get me out of here will you, butty?' Guto called out.

There was a bit more whistling and a faint chortling laugh.

'Don't just stand there,' Guto called out yet again. 'Give me a hand, will you? I want to go home to my house.'

Chapter Seventeen

Summer drifted into autumn, and the air was full of floating pollen and dandelion seeds. The walls of the Valley turned to ragged patches of gold and dark orange. Even the sheep were finally rounded up and taken in for the annual count. The winds became colder too, scissoring through the thin summer clothes and making the people of Bont ransack their cupboards and drawers for the old winter flannels and woollies which had served them so well in so many past winters.

The village continued its way with the tenacity of a life-long believer. The Buffs still met every Tuesday night in the Hall basement to celebrate the sacred mysteries. The Hall committee still met every Sunday afternoon to quarrel and bicker about crimes and their appropriate punishments. Though the pit still kept producing coal, maddeningly the board had withdrawn its earlier closure date and was now saying nothing at all. This move infuriated Emlyn Kremlin and the boys of the N.U.M. lodge since, as the board well knew, they did not have a date around which to orchestrate their anti-closure campaign.

Rev. Mordecai came out of his seclusion long enough to enter his hernia-inducing leeks and cannonball cabbages into the Horticultural Society's annual show. But the bronze commendation for his cabbages so enraged and disappointed him that he returned to his seclusion and his great literary and historical work on revival which was now running to some seven tomes and encompassing every single revival since 1700.

On other levels Snipe Wilson was picked up one afternoon on the bench in front of the clock and taken to the police headquarters in Pontypridd for questioning about a stolen video. Mrs Oboe Parry went into Church Village Hospital for sterilisation and Ted Milk was given instant dismissal by the

Co-op dairy for watering down his milk. The housewives were complaining that he was putting water in his water.

After his brush with death, and the even more perplexing problems of life, Guto temporarily abandoned his search for Bomber's millions and went home to his house where he took to his bed, overcome by what felt like a terminal bout of melancholia.

Meanwhile, the passion in Glynmor and Maggie's marriage had packed its bags and caught the next bus to Cardiff. There had been no fights or ringing arguments. The relationship just seemed to fall face forward, dead in the middle of the road, like an old miner who had finally run out of puff.

But it was quiet enough, until Maggie had her first real inkling of the coming storm when Glynmor went over to Aberdare to have his hair cut only to return with his hair permed and curled in a style that had been made fashionable by the footballer Kevin Keegan. What is more he was wearing a ear-ring.

Huw Bungalow was eating a plate of chips and Maggie was preparing some sprouts when Glynmor walked into the kitchen with one of those broad silly smirks on his face. She took one look at the curls and ear-ring before dropping her peeling knife into the sink and running out into the backyard. There she had to sit in the outside lavatory for a few minutes before she managed to compose herself.

'What's the name of this barber then?' she asked when she came back into the kitchen. 'I'll go over and break his arm.'

'It's the new style,' Glynmor shouted, sitting in his armchair with his feet up against the mantlepiece. 'All the boys in the pit are having their hair curled now. We're not the apes in Wimpey jackets of old, you know. The modern miner has got style ... class.'

'Glynmor, there's more style in a sack of nails. Go and have your hair cut proper will you? I can't go out with you looking like that.'

'I had it done like this because I like it like this.' There was a coldness in his voice that Maggie did not like at all. 'What's more I haven't asked you to come out with me, have I?'

'You'll be wearing one of those gold medallions next.'

'It just so happens woman ... ' He stood up, opening his shirt buttons and displaying a huge gold sovereign hanging on a gold chain. Medallion Man. She looked at it, appalled, but said nothing. Perhaps all these idle days were having an effect on his brain.

His compensation offer was going to come through at any time now, Emlyn had said. He was confidently expecting something in excess of thirty thousand pounds – though the real problem, which had yet to be resolved, was if he was too disabled to go back down the pit. The N.U.M. was claiming a 60 per cent disability on his behalf but the N.C.B. was claiming that it was more like 15 per cent. Somewhere between these two claims there was also the problem of a hardship pension. Meanwhile, he was drawing social security which, in real terms, meant that he was as well off as ever.

Perhaps it was only Maggie who had seen how much it had really affected him; the way he sat around watching television and neurotically trying to gnaw the space where his thumb had been; the way he kept on blowing on his stump and complaining about the pain which got worse after he'd had a couple of pints. *Duw* she could even feel him sweating and shivering in his sleep. It would not be so bad if he would talk to her about it all, but he wouldn't even say boo, baa, bob's your arse.

Now, as if there weren't troubles enough, he was becoming as flash as a poodle with diamond fillings. Maggie sighed and returned to the sprouts. The sooner he got back down that pit the better. To hell with the hardship pension – and any compensation money, come to that.

The next morning he drove off to Pontypridd in their old Cortina car and came back driving a sparkling new Toyota estate car with an enormous dashboard bristling with rows of buttons and space-age dials.

'Glynmor, what've you done?' Maggie asked, coming out of the front door holding her hands to the sides of her head.

'I've been to see the bank manager. He says I can have anything I want till my compo comes through.'

'But this car … look at it … it must have cost millions. We were going to save your money.'

'Save for what?'

'Save for a rainy day. You'll need all that money if you don't get your job back.'

'We'll worry about rainy days when they come. You fancy a ride?'

'No, I do not.'

'Please yourself,' he said and accelerated off up the road towards the pit.

Maggie ran back into the house in tears. She could see what was going on clearly enough. Retaliation was the name of this game. He was needling her because she was sticking by her Huw. He was hitting back at her as well as trying to make himself look big and more fanciable in her eyes. But the more he acted like this the more ridiculous he became. She fancied him well enough as he was. If she had wanted perms and ear-rings and fancy cars she would hardly have fallen in love with him in the first place. Well, would she?

But all that week it continued to get far worse since him and his fancy car were now staying out until three, four and even five o'clock in the morning and, what was even worse than that again, he was not coming home drunk and smelling of the beer either. He said he just curled up in the back of the car and slept off the drink rather than drive home, when she challenged him about it.

Although frantic with worry she tried to stay calm, always waiting up until he came home, leaving out little peace offerings like cheese or corned beef sandwiches with Branston pickle, even making tea for him as he chattered on freely — rather too freely? — about what fun he'd had in this unspecified pub in this unspecified Valley, usually with Tom the Nutter.

He was not acting happy enough, that was for sure, so she supposed it wasn't for her to interfere with that. But it was terrible hard for her. She just wanted to make sure that he knew that her love was forever; to make him understand that there really was enough love for both of them and, when he accepted that, perhaps everything would become fine again. As he stayed out she sat staring at the fire and listening to her records with her belly knotted into a dozen knots until he came home again. Then she made him feel welcomed, loved, reassured. But it was terribly hard.

'I'd like to come to this pub with you sometime,' she said as he sat eating his sandwiches. 'I'd like to see a few new faces. And it must be boring for you being with Tom the Nutter all the time.'

'Oh aye,' he said, looking shifty.

'Huw doesn't need to be baby-sat all the time now does he? It'd be nice for me to get out a bit more. It'd be nice for both of us wouldn't it?'

'Aye. It would. Is there another cup of tea in the pot is there?'

Maggie could see that she was losing, though quite how much she only discovered one morning when she was cleaning out the bedroom and discovered that their sex book in the brown paper bag had gone missing from under the wardrobe. She was truly astonished at how much that hurt. It was *their* book and he had gone and taken it to someone else. It was as if someone had punched her half a dozen times in the belly. She sat on her knees on the bedroom carpet, her hands shaking, practically doubled up with pain. Oh Glynmor, how could you do that? *Our* book with all that *our* bodies have done together.

There were a couple of inches of vinegary wine left in the bottle and she poured it into a cup and swallowed it in one gulp. At least he had not taken that to his fancy woman though, come to that, he was probably buying her champagne. But even as she finished it and stood looking at her shocked, haggard face in the dressing-table mirror, she resolved there and then that, painful though it all was, she was just going to sit it out. There were going to be no rows and no bitterness. She had seen far too many hasty divorces in the Valley. She wasn't going to be like her sister Daisy. She'd divorced in five seconds and look what had happened to her – camping in the mud in Greenham Common and a son who had gone rotten and ended up in the clink.

When you were married, you were married for life and that was the end of it.

The next day there was a brilliant autumnal afternoon of bright crisp sunshine and thin shadows. Ghostly, purple mists were sliding along the rims of the Valley when, as the police were to record in their notebooks, there was an incident outside the Welfare Hall just after four o'clock. As an event it shot through the parish precincts like a giant electric shock, adding considerably to the lustre of the gossip for weeks to come.

The 4.10 X6 bus to Upper Boat had been standing outside the Welfare Hall, filling up with about a dozen old age pensioners and mothers with armfuls of babies and shopping. Inside the Hall the driver was having a smoke and catching a quick pint at the bar.

There was a particularly raucous group in the corner of the bar including Snipe Wilson who, only that day, had completed his suspension from the Hall for using obscene language in front of the committee chairman's wife. To celebrate his return to the fold it had been drinks all round with Snipe even doing a turn on his spoons.

When the bar steward pulled down the wooden shutters to signify the end of the afternoon session, Snipe lurched slowly up the Hall's corridor and stood outside on the pavement looking up at the half-full X6 bus. Now everyone knew that Snipe was as brainless as a waterfall – even when sober – but no one could ever work out quite what had wandered through his beer-addled mind at that moment. At 4.05 on this bright autumnal afternoon he just climbed straight up into the bus' driving seat, switched on the ignition and accelerated down the road with a furious roar of cylinders and a long screech of speeding tyres.

At first none of the passengers, all busy gossiping to one another, noticed anything wrong. But, instead of following the road straight down the Valley, the bus turned right by the village clock and began rattling and bumping up the mountain road, flattening the village sign and sending the frightened sheep running helter-skelter in all directions.

Pained shouts of anguish echoed up and down the pavement outside the Hall. Women ran towards the shocked driver shouting dementedly. Sister Betty was expecting a baby any moment now! She shouldn't have come out anyway! Uncle Fred had this heart trouble and couldn't stand any excitement! Snipe had drunk at least sixteen pints and couldn't tell his right from his left at the best of times!

'Well it's no good shouting at me, is it?' the bus driver kept repeating before going back into the Hall to phone head office. Someone else called the police.

Glynmor, who had been dozing in his armchair in front of the television, pricked up his ears at the agitated noises going on outside the Hall. He wandered down to investigate and soon found out what had happened. Snipe Wilson had hi-jacked the X6. Recalling the chase scene in *The French Connection* when

Gene Hackman had pursued the hit man in his car, Glynmor ran back to his new car and was off up the mountain road in hot pursuit.

Even as the Toyota sped past the flattened village sign there was a quick burst of movement in his own house. Huw Bungalow had come in through the back kitchen door and spotted that the television had been left on. He ran across the living room, unplugged it and heaved it out onto the pavement along with the empty milk bottles. He permitted himself a few joyous giggles and promptly hurried out through the kitchen door again.

By now a whole cavalcade of cars, police cars, ambulances and trucks were careering up the mountain road in pursuit of the hi-jacked bus. Wheels were screeching through clouds of dust, the windscreens brilliant blazes of light in the sunshine.

Inside the bus, the mothers were weeping and clutching their babies tight. All bloodshot eyes and hiccups, Snipe trampolined up and down on the driving seat arbitrarily flinging the huge steering wheel one way and another as they crawled along on the old road, bashing the trees on the edge of the pine forest.

'Snipe Wilson, I'm going to tell your mother about all this,' one of the women shouted from the back of the bus. 'She's going to box your ears proper when she gets hold of you.'

The wheels of Glynmor's car went scything through a patch of shale as a police car tried to pass him on the narrow trail. Headlights blazing they both jostled for possession of the mountain road. But it was the Toyota, with the benefit of the curve and the maestro at the wheel, who won. Nose to tail, they scorched along the path of those broken trees until they finally came across the missing X6 bus in a Forestry Commission car park. There, next to a sign warning about forest fires and a wooden paddle to put them out, sobbing mothers were coming shakily down the stairs of the bus and frenzied cries erupting from inside that Sister Betty was about to have her baby at any second. Worse, Uncle Fred seemed to have chosen that moment to have another of his pulls, his face a pilchard red as he gasped for air.

Meanwhile the still centre of this storm, Snipe Wilson, had sobered up enough to take off on foot through the pine forest pursued by Glynmor and a policeman anxious for Snipe to breathe into his breathalyser. Just behind them were two brolly-wielding mothers anxious for revenge and a few kids anxious to see what kind of walloping they gave Snipe when they caught him. Snipe leaped across two gullies and a stream before running out of puff and being caught behind a woodman's hut.

'I think we'd better start with this breathalyser,' the policeman said when he got hold of him to start helping with their inquiries.

'What's that?' asked an out-of-breath Snipe. 'Some kind of new cocktail is it?'

'It's a new kind of brain you're going to need,' said Mrs Palser, raising her brolly and belting Snipe a real brahma with it.

Even as another woman began belabouring Snipe with Glynmor egging them on, yet another crime was being committed back in the streets of Bont. An unmarked blue van pulled up outside Glynmor's house and, faster than diarrhoea with daps on, which is Valleyspeak for very fast indeed, a man leaped out, picked up the television among the empty milk bottles, flung it into the back of the van and drove off.

Mrs Pritchard, standing in her doorway in the next but one house, actually witnessed the theft, but the van was just about out of sight by the time the penny dropped. Maggie was coming back down the road from the shops when Mrs Pritchard broke the news.

'It's *Coronation Street* tonight as well!' was about the height of Maggie's outrage. 'Glynmor do love his *Coronation Street* he do.'

After they scraped Glynmor off the ceiling he was practically speechless with rage. 'It's *Coronation Street* tonight as well,' were about the only words he managed to get out after he returned from the chase to find that his television set had been stolen in broad daylight. 'I'm never going to find out if Len Fairclough gets off with that piece now,' he wailed.

'Well that's not really the end of the world, is it Glynmor. I'd hardly call that the end of the world.'

He looked truly comic with his gold medallion and poncy long curls, standing there, foaming at the mouth about

Coronation Street, of all things. Unforgiveably, she laughed.

'It's funny is it?' he snapped. 'You think it's bastard funny do you?'

She could see by the white fury in his face and the trembling of his fingers that he, at least, did not find it funny at all. Far from finding it amusing he seemed to be alarmingly close to frenzy.

'I've nothing, have I?' he screamed. 'I'm disabled out of the pit with no future and I enjoy television. Where's the harm in that?'

'There's no harm in it Glynmor.' She was trying to stay cool in the face of this storm of self-pity and bluster. 'It's just that Huw can't stand television, that's all. You probably left it turned on when you went out, so he put it out into the street.'

'Well if this goes on he'll just have to go and that's the end to it.'

She could feel her blood pressure rising and actually saw a few spots but managed to control her temper.

'How can anyone live with someone who keeps putting the furniture out in the street?' he went on. 'Next he'll be putting out the beds and chairs. It's time he went away to a home. Do you hear?'

'No Glynmor. Huw's not going into any home. I've told you. I've told you before. Huw stays here with us.'

'He stays here with us,' he mimicked. 'He stays here with us.' His eyes darted around, his face taut with fury. For a second she thought he was going to throw something but, unmoved, she stood her ground.

'I really do think it's time he went into a home,' he said. 'I mean how can anyone live with a sledgehammer like that?'

'If you find it so difficult to live with him,' she replied evenly and calmly, 'why don't you go and live with your fancy woman if you find it so bad living here? Well, why not? She'd let you record *Coronation Street* on a video, no doubt, and you could play it all night as well. You'd like that wouldn't you? You could watch Len Fairclough while she was giving you love bites on the neck. That would be lovely for you, wouldn't it?'

She stood glaring at him impassive, hardly able to believe that she had finally blown her top. So she had done it now. The question was what was he going to do?

He didn't know. Her words had cut into him like darts and

he'd seen the way she had diced him up before. Somehow she had managed to turn his self-righteousness about his loss of his television against him; somehow taken out a completely different hand of cards while he had not been looking. He felt raggedly exposed, unsure of what his position now was.

On the matter of his fancy woman how much did she really know?

'You're talking through your arse again,' he said lamely.

'Oh I am, am I? Well you should know all about that shouldn't you? Tell me, does your fancy woman like *Coronation Street*? Do you talk about Len Fairclough while you're screwing the arse off her?'

'Don't be so disgusting.'

'Me! Disgusting? Glynmor, you invented the word.'

He stood glaring at her for a few seconds then, without saying a word, strode out of the room, slamming the door so hard the noise exploded right through the house. She knew that he was standing out in the hallway and wondered what he was going to get up to next, now really regretting that she had opened her big mouth. He opened the door again.

'I'll be taking my things,' he said quietly with tears pouring down his cheeks. Tears! 'I'll go and lodge with Aunty Phyllis.'

'Oh Glynmor don't. Don't do this to me.'

'I've already spoken to her about it. I'll have the back room. At least she likes television.'

'Glynmor, if we're going to split up let's do it about something proper is it? Not over a bloody television for goodness sake.'

'I'll take my things later.'

'Don't Glynmor. Don't do this to me.'

She heard the front door slam and him start up his hateful car as she sat down on her armchair and stared at the space where the television had been. Oh that damned television. It seemed to ruin and cheapen everything it got near. And who was this Len Fairclough anyway?

Autumn was busy colonising the Valley with long tall shadows and russet-coloured leaves. After the long sumptuous days of summer it was if, just after five o'clock, a hand had been rolling down a curtain of murk. Shadowy figures moved, black on orange, past the brilliantly-lit shops. Figures shuffled through the patches of sodium lights on the pavements outside the terraces calling out 'Good night' or 'All right?' to one another as they crossed paths: a custom passed down, perhaps, from the times when there were no forms of street lighting in the Valley and such greetings provided a form of security insofar as everyone was then instantly recognisable.

The thickening darkness also told Huw Bungalow that it was time for him getting back home. In his usual state of animation, and chewing a jelly baby, he was loping down the hill past the Libanus Chapel when the Rev. Mordecai called out to him 'Huw, Huw! Come over here! Come inside. I want you to look at the chapel.'

Huw just stood there chewing and made no move. Then the Rev. walked out to take him by the wrist and led him up the chapel steps. Inside the vestry he switched off the main light and, still holding onto him, escorted him down the chapel aisle where strange brilliant lights shone in the shivering darkness. In its atmosphere and protective magic it was like nothing that Huw had ever seen and he was immediately drawn to the place. Just being there was like putting on an old and well-fitting glove. As his eyes became accustomed to the strange shifting light he could make out some of the features of the place. Just above the pulpit on the wall, an inscription in gold letters on a green scroll read: 'Enter into his gates with thanksgiving and into his courts with praise,' Next to the pulpit was a hymnary. In one corner an old pedal organ, dead now from mildew in its bellows. But the reason for the shifting light in this deserted place of worship was that the floor had been taken up from the dais in front of the pulpit and the baptismal font had been filled up with moving water with lights submerged just beneath the surface.

It was the light swimming in the font water which was making the whole building tremble with the promise of something new. The very waters spoke of the renewal that is at the heart of the Baptist belief; the statement that, in these waters, it really was possible to have a new start in the cleansing hands of the Lord.

Huw walked up to the water and looked down into it, turning his face to Mordecai and laughing softly.

'Here is where we Baptists perform our most sacred rite,

Huw. If you'd care to come down into those waters with me I could cleanse you of all sin.'

Huw went down on one knee, putting one of his hands into the font and letting the water trickle down through his fingers.

'Water. The symbol of all things holy my beloved Huw. Water, with which the Lord washed away all sin. Water, the giver and sustainer of all life. Water, God's most precious gift to us all.'

Huw stood up again, showing no indication that he had understood Mordecai's invitation to the Baptism, now walking back to the deacons' Big Seat at the front of all the other pews and smoothing it before looking up at the rafters where the lights from the font danced in his dark eyes. Despite the chapel's dank coldness he still felt very warm indeed.

'I thought you would like it in here,' said Mordecai. 'Evan Roberts once spoke in this chapel you know. Have you ever heard of this mighty man of God have you? He stood in this very pulpit.' Mordecai walked up the steps. 'And he spoke to the congregation for five hours and, in turn, to the world. Huw, it was fantastic. All the pews down there were packed, the gallery was packed and out in the streets you just couldn't move.'

Huw, nodding his head and smiling all the while, looked back at the vestry and then up at Mordecai again.

'And the people came from every Valley to be saved Huw. Evan Roberts would work on them with all the powers of the Holy Spirit until they yielded their lives and hearts to God. His lady singers were the greatest singers the world has ever known and, between them all, they brought thousands, no millions, back to the arms of the Lord.

'And all from this pulpit Huw. This pulpit was one of the pulpits from which Evan Roberts launched one of the greatest revivals that the world has ever seen. Can you hear them singing now Huw? *Diolch Iddo*, thanks be to him for remembering the dust of the earth. I can hear those voices myself sometimes. And the people from every Valley were bound up in the great golden chains of love.'

Mordecai came down from the pulpit and held up a key, smiling perhaps his first smile for years. 'God has told me to give you this key Huw. He wants you to come here and spend some time with him.'

He put the key into the top pocket of Huw's Edwardian

suit. 'Look on the key and this chapel as yours,' he said putting his arm around Huw's shoulders and leading him back up the aisle. 'I know that you are not good at understanding but let this house be your house too. I see you out on the hillsides on your walks, so use the key and come in here whenever you feel in need of a rest. Some day, perhaps, you will let me take you down into those lovely baptismal waters since, just like those waters, there are clear marks of holiness on you Huw. You are a child of God and there's something in your soul which is going to save the Valleys.'

You know I just can't understand, for the life of me, what's got into Glynmor these days, said the boys in the bar. All those years he was quiet and faithful to Maggie. There was no other star in the heavens was there? An' now it's got that he's a'willing to fuck anything at all. I heard he was even dicking that horrible Chinese piece over in Ferndale. Aye.

An' I heard that Oboe Parry's wife has gone into hospital for an abortion. That's got to be Glynmor's for sure that has. He's been seen coming out of the back lane when Oboe's been on mornings. It's more than a cup of tea he's been having with that Brenda I'll bet a pound.

Do you think it's something to do with him losing his thumb? He's never been right since he lost that now, has he? He was a wild bad bugger when he was young but he settled down sweet as a nut after he got married di'n'e? But ever since he lost his thumb he's been busy shafting everything that moves.

Well he's going to lose more than his thumb the way he's been performing. I hear that he's been shafting that Xenia in his new car up in the sidings. And you know all about those brothers of hers. Right mad bastards they are when they get moving. They'll tear him apart they will if they catch him at it.

Aye an' Maggie will tear apart anything that's left. That's a racing certainty that is.

Late that night Huw was splashing about in his bath while Maggie made his tea. She was still dreadfully upset. Silent tears continually ran down her cheeks and onto the bread as she buttered it. When she had finished the sandwiches she went and hauled him out of the bath, wrapping a towel around him. He could sense her mood but his sympathetic hugs and touches only seemed to make her worse.

'I'm going to start making you less chips,' she said through her tears. 'That's a real pot belly you've got growing there.'

Lucky to be born alive at all, Huw had spent the first few months of his life in intensive care and then it was not at all clear quite what was wrong with him. He had been to see several specialists and although they all diagnosed a form of brain damage from the moment of his birth they were not at all clear what it was and neither extensive tests nor X-rays brought them any closer either. Since they did not know what it was, they did not know how to treat it though, for a few years, Huw was daily bussed to a Mencap school where he quickly learned how to do such basic tasks as make beds for himself, use a knife and fork and tidy away his clothes. The real puzzle was that, although his speech was impaired and his movements uncoordinated, he often showed signs of having a quick and agile intelligence. He even showed a nifty bit of pace and skill on the rugby field until Maggie put a stop to it after he got a bruise one afternoon. He was also quite good at snooker, all of which continued to bamboozle the specialists who had, by now, given up trying to work out what was the matter with him. If, indeed, as Maggie reminded them sharp, there was anything the matter with him at all.

She got his pyjamas on and he sat at the kitchen table, eating his sandwiches and sipping his cocoa. She ran a comb through his damp hair, patting the fringe into place. 'We should get you a more up-to-date hair-cut, I suppose. The Beatles are a bit old-fashioned now but it suits you, in a way.' He looked up at her and winked.

What she could never get over was how good he was, particularly compared with the other teenage thugs of his age who were always running about the village vandalising things. He was also marvellous to have about the house, getting in the sticks and coal every morning, even managing to go shopping down the Co-op as long as he had a note. Not only did he never complain about such jobs he actually seemed to enjoy doing them.

Everyone in the village seemed to love him as well. He could hardly walk down the street without someone giving him a sweet. He only had to show his nose in the Hall and one of the boys bought him a pint. Even that smelly old tramp who never said anything, Guto, had brought him an old miner's lamp as a present the other day.

So what had Glynmor, his very own father, got against him? He should be proud of having a son so good and so loved, she told herself. All right he didn't look like Mr Universe but, in his own way, he was more beautiful than any person she had ever come across. Often she could not bear to be parted from him for more than five minutes and that, of course, was a large part of the trouble. She did understand that.

There was the sound of some shrieks and argument out in the street so she rushed out to the doorstep expecting that Glynmor had come back and was up to his old tricks again. But it was young Audrey, Mrs Pritchard's ten-year-old daughter, who was standing out on the pavement in the sodium darkness, crying and holding her new puppy. Mrs Pritchard was yelling that the dog had to go and Mr Pritchard was yelling back at her to leave the girl alone. It appeared that the dog had gone and got Mrs Pritchard's false teeth and she was even now screaming that she couldn't go out for weeks until they got fixed.

'Leave him here with us,' said Maggie bringing the crying girl and her puppy indoors. 'You can come and get him in the morning when it's all blown over.'

The puppy was shivering with terror, with its big brown eyes looking up guilty and head lowered, when Maggie took him off Audrey and put him into Huw's hands. 'All the animals love Huw,' said Audrey. 'Even the sheep and pit ponies follow him around. You should get a puppy for him, you should.'

Huw chuckled into the puppy's ear as the dog kept licking Huw's nose and cheeks. He put the dog down on the carpet to let him run around, dashing here and there, yelping as he sniffed out exciting new smells.

'Oh Glynmor would never allow a dog in the house,' said Maggie. 'He never liked dogs since he was a kid and got bit by one when he was scrumping apples over in Mountain Ash.'

'But Mammy said that Glynmor had left home.'

Huw was down on all fours and barking at the dog as Maggie looked straight at the girl's guileless face. Such innocence. There was nothing like a child for getting straight to the heart of the matter. 'Oh he's only gone for a bit,' she said brushing her skirt down with her hand. 'He'll be back soon.'

'But you could have a dog, if Glynmor didn't come back, couldn't you?'

'I could, yes. But Glynmor *is* coming back. Your Mammy got it wrong. Now let's put the puppy out in the kitchen 'cos it's time for Huw to go up the wooden hill. Come and get him back in the morning. Your Mammy will have calmed down by then.'

She tucked Huw into bed and, as was her habit, read him a few verses of the Bible before holding one of his hands and reciting the Lord's Prayer very softly. She had never told Glynmor about the tramp John who she had once met in Cardiff – never told anyone come to that – and how he had asked her to surround Huw with prayer. She had often wondered what had happened to John but had never gone back to Cardiff to look him up. The Lord's Prayer was the only prayer she had ever known but Huw seemed to like it well enough, smiling and closing his eyes just when she reached the end. She kissed his cheek and sat watching him for a bit, the light from the street lamp filtering through the curtain and making him look just beautiful as he lay there like a smile from God.

Downstairs she put a record on the turntable and let the puppy back into the living-room to scamper around. She liked the noise it brought to the empty room, quiet for a change without television and Glynmor. She really did want him back though. She was sure of that. She would never let him go without a fight.

Diana Ross was singing about how she wanted to be touched in the morning as Maggie sat gazing into the coal-fire remembering the way, when they were kids, they used to flick bits of orange peel into the glowing coals and watch their small phosphorescent explosions. She liked old things. She was an old-fashioned girl all right and perhaps it was the chapel in her blood but she would never agree to a divorce. Never. The puppy put his nose near the fire and she pushed him away from the grate.

She had even got on the phone to the Rediffusion people in Pontypridd that afternoon and asked them to send up the biggest television they had. That's how much she wanted him back. Huw would just have to learn to live with it and that was that. They could always bolt it down if necessary.

Out in the Valley, a crescent moon was throwing a bright

fluorescent sheen over the roof-tops with the black lines of the pit edged in a silvery glow as Xenia Prosser was busy undressing in the back of Glynmor's Toyota, parked down by the railway sidings, just above the gurgling river.

Glynmor had never quite seen such a performance and had to work hard not to laugh as he remained in the driving seat and she scrimmaged around in the back, bent double as if working a two foot seam, while taking off her clothes and hanging them up tidy. With most of the girls that Glynmor had grappled with in his new passion wagon he usually half-ripped the clothes off. But not with Xenia Prosser. She always brought a carrier bag with a bundle of wooden clothes hangers, first hanging up her coat on the safety belt hook, hanging up her skirt on one of the passenger hooks, then her blouse and now folding up her underslip all as if getting some C. & A. shop ready for its January sale.

'Why don't you just wear jeans and a sweater like every other girl?' Glynmor asked.

'Because I always like to look smart,' she said, rolling down her tights. 'Anyway I do tell him I'm going to play bingo with Jennifer over in Aberdare so I can't go out wearing jeans and sweater can I?'

'Don't see why not.'

'He'd smell a rat straight away, fathead. He knows me. I won't even peg out the clothes on the line unless I'm looking tidy. Anyway I could never wear jeans. My legs are too fat for jeans.'

'How much longer ... '

'All right. Keep your hair on is it? Right. I'm ready for you now Glynmor. As ready as I'll ever be anyway.'

He sort of vaulted over his seat and grabbed her goosepimpling flesh. 'Hold on there lover boy,' she puffed. 'After all that complaining aren't *you* going to take anything off?'

'Aye.' He unbuttoned his belt and pushed his trousers down his knees before jumping on her and trying to get straight down to business.

'No, no, no,' she squealed. She pushed him off, dusting her hands together as if they had become covered in dirt. 'What kind of behaviour do you call that then? I had a rabbit who used to act just like that. He jumped on anything that moved. We're

274

not animals, Glynmor. I want a bit of magic with my sex. What I want ... what I want is for you to lick me all over for an hour an' then we can make love slow. The bingo doesn't throw out till half past ten so we've plenty of time.'

'An hour!' He swallowed hard. 'A whole hour?'

'Well half an hour maybe. I do like my nipples to be licked first. Then I'll lick you a bit, if you like, and we'll move on from there.'

He was squatting with his trousers down around his ankles while she was lying in front of him with her legs apart and her pudenda gazing up at him like a cat that had just had its throat cut. He was not at all certain by now if his old boy wanted to perform or not. He was not certain of anything by now. All he kept seeing was his Maggie and all he kept aching for was Maggie's body. He wished he wasn't here doing this, anything but this. He had never enjoyed himself so much as when he was in bed with Maggie so why was he throwing it all away by being here with this bingo bitch now? Word would get out soon and that's a fact. He might have been able to get back with her as it was but if she found out about this, that would be that.

'We girls do love to be licked Glynmor an' I don't care what any of them say. That's probably what went wrong with your marriage you know. Not enough licks. Me? I love being licked. I could be licked all night I could. Did you lick Maggie much did you? Different positions are all very well but the tongue, Glynmor. The tongue's the key to it all.'

Now his old boy knew one thing anyway. It didn't want to get erect after all. If he wanted to go in for all this licking he'd go and buy himself a lollipop. He pulled up his trousers and turned away from her.

'What's the matter my lovely?' He felt sick again. Maggie had always called him that. Somehow it sounded obscene in Xenia's mouth. 'Are you upset about something?'

He nodded. 'It's Maggie. I've gone and left her.'

Sensing a good gossip she sat up and rolled onto her side. She preferred a good spicy gossip to a good licking any day of the week. 'Now what did you go and do a daft thing like that for?'

'What do you care? You never liked her. She hit you once didn't she?'

'Maggie's a girl of passion. Like me. Anyway I never bear

grudges an' I've never liked to see couples break up.'

'So what are you doing here now then?'

'A bit on the side? That's different. That's nothing. That can be good for a marriage that can. But you'll never find another girl like Maggie, you know. I've never known a girl love anyone the way she loves you.'

'It's not that. It's not like that at all. It's 'cos of Huw, really.'

'Huw Bungalow? But everyone adores Huw Bungalow, Glynmor. He's the joy of the Valleys. Why don't you get on with him for heaven's sake?'

His mouth went completely dry and he just stared at her saying nothing. When he saw that she was going to say nothing until she had a reply he finally said 'I can't get on with Huw 'cos he takes Maggie away from me.' His eyes opened wide and he continued staring at Xenia, barely able to believe that such words had actually come out of his mouth. So he had finally admitted it out loud. It was nothing to do with the loss of his television or anything like that. It was because Huw took his wife away. It was because he was jealous of his own son.

'Poor dab,' said Xenia, understanding it all immediately. 'This jealousy is a terrible thing. That's why you're here with me now I 'spect. Trying to get back at her, trying to work the old knife in.'

'I'm here 'cos I want to be here. Not 'cos of her.'

'I've seen whole families destroyed by jealousy I have,' she went on, unconvinced by his feeble protest. 'There was that Tibbs family down in Ferndale. Everyone was jealous of everyone else in that house. If the husband went out the wife would follow him all the time – even down to the pit gates to see him in. Then back at the end of the shift to see him home. The kids were the same and the funny thing was they all hated one another. It was terrible seeing them jostling against one another all the time. Everything was some sort of a competition with them. Freddy Tibbs killed himself in the end. Put a pipe over his exhaust and gassed himself in his car. Couldn't stand it no more.'

'Aye, I remember the story. Didn't he kill himself outside his first girlfriend's house?'

'That's the boy. He had to die making the big gesture. You know how they always love making big gestures in the Valleys.

Here. Turn up that heater will you? I'm getting goosepimples on my goosepimples.'

He leaned across to the dashboard and turned up the heater, making the windows cloud up as she, as unselfconscious as a fanfare, stretched out her long fleshy body. He lit a cigarette and they took it in turns to smoke it.

'Funny thing is I've never felt anything like jealousy before,' Glynmor said, the smoke coming out of his mouth and nose alternately.

'Well you've never found anything you've cared about much have you? But you must fight it. It'll kill everything in time. Not just you and Maggie but everything. It'll kill everything that ever came your way. Everything walks out when jealousy walks in.'

'Quite the little thinker aren't you, girl?'

'We Valley people always have trouble with our emotions. They're stormy, difficult to subdue. Our chance is only through thought, to try and reason our way out of our passions. And with jealousy you've got to get your brains and stamp on it hard. Jump on it like a slug.'

'But it's not always as easy as that, is it?'

'Perhaps not as easy as just saying it. But it's like these fags here. They can be given up if you work on it, convince yourself how bad they are like. It's easy for me, of course. I've never felt a flicker of jealousy in my life. My 'usband could have a dozen women all at the same time an' I wouldn't feel a thing. I'd just be happy that he was happy. Proud of 'im, in a way, if he could get away with it.'

'What about him?'

'If he caught me at it? Oh he'd get upset right enough. He'd get upset all right but he'd get over it. We get over everything in time.'

'You should work for some marriage advice bureau you should.'

'Aye. My friends always said that. I do love chopsing and my Dad always said I was the only one he could ever tell anything to. The problem is I'm into adultery. It's good to get fucked a lot.'

'I like fucking too,' said Glynmor suddenly remembering why they had come there in the first place. 'You know when I come my whole body rattles.'

'You rattle when you come do you? Another of those rattlers eh? It's a bit like a car when the big ends goes I've always thought. Come on. We're here now. Let's try a friendly one is it? Just a bit of a cuddle like.'

'You're not going to worry if my big end goes then?' he asked rolling down the window an inch before flinging out the cigarette stub and rolling it back up again.

'No, but I must warn you that when I come I do sound like an emptying bath.'

'What does an emptying bath sound like?'

'If you stopped chopsing and got on with it you might find out, mightn't you?'

He slipped off his trousers and rolled over on top of her, cuddling for a while as she slipped off his shirt before pushing it in and riding her home slow. She kept making little gasps and her legs moved around gently like long white tentacles. It was odd but he felt a little closer to her now that they had had their little chat. The thought of betraying Maggie wasn't burning into him so fiercely either. Her face was even moving away into the distance for a while as his lips looked for a soft kiss. Then his hip movements became a little quicker and a little more urgent. Quite soon now his big end was going to bust.

'Not too fast now Glynmor,' she said softly. 'Remember the bingo doesn't fling out till half past ten.'

'We'll have six more before then.'

'Oh, bragging are we? I must say that dick of yours was always something of a legend in the girls' bog back in school.'

'A legend in its own nightshift this thing here.'

Outside in the crescent moonlight five men in flat caps and baggy trousers came running out from behind the coal wagons on the sidings. They were not actually talking but pointing their agitated fingers at Glynmor's misted-up Toyota which was rocking gently on its chassis.

Xenia was gurgling like an emptying bath and Glynmor's big end was knocking badly when the five men tipped the car up on its side and rolled it over the bank. With a great concerted heave they then sent it spinning down towards the river.

Carried along on a breaking surf of their surging lusts the two adulterers were not at all sure what was happening. They grunted and gasped and had the vaguest idea that they were rolling over and over – naked limbs, ash trays and clothes

278

spinning around and around as if they were inside some giant tumble drier. He floated upwards and she sailed past him in a swoosh of mammary glands. He hit his side and she gave her head a nasty crack. There was going to be no more playing around for him, he decided as they both landed in an untidy painful heap with the car on its side in the middle of the river, two of its wheels spinning slowly.

Glynmor, fortunately still with his shoes on, kicked his way out of the shattered back window, standing up to his knees in the freezing water with Xenia's brassiere half-wrapped around his neck. Blood was trickling down the side of his head. Looking a little like a half-murdered crazy in a Hammer horror film, he just stood there screaming wild obscenities at the moon.

'What the hell was that?' cried Xenia, trying to crawl out of the shattered car.

'My car! My fucking car! Three weeks I've had this car. Three fucking weeks.'

'Never mind about your car. What about my clothes? This water's freezing. Where are my clothes?'

'Here's your bra anyway,' he said flinging it towards her, only to see it floating off down the river like a couple of mating jellyfish.

'Look, are you going to help me out of here or what?' demanded Xenia her wrist throbbing badly as if it had been sprained.

'Perhaps we should have kept our seat belts on,' he said, reaching down to help her out of the shattered window.

'You can't fuck in a seat belt can you? Oh I've done something awful to my hand, I have. I've broken it, I have.'

Even as they helped one another up the slope a police car, with revolving flashing lights, pulled up in the sidings. 'Now what precisely have you two been up to?' the policeman asked, flashing his torch on the naked, bedraggled pair. 'We had a call that someone was out here pinching coal.'

'I work in the pit and get my coal free,' Glynmor puffed piously. 'We were just out having a swim we were.'

'I see,' the policeman replied with a bright note of disbelief in his voice. 'A sort of midnight dip was it?'

'Aye. You could put it like that.'

'Mrs Jones? I've come to tell you that your husband's been in an accident. There's nothing to worry about, but he is in hospital.'

Maggie could feel the blood drain out of her face and the strength going out of her knees as she looked up at the policeman on her doorstep. It was dawn. Since midnight she had sat dozing in her armchair, the puppy sleeping on her lap. She had woken when she had heard loud knocking on the front door.

'He was in a parked car up by the sidings,' the officer was saying. 'Five men rolled it over and down into the river. We've picked up the men involved in the incident and are questioning them down at the station.'

'Do you want a cup of tea or something?' she asked, ushering him in.

'No thank you, Mrs Jones. But it is my unpleasant duty to inform you of something else since it is bound to come out in any court proceedings later. You might as well know now that your husband had a woman at the time of the accident. We have grounds to believe that it was the woman's husband who ...'

At this point Maggie's knees gave way. White as the milk bottles on her doorstep, she fell into a swoon. The policeman just managed to catch her before she slumped to the ground. He carried her inside and stretched her out on the sofa. 'Better send a nurse or something,' he said on his radio, to the Police H.Q. 'I told her what had happened and she just flaked out on me. Of course I told her about it. It'll all come out in the trial won't it?'

Later that morning, after a visit by the doctor, Maggie felt well enough to make a couple of telephone calls and a decision.

She rang Brian Jones & Co., the Cardiff solicitors, to make an appointment to discuss a divorce. Then she rang Rediffusion in Pontypridd to cancel the incoming television set.

About half an hour later little Audrey, from next door but one, came into the house in a flood of tears saying that her Mammy would never allow the dog back. There and then Maggie decided to keep it. She hoped that it would grow up to be very big and fierce. She hoped that it would bite any Bont miner who came near her. She particularly hoped that it would take a big chunk out of that Glynmor Jones.

Chapter Eighteen

After the loss of his thumb and the car-rolling incident, Glynmor's confidence crumpled like a paper bag. For the next few weeks he rarely ventured from his bedroom in Aunty Phyllis' house. Instead, he listened to the radio, watched the little portable television, or just sat at the window looking at the comings and goings in the street.

It was an unhappy time for him, never more so than when he saw Huw going to the shops or Maggie, with that new puppy of hers on a lead, going down to the hairdresser's. She walked past the house with a cold, distant look on her face but with her heart pounding. But he could not read her mind and her apparent coldness always managed to bring his spirits right down.

The police came one morning and explained to him that Xenia Prosser's five brothers-in-law would be charged as soon as they had decided exactly what to charge them with. Glynmor said that he didn't know what they were talking about. Flatly contradicting what he had said in earlier statements he now insisted that he had just stupidly left the handbrake off and this had led to the plunge into the river. With Xenia coming out with a similar story, the police were clearly going to find it difficult to bring a successful prosecution against the Prosser brothers. After making various threats about the penalty for perverting the course of justice, they went away again.

More worryingly, though, the car insurance man had called about the written-off Toyota. When Glynmor told him what he had already explained to the police – that he had simply left off the handbrake – the insurance man warned that this might affect his claim since, as he only had third-party cover, he was not insured for personal negligence. Glynmor then began to have grave doubts about the virtue of letting the Prosser boys get away with it. Not that he had decided to let them get off scot free. In his own way, and in his own time, he was going to beat twelve different colours of shit out of each of them when he caught up with them. No one was going to roll him and his new car down into the river and get away with it. Not even if he was screwing their sister-in-law at the time.

To add to his woes the stump of his thumb was giving him murder. The doctor gave him a variety of pills which did nothing to soften the pain. And he was having dreams of the black tide of Aberfan. Come the nights, while watching the portable television, he would sit drinking whisky to enable him to sleep. But no matter how drunk he got, those bad dreams came swirling back. Everyone was being swept away by the black waves: Maggie's face was often there, the terraced houses, Huw's teddy boy suit, the insurance agent, the committee chairman ... friends, enemies and homes all being swept away by the same killer tide.

Some nights he woke in the dark, covered in sweat and believing that he was drowning. Then, still shivering, he would sit chain-smoking and looking out onto the empty street, lined with parked cars and silent shadows, when everyone else was in bed, doubtless enjoying great dreams of sex, money and power. Not that he was so lucky. He was a prisoner in a cell which he could not quite understand.

There were some mornings when he did sit with Aunty Phyllis down in the kitchen next to the range fire, but then Enid would come in and they would drive him daft with their continual gossip, usually about ailments ...

Marjorie's found that she has got another lump again and she's ever so pleased about it. Gwyneth has been in twice with the fatty lump she's always been worried about. It's a sort of sprout it is. She says it's a gall-stone but they keep saying they can't find anything wrong. She's off to hospital for more tests next Wednesday. That Brenda Parry has found out she's got bad blood pressure and the doctor can't seem to get it down. They've tried everything on the poor dab but she's on the turn she is. On the turn. You get some terrible things when you're on the turn.

Sometimes Glynmor felt that he was going to drown in all this infernal gossip. He longed for the compensation money for

282

his thumb to come through but nothing came and nothing had yet been resolved with his continuing dispute with the board. Since the loss of his car, the bank manager had stopped 'that overdraft lark' – as Maggie had once scornfully called it – and, since he was still giving Maggie most of his social security money (delivered in an envelope every Friday by Aunty Phyllis), he had virtually nothing for any reckless spending now, even letting his curls grow out. What he had, he spent on whisky, looking for the concussion which never quite seemed to come.

He was quite sure that Maggie would have him back when his compensation money did come through. He would bump into her one night, by accident perhaps, in the Hall after a few drinks, and offer to take her away from all this. They would go to Cardiff and start again or even go to London. She would agree straight away and they would pack and disappear into the night, first signing into a hotel in Porth where all their differences would be settled by a night of warm passion in a soft bed. He missed her body terrible. He was almost physically sick when her lovely limbs crowded into his mind in the lonely darkness.

Such escapist fantasies came to an end when he received a letter from Brian Jones, the posh Cardiff solicitors, informing him that his wife was suing for divorce on the grounds of his adultery with Xenia Violet Rose Prosser of 18 Taff Street, Bont. Who could commit adultery with a bastard flowerpot?

He put the letter into his pocket and promptly took it out again, hardly able to believe the cold, dismissive message of farewell the legal words contained. Surely not after all these years? And just for one night? Well, the one night that she had found out, anyway. How much worse could it all get? He didn't want to play this silly game any more and, plunged into the deepest despair, went upstairs to his bedroom where he wept, silently and copiously, until his eyes stung red.

But there was one incident in this period of desertion and misery which was to turn out to be significant. One afternoon, while sitting staring out of his bedroom window, he spotted the mobile library which came around twice a week. Tiring of the persistent fatuities that seemed to drip constantly from his portable television he went over and signed up with the library, and then looked for a suitable book. The one that took his fancy was *Martin Eden* by Jack London. That book was the start of a long socialist rapture which deepened with every book by Jack London that he could lay his hands on. He wondered at the commitment and humanity of the great writer, the sheer strength and tenacity of his beliefs. *The Iron Heel* overwhelmed him and, together with his domestic misery and a whole new range of ideas, this was clearly a time of deep and lasting change, even if he didn't quite understand it himself at the time.

Unaware of even the possibility of any change, Maggie was surprised at how fast the divorce proceeded once it had been set in motion. She hardly felt a part of it at all, just signing statements sent to her through the post or filling in forms for legal aid. It was like signing things about someone else's life altogether. And when they told her that she had to list all Glynmor's bad behaviour over the past fifteen years and she said she didn't want to do it, she was assured that this was the way the law asked for it to be done. A funny old law that seems to me, she thought. Who would think up a law like that?

The emotional strain of it all had made her go as thin as a lath and, in the process, even more beautiful. All this had not been lost on the boys in the Hall. There was never any shortage of drinks if she went there for a quiet half of lager with the girls. Not that she was interested in any of the boys, as she had to make clear more than once. All she ever seemed to want to do was to sit with the girls and talk about Glynmor. Had they seen him? What did he look like? Who was he with? Had they heard if he was eating proper?

The girls did their best to try and smooth the ruffled waters of her anxieties but then it was 'do you remember' time. And do you remember that night when the two fire engines came when Glynmor was in bed and he was going around bragging about how he was clearly the hottest thing in the Valleys and they had to send out two fire engines to cool him down? And do you remember the time when Glynmor ...

A time of divorce was awful hard for any woman the girls would say to one another when Maggie was not around. But if I hear any more of Glynmor this and Glynmor that I'll scream I will. She was mad enough about him when they were married but listen to her now. And I'm worried she's beginning to neglect poor Huw Bungalow too. She's not been ironing his suits the way she used to. And there were holes in his socks as well. Perhaps she's cracking up. I hear Glynmor's in a terrible mess too. Drinks in his room all night, he does, but you couldn't tell her that could you? What a bloody mess it all is. Still you couldn't expect much else with that Glynmor could you? I've always said he's as odd as a bottle of crisps.

Maggie and Glynmor did bump into one another one sunny Saturday morning outside the Co-op and had their first chat for a month.

'Better be careful you don't fall over with all that stuff in your bag,' said Glynmor, smiling while his eyes misted over.

'What do you care?' she asked with her insides going all funny.

'I've just been for a walk up the pit to see the boys.'

'Really? A nice walk, was it?'

'It was. Nice to see the boys anyway.'

'Nice.' She showed her teeth in a sort of smile though it looked to Glynmor more of a snarl.

They both stood there awkwardly for a few more seconds, she looking inside her bag of shopping, as if she had forgotten something important, and him looking over the road. 'I'd better get on,' he said. 'Aunty Phyllis will be having the dinner on.'

'Well, you'd better not be late for that, had you?'

'No. I'd better not. See you.'

'Aye ... see you.'

She half-walked and half-ran back to her house, bursting in through the front door and letting out a fearful wail as she flung herself on the sofa, with the puppy making her worse by coming over and licking her face. Even Huw got out of his chair in the kitchen to give her some reassuring pats.

'Oh leave me alone,' she snapped at him and, more amazed by her tone than anything, he returned to the kitchen followed by the puppy. Now she felt really awful. 'I'll make you some hamburger and chips in a minute,' she called out. 'I've got some ice cream too.'

It was a damp arthritic morning in November when Emlyn Kremlin and five of the boys from the lodge went in Ted Jones' mini-bus down to the Llanishen headquarters of the National Coal Board.

'How much coal do you think we dug to pay for this place then?' Dai Prosser wondered as they entered the great neon and glass edifice where the smell of polish bounced off every wall.

'How many men's lives more like?' asked Emlyn.

It was time for the six working miners of the Bont lodge to meet over the conference table with six officials of the board, or best-suited capitalists, Emlyn always decided, with tailor-made brains, who sat in unsmiling line, taking out yellow folder after yellow folder and explaining that the pit was continuing to make heavy and unacceptable losses. The usual game.

'So what are you trying to say then?' Emlyn demanded.

And that was precisely the trouble. The board wasn't really saying anything. This murky cloud of statistics was just another of their ways of dispiriting and demoralising the miners, who were not economists after all; another part of the steady process of softening them up and pulling a few teeth before finally putting the boot into the pit.

'The South Wales coalfield lost seven per cent of the market availability last year ... '

'We know all that. So what are you trying to say?' Emlyn asked again, dogged in his pursuit of plain meaning and motive.

'We don't necessarily have to say anything. We just want to make sure that we have painted the fullest picture of where the Bont mine stands.'

'But, if you stopped painting pictures and told us what was on your minds, we'd all know where we were.'

'Well, we're not really anywhere ... '

And so it went on but – apart from suggesting that the miners might improve the pit's productivity, which they might, agreed Emlyn, if the geological conditions were with them – they still wouldn't say what was on their minds. It was all as you would expect, Emlyn thought, from men who drove Volvos, had expense accounts and went to B.U.P.A. hospitals; men who barely knew where the Valleys were, let alone ever having visited them. Such men spent their days standing on shifting sands and, when the sands shifted, they shifted with them. These were the real barnacles on the ship of coal, not the struggling pits and their decaying communities. Emlyn had watched such men become more arrogant and offensive in Margaret Thatcher's Britain. There was a time when the board seemed to be on your side, but no longer; these were steely, plump men with short hair who would knock you down sooner than look at you; yet another part of the Thatcherite enemy dribbling on about economic efficiency while the Valleys and their communities rotted away.

'Next time you gentlemen call us up here,' Emlyn said finally standing up, indicating that the meeting was over. 'Try and make sure you have something to say will you?'

When Emlyn stood up, everyone else stood up too – even the members of the board. The old communist warhorse had some of that old-fashioned quality that inspired a form of respect – even among his enemies. It was always interesting that very few men ever swore in front of him. He was one of those big, learned men, with a quiet committed passion, who, in another life and with different political ideas, might have been a Member of Parliament or even a Prime Minister.

He felt very old and tired when they got back into the waiting mini-bus. What he had really wanted to find out was the date the board intended to try and close the pit. Only then could they get their campaign properly organised; a stratagem which the board recognised all too well which is why they clearly weren't going to give them a date. Instead they kept shuffling around on their shifting sands, speaking their mealy-mouthed platitudes which meant nothing.

And in such a mood they drove silently back to the Welfare Hall, a weary and dispirited group, frustrated at fighting with an enemy who would not fight properly. 'You know, boys, talking to them is a bit like shouting down an empty oil pipe,' Emlyn said. 'You get plenty of echoes but you never get a reply to anything.'

But, after a few pints in the Hall, always the pit rhetorician, he began to get a little rhapsodical. 'You know, I've always hated these new steel pit props,' he said, his back straight and one burly hand clamped on his knee. 'They snap sudden they do and never give you a warning about anything. Now those old wooden pit props would tell you all kinds of things. You could tell if there was water about. You could see in the way they sweated, how hard the rock was coming down. But, most of all, they told you when a fall was coming. They squealed and moaned in a way which told you that you had better make a run for it. And run you did. These days the air is full of creaking pit props. But we just sit here and don't know what to do. We just don't know whether to fight or run. That's the way they've got us now.'

Later still in the afternoon Maggie came and sat with the group. Emlyn shifted around in his seat uneasily and already some of the boys were drifting away. Maggie was becoming notorious for going around the place boring everyone senseless with her talk about Glynmor and, when everyone else failed her, Emlyn's was the one broad shoulder she often ran to for sympathy.

He was good at sympathy too was Emlyn. Even when his very veins were clogging up with boredom he never showed it. Perhaps it was something to do with his natural feeling for the suffering of others, or perhaps it was something altogether different, but many beat a path to his door when they were in trouble.

Barely had Maggie got her behind down on her seat than she was going on about Glynmor. Emlyn wouldn't have minded so much if he could have done anything, but Glynmor had refused to speak to him at all about the break-up and all Maggie really wanted to do was talk to herself. He smiled faintly to himself as Maggie prattled on. What he really ought to do was turn her loose on those men from the N.C.B. They'd all be agreeing to anything, then running down the road crying with their hands over their ears.

'Look I've told you before,' he finally interrupted her and getting quite sharp. 'You've got to call off this divorce thing. He might talk to you then. He might.'

'He doesn't give a rat's arse for me, Em. He never did.'

'What nonsense you do talk sometimes. You were the only star in his firmament. But you can't really expect him to come rushing up to you and kissing you in the street can you?'

'I don't see why not.'

'You don't see why not? Because you're divorcing him that's why not. It stands to reason. Men don't like it when their women divorce them. They get upset.'

'But he doesn't love me any more does he?'

'Of course he does. But he's like all the other men around here. He doesn't like to show it. Valley men never like to show their feelings. They're afraid of being thought pansies.'

'But, if he'd loved me, he wouldn't have gone off in his car with that cow Xenia Prosser would he?'

Just then Emlyn was caught short of air and just sat there for a while, with his mouth opening and closing, waiting for his lungs to catch up with his body again. 'Who's to say why a man like Glynmor does anything?' he said finally. 'Someone like him has got more layers than a prize onion. Beneath all that wide-boy, dirty talk there's a man of exceptional tenderness who lives in a cloud of terror. That's probably why you fell in love with him. He's not a robot and he's different from the rest – childish often – but angry and sharp too; someone who I wish would join us in the lodge. Oh I'd love to have him in with us. I've always wanted that.'

Maggie loved Emlyn and the beauty of his words. It warmed her that someone could speak like this about her own husband and even made her ashamed of her own low opinion of the philandering old bastard.

'Who's to know why a man like Glynmor started playing around with that Prosser woman,' Emlyn continued. 'It might have been because he lost his thumb. It might have been because he thought he was losing his attractiveness to women. I think it was because he was jealous of all the attention that Huw gets. A man like Glynmor needs warmth and praise. He needs to be at the centre of the comedy. He just can't live with any form of rejection, so, if you really want my advice, call off the divorce and see where that gets you. One thing's for certain – he won't talk to you proper again till you do.'

'I've got to go down to the solicitors in Cardiff on Tuesday,' she said through her tears. 'Should I tell them to call it off then do you think?'

'I do. Put it on ice for a bit anyway. Look, if you're going down to Cardiff, take some fags to Bobby in the prison will you? I'll get you a visiting order. I'd go myself but I'm too busy to get there next week.'

The bus journey down to Cardiff to see about her divorce was something of a family affair, since Maggie took along Huw Bungalow and the dog. It was one of those tiring stop-start journeys with the bus filling up with cigarette smoke and body odours as doddery old ladies with varicose legs got on at every stop and took an age to pick the correct fare out of their purses. At one stop, at Llwynypia, an old man lit up a pipe which led to a storm of protest and complaint from the nearby passengers.

'What are you smoking in that, then? Smells like dried shit and bus tickets it do.'

'Leave me alone,' the old man squeaked, putting another flaring match to his pipe. 'Just leave me alone, is it?'

'I'll leave you alone with my umbrella if you don't put that thing out.'

And so another quarrel broke out, giving Maggie a right old headache. Any excuse for a quarrel with this lot, she thought, looking out at the moody day which was neither sun nor rain, a nothing day, almost regretting that it had to make any kind of appearance at all. If you told them black was black they would start quarrelling about it.

Her Huw was enjoying the journey immensely though and, at times, she could feel him quivering with delight as he looked out through the window. Even now he was trembling with happiness as he looked up at the old Thomas and Evans Welsh Hill Works in Porth. What he found so enchanting about an ugly and derelict pop factory, with weeds growing out of the walls, she could not think. Indeed she would have been truly astonished had she known that his imagination had transformed the broken-toothed building into a bright fairy castle with turrets and a drawbridge, all burnished with lots of small bright rainbows. Huw's bright black eyes never beheld such things as ugliness and decay. Whatever he looked at made him joyful.

Duw, even the dog stood on his lap and seemed to be enjoying everything he looked at too. What with Huw's laughter and the dog's squeaky barks the pair had now established themselves as a sort of comic double act around the village and, if ever Huw went into a shop or house, the dog just sat down on the doorstep and waited for him to come out again.

Maggie's belly tightened and headache thickened as the bus roared down past the misty steel shapes of Nantgarw colliery and into the sprawling semi-detached suburbs of Cardiff. She had never got on with the city, finding it gigantic and full of threat. Even as the bus jerked into the sprawling bus station, with its massed queues and shelters, she took hold of Huw's hand for comfort. When they got off, seagulls sailed through the grey skies overhead as whole marching bands of people went crashing through one another in the shops and pavements. *Echo* sellers cried the latest bad news and babies cried in their prams as she skirted around an omelette of dried vomit just outside the Boots chemist shop. The very roads were jammed with traffic of all shapes and sizes while the Castle clock chimed dolefully, telling the populace the dismal story of the passing hours.

She just felt so menaced as they made their way to the solicitor's office in City Road. All this noise! All this filth! She couldn't understand how anyone could live here. Glynmor had often said that he wouldn't mind living in Cardiff but she had never fancied it. She was a mining village girl who liked living in a mining village. She liked one chip shop and one Welfare Hall. She liked people to be where they were yesterday and would be tomorrow. She wished that Glynmor had been there yesterday and would be there again tomorrow.

Huw and the dog were made to stay in the reception room when Maggie went in to see the solicitor who, with his large mahogany desk and fitted carpets, only added to her sense of inferiority. But he was likeable enough and had a smile, which she took to immediately, even if it did waver when she announced that she had decided not to press on with the divorce.

'I'm glad, because I've always hated divorce myself,' he said straight away and she nodded, relieved that he wasn't going to throw a wobbly about it and send her huge bills for wasting his time. 'But if you are still estranged from your husband, by which I mean living apart from him, I must warn you of certain difficulties that may lie ahead for you.'

He then, with great patience and clarity, outlined the problems of her maintenance, living accommodation and the custody of Huw while her matrimonial status remained unresolved. If there was not a divorce, or at least a legal separation, the court would be unable to set a proper level of maintenance and her husband might get away with paying nothing. Although she had certain common law rights to half the house he could legally argue that he had inherited it and that it was his alone – if there was not a legal and proper divorce. Her husband could also claim custody of their son.

'He wouldn't do that. He can't stand the sight of him.'

'Well that's what he might be saying now. But there's always strange, bad feelings when marriages break down.

People start saying and doing the oddest things. Huw is due for a disability pension next year. That could be a lot of money and your husband would enjoy certain legal rights over it.'

Maggie was quite dazed by this barrage of advice and legalisms but was considerably unnerved by the thought that anyone – let alone Glynmor – might be able to take over custody of her Huw. 'What do you suggest then?' she asked.

'Keep the divorce process going but look for a better basis for calling it off.'

'Better basis?'

'A better basis would be if your husband came back to live with you. But you are saying that you are not even talking at the moment so, while the prospects of reconciliation are dim, you should – you must – keep the divorce process going, if only to protect your future rights. The best we can do, on our side, is slow everything down which will, at least, give any reconciliation plenty of time.'

'All right, if you say so.' She frowned hard and felt that she was being led somewhere she did not quite want to go. It now rather looked to her as if it was going to be easier to get a divorce than to actually call it off. It was all beyond her. There had been no mention of love or anything like that. 'All right, if you say so,' she repeated, uncertain.

When she left the offices with Huw and the dog she was not even very sure what she had agreed to in the end. She just had a dim idea that she was going to wake up one morning and find herself divorced and that would be it. Emlyn was going to be furious with her. That was certain, that was. And what was Glynmor going to say about it all? Her mind was whirling with so many colliding thoughts and anxieties she was almost sick as they walked down the road towards the prison.

The prison officials were not at all happy about the dog coming inside their high stone walls but finally relented when they saw that Huw Bungalow was do-lally and very reluctant to part with the thing. They were also much taken by Maggie's good looks and there was a fair bit of uniformed jostling to escort her down to the visitors' room. Glynmor had often told her about this and how the screws often knocked off visiting wives, working on the assumption that they were desperate for it with their men locked away inside. That was just the dirty kind of information you would expect from him.

Young Gnasher actually seemed very pleased to see her and even more pleased when she produced the carton of cigarettes that Emlyn had bought for him. Although he was her nephew she had never had a great deal to do with him in the past. Oh, she had done what she could, in the way of meals and spare cash, when Daisy had upped and left for Greenham Common but, like so many others, she had flung up her hands in horror and turned away when he had become a fully-fledged skinhead at war with society.

Not that he looked terribly ferocious now, she was pleased to see, since his hair had grown to a normal length and he looked almost human in his blue dungarees and polished black shoes. Those horrible home-made tattoos were still on his fingers though and she had to keep looking away to stop herself from staring at them in disgust.

'There's talk I might be sent to Dartmoor,' he told her, with a hint of pride.

She looked at him appalled, visibly shaken by the picture of some dark Victorian fortress where they toiled, breaking up rocks all day.

'Oh don't worry,' he reassured her. 'They've got good teachers in the Moor. You can learn things there.'

'Things like what?'

'Business things and trades. I could become a plasterer.'

'That would be good, wouldn't it?' She did so hope he would do something useful when he got out but, again like so many others, she had the gravest doubts.

'Might keep me out of trouble for a bit init?'

The visitors' room was high and wide with plain, white-washed walls and thin strips of neon hanging on chains from the ceiling. The visitors and prisoners sat around small tables, many holding hands as they were watched by the warders who stood near the doors. Odd prison sounds like the hooter or the slam of a metal door, penetrated the room, but this afternoon, most of the sounds were the sounds of laughter as Huw Bungalow and the dog went around the tables entertaining everyone. It was just the sheer unlikelihood of the act that amused everyone; a whistling, laughing teddy boy in bright gaudy drapes with a dog that kept barking and running around his blue suede shoes.

'Still as dull as ever then?' Gnasher asked nodding towards Huw.

'Aye. An' if he had two heads he'd be twice as dull.'

'Glynmor is all right, is he?'

'Yes, he's fine. Are any of your Clay Class butties still in here?'

'Not any more they're not. Cocoa has gone off to an open prison. And Nipper and Iffy. But they wouldn't send me to an open prison would they? After what I've done like.'

'No. I don't suppose they would.' A wave of sadness washed over her. Such a youngster and everyone was treating him like a hardened criminal. But he was still just a kid really, wild and footloose like every other kid in the Valley. Now that he was out of his skinhead uniform, and holding his carton of cigarettes like a baby with a new toy, he didn't even look terribly tough.

'I was talking to that Snipe Wilson in here the other day,' he went on. 'Sitting on the bog eating a bacon sandwich he was. He's in here for pinching that bus. I had to laugh. He said he'd only borrowed it for a little ride and just took the wrong turning. One of the screws was saying that there's always been a fair few of us from Bont in here.'

'Must be something in the air.'

'Aye. One of the screws said it was something to do with us all living at the end of the Valley. He said that they always get madder if they live at the end of the Valley.'

She looked around anxiously at Huw again but now even the stone-faced warders were beginning to laugh at his antics. She shook her head in mock-sorrow. 'It's like living in a circus with him sometimes. I don't know where he learns all his little antics. Oh well, time to go. I'll come and see you again soon. I don't suppose you get too many visitors do you?'

'My Dad came in to see me a few weeks ago. He was my last. He's given up the building and works for Rentokil. The money's great, he says an' now he's the champion rat-catcher in South Wales.'

'Really?' She would have laughed out loud at the thought of Denzil becoming a champion rat-catcher except that she felt an even stronger urge to cry. So she was Gnasher's first visitor for a few weeks. A few weeks! And even that great lover of men, Emlyn Kremlin, hadn't been here for ages. She was going to be sending off some scorching letters – to her sister for one – when she got home. 'I'll come and see you again next week,' she promised.

'It's all right. You don't have to.'

She looked at him with crouching eyebrows. Rough he might have been but thick he never was. He saw things as clearly as anyone. 'I promise,' she said firmly. 'And when you do get out you're going to come and live with us.'

'Glynmor wouldn't like that,' he laughed.

She decided then that there was no point in trying to explain anything to the lad. 'He might, you know. You can never tell about anything with Glynmor.'

Chapter Nineteen

It was the pounding bass guitar of the rock 'n' roll band from Swansea that told the Valley that the Saturday night hop was well under way. It had the throb and authority of tropical thunder did that bass guitar, shaking the flaking walls and rotten rafters of the Hall, filtering out through the adjoining terraces, rattling the dustbin lids and banging into the dry stone walls of the gardens, throbbing through the damp night air as pervasive and insistent as a giant hangover and even making the sheep look up from their eternal munching before they moved off with a jerk and a melancholy inaudible bleat, hoping to find a patch of grass where it was not quite so loud.

As the bass thumped on, the volume knobs of the televisions were turned up very loud. Some jumped into their cars and drove off to spend a few hours with some distant relative in some distant Valley. Others, like Aunty Phyllis, went through their little rituals of plugging up their ears with screwed-up lumps of Kleenex or penning yet another letter of complaint to the committee. But they were all just futile, empty gestures against the world colonisation of rock 'n' roll. Even the bolshiest members of the community accepted that, just like the rain and the rent, they had to learn to live with rock 'n' roll.

The music even penetrated those houses well up the hill, forcing the Rev. Mordecai out of his manse and into the chapel whose walls were just thick enough to make the pounding of the bass guitar bearable. He hated rock 'n' roll with a particular ferocity, seeing it as the dead marching music of a dying tribe.

Most in the village, however, saw that the only way to beat the band was to join them, which was why, as usual, the dance was packed with huge groups standing around near the bar with even more either dancing or sitting at the tables, pens and pencils at the ready, with their bingo tickets in front of them, waiting for the game to begin in the interval.

Maggie was sitting at her usual table with the girls. For some of the livelier numbers she might have had a dance with Cynthia but, most of the time, she stayed seated at the table, singing and clapping along with the others. They were much the same group of girls as had sat together for most of their lives, singing and clapping along to the music every Saturday night, supportive in times of marital strife, despairing over the inequity of bingo, celebrative in times of anniversaries, mournful in times of bereavement. For Saturday nights in particular they were the closest of friends and, in this group, there were hardly any of the ordinary breakdowns of ordinary marriages.

'Don't look now Maggie,' said Thelma. 'But I've just seen Glynmor come in.'

Maggie had already spotted him, talking with that Graham Mainwaring just near the door to the Gents. She had seen him as soon as he had walked into the dance, not as cocky as usual maybe but cocky enough, going over to the bar to buy a pint, smiling at that boss-eyed cow from Aberdare, nodding at Oboe Parry then going over to chat with Graham. He was wearing a white shirt, which seemed to have been nicely ironed, and had just had a hair-cut too, by the look of it from here. He still had those poncy curls with that silly gold medallion around his neck.

Now, pint in hand, he moved away from Graham and sat down at a table with the two Costello brothers and their wives. What was he sitting with them for? He had never had anything to do with them. He had spent much of his youth fighting with the Costellos and not always winning either.

'I wish I'd stayed in the house now,' she sighed, overcome by a feeling of gloominess. 'I just can't seem to relax when Glynmor's around. I do get this feeling he's watching me all the time. You know how jealous he gets.'

Take no notice of the silly sod. Come and have a dance is it? You know I still think that Lenny Fox has got his eye on you. All those years and you're still sparkling his fancy. She doesn't want to be bothered with Lenny Fox. Don't talk soft.

He's all right. Lenny's all right. Well go and have another dance with Cynthia.

'I don't want a dance with Cynthia. I just wish Huw would come.'

'Where is he anyway? It's not like Huw not to be here.'

'He'll be along. He fusses around for hours in front of the mirror on Saturdays so he can look lovely for the dance. He's as bad as Glynmor when he gets going.'

'Stop it now, Maggie.'

'Stop what?'

'Stop what you're doing to yourself is it?'

One of the Costello brothers got up with a tray, buying three pints and two gin and oranges. Why was Glynmor sitting with them of all people? Well at least he wasn't out with another woman. She doubted if she could have put up with that. Anything but that. Well he looked as if he was eating proper anyway. That Aunty Phyllis was probably throwing tons of food into him. He was laughing at something one of the Costello boys were saying. She had always fancied him for his laugh with those lovely teeth of his and the way he lifted his head back.

'Stop it now, Maggie.'

'I'm not doing nothing. I wasn't even looking at him.'

She began sipping her Bacardi and Coke morosely when the band began a medley of those great old numbers by such as the Crystals, Shirelles and Ronettes. It was the very music that she had courted Glynmor by – the sounds of their love – and she was almost furious she couldn't just go over there and get him up on the floor. She finished her drink fast with bits of her insides collapsing with the sadness of it all. *Why don't you beeeeeeeeeee my babeeeeeeeeee* ...

It was just after nine with the bass guitar still throbbing along the terraces when Huw Bungalow, all spruced up in his Saturday best, and with the dog at his heels, was ambling down the road to the Hall. Five skinheads were playing the new Space Invaders machine in the chip shop and a bus was turning around the clock. Huw stopped walking and looked up the hill.

Normally, the Libanus Chapel, as befitted an empty tombstone on the grave of a dead movement, was dark and silent but tonight its lights shone out like a lighthouse on a sea of black rock, huge golden shafts which sprayed out onto the walls and roofs of the outlying houses. It was almost like some joyous and miraculous oasis of light and Huw found himself irresistibly attracted to it.

Gaudy rock 'n' roll was still thundering out of the Hall as he walked up the hill towards the chapel, the dog still running around his feet, snuffling under stray newspapers and stopping to investigate the odd stale patch of dog piss on a lamp-post. Now Huw stood in front of the chapel, grasping the iron railings and looking up at the light filtering through the dirty windows and over the rotting wooden door and decaying noticeboard with its posters long since faded. At the foot of the noticeboard was a rubble of stained polystyrene chip trays.

He paused, unsure of a certain atmosphere in the air. He was about to return back down the hill when his ears caught the sound of music coming from out of the chapel, a compelling, sorrowing sound that made him walk up to the wooden doors and push them, only to find that they were locked against him. The dog was still snuffling around the pillars of the noticeboard as Huw took out the chapel key that Mordecai had once given him, unlocking the door and closing it behind him.

All street sounds stopped as soon as he moved through the vestry, half a smile on his face, past a table piled high with mildewed hymn books and the dusty pews leading to the wooden pulpit where the Baptismal font had been sealed off again.

Then the sound of many voices singing a hymn broke out of the very air as sudden and striking as blood from a savage wound. It was the hymn of a people singing the praise of God, the many-layered harmonies soaring and breaking over Huw's head in the sweetest waves. He looked up and around the chapel rafters, his smile getting wider and yet wider, as if he had just been made a personal gift of the sun.

Abide with me; fast falls the eventide;
The darkness deepens; Lord with me abide
When other helpers fail and comforts flee
Help of the helpless, O abide with me.

A man's voice, powerful in strength and resonance, interrupted the singing of the second verse and Huw kept looking around trying to locate its source.

'Though he may send thunder and locusts we will still love God. Though we be thrown into burning bushes or pierced with swords we will still love God. Though misery and darkness and the slime of Satan overtake us we will still love God. Even though we have lost our eyes and ears; even though every bone in our bodies be broken; even though the blood pours from every vein and we have fallen as low as it is possible to fall ... we will still love God. Always love God, my people, and be certain that he loves every second of our adoring praise. Know the world is round and day follows night so that the sound of our prayer and praise will always be in his ears. The only command is to love him.'

The speaking stopped and fell away to singing again, the massed voices of the congregation being lead by the strong direct voices of a group of women. *Diolch Iddo*: thanks be to him for remembering the dust of the earth.

> Thank you Jesus.
> Praise you Lord.
> Hallelujah. Amen. Hallelujah.
> Bless you Jesus.

Outside the chapel nothing moved in the village streets except light through shadow. The rock band had given way to bingo. The pale deathly glow of television sets flickered in the blinds and net curtains of the terraces. The orange street lamps shone on the silvery tops of the cars and, down at the mine itself, the great wheel was black and motionless above the huge pool of naked light in the empty windows of the canteen.

In the sepulchral silence of the Welfare Hall the bingo caller was reading out the all-important numbers from his glass box of bouncing balls. Everyone was rapt and attentive, their pens jerking around the blue cards. *On its own number eight: all the threes, thirty-three: old age, number sixty ...*

The bingo numbers carried out into the deserted streets as distinctly as had that bass guitar. Even the starlings dozing in the eaves seemed to heed the numerical progress towards the flyer of fifty-eight pounds. *Five and nine, fifty-nine, two and six – was she worth it: all the sevens, seventy-seven ...*

A police car turned a corner and accelerated down the Valley. The staccato, electronic gunfire of the Space Invaders

300

spat out of the chip shop as the skinheads continued trying to gun down monsters from outer space, kicking the machine hard when they failed. The face of a woman appeared in one of the windows before she drew the curtains on herself. *Top of the shop, number ninety: one and six, sweet sixteen: all the sevens, seventy-seven* ...

In the back room of Walford's video parlour some six men were sipping cans of beer while watching a blue video. Sweating, slithering flesh climbed over yet more piles of sweating, slithering flesh. When they were not actually grappling with one another they were torturing one another in various ways. One of the men sitting in the darkness at the back of the room was masturbating discreetly. *One and eight, eighteen: all the fives, fifty-five: two and three, twenty-three* ...

Around the back of Lipton's shop there was a lot of cussing and swearing in the darkness as two youths tried to jemmy off the back door. Long experience of break-ins had encouraged the management to smother the door with bars and bolts but still the two continued ripping off the steel strips, swearing when their fingers got caught, now scraping and scratching around a long bracket. Even when a window went up and there was a shout they kept up with their scraping and scratching like starving rats knowing that they were on the brink of a load of food.

Down in the floor of the Valley the river continued washing over the unruly rocks and swirling around the dumped prams and old fridges. In the Hall a loud cry of dismay went up when someone called 'House'.

The next house is your snowball accumulator which stands this week at three hundred and twenty-four pounds ...

Thunder cracked like giant cannoning snooker balls over the heads of the Valleys as dark, fat clouds were being shunted together by speeding winds. Sheets of white lightning stammered again and again followed by slashing rips in the skies, all telling of one hell of a storm about to arrive on the doorstep.

Huw Bungalow had mounted the pulpit and was just standing there with his hands on either side of the lectern as the lightning flashed through the windows and the thunder cannoned closer. But, even with the air full of a coming

301

commotion, he could still hear the words and music of older, more precious, times seeping out of the air. 'In the last days, we are told, certain things will happen. I read my Bible to mean that we are coming to the last days when the old men will dream dreams and the young men see visions. There will be bloodshed on the moon, a great darkness over the land and signs writ large on the sky ...'

That singing filled up the chapel again; singing like Huw had never heard. He stood there smiling, still looking around him as the great groundswell of voices came together in scalp-tingling harmony, shaking the chapel rafters with the warmest emblems of power.

> Love divine, all loves excelling,
> Joy of heaven, to earth come down,
> Fix us in thy humble dwelling,
> All thy faithful mercies crown.

A pink slash of lightning tore apart the sky and the Valley walls shook with fantastic hammer blows of thunder as clouds built up into huge mountains of black shadow, now disgorging torrents of rain. But, even in the angry hissing of the rain and repeated rolls of thunder, it was the winds which screamed the loudest; a savage, siren wind, thick with obscenity and hate.

Such was the fury in the sky, the chapel lights dimmed and Huw's eyes darted around anxiously, worried by the dark that was falling everywhere.

'He is coming then and will engulf the world,' a soft voice muttered in the darkness. 'Satan and all his dark angels have escaped from hell. Beware, my people. Arm yourselves with holiness for this hurricane of destruction is coming down on you with a terrible force.'

Lightning the whip cracked again as Rev. Mordecai stepped out of the flashing shadows, stopping at the foot of the pulpit stairs and blocking Huw's way out. Huw looked down at the Rev., his eyes wide with fright.

'This invading force of evil will come as organised intelligence,' the Rev. spat soft, holding up a rope in both of his hands. 'He will come anxious to serve you and even able to convince you that Satan does not exist. But he does my people. The tongues of the old Welsh prophet has been fulfilled and even this very hour he has thrown a cloak of violent perversion all over the face of the world.'

The storm continued to rage, making the domestic lights stutter and dim. Walford's blue video even jerked to a halt and the electricity supply to the Hall itself failed, making the band's amplification whine and twist before it too went dead. There was a short dark silence but then the supply was restored and the hop was quickly back to its normal buzz.

Here Maggie I've heard they've got a great group from Manchester here next week. You remember that one from Manchester? Winston weren't they called? Wasn't he the singer who was always making eyes at you? Gorgeous he was an' all. What wouldn't I give to meet him down a dark alley.

But Maggie still wasn't listening to the girls' chatter, she was still watching Glynmor who had now left the Costello brothers' table and was back talking to that Mavis Nipples, a very fat and totally boss-eyed cow from Aberdare. What he saw in her she couldn't think. She even danced like a hippo with arthritis. He was keeping his left hand in his pocket all the time too. He could never get used to not having a thumb could he? He'd just worry about it for the rest of his life he would. He wasn't the sort who could just shrug it off and learn to live with it. Not Glynmor. He was far more sensitive than most people ever gave him credit for and there was a seriousness about him that he kept well-concealed too. She'd heard about all the socialist books he'd been taking out of the mobile library and had started ordering some of them too. Just to see what he was reading and thinking about. That Jack London was one hell of a writer and she longed to have a chat to Glynmor about it all, longed to discuss that Martin Eden and how he stayed up all night on that boat educating himself. She had cried along with Martin Eden's frustration, was sure that there was enough in Glynmor for him to become a writer too.

But now she was almost crying in frustration about something else too since that fat cow was drooling into his ear and he was responding happily too. He was going to need a new set of glasses as well as a new thumb the way he was going.

Maggie's back stiffened and she took in a sharp intake of breath. The fat cow was going off to get her coat. Now Glynmor was finishing his pint and following her out of the dance. She saw that all the girls had gone silent and were looking at her, curious. She was engulfed by a feeling of total despair and began weeping uncontrollably. She just couldn't see how she was going to cope with all this pain. The band was playing some jubilant rock 'n' roll totally at odds with her mood. 'Where's my Huw?' she wailed. 'I just want my Huw. Why doesn't he come to see me?'

Oh Maggie it's all right. Huw will be along any second won't he Cynth? Do you want another drink do you? Shall we go to the ladies shall we? Glynmor's only going off with that piece to get you all worked up. Just look at the size of her. You'd need a block and tackle to get on top of her.

'Huw. I just want my Huw.'

With everything bleeding and crumbling inside her, she picked up her handbag and ran out of the Hall, leaping down the stairs three at a time and hurrying home in the driving rain. She hardly cared about the storm though and her eye-liner had been blotched and smudged as much by her own tears as the raindrops when she burst in through her front door. 'Huw? Where are you my lovely?' she called in desperation.

The house was worryingly, and obviously empty. She walked out into the kitchen, picked up a tea-towel and dried her face with it before going upstairs. His bedroom was empty too, his best suit and shoes gone. She so hoped he wasn't outdoors in this storm or he'd be getting a terrible cold. She so hoped he would just come home now so she could hold him tight and take some comfort in her wretched misery.

Once back downstairs she stood in the window of her living-room looking out onto the Terrace where the rain was still pouring down on the parked cars and filling up the gutters, making empty cigarette packets and lollipop wrappers dance around. The band had stopped playing now, she could tell, with the people running home fast: the men, with their shoulders hunched forward and their jackets pulled up over their heads: the women bustling along the pavement, with grim lips and eyes half closed, in a clatter of high heels.

After a few minutes Maggie put on her raincoat and braved the storm again, going back down to the Welfare Hall and finding a sort of fight in progress on the stairs, though not so much a fight as a rolling maul with lots of shoving and pushing by some men she did not recognise.

'Boys, boys,' Max Million, the chairman, kept shouting. 'Let's have some order now shall we?'

Maggie sidestepped the maul and hurried up to the dance hall where, already, the tables were deserted with the band shouldering out their equipment and just a few committee men picking up the empty glasses.

'Stan. Have you seen my Huw?' she cried out to someone behind the bar.

'No girl. Haven't see him all night.'

She ran back down the stairs and out into the rain again, her hair by now but long dripping ringlets as she walked to the bus shelter where Curly and Idris were sitting sharing a bottle of cider with Danny Bits and Pieces.

'Have you seen my Huw anywhere, have you boys?'

'I seen him,' chortled Bits and Pieces. 'I seen him a few days ago. In the chip shop, wasn't he?'

'No, we haven't seen him,' said Idris. 'Do you want a swig from this, do you?'

'If you see him send him home, will you?'

'Aye. For certain. C'mon Maggie. 'Ave a drink of this.'

She turned into the rain and began running again – where she was not at all certain. She just ran on in a blind panic up the road towards the pit. She passed a huge tip drainage pipe which was gurgling and foaming with torrential swollen streams when a great roll of thunder stopped her dead. She looked up at the quivering sky, half fearing that it was all going to collapse on her head when lightning lit up the whole Valley, with the mine and surrounding tips looking like some strange wet moonscape with just a few black shapes of sheep moving around. Then everything turned to darkness and rain again.

The rain had seeped right through her raincoat and seemed to have got right into the very marrow of her backbone as she turned and turned again. Perhaps Glynmor had not gone off with that fat cow from Aberdare after all? He didn't have a car these days and that piece was too fat to get into any car of her own. Perhaps Glynmor had taken Huw home to Aunty Phyllis just to upset her. That would be just the kind of thing you'd expect from someone like him isn't it? Anything to get back at her for what she'd done to him.

But she could find no sign of Huw. Tired and out of breath, she strode back to the village, knocking on the door of

Aunty Phyllis' in No. 3. When there was no reply she knocked again so furious it was as if she was about to bash it in.

'Who's there?' Aunty Phyllis called out. She had long given up opening the door at night.

'It's Maggie. I want to speak to Glynmor.'

'He's not here. He hasn't come home.'

'Did he say if he was coming back?'

Aunty Phyllis opened the door and her plump frame, in her dressing gown and curlers, seemed to fill up the whole doorway. 'I'm not sure where he's gone,' she added. 'He did say he might not be coming home.'

'It's Huw. He's gone missing. I've been looking for him everywhere I have.'

'Called the police have you? You'd better come in and do that straight.'

The police could not have been less helpful when Maggie told them that her son, seriously handicapped, had gone missing. They took his name – 'Oh that's young Huw Bungalow is it?' – and suggested she went home and waited for him. If he didn't turn up she was to ring them again in the morning. 'He might just have got drunk somewhere,' the policeman added.

'He doesn't get drunk,' Maggie snorted.

'Or just fallen asleep somewhere.'

'He always likes to sleep in his own bed.'

'There's always the simplest reasons for these things, Mrs Jones. And it's far too soon to put him on the Missing Persons' List.'

'Well a fat lot of help you are, I must say.'

'Do ring us again in the morning, Mrs Jones,' the policeman said, putting down the receiver.

'Useless bastard,' Maggie replied, putting down hers.

'Do you want a cup of tea?' Aunty Phyllis offered.

'No. I just want my Huw. I just want to know what Glynmor has done with him.'

'Glynmor wouldn't harm a hair of that boy's head.'

'Well, you don't know Glynmor then do you?'

'He never would.'

'But you don't *know* do you? You don't know him like I do.'

In a state of high dudgeon she stormed out of the house,

306

hurrying first to re-check her own before continuing her search in the rain. She followed the gulley along the back of the terrace, peering into the dark sopping places but hardly able to see anything at all. Down by the garage the barking of a Doberman reminded her of something that made her stop still. She had been so distracted by Glynmor's behaviour and then worried about Huw she had quite forgotten about Huw's dog. What had happened to him? And, if they had both disappeared together, should she be comforted by that or worry even more?

Yet more furious dodgem cars of thunder were crashing against one another as she strode on up the hill, past the council houses of Giro City with its broken street lamps and cardboard windows. How could anyone live in houses like that? A dog was howling miserably inside a garden shed and she hurried over, but it sounded far too big and savage to be their dog. Now she had reached the outskirts of Bont and she didn't know where else to go. She stood on a patch of waste ground near the tip, wondering what to do. 'Huw!' she called helplessly into the rain. 'Huw, where are you?'

But, even shouting as loud as she could, through cupped hands, her voice didn't seem to carry anywhere in the rain which just kept falling – steady, determined, inhumanly mocking her human anxiety.

Her stumbling, calling search carried on for the remaining hours of the night, taking her up around the huge forests of pine trees and back around the reservoir. She moved slowly but relentlessly – over brambled fields and dry stone walls, up gulleys and into brown beds of bracken, across the swollen rivers and around the sides of the giant tips. She went down the Valley as far as the next village then crossed the river by the Banana Tip, finally arriving back in Bont unable even to feel her muddied and scratched legs. Not the athletic type at the best of times it was only some dark crawling fear that kept her going.

A grey, weeping dawn finally broke over the village when she returned from circling the reservoir yet again, fruitlessly checking her house once more. By now she was so dirty and dishevelled, Emlyn Kremlin did not at first recognise her when he opened his front door. She was so tired and overcome by shock it took him a full quarter of an hour – and a good three cups of tea – before he managed to extract the full facts of the disappearance out of her. She was chattering and shaking so much she actually dropped one of the cups of tea onto the kitchen floor.

He made her take a hot bath and put on one of his thick, blue-striped nightshirts as he hung her sodden clothes up on the range before putting her into his own bed where, still shivering and chattering incoherently, he promised he would sort it all out, providing she stayed put.

There wasn't a better man in the Valleys to meet such a crisis than Emlyn, the old N.U.M. warhorse, who had spent most of his life leading teams through fire and gas, to rescue those who had gone missing. Where others merely panicked, Emlyn became calmer. Where others dived off in all directions, Emlyn actually sat down, as he was doing now in his kitchen, studying the face of his job watch, thinking the rescue syllogism through from known premises.

He might have been studying his watch for a full five minutes and some would have said that he was just taking it easy. But those who knew him would know that he was thinking it through. There were none of the usual premises here – this was not some unfortunate miner trapped in a known position deep in the bowels of the earth. This was the mentally handicapped child of a broken marriage whose father had gone missing and who, given his love of wandering the Valley, could be almost anywhere.

When he did act, he did so decisively, picking up the telephone and first ringing Ted John North, the mountain rescue specialist. 'Ted, it's Emlyn. Get the rescue team together and down to the Hall now. Huw Bungalow has disappeared.'

'Dai, it's Emlyn. Open up the Hall. We've got to mount a search of the Valley. Huw Bungalow has disappeared.'

'Oboe, it's Emlyn. Get word to the boys of the lodge to get to the Hall. Huw Bungalow has disappeared.'

He put down the receiver and looked up to see Maggie standing in the kitchen doorway. She looked dreadful with her twisting, anxious mouth and black sunken eyes which were even more pronounced on the white mask of her drawn face.

'Couldn't sleep,' she explained feebly. 'Any news is there?'

'None. I forgot to ask but does Glynmor know about all this?'

'Glynmor's not been around. I thought he might have

308

had something to do with it but now I'm sure he hasn't. He's … oh … gone off with some fat cow from Aberdare.'

'Typical. But he could, of course, have gone off with Huw somewhere. You don't know do you? It would make some sense. Just to get at you over the divorce. I told you before. He wouldn't like any of that solicitor stuff.'

'Glynmor wouldn't go anywhere with Huw. He can't stand the sight of him.'

'Well maybe the pair of them'll show up. Let's hope so anyway.'

'Yes. Let's.'

She went home, alone.

It was still sheeting with rain and not yet eight o'clock on Sunday morning when Emlyn had chalked a map of the Valley on a blackboard on the stage of the Rainbow Room as his damp, bleary-eyed troops, still stiff with stale breath and hangover, filed in through the doors and dragged chairs up near the stage. Stan Swansea, Graham Mainwaring, Dai Box, Ted John North … None of them spoke or bantered with one another in their usual manner and just sat there with their arms folded, waiting for the word of command. Oboe Parry, Tony Chef, Tom the Nutter, Dai Prosser, John Abdabs …

Although he never said as much, Emlyn was always proud to be a man among men on such occasions. These were the men who had fought long and hard to save a dying pit and who would even now fight just as hard to find a missing boy. Somehow they always *responded* when they were needed; always faithful to the call of distress; ordinary, decent men, primed and ready to do whatever was necessary.

'This might be a short one since Huw Bungalow might turn up at any minute,' Emlyn told the men. 'But let's tackle it from the start as if it was going to be a long one. Huw was last seen at about seven last night so, first off, I just want to mount a general box and sweep search of the Valley. Everyone is to report back here within two hours. If the general search fails, we'll just have to plan a particular one. Ted, take a few men up to those steep gullies opposite the Banana Tip. Abdabs, take the res.; Graham, the forest; Tony, the mine – just the surface workings, he couldn't have got down below; Dai Box, the tip over on the council estate. Huw's got his dog with him somewhere too. Remember now, a fast search then back here and, if we haven't lifted him, we'll send out more men.'

Even as they left the Hall, the men hurried across the village streets, knocking up their butties to join the search and, within minutes, a small army of men, many in brightly coloured wellingtons, capes and sou'westers was marching out into the drifting rain.

The thunder and lightning of the night had stopped by now – as had the savage siren winds. All they could hear now was the steady hissing of rain. Lots of rain.

John Abdabs and two others jumped into a van and drove up to the edge of the reservoir, which was as quiet and as still as the marbled moat of a ruined Norman castle. Fanning out into a corridor of some ten yards they worked around the brown rocky shoreline, prodding their sticks down holes and into the scummy froth trapped in the small pools. Nothing moved except the odd trout, swimming away and leaving a V-sign on the surface of the rain-speckled waters. Way out on the middle of the lake two abandoned fishing skiffs sat, black on grey, with the muted sounds of a flock of wintering geese gabbling softly to themselves somewhere in the distant mists.

'We used to catch frogs up here when we were kids,' said Abdabs. 'We'd get straws and blow up their arses.'

'What did that do?'

'It made 'em blow up like balloons. Then we'd throw them into the water and throw rocks at them.'

'You were nice as a kid then Abdabs?'

'Nice? Aye. As nice as any of us were.'

The rain had swollen the river so high that Oboe Parry was taking no chances with his river search, holding hands with Dai Prosser and Roger Williams as they waded up it. Actually being in the river was the only way to see what was in it and they could stop together and pull away a mattress or sheet of lino to see what it hid, usually something in the way of more rubbish – empty processed pea tins or Coca-Cola cans.

'We ought to get together and clean up this river one day,' Roger Williams shouted above the swirling roar. 'I do get sick every time I look at it.'

The river charged against their thighs and legs, as relentless as Llanelli rugby prop forwards, hungry to get the ball back. But the trio held solid as they waded up through the railway sidings next to the pit, the two of them standing steady if one of them lost his footing on the slippery rocks. 'If Huw Bungalow has fallen in this he could be in the Bristol Channel before they find him,' Oboe called out.

The trickiest job in the search had fallen to Ted John North who, with Dai Blades and Dan Corduroys, had to climb over the deep slashes of the ravines opposite the Banana Tip. The bright, even fluorescent, colours of Huw Bungalow's suit had often been spotted out in the ravines. It was, of course, unlikely that someone even as do-lally as Huw Bungalow would go out climbing in the dark in the middle of a storm. But, as a veteran mine rescue man and expert at pulling sheep and dogs out of these gullies, Ted understood that any search had to cover the whole area: that you just could not miss out parts of the search area just because access was difficult. The fissures were unstable at the best of times and the rain had opened them up, dislodging small stones and sending them tumbling down the Valley wall. He leaped across one of the gullies with the sureness of the local sheep. Wet rock was always murder to grip.

If Ted had fallen he had been taught to relax and just enjoy the fall. You would only get a few broken bones and they would dig you out soon enough. The trouble was, you never quite knew how deep some of the gullies were. Dislodged rocks seemed to fall down them forever before any sound came back again. Sometimes if you stopped and listened hard, the infernal noises inside some of them sounded even more destructive than the seven furies trapped inside large seashells.

Seagulls always gathered around the village tip in the heavy rain since it made the foraging easier and the maggots more plentiful. They took off in a squawking cloud of flapping wings however when Dai Box and Dibber Williams came tumbling down the rubbish slopes, cussing the rain and kicking out at the exploded plastic bags of rubbish which, even in the freshening rain, released their foul smells of mildew and rot. Dibber, who had already been belching and tasting last night's beer, began puking over a rubble of potato peelings. 'Why couldn't you have got the reservoir or something Dai? These smells mun. You know how I get first thing in the morning.'

'Better you puke up here than in the reservoir. We wouldn't want the village drinking your puke now would we?

311

It's bad enough getting it over our boots in the cage.'

'I haven't done that for weeks.'

'You did it last Thursday you bastard liar.'

'So I did. I must 'ave one of those ulcers you know, Dai. No one else goes about puking all the time like me. Now do they?'

'No. Thank God.'

'But I've been to see the doctor and he keeps saying it's indigestion. Then I'm taking some of his medicine and that's making me puke as well. How can it be indigestion?'

The mine itself was abandoned and silent this Sunday morning, the roofs of its many buildings and outhouses weeping along with the rain. Tony Chef toured the workshops and changing rooms scrupulously, even looking inside the large refuse bins next to the canteen. The rain pattered on the corrugated iron roofs of the foundry and on the huge ten-wheeled Arctic lorries. The rain danced off the gutterings and fell into the brown muddied pools rainbowed with whorls of oil. The rain washed over the wheelhouse where a deputy was sitting with his feet up and smoking a Woodbine. Who would want to go missing in the rain? Tony Chef asked himself. Why be out in all this when you could be home in a warm, dry bed?

Glynmor was happier than the smallest baby as the first Aberdare bus of the morning came toiling up the Valley. This was more like the Glynmor of old; an old woman kept turning and glaring at him as he sat looking smug. He had spent most of Saturday night clambering over the extremely pneumatic frame – and poking his tireless winky into the various orifices – of Mavis Nipples and it had been like scaling a mountain so big it even made the Himalayas seem like a row of beans. All night his whole body seemed to have been trampolining over those giant tits capped by nipples the size of apple tarts. He had gone snorkelling down into her cabbage patch too before having a rest and returning for air around the whereabouts of those amazing nipples. Even her appendicitis scar was vivid with torment.

And after all this sporting activity – which clearly needed a kind of sexual decathlete – he had, not surprisingly, slept the sleep of the dead. Aye boyo bach, there was gold in them thar hills and that was a fact. Clearly the lakes and mountains of Mavis Nipples were going to be explored again very soon.

Even more unusually his missing thumb was not playing him up either. If it was sunny or rainy; if he was drunk or sober; even in the middle of the night in bed or just sitting quietly on the lavatory trying to get a big one out, his thumb would suddenly start romping with pain and he would spend hours sucking or blowing on the stump. But, today, it was purring away as happy as Larry which suggested to him what he had long suspected: everyone should fuck at least twice a day and, in the absence of that, wank often. A pox on what the doctor said.

Those marvellous nipples floated through the clouds of his consciousness again like a couple of sexual flying saucers. Ah me. And that appendicitis scar, as fat as a clap of thunder ...

As the bus pulled into Bont he could see that men were moving about in the surrounding countryside in the rain, which was unusual on a Sunday morning, even in fine weather. But he thought no more of it as he leaped off the bus and ran down to Aunty Phyllis' house.

'Everyone's been looking for you,' she told him sharply, standing in the doorway. 'There's been mischief there's been.'

'Oh aye. Well they can't blame me for once. Are you going to let me in out of the rain or what?'

'Your Huw has gone missing he has. Emlyn has got men out searching for him.'

'Where's Maggie?' he asked, his good humour draining away as those flying saucers went whirring off to another galaxy.

'Home. Waiting to see if Huw will be coming home I expect.'

He ran down the terrace and, pushing open the front door, walked inside calling out Maggie's name. The living-room was cold, and there was no fire. He turned when he heard someone in the hallway. It was Mrs Pritchard from next door but one. 'Huw's gone missing Glynmor,' she said quietly, with no hint of reproach.

Glynmor just stood there, the raindrops hanging in his black curls as he wiped his nose with the inside of his palm. He kept staring at Mrs Pritchard but said nothing.

'He didn't get to the dance and he's been gone all night.

The miners have started a general search of the Valley.'

'Where's Maggie?'

'She's at Emlyn's. Emlyn is organising the search from the Hall. She sent word for me to keep an eye on the house in case Huw came back of his own accord.'

Glynmor ran down to Emlyn's in Richard Street, knocking on the door hard and surprised that Maggie opened it almost immediately. She was ghostly pale. 'Have you seen Huw?' she asked without asking him in.

'Where would I see him? I've been over in Aberdare.'

'Oh had a good rub with that fat cow did you?'

'I went over with a few of the boys and found this wine bar that stayed open all night.' He wasn't sure why he was lying to a woman who was on the verge of divorcing him but there you are. 'Where could Huw have got to?'

'What do you care? Get back to that fat cow of yours. Go on.'

'I told you. I was with the boys.'

She slammed the door shut and he knocked on it again. 'Come on Maggie. We can both get on out and look for him.'

'What do you care about him? Go on. Piss off back to that fat cow of yours.'

'Come on Maggie.'

'Go on. Piss off out of it.'

He ran back to the Hall finding Emlyn talking with Billy Discordant and Morgan Moses in the Rainbow Room. 'Come home have we?' Emlyn asked with a faint censorious sneer as he walked towards Glynmor. 'Have you any idea at all where Huw might have got to?'

'None. Maggie just asked me that. What do you think I might have done with him? You think I'd run away with my own son?'

'Just asking Glynmor. Just asking. You'd both gone missing at the same time. We put two and two together ... '

'And made six. Aye well I didn't. So what are you doing now? Have the police been called?'

'Not so far. They were told last night but we've got far more men than they have. Miners are always best looking after their own.'

'The police, Emlyn mun, have got dogs and helicopters. They've got frogmen for dragging the reservoir. They've got

314

communications with the other Valleys. If Huw's been found in some other Valley he's been reported to the police. This is not one of your underground rescues. Let's get the police in.'

Emlyn's eyebrows raised in the face of such unanswerable logic. He was bound to agree.

'Where are you searching?'

'A general box and sweep of the Valley first. The pit, the res., the tip, the river.'

'Right, well that's a start,' said Glynmor. 'Morgan, I want you and Billy to send out a general call to the village. Knock on every door and tell them to do the same. We want everyone here at one o'clock and we'll cover every square inch of the Valley by nightfall. Just send out the word that Huw Bungalow has gone missing and his father needs all the help he can get.'

Morgan and Billy glanced at Emlyn who nodded. Glynmor had now taken effective charge, just as Emlyn had always wanted. He had, in Emlyn's view, a most unusual combination of brains and courage. When properly motivated, there was no telling where he would lead the men. There was never any better motive than the protection of your own blood. Emlyn was happy to hand over the torch for other reasons too. He had always wanted Glynmor to get a taste for leadership. He still longed for a new leader to emerge in the Valleys and was perhaps alone in believing that Glynmor might be the one.

Emlyn and Glynmor were deep in conversation in front of the blackboard when Maggie walked into the Rainbow Room. 'So what are we going to do next?' she asked, walking over to them, her hands thrust down into her raincoat pockets.

'We're going to get the village together,' said Glynmor without turning around. 'Then we're going to turn this bastard Valley inside out. That's what we're going to do.'

Emlyn's blood surged hot and, slightly overcome, he had to turn away. It had been a long time since he had heard any fighting talk around the place and what sweet music it was to his tired old ears.

The general box and sweep search of the Valley produced nothing but the general call to the village produced the largest public meeting that anyone could remember. The Rainbow Room had been filling up long before one o'clock but, just on one o'clock, the room was packed to the point of suffocation with the people standing on the chairs at the back, others sitting on the floor at the front and yet more trying to push in through the swing doors. Huw Bungalow had brought everyone together.

Among the first to arrive were a gang of skinheads from Giro City, all chewing gum and twitching a bit at the outrage which had befallen Huw. Then there were many of the miners' wives, who had always taken a back seat in times of emergency, grim-faced and talking to one another. Schoolchildren milled everywhere, a few with their dogs who, they said, would spot Huw for miles. The committee chairman, Max Million and his wife, were among the earliest arrivals too – already in oilskins and with walking sticks – as were Bits and Pieces, Idris and Curly from the bus shelter.

The more Glynmor studied their faces the greater his surprise. The two Pryce sisters from the big house on the corner had both come and they hadn't been seen outdoors for years. Billy Smiles had come from his farm down at the other end of the Valley. Even more interestingly, two of the Prosser brothers – who, not many weeks ago, had rolled Glynmor and his new car into the river – were sitting there too. Old Guto had come out from under his stone as well, the crowds making a big space for him and his smell as he just stood there, apparently uninterested in everything, and just glaring at Glynmor.

No one could remember when the Rev. Mordecai had last been seen in the Hall – or indeed at any public meeting anywhere – but there the mystic nitwit was, large as life and twice as puzzling, looking positively buoyant in his duffel coat and brandishing a furled multi-coloured golf umbrella. It was the way he was forever nodding and smiling at everyone as if they were in chapel that got up Emlyn's nose. Just where did he think he was?

Emlyn was even more surprised at the turnout than Glynmor and just sat there on a chair on the stage with his fingers interlaced and his thumbs circling one another. He had never understood why his maddening people so often managed to fill him with such pride. Most of the time they just drove him crackers but, boy, could they be there when you needed them. Such a motley crowd was a sign of their concern that one of their children had gone missing and had to be found. You could reach out with both hands and shape the anxiety in the air. But it was their concern and sense of purpose that was the most real; the love for Huw Bungalow that had made them as one.

'We have but three hours of daylight left so I want groups of you to fan out in different directions and search the whole Valley,' Glynmor said from the stage. 'We've already done a general search so now I want every inch covered. I won't give each of you a precise area but, if you come close to anyone, just move away. Just keep fanning out and looking for any holes; anything at all down which Huw might have slipped. He really could be anywhere.'

Maggie just stood next to him staring down at her feet as Glynmor continued, pausing only occasionally to think out his next words. 'If we have no luck by the time it gets dark come back here to the Hall and we'll already have got the miners' helmets up out of the lamp room. They'll be good for searching through the night. We'll keep going for as long as it takes till he's found.'

Emlyn was mildly surprised by the raid on the pit's lamp room since he had not been consulted but gave no sign of this surprise. If John Walsh, pit manager wouldn't allow the use of his precious lamps, they would just take them.

'The great likelihood is that Huw is in some house or building,' Glynmor went on. 'And we've not yet found his dog either. So, if we're still out of luck after dark, we'll start in Richard Street down near the river and work up through every house and building in the village. Check any sheds and garages. Look in any rooms you haven't looked in lately. Most of all, use your commonsense. If you see anything or anywhere that Huw might be, then check it out. The more thorough the search, the sooner we'll find him.'

Glynmor stepped down off the stage and there was an outburst of clapping with cries of 'We'll find him' and 'Don't you worry now.'

He stepped back up onto the stage again. 'Maggie and me thank you for your help,' he said, humbled and embarrassed. 'You will know that we have had our problems but today we are together. The whole village is together. We are all anxious to find our beloved son.'

Everyone clapped again and Emlyn smiled with a quiet admiration. Glynmor had tapped the emotion of the meeting and mobilised it with an instinctive political skill. If only the

317

lad cared to he could certainly become the leader the Valleys were waiting for.

A police inspector in full uniform stepped out of a car outside the Hall and asked for whoever was in charge of the search as the crowds filed out and peeled off into the rain. Even as they reached the outskirts of the village they broke up into smaller groups, fanning out on the Valley walls as they climbed higher and yet higher.

The one searcher who had moved faster than almost anyone was Guto, rope coiled around shoulder and old Davy lamp in his hand. Even when the others stopped to prod around the tip or under the huge iron sewage pipes, Guto strode on resolutely until he had gone well past the Banana Tip and the bend in the Valley, fording the river and coming to a stream bounding out of a gulley.

He followed the narrow shale bank of the stream and squeezed through a narrow opening before coming to the old mining cavern with its forecourt still strewn with rusty rails and drams. He lit the Davy lamp and stepped over a pile of old pit props, pausing only briefly to look at the scene of his emergence from a hallucinating hell. Just near the huge stone he hoisted his lamp up into the air and took in two deep breaths of air. If Huw was anywhere he was in here, Guto decided as he stepped into the darkness of that fearful, dripping tunnel.

The police inspector was in the Rainbow Room talking with Maggie, Glynmor and Emlyn when a skinhead burst in through the swing doors, holding a small dog in his hands. His eyes were red with running tears and his nose was dribbling too as he carried the dog over to the group. He was crying because – as he knew and Maggie had seen immediately – it was Huw's dog and it was as dead as mutton.

'He's had his neck pulled,' the police inspector said, holding its head up by one of its ears. 'This dog's been killed.'

'Oh Glynmor!' Maggie bawled, her arms reaching out for him as her vision swam and all the strength began draining out of her legs. 'What's happening to us? I can't take this any more. I can't.'

The discovery of the dog in a backyard next to the Hall sent a spasm of dry fear through the community and even more joined in the search, with Emlyn himself going up into the Hall's rafters and searching through all the Lodge banners which were stored there. The huge red and gold tapestries – honouring such as Horner and Ablett, the great trade union leaders of old, as well as extolling the virtues of brotherhood, unity and strength were now brought out once a year for the Miners' Gala Day in Cardiff.

But, just that minute, they seemed very sad indeed to Emlyn as he stood with his head bowed to avoid the beams, wondering quite what it was that had got loose in their small village. The creeping dereliction and loss of pride were bad enough, but murder too? He took out his fob watch and looked at it and could just feel the ghosts of Ablett and Horner standing there next to him, their spirits crying along with the rain that was still pattering on the grey slate roof.

Maggie had been put to bed but it was not long before, refusing all offers of any sedatives, she was back in the Rainbow Room again. So many people were now moving in and out, past the glittering one-armed bandits in the corridor that some of the women had set up a silver tea urn, dispensing hot tea and corned beef sandwiches off a trestle table. Clearly, the news of the disappearance had now travelled further than anyone had ever imagined. Dan O'Neill from the *South Wales Echo* had turned up. And he was sober too. 'Yes but I'm still not quite sure what was so special about this Huw Bungalow,' he kept saying as, notebook in hand, he went from tired, blistered group to tired, hungry group.

Down in the square, the rain had stopped as Abdabs and his butties were handing out the miners' helmets with the silver batteries and, quite soon, the dark Valley was scoured with hundreds of shafts of light; not just from the miners' helmets but from the myriad torches, flares and hurricane lamps that were now travelling in floating processions everywhere, criss-crossing one another as they moved up and down the Valley walls.

'It was much like the funeral of a Ming emperor,' O'Neill was later to write in the *Echo*. 'Everywhere there were flickering lights as far as the eye could see. It was almost as if the whole world was out and sorrowing for the loss of its king.'

Lights winked through the black needles of the pine

forests and glazed the still cold depths of the reservoir. Orbs of light moved around the high pyramids of the tips, like floating, magical glow-worms. Golden funnels of light waved along the dark gulleys and danced on the hurrying waters of the river. The Valley had become a vibrant symphony of moving golds on a black velvet, with half-formed, shouted words or the cry of disturbed sheep carrying through the damp air as the people, frightened by this awful glimpse of hell where love had gone, tramped the slopes in their search for their lost king.

Guto stumbled and cussed softly as he emerged from the old mine-working, holding up his flickering Davy lamp and staring up at the huge boulder. He had found nothing but flooding water in the cave. There had been no sweet whistling in the air. The song of the cave had fallen silent. Huw Bungalow had gone. The king had risen.

Chapter Twenty

Maggie was sitting on the stage, sipping at a mug of tea next to Glynmor when Rev. Mordecai went up to her and said that he was sure that Huw would be found soon. 'That which has been lost will always be found,' he added.

Maggie, in no mood to get provocative, merely nodded and Glynmor looked away.

'It comes to something when you have to search the houses doesn't it?' the Rev. went on. 'When are you going to start all that?'

'I'm not sure,' said Glynmor, vague. 'I should think they'll be starting in Richard Street now. Tony Chef is in charge of that side of it.'

By now, so many were coming in and out of the Hall a committee man had been posted on the door to keep out outsiders and, unusually, the bar had not been opened either. 'We'll drink our fill when Huw has been found,' the committee chairman had decreed. 'But not till he is found.'

Rev. Mordecai left and Maggie just sat there asking herself the same single unanswerable question. Who would want to kill a dog? But Glynmor was holding up well under it all, she was relieved to see. It was that unpredictable side of his personality with which she had first fallen in love with, she guessed. No matter how regular the play, you were never quite sure how he was going to play the part. Just now he was coming through as strong as a brick.

It was Oboe Parry who came in and told Maggie that there was a man out in the bus shelter who wanted to see her.

'Can't he come in here?'

'The committee is stopping everyone. He seems a bit of a strange one but he says it's important.'

She looked at Glynmor who nodded. 'It might be something. Better go.'

Oddly, in the circumstances, she had a presentiment that something valuable might be breaking out of the gloom. Even as she walked across the road she knew who her visitor was. And she had not seen him for fourteen years either. 'Hello John,' she said, her spirits singing sudden. 'Can't you come over the road for a cup of tea?'

His head turned and a smile broke out in his bushy beard. Even in the light of the street lamp she could see the intelligence in his big brown eyes. A police car went speeding past with its blue light flashing and they both turned to look at it.

'These are bad times Maggie,' he said. His voice had lost none of its warm and consoling power either. He was still the only man she had ever met who, despite his appearance, was immediately trustworthy. 'There are evil shadows everywhere and your people are under fierce attack but I just came up to tell you that joy will return to your breaking heart. You must trust that.'

'Trust what though John? Trust what? And where's my Huw? Just tell me that will you? I can't live without him John, don't want to live without him.'

'I can't tell you just yet, Maggie. But your heart will be full again. Joy will return to your household. Believe that and you must still pray.'

'But I do. Oh John I do.'

Angry shouts came from the end of Bont Terrace. It might have been a scene from some scabrous nightmare of end times as the house search party, some holding hurricane lamps out in the street, entered each home, whether the householder was a'willing or not. People were screaming their outrage at not being trusted but Tony Chef kept shouting that every house – without exception – had to be searched from top to toe. *Without exception now, boys.*

'I shiver when I think of all the evil that has come to our homes, Maggie,' said John, turning back to her. 'Even that which was once good has gone rotten. The people are ill, they are physically breaking down, they are crying out in pain. But keep praying to God now. He needs every single prayer He can get, since He is alone and embattled, fighting hard to hold onto

322

his power and authority. He does not work like tyrants and despots, murdering to have and hold. He just works through love and prayer. Those are his only weapons. He is suffering the most enormous pain. But be glad. Your Huw is important to Him.'

'I can't be glad though John. You see there's this enormous pain with me too. It's a mother's pain it is. There's only one thing I want to know. When will I see Huw again?'

'I cannot say Maggie. I cannot say because I do not know. But what I do know is that God needs Huw for the struggle that's coming to this Valley. Your very home is going to become a battleground between good and evil when God himself will be fighting for His own life. So remember your prayers. There are but a few faithful left and even a second of prayer is important to Him.'

'Oh John, I don't like any of this. I'm just a mother who wants her son back.'

'God wants His Son back too, Maggie. That's why there's so much death and pain in the Valley. The people have lost His Son and God is desperate to find Him again. He's searching far and near. Huw is important to Him.'

'I don't understand any of this. Why don't you come over and have a cup of tea with us?'

'Not tonight Maggie. Not tonight.'

After the wind had shunted away the rain clouds, moonlight broke over the whole length of the Valley. But still the searchers' lights kept travelling its length and breadth. Huge arc lamps had been set up on the dam wall of the reservoir, where the eerie silence was broken only by the soft splash of police frogmen as they toppled backwards off their boats, to sink deeper and yet deeper into the still, cold water. On occasion a flicker of light appeared beneath the surface, breaking into a small golden pond with the black-masked head of the diver bobbing in the middle of it.

'What happens when we find him Uncle Billy?' asked a watching child.

'That depends. If he's fine, we'll be happy. If he's not, the Valley will die of a broken heart.'

'But we will find him, won't we?'

'We'll find him all right son. If he's anywhere on this earth at all. We'll not rest till we've found him. Have no fear of that.'

'What's so special about Huw Bungalow, Uncle Billy? I mean everyone seems to be concerned about him don't they? Why's that then?'

'It's terrible hard to explain. Huw has become special to us 'cos we find it easy to love him. Love is never easy but Huw makes it easy for us 'cos he's without blemish or sin. Love has always been important in the valleys. We built our homes on love we did. We had everything we did, with this love. It kept our babies safe an' warm, it brought us close to our brothers, made us honour our parents. But there's too much hate now and we've lost what we had. Huw is all we've got left now. He's all of the past that we've got left so that's why everyone is up and out looking for him. They're scared. Everyone is that scared.'

A single, dusty 40 watt bulb dangled from a rafter in the cellar of the Libanus Chapel as Rev. Mordecai sat face to face with Huw Bungalow. He had been gagged with a cravat and his hands and feet were tied up with a thick rope.

Huw just sat there in an old chair looking directly at his captor but there was no fear in his wide, innocent eyes and neither did he make any sound when the Rev. took off his gag. Even despite the dirty stains and scuffs on his new canary-yellow jacket there was an immense dignity about him as he sat, slack-mouthed and uncomprehending, staring unflinchingly at old Mordecai. His black eyes looked down at the bread that Mordecai was breaking and now holding out with a trembling hand. But his mouth did not open to receive it and the accusing stare continued.

'Not hungry then, my boy? That is a pity. Everyone should eat well. Food is one of the very greatest blessings, as is water. You must allow me to baptise you Huw, before we do what we have to. I am very sorry about this Huw but the times demand that there must be a sacrifice. And you were the only possible one. You do understand that, don't you? You were the only possible one.'

Huw looked down at the bread in Mordecai's hand and then back at the minister's tired old eyes.

'It's no good looking at me in that tone of voice Huw. I had to do this. And I was left with no alternative but to kill your dog. He would have led the people here to you now wouldn't he? He knew where you were. And with us the stakes are too high to worry about a mere dog. Since we are in the business of saving people's souls, Huw, making them well for eternity.' He picked a small lump off the bread and chewed it slowly. 'You see, Huw, when you study the pattern of Welsh revivals, you begin to understand that the Welsh only ever react to an emergency. Look at the Cholera Revival of 1849 – noted largely for the fierceness with which it grew at first and suddenness with which it disappeared again when the disease lifted. Look at the great 1904 revival and, when you dig around in the roots of that, you find that there was a train crash next to the village where it started, the Welsh lost to England at rugby, then the great Evan Roberts stepped in and tapped the general mood.

'The general mood, Huw. That's the key to Revival in the Welsh history. Get the right general mood, followed by an alarming emergency and there is almost always a return to the chapel. Well, today, the mood is right. Everyone is guilty and depressed about something or other. So what I've now done is create an emergency. I've taken you off them, Huw. Your disappearance is going to make the whole of the Valleys get up and look for its soul again. That which has been lost will be found. It *will* be found, Huw.

'That's why I've done this, as I'm sure even you, my broken, handicapped angel, will understand. I want to see if there's anything that's decent left in this Valley home of ours. I want to galvanise and goad it into life, make it a force to be reckoned with. I'm the new Evan Roberts you see, Huw. One day the people will give thanks to me for making them come awake again.'

He stood up and climbed the cellar stairs which came out into the vestry. Then, standing in the chapel doors, he looked down the hill, noting that the house search party had come to the end of Bont Terrace. He climbed back down into the cellar again.

'I'm going to have to put the gag back on you, Huw. They will be coming to search the chapel soon so I will have to move you somewhere else for the moment. Do not be uncharitable in your thoughts to me. If there has to be a sacrifice for the soul of the people it could only be you.'

Later that evening, Mordecai took three men down into

the chapel cellar and then through the manse. They found nothing, of course. It was nearly four o'clock in the morning before every house and building in Bont had been searched. A few stayed out on the moon-grazed slopes but most were grateful for at least a few hours shut-eye. But not Glynmor and Maggie. Fortified by tea and some hot bowls of cawl from Mrs Pritchard, they stayed the long night through sitting on the chairs of the Rainbow Room, smoking cigarettes and chatting about this and that in the casual way that well-established married couples do.

It was Maggie, mostly, who was fond of sentimental reminiscences, even going back to the night they had got married and he had taken a shower fully-clothed in that hotel in Barry Island. Then, do you remember, that time when you came home pissed out of your brain with that parrot on your shoulder claiming that you were Long John Silver? Aye and there was all that white shit over my best suit. And do you remember when you thought there were fleas in the bedroom and you bought all that sulphur stuff in the ironmongers? Aye an' it didn't get the fleas but all but finished us off.

Neither of them mentioned the landmines of infidelity and jealousy that had blown up so many marriages, including their own. With so many other real problems to cope with there seemed no point in adding to them and, anyway, their past problems seemed to have floated away just now, like dead leaves coracling down a stream. Just now they needed one another badly. They needed that long experience of one another – that collective, yet individual, memory of joy and laughter of a long marriage – to sustain and nourish one another in this time of anxiety and pain.

'You've been reading Jack London, I heard,' she said.

'Who told you that?'

'You know this place. I know more about you than you'd think. I've been reading him too. Aye. All that passion and honesty. It's almost heart-breaking.'

'Aye, he gets to you like that, don't he? *Duw* he makes you care. I can just feel my insides changing as I turn the pages. Needless to say Emlyn thinks he's marvellous. He says I should read some of Shaw's earlier stuff. Shaw was a good, hot radical, Em says.'

*

Dawn, the next morning, was so ravishing and so full of clear, ebullient sunshine that the people already milling around outside the Hall had to shade their eyes to look up at the sky.

But they were also shading their eyes to look at something else since, just where the light was breaking over the rims of the volcano, there were also hundreds of people swarming over the rocks and coming down the cliff paths. News of the search had carried into every Valley and they were coming from everywhere; a motley collection of odds and sods, many wearing walking boots and others daps; some with cameras and others with sticks; children with dogs and a gypsy with a horse; skinheads in Doc Marten boots and girls in school uniforms; a priest mumbling his rosary and many, many old-timers with their flat caps and shonny scarves.

Some were wandering up the main road and yet more were coming from the road leading up to the reservoir. But mostly they were trickling steadily over the volcano walls like blobs of wet paint falling off the outside of a tin; a dozen here, a pair there, one over there, a few coming up here …

Who would have guessed that so many had heard of the disappearance of Huw Bungalow? Even more unfathomably who could have guessed that so many people cared enough about him to get up at the crack of dawn and tramp miles over these ancient hills of coal? The way the village streets were filling up it was as if almost every community in the whole of the South Wales Valleys had come, if not to find Huw, then to pay their respects to a boy everyone had loved.

The Hall could only hold a fraction of the massing crowd so Glynmor stood on the back of a beer lorry in the square to address them. 'We know Huw is here somewhere,' he shouted. 'We all want him home. Even if harm has come to him we must have him home. We've already searched the Valley and the houses. We didn't find him. So today we are going to have to do it all over again. I want men to go down the pit and look everywhere, even the old workings – particularly the old workings. By nightfall I want every single inch of this Valley to have been looked at and scratched and poked until we … we …'

He stopped speaking suddenly. 'Well kiss my aunty's cat's arse,' he muttered to himself. It looked as if the whole south

327

western corner of the Valley had blackened and was crumbling before his very eyes. Virtually the whole of Penrhos – which over the years had expanded to become one of the largest council estates in Europe – was pouring down on Bont like some medieval army come to lay siege.

'If that lot come to search our houses,' a warning voice shouted, 'we'll be lucky to have any chimney pots left by the time they've finished.'

'They once took the whole garage down in Ferndale,' someone added.

As the Penrhos army approached, a police helicopter came chattering overhead, its rotor blades chopping up the air into the finest slices, its fat body swerving one way and another above the approaching mob before lifting off up over the reservoir.

Glynmor drew himself up to full height like Adolf Hitler gazing down on his least-loved stormtrooper. It was Dan Bag O'Shit, former drinking butty of Tom Jones' bodyguard, former market gardener until the police examined his plants and locked him up, even a former Bont miner until he was caught stealing scrap from the pit and sent packing. Later sent to the new council estate of Penrhos – together with most of the other problem families of the Valleys – he was probably responsible for most of the trouble on that crime-ravaged estate.

So he had come back, his ratting cap set at a jaunty angle and a broad smile which suggested that he had never once told the truth or, if he had, it had been accidental. Glynmor had always been very fond of Bag O'Shit even if he was less sure of all the dole artists and ne'er do wells he had brought with him. You could even hear them all belching and farting when they were still half a mile away.

'Well, Bag O'Shit, it's been a few years since you honoured us with your presence in Bont.'

'Too long Glynmor. I came to your wedding, remember?'

'I remember all right. You haven't brought those bastard wooden spoons with you have you?'

'Left 'em home, Glynmor. But I've always loved Bont an' I never pinched that iron down the pit either.'

'Thousands would believe you Bag O'Shit,' a voice shouted. 'An' millions wouldn't.'

328

'I know who stole that scrap,' Bag O'Shit bellowed back. 'An' it wasn't me. I was framed for that job I was. A year in the nick I did for that. An' I lost my job down the pit.'

'All right, boys, we're not here to debate Bag O'Shit's innocence,' Glynmor shouted out. 'But I say he done it.'

'Guilty as hell, Abdabs shouted above the cheers. 'They said he was going to pinch the pit wheel next.'

'Pity he didn't.'

'I never done this ... '

'All right, all right,' Glynmor chimed in again. 'Well, Bag O'Shit, I suggest you take you and your lot up to the pine forest on the west slope. People here wouldn't be happy with you lot searching their houses.'

'No, they fucking wouldn't,' shouted another voice.

'Your fucking language mun,' Bag O'Shit protested. 'There are women around aren't there?'

The search continued throughout the day, the pine trees resounding to the farts of Bag O'Shit's army, as yet more searchers came in from other valleys, kicking over stones and nosing into dustbins, peering and prodding down holes that had been peered down and prodded a hundred times before, opening doors uninvited and getting shooed away by irate housewives.

There were just too many enthusiastic volunteers to organise anything properly. When a search party of four miners tramped two miles underground just to check out the face of the old Trelewis Seam – abandoned as clapped out three years earlier – they met another group walking back.

'No sign of the boy there then?'

'Nothing except a load of good coal we could still get out if they let us.'

By midday many came drifting down the slopes to the Hall in search of a pint of beer. But soon they were wandering off again, thirsty and disappointed, since the committee chairman was still insisting that the bar remained closed until Huw had been found. One itinerant hot dog van was doing a brisk trade in the square and, in the chip shop, there was a long queue for fish and chips, bowls of curry and faggots and peas.

Glynmor and Maggie walked up to the reservoir and watched, with arms linked, as the frogmen continued diving into the cold lake. 'I saw the body of Stan Hughes pulled out of there once,' Glynmor said. 'Well, it wasn't a body really. It was a skeleton an' I'll never forget – his knee-cap fell off when they lifted him out of the water. A baker he was.'

'Oh I remember. I went to school with his sister. She was always falling asleep in the class she was. They used to call her Rip Van Winkle.'

'They say they're going to stop diving soon 'cos they've covered the whole of the reservoir.'

'I think I'd prefer not to see him again if he is, you know, dead,' she replied hesitantly. 'I'd like to remember him as he was. Always laughing. He always had some sort of smile on his lips didn't he? Even in his sleep he had that silly smile. I just couldn't look at that face if his smile wasn't there. Oh Glynmor.'

They had never once discussed that, at the root of their break-up, was Glynmor's wish to put Huw into a home. This conflict had floated away and disappeared like a long-forgotten argument. All they both wanted now was to have Huw back home again. That went without saying.

Neither had Maggie said anything about her visit from John. She wouldn't have known how to start explaining him to Glynmor. Anyway his visit now seemed more and more like a dream. The more she thought about it, the less sense it all made. But she was still praying, albeit secretly. She was still doing that. But Glynmor wouldn't understand, so she kept quiet.

For his part, Glynmor had been astonished at how forcefully his view of his son had changed over the past few days, how really desperate he was to find him again. Perhaps this reconstruction had come from the realisation that Huw was loved so completely by so many and perhaps the ideas of Jack London had begun to gnaw away at the inviolable citadel of his traditional selfishness. Perhaps it was merely the relief – and it was an immense relief – to be able to hold Maggie's body again, and perhaps it was because of other factors that he had not even thought of, but the sheer desperation of his desire to find Huw was something at total odds with all the previously-known features of Glynmor Jones. The shadows of a deep-rooted personality change were falling everywhere.

They turned and walked back to the village again, the air

blackening and the orange street lamps winking on throughout the length of the Valley. 'There's not much more we can do now is there?' she asked.

'No girl. We've all run out of ideas now. No one seems to know where he is. He's gone and left us.'

'Don't say it like that Glynmor.'

'How else can I say it?'

'Well you say it as if he wanted to leave us. He wouldn't go anywhere without me. He's been taken.'

'But taken by who? Who would want a handicapped teddy boy who goes around laughing all day?'

'Oh I don't know. I'm so tired I don't know anything. I don't think I'll ever sleep again.'

The dark thickened up quickly and the last of the searchers' lights soon floated out of the Valley as they both walked back into the empty Welfare Hall where Emlyn was sitting alone in the Rainbow Room reading the *South Wales Echo*.

'We're going home,' Glynmor told him. 'We'll be having some tea I expect. You want to come?'

'I'm all right here,' Emlyn replied. 'I'll stay here. When you've gone through what I've gone through you get to be good at waiting.'

'Nothing turned up I suppose?'

'Nothing.'

And so another empty night came to Bont – the third night without Huw Bungalow being among them – and almost the whole of the village had withdrawn indoors to their hearths, sitting silently watching their televisions or going to bed early to catch up on their sleep.

The early excitement and hysteria of the mass search had faded away. The police and their helicopters had gone off in search of other emergencies. The frogmen had gone away to dive in other lakes. The visiting armies had returned to their own Valleys leaving the streets and terraces of Bont full only of dead sounds; sounds without echoes, this winter night in this Valley volcano home.

The chip shop, after a record day of spitting fat and jangling till, had run out of potatoes and closed early with the Space Invaders switched off and its electronic guns silent.

331

Nothing stirred in the Libanus Chapel either while the only living soul outdoors was Danny Bits and Pieces sitting on his own in the black shawl of the bus shelter, eyes half-closed and nothing by way of a hymn on his lips. Even the skinheads of Giro City had forsaken their favourite corner where nothing moved except the night wind blowing a newspaper past a vandalised telephone kiosk.

No matter where you walked in the Valley, this wind was moaning sorrowfully. Up in the reservoir, down by the pit, up by the sides of the tump ... that wind was moving around trailing its coat on the earth behind it, wandering around and around, unloved and weeping, as if searching for a friendly shoulder to cry on. This wind was singing of the innocence which had been lost and would never be returned ... the days of the Penny Readings and the meetings of the Hearts of Oak; the Rechabite pledge of abstinence and the massed choral singing, the proud march of the Knights Templar and the defiant rhetoric of the first early prophets of socialism ... all gone now, this shadow-haunted night, when all that could be heard was the wind lamenting its lost and fallen tribe and everything had fallen so low in the volcano that murder had finally come to the terraces and even God was preparing to do battle to retain His throne and crown.

It was approaching five o'clock in the morning, the darkness just beginning to break up over the sleeping village, when Guto groaned in his sleep and turned on his side. All his bedclothes were black with filth. On his bedside table, there was a jar of Branston pickle and a half-finished packet of Jacob's cream crackers. Downstairs there were boxes and newspapers strewn everywhere and there was the sound of pigeons warbling and fluttering their wings in the white-spattered scullery. Guto always left one of the scullery windows open and the same small group of birds always fed and roosted there.

He groaned and turned over again when a sound carried through the darkness and hung over him, vibrating and steady, like the humming of a tuning fork. Although pitched quite softly the sound was enough to wake him fully and he sat up with a start, his eyes looking around him. He was still fully-dressed – blankets alone were not warm enough for him – and his hands went down into his jacket pockets as if he was looking urgently for some long lost object. Now he sat upright again, listening to the sound which was just lying in the air, sweet and mysterious, trying to tell him something. He coughed and spluttered, then began ransacking his pockets again.

The sound stopped and he cocked his head to one side and lifted his chin in the manner of a hunted fox. He looked down at the cream crackers on his table, at the jar of pickle and over at his bed-pan, overflowing with circles of rancid froth, sitting next to the broken wardrobe. The noise of rustling wings came up from the scullery and he moved his buttocks around on the bed.

The sound returned, warmer and more powerful now, tantalising him with a form of promise. And it was not any old sound either. It was a sort of whistled song which he had heard once before when, with his legs broken, he had been lying in a stone-enclosed darkness, counting his final heartbeats and waiting to die.

This was the song of the cave.

He bounded out of bed and half-fell, half-ran down the stairs out into the scullery and into the grey darkness of his backyard. He peered around anxiously. The whistling came back to him, striking even his old heart as a sacrament of beauty. Laughter broke his sad, stiff face into a smile of recognition.

Returning into the house he picked up his old Davy lamp, his fingers trembling so much with excitement that he broke match after match until he finally managed to light the paraffin-soaked wick. He ran out through the scullery again, the light from the lamp swinging around the backyard, seeming to make the very darkness dance as he raced past yet more boxes piled high against the dry stone walls.

He came out into the back gully which sloped down to the bottom of the tump on one side and rose to the start of the allotments on the other. There he heard the whistling again, so close and loud it came almost as a smack on the ear. He jumped, believing that someone might actually be standing next to him. Then the sweet sounds became softer and he followed them until he reached the allotments' high barbed-wire fence covered with tiny shanks of sheep wool where the scabby marauders had come to give themselves a good scratch. He held up his lamp and his warm breath plumed in the coldness of the morning as he gazed out over the allotments with their tiny tool sheds and the dark shadowy scaffoldings of the bamboo canes waiting again to carry the twisting beans. He scrambled up over the allotment gate, hurrying down the central path and veering off towards a corner plot until he came to a small creosoted shed with two large padlocks on the bolt. He put down his lamp and listened to the music, very close now. Then he picked up an iron bar lying by the side of a broken marrow frame and smashed it down on the padlocks again and again.

He not so much tore off the padlocks as broke in the whole door. It was all but ripped off its hinges when he stepped inside the shed, lifting his lamp high to reveal a big pile of seed boxes, some sacks of fertiliser and a scattering of gardening tools. But there was a human being in this shed and no mistake. He could sense it. He moved some of the seed boxes and looked down to find a pair of blue suede brothel creepers attached to a pair of luminous pink socks sticking out from beneath a pile of sacking. The ankles had been tied by rope and, as he picked up the sacking further, he discovered a pair of legs covered with canary yellow drainpipe trousers and two tied hands. Next came the jacket with its red velvet collar and then, lo and behold, the face of Huw Bungalow himself, his eyes squinting up into the light of Guto's lamp and his cheeks still full of his sweet whistling.

'Huw, mun,' was all Guto could say in his excitement. 'Huw, mun.'

Guto put down his lamp and untied Huw's hands and feet, helping him up and out of the shed. When they both got outside Guto kept going from one side of Huw to the other, touching his arms and tugging at the bottom of his drapes, still hardly able to believe the great treasure he had discovered at last. Huw seemed remarkably cheerful after his ordeal, even laughing a bit as they crossed the allotment, now going up the gully and coming out onto Bont Terrace where Guto led him down the middle of the road.

Although it was still more dark than light, Guto could contain his excitement no further and shouted his thrilling news into the lamplit, sleeping sky.

'He's come home!' he shouted. 'Huw Bungalow's come home!'

A short silence rolled up and down the terraces. Then

bedroom lights flickered on and a window went rattling up.

Heads came poking out into the cold black dawn. There was a terrific scream from one of the windows, then another and another. Quite soon every light in the terrace had flashed on and people were coming out onto the doorsteps in their nighties 'and pyjamas.

'Huw Bungalow's come home!'

The cry was repeated again and again, now being taken up in the other streets running off Bont Terrace until it became a great rolling roar of joy. Spasms of goosepimpling emotion went swirling around and around the grey crouching rooftops. Yet more doors burst open and yet more pyjamaed people hurried to surround Huw who just stood laughing and looking around him in the light of Guto's lamp.

'Huw Bungalow's come home.'

Maggie came tearing out of her front door like a greyhound out of a trap. In her night-dress and barefoot she rushed up the street towards the groups of people who had already gathered under Guto's lamp.

'Huw,' she cried, her eyes shining and her lips trembling. 'Is it you? Have you come home?'

Huw jerked his head around at her voice. Then he held out his arms wide and let out a great golden gale of laughter. Her whole body stiffened and she could not move at all. It was Glynmor who got to Huw first, taking him by the hand and leading their prince back to the sorrowing queen.

She ran to him, grabbing hold of him tight, now kissing him on his nose, eyes, mouth … his nose again. More gathered around, some touching him as if unable to believe that he had come back. 'Oh Huw,' Maggie sobbed. 'If you ever leave me again I'll break your neck I will. I swear it. I'll break your neck.'

Huw laughed and laughed in his finest Woody Woodpecker laugh and she just held onto him weeping inconsolable. Many of the onlookers were weeping too – men as well as women. 'He's come home!' the cry was still going up everywhere. 'Huw Bungalow's come home!'

The word swept through the sleeping terraces like flames dancing through petrol, bringing almost the whole of the village hurrying up the hills and down the slopes. Some had managed to put their slippers on but a lot more were barefoot.

Stan Waterboard actually fell over as he came bundling down the slope, fetching his head a fearful clout against a lamppost. Annie Sugar Lump, a few of the boys were pleased to see, had nothing on at all. By now dozens upon dozens were thronging through the square, some with blankets around their shoulders to keep their bodies warm as they ran to celebrate Huw's return – others with coats over their nighties or in their pyjamas, oblivious to the freezing cold of this winter morning.

Maggie was still hanging onto Huw as if he was going to disappear at any second when Max Million, resplendent in a thick serge nightshirt and gartered socks, ordered the Hall and the bar to be opened. No sooner could anyone say 'Pints all round' than Bont was in the middle of its first pyjama party in the Rainbow Room. Huw, as the honoured guest, was sat down next to the stage where his table was piled high with drinks as yet more people came pouring into the room to see him with their own eyes.

They always said that the Bont lot would have a party for the death of a cat but, even at such an ungodly hour – *duw*, the milk hadn't been delivered yet – they were clearly shaping up for the party to end all parties. Since the bar had been closed many of them had not had a drink for three days, an astonishing feat for a Bont miner. More than a few of them had got quite ratted already on just a few pints – and dawn had not yet fully broken in the Valley.

Perhaps it was the excitement of Huw's return – and perhaps it was merely that the bar had opened at last – but the good news went straight down to the mine's nightshift. The face workers switched off the Dosco and let the Panzers fall silent before running – running! – the few miles to the cage. They didn't even bother showering either and were still in their coal-blackened dungarees as their boots clattered down the pit road.

'Where do you think he's been then?'

'Who can tell? The thing is he's back.'

'But back from where?'

'I don't fucking know. What you asking me for? You think I carry a bastard crystal ball in my tommy tin?'

'I could murder a few pints I could.'

Even Bits and Pieces – on yet another committee ban for bad behaviour – had been allowed into the Hall to join in the celebrations though, unfortunately, the committee chairman had ordered Annie Sugar Lump to cover up her fleshy folds by putting on one of the raincoats left in the cloakroom. No one was bothering with the one-armed bandits either. The black-faced miners came pouring in, taking their pints and going over to toast Huw who was already on his fourth pint and dribbling a bit while Maggie, relaxed for the first time in days, was holding his arm, and fast asleep with her head on his shoulder.

As the party got under way Glynmor and Emlyn had gone off with Guto to look at the allotment shed where Huw had been found. It had taken them all of five seconds to work out that all this was the dirty work of the Rev. Mordecai Hughes. Preacher or no Glynmor really was going to stick the head into him when he caught up with him.

'I will, I will. I'll bastard throttle him when I get my hands on him,' he cried.

But even as he stood there fulminating, a small precise figure, dressed in a black overcoat and carrying a Gladstone bag, was hurrying along the mountain road past the pine trees.

'I just set out to save their souls,' he muttered to the trees. 'They'll see that one day, how I just wanted to save them for the Lord. But they won't see it now. They'll just have a party and come looking for me, come looking for revenge. I know these poor, fallen people all too well. They won't be returning to chapel now.'

Within the hour Emlyn, Guto and Glynmor had got back from a fruitless search of the manse and chapel to find that the party in the Hall had moved into overdrive. The music was at full volume and everyone was dancing like crazy. Scratch choirs got together in one corner and did battle with scratch choirs from the opposite corner. Emlyn and Glynmor sank three pints in quick succession with Emlyn's Adam's apple barely moving as he poured the first of his down the hatch. Mrs Pritchard got up and showed her knickers. Annie Sugar Lump got up and showed that she'd left hers at home. Even old Guto was pouring it down like a Guinness drought was about to sweep the land.

It was all going more or less handsomely when disaster struck. Aunty Phyllis brought in a dozen bottles of her home-made punch. The very smell of it was enough but, poured on empty bellies too, almost everyone was soon as pissed as parrots and falling about all over the place.

Glynmor sang the only song that he had ever learned – *Tell Laura I Love Her* – and there was almost a full-scale riot when who should come dancing in through the door and over the floor but Dan Bag O'Shit playing his spoons. 'Oh not those bastard spoons,' Glynmor complained loudly, holding both hands over his ears. 'Anything but those spoons.'

Maggie continued snoozing and Huw continued enjoying the entertainment as everyone sang *Old Macdonald* followed by *Cwm Rhondda* – or it might have been the other way around. Stan Waterboard was sick over Annie Sugar Lump and then a fight broke out – or it might have been yet another sort of dance. Then everyone began dancing the *Breakaway Blues* followed by a game of dead ants. You just lay on your back when the music stopped except that, by now, most of them were too paralysed to get up when the music started again.

Emlyn had somehow got hold of a whole bottle of Aunty Phyllis' punch and, four sheets to the wind, walked slowly and carefully over to Glynmor who was having a laugh with Bag O'Shit. 'All right you two,' Emlyn said swaying dangerously and taking another swig from the steaming Molotov cocktail. 'What I want to know ... and what I want to know right now ... is ... is going to stopthebloodyclockoutthere.'

'Stop the what?'

'Stopthebloodyclockoutinthesquareoverthere.'

'Just what are you talking about, mun?'

'Who?'

'Yes.'

'Who is?'

'Yes, yes.'

'Who is going ... to ... stop ... the ... bastard ... clock?'

'You mean you haven't stopped that bastard clock after all these years?' Bag O'Shit asked incredulously. 'What are you here in Bont? Men or mice? *I'll* stop that bastard clock.'

'You couldn't stop that clock,' Emlyn slurred prodding Bag O'Shit in the chest with the neck of his bottle.

'Yes, I could.'

'No you couldn't. No one could stop that clock. You hear me? No one.'

'Well I'll stop it,' Glynmor offered.

'Can you throw straight without your thumb?' Bag O'Shit asked deadpan.

'You just wait and see butty. Just you wait and see.'

'I'm telling you now,' Emlyn began again. 'No one could stop that ... what was it again? ... that clock. No one at all. Not even all you wankers from Penrhos couldn't. No one at all.'

So, ritually, the three of them began picking up empty bottles off the table and gathering them in their arms. There were excited whispers of 'The clock. They're going to get the clock' followed by loud anguished cries of 'not the poor old fucking clock'.

And so it came to pass that, yet again, half the village shuffled out into the square to hurl missiles at the poor old fucking clock. Stones, bricks, bottles ... anything at all that could be hurled went smashing, tinkling and bouncing off the clock face. But it was no use. Yet again they all failed and still those black iron hands continued to revolve around themselves, still they kept going in the face of all this grievous bodily harm, still they kept marking off the minutes and hours in the life of this village, deep in the ancient hills of coal.

Did you hear that they're blaming me for everyone getting drunk, Aunty Phyllis said, over the fence, to Enid, the next day.

Never to God.

They are. You'd think I went around forcing it down their throats with funnels wouldn't you? Someone was saying I was going to be up before the committee. I can't help it if they can't hold their drink. Even Huw Bungalow's belly is so bad he can't get out of bed.

Why they're getting their hair off, Phyllis, is because you never drink the punch yourself.

I'd never touch the stuff. Never. And there's Glynmor saying he's got six hangovers *and* blaming me for the attack on the clock. I told him straight. I said I've got nothing against that clock so it's no good blaming me. Well is it? The whole village was throwing things at that clock and they couldn't have *all* been drunk on my punch well could they?

They might have been. They do say it's awful strong.

Fiddlesticks. Anyway Glynmor's gone home for good now. And they had their divorce through the post yesterday an' all. Marvellous isn't it? You can get a divorce in five minutes these days and you don't have to turn up either. He had his hair off about it all though. Said he wasn't going to pay no legal bills for a divorce he didn't want. But I'm glad he's gone home to Maggie. She's much better for him and his socks did smell something terrible. I had to put a peg on my nose before I washed them. He's also saying his thumb doesn't play him up so much when he's with Maggie. He gets some terrible pain with it.

But not so much when he's home with Maggie it seems. He's starting back down the pit next week as well.

Never to God. I thought he was going to pick up compensation.

That's what he thought too. But the board doctors put his disability at only 22 per cent. That's not fully disabled for a pension but it meant he got just seven thousand in compensation which he had to pay out for his car 'cos he wasn't insured.

So he's not going to end up with millions and an island in the Bahamas then?

He's not ended up with a pot to piddle in and he's back down the pit 'cos there's nowhere else for him to go. Trouble is I can't see the pit lasting much longer now. They do say the face is coaling great but they've been getting more water in there. It's always something init? It'll be just as well when they do close the place if you ask me.

Part Three

The Canary Falls

They have broken our bodies
They have leached our blood
But they cannot steal our spirit.
So go forth my scarlet warriors
And do battle for our
Fathers' fathers and
Our sons' sons, keep the
Flame of our people burning.
For we are not defeated.
We wait. And I will sing
For you – but softly.

Gwaed, Bob Reeves

Chapter Twenty-One

The winter of 1984 came screeching into the Valley, flinging out great armfuls of frost and snow, freezing up water pipes and cracking radiators. Even well into March the old harridan was still jabbing her ice pick into the Valley slopes, still turning cheeks blue and making noses drip like taps, still making the villagers creak with cold as they shuffled about the streets like dummies in an Oxfam shop beneath their veils of old scarves and layer upon layer of winter woollies.

But then, almost overnight, this vicious old harridan was vanquished by a brilliant cross of holy sunshine. It was still more cold than warm but no longer did every joint creak with the pain of movement. The coats of frost disappeared off the car windscreens and bandy-legged lambs made their first wobbly steps out of their warm wombs.

Yet, as the sun daily climbed over the volcano wall, making the opposite slope sing with warmth and surging weather, even a casual visitor would have been astonished by the stain of sadness all over the village. Each year now you could almost see the colour and vivacity continuing to drain out of the houses and buildings. You could almost smell the clogging aroma of decay curling above the terraces; almost feel the arrival of death among such life as was left.

There was terrible music in those padlocked streets. Two of the shops had been closed down and boarded up. The Co-op was festooned with iron bars and aluminium roll shutters. Whole sections of the roof of the deserted police station had been vandalised, and litter spilled out of the rubbish tip and over the outlying fields in ugly, haphazard avalanches. The Welfare Hall, once the proud heart of the community, was also visibly puttering towards death. Practically every window frame was rotten. The roof beams had been condemned as unsafe by the council. Even the one-armed bandits just inside

343

the main door were locked inside cages to stop people robbing what robbed them. Such fresh faces as anyone saw these days belonged to marauding Jehovah's Witnesses or hopeful sellers of double glazing.

Soon after the disappearance of the incumbent, thieves and vandals had ripped the very heart out of the Libanus Chapel. The lead in the roof was the first to go followed by the pulpit and pews. Even the old organ had been unceremoniously chopped up for firewood. There were no sounds of old in the place any longer either; not a whisper of Revival in any of its dusty corners – just the steady drive of cold draughts whistling past damp patches and jagged edges of broken windows. Of Rev. Mordecai himself there had been little to go on. Once he had been spotted walking, as neat as a wren, down a pavement in Chepstow. But, despite a prompt visit by Glynmor and the boys, old Mordecai continued to elude them and the police.

The days of the pit were clearly numbered too. The miners were still struggling to maintain their quotas; still battling against immoveable sandstone, flash floodings and sudden squeezes. It even looked, at one stage, as if they were winning. Then, right out of the blue, the pit manager, John Walsh, sent every Bont miner a letter.

Dear colleague (the letter ran),

The National Coal Board is running at an operating loss of £410m. a year. Our new chairman, Mr Ian MacGregor, is looking at ways of taking out 4m. tonnes of uneconomic capacity. This will entail a total loss to the coalfield of around 20,000 jobs.

The plain fact is that Bont Colliery is currently losing £200,000 a week. It costs us £82 a tonne to bring to the surface coal which would never earn more than £47 a tonne in the market place. In fact Bont coal – once primarily used in steel production at the now-closed East Moors Steel Works in Cardiff – is probably unsaleable anywhere. Even if all the faces were now developed and worked they would be exhausted by 1991. In the circumstances it is my regrettable duty to inform you that the board intends to close Bont Colliery as soon as possible.

Yours etc.,
John Walsh, Pit Manager.

The letter came as a considerable slap in the face to the boys in the pit, particularly as they disputed every fact and figure of it. 'Well, what do you expect if you put a bastard Englishman in charge of a Welsh pit?' Glynmor shouted at the next meeting of the lodge. 'Next thing he'll be joining those bastard Buffs.' That same day the lodge called on the said Englishman in his office demanding an explanation of his figures. But he had none. More maddeningly, he did not have a date for the proposed pit closure either.

Having failed to convince the board's doctors that he was a chronic invalid Glynmor had finally gone back down the pit and, within months, had become the disciple that Emlyn had long been looking for, quickly rising to lodge secretary where he surprised everyone by showing good organisational promise too. He was more than willing to pick up the telephone and send off letters. The pit manager was also scared of him which, Emlyn thought, was a very good omen indeed.

It was also especially important for Emlyn to have a good man at his side since, allied with their own local struggle to keep their pit open, a national struggle was beginning between the N.U.M., under the leadership of Arthur Scargill and the N.C.B., under the chairmanship of Ian MacGregor. Each day now Emlyn was travelling to union meetings in various parts of the country and each day now a confrontation was becoming inevitable between a monetarist board who wanted to see profits and the miners themselves who were pledged to fight for their jobs, pits and communities.

Each week now Scargill, the fiery young gunslinger at the head of the most militant union in the land, was having some sort of skirmish with MacGregor, the ageing American sheriff, brought in by the Prime Minister to restore law 'n' profits to the coalfield. With every newspaper report it became clearer that a showdown was inevitable and it came sooner than anyone expected.

The catalyst of the conflict was the proposed closure of a pit in Cortonwood, Yorkshire, deemed by the board to be exhausted after losing £10m. between 1977 and 1983. There were many parallels between Cortonwood and Bont but it was the Yorkshire mine which became the centre of a national row after the local unions met the management only to storm out and prepare for battle. The unions called a meeting in the small parish hall of Brampton Bierlow where the branch secretary warned everyone present that the pit could have turned its last bucket of coal. Their pit of 111 years was now on the operating table and heading for the morgue. The meeting decided to fight the closure tooth and claw, asking the rest of Yorkshire for its support. Half the local pits fell in immediately and, within days, the whole of the Yorkshire coalfield was grinding to a halt.

Then, on Thursday 8 March, Scargill told his executive that, following the case of Cortonwood, the board clearly believed that 115 of the country's 179 pits were uneconomic. Now was the crunch. 'We are all agreed that we have to fight.'

A national strike was duly voted on and announced. And so began the longest industrial dispute in Britain's history.

The dance floor of the Welfare Hall was packed again that afternoon, not by the devotees of Smokey and his Sounds, but by the men from the Bont mine. Almost seven hundred of them crowded in for their first lodge meeting of the strike. Glynmor sat at a table on the side of the stage, preparing to take the minutes. Emlyn was shuffling with his papers, waiting for the men to settle down. A shaft of sunlight burst down through one of the dusty windows, dancing in the blue swell of the drifting cigarette smoke and the men's excited faces.

The news of the strike continued to make new blood surge through Emlyn's old Marxist veins. This was the right fight at the right time. Even as he stood there, checking the time on his fob watch and looking out over the smoky sea of all those familiar faces, he could feel his throat drying up and the flames of defiance flickering warm once more inside his belly. At last they had been given a chance to engage Milady Iron Drawers, Margaret Thatcher and her geriatric hatchet man, MacGregor. Emlyn had long thought that the old hated Tory coal barons had burned in Hades. But here was yet another, very much alive and kicking. *Duw*, the miners had brought down the last Tory government and they could do it again.

He tapped the microphone with his finger and stood waiting for quiet. His speech was extremely important, he knew. It was how the men would remember the start of the strike. It was his first opportunity to fire them up and he would clearly have to do that more than a few times before it was

346

over. But he was up to it. He drew himself up to his full height. When I open my lips let no dog bark, his look said.

'Well the fight we've always wanted has come,' he said into the microphone, his voice thick with a musical power. 'And let it be known right at the start that when the history of this strike is written it will be recorded that the men of Bont – *all* the men of Bont – were there right at the very guts of it.'

His next words were drowned in ecstatic cheers. 'One thing is very certain,' he proclaimed. 'Bont will be rock solid. First in, last out – that's Bont. There will be no scabs here in Bont.'

Such words, the very manna of the socialist tribe, provoked a further outburst of cheering and clapping among men as diffuse as their multiple nicknames. Here they were, day shift and night shift together now: large, beefy types, force-fed by beer and black pudding, with bobble caps and round, generous faces; ratty faces with small mouths, devoid of mirth or charm; thoughtful types with soft voices and a copy of *Marxist Today* in their back pockets. Some had a surprising fairness, at odds with the more normal thick-set dark Celts.

'There are some fights which are over quickly,' Emlyn continued when the applause had abated. 'In 1912 the Bont miners gave the agents six hours' notice that, unless their demands were met, they would destroy the pit by pulling down the wheelhouse and filling in the shaft. And that, boys, is the real art of negotiation. Three hours after the delivery of that threat, the agents gave in and all the demands were met.'

The men all laughed and looked knowingly at one another.

'But this fight will not be like that,' continued Emlyn. 'Some of you must be wondering if this strike will be long. It will be long. Some of you may be asking if it is going to be a tough fight. It will be the toughest.'

He paused and raised a finger into the air, corkscrewing it around slow. 'This fight will be the longest and toughest ever. This Tory government has been preparing for it for six years. They planned this fight with the Ridley Report six years ago. We overthrew them once but then they began planning their revenge. They built up coal stocks. They planned coal imports. They adapted power stations to burn oil. All these years they've

347

been planning the destruction of the National Union of the Mineworkers – the greatest and most powerful union in the land.'

He stopped speaking and raised both hands into the air like a champion boxer. 'This Tory government wants to whip us into the ground ... but we will never surrender ... they want to take our pride but the rank and file of this union will never bow the knee ... no matter what the cost – and the cost will be high – we will win in the end. Because the N.U.M. will never give in ... the N.U.M. will never hand over its pride ... never ...'

As each sentence rose in power the cheers of the men mounted until Emlyn's words were barely audible in the rolling crescendo. One man after another stood up to applaud the veteran warhorse. A few had tears rolling their cheeks – this was fighting talk such as the Valley had not heard for years. If there'd been more men like Emlyn perhaps it would not now be floundering so badly towards an early grave.

'But before we go out there let us be clear about one thing,' he went on. 'Let us be clear in our minds that this is not just a political fight – not just a scrap between Maggie Thatcher and Arthur Scargill. And neither, for once, is it a fight about wages. This strike is our very last chance to keep this pit open. This is our last chance to save our community. When our pit goes our community goes with it. This strike is about our right to life.'

More cheers and clapping interrupted his flow for a few moments.

'Half the South Wales coalfield is under threat at the moment by Thatcherism. The Tory proposal is to cut our coalfield in half, so we have to fight.' He paused and gave a hollow sardonic laugh before shouting 'We have to fight because we have no other option open to us. We have to fight because we are redundant already. We have to fight because, when you've got nothing, you've got nothing to lose. We have to fight because otherwise we're as dead as dogs. And we're not dead yet are we? Well are we?'

The men, all still standing, cupped their hands to their mouths shouting a great gale of defiant 'No's'. Emlyn stood back from the microphone and looked over at Glynmor, the lodge secretary who had found the polemic so pulverising he

348

had not even taken any notes for the minutes. He had always known that Emlyn was good but never quite this good. He was proud to be at his side. The magician of oratory was still magical. Perhaps the old Marxist had finally met his moment.

Emlyn was not a man of God but had he been he would have given daily thanks for the life of Jack London since, no sooner had Glynmor stuck his nose into the old lefty spell-binder's novels, than he just seemed to wake up more and more by the hour. It was then a simple journey through George Bernard Shaw's Fabian days, then to Nye Bevan and the earlier works of Keir Hardie which had contributed so much to the birth of the Labour Party in the Valleys. After that Glynmor read more or less anything he could get his hands on and, oddly enough, Maggie seemed to join in with him too. Already Glynmor was puzzling out rosters for the flying pickets and talking of ways of fund-raising, while Maggie had already made the first few phone calls with a view to setting up a women's support group in Bont.

'And if anyone thinks he's going to sit out this strike in the bar he'd better think again. My branch secretary Glynmor Jones is going to be in charge of the pickets and, by the time he's finished, the pickets of Bont are going to be flying all over the country. And, boys, remember another thing – Bont pickets are like draughts. They can get in anywhere.'

The men were all laughing again now. Within the fishing net of his rolling rhetoric Emlyn could have got them to do anything.

'So let's remember the spirits of Ablett and Horner. Let's think on Senghenydd and those of our own families lost in underground explosions and floods. Let's think on history and remember history. The whole world came to this Valley to help keep themselves warm. The world came to plunder and exploit us. Now it's our turn to turn and say to the world and say, "You owe us now. But it's not much that you owe. You just owe the dignity of work, not the insult of your social security handouts. All we are asking for is the right to life, both for us and our families." So, boys, let's get out there and do it.'

As he sat down all the men raised their hands into the air in salute, shouting and cheering, stamping their feet so much it reverberated down into the rotting foundations of the Hall. It was a thundering roar of triumph: the roar of a defeated people who had begun a victory march at last.

'Well, boys, that was something, wasn't it?' It was Glynmor's turn on the microphone now. 'I'm going to be in touch with every one of you about picketing duties but, before we break up, the union has asked every lodge to take their own vote on the strike.'

'When did *we* ever need to vote?' shouted Danny Kettle. 'First out, last in, that's Bont. What do we want to vote for?'

'Well, if for nothing else, for the fucking minutes,' Glynmor replied, exasperated. 'I've got these minutes to write up. If you don't vote on it what am I going to do? Well, what am I going to do?'

'Sing us a song.'

'You can buy us a drink if you like.'

'As a striking miner with a missing thumb and a family to support' ... ironic jeers of commiseration here ... 'I can't afford to buy you all a drink but, if it's a song you bastards want, I've got a song for you. It's simple enough, even for you, and we'll sing it to the tune of *She'll be Coming round the Mountain*. You ready?' He unscrewed the microphone and lowered it a little before singing 'Oh I'd sooner be a picket than a scab: I'd sooner be a picket than a scab. Right now you sing it.'

The men soon picked it up too. 'Oh I'd sooner be a picket than a scab,' they sang. 'I'd sooner be a picket than a scab.' They repeated it again and again, dancing about and clapping, hardly knowing that they had just given the first rehearsal to what was going to become the national anthem of the Welsh striking miners.

Huw Bungalow stood back from his drawing board, lifting his brush into the air and staring hard at his almost completed painting. It was a simple Valley scene, full of ravishing sunshine and thick shadow, with a blue river pouring out of a blue sky through a green field and past a small white house. What he lacked in craftsmanship he made up for with the exuberance of his colours, particularly his marigolds, such fierce daubs of yellow they might even have made Van Gogh think again. Large black eagles soared across the Valley.

Maggie, holding a mug of tea, came across the room and stood next to him. She was so glad that they had sent him to the

Mencap art classes over in Mountain Ash since he had taken to the oils immediately, constructing vast and colourful edifices which, although child-like, made the heart sing with their happiness and purity. Nothing, in Huw's eyes or indeed his art, was dusty or broken-down. The rivers were always pure and the buildings as fresh as a drying coat of paint. Even the pit looked lovely and he managed to make the tips a mountain range of extravagant beauty by the time he had finished with them. It was her first tangible insight into what was going on inside her son.

But it was his concentration that everyone found extraordinary. Give him a brush, a fresh sheet of paper and a few tubes of paint and he would stand there for hours, sometimes just staring at a detail before, in the manner of a great master, making the smallest adjustment and then carrying on with the broader work again.

'He gets so fussy you'd think he was Michelangelo painting the bastard roof of that chapel of his,' Glynmor would say.

'He might turn out to be greater than Michelangelo,' Maggie responded, always half-defensive when there was any suggestion that there might be something not quite right with Huw. She still believed that Huw had some great historic destiny yet to be worked out. Perhaps he had found it as a painter.

The nature of the living-room had changed yet again, now rather more suggesting the home of a pair of rumpled intellectuals who have given up appearances. Everywhere was a pleasant and warm jumble with papers and books scattered in alcoves and over floors; lots of Athena prints, mostly of Matisse and Picasso, festooned the walls. The furniture was still the same but frayed now with bits of horsehair and the odd spring poking out of the arms. There was no television but there was still a radio since Maggie still liked to listen to pop songs on Radio One.

The front door slammed and Glynmor came in, humming to himself. Dropping his carrier bag full of papers at his feet he kissed Maggie on the cheek before going over to stand next to Huw and admire his new creation. He marvelled at this outbreak of artistic endeavour as much as Maggie. 'Oh aye. Back on sodding landscapes are we? It's those birds of his that get me. Just like sodding eagles they are.'

'Perhaps that's because they are sodding eagles,' Maggie pointed out.

'But when did you ever see an eagle in the Valleys? Any eagle that showed its beak in the Valleys would get stoned straight away. The kids around here can only understand beauty when they're destroying it.'

'Not all kids are like that.'

'Most of them are. Most of those little fuckers would destroy anything they could get their hands on.'

'Look, stop using that bad language in front of Huw will you?'

With hand clamped on mouth Glynmor went out into the kitchen to make himself a cup of tea. 'The meeting was brilliant,' he shouted out to her. 'Emlyn spoke like he was on fire. I've never seen the boys so wound up. There's a revolution going to come tearing out of this Valley by the time this strike is over you mark my words. One great bastard revolution and it's not going to be a minute too soon.'

He brought in the mug of tea and flicked some papers off the old armchair before settling down in it, letting his legs splay out in front of the firegrate. 'But there's so much to do first. There's sixteen or so Welsh pits still working so we'll have to picket them out first. That'll be no problem. But then we're going after the big power stations like Aberthaw. Then we'll be looking at the really big ones in the Trent Valley. We're going to have to educate those fucking power workers, get right in there and tell them what's what. They're the key to this strike. If we can close down the power stations we'll bring down Margaret Thatcher just like that woman in the burning house who had two wooden legs.'

'Two wooden legs? Just what are you talking about?'

'You know what happened to the woman with two wooden legs in the burning house don't you?'

'No, I don't.'

'They all burned to the ground. Get it?'

'You and your jokes. You know I do get this awful nightmare sometimes that I'm being lowered into the ground in my coffin an' you hold up the ceremony by leaning over the hole and taking off the lid of the coffin to tell me, just one more time, that one about the queer who was raped by the gorilla.'

'But I haven't told you that one for ages.'

'Thank God.'

'You want to hear it again then, do you?'

'No I do not.'

'I will if you like.'

'No, no, no. But tell me one thing. Are you going to put a picket on the Bont pit? Some of us women have already been talking we might do something like that.'

'Don't be so soft. There won't be any scabs in Bont. If anyone tries to work here we'll throw him down the bastard shaft and bury him in the gob.'

Though it had been years since the abduction of Huw and the first intimations that Glynmor was shaking off his old ways Maggie still almost had to pinch herself when she heard her own husband talk like this. She had always known that he was mercurial but who would have expected him of all people – him! – to have turned out like this? Most normal young people lost their ideals as they grew older, ending up as fully-pensioned cynics. But with Glynmor it had been the other way around. He had even been travelling to other lodge meetings in other Valleys, warning them of the coming fight in the coalfield and the dangers of being unprepared.

'But there is one thing about Emlyn that always gets right up my nose,' Glynmor said after staring at the fire for a while. 'He's forever looking into the past. Today he was going on about the 1910 lock-out again. And if he mentions Senghenydd again I'll scream. It's the future we should be looking to now.'

'It's just Emlyn's way of looking at things,' Maggie replied evenly. 'Someone like Emlyn can only understand the present by thinking about it through the past. You don't think like that because you have no past as such, no past that you want to boast about anyway.'

The other part of his past which he certainly never boasted about was his poor relationship with his son Huw but that had all changed now, Maggie was the most relieved to see. Glynmor sometimes took Huw off to the lodge meetings where he always sat, happily and quietly enough, until the proceedings were over. The father and son often drank together in the Hall and it was Glynmor who had first suggested the Mencap classes in art, even driving Huw over to Mountain Ash for them for the few hours each week.

After another long period of staring at his masterpiece Huw kneeled down and carefully washed one of his brushes. He was extremely fastidious about that, washing all of them before he packed up for the night. Now he squirted out a wodge of yellow onto the pallette, his tongue sticking out slightly as he concentrated hard on the task at hand.

'We'll have to make young Michelangelo here our official artist,' Glynmor said, nodding at Huw. 'Like them war artists in the Falklands. I'd like to see what he made of the flying pickets of Bont. But, the next move now, we've got to take over the basement of the Hall as our strike centre. We'll be doing that tonight. We'll get a 'phone in there and a map of the country so that we can see where our pickets are.'

'It's map of all the pubs you're going to need for that.'

'Not this time girl. We're all very serious this time. There's too much at stake this time and everyone is off their chumps with the excitement of it all. Even Tom the Nutter is going around saying it's serious so it must be very serious indeed.'

'We women are going to do a lot this time,' said Maggie with a firmness that was more statement than question. 'The days of the women taking the backseat are over. We've already got a few ideas together.'

He glanced at her oddly. 'I've no objection,' he said softly. 'It would be good for the women to get involved in this one.'

But she could see that, pushed a bit, he would find all kinds of objections to the women getting involved. He may have changed a lot but there was one side to him – and the Valley – which would never change. Deep down him and the rest of the boys were all male chauvinist pigs and always would be. Deep down they would always be expecting the little wifey to be sitting at home stirring the cauldron on the fire while the hairy-arsed men moved off into the forest, scratching themselves with their clubs as they hunted for some dinosaur for tea.

'You've got to have our help with this one,' Maggie insisted. 'Even you would be amazed at what women could achieve. I'll tell you one thing. You won't win without us and that's a fact.'

'Oh, that's a fact is it?' he replied, amused. She was even beginning to talk like him in her old age.

'Yes, that's a fact. Without us you're dead. The whole lot

of you. I bet Emlyn never spoke about the women. Well did he?'

'Maggie don't go getting your knickers in a twist now. I said didn't I? I said the women should get involved.'

'But you didn't say it as if you meant it.'

'What do you expect me to do? Get down on my knees with a fiver in my teeth? I said. What more do you want me to say?'

'I've been talking to Thelma and Jackie. We want to start a women's support group, a proper one with meetings and an organisation. There'll be others all around the country.'

'Fine. A tidy idea. What're you going to do?'

'We'll start small, I thought. Easter's coming up so, first off, we'll get onto the chocolate people and get in some eggs for the kids.'

'Great. Get in some eggs for the flying pickets too.'

'You lot can get your own eggs.'

John Walsh, the pit manager, stood in the middle of the dusty parquet floor of the Hall's basement with his hands tied behind his back and his blindfold head bowed. He was flanked on either side by the officials of the Captain Laggard Lodge and about to be inducted into the highest office of the Royal Antediluvian Order of Buffaloes.

On the wooden throne in front of him sat Worthy Primo, gavel in one hand and ceremonial wand in the other. Two burning candles smoked and stammered on either side of him. The rank and file Buffs were sitting at their tables with beer mats placed over their pints, the ultimate symbol of respect for ancient traditions.

The door was rapped three times and the City Tyler peered through the spy-hole calling out 'Known brothers requesting entry to the lodge Worthy Primo.'

'Open the door City Tyler.'

The door swung open to allow in a great and glittering phalanx of officials, all dressed in dinner suits with huge pantomime gold and green cuffs, green sashes with yellow diamonds and embroidered aprons with bright gold tassels. They marched, slowly and solemnly, to take their positions in front of Worthy Primo's throne. 'We are here to follow the way of Juniper,' Worthy Primo intoned. 'And tonight there can be no greater way than an induction to knighthood of our great order.'

The bemedalled and tasselled officials, come from as far away as Aberavon and Treforest, moved to another set of positions, preparing for this, the most sacred ceremony in the Buff calendar: Brother John Walsh was about to be initiated as a knight of the order. Already he had been issued with the new secret passwords of the knighthood – Beverly, Onion, Battle – for use at further exclusive meetings of the knights. Now he was preparing to take the most solemn vow of this new order which took him to the very highest and distant social order in the Valley dedicated only to the protection of their own.

Just above them a huge pair of buffalo horns skewered the air. At the far end of the room was a trestle table covered with what the Buffs were pleased to call graze – faggots, slices of cheese, raw black pudding and jars of pickled onions. Buff wives were pleased to call such graze 'fart food' on account of the deadly, rip-roaring farts that Buffs – full of their graze and gassy All-Bright beer – let rip right through the night after such ceremonies.

'We hope that, by his example and devotion, he will be able to work for this and other lodges ... we hope that he will never deviate from the paths of justice, truth and philanthropy ... we invite you to partake of the tray of Juniper ... '

The sacred ritual was moving swiftly to its most holy climax when there was a furious banging on the door and a look of the most abject woe flashed over the City Tyler's face. The ceremony stopped dead. Buff heads looked around in consternation as the City Tyler opened his peep-hole. 'You can't come in here without the right knock and passwords,' he shouted at someone on the outside.

'You'll get a knock on the nose if you don't open this bastard door,' an angry voice shouted from without.

'It's a group from the N.U.M. Worthy Primo,' the City Tyler explained, still without opening the door. 'They say they're going to take over the basement.'

'Tell them we're in the middle of a ceremony, City Tyler. Tell them to come back in an hour.'

The City Tyler explained Worthy Primo's orders through the peep-hole when there was yet more hooligan shouting and kicking.

'Better let them in, City Tyler. City Chamberlain, put the meeting on Liberty Hall. Alderman of Benevolence, look after our distinguished visitors.'

Glynmor was first in through the door, followed by a motley bunch of the N.U.M.'s finest and brightest – Tom the Nutter, Oboe Parry, Dan Box and Danny Kettle – who, in their dirty windcheaters and flat caps streaked with dirt, with their torn jeans and big boots, made a startling contrast to the bejewelled brilliance of the Buffs.

'So this is what you bunch of perverts get up to,' Glynmor roared as he looked around him. 'All done up in drag and gang banging that poor bastard there. Hang on that's no poor bastard. That's the fucking pit manager. Well that explains a lot that do. No wonder the poor old pit has gone to the dogs. There's a bastard Buff running it.'

The pit manager, who had taken off his blindfold, shuffled around sheepishly but said nothing.

'Look, Glynmor, just leave us alone for a bit, is it?' Worthy Primo pleaded. 'Tuesday nights is always our night.'

'Listen you bunch of perverts,' Glynmor roared on defiantly. 'There's a strike just been called, in case you haven't heard. We need this basement for our headquarters.'

'Can't you hang on for an hour?' Worthy Primo wondered.

Glynmor looked around at his boys and smiled. 'Cop for old King Canute there trying to tell the tide of shit to go back.' He shook his head in sorrow. 'And old Walshy, the manager in the middle of it too. Look you Buffs we've got a serious strike on our hands. This is a miners' Welfare Hall, built through the levies of miners remember? So pick up your crowns and jewels and piss off, the lot of you.'

Grumbling and mumbling amongst themselves, but unwilling to make much of a fight of it, the Buffs packed their medals into their cases and folded up their tasselled skirts. Then they made their way disconsolately to the bar upstairs.

'And take that daft pair of Buffalo horns with you,' Glynmor called after them, as Worthy Primo came hurrying back to lift the horns off their nails and cart them up into the bar too.

'If there's one thing I've always hated it's those bastard Buffs,' said Glynmor going over to the untouched graze and helping himself to a few slices of the cheese. 'All they ever seem to think of are their secrets and dopey ceremonies. I might have known that pit manager was in the middle of them. If there's anything secret or undercover going on in the Valleys you can be sure the Buffs are around in somewhere. Now I know why we never know what's going on in the mine. It's a bastard Buff secret that's why. Here now. You'd better get stuck into this, boys. You might not be eating again for a long time with this strike so we don't want it to go to waste now do we?'

'When're we going to get our lodge banners down from the loft?' Tom the Nutter asked.

'We could go and get them down tonight,' Oboe Parry thought, taking a great handful of black pudding and packing it into his mouth.

'If not tonight, then first thing in the morning,' said Glynmor, crunching on some pickled onions. 'Emlyn is going to handle all interviews with the media. The BBC has already been on so we'll want a banner as a background.'

'My missus has been saying she wants to help,' said Dan Box helping himself to some more cheese.

'Aw I've got all that shit too.'

'Maggie's the same. We're just going to have to let them do something.'

'I don't know what's got into these women,' Dan Box elaborated. 'There was a time when they were happy to stay home an' now look at 'em. They want to get their fingers into everything.'

'It's the times mun,' said Oboe. 'It's all this bloody feminist shit it is. There's just no pleasing them with anything now. There was a time when all you had to was give them a washing machine and a good fuck now and then and they were as happy as lambs they were. Now you make some remark about how they've got lovely big tits an' they want your guts for garters.'

'Boys, boys,' Glynmor intervened. 'Times have changed it is true but we've got to change as well. We've got to let the women get involved this time. They're going to be a big help too.'

He reached down for another slice of black pudding while the others were still stuffing themselves as if a famine was about to break out in the land at any second. Tom the Nutter belched and Glynmor lifted his leg a bit and farted. '*Duw* this stuff really is thirty farts to the ounce,' said Glynmor shaking his head in wonder. 'I always said that the Buffs supplied the rocket fuel for the Houston Space Centre. This is the real stuff this is. Sit on the bog and, next thing, you've rocketed through the roof and you're shooting through space just behind the Space Shuttle.'

'But what can women do?' Oboe asked, bringing the conversation back to terra firma again. 'They can't picket can they? Women can't man a bastard picket line can they? They can't fight with the police. They can't intimidate the lorry drivers. They can't do fuck all.'

'Oh yes we can. We can picket as well as any of you bloody men.'

It was a woman's voice and the boys, still busy picking over the Buffs' graze, looked at one another without looking around.

'You men have gone so soft the women can out-run you, out-fight you and out-fuck you,' the woman's voice continued as a big lump of black pudding fell out of Dan Box's mouth.

'Well, just look at what the cat's dragged in,' said Glynmor turning to look at the basement door which framed the tiny, combative shape of his sister-in-law, Daisy. She was in her mid-forties now but there was still a rough kind of poetry about her with her sparkly black eyes and hair the colour of ripening corn. Her figure had lost none of its bounce either, still in evidence beneath a canary yellow T-shirt with COAL NOT DOLE printed on it in big red letters.

'So it's the original mouth on legs back from Greenham Common,' Glynmor added. 'So what're you doing down here then?'

'I heard you were having a spot of bother with that MacGregor so I thought I'd come and help you out. Daisy Three Balls and Maggie are going to organise the women.'

'Well that's fucked it then,' Oboe Parry muttered. 'We might as well call off the strike and give in now.'

'You're taking over this room I hear,' Daisy said walking over to them and helping herself to some cheese. 'We'll take the old store room then. We're going to start a proper soup kitchen in there. Food, funds and fun. That's what the women are going to raise.'

'Well that's really fucked it that has,' Oboe muttered to himself again. 'Finished before we've begun. It all went wrong when they gave the women the vote.'

'You just wait,' Daisy said thrusting out her chin pugnaciously. 'You just watch us. The women are going to win this strike for you. You just wait and see.'

Chapter Twenty-Two

After the sharp-edged Spring, a long, hot summer – sunny and bird-loud – came tumbling through the Valley. White butterflies danced and bobbed in the shivering heat hazes over the tips; blackbirds settled on the still wheel of the strike-bound mine; children waded around in the cool river, constructing a small dam just past the tump.

The long voluptuous days of sunshine were followed by lazy and gorgeous nights with children whizzing around in the darkness on their chopper bikes while Idris and Curly sat out late, drinking cider and quarrelling with each other, on the bench near the clock. The upstairs windows of the terraces were left open and the silky night breezes made the lace curtains flap around softly. Down in the long grass young lovers lay together feeling for warm places.

When the Hall had finally emptied and the last drunks had ricocheted home down the gullies, the village slept in silent warm streets, with just the odd cry of the sheep lifting into the darkness, until yet another Valley dawn broke, strident with the yodelling of cockerels and the first rays of the sun doing a magical square-dance high on the east volcano wall.

There was very little boredom or even any particular anxiety with the Bont miners in that first thrilling flush of summer. They *knew* that were going to win soon, that it was only a matter of days before the Government would crumble. Meanwhile, in their boxer shorts and tanned perhaps for the first time in their lives, they played football and cricket; they fished and they dug over their gardens; they even cut down on their drinking and spent a lot of time with their kids, taking them on day trips to Barry and Porthcawl.

No one was hungry or short. With memories of bitter

strikes still very much alive in the collective memory, the village, like the amoeba, merely changed its shape; it geared itself a little more finely to the matter of survival. Those with jobs outside the pit – and those with savings – just kicked in what they could afford. Families and relatives in other parts of the country sent what they could as well. No one even thought about it.

Not that it was long holiday for the striking miners – far from it. It was a rare hour when a van or mini-bus was not pulling away from the Welfare Hall, taking the pickets somewhere or other. Emlyn spent a lot of time travelling to the various N.U.M. executive meetings but it was Glynmor and his pickets who were making the most speed and noise. Sometimes they travelled up to two hundred miles on a single night, so that twenty or thirty of them could fall out of a bus in a grey dawn and confront a steel or power worker about his responsibilities to the working class.

The Welsh pickets were always listened to with respect – they pleaded their case with passion and wit – and yet what the strangers could never quite understand was why a smiling and clearly bananas Teddy boy should always be bobbing around in their midst. Right from the first picket at the Aberaman drift mine, Huw Bungalow – in a variety of Edwardian drapes with boot-lace ties and brothel creepers – was usually next to Glynmor on the picket line.

'He's the manager of our pit,' the boys always said to anyone who did ask. 'He's got so little to do now the pit's on strike he likes to come picketing with us. It gives him something to do.'

In a matter of weeks Huw became the talisman of the South Wales striking miners, often photographed with the Bont boys as they made a swift sidestep around a blue line of policemen and managed to stop another vanload of scabs. In an odd sort of way Huw became something of their leader too since, in the constant games of tip and run with the police, Huw always showed a surprising fleetness of foot and could spot a way through the blue line – sensing where the break would come often before it did – and, next thing, the boys were all streaming through the break after him.

The police would never touch Huw either. It was almost as if they knew that anyone who laid a finger on Huw Bungalow would get torn apart.

On such outings Glynmor and Huw were inseparable – Butch Cassidy and the Sundance Kid – the fastest guns in the coalfield, with their ragged bunch of outlaw pals, in a ceaseless search for blacklegs and scabs who would then be gunned down with the deadly bullets of their Welsh eloquence.

Some mornings Glynmor would send up to six different groups of pickets from the Hall – each with a bit of money for petrol and a pint – but Huw always travelled with Glynmor's group, the father and son able to communicate with one another in their own private sign language as they proceeded to run rings around the police.

'He's just like some bastard whippet with his arse on fire when he gets moving,' Glynmor would say of Huw. 'He just looks around for a bit, then he looks at me and, next – wham! – we're all running after him like mad till we've lost the police and found the scab. I tell you what. If that General Custer had my Huw he'd still be on the Little Big Horn today.'

The Bont pickets did not always picket as planned though.

It was still dark and drizzling when Huw and Glynmor leaped off the charabanc – on free loan from Evan Jones of Tylorstown – outside the Aberthaw Power Station, followed by some thirty of the boys, many just in shirt sleeves or COAL NOT DOLE T-shirts.

The sound of lazy waves collapsing on the shore roared through the shadowy morning with the odd squawk from a seagull as the boys set up an official N.U.M. picket line – complete with placard and the Bont lodge banner – while Huw Bungalow was busy taking coal out of the boot of the charabanc and setting up a brazier for the brewing of the official N.U.M. tea.

Glynmor's strike H.Q. had been given some good unofficial intelligence that a convoy of coal lorries was going into the power station that morning but, as the boys continued to jump around to keep warm with a few of them even kicking a tennis ball around in the middle of the road, an even greater mystery than the non-existent convoy was the non-existence of the police. Even more perplexing than that were the non-existent power workers. Cars had whooshed past them in a surge of speed and flaring headlamps but none had turned to confront the massed muscles of the Bont picket line.

The night was breaking up with Huw blowing into the

faintly flickering coals of the brazier and the sea continuing to roar lazy on the shore when a car did pull up and the driver wound down his window. 'What're you doing here then?'

'Official N.U.M. picket,' Danny Kettle explained leaning on the car bonnet with his forearm to discourage any rapid acceleration into the plant. 'We are in official dispute with the coal board and we're asking you not to cross this picket line.'

The driver looked at the back seat behind him as if Danny Kettle might be talking to someone else. 'You've got the wrong place,' the driver said finally. 'This is the cement works. The power station is down around the corner.'

'And a merry Christmas to you sir,' said Danny Kettle getting up off the car bonnet and walking away shoving his hands down into his pockets. 'Glynmor. We've been picketing the bastard cement works.'

'The what?'

'The bastard cement works. The power station is down the road.'

'Well isn't there anyone here who knows the difference between a fucking power station and a fucking cement works?' Glynmor shouted as he turned and turned again, the veins bulging thick on the sides of his neck. 'Well isn't there?'

'There's no point in shouting at us.'

'Well who do you suggest I shout at? The fucking sea? There's more sense in that sea than you lot.'

'Glynmor, you're supposed to be the gaffer,' Dan Box pointed out. 'Don't *you* know the difference between a power station and a cement works?'

'I've never been to Aberthaw before.'

'I made sand castles here when I was a kid,' Tom the Nutter chimed in. 'I don't remember any cement works. But I do remember the power station.'

'So where is it?'

'It's up the road, just around the corner.'

'Well why didn't you tell us?'

'I don't know. I just thought we were on the cement picket today.'

'It's cement in your brain you've got. C'mon let's get packed up. And someone piss on the fire will they?'

Stan Swansea and Dibber Williams pissed on the brazier as they packed up their placard and banner while Huw

Bungalow loaded the stocks back into the charabanc boot. By the time they had all settled down into the bus the sun had climbed high into the sky giving them all a clear view of the cement works, covered from top to toe with a thick powdery dust which was as thick as drifts of dirty snow on the ground, spilling out of the compound and even coating the leaves of the surrounding trees and hedges.

'See that there,' Glynmor shouted waving his bunched fist around. '*That* is a fucking cement works. And *this* is going to be a punch in the eye for any bastard who breathes a word about this when we get home.'

The sun was still climbing the blue sky when the Bont pickets tumbled out of the charabanc again to face a blue and silver-buttoned phalanx of police formed outside the power station gates.

'They've finally made it have they?' Police constable 47 muttered to Police constable 91 as the Bont boys waved at them before proceeding to unfurl their lodge banner for the second time that morning. 'They must have found a pub open on the way.'

'Did you hear the one about the Bont picket who fell into a vat of Brains beer and drowned?' asked Police constable 91. 'Terrible death it was. He had to get out three times for a piss as well.'

'I hope there's not going to be too much shoving and pushing this morning,' Police constable 47 continued. 'Just look at the size of some of them. Just look. Talk about being built like a brick shithouse. There was one of them yesterday. I still don't know who he was. But we were all shoving and this dirty bugger reaches his hand through the ruck and starts tickling my knackers. Aye. Whoever heard of tickling a policeman's knackers on a picket line? Kicking them maybe. But never tickling them.'

'That's the way this lot are. It's all a bit of laugh no matter what they're doing. They wouldn't harm a fly any of them. There's that famous Huw Bungalow over there. I recognise his photo from the *Echo*.'

'My family all came from the Valleys you know. I really hate being on the opposite side to them but, when they're pushing and shoving, I just keep repeating the word "overtime" to myself again and again.'

'Aye. And there was me thinking we wouldn't get another holiday in Greece again this year.'

'Eyup. The one with the big mouth is coming over.'

The Bont boys had now lined up face to face with the police, leaving the standard ten feet alley-way between them, as Glynmor stepped up for the ritual smiling inspection of the police line. He peered at their collars and down at the shine on their boots, occasionally pulling out his braces like a circus clown.

'Well they've sent toddlers from the kindergarten to face us again and that's a fact,' he shouted back at his men in a voice so loud all could hear. 'When those scab coal lorries come we're not going to have any trouble from these toddlers. Look at 'em. There's some who haven't even started shaving yet. And a few, I daresay, who are still in nappies. So, when those scab lorries come, I want you to keep your arms linked tight and those shoulders down as low as you can. Then we'll push the whole bastard lot of them into the sea.'

Smirks and sardonic guffaws broke out in the police line at this point, only cut short when an inspector, with lots of silver leaves on the peak of his cap, walked up to Glynmor and asked him to get back in line with the rest of them. 'No one will interfere with a peaceful and orderly picket,' he promised, taking Glynmor by the arm and leading him back to the men with an exaggerated politeness. 'We just want good clean shoves then no one will get hurt and no one will get arrested.'

'But why don't you send some real men to face us?' Glynmor protested. 'Just look at them. They couldn't shove a sack of feathers.'

'Well let's wait and see shall we?'

Huw Bungalow was busy relighting the brazier as the miners and police stood cheerfully facing one another waiting for the appearance of a coal lorry to signal the start of a massed scrum.

Nothing had happened twenty minutes later and the miners were breaking ranks, leaning their lodge banner against the power station's fence and going back to the glowing brazier to help themselves to a mug of tea. The police were very relaxed too, talking amongst themselves, some even taking off their helmets to give their sweating heads a bit of air.

A reporter from Cardiff Radio sidled up to Dai Scraggs

and asked how he was managing during the strike. Dai Scaggs was always a bit of a silent type, and no one could have foretold how he would prove to be a great and inventive liar, particularly when there was a microphone near his mouth. But even Glynmor congratulated him after his finished his first performance.

'Well my kids are all very hungry and were crying last night they were 'cos they're down to the last pair of daps between the lot of them,' Dai told the microphone. 'Six I've got. All boys. My wife was up at the crack of dawn digging coal down the tip 'cos the house is so damp even the snails are complaining of arthritis. Pitiful it was, watching her this morning struggling down the road to the tip, what with her surgical boot an' all. She suffers from angina she do an' lies awake all night struggling for breath.'

'I'm very sorry about this, Mr Scaggs. Anything else is there?'

'There is. The man from Radio Rentals came last week and took the television back. He even tried to get me to help him to carry it out. I told him to hop it and carry it out himself.'

The boys nodded and mumbled mutinously at the cheek of the man from Radio Rentals. They sighed even more when Dai started on about how he had taken his six boys to the Social Security offices to try and get them another pair of daps. 'There's nothing we can do about it,' they said. 'Six boys in bare feet an' I've got to get a form.'

The gullible radio reporter was happy enough though. 'We'll be using all this,' he said slipping the boys a fiver before hurrying back to his car and back to the studio where that morning – between pop records and messages about lost dogs – he all but broke the city's heart with a Dickensian tale of the poverty and suffering of an average striking miner.

There was still no sign of any scab coal lorry though. A van painted in bright psychedelic colours had pulled up, disgorging a pile of students who went around the miners shaking their hands and giving away cigarettes. Later still a mini-van rolled up containing some very shady characters in black coats and black balaclavas who proceeded to unfurl lots of black flags with ANARCHY painted on them in silver letters. A spotty young girl was trying to sell *News Line* to the police while yet another youth was handing out leaflets in support of the Animal Liberation Front.

Everyone was welcomed on the Bont picket since Glynmor, in particular, saw it all as a steady process of building up a broad church of the left which would not only carry the miners through triumphant in the end but also bind the various radical groups which, in their turn, would help to radicalise the ailing Labour Party, the leader of which had yet to show his nose on this or any other picket line.

And triumphant they would be in the end. No one had any doubt about that in those early, sunny days of the strike.

It was getting on for noon with not so much as a glimpse of a lorry when a police helicopter came chattering over the giant chimneys of the power station, hovering for a minute or two above the swirling crowd before breaking away towards Barry town.

Danny Kettle took out a packet of cigarettes and Eggey tried to take them off him. 'What's the matter? Have I given them up or what?' he exclaimed.

'I thought you had bad hands.'

'You'll be getting a bad lip if you don't watch it.'

'When're you going to buy a packet anyway? I've had a real bellyfull of all your cadging I 'ave.'

'I'm a striking miner mun.'

'Well, so am I.'

Down in a glade on the opposite side of the road to the power station Dibber Williams was busy being sick into a bunch of nettles. His belly heaved again and again until it was quite sore but nothing came out except thin dribbles of sputum. Dibber was being sick as much as three times a day now but the doctor repeatedly assured him that it was merely alcoholic gastritis which would disappear as soon as he gave up the booze.

Even further in the glade, Huw Bungalow was wandering around picking wild flowers. Dandelions, cow parsley, dog rose ... he picked them all, on occasion stopping still and, with his nose close to the flower, peering intently into its beautiful, fragrant heart. For minutes at a time his black eyes followed the tiny insects stumbling around the stamens or studied the architecture of the leaves. Sometimes he took one flower and compared it to the other, almost as if he was adjudicating at a flower show. But what he found most attractive was simple perfection; the way in which they just could not be improved on.

Gnats danced in the shafts of sunlight as he moved further on into the glade, now stooping to stare into the trumpet of the convolvulus weed to marvel at its shape and the quiet serene tune that came out of it. Even the ugliest flowers had the sweetest tunes in Huw's ears and he could sometimes just stand still among the yellow puffs of dandelions and the bright red bursts of the poppies, listening to a whole symphony of flower music bursting out around him. It was a lusty creation singing a song of life and he would laugh quietly along with it.

Ten minutes later something happened outside the power station.

There was the roar of a lorry coming down the road and bedlam broke out as everyone ran to their action stations; the policemen nipping their fags and putting on their helmets; the anarchists leaping around and waving their black flags; the lodge banner being picked up off the fence; the pickets all linking arms and shuffling forward to engage the police.

'Now keep your shoulders low and we'll shove them all the way back to Cardiff,' Glynmor was shouting. 'Just hold together now and keep low.'

As the lorry roared closer the boys began a Maori war chant of 'Scab, Scab', their shoulders clashing and heaving against those of the police. Stan Swansea actually made a salient in the blue line largely thanks to Abdabs who had fatally weakened the opposition by stretching his hand between Stan Swansea's legs and tickling the policeman's knackers.

More police reinforcements were running to shore up the breaks in their line when the lorry approached and roared straight past them with its smoking exhaust disappearing up the road. It wasn't a scab coal lorry either but loaded with scrap iron and driven by a gypsy wearing a gold ear-ring.

Twenty minutes later the pickets had a victory of sorts when a power worker, on a bicycle, dismounted and proceeded to walk it back up the road away from them. Eggey ran after the power worker who explained that it was not that he was intimidated by the pickets but that it was just that his bike brakes were not working proper and, with all those police

369

around, he was afraid of being booked.

Someone had pinned an old print onto the wall of the new Bont soup kitchen in the Welfare Hall. It was a grim sepia study of the same soup kitchen in the 1926 strike. There were small mountains of potatoes next to a simmering pot. A queue of thin raggedy children was standing outside, waiting for this, their only meal of the day. Fat women in black dresses were standing behind the pot with unsmiling faces and beefy, bruised arms. The sheer isolation of their position reached out and grabbed you by the throat.

But, in the soup kitchen of the 1984 strike, nothing could be less likely.

Under the inspirational leadership of Daisy Three Balls, enthusiastically supported by her sister, Maggie, the girls had created a palace of wonder and surprise almost unknown in the whole history of the Valleys. The pop music of Radio One blared out all day as the vans arrived, almost hourly, with deliveries of this and that. Nothing was predictable. It might be a dozen cases of Coca Cola or a tray of frozen turkeys. Some mornings might bring a mountain of corned beef or a couple of miles of fresh sausages. All were gobbled up.

What no one had foreseen at the start of the strike was the immense amount of goodwill that there would be for the miners in their stand against MacGregor and the Government. Certainly Maggie had not foreseen it. She was surprised as much as anyone, when she had written off to the chocolate manufacturers that Easter, by the avalanche of chocolate that had poured into the village. *Duw*, for the first time ever the kids of Bont had seven eggs each and the little sods were actually complaining and threatening to throw up if they so much as saw another chocolate egg.

Then Maggie and the girls had begun making soup and sandwiches for the men when they came back from picketing. It had been a casual, spontaneous gesture, but it was Daisy Three Balls, with her broader knowledge of organisation learned from the Greenham women and her wide range of contacts, who had quite soon set up a system of fund-raising around the area. Before long she was sending the wives out into the larger towns and cities of Wales, to raise money with the help of collecting boxes and buckets.

They needed to raise some £7,000 a week to ensure that the 650 families were never without a steady supply of basics: potatoes, milk, butter, bread and sugar. They were never far short of this target either. A mistress of the dunning letter Daisy would write to anyone – or ring anyone up – if she decided they could advance the cause of Bont's soup kitchen. No one – not even Tom Jones in Los Angeles or Richard Burton's ex-wife, Elizabeth Taylor in New York – was immune to a sudden call from Three Balls, often in the middle of the night, asking for moral or financial help. It was Daisy who also set up links with the other mining support groups which were springing up in the Midlands – the girls sometimes taking off in a mini-bus and leaving the slightly bemused men to look after the children while they spent a few nights with their new-found friends in Birmingham, Coventry or Manchester.

Maggie did not quite have her sister's chutzpah but she still threw herself into it all with tremendous enthusiasm. The women even mounted a token picket on the Bont mine, and a fearsome lot they could be, Sherman tanks in Duffel coats, COAL NOT DOLE stickers on their labels. NACODS, the safety men, were still working in the mine and sometimes the women would stop their cars when they came out and, if they found sacks of complimentary coal in the boot, they would take them out and throw them into the river.

Despite all this toing and froing, Daisy began to find time to visit her son Gnasher who was due to be released on parole soon. She seemed determined to make a better effort by him too, never missing the visiting hours and even once managing to smuggle him in a new Sony Walkman, with some tapes of Iron Maiden and Status Quo to enable him to headbang away a few of his last hours in the cell.

'We're going to catch up on all our lost hours when he comes out,' Daisy told Maggie. 'I must try to be a better mother and find him a job or something.'

'Aye but a job doing what?' Maggie asked. 'It's all this unemployment that's getting our kids into prison in the first place. I'm often glad Huw is as he is. If he'd been normal he wouldn't have got a job like everyone else and probably ended up in the nick as well.'

'There must be something he can do.'

'There's nothing Daisy. You've been away. You haven't

seen how bad it's got. We've been left with nothing. That's why we're out on strike. If only people could see that instead of thinking it's some attempt at bloody revolution led by Arthur.'

As the girls got the soup kitchen better organised – and the range of their contacts kept increasing – some of the strangest stuff began arriving there. One morning a huge lorry turned up from Italy piled high with tagliatelli and other unpronounce-able forms of pasta which the women were not at all sure how to cook. Then came a ton of tinned turtle meat which no one – not even the dogs – would touch at all. One afternoon a van came from Austria with a load of second-hand clothes and, faster than blinking, some of the Bont boys were going off on picket duty yodelling in their Tyrolean hats and wearing lederhosen.

Foreign trade unions were also constantly sending over invitations for the miners to come and address them. Emlyn was soon despatching some of his boys to meetings in Italy, France and Belgium. Glynmor was learning the hard way how to address an audience but the surprise discovery of the summer was the endlessly inventive eloquence of Dai Scaggs. He was also a popular choice to go abroad, particularly after his triumph on Cardiff Radio. A few days after his broadcast a sack of daps had arrived at the Welfare Hall, all sent by listeners of the station, for the Scaggs boys. There was a note attached to the sack saying that they had also received half a dozen offers of surgical boots for Dai Scaggs' wife. What size boot did she have and which foot was it for?

The ladies and gentlemen of the media, sensing a strong story, turned up to the Hall in a steady trickle. Emlyn chose to handle the most important ones, which usually meant the ones who had not upset him in the past. He liked to take the cameras down into the room behind the stage and show them the hooks where the striking miners used to hang up stolen sheep, to let them bleed, during the 1926 strike. He would describe, with great gusto and flair, how the hungry men would lure the sheep into a hut, often with a trail of bread, then jump on the poor beast with two actually sitting on it while another slit its throat.

He was also brushing up his lines about the sacred dignity of work and the way in which the past still lived in the collective consciousness of the community, the way in which the typical Welsh miner needed his past to make sense of the present. He took a liking to standing in the street in front of a camera, one thumb stuck in his waistcoat pocket, as he described the dread sounds of the hooter down the mine after an accident and the way the whole village would run up the road to gather around the pit gates to see who came up alive.

It was strange, and almost magical, how the spirit of rundown Bont was reinvigorated in the fresh air of that first summer of the strike.

You could almost see the spirit of the place stepping up out of its coffin, lifting it up on its back and walking away on spritely footsteps. Old enmities were forgotten and new alliances formed. New ideas went spinning through the Valley like the first swallows of summer. At the miners' lodge on Sunday mornings and the women's meetings on Thursday nights, mouths were sparking with excited chatter. When they won this strike, they were going to get back the railway station and restore the school; when the strike was over, they were going to insist on the reopening of the police house; with the future of the pit assured, they were going to build an arts centre and get the Welfare Hall sorted out and painted too.

When the strike was over decades of neglect and decay were going to be arrested overnight. There were going to be murals painted on the walls at the end of the terraces and a choir was going to be formed and attached to the Hall. They were going to get back all the books that had once formed their library and been loaned to the University of Wales, and start another of those great miners' libraries ... they were ... they were ...

But, in spite of all this talk, the main body of the village carried on much as normal that summer.

Mrs Oboe Parry, Brenda, found that, a year after her sterilisation, she had become pregnant again; Billy Smiles' wife ran off with the lodger; Walford opened up two new video parlours in Penrhos and Ferndale; Mrs Pritchard's sister died from a stroke while pegging out the clothes; the two Pryce sisters, in the big house up on the hill, had an argument and one of them moved out and went to live with her friend in Upper Boat.

Also, in the last week of August, all the homes in Bont

373

Terrace were in the process of getting – or being about to get – a new roof. No one was absolutely sure what it was all about except that it was called the Envelope Scheme and that it was something to do with the European Economic Community.

Earlier in the month a man with a clipboard had called on every home in Bont Terrace asking if they wanted a new roof free. Naturally they all said 'Yes please' and, within weeks, perfectly good roofs had been stripped off the terrace and new ones fixed on. It was another of those schemes it was. Another Valley scheme. A Bont scheme.

The coach sped over the high formal architecture of the Severn Bridge, past the narrow white boxes of the toll booths and on up the M4 to London. Maggie and Glynmor sat in the front passenger seat holding hands. Huw Bungalow was in the seat behind them, quiet for a change and looking out of the window as the motorway unwound beneath them and the coach roared down the centre lane.

It had been raining for much of the morning, the spray dancing around the wheels of the lorries like trapped and angry ghosts. Tiny rainbows formed in the spray as the sky above them changed form and colour: now with huge shafts of sunshine rolling down past speeding clouds, then everything stacking up into an endless panorama of gunmetal grey going on for storm black.

Another shower of rain fell and the giant windscreen wipers of the coach swept back and forth in steady and perfect time, piling up the rain in running banks of rivulets on the bottoms of either side of the windscreen.

'I haven't brought my umbrella with me neither,' Maggie said, getting increasingly agitated as the journey progressed.

'Don't worry girl. We won't be out in it much.' Glynmor leaned across the aisle and asked the driver how far they had to go.

'Depends on the traffic. Less than an hour I'd say.'

Maggie's grip on his hand tightened and she closed her eyes, letting the images and faces of that summer dance through her mind. It had been the most exciting summer of their lives and she still could not actually believe that it had all come about. As chairwoman of the women's support group there had hardly been a day when she had not been invited somewhere. Yet, in all that time, and despite all the travelling, she had always tried to meet Glynmor wherever and whenever possible, sometimes in a Cardiff pub or even, just recently, in a seedy bed and breakfast behind the Bull Ring in Birmingham.

Most of the women's contacts were in the Midlands. When they were not visiting up there, the Brummie women came to Bont where, when not enough beds were available, many of them slept on the floors of the soup kitchen. The South Wales pickets were concentrating on the big power stations of the Midlands so Maggie and Glynmor were often meeting in the strangest of places somewhere around the centre of England, more often than not falling asleep in one another's arms, sometimes in the back of Trevor's mini-bus or indeed in any bed that might be available, both exhausted by the whirls of picketing and running from the police; the meetings with the activists and the thrilling flights of rhetoric; the strange beds and the ceaseless strain of meeting new faces and learning so many new names.

But no matter how tired they were, they always found the time to make love since, in such stirring times, it was only their naked bodies which brought them much-needed relief, only their strong physical passions which, when satisfied, enabled them to face and chase around in a chaotic changing world. In their bed nothing ever changed. It was only ever blessedly the same when they clambered over one another gently and greedily knowing that quite soon they were going to be released from all their worldly cares, released from picketing rosters and writing up the minutes, to enjoy the simple warmth and smell of one another, to nuzzle into one another's neck and hair, knowing that here, at least, there would never be any conflict of interests, shouting pickets or marching lines of police. Here they were made fresh and new again. When they were apart, Glynmor could only last for about three days and then every fibre of his being was crying out for her, while Maggie could just manage five before she too got into a frightful state. Once they were apart for six days and he hardly managed to get in through the front door before they had it off on the stairs.

One of the favourite misconceptions of the media – with which they persisted tirelessly – was the way in which marriages were breaking under the strain of the strike. Yet Maggie and Glynmor had never been stronger. And neither had most of the marriages in Bont. In more senses than one, the women of the Valleys had finally stepped up to be counted; they were providing energy and reassurance, not simply, as in the past, in the home, but out in political meetings and on the picket lines.

Oh, they were heady days indeed. Who of them was not in love, with their minds stirred with new ideas, the warm fires of a new-found radicalism pouring through their blood? This was the long-awaited summer when they were all waking up at last; when they were really going to seize the time, equal and as one, with their souls renewed in this brave new dawn in the ancient hills of coal.

Huw Bungalow, in particular, had come into his own during the strike. He often travelled with Maggie but mostly he went with Glynmor because he found the picketing more fun. He positively seemed to flourish within his parents' love of one another but what was beginning to happen more and more was that, in some strange but definite way, he too was becoming a leader, often to be found at the head of the flying pickets and, when necessary, leading them through the police lines.

Today they were all going to London together and, as the coach passed the Uxbridge exit, Maggie could actually feel the pulse of the approaching metropolis. The very rhythms of the motorway were becoming more intense, the cars and lorries becoming thicker and going that much faster. She kept looking around beneath a thin veil of terror. She had never been to London before.

They had chartered a coach to go and lobby Parliament and then, later that day, they would be going to a miners' benefit concert featuring their very own Donny Hughes, Donny the Ding, at the Royal Festival Hall. Donny would be sharing the bill along with a half a dozen top-name bands who had each waived their usual five-figure fees to appear. Donny had been enjoying something of a success lately, even making it into the bottom section of the charts with his new song, *The Cost of Coal*, a powerful song about the pain and suffering of a coal-mining Valley which was thought not to be a million miles removed from his Glamorgan Valley home. So now, keen to promote their Welsh boy and 'make a few bob for the miners' Donny's management had picked up the bill for the coach, though the Bont contingent had been told that they would be expected to meet the media and all performers at a small party before the show.

'I hope Donny is not just using us as a publicity stunt,' Maggie had hoped.

'He wouldn't do that. We'd kick his arse from here to November if he did that.'

'Why can't we just go and enjoy the show. All this media stuff is beginning to get me down. It's got we can't go anywhere without facing a camera or talking into a microphone. It would be nice for once if we could just put up our feet, relax an' enjoy ourselves.'

'Let's face it, it's the age of the mass entertainer,' said Glynmor. 'Every age has its God, be it the chapel or socialism. But now it's the mass entertainer we worship every night. He occupies the centre of the shrine now and we're all there, in love and on our knees. It's crazy when you think about it but there you are.'

Just where did he get it all from? These insights surprised Maggie. He seemed to be thinking about things so differently these days. She still had not quite got to the bottom of why he had thrown himself so whole-heartedly into the strike. Becoming a lefty had been easy for him but now he was acting as if he was about to challenge for leadership. He was different in so many ways. Heavens, he wasn't even unduly concerned about going to London, even if he had made various drunken forays with the boys there for international matches at Twickenham, including one famous weekend when he had ended up in Bow Street Magistrates' Court and Bobo Rees, who had also gone with them, had disappeared, never to be seen by anyone ever again.

The coach gears whined and screeched as they stopped and started through the traffic jam in Cromwell Road. Maggie stared at women in their fashionable clothes, walking manicured dogs past the huge hotels and shivering shopping windows. There were Arab women with black-veiled faces and giant Africans in gaudy coloured clothes. Punks with technicoloured Mohican hair-dos and safety pins in their ears clattered past a Chelsea pensioner. Squat black taxis weaved in and out and she saw a traffic warden put a note on the windscreen of a parked car.

'Look Glynmor! There's Harrods. They do say you can

buy anything in there. I've always wanted to go to Harrods.'

'They don't sell anything in Harrods any more, I heard.'

'You're joking aren't you?'

'No. Those bastard Arab women have pinched so much there in the past everything's locked and screwed down in there now.'

'Don't be so soft.'

The coach went past Westminster Abbey and into Parliament Square where the miners and their wives let out a spontaneous burst of applause. Even Huw Bungalow became excited at such a famous sight, standing up and squeezing Maggie's shoulder with the purest delight. They pulled up by the Houses of Parliament, a giant, black Gothic birthday cake of a building with its thousands of tiny arches and crenellated spires, topped by the most famous clock of them all, Big Ben. The sun was shining on the crowds of tourists milling around St Stephen's Gate.

Maggie was feeling quite nervous as they alighted from the coach, taking Huw by the hand as she looked over to the House of Lords and the Victoria Tower. So this was the Mother of Parliaments, where all the decisions that were making their lives so wretched were being taken. She gazed up at Big Ben, feeling remote from the building, somehow offended by its great and fancy panoply. Just a pile of airs and graces, her Mam would have said. How could something like this have anything to do with the Valleys? Did they even know where the Valleys were? Did they care?

She would have preferred a small legislature about the size of Pontypridd market, where the members were directly elected from the towns and villages of the Valleys and who would then run the place in accordance with the needs of those towns and villages. What's what she would have liked. Not this. Anything but this.

Glynmor had gone off to see about entry to the Lobby and they were all standing around as dozens of pigeons came wandering over to Huw Bungalow, their heads clockworking around his blue suede shoes and others fluttering up onto his hands and shoulder-pads. He was making strange noises in his throat as if he were communicating with them. Maggie wondered yet again what it was that made her son extraordinary.

Certainly the passing crowds found Huw's Teddy-boy gear quite compelling. Some Japanese tourists started taking photographs of him as he became increasingly smothered in pigeons, until Maggie shooed them away. Not that Huw ever minded such attention. There was never anything terribly introverted or extroverted about his personality; now everything about him was in perfect balance.

Glynmor finally led them all into the high whispering corridor of the Lobby where they stood around in groups waiting to exercise their most basic democratic right – button a passing Member of Parliament and give him an ear-full about whatever it was that was giving pain or offence. The trouble was most members seemed to have enough of their own pains and offences without looking for any more in the Lobby and, within half an hour, virtually no one had come past, merely confirming Maggie's view of the worthlessness of such a remote parliament.

Notes had been sent to all the Welsh M.P.s with none turning up, including the Labour Party leader Neil Kinnock. Glynmor did manage to nobble a Tory M.P. who made some withering remarks about how the miners always expected the mines to be run as some sort of expensive social therapy for them. Indeed he then began to get even more insulting particularly about Arthur Scargill and it was only Maggie's speedy intervention that just managed to stop said M.P. from getting a kiss from Glynmor's famous flying head butt. 'Not here Glynmor for goodness' sake. This is not Bont Hall. They'll hang you if you lay someone out in here.'

Glynmor finally managed to calm down and they waited for a further half an hour but still managed to see no one of any importance. It was Glynmor's first real insight into how alone the miners were in their struggle; how they had been dumped by the trade unions, politicians and media alike.

'Any sign of Kinnock is there?' asked John Abdabs.

'Not a sniff,' Glynmor growled. 'We've sent in some more notes but they do say he's not around. What's the matter with him? He's a Welsh boy from the Valleys like us. All his family spring from the mines and coal. He's one of us! But he won't come and see us, won't picket with us, won't do fuck all. Just what's he playing at? Nye Bevan would never have done this. Nye would 'ave been with us from Day One.'

*

379

The Press conference before the benefit show that night was an amiable, boozy affair. Glynmor, by now slightly more drunk than sober, was swigging beer and managing to hog the cameras as he told reporters how they used to get Donny to stand on an orange box in the local shop and make him sing all the women a song. 'He sounded like a rope under the door he did. We always said that he would never get anywhere.

'One thing we always tried to do as kids was to catch those scabby valley sheep. They're murder to hold onto they are and do kick like mules. Anyone who couldn't hang on had to take their punishment, Licky Locky. Everyone pulled your hair twice and that's why Donny's head is as bald as a badger's arse and he always wears a cap. He never could hold onto those sheep. Scared of 'em 'e was.

'Now people always wonder why Donny never had a girlfriend ... '

More and more media people were gathering around Glynmor, whose indiscreet stories were natural tabloid fodder. Maggie sat on the other side of the foyer having a bit of a *cwtch* with Huw. They had been drinking most of the day and, what with the interminable walking around the streets, were dog-tired too. The rest of the miners and their wives milled around.

It was just then that Maggie found that she was sitting next to the star of the show, the great Donny Hughes himself, who was laughing along with the rest of them at Glynmor's remarks. She had known Donny since he had been knee-high to a duck's beak and it was odd sitting next to someone you knew so well who had then become so famous. 'Hello Donny. How's tricks?' she asked, greeting the star as though she had just bumped into him in the Co-op.

Donny turned to face her. 'Maggie!' he exclaimed. 'I haven't seen you when – since the day of your wedding. My God that was a piss-up and a half that was.'

'Aye. And our Glynmor hasn't sobered up yet.'

There was another roar of laughter and they both looked around. 'I've never known anyone to tell stories like Glynmor. He should be on the stage with me.'

'Aye. They always did say that Glynmor had a bell on every tooth. All jaw and no do he is.'

'Oh Maggie it's good to hear Valley talk again. No one

speaks like Valley people. I should come home I should.'

'We're all still there Donny. You'd be welcome any time. You *should* come and live with us again. It would be good for your work it would and we need people like you back in the Valleys. We need you to come home and tell the world what we're going through.'

'A lot of my work is about that, of course.'

'I know that Donny. And we're proud of you, we are. But it's getting worse every day there. It's getting so that when you walk out through the front door you just want to burst into tears. Aye. Come home, Donny. Come back to the Valleys, kid.'

After Madness and Bananarama Donny topped the first half of the concert, receiving a huge round of applause when, dressed in leather thigh-high boots and a black cloak, he shambled onto the huge darkened set with a glittering silver terrace of houses and the slowly spinning pit wheel being picked up with silver lasers. A few real sheep wandered around inside a pen with a silver blue night shifting in yet more laser effects.

Donny nodded acknowledgement to the applause before beginning a neo-surreal monologue about his mining village home and the characters who lived in the various houses. In the background his band's synthesisers quietly hummed and soared, now like a male voice choir, now like clanking industrial machinery.

'Poor old Wendy Pugh, in No. 17, has just had another baby she has. And she's nearly into her fifties too – caught on the change, poor dab!'

'Will Roberts lived right up on top of the hill … it's one hell of a pull to get up there … and one night he was so drunk he had to get one of his whippets to pull him up there … '

'Dan Box has just bought a video with all the great Welsh rugby tries since 1959 – watches it every night he do, with his scarf and rattle in bed … '

And so his extraordinary rock drama continued – a sort of *Under Milk Wood* meets *Tommy* – with sobbing guitar riffs and moody cries on the synthesisers breaking into the charming word pictures of a coal-mining community taking trips to Porthcawl on the Costa del Hiya-Butty and the miners working reg'lar in the pit; of rugby fanatics drinking too much and the marathon fist fights on the mountain. Occasionally he would pick up a guitar and sing unaccompanied one of the old mining ditties:

> He's barmy, he's barmy, he's fairly off his dot –
> He's drunk a pint of paraffin oil and thought it was
> whisky hot.

When he finished his performance the applause was deafening. Donny and his band trooped off, but, within minutes, the stamping, clapping audience had brought them back. To close the first half he reworked such old sentimental classics as *My Rhondda Home* and Tom Jones' *Green Grass of Home* before climaxing it with his own *The Cost of Coal*, full of memorable images of dead miners being taken home in sacks to their widows and children queuing up at the soup kitchens.

By now the concert was running very late indeed and the Bont contingent had to leave, happy enough anyway with what they had seen. Happy enough, that is, except Glynmor who, Maggie could tell without even asking, had hated Donny's performance and was tamping mad about something or other. Perhaps he had caught an early hangover from all the beer he'd been guzzling during the day. Perhaps all that loud pop music had given him a headache but whatever it was he had left the theatre, silent and grim-faced, going over to the pre-appointed spot where they had been told to pick up their coach and just standing there, daring anyone to so much as say a word to him.

But Maggie could read the tea leaves and said nothing, knowing of old that, if she said nothing, then he would have nothing to argue with. She merely stood there hanging onto a half-dead Huw while the others milled around, still buzzing with pleasure and saying how great the concert had been.

It was Dibber Williams who made the grave mistake of asking Glynmor what he thought.

'Well it was all very pretty I'm sure,' Glynmor said. 'It was all very pretty but it was just bugger all, wasn't it? Absolute bugger all. It's that wanker Dylan Thomas I blame. He's infected everything in Wales he has. Fuck all about fuck all, that's all his stuff ever is. A flood of pretty words in search of just one bastard idea. Even *The Cost of Coal* is about the 1926 strike. That's why old Emlyn Kremlin likes it so much.'

'There's a lot more than Emlyn who like *The Cost of*

Coal,' Dibber pointed out as the rest gathered around.

'Aye, because there's a lot more like Emlyn who like living in the past,' Glynmor exploded. 'And there's politicians like Kinnock who like living in London. And there's singers like Donny who wouldn't come near the Valleys, not if you gave them a million pounds they wouldn't.'

'Glynmor you're just talking a load of balls as usual.'

'Oh it's balls is it? What about the Valley today? Eh? What about unemployment? What about those poor bastard skinheads they keep on locking up all the time? What about the stretcher cases in every home? How do you get a doctor? Where's the police when you need them? Why are the streets filthy? Just what is it that we are fighting for in this bloody strike? Eh? What? Why isn't anyone talking about that?'

''Cos it's not all like that mun. It's not all like that.'

'It's not all like that. Well, well. It's all fucking lovely and cosy is it with funny people with funny voices going around and having a funny time all day. We're *dying* mun. We've already started picking our kids out of the gutters and putting them in coffins years too soon. And there's Donny going on about how hard it was in 1926 as if, somehow, it's suddenly all got better.'

Maggie turned away and watched their coach pull up with the air locks on the swing doors hissing and sighing. She held Huw very tight. Glynmor was changing all right but it was a change that was going to turn everyone against him. It was frightening, the way he seemed to be prodding at the bare truth of everything. Much as she agreed with him, it just meant that he was going to end up disliked, a misfit, the social leper that everyone avoided. They preferred him when he was telling dirty stories; they certainly would never accept what he was saying now. They really did believe that it was still all warm and lovely in the Valleys, that it was exactly the charming way that Donny had portrayed them. They believed it because they wanted to believe it and there were none better at kidding themselves.

All of which left her Glynmor, the lone stag, baying his anger at the moon.

Chapter Twenty-Three

Autumn drew close and the colours of the Valley changed from bright green to dark brown. As had happened from time immemorial, the sheep were rounded up and counted and the reservoir drained and cleaned. Almost every day it was picking with rain, the thick banks of mists travelling up and down the Valley walls. It had been chilly for most of September but, come October, the Autumn foreclosed in full and sank teeth of ice right into the neck of the village.

With the freezing mornings came the problem of keeping warm. The strike-bound pit meant that everyone had run out of coal. Quite soon the dole boys were out on the tips, scratching and riddling for small lumps of coal which they sold from door to door at £1.50 a sack. Everyone was amazed at their industry and inventiveness as they turned the black, half-grassed slopes of the tips into a sort of black Aberklondyke, the scrape of shovels and the shaking of riddles rising up out of their dark little bunkers, which they protected with an extraordinary ferocity.

Within days every supermarket in the Valley was complaining of a shortage of trolleys. The dole boys had found that they made ideal sieves for their coal. Anything – from newspaper delivery bags to Post Office sacks – was hauled in to help in the transport of coal. Even children's prams, built for small dolls, were commandeered to carry a hundredweight or so of nutty slack. As often as not, the axles would collapse or the wheels would buckle hopelessly as its owner toiled and puffed, trying to push it up the ragged slopes back to the village.

It was on a day late in November, when the sun sparkled in the early-morning frost, that Daisy borrowed Trevor's mini-bus and took a few of the old Clay Class down to Cardiff prison to meet Gnasher on his release. They all sat in the mini-bus outside the prison gates and had a little party with the help of a few flagons of cider. That night they had an even better one in the Hall. Committee chairman Max Million came around telling them that they were all welcome back but, if they didn't behave tidy – or if they started any bother at all – they would all be boxed for life.

'You'll not be getting any trouble out of me Max,' Gnasher had assured him. 'I've learned my lessons now I 'ave an' now I'm going straight.'

He spent his first few days of freedom wandering around the place with Nipper and Cocoa, watching the dole boys enlarging their network of tunnels and holes, seeing how they went about their business, noting where the keenest customers could be found.

I think that Cardiff prison must have shaken Gnasher rigid, Aunty Phyllis told Enid. 'E's not so slummocky somehow an' there's talk he might be going up to London to get a job. 'E's been saying 'e wants to make something of his life an' that 'e's heard you can get a job up in London. 'E's made some contacts in prison he has. Bright contacts they'd be as well, if you ask me. But 'e'd only get into trouble again if 'e stayed around 'ere wouldn't 'e? The police would still go after 'im after what 'e did all those years ago. Stands to reason donit?

Within four days of his release, Gnasher – who must have learned a thing or two in Cardiff prison despite what they were always saying about the place – began getting a bit of a business organised. He took over an empty yard behind the chip shop and, the same day, got a dozen or so of the boys wheeling their prams and trolleys up to the tip and then back to his yard. Up and down the great slopes they trooped; an endless procession of skinhead worker ants, leaving the yard with their trolleys empty and rolling back with them overflowing with small lumps of nutty slack.

Somehow Gnasher had acquired a pile of polythene bags which took 28lb of coal. Soon he was selling them around Bont for 80p a bag. As far as profit went, this was a vast improvement on thier £1.50 for a sack which held some 100lb. As word got around Aberklondyke, all the dole boys began taking their coal to this wily jailbird who was paying them twice as much for their labours and relieving them of the problem of trying to sell it from door to door.

Right from the start Gnasher established himself as a boss who wasn't going to take any messing about. If any of the dole boys came back with any bricks, stones or shale in his coal he was given a good kicking and sent back to dig some tidy coal. Any freelance competition on the tips was also quietly disposed of, though if any of them looked bright enough to tell the difference between a decent lump of coal and a poke in the eye, they were also invited to join Gnasher Enterprises Inc.

The strange thing was that the business began coming together with the speed of light. In his second week Gnasher acquired an old coal lorry from down Pontypridd way. It rumbled and groaned belched a lot of black smoke, and its wheels seemed to be pointing in different directions, but it did somehow go forward and was a great boon to his customer sales service.

An even stranger thing was that no one objected to the rise of his empire or even tried to give him a bump on the nose when he declared the whole of Aberklondyke his own. The truth of it all was that, despite nearly four years inside, his reputation for violence and brutality was as vivid as ever. *Duw*, everyone still spoke of that night when he had just ripped up that policeman's dog like an unwelcome gas bill. No one – least of all those scrabbling about on the coal tips – was inclined to test the legend and risk getting themselves ripped apart too.

Even the police stayed well clear, though tongues had been buzzing in the Valleys about the sheer size of the illegal business. Why, twice a week, they even loaded the lorry high and went over to Penrhos and Aberdare. The biggest mystery of all was how they got all those idle skinhead bastards working so hard. They were at it day *and* night. Even the striking miners marvelled at the work they put in, particularly at night when great arcs of black silt were being thrown up out of the bunkers and into the moonlight as if by dozens of furious great dogs who had lost their favourite bones.

Yet, after three or four days of frenzied effort, the skinheads seemed to go to pieces, collapsing on the job and having to be wheeled home to sleep around the clock.

It was Dan Box who raised the matter of Gnasher

Enterprises at the next lodge meeting, wondering if the boys were happy about this sudden outbreak of capitalist endeavour in their midst while they themselves were fighting to bring capitalism down.

But they grumbled and puffed. Then they oohed and aahed. But no one could come up with any really coherent objection to Gnasher's new activity. 'It's good to see the dole boys finding themselves a bit of work,' Emlyn said. 'We can't find it for them so we can hardly stand in their way now they've found it for themselves. Between you, me and the gatepost I hope young Gnasher makes a million.'

'I tell you what, Mr Chairman, there's men in this room who've never worked as hard as those skinheads. I don't know what Gnasher's secret is but, if anyone ever finds out, just make sure he keeps it away from MacGregor, that's all.'

Gnasher's secret was contained in a huge sweet jar, judiciously hidden inside a biscuit tin, under his trestle table down the yard. Far from being reformed and on the straight and narrow Gnasher had learned some very useful things while in the nick. Right from the start he had been supplying his skinhead staff with high octane amphetamine pills which kept them permanently hopped up and moving – day *and* night.

Bursts of whistling came from the opposite sides of the field as black shapes went skirmishing through the thick white mists. There was a squeal of muzzy static on a CB radio as yet more figures came swooping through the swirling white clouds to stand, in a disorganised line, and peer out over the barbed-wire fence into mist so thick and damp it could almost have been rain.

At one end of the fence, standing on a mound, was the bent awkward shape of Huw Bungalow straining himself erect. He gave two long whistles and waved at Glynmor before pointing down the country lane. Glynmor ran along the length of the fence where the mist had lifted enough for him to see, parked at a cross-roads, a police Range Rover with a group of some ten policemen, smoking cigarettes and chatting to each other.

Glynmor came scurrying back holding his finger over his lips and signalling the boys to retrace their steps until they came out into a lane next to the farmhouse. There was the sound of an alarm clock and a light went on in an upstairs window. Huw pointed at an open gate on the other side of the line.

They crossed the lane as silently as Red Indians setting up an ambush, twenty-five of them, bent low and running in single file across the field. The only sounds came from their boots which squished and squelched in the muddy grass.

'I'm going to catch a fresh cold on top of the one I already 'ad after all this,' whispered Abdabs, skidding through on the thick cow pats.

'*Duw*, this cow shit don't 'alf pong donit?'

'Cool head boys. Watch out for Huw now.'

Huw had found another high vantage point and was waving them on again, as they ran around the back of a country pub where a chained dog was snarling and barking at them. Then Huw scampered up another high dry stone wall and walked along its length, looking out over the fields in the direction of the mine. He looked down at Glynmor and raised his thumb upright whereupon all the men went running over the road.

As they crossed the next field they found themselves running alongside a group of Kent miners who had somehow found a way in direct off the motorway. The Kent and South Wales miners had become the leading flame-throwers in the flying picket game and they fell on one another like long-lost brothers, hugging one another without any sounds and dancing around the cow pats, as if they were at some strange party where someone had just pinched the record player.

Stan Swansea went down on his knees to see if he could pick up any messages on the CB radio but it was Huw's whistle that got them all moving again: about a hundred of them by now, with their brightly coloured bobble caps and donkey jackets festooned with metal badges, all more visible now as the dawn sun began to burn away the early morning mists.

The communication that Glynmor had established with his son Huw was both uncanny and unerring. At times like this, the boys followed without question whatever directions the pair gave them. They followed Huw in particular since he had clearly developed the soundest instincts in taking the Bont boys through the police lines. His ability to read a dangerous situation was positively forensic. In all the long months they had been picketing the coalfields in search of scabs, the outlying police patrols had never so much as seen them, let alone laid arresting hands on them.

Grey streaks of light were shivering past the bare branches of the trees as the first birds of the dawn chorus began clearing their throats in readiness for their daily choir practice. A few cows began lowing moodily, doubtless bemused by all these miners running through their field. Something small – as in rat or rabbit – went squealing past Oboe Parry's boots and all but made his heart stop.

'Gawd mun. This is going to play up my angina something terrible all this is. You see if it don't.'

'What're you wearing that stupid hat for? You'll make it rain you will.'

It was just after 5.15 a.m. when they huddled together against a high embankment which overlooked Ackerton pit, four miles outside the scab capital of Nottingham. The motionless, black wheel of the pit was suspended on invisible strings above a thick bank of the whitest mist. Heads bobbed up and went down again. They had about twenty minutes to get to the pit main gates to confront the scab morning shift.

'I've just got a message from our Yorkshire butties on the other side,' Stan Swansea told Glynmor. 'They say they're going in in ten minutes and hope we've brought our Meals on Wheels with us.'

'Tell 'em we'll give 'em a cup of tea as long as they've brought their racing pigeons with 'em.'

At Huw's whistle they went over the embankment and across another lane before hiding again against the opposite bank while Glynmor checked the time and Huw shinned half-way up a telegraph pole.

'They say they've got their racing pigeons an' they've got plenty of whisky,' said Stan Swansea.

'Tell those drunken bastards that Arthur Scargill is most firm that miners shouldn't drink on the picket line,' said Glynmor with half a smile. 'Tell 'em to give their whisky to their pigeons. It'll help 'em fly straight.'

Suddenly Huw raised a hand. There was a stretched-out silence with just the sound of the boys, panting and dragon-breathed, against the grassy bank. Then there came the sound of marching boots and Huw raised his thumb, giving three short sharp whistles.

Without a murmur the Welsh and Kent pickets stepped forward onto the road, finding themselves about a hundred yards away from the pit gates and some fifty yards from the scab morning shift who were marching down the road towards them flanked by a few police officers.

It was the silence of all these men that was the most eerie. The marching scabs, carrying their Tommy tins and tea jacks, just stopped and looked at the pickets milling about in front of them. Down at the pit gates groups of around a hundred policemen also stopped chatting and turned around to look. All eyes continued to stare as the Yorkshire pickets came drifting out of the woods on the opposite side of the road. As the scabs surveyed the hostile armies massing all around them, they must have had a new understanding of what it must have been like facing all those hostile Zulus at Rourke's Drift.

'This be eleventh hour business,' shouted a Yorkshire picket. 'A hob-nailed boot job. So, boys, here we go!'

           'Here we go!'

'Here we go!'

               'Here we go!'

     'Here we go!'

                  'Here we go!'

The police began running from the pit gate and the pickets began running towards the scabs who, in their own turn, began running back the way they had come. The pickets, whose objective was to disperse the ranks and give them a bit of a roughing up, hurled stones and clodges at their fleeing backsides.

Glynmor managed to catch hold of one of them, dragging him, squealing like a piglet, off the road and flinging him into a nearby stream. As he tried to get hold of another scab three policemen pounced on him but even as they were trying to get him down to the ground he caught sight of Huw streaming past him like a one-man cavalry charge. The next thing he was free and running back down the road to regroup the Welsh forces.

    'Here we go!'

       'Here we go!'

             'Here we go!'

                   'Here we go!'

But now yet more police were marching down the road and the Bont boys were beginning to think about a tactical retreat. Before they could organise themselves Huw's head bobbed up over some blackberry bushes in the nearby wood, whistling frantically. He waved for them to follow him down a twisting muddy path and some thirty went stumbling and sliding down after him until they came out onto another road where a gang of some twenty scabs were standing waiting, surrounded by a thin blue line of policemen.

They never had a chance since the Welsh sent a flying wedge straight into them, bodies sailing in one direction and helmets going in the other, fists going into jaws as yet more bloodied faces rose up and bruised shins were bruised some more in another of those blustering cartwheeling mauls that were as familiar on the picket lines as they were at the Arms Park.

Again Huw began whistling and beckoning so all the boys went slipstreaming back into the wood again, this time taking a path which led them directly out in front of the pit where but two solitary policemen stood. On seeing the battered and bloody Welsh coming out of the wood, led by a Teddy boy with mud all over his brothel creepers, the police simply turned and walked away.

Huw left them as Glynmor set up a line of his own boys across the pit gates and, about a minute later, Huw returned with many of the Kent contingent.

'This boy can't half move, can't he?' said one of the Kent pickets.

'Aye. The Barry John of the picket line is our Huw.'

Some more of the Yorkshire pickets came trooping down the road but what no one could understand was what had happened to the police. Or, come to that, all those bastard Nottingham scabs.

There had still been no sign of the boys in blue when an old van came bumping over a field driven by an old lady who promptly got out and began handing around cups of tea and steak and kidney pies. A few students from Nottingham University rolled up on bicycles and unfurled a banner announcing the students' solidarity with the striking miners. A Granada television crew began setting up their equipment.

But there were still no signs of the police until an inspector appeared, walking slowly down the middle of the road towards the waiting pickets. 'You caught us on the hop this time,' the inspector told them. 'We've advised the morning shift not to go into work today.'

'Does this mean we've won?' Glynmor asked.

'This means we have advised the morning shift not to go to work today. But, remember now, we'll be ready for you tomorrow.'

'We've won boys. We've bloody won. It's surrender!'

The boys all let out a great cheer, many flinging their pies into the air as others hoisted Huw aloft, marching him up and down the road. 'Surrender! Surrender! Surrender! They had out-gunned them. Surrender! Surrender! Surrender!'

Just a token picket was left on the pit gate while the rest, arms around one another, went off to see if they could get the local publican to open his bar. With the bill on Granada television.

Even as they walked off a great fluttering of racing pigeons rose up out of Ackerton Wood, circling around and around the pit before making off in the direction of their Yorkshire lofts. The Grimethorpe pickets had, as usual, brought their own racing pigeons to send home the news. That was the way the Yorkshire people liked to receive their news these days. If you'd just relied on newspapers or the evening news, you'd never have known that the shock troops of the mining movement had just won yet another famous victory, at Ackerton, by stopping the scab morning shift.

'Oh 'ello lovely. I miss you I do. How are you?'

'I'm tidy. We're all tidy. Did you hear about us in Ackerton? Routed those scab bastards we did. Bloody routed them.'

'There was just a few seconds on the Welsh news. It didn't seem as if much was happening. We saw Huw we did but the television news has been full of that Oak Dale pit. Glynmor it was terrible. Horses an' tear gas an' I don't know what. Knocking them down everywhere they were. They're going to be shooting the pickets next. The sooner you're both home the better.'

'We're scaring them we are. The more police they pour in the more scared they are.'

'Huw's all right is he? I do worry about him.'

'He's as bright as ninepence. He's only a little *dwt* but he's running here an' there an' getting us out of all kinds of trouble. They do say they're going to have him in the Welsh team when the strike's over. He's been craftier than ever Barry John was in his prime.'

'How are the rest of the boys?'

'They're all great. There's been none of us hurt so far and none of us arrested. Even Dai Scaggs twisted 'is ankle an', five minutes later, it was better. In a funny sort of way Huw seems to be looking after us.'

'I'm sure he does. I'm sure he does. Oh I miss you both so bad. Can you get home before Friday?'

'Wish I could 'cos my thumb's romping it is an' we know what that means don't we?'

'Well we can't do much on the telephone can we? Nip home for an hour, if you can, an' we'll fix it up quick enough.'

'Can't girl. We're on another of those big power stations in the morning. 'aven't heard which one yet. They only tell us late the night before. 'Ow's the soup kitchen anyway?'

'It's all right. We 'ad another ton of turtle meat in there this morning. No one knows what to do with it. It's been terrible weather, picking with rain all week. Oh an' Daisy is under the doctor.'

'Hasn't she found herself a man yet? That's all that's ever wrong with 'er an' her hungry fanny.'

'She says she doesn't fancy any of the boys around 'ere but I've got my own ideas 'cos I'm certain she's having an affair with some man she's met in Birmingham. Something to do with the N.U.M. 'e is an' all. Married? Course he's married. Aren't they all? You know Daisy well enough. She wouldn't want anyone who was easy to get. Hang on. Emlyn's just come in an' he wants a word with you.'

'Glynmor, things are getting bad they are,' Emlyn said. 'On television today there was horses an' CS gas an' blood all over the shop.'

'That's just television Em. You know how they are.'

'I know how they are Glynmor but I don't want our boys getting into any punch-ups with the police. Specially if those television cameras are around. You hear me Glynmor? I know you. You'll fight anything when you get going.'

'Emlyn mun. A little bit of violence never hurt anyone.'

'Glynmor, we've got to fight this thing with discipline. This battle of ours is not just about picket-line violence which is all we ever get on the box. It's not some re-run of some old cowboy film. It's about pit closures and our communities. So let's remember that now.'

Thick black clouds came scudding in over the brow of the hill as Glynmor stood there blowing on the stump of his thumb while watching the gathering forces around the Wensley Hill Power Station.

The Bont boys were tired and cold as they had been dodging around fields and back lanes to avoid the police blockades since four in the morning. Now, with their feet pure lumps of ice, they all just stood there watching line after line of police marching up the road and taking up their positions outside the power station. A few pickets had managed to get near the power station whistling a Laurel and Hardy tune or throwing the odd clodge as the police marched. But if possible, the sight of all those policeman was making the cold bodies of the Bont pickets run even colder since, even so high up here on the hill, they could see that there was no jocularity about the police ranks today. They were wearing all-black uniforms with NATO helmets, carrying long riot sticks and body-length Perspex shields.

Glynmor continued standing there blowing on this thumb. The sight of this new, well-armed police force had come as something of a shock to the boys. Oh they had expected it long enough since, in foray after foray, they had suspected they had got the police on the run and that they would do something soon. So here it was – the Thatcher response – give them a more military uniform and let it be known that, if it was a war the miners wanted, then it was a war they were going to get. It was all a natural response to the way they were being presented on television really. Glynmor saw that but still found it difficult to believe what was going on down there in front of him.

The dark clouds began spitting with freezing rain with a siren wind moaned up out of the wood behind them. Huw tugged at the bottom of his father's jacket, pointing down at the marching police and shaking his head as if to say that they had no chance against them.

'We'll see them off,' Glynmor said with little conviction. He turned and looked around at the boys who were still just standing there and looking down at the power station. He couldn't but help note the difference between the disciplined, military turn-out of the police and his own gang with their tartan windcheaters and leaky trainers, their sweat-stained headbands and baseball shoes, their N.C.B. donkey jackets and muddy jeans with holes in the knees. Not that he was worried about any of that. His side might be a ragged-arsed bunch but he would far prefer to be with them in any foxhole. They might not be very pretty with polish on their shoes and creases in their trousers; they might fart like thunder and get as pissed as parrots but they had more guts and fire than a thousand bastard police forces.

Just behind the police line, on the left of the entrance to the power station, a large green van was parked with three television cameras mounted on its roof. There was a distant bugle call and a flag of flame came spinning up from inside a wooden hut on the opposite slope – lit by the Yorkshire pickets perhaps – sending a high pall of thick smoke drifting, black on grey, across this colourless and cold winter morning.

'We'll stay here for a bit, boys,' said Glynmor. 'Stan, see what you can pick up on the radio.'

Huw was shaking his head again.

'Don't worry mun. Don't worry.'

A group of some two hundred pickets came running out of the opposite wood just above the other side of the power station, disturbing a murder of crows as they went tearing down towards the police line. After another minute another group of a hundred or so came running out of the same woods but in the opposite direction, grouping directly outside the main gates. Clearly the aim was to stretch the police line as thinly as possible; to run and poke around looking for weaknesses.

'Our Yorkshire butties are on again,' said Stan Swansea. 'There's going to be a scab lorry in a few minutes and, when it comes, they want us to attack the line by that huge oak just next to the television cameras. Don't worry, they say. There's going to be a sodding great hole in the line by the time we get there.'

'Oh aye. The police are just going to put down their

weapons an' wave us through are they?' asked Glynmor. Like a First World War veteran he had acquired a pretty shrewd notion of what was possible and what was not.

Small isolated squads of pickets were marauding fast along the front of the police lines, some taking the odd kick at the Perspex body shields or flinging a brick or bottle. Now and then a pair of police would break ranks to try and grab the odd picket but, more often than not, they were too fast for them. The nip and tuck kept up for a further five minutes when there were rising chants of 'Here we go!' mingled with drifting lines of 'Arthur Scargill, Arthur Scargill, we'll support you for ever more.'

'Yorkshire wants us to get down about a hundred yards from the police line and to stay ready,' hissed Stan.

A handcart loaded with bales of hay appeared at the top of the hill with a hand carrying a flaming petrol rag just next to it. In the far distance some ten men emerged from out of a knoll carrying a telegraph pole. Even as they stood there poised for the attack Glynmor could see that the plan was to frighten the shit out of the police on one side so that they would double up over there, leaving the Welsh boys to make a salient on the weakened flank so that they could get to the lorry before it made the gates.

'The lorries are coming Glynmor. There's three of them an' they'll be coming 'round the bend any second now.'

'Everyone keep well in around me now,' Glynmor shouted, taking Huw by the arm. 'All this is going to be a question of timing so, for fuck's sake, don't move till I say so.'

A brilliant maroon flare exploded in the sky to the left of the power station, just above the motorway. The hay-cart was set alight and the flaming pyre sent rolling down towards the police line. The miners with the telegraph pole began shouting and chanting and charging down the slope. The police wheeled to meet the battering ram while others came running up behind to fortify them.

On the other side of the power station the three lorries appeared just at that moment as the Bont boys went dashing down the hill towards the line of glittering Perspex shields, weakened – as predicted – by police panic.

'Here we go!'   'Here we go!'
'Watch it. Brick up!'   'Brick up!'
            'On your left. Brick up!'
'Here we go!'

With Huw pointing slightly to the left of the police line they went hurdling with a great whoop straight through the thin blue cordon, ricocheting around before preparing to face out the oncoming lorries. A rock was hoisted in the air and smashed the windscreen of the leading lorry which had braked and was inching towards them uncertainly. The boys were still running towards it when the heavens farted and there was a lot of loud snorting and seven police horses came galloping from nowhere, the riders in their billowing black jackets, looking like avenging demons of the apocalypse as, with truncheons raised, they bore down on the miners.

The flaming hay-cart had fallen over on its nose by this time and fat, fiery lumps of blazing straw drifted above the battling bodies as the horsemen rained truncheon blows down on the heads and arms of the men. It was the sheer size of the horses that was the most frightening, even more than the fearsome thunder of the hooves on the ground.

'Well kiss my aunty's cat's arse,' Glynmor said softly when Huw came skidding past, grabbing his arm and towing him out of the path of the destroying horsemen towards the shelter of one of the power station's fences.

Now a few hundred Kent pickets – who had been called in from a nearby pit – were streaming down the slopes. Rocks and stones came showering down on the horsemen. There was fierce hand-to-hand fighting everywhere. Some of the Yorkshire pickets had made another break in the Perspex line and were scattering ball-bearings over the road, making the horses rear up, their eyes wide with fright and their foam-flecked mouths whinnying in fear.

A dislodged NATO helmet bounced near Huw's feet and Glynmor picked it up and lobbed it at the backs of the horsemen who wheeled again and were now trying to contain the Yorkshire breakthrough. One of the horses limped uncertainly away; he could see the anxious look in the rider's eyes. Now the acrid stench of CS gas drifted white around and around them, making the eyes sting so hard both the police and pickets could barely see the bleeding and bloody confusion all around them.

Heads had been bashed raw, blood running warm down the sides of their necks. One miner was caught by four policemen and flung around like a rag doll. A petrol bomb curled over the struggling bodies to burst against the radiator of the leading lorry, scaring the already-scared driver so much he jumped out and made a run for it.

Glynmor was standing with Huw, Oboe Parry and Dibber Williams in front of the fence when he shouted, 'The lorry. We've got to get the fucking lorry.'

Two more horses went galloping past when the four of them went bobbing and swerving around the fighting groups until they got to the still-smouldering lorry. Glynmor leaped inside the cabin, kicking out the shattered windscreen, before turning on the ignition. Oboe and Dibber were hanging onto the running boards while the ever-agile Huw was on top of the cabin, riding shotgun and whistling for the other Bont boys to jump on with them.

More climbed on and there was the screech and clash of gears as the lorry reversed into the one behind before Glynmor managed to find first gear and, with a loud blaring of his horn, he stamped on the accelerator and went roaring straight into the heart of the battle-field. Much of the fighting stopped with the warring armies parting like the Dead Sea for Moses as the three television cameras followed the path of the hijacked lorry. This path was spectacularly short however since, after crossing the forecourt of the power station, the lorry ran out of road and broke through a fence, ending up in a ditch where it shed its combined load of Grade B anthracite coal and eleven Welsh flying pickets.

In that instant the television cameras caught the image of a gang of bloodied and blackened miners pulling a laughing Teddy boy out of a pile of coal and hauling him up onto their shoulders victoriously. Huw lifted his arms up towards the sky in triumph as the smoke of battle curled all around him.

That vivid and memorable image was to shoot straight around the world. The media had found a new hero.

LORRY HIJACK: TWELVE FINED.

Wild scenes broke out in a Nottingham court yesterday when pickets from Bont appeared on charges of trespass and theft, according to the Valleys edition of the *South Wales Echo*. The singing of *Cwm Rhondda* and the chanting of 'Here we go!' broke out repeatedly in the public gallery and the magistrate threatened to clear the court three times.

The Bont lodge secretary, Glynmor Jones, took an abandoned lorry and drove it recklessly through police lines without care for life or limb, according to the police solicitor. The others, he alleged, climbed on the hijacked lorry and threw lumps of coal at the police who could have been seriously injured.

Jones, aged 40, of Bont Terrace, in his defence, said that he had only moved the lorry because it seemed to have been badly parked and was stopping the other lorries going into the power station. 'The boys threw coal at the police because they thought they might be short because of the strike,' he added amid further roars of laughter from the public gallery.

Each of the eleven defendants were asked, in their turn, if they had anything to say in their defence. One started to make a speech about Thatcherism but was cut short by the bench. Glynmor Jones' son — known to all as Huw Bungalow and a popular figure in the valleys — could not say anything at all on account of a handicap. 'He must have thought the lorry was a taxi,' said his father.

Each of the defendants was fined £150 each with Jones disqualified from driving for 18 months. Huw Bungalow was given an absolute discharge since the magistrate was satisfied he had been led into all this by his father who 'should have known better than to take a handicapped person onto the picket line'.

After the hearing the court room was mobbed by hundreds of chanting miners and sympathisers. Later, on the court doorstep, the defendants led several choruses of: 'I'd sooner be a picket than a scab.'

That weekend Bont was three overcoats colder than any other village in the Valley. Ice had got into every car engine that chattering, grey Saturday and the terraces were alive with the sounds of cars unable to start.

Even in such freezing conditions, with cold winds trying to

slice the very skin off your cheeks, Gnasher's dole boys and skinheads were out digging in the high frozen tips. But now other villagers had joined them too and they all laboured together in their balaclavas and old army greatcoats. They might have been a medieval army settling down for a long winter siege. Like the echoes of long-forgotten sword fights the scrape of shovels and the rattling of riddles seemed to carry all the louder in the cold stillness of the afternoon.

Gnasher's business was visibly prospering. Even in the few short weeks in which he had been operating he had left the small yard behind the chip shop and moved – lock, stock and barrel – down to the old waste-paper yard next to the river. The yard had an old brick shed with weeds growing out of the disintegrating cement. Its gate had to be lifted off its hinges and opened backwards. The office had a lavatory, however – even if it was always blocked – but it was the old hopper which was the chief attraction since, with a few adjustments, it would shake down 28lb of nutty slack into polythene bags at the rate of five a minute. Gnasher Enterprises Inc. had got itself mechanised.

Later that Saturday afternoon the sun staged an unexpected explosion of brilliance in the enfolding darkness, kissing a few distant peaks in the bend of the Valley and gilding them with a strange golden haze, as if a couple of passing angels had dropped their halos.

Emlyn Kremlin liked to stand in his back bedroom window to watch the last of the day on such afternoons and even his pragmatic soul was stirred by these magical bonfires of light up here in the ancient hills of coal.

But Emlyn was far from a happy man these days. The strike was entering a new and very bitter phase and the boys did not seem at all aware of it. They had come back cock-a-hoop over the lorry hijack, as if that had meant anything at all, except a brief explosion of publicity on television. There had been no substance in it at all, it hadn't made anyone more aware of what the strike had been all about.

Now they were even banging on about picket-line violence in Parliament and the papers were full of it every day as if all this soccer hooligan nonsense had anything at all to do with the issues. All these punch-ups really did was to fudge the real issues and give the government the opportunity to send in the riot police against his boys and beat the hell out of them because they were posing some sort of threat to the public order.

And it was getting worse all the time too. Two men had now died on the picket lines with numerous more being injured and even more being sacked. And for what? Their deaths had not made anyone any more aware of the central issues of mining communities struggling for their very lives.

Only that afternoon Emlyn had been in the Welfare Hall where he had learned that the council surveyors had been up in the roof again and were making noises about closing the Welfare Hall down because of the rotten rafters. The number of young people unemployed in the Valley was rising astronomically – as were the crime figures. The new health figures were little more than a sick joke but who knew anything about them? How did pictures of the boys on the top of a hijacked lorry help any sort of understanding of why people in the Valleys were more likely to die at a younger age than anywhere else in Britain.

Well there were a few signs that all was not lost. Any time now the deputies' union, NACODS, would throw in their hands with the miners and close down the scab pits. General Winter would soon be entering the battlefield. Soon there would be wholesale power cuts. Soon the country would be slithering and sliding to a halt with the white flags of surrender being waved all over Whitehall. All the pits threatened by MacGregor's axe would be saved then and even Milady Iron Drawers would have to give in. Not even she would be able to stand up to General Winter when he mobilised his great armies of snow and ice.

That night the Welfare Hall was throbbing with activity. Daisy and Maggie had invited representatives of women's support groups from all over the country to come to the Valleys for the weekend to meet and get to know one another. And they had come from everywhere too: a laughing, garrulous, slightly intimidating crowd from as far apart as Clydebank, Sheffield, Birmingham and Southampton. They were not necessarily connected with the miners either. Many of them were politicised women – the feminists, activists, anti-this, anti-that – all seeing the coal flag as the one which they could all rally around and get themselves organised.

Tonight a concert and dance had been arranged – with the

Birmingham contingent even bringing their own band – but there was little doubt that Huw Bungalow and Glynmor were the heroes of the hour after the hijacking of the lorry which was still being talked about in the news and even reconstructed the following Sunday, by *The Sunday Times*. Indeed the two hijackers received a standing ovation when they walked into the dance with Glynmor waving back happily. Huw, who had acquired a new purple and pink Edwardian suit, didn't mind the applause either, even if Maggie was less sure of it, holding onto his arm tightly. She took no pride at all in the new media status of her two men. As far as she was concerned they were big enough stars already.

Aunty Phyllis was in the cloakroom taking in the coats that night, but there was nothing for her to do since the Hall had not not escaped the effects of the strike and had run out of coal. Consequently some of the rooms were almost as cold as outside in the Valley. Many of them kept on their coats throughout the evening, even when they were dancing. *Duw*, even the bottles of Newcastle Brown had frozen up and had to be put in the pasty warmer to thaw out. Double glazing, in the form of polythene sheets, had been tacked over all the windows.

Yet, incredibly, everyone was in the highest of spirits, overflowing with laughter and drinking their fill, almost as if they were about to win a war which, in a sense, they believed they were. Everyone got up and danced their socks off – if only to keep warm – while a lot of the girls were comprehensively and warmly groped by the boys, beneath their layers of winter woollies and coats, during the slower numbers.

Even the compère took to the stage wearing a duffel coat with the hood pulled so far over his head you could not actually see his face as he told his jokes into the microphone.

'There was this man came over to the club in Merthyr saying that Maggie Thatcher had a face like a sheep's arse. He was hit sick he was and kicked something terrible. "I didn't know you lot were Tories," he moaned as he lay on the floor. "We're not mun. We're shepherds." '

'What shall we do with Margaret Thatcher, what shall we do ...
Sling her down the nearest shaft ... early in the morning.
What shall we do with that MacGregor. What shall we do ...

Burn the bastard burn ... early in the morning.'

Later some records were put on and Maggie smooched with Glynmor as Stevie Wonder sang about how he had just called to say I love you. Later still they all danced around the floor singing 'I'd sooner be a picket than a scab'. Maggie, in particular, enjoyed it all, savouring the Welsh spirit of *gwerin*, the community of the common folk. It was this *gwerin* for which they had all been fighting. And its heart was beating still. Maggie Thatcher and the combined forces of Whitehall and the N.C.B. had brought them all together. Times were a-changing, aye, but the Welsh spirit of *gwerin* would live for ever.

Downstairs in the bar, Dibber Williams was sitting with a group at a table when he suddenly started swallowing and breathing hard through his nose. 'I shouldn't think ... ' was about all he said when his belly gave a sudden heave and he brought up a thick mouthful of blood which went slapping onto the aluminium ash-tray and around the beer glasses on the table.

The boys, accustomed to Dibber and his habit of throwing up everywhere, were already moving away from their seats when his belly heaved again and more blood came pouring out of his nose and mouth. He looked at the rich blood foaming around the half-finished pints on the table and up at the faces all around staring at him. He could feel his underpants going wet and warm too. He reached his hands down between his legs finding his fingers going red and sticky before looking up again at the alarmed faces all around.

He was still sitting there and trying to say something but, instead of words, more blood came mumbling out of his mouth. What he couldn't understand was how completely peaceful he felt sitting there coughing up all this blood. It was all so silent too in the rising panic all around. People were clearly talking and shouting. But their words seemed like those distant underwater sonar pings you always heard in those submarine films on television.

He sniffed a sort of smile and looked down at the bloodied table in front of him. He could see everything in oddly clear detail. There was a crack in his pint glass. You could get germs from cracks in glasses, he had been told and he wondered if he could take it back and claim a fresh pint in a *proper* glass. A photograph of a semi-naked nude sat on one of the beer mats; he would have liked to have had a bit of a rub with her – blood or no blood.

'I'm sorry about this boys,' he said.

Dan Box was on the telephone dialling the new emergency number in Pontypridd. After two engaged tones and a wrong number, he learned that both ambulances were out in the neighbouring Valleys. He rang the local doctor's number only to be referred, via an answering service, back to Pontypridd who said they would try and raise another ambulance from Cardiff.

The boys stretched Dibber out on one of the seats but he still continued to throw up blood. 'Sorry about the mess,' he said again, his face as white as a bottle of milk. And then, after bringing up another mouthful, he shook visibly and died.

Word of the tragedy spread quickly through the Hall. It was Emlyn who took to the stage and brought the concert to an abrupt end. 'One of our miners has just died of a burst ulcer in the bar,' he said. 'I think it would be fitting if we just left the dance right here. But stay by all means. We're still waiting for the ambulance.'

Glynmor swallowed and looked very old indeed as he looked at Maggie.

'It was Dibber I think,' she said soft. 'I heard them saying by the bar.'

'But he wasn't old was he? He wasn't forty yet?'

Dibber eh? Glynmor reached out and took hold of Maggie's hand. He had gone to school with Dibber, once had a fight with him over a tanner. Only that week they had been picketing together in the Trent Valley. They had shared a sausage roll for breakfast one morning and then he'd been complaining how it gave him indigestion. So now he was dead.

He looked down at Maggie's hand, turning it over and over. How would it have been if his beloved Maggie had died instead. How could he ever take hold of this hand and feel it cold and without life. But it didn't look as though it was going to be long before they were all dead and flung down the shaft of that dead coal mine.

He looked up and saw that Huw was watching him closely

and their eyes held one another's for a few moments. There was something, a certain air in those big black eyes that he was going to carry with him for a long, long time. He didn't know what it was. They weren't so much big black eyes as deep pools of sorrow – there was clear understanding in them but a melancholy too. It was the melancholy perhaps of the prophet who told the truth ceaselessly but knew in his heart that no one was going to listen to his words in the end. The people would only ever finally listen when it was too late. The days of *gwerin* are coming to an end, those eyes seemed to say. Keep the faith since you are now riding into the valley of the shadow of death. Every heart will soon burst with pain. Prepare for the great lament.

An ambulance finally arrived from Cardiff – to a chorus of boos and catcalls – a full hour and a half after Dibber had died.

Chapter Twenty-Four

Dibber's death took a lot exuberance out of the boys. All that week, right up to the time of his cremation at Glyntaf the following Saturday, an increasing number of them were not turning up for picket duty. Some had been spotted in different places doing various little hobbles like house painting or roof repairing.

Glynmor, however, was more committed to the cause of the strike and, implicitly, of the Valley than ever. He was full of the most bitter thunder at the manner of Dibber's death. The doctor had only ever told Dibber that the reason for his continual vomiting was that he drank too much booze. But then, when blood was spouting from every part of him, the ambulance took nearly three hours to arrive after Dan Box's first telephone call. Somehow, Glynmor could not quite see anything like that happening in the corridors of Whitehall or even in the offices of the N.C.B.

Emlyn had acquired some World Health reports on the Valleys which he had passed on to Glynmor. And the grimmest reading they made too. The Valleys had the highest premature death rate in Europe: cancer, heart attacks and respiratory diseases from lung infections caught down the mines were the main illnesses. The University of Southampton's *Atlas of Mortality* actually put the Valleys bottom of the table. The classic diseases of poverty like malnutrition from poor diet and arthritis from the damp were also cropping up in every corner of the Valleys. Indeed, with its depressed economy, high unemployment and poor housing, there was poverty in abundance.

Hypertension also contributed to the appalling death rate. Here in the valleys some 10,000 a year were dying of heart attacks – the equivalent of a jumbo jet crashing into an airport every two weeks. Many thought an impending heart attack was just indigestion and, when they did realise what it was, it took an average of five hours to get to hospital.

But, even if a thousand reports had listed the Valleys as being bottom of everything in the world, there was little Glynmor could do about it. Oh, he could do a poor man's Hamlet, raging and foaming at the evil winds gusting down the Valley slopes but almost a greater problem was that no one cared to listen to anything serious at all. They loved the fantasy worlds of bingo and one-armed bandits and the totes. They liked to watch the soap operas and game shows on the television. They liked to drink and dance. They liked to do almost anything but *think* about the extreme peril that their apathy and lethargy was going to bring to their children. Reports by the World Health Organisation which showed the Valleys as being bottom of the league were clearly drawn up by men who hated the Welsh. When they spoke of malnutrition they were clearly just far-back snobs who had something against hamburger and chips. And when did a bit of damp harm anyone? *Duw*, we've got a few problems here like, but nothing that's worth getting crazy about.

One night Glynmor was sitting at home with his feet up on the mantelpiece when he announced to Maggie that he might have a go at Parliament. Wasn't that where the real power to change lay?

'I shouldn't think that place could change anything,' thought Maggie. 'It's too far away for one thing. Anyway you couldn't go to Parliament. You'd have to stop swearing and telling all your dirty stories if you went there and I don't see you doing that.'

'I wouldn't tell any dirty stories if you must know. I'd get up there and tell them the terrible story of the Valleys. I'd tell them what Kinnock should be telling them if he wasn't hiding away somewhere, hoping this strike would somehow go away in case it effected his election chances. There'd be no mincing of words with me.'

'No, I don't suppose there would. You wouldn't start by telling them the one about the queer that got raped by the gorilla would you?'

'No, I would not. I'd tell them about Dibber dying years

before his time. I'd tell them about teenagers rotting in prisons. I'd tell them how you can't get an ambulance or a fucking doctor when you need one.'

'All right don't take it out on me. There's no point in shouting at me now is there? Go and make me a cup of tea if you want to do something.'

'There you are. You're as bad as the rest of them.'

Such arguments were almost everywhere that week. The lodge meeting on Sunday morning was a bad-tempered affair too with Emlyn only just managing to keep control. Nothing at all seemed to be going right for the miners. Following repeated collisions with the High Court over a refusal to pay a £200,000 fine the N.U.M. had been stripped of three of its trustees and its funds handed over to a receiver. Scargill had spoken out against 'this unprecedented attack on the trade union movement' and promised that the miners were going forward to the 'greatest victory in history'. But, somehow, even his most committed supporters were beginning to have their doubts. That very day, even the *Sunday Mirror* had likened the miners' actions to the Charge of the Light Brigade.

Worse still, there had been none of the promised power cuts yet and the miners were banking on them to exert the same leverage that had helped to topple Heath's government in 1972. Even worse than that, the N.U.M. had swiftly transferred all its funds to Luxembourg, meaning that the union no longer had any immediate cash to give the boys their bit of daily picket money. And, as if this wasn't enough for any one lodge of striking miners, the women's support group was on at them too, coming to their Sunday morning meetings and urging them to get *more* militant.

Ever since the start of the strike, the Bont lodge had been careful to see that complete safety cover was maintained in the mine. Where necessary, one or two members were getting paid the odd shift to co-operate with the NACODS men by helping to install pumps in flooded shafts or shoring up roofs threatened by a new squeeze.

Now the women – with Daisy in particular making the most noise – were arguing in the meetings that the boys should picket out NACODS from this and other mines, thus withdrawing safety cover altogether. 'If those NACODS bastards won't come out and help you then you've got to put the boot into them an' get them out yourselves,' was the way Daisy put it.

In their present mood – and with so little going right for them – the men bitterly resented such advice and there was lots of 'For fuck's sake, woman, shut your gob will you?'

Or there was Tom the Nutter's pungent: 'Haven't you got any Sunday dinner to cook?'

'No, I haven't,' said Daisy, drawing herself up to her full height like an embattled budgie. 'Those days are over for all us women in case you haven't heard. Oh aye you can moan and shout, but they're over. And there's no slippers warming for you by the fire either. We're all men now an' when we're telling you to picket out NACODS you can't stand it ... you can't stand it 'cos it's the women telling you to be bigger men than you are.'

'For fuck's sake, woman, give it a rest will you? Mr Chairman, do we have to have these women in here?'

'I'm afraid so,' said Emlyn. 'There's no slippers warming for anyone at home any longer. Let's face it. There's no damned fire either.'

Emlyn was not at all happy about withdrawing safety cover from the pit, since it would certainly never open again in the event of fire, flood or major squeeze. But, as was usual with anything he was not sure about, he managed to change the subject of debate without anyone ever actually voting on it: his version of democracy.

They discussed various new initiatives for fund-raising – 'a sponsored skateboard ride down the motorway' was one suggestion – when Emlyn banged the table for order and drew himself up to full height saying that he had an important announcement which he had been keeping until last. 'Yesterday,' he began in a sonorous tone, 'I was approached by a director who wants to make a film about us for Channel Four. What we now have to decide is if we ourselves want him to.'

General cries of 'Aye' and 'Not fucking likely'.

'But, remember now, if you say "Yes" he's going to be with us night and day. He will be out picketing with us and around here, in our spare time, in the Hall. In the end we might not like what he says but I think what we're going to have to decide now is if we are going to take a chance on that. He's outside now and waiting to speak to us. So, boys, what's your pleasure?'

'Why bother with 'em? They're shitting on us every day they are. Even the *Mirror*'s gone against us.'

'Daisy here is saying she'll only be in it if she can play the part of Samantha Fox.'

'She'll have to grow bigger tits first.'

'Do you think you could leave my tits out of this just for once?'

'Are they offering to pay us any ackers for this film?'

Glynmor, who had been uncharacteristically silent for all of the meeting, spoke out strongly in favour of the move.

'We're not going to win this strike through force, Mr Chairman,' he argued. 'If we're going to win anything at all it's going to be public sympathy, won through the media, with the true facts of our case. We've got to get our case over in any way we can and, say what you like, the media is a powerful argument. I say we should welcome this opportunity with open arms. At least let's listen to him.'

'If we agree to this film, Mr Chairman, do you think we could also agree to keep Glynmor out of it so the rest of us would have a chance to say something?'

'I would think the chances of that are nil,' said Emlyn. 'Worse than nil in fact.'

And with that he introduced Jack Young, who walked into the room accompanied by his female production assistant. The would-be director was small and intense wearing a dark, scruffy suit making him look rather more like a bank clerk than a trendy film-maker for Channel Four. He also kept looking down at the floor, giving him the slightly shifty air of a second-hand car dealer, though he addressed the lodge loudly and directly enough.

'Let me say from the outset that I've never believed in balance in films. Balance is always banal, often flat. A film-maker should be brave and audacious – not just stand behind the police lines and accept whatever the police tell them. So I'm proposing a film weighted in your favour, giving your point of view alone and to hell with the police and the coal board. We're all in the business of propaganda so, if you could do with a lively and powerful piece of propaganda, I'm your man.'

As he continued speaking a few of the boys were gazing at his production assistant, sitting on the stage next to him, not the least because she was wearing a sixties' mini-skirt and kept crossing and uncrossing her legs. She also had huge ear-rings which somehow matched her enormous knockers. Her air of exotic perculiarity was also heightened by her large red spectacles, the stop-watch around her neck and clip-board in hand. Bridget Danser was her name, it seemed.

'Bont is an ideal place to make a film like this not only because of its importance in the social history of South Wales but because there are also lots of interesting characters in this lodge like Huw Bungalow and his father Glynmor.'

Jack did not quite understand the reason for all the moans and groans at this point.

'We would also want to focus on the work of the women's group and, of course, Bont's history when it became known throughout the land as Little Moscow. There would be some sort of facility fee – but not a lot – paid into your strike fund. But I need hardly tell you that, to pay for such exposure on television – even if it were possible – would cost millions.'

The two of them were invited to leave the room and, after a brief discussion, in which no one had any real objection, they voted, almost unanimously, to allow the cameras into their midst. Only Maggie and, surprisingly, Emlyn voted against.

The following Wednesday a snow shower fell on Bont, putting thick, white carpets on the slate roofs and pigeon coops, edging the walls and icing the fences, making them unusually fluffy and incandescent. The sun rose over the motionless ducks on the cold reservoir and hammered down on the Valley walls, which glittered cold as if dusted with powdered diamonds. The pointed daggers of icicles hung off the eaves of the terraces as kids went out on sledges and shrieked with delight as they caroomed down the tump. All along the railway track there were frozen pools, many with bright cobwebs of frozen ice in them where boots had walked. The triangular footprints of birds and the hoofprints of sheep lightly marked the snow too and the streams, which normally gurgled out of the tips, froze up into many still and silent tongues. Down near the pit only the odd iron dram, poking up from beneath the white carpet, gave any sign of the debris that was always scattered around the

411

washery. even the shattered old mine itself looked spruce and tidy with snow banked up against the wheelhouse and just the wheel poking up, like some giant spindle which had lost its way in a blizzard.

Down by the river a grey van pulled up near the bridge and the television crew were busy mounting their cameras as they took a series of establishing shots of the Valley.

Just out of the range of the camera Huw Bungalow was busy pushing a supermarket trolley up a slope. When he stopped to look around this kingdom of snow, the very whiteness of the surrounding landscape caught in his eyes like white flames flickering deep inside black mines. He loved the purity of the snow and it made him full of joy. Today he was doing work of sorts, taking an urn of tea to the people as they laboured, digging coal out of the glacier tips, their working holes a surrealist study in black mouths on a white canvas.

Everyone stopped and smiled when Huw called at their holes, their cheeks ruddy and their breath pluming as they held the plastic cup in both hands, alternately blowing and sipping on the hot tea. Sometimes he brought sandwiches from the soup kitchen – made up by the women's group in the mornings – though today the bread had inexplicably failed to arrive so the coal pickers had to make do with a couple of biscuits instead.

These days the Aberklondyke was far from the exclusive reserve of Gnasher and his skinheads. By this time in winter, almost everyone had run out of fuel and anyone who could tell one end of a shovel from the other was out digging and riddling in their little holes. In one run Huw could do anything up to two hundred cups of tea, handing over his cups to everyone from Mrs Pritchard from next door but one to some of the striking miners themselves. If not away picketing, many had been sent out by their cold wives to keep in their hand at digging out coal by bringing home a few grateful.

Almost anything that could provide some sort of warmth was ripped apart and plundered. Old railway sleepers were prised up and sawn to bits. Whole sections of fence disappeared overnight. Wooden cable wheels from the pit were jemmied apart. Fortunately there were no trees to be cut down since the Valley had already been stripped of all of them during a shortage of pit props in the Second World War. Very unofficial estimates were that half the electricity coming into the village was now going through an illegal spare meter. *The man from the electricity board will call at your inconvenience.*

But here, out on these glacial slopes, was where the real source of warmth was – as it had been for over a hundred years now – in the coal on the tips; in the black sunlight of an antediluvian forest.

Down in Gnasher's yard they were having trouble with the machinery. The gaffer had just acquired a third-hand JCB to load the coal into the hopper and, it being so cold, the tractor was refusing to load the coal into anything. To get it started they had to tow it with a lorry but the trouble was that the lorry wasn't very keen on starting either. After a lot of cussing and aimless kicks into lifeless carburettors they managed to borrow Stan Swansea's big old Granada to give the lorry a pull which, in its turn, then gave the tractor a pull. At one stage, there was a whole cavalcade of clapped-out vehicles belching black puffs of exhaust smoke as they stuttered, stopped and started up and down the road next to the river.

Gnasher actually caught the television cameras trying to film his worn-out machinery and came out waving his fist and telling them to fuck off out of it. He didn't wany any television cameras poking their noses into his business which by now was making him a small, if undisclosed, fortune. The yard, with the skinheads still working at a level almost unknown in the Valley, had stockpiled a small mountain of valuable coal. And now they were delivering bags of coal – at such handsome prices they would even have delighted the coal barons of old – to shops and garages throughout the five Valleys.

Indeed there was so much coal going out of the yard that the Bont lodge had sent over an official delegation to find out where all the coal was coming from and if it had anything to do with scab labour – or, perhaps, coming in from those Communist scabs in Poland. On being reassured that it was all being picked out of the tips by the dole boys, the delegation reported back that there seemed nothing to object to.

Had they discovered the real commercial secrets of Gnasher Enterprises Inc. they probably would have found much to object to. His army of shovellers was now taking so much speed that Cocoa was having to make a regular weekly trip down to Cardiff to get fresh supplies from The Man.

Then one morning old Guto – who had been watching the business boom along with everyone else – had wandered into the yard to tell Gnasher of a large outcrop of coal he knew about which was just sitting there waiting to be taken away. In return for a slice of the action Guto had offered to organise the mining of the coal and, after a great deal of hesitation, Gnasher had agreed.

Then the pair of them had gone down to the little-known old mine working opposite the Banana Tip which had once very nearly become Guto's final resting place. After pushing away a pile of rocks and taking him a hundred yards or so into the old roadway, Guto showed Gnasher a three foot deep seam of the finest anthracite. They decided there and then that it would be best if they worked the face and carted the coal away by night, to avoid any aggravation from the N.C.B. or the striking miners. Then they could pretend that they were still just picking coal from the tip during the day.

As it happened the gossips began working overtime when they saw Gnasher smoking cigars and taking the odd swig of brandy with Guto. Who could want anything to do with the smelly old git? But they never even started to even suspect the real truth of the matter. Daisy, for the first time ever, was actually going down to the yard and borrowing money off her son. She always, somehow, forgot to pay it back and, somehow, he never seemed to care.

By early afternoon, Huw had emptied his tea urn and was pushing his trolley back along the path next to the railway line. The dying sun had now given the Valley a curious lop-sided look, since it had melted all the snow on the eastern side so that the dead gorse mixed with the drifting slush to make huge brown whorls. Yet the snow on the western side, untouched by the sun, had stayed deep and firm so it was as if the twinkling river had become the junction for two separate countries each with their own different climates; one a shapeless brown and the other as white as a virgin bride walking up the aisle.

Huw left his trolley outside Gnasher's yard and went inside to play with the guard dog and give him a biscuit. Apart from Gnasher, Huw was one of the few who could handle the dog to the degree that, if Gnasher wasn't around, even the skinheads were too afraid to go into the yard and they would fetch Huw to come and calm the slavering beast down.

After a little chat with the dog Huw went over to stand with the blackened skinheads as they stood around bagging coal in the hopper. *Chug, chug, chug* went the conveyor belt. *Tinkle, tinkle, tinkle* went the coal inside the hopper. *Chug, chug, chug, tinkle, tinkle, tinkle.* Down the conveyor belt the coal tumbled, falling into the polythene bag on the weighting scales then being stacked in readiness for a big order from Penrhos. *Chug, chug, chug – tinkle, tinkle, tinkle.*

The skinheads were all pleased to see Huw, going over to him and poking him playfully. One tried to get him to bag some coal but he would have none of that since it might mess up his suit. Huw pointed at some stones on the conveyor belt and shook his finger in gentle admonition. The jokes and laughter hung over the yard in a bright ring of warmth as the sun bowed out of the Valley before the long cold shadows of darkness moved in. *Chug, chug, chug – tinkle, tinkle, tinkle.*

The long necklaces of street lamps were switched on throughout the Valley as the darkness thickened, their bulbs glowing fierce on the white roofs of the terraces and piles of dirty slush in the gutters. Houses and streets alike turned the same dark tone of orange. The last coach from Cardiff came whining up the surly slopes, its huge tyres crunching into the blackened piles of snow, its gears droning lower as it slithered and struggled to keep its footing.

A dog was howling miserably as the bus dropped its remaining passengers outside the Welfare Hall to pick their shivering way home up the slopes. Only the chip shop was still open, the smell of frying drifting out into the orange darkness and across the Valley whose snowy summits were still visible in the murk, high and poised, like an avalanche ready to fall.

'*Duw*, I do feel like that brass monkey out looking for a welder,' Ivor Llewelyn told Tony Chef as they both shuffled around together on the bus stop waiting for the bus to turn around.

'Aye. Here's weather for you init? Nasty I do call this. How long'll it last do you reckon?'

'Well it couldn't last long enough for the boys on strike could it?'

'The sooner it lifts the better I say. My whole family is under the doctor they are. Aye. The whole bloody lot of 'em.'

*

Deep in the bowels of the Hall, Maggie and Daisy were the only ones left in the soup kitchen, having a laugh and sharing a cigarette as they sat together on the piled sacks of potatoes. Just next to them was a weighing scale surrounded by small stacks of sugar, corned beef and boxes of butter. Behind them was a mountain of pasta and turtle meat with a poster of Margaret Thatcher pinned to the wall. 'Let them eat turtle meat,' said a bubble coming out of her mouth.

'I still think we should picket the pit,' said Daisy. 'We should show a lead to the rest of the women in the country.'

'The men are worried about losing safety. They do say a flood would finish the pit.'

'Well, the men would wouldn't they? That's men for you that is. But the snow's here now so we really should be thinking about a quick end to it all. If all the women got off their fannies an' took out those NACODS bastards it would soon be all over bar the shouting.'

'There's no reason why we should wait for the men, of course.'

'No reason at all. It's what I've always said. If we'd been running this strike it would have been all over in a week.'

They passed their cigarette back and forth as they spoke, with grubby hands that might just have finished working a shift down on the face. Their fingers were ripped and torn from weighing and bagging the potatoes; their very arms ached from heaving all the sacks around. But in an odd sort of way they were proud of their dirtiness; it had always been a traditional emblem of work in the Valley and, during the day, they hardly ever washed at all.

'Ah, there you are. I've been looking all over for you.'

The girls both looked up as Bridget, the production assistant, walked into the soup kitchen. 'I've just had Jack on the 'phone,' she said as she came over and stood in front of them. 'There's been some awful fighting with the police again today in Nottingham. Eggey an' Stan Box have been hurt and they've been taken to hospital. Five have been arrested too. Don't be alarmed. Glynmor's all right.'

'He would be, wouldn't he?' Daisy said without rancour. 'Glynmor is better than Arthur Scargill for walking on water.'

'When're they coming home then?' Maggie asked. 'Have you heard?'

'Tonight. They had such a bad time with the police they're coming back tonight. Jack was wondering if we can use tomorrow to film the women at work in the soup kitchen. Preparing for Christmas and all that.'

'We've no objection. There's lots we've got to do at the moment,' said Maggie. 'How many injured in all?'

'What Jack had in mind,' Bridget went on undeterred, 'was to show you all preparing for Christmas, struggling to feed a family of five with just one small chicken. You know the kind of thing.'

'But we've got plenty of food. That's been the great success of the soup kitchen. People have helped us marvellous.'

Bridget chose to ignore this.

'Then he heard that the women were threatening to picket someone's house if the electricity board called to cut off the supply. We'd like to put some women around a miner's house. And Jack asks that they don't have their hair done either. Just for them to picket the house as they are in their ordinary clothes and with their hair untidy. They've started putting their best on again and that really pisses Jack off that does. Jack says you can't show a community at war when they're going about the place all toffed all the time. Anyway, he thought the picketing of the house would make a good sequence.'

'It would be good all right,' Maggie agreed. 'Except it hasn't happened. The electricity bill was paid after a whip round.'

'It's not so much what's happened that Jack's interested in as – how can you say? – what *might* happen, or could have happened, if the circumstances had been different.'

Maggie looked at Daisy and wrinkled up her nose in a sort of question mark. This Jack wasn't making too much sense and more than a few of the women were beginning to wonder aloud if they hadn't made a mistake by allowing him into their midst.

'Do you have any more information on the injured?' asked Daisy.

'Oh and there is one aspect of the film that Jack is very worried about, Maggie, and that is your son Huw.'

'What about him?'

'Jack's a bit put out that Huw does not go out picketing any more. In his own way Huw has become famous, you see,

417

and Jack thinks it's very important to have him in the film. In fact Huw is one of the main reasons why Jack picked Bont in the first place.'

So that was it, thought Maggie. They just thought of him as a character in a film. Or as some kind of freak show.

'I'm very sorry I must say,' she said, not looking sorry in the slightest. 'But I don't force Huw to do anything. He took one look at the cameras in the bus that morning and went straight home. He may look do-lally but he knows what he doesn't like and anything to do with television is one of them.'

Bridget frowned, making her huge spectacles rise up on her nose. How could anyone possibly object to anything to do with television, the great new school of the masses? 'But just *what* is it that he doesn't like?'

'I'm sorry but I just can't tell you 'cos I don't know myself. All I do know is that he now likes taking the tea out to the people picking coal. And he spends a lot of time here with us girls. I prefer him here with us if you must know. It's getting more and more violent on those picket lines it is. We're seeing it get worse and worse on the tele every day now aren't we?'

'Could we film Huw here in the soup kitchen then? Or even out in the snow taking the tea around?'

'Well, let's put it like this. You can *try*. But, ever since he's been a little *dwt*, Huw would never have anything to do with television. He wouldn't even have it in the house – kept putting it out with the milk bottles he did an', one day, it was pinched. Honest. Anything to do with television always gives him a bad belly. I'm not joking either. So you'll have to do what you can an' I won't be saying anything one way or another. All I want is for him to be happy. It's just the way it is with him.'

'What sort of money do you get for doing this?' Daisy asked Bridget. 'Tidy screw is it?'

There was more than a hint of exasperation in her voice.

When the charabanc came back to the Hall that night Maggie was out on the pavement waiting. It soon became clear that the boys had been given a right old hammering. Some came limping off the bus, others had their arms in slings. Even Glynmor had a beautiful black eye and a cut down the side of his left cheek.

'Hello, lovely,' said Maggie, with a bit of a smile. 'Run

into a door again have you? You should open 'em first.'

Maggie could feel Glynmor's arm stiffen with anger. 'Oh let's go home straight,' she said, knowing the signs. 'I've got a few bottles in and that thumb of yours needs sorting out quick by the look of you.'

Glynmor nodded and she could feel his arm relaxing again as they walked back to the house in silence. When he was in this kind of mood he was best left alone. He would tell her all about it in his own time.

When they got indoors they found Huw, in his pyjamas, busy painting. Glynmor went over to him and gave him a hug. 'We're missing you awful bad out there butty,' he said, ruffling Huw's hair with his hand. 'The police are hitting us sick. But they never laid a finger on us when you were around, did they? All the boys have been asking after you, wanting to know when you're coming out with us again.'

Huw reached up and finger-tipped his father's black eye and cut.

'Every move we make they're 'aving us. They've got riot shields, truncheons, CS gas, rubber bullets. An' all we've got on our side is snowballs. Aye. Bloody snowballs. You can't even find a decent rock to fling in all this snow. They've sent all the legions of hell against us miners who only want to talk to someone; talk to anyone about the death of their village. Crazy init? Aye, Huw boy. It's a crazy bad world you've been born into all right.'

Huw, clearly concerned about the injuries, wiped his fingers across his father's eyebrows again. He just kept bringing his face closer too, his throat swallowing hard as he examined every cut and scar. There was a strange, naked display of emotion going on between them and Maggie had to look away.

'But don't worry my butty. I wouldn't take you out with us now. Not even if you wanted to go I wouldn't. It's getting too tough for man and beast now, it's the miners they want bad.' He paused and kissed Huw lightly on the nose. 'What're you painting this time anyway?'

They both walked over to the easel and it was Maggie who spoke. 'He's been at it for a few days I can't make it out. It's not one of his happy ones that's for certain. It's something dark he's painting – just like that bastard coal.'

Glynmor looked up from the painting with a raised

eyebrow. It wasn't often that he ever heard her use bad language.

'How can something that's so dead cause so much trouble?' she asked. 'Here you are out fighting pitched battles with the police. And for what? Eh? For what? Just 'cos you want to keep going miles down into the earth to keep digging that bastard coal. Where's the sense in that for God's sake? I don't understand anything sometimes … nothing … oh come on, let's go to bed. My thumb's beginning to hurt too.'

After they'd put Huw to bed they undressed quickly, but they were in such a state of brittle anxiety their bodies were as taut as violin strings. Bumping and banging into one another beneath the sheets. It was hopeless it was. You would swear they had never done it before. They both wanted to be active and passive at the same time. One wanted to go one way and the other wanted to go in another.

There was no real reason for all this honeymoon fumbling, of course, but now they were almost acting like the last lovers in the world, with only their love to redeem themselves before they were hung at dawn. They were so desperately anxious to make it all right it was all going wrong.

He finally lay back on his side of the bed looking up at the ceiling. 'We should have had a drink or two maybe,' he said. 'I'm wound up tighter than a bastard cuckoo clock and that's a fact.'

'You're wound up? You've got me jumping about like a cat on a hot tin roof. Better have a fag. I've got a couple around here somewhere.'

'You had any good parties while I've been away?'

'Any good parties? What kind of question is that?'

'It's a nothing question. I'm just trying to calm down I am.'

'Since when did nothing questions calm you down?'

As they spoke the sheets slipped off her long, spreadeagled legs as she leaned sideways rummaging in her jacket pocket on the floor, making her pelvis rise up with her pudenda invitingly framed by the street lamplight pouring through the white gauze curtains.

'Just hold it like that,' he said wriggling down into the bed and holding her buttocks on either side as he put his tongue into her barbed curly hairs and began to lick her softly.

'I can't hold it just like that,' she said, holding up the whole weight of her body on one arm. 'Lemme get back into bed will you?'

She managed to get back and, as he continued licking her out, let the palms of her hands lie on the back of her head with her eyes closed. The more his tongue kept working in and out of her, the more relaxed waves kept breaking inside her and she was almost purring loud like a contented, warm cat. She thought of her day and of her work and how the women were now trying to make sure that every striking family had a turkey each for Christmas. Daisy had to ring up Elizabeth Taylor that week as well, to see if she would come up with some cash. That one had a tidy bit in the bank that was for sure. Then she remembered how she had stood with Daisy that afternoon admiring the sun on the snow and how they'd had that delicious warm cup of tea together as they wondered aloud what the pickets had been getting up to.

And then … and then … she felt nothing much at all – just a lovely warm smile all over, as all her worries and fears dribbled out between legs with her going down on him now, taking her husband into her mouth, sucking and licking his helmet, snorting softly through her nostrils as she moved about on her knees keeping a warm tight purchase on this which was part of her too.

His mind was still crowded with the yelling of pickets and the thundering charge of the police horses and the black flashes of painful truncheons as the ship of his body rose and fell on the warm, right anchor of his wife's mouth. All the while his belly kept sucking gallons of blood in on itself as his heart pounded like a man driven by a terrible obsession.

'Run Glynmor,' Tom the Nutter was shouting. 'Run, mun.' He was looking one way when a police horse came pounding past on the other with a truncheon smacking against his hip, causing his whole body to be temporarily paralysed. Unable to move he just stood there uselessly when he caught another blow just above the eye and, just swaying around, he was then flung forward by a blow on his shoulder that he had not even seen coming.

Next he was up on all fours, the police horses charging all around but, with his vision all runny, able only to see one thing: the lens of Jack Young's television camera trained straight at him.

She could feel that he was going to come soon and trailed

her wet tongue up his belly, rolling his body over on top of hers and putting him inside her, believing that this was the way that the sacrament of love should always end: unified and as one, as close together as possible.

He went up and down into her, his hands feeling the marble smoothness of her lovely body, his wet lips kissing the side of her neck and her shoulder-blades, still riding up and down into her when his mind was also cleared of the day's violence and a liquid warmth spread out to every part of his body as sunshine came dancing down the Valley slopes with him, Maggie and Huw walking together along the path next to the river, finally coming out at the top of the reservoir where the still surface of the water was only broken by the jumping of the odd trout.

His fingers spread out and he stiffened a little before the whole loveliness of the day liquefied together and he poured it all into her – all! – coming again and again with his hips bucking softly as he pumped her full of his sunshine, happiness and love.

'How's your thumb feeling now then?' she asked when he rolled off her.

'Fine. It's just fine.'

'Well, that's all right then init?'

The very next day, General Winter sounded the retreat and withdrew his armies of ice and snow. Sunshine powered down the Valley slopes so hard it was as if it was the height of the summer and not the few weeks before Christmas. In every corner there was the continual drip and trickle of thawing ice with patches of the grassy slopes steaming like Turkish baths. It was *not* the kind of weather the striking miners had been hoping for.

On a national level the leader of the Labour Party, Neil Kinnock, accused the miners' leaders of wanting a 'glorious defeat' and his deputy Roy Hattersley again called on the N.U.M. leaders to ballot their members about the strike. Later, on a trip to Russia, Neil Kinnock had said that Press reports of starving miners being beaten by the police had been exaggerated. 'I told them that while enduring very great hardship there was no hunger, and that reports on that scale were somewhat misleading.'

On a local level Eggey James was let home to Bont after treatment for concussion but Stan Box had been detained in a Nottingham hospital with a fractured arm and leg. Had it not been for his bad leg he would have been out in a winky since lying there in the heart of scabland wasn't doing his morale any good at all. Eleven of the boys had been fined by the magistrates on a variety of offences, ranging from breach of the peace to obstruction of the highway and trampling on winter barley. All had refused to pay but had not been locked up since the Bont lodge paid their fines for them.

Other bits of news of the day were that the remaining Pryce woman in the big house on the hill had been put under the doctor with a touch of pneumonia so her sister had returned from Upper Boat to nurse her; Gnasher and his new partner, Guto, were making so much money from the coal yard they had bought a second-hand lorry; and Tony Chef's son, Peter, had written to the Queen in Buckingham Palace complaining that his Mam and Dad were always picking on him.

But, in other ways, the village was much as it had been the week before – and the week before that. Whole armies were still drifting out each morning to pick coal from the tips; the women's group was still collecting money for turkeys and toys for Christmas; the committee chairman, Max Million, was still worrying about the rotten rafters in the Welfare Hall and Aunty Phyllis was still relating the gossip to Enid over the fence.

With the day being so mild the old-timers found they could sit out on the bench near the clock again where they liked to jaw and drink rough cider.

'I'll be glad when this strike is over so I can get my free coal again,' Idris said.

'I didn't know you got free coal,' Curly replied. 'How come you get free coal when I don't? Eh? How come?'

'What're you asking me for? You were down the hole as well as I was. Perhaps you didn't fill in the right form when you retired?'

'They said I wasn't 'legible with my two brothers still working down there an' all.'

'Well there you are then.' Idris held his brown cider bottle up to the sky to see how much was left in it. 'That's why you don't get free coal. Stands to reason donit?'

'But if you got it I should have got it. Why should I stay

cold when you're sitting in the bastard warmth?'

'I don't stay warm mun. I do sell the coal to that Therese Williams. She did give me twenty pounds for it. It's the money I miss, not the coal.'

'Well don't that beat all? Don't that beat bastard all? It's because of grabbing bastards like you the coal industry is wanged out.'

'How do you work that out? I didn't do nothing.'

'If it weren't for grabbing bastards like you that Arthur Scargill wouldn't have to pull all the boys out on strike.'

'How much cider have you been drinking? It's only twenty pounds' worth of coal mun.'

'Oh aye. That's what they all say. That's what they all fucking say init? Twenty pounds here an' twenty pound there. Next thing it's a 'undred pound here an' a 'undred pound there. Then it's a million pound here an' a million pound there. That's why the Board has lost all its money an' they're closing all the pits 'cos piss brains like you have made off with all the money.'

'Twenty pound. Who's worried about twenty pound?'

'Twenty pound is a tidy lot if you haven't got it. A very tidy lot. Look at that pit. Just look at it. Stinking dirty it is. If the manager had that twenty pound spare he might have painted it.'

'I don't see that would make any difference.'

'No, you wouldn't, would you? Selfish, thieving bastards like you wouldn't would they? They're too busy thieving to think. That's always been the trouble with brains made of piss. That's the trouble with this fucking Valley come to that. Every bastard going around the bastard place pinching every bastard thing that moves. I've even got to sit out the back watching my clothes after they've been washed in case some bastard pinches them. It makes me bastard sick it do. Now there's you thieving off the Board and those boys will be out on strike for years and their families starving to death. And for why? Shurrup mun. I'll tell you for why. 'Cos grabbing bastards like you go out an' sell their free coal for twenty pounds. It's robbing bastards like *you* that I blame for this strike.'

A short silence.

'The cider has all gone in this bottle,' Idris announced. 'I s'pose now you're going to say it's my turn to buy one.'

'I wouldn't take a drink off a thieving bastard like you,' Curly spluttered in self-righteous outrage as he stood up dusting his hands together. 'And I'm going to sit on that seat down by the bus shelter as well.'

'Suit yourself.'

Emlyn kicked the door open with his foot and walked into the committee room carrying a tray of twelve foaming pints of beer. The boys were already sitting around the committee table, chatting and smoking cigarettes as Emlyn handed out a pint each to Dai Scaggs, Tom the Nutter, Danny Kettle, Eggey James, Oboe Parry, Dai Blades, Dan Tibbles, Jones First Aid, John Abdabs, Stan Swansea and Glynmor Jones.

'Daisy said she'd get some sandwiches sent down later,' Emlyn said, as he eased his huge bulk down into the chairman's seat. 'Now don't worry boys. They're not going to be turtle meat sandwiches. They had some more turtle meat in last night but the women think they've got someone down in Cardiff to buy it all.'

'They'll eat anything down in Cardiff, Mr Chairman,' said John Abdabs. 'Pit pony sandwiches and Kit-e-kat curry they do serve in the cafes down there.'

Laughter flared and died quickly as sunshine slanted down through the dusty window, catching in the foaming bubbles of the beer and the twisting cigarette smoke. All faces turned and looked at Emlyn; troubled faces they were too, worn down with work and blue-scarred from accidents in the pit, stiff with the worry of having no money for their families for getting on for twelve months now – three months longer than the '26 lock-out. Life was hard and getting harder. Emlyn had recently sensed a rising panic and, with so many uncertainties around, had called the central lodge members together for an informal talk. These twelve boys were the keepers of the culture; if he could nourish them with his ideas he would nourish the whole membership.

'Christmas is coming down on us, boys, so I thought we should meet and have a bit of a talk about where we stand,' Emlyn said. 'Trouble is it's very difficult to work out just where it is that we do stand. The miners of old had this pit sense and always knew what was going on by the shape and colours of the flame in their lamp. They were taught to study the flame since certain levels of gas made it turn into different colours. Bad air would make the whole flame shrink in size. Then you would look to see if it was holding steady or flickering, perhaps, or even guttering with a thin carbon stream coming out of it. Men's lives were saved by knowing what the colour of the flame meant; by seeing in what direction the air was blowing those thin carbon streams.'

He stopped speaking and took a few moments to catch his breath. His mouth opened and closed silently as he took his pint in his two great ragged hands. Part of his fingers were twisted with arthritis and other parts were scarred, but his wrists were still thick and strong, still redolent of their power to rip long holes through the very bowels of the earth. The finger-nails were going dark around the edges but – as befitted his new role of travelling the country to N.U.M. meetings – were neat and clean enough. But it was only when he bunched his fists that you really saw the awesome strength that still resided in them; this unwavering firmness which was matched only by the wisdom and clarity of his mind.

Emlyn Kremlin was the Old Hewer and, even as his dust-raddled lungs continued struggling to find some relief, the boys waited in silence, their pints untouched, until The Old Hewer was ready to speak to them again.

'The trouble is, from where I'm standing, I'm having great difficulty in making out what the flame is telling me. All I can feel is some terrible bad air coming up out of the hole. I just look around and see our small community being pulverised by the slow work of the hammer and anvil. I just can't see where we're going and, with all this darkness, I'm licking my finger and putting it up to locate the fresh air but there seems to be no fresh air around.

'I was walking home up the hill last night and there was this boy just running along the terrace flinging stones through windows. They were not empty homes either. There were people living in those homes and this boy was flinging stones into their parlours. Every night now there's a fight in the Hall. Six women were at it for over half an hour in the bar the other night and that was just over a spam sandwich. The weighbridge down the pit has been torn apart. Rocks are being thrown at passing police cars.' The tone of his voice changed and it became deep and angry. 'All this violence and destruction is not Welsh. All this hate is nothing of us.' He banged his fist down on the polished table. 'This is not what a generation of miners gave their blood and very lives to build.'

He was caught short of breath again and just sat, snorting and staring into space ahead of him. The boys remained silent, almost as if Emlyn had been tearing a strip off them. It was Dai Blades who first broke the silence.

'It's television that I blame for a lot of this,' Dai said to a chorus of 'Ayes.' 'The news in particular has got the world believing that all this strike is about is a punch-up between us an' the police. And not just the world either, Mr Chairman. There's some around this table who believe that as well.'

'I never wanted it to get like this if you're pointing the finger at me,' said Glynmor. 'I agree the violence has gone beyond and, while we're on the subject of television, I'm not happy about that Jack Young being out with us either. Yes, I *was* for it. But no more.'

'It's the women he's driving daft,' said Danny Kettle. 'They don't like it 'cos he's always shouting at them for having their hair done an' dressing tidy. 'E wants them to look all slummocky like.'

'He's a pain in the arse, Mr Chairman,' said John Abdabs. 'He just wants to set everything up all the time. There's only so many ways you can shout the word "Scab".'

'Aye. That's the real problem and that's a fact,' said Glynmor. 'Last week Jack had all the boys fitted up with microphones an', I don't know, they seem to get fighting mad when they're fitted up like that. An' when the cameras are trained on them they do seem to go berserk. I don't understand it. I've always said a little bit of violence never hurt anyone, Mr Chairman, but the problem now is our boys are fighting like it's closing time in the Top Rank down in Cardiff. An' now the police are wading into us too. Where it was all a bit of a laugh and a joke the police have started lashing into us – even tying us to fences an' gates.'

'Fences an' gates?'

'Aye. When it gets out of hand they handcuff four or five of us together to form a shield against the bricking. Anyone who bricks them now bricks their own as well. An' when they're catching us they're hitting us sick.'

'Well if you're saying Jack is stirring all this up then we really had better give him the elbow.'

'The camera is not making any difference,' Oboe Parry chimed in. 'It's only recording what's going on. They'd be hitting us sick even if the camera wasn't there. Myself I think the camera saves us from getting a bigger 'ammering than what we're getting. They're careful what they do when the cameras are around.'

'Why doesn't the camera ever show the police waving their pay packets at us?'

' 'Cos they don't do it when the cameras are around. That's why.'

The door opened and Huw Bungalow came loping in carrying a plate piled high with ham sandwiches which he took to each of the men in turn.

It was Emlyn who noticed how the spirits of the boys visibly raised when Huw came near to them, how they liked to tease him and reach out to give his ribs a bit of a tickle. It was strange the way Huw seemed to generate love wherever he went: how he had become both the talisman and comforter of a strike village.

'We do miss our Huw out on the picket line, Mr Chairman,' said Dan Tibbles. 'We never seemed to get hurt nor nothing when Huw was around. Isn't that right boys?'

'Aye. Not a bloody scratch when he was around.'

'Well, we can't force him to come out with us can we?'

'He won't have anything to do with television, Mr Chairman,' said Glynmor. 'Never has.'

'Yes, well, perhaps he's got more sense than all of us put together,' said Emlyn. 'Perhaps that's another good reason for getting rid of Mr Jack Young.'

Huw acted as if he was unaware what they were talking about and, when he had finished handing out all the sandwiches, he sat down on his father's knee. The boys ate their sandwiches and swigged their pints. Apart from the munching they were all totally silent with just sunshine and thin wisps of cigarette smoke massing around their faces.

They may have been uncharacteristically silent but it wasn't too difficult to see what was weighing them down: the terrible uncertainty of the times and the smouldering panic induced by all the great and implacable forces that were being lined up against them. Something awful was going to happen soon. Everyone sitting around that table knew that as sure as

428

they had a pint in one hand and a ham sandwich in the other.

Emlyn sensed that he should reassure them with something strong and optimistic but, whichever way he thought, he could think of nothing helpful and had never been in the business of telling lies no matter how noble the motive.

'Well, in my capacity as treasurer – just to cheer everyone up – after we paid the Nottingham fines, there's just two pounds left in the strike fund,' said Dai Blades. 'So don't anyone go getting picked up by the police 'cos we can't pay the fines any more.'

'Have you got any other good news for us Dai?'

'No. That's all for now.'

They all relapsed into a silence again, like a gang of workmen gazing down a newly-completed hole that had taken them a month to dig.

'Tell me, Mr Chairman, what happened to the funds from that Donny Hughes' concert?' asked Tom the Nutter.

There were more sighs but nothing was said as they all continued to stare down their hole. That was one very sore nerve that everyone had hoped would not be prodded.

'Well is someone going to say something or what?'

'Tom, we know you can't read but, if you'd read the *Western Mail*, you'd 'ave read what happened to Donny Hughes,' said Glynmor.

'What 'appened to him?'

'Our Donny Hughes got locked up.'

'Never to God. Whaffor?'

'For possessing cocaine, that's whaffor. Drugs mun. He's been sent to prison for six months and no one knows what happened to the money from the concert. We've called his manager but he seems to have gone missing too.'

Another silence followed as Huw reached out and picked up his father's pint, taking a few sips out of it before putting it back on the table. Glynmor just sat staring into space, not taking the slightest bit of pleasure in the fact that he had been right about Donny all along. He was just another wanker jumping on the bandwagon, hoping to make a quick few bob, as if there weren't enough of them bleeders around already.

But it was Emlyn who was feeling the most pain, the bitterness of betrayal flowing hot through his veins. It was bad enough having to battle against the combined forces of the

429

state, police and government but there was nothing quite so painful as when one of your own came to you, posing as a friend and ally, then turned and stabbed you in the back like this. He had known Donny since he had been a little kid and even loved him more than most kids. Now he done this to them. Used them to support his evil drug habit. Sometimes the world threw at him more than even the Old Hewer could take.

Emlyn looked around the table with eyes that were like shattered marbles. Everything was indeed running away from them ... their jobs, their homes, their friends. All these enemies and not the strength to fight one of them.

He didn't even feel that he could hold out any reasonable sort of hope to his boys either. He might even have been a prophet of old, studying the sky for rain clouds but finding none. He had called them together to nourish them with new ideas and fresh plans but all he had really done was to invite them to share in the same chalice of bitterness.

'Tomorrow we will doubtless fight on,' he said. 'But, for today, I declare this meeting over.'

Chapter Twenty-Five

Despite the encircling gloom, Christmas in Bont – as organised by the women's group – was a brilliant success. Daisy and Maggie, in particular, had worked tirelessly to ensure that each family had a turkey and all the children in the village receiving at least three beautifully wrapped presents each.

Gnasher donated ten cases of Sainsbury's wine to the soup kitchen while lorries – financed by fellow trade unionists in Europe – continued to arrive at odd times in the night outside the Hall. Everything was coming in – BMX bikes, construction kits, dolls, Action Men, food of every kind and, perhaps inevitably, yet another consignment of turtle meat. 'Perhaps the E.E.C. has decided to start a bastard turtle mountain 'ere in Bont,' said Glynmor, helping to unload the boxes.

Someone in America had sent £100 to the soup kitchen so that every strike child could have a new pound coin. An anonymous businessman drove up the Valley and left a case of whisky on the steps of the Welfare Hall. The police on picket duty sent £350 towards the cost of a children's party. Even the thieving stopped for a few days and there were no reports in the Valley of broken locks or of videos that had walked off into the night.

To the relief of many, Jack Young announced that, due to a tight budget, he was pulling out his cameras over the Christmas period and would come back in the New Year. He did, however, leave Bridget behind. She was now living with Daisy and it was her duty to record everything in her diary which, if necessary, they could reconstruct when he returned. 'I don't know why he doesn't reconstruct it all in some London studio,' said Daisy. 'If something really happens he's never interested, is he?'

On Christmas Eve there was a huge dance in the Hall and Smokey and his Sounds again came down to put on his fabulous disco and light show. It was one those whooping, legless dances too with heaps of people coming, balloons bouncing around and streamers streaming everywhere. Maggie wouldn't let go of her Glynmor for as much as a second, hopping through the fast numbers and smooching through the slow ones.

'Look at those two now. Lovely I do call that,' said Thelma, sitting at the girls' regular table. 'I tell you it's been a long time since my 'usband put 'is 'ands around my bum like that.'

'They're going to eat one another the way they're going,' said Jackie, taking half a bottle of gin out of her handbag underneath the table and replenishing their drinks. 'Ach y fi. He's sticking 'is tongue into her mouth now. 'E'll 'ave the committee after 'im less 'e's careful.'

'I could never get Ted to put his tongue into my mouth. I could never get that fat slob to put it in anywhere come to that. Ooooh loook there's that Stephen Ducks. 'Aven't seen 'im f'r ages. Hiya.'

'I got Peter to put 'is tongue down there once. You know. There. Smashing it was too. But 'e was so drunk 'e didn't remember doing it an' the next morning when I tole him 'e ran out to the lav and was sick as a pig. Aye. Straight out to the lavatory an' I never got 'im to do it again – no matter 'ow drunk he was.'

Huw Bungalow had clearly located a plentiful source of free festive drinks since he was already three sheets to the wind and dancing with every girl in sight. Even so far gone he could still bop, however, sometimes jiving with two girls, one in each hand and keeping them spinning too.

They all finished dancing to the current favourite, Bruce Springsteen's *Dancing in the Dark* but, as it had ever been, it was the gaudy, strutting flash of the great old rock 'n' roll anthems that had everyone clapping and whooping and running onto the crowded dance floor. For the umpteenth time it was the Shirelles and the Ronettes and the Crystals who sang to them about the adolescent happiness that was once their lives on the mining terraces; those golden days when they were all being each other's babies and breaking one another's hearts as they were being stood up on the corner; those marvellous hours of pony-tails and dancing white socks when God was in His Heaven and all was right with the world.

You never knew you could dance at all until you danced to those songs but, no sooner had you started, you were ready to keep dancing until you keeled over and could dance no more. Certainly there were now only two old miners sitting down at their seats, as song piled on song and, oh boy, the world became a heaving, multi-coloured sea of love and pain, of laughter and tears, as those golden harmonies surged around and around the Hall before drifting out into the cold, snow-flecked night.

The snow was coming down thick and fast when the dance finally ended. Later still, drunken groups stood around the clock in the square singing hymns as snowflakes dissolved in their eyes. Then they formed a stumbling conga and a few hundred of them threaded around and around the square singing 'I'd sooner be a picket than a scab.' Later still they all began throwing snowballs at the clock but, as usual, it defied all efforts to bring it to a stop.

When the assault on the clock had finished, Maggie and Glynmor had to carry Huw home where, just outside the house, he committed the ultimate blasphemy of being sick all over his blue suede shoes.

Mothers are not supposed to laugh like drains when their own sons are being sick over their best blue suede shoes but laugh Maggie did as Huw continued to bring up bits and dribbles of everything that he had drunk all that day. She laughed until tears poured down her face and her laughter turned to weeping since she was pretty far gone as well. It was the last completely happy night she was ever to know.

That Christmas Day every strike family had a turkey and a bottle of wine. For many it was their best Christmas ever. That day the television news took a rest from picket-line violence — there was no violence to report. Instead it showed a group of men, bloodied but unbowed, standing with a Christmas tree outside their rickety makeshift shed, the Alamo, at Cortonwood in Yorkshire where the strike had first begun. That day Huw spent the morning in bed with a bad belly while Maggie and Glynmor cooked the dinner together through thick hangovers which got thinner as they made inroads into the wine. But when they did manage to get Huw out of bed, and ate the meal as a family they knew that the success of the women's efforts could have been the worst possible thing to have happened to them; that, in the field of their most marvellous victory, they had sown the seeds of their own defeat.

Even as the three of them sat bloated around the fire, with coloured paper hats on their heads and a glass of wine in their hands; even as the Queen was addressing them about her problems with the Commonwealth on the wireless; both Glynmor and Maggie were afflicted by an intense melancholy since they knew that now there was nothing to look forward to; that, from now on, it was all going to be downhill.

In fact there was so little said that, after an hour or so, Huw took to his painting while Maggie and Glynmor went back to bed. 'I'm getting so scared Glynmor,' she said holding him tight under the bedclothes. 'I can't see where we're going and I do get scared when I don't know what's going on.'

'Shush girl. It'll work out fine.'

'You know I often think of all our times together an' the way we've been reared together here in Bont an' I ask myself if it could be all for this?'

'What's all this then? Christmas blues is it?'

'Oh just sadness for all of us. Since Daisy came back she's made me more aware of things. *You*'ve made me more aware. Then there's been the women's group. All of use have changed and we want to do something but it's like it's gone too late.'

'It's never too late.'

'It is Glynmor. Everything we're doing now is too little too late. An' there's no one on our side. Well, is there? I get afraid of all this hostility an' I want Huw safe and out of it. The strain is getting him down as well. He's much quieter than he used to be. Sometimes I think we should go an' live somewhere else an' start again.'

'Where would I get a job? Me, a forty-year-old miner with one thumb?'

'Don't be so soft. You've got plenty of work left in you yet.'

'Aye. Perhaps. But down the hole. That's all I know about. We can't go anywhere Maggie girl. We're a mining family and here's where we'll stay – on strike and out for ever, if necessary.'

'Don't say it like that, Glynmor. It's got to end sometime hasn't it? This really can't go on for ever, can it?'

Within a week of Christmas the strike really did begin breaking up. Throughout the coalfield, once-staunch men were throwing in the towel and drifting back to work at an alarming rate, particularly in Yorkshire. According to the *South Wales Echo* there were now twenty-four pits working normally, eleven producing some coal, forty-two with men reporting and fifty-one strikebound. On Black Monday 5,170 scabs crossed the picket lines.

The striking miners bitterly contested these figures. 'Every time the canteen cat walks in twice the Board counts it as two men back at work,' sneered Arthur Scargill.

But, as the drift back continued, the South Wales coalfield was still almost a 100 per cent solid. Almost every man was ready, if necessary, to stay out for the rest of his life. There was a nuclear war, see, said the joke, so Margaret Thatcher and her cabinet went into a bunker and stayed down there for five years. When they did finally come out they met a group of Welsh pickets coming down Whitehall. 'The strike's still on,' they shouted.

There had never been any scabs in Bont's long history but, after Black Monday, the strain of siege was visible in almost every corner of the village. For reasons that were never very clear, NALGO called a refuse strike which resulted in bins overflowing down every gully and the sheep scattering refuse all over the roads. The refuse men even picketed the public refuse tips, turning away anyone who came in to dump their own rubbish and telling them to take it home again. Some dumped theirs in the fields around the tips or into the river. Down around the foot of the tump exploded black bags were lying around everywhere, bleeding great streams of rubbish and making the Valley look appallingly ugly.

Snow came again and briefly covered the litter, making the Valley look spruce and tidy, with just the barbed wire of dead brambles poking up out of the snow and, here and there, the smooth black olives of the sheep droppings scattered over the glittering white drifts. *Chug, chug, chug – tinkle, tinkle, tinkle* – went the hopper still working tirelessly down in

Gnasher's yard with the skinheads still labouring down the old mine and out on the tips. *Chug, chug, chug – tinkle, tinkle, tinkle.* The secret of Guto's mine had long got out but Gnasher bought off any objections he couldn't handle with a good kicking or private deliveries at the objectors' homes at night.

But then there was a quick thaw. The dirty brown slush and house refuse mingled together to make stinking ponds dotted with rotten vegetables and food cartons which the sheep trawled through again and again. Three old armchairs and a stolen car had been dumped in the river. Someone even broke into the soup kitchen and made off with all the corned beef. '*Duw*, I'd give him a right good lambasting if I caught 'old of him,' Daisy exploded. 'But don't you go saying any of this to Jack,' she told Bridget. 'There's some things we don't want to get out.'

The very next morning, Jack Young and his crew did turn up again but nothing was said as they got back to work, poodling about the place taking a shot of this and a shot of that. Jack's real problem was the lack of any real 'visual texture' – as he put it. All the N.U.M. funds had been sequestered by government accountants and, for the moment, no one seemed to be doing anything. Few wanted to co-operate with him now anyway since there was a growing conviction that he was going to be filming the time of their defeat rather than their victory.

The final indignity came when a council surveyor discovered that pit subsidence was beginning to distort the foundations of Bont Terrace. If you looked carefully you could see some walls sagging forwards, others going backwards and more than a few bulging portentously, as if in early stages of pregnancy. A letter was sent to all the residents warning them that they might soon have to move out while underpinning took place. The job might take up to a year.

In the same post there was yet another letter from John Walsh, the pit manager and distinguished Buffalo, outlining how much a miner could make tax-free if he returned to work now. He also assured them that they would have safe transport to the pit if they decided to return and invited them to fill in a confidential form if they were interested in doing so.

It was Glynmor who stormed down the pit, all but kicking the door off the manager's office as he went in. 'If you send out any more letters like this you'll end up with your bastard Buffalo teeth kicked in,' he shouted, waving the offending letter under the manager's twitching nose. 'There will never be any scabs in Bont.'

Later Glynmor told the Sunday morning lodge meeting that the manager had apologised and said that he wouldn't do it again. 'And that, boys, is the art of negotiation,' he added, still with a twinkle in his eye.

That night a cold winter wind went howling around and around the terraces, grating and insistent, like a baby hungry for his mother's milk. Down around the back of the Co-op this persistent howling mingled with the cauterwauling whines of cats busy having a bit of a rub; the cats and the wind created a small harsh symphony of nerve-grating discords which brought windows flying up with avenging milk bottles and boots flying out into the howling darkness.

In the front parlour of his house in 49 Bont Terrace a whole spectrum of emotions passed across Oboe Parry's features as Jack Young sketched out the role that he saw Oboe playing in his film.

'You see what I am looking for, Oboe, is some way of humanising my story and, the more I think about it, the more I'm convinced that you're my man.' *Pride*. 'What I want is a typical family right at the centre of the combat zone; someone who'll flesh out the real meanings of the larger war going on between Scargill and MacGregor.'

'Just what exactly have you got in mind, Jack.' *Curiosity*.

'What I've got in mind is that I follow you around for some time – down to the soup kitchen to pick up your bread and veg, over to the tip to pick some coal, to the lodge meeting to discuss tactics, then back here to talk with your wife and kids about money. You are running low aren't you?'

'Running low!' *Anguish*. 'You're joking are you? You *are* joking I hope. I'm seven months behind with the mortgage. Can't pay the gas or rates. The 'lectricity is coming in on a fiddled meter, if you know what I mean. This strike has been terrible long. Terrible long.'

'I could perhaps do something about that.'

'Are you talking about paying me, are you?' *Avarice*.

Jack Young looked down at the brown threadbare carpet.

A bright red spark exploded and faded on the single red bar of the electric fire. Somewhere in the house there was the sound of a television.

'I asked. I asked if you were talking about paying me?'

'It would be a private deal,' Jack said, picking his words carefully. 'Strictly between the two of us. Nothing going into the strike fund or anything like that.'

'How much were you thinking of?'

'Depends on what you do. It depends on how much of your time I took up.'

'I've got all the time you need, Jack. So 'ow much were you thinking of?'

Jack took out a thick bundle of five-pound notes from his pocket and peeled off ten, handing them over. 'Just regard this as a down-payment.'

'Aye,' said Oboe without actually holding out his hand and accepting the money. 'But a down-payment on what?'

'Your part in my film. Go on. Take it. There could be a good bit more where this came from.'

''Ow much more?'

'That depends. That depends on how what you actually do and how much you help the film.'

'Tell me now then Jack … what would you pay me … how much would you give me if I became a scab?'

Now it was Jack's turn to register emotion. Though he feigned surprise, his true feelings were excited relief. He had long seen that his film was in danger of becoming predictable, boring even, since the protagonists had become so inactive and even hostile to his cause. What he really needed was a dramatic catalyst on which he could fashion a film based on conflict which would both explain and underpin the pressures and tensions of the strike. And that dramatic catalyst, he had quickly seen, was a scab who would turn the situation inside out.

Before he had left for his Christmas break he had asked Bridget to scout around for a likely name. From what she had subsequently heard in the gossip, she had come up with the name of Oboe Parry – with his odd mixture of weakness, pride and poverty – as the most likely contender for that unhappy role. So now Jack was here, in Oboe's house, tapping patiently on the oyster shell and watching it open bit by bit.

'Are you saying that you might go back to work down the pit Oboe? Here in Bont?'

'I might be.'

'If you did return to work I could find you a lot of money. A lot of money, Oboe.'

'Aye, aye. But 'ow much?'

'Providing no word of our agreement gets out of this room an awful lot.'

'Aye. But 'ow much mun?'

'On an agreement like this which, I must warn you now, is unethical and possibly illegal – and would perhaps end up in a prison term for each of us if it got out – I could manage as much as a thousand pounds.'

'A thousand pounds! One thousand pounds. That's chicken-feed. I've lost at least three thousand since the strike started. I'd want at least that to go back.'

'I couldn't find that much, Oboe. Not even Terry Wogan gets that.'

'I tell you what. Terry Wogan would want far more than three thousand pounds before *he* became a scab in Bont. What you're offering wouldn't cover my bill for bandages and sticking plaster after they'd finished with me.'

'A thousand is the most I could find Oboe.'

'Well three thousand is my price and not a penny less.'

Jack Young had no difficulty at all in squaring his conscience about the highly suspect deal he was trying to make. He was a revolutionary film-maker in every sense, one who had never seen his camera as being a passive observer but as a highly active protagonist in the conflict. He dismissed notions of objectivity in the same way as he dismissed notions of balance. He knew that the only real drama came out of what the Greeks called *agon* or struggle and, in the absence of such elements in the real world, he saw no contradiction in injecting his own. He needed no crystal ball to work out that a scab flung into Bont would hit the village with all the force of an anarchist with a bomb. All falsities and half-truths would then be ripped aside in the ensuing, often violent struggle.

He, the revolutionary film-maker, was an essential part of the dialogue which is why he always wired up the boys on the picket line just as he would also wire up Oboe when he began his long lonely walk to the pithead. It was for such audacity

439

and boldness that his London media associates spoke about him in the wine bars and Greek restaurants of Charlotte Street.

'But you wouldn't be going back just for the money – even if I could find what you're asking – would you, Oboe? When you are asked you must be very clear about your motives and never, of course, mention anything to do with money.'

'Motives! You want motives? I've got a million motives and it's nothing to do with money either. This strike has been political from the start. It's just the same old Red army trying to pull the government down again. We should 'ave 'ad a ballot. The timing was all wrong as well. You don't call a strike in the middle of summer.'

'Yes, yes. That's the kind of dialogue I'd like to use.'

'That's not dialogue. That's the truth about the way I feel about this damned strike. The way I feel inside me, in my heart. But the strike is breaking up now. We've been out too long an' I'd like to lead the more moderate men back.'

'It could be dangerous, of course.'

'Not really. There'll be a few punches thrown. But I know these boys. They're not killers. They're all jaw most of them. If jawing could dig coal there'd be none left anywhere in South Wales.'

'You might have to leave the Valley and go and live somewhere else.'

'You're saying you're going to pay up are you?'

'I might.'

'Oh well.' *Visibly brightening*. 'If any man goes back to work the N.C.B. has promised that they will look after us. They might even get us a new house. You wouldn't get anything for this old house now anyway. They've found subsidence around here they have. The old mines around here. Aye. The people of Bont wouldn't like it at first but, in time, they'd agree that I 'elped them to get out of the hands of the Reds like.'

'You're not too worried then?'

'Not too worried? I'm worried sick I am but there's some things a man has got to do. I can't see my wife and kids suffering like this any more. I can't take it myself either. Arthur's Red army has put us through too much.'

Outside, the cold winter wind was still wailing around the terraces. It howled over the face of the cold Valley walls and down along the shivering grass on the river banks. It howled around every corner and through the icicled eaves of the Hall. It howled down through the machine shop and washery of the deserted, silent mine, so intense it was as if the winds themselves were full of sorrow and pain at the betrayal of the land.

Was Oboe just an ordinary miner who, in his heart, had seen his family suffer enough?

No, no, no, the winds howled back. Oboe Parry is just a scab who will fill his people with crying and shame. Oboe Parry is a scab whose family will turn their back on him. Oboe Parry is the slime of the slug who will be remembered as a scab for ever, someone who stamped on the hands of the people when they were trying to struggle out of a swamp and reach for life.

Emlyn Kremlin was just leaving his house the next morning and locking the door behind him when the frying range in the chip shop burst into flames.

Cocoa and Nipper were playing the Space Invaders at the time and the shop owner, Bernard James, was reading the *Sun*, his chips all peeled and ready, waiting for the fat to warm up. His first indication that something was wrong came when he heard a hissing sound and looked up from his newspaper to see a long wavy spurt of yellow flame darting out past a pile of deep frozen plaice.

The flame was so fierce Bernard did not even stop to look at it a second time, let alone tackle it. He ducked out beneath the counter flap and followed the skinheads out through the door. The three of them only just managed to get into the street when the whole shop was engulfed in a ball of flame. They glanced back at the red and orange inferno rising up inside the shop window looking, briefly, like an aquarium for something very wild and terrible. Then there was a huge explosion which blew out the window followed by yet another explosion which seemed to blow out most of the fire.

Neighbours came running with buckets of water and hurled them into the shop making steam clouds hiss and spit. Soon a whole crowd of children, women and sheep had gathered around gazing into the charred, smoking mouth of what was once their fish and chip shop.

'Burned the chips again have you, Bernard?' Emlyn asked

as he came and stood next to the owner of the chip shop.

'Em. It just went whoof! No warning, no bugger all. Whoof!'

Emlyn walked over and looked inside the shop where a Space Invader was still bleeping as if in pain. 'You won't be salvaging much out of that,' he said. 'Phoned the fire brigade have you?'

'Well, someone must 'ave mustn't they?'

'It doesn't much matter. As I said you won't be salvaging much out of that.'

Emlyn continued walking up towards the Hall when he stopped walking again to look up the hill where a demolition ball was knocking down the old Libanus Chapel. The children of Bont had plenty to look at that morning with yet another crowd watching intently as the huge iron ball swung through the air like a giant avenging conker. It smashed against the old chapel wall which was so rotten it collapsed almost as soon as it was touched.

The old N.U.M. warhorse had never been a follower of the pulpit – particularly when nutty old Mordecai had been ranting in it – but he felt a definite heartburn of sadness at seeing the old chapel finally fall. Such buildings had played a tremendous role in the formation of the early culture of the Valleys – even sustaining the Labour Party – and the two philosophies had grown together. But no longer. The Labour Party had lost its way and now the old buildings, along with the great spirit which had once informed them, had got lost too.

He took out his fob watch and checked the time, turning on his heels and walking towards the Hall. He had long sensed that a plague had been sweeping through the Valley, that their village had been dying as if of some mysterious illness. But this morning, in the new year of their longest and most bitter strike, everything actually seemed to be falling down or bursting into flames before his very eyes. The long, invisible process of dereliction was reaching its end. Even the Welfare Hall, the very heart of the community, was under threat of being condemned unless the committee could find enough money to replace the rotten roof rafters.

All they had left was the pit and, in the age of computerised and super-pits, the days of that damp, dark hole were clearly numbered too.

Emlyn walked past the caged one-armed bandits in the corridor of the Hall and went down into the basement, pausing to look into the soup kitchen where Daisy had her feet up reading the *Guardian* and Maggie was entering some figures into a ledger. With its blue shadows and bursts of very thin light settling on the piled sacks of potatoes and boxes of butter, the room had the atmosphere of a First World War bunker waiting for some war artist to come along and immortalise it. For this, surely, was the ultimate cell, indivisible and at war, into which all society was going to be atomised under Thatcher's capitalism. Way above there would always be the rich and powerful enclaves. But here, down below, there would be makeshift soup kitchens like these keeping the tattered flags of resistance alive.

But now that the miners had been defeated – as even he now privately accepted – such places had become inevitable. With the continuing cuts in D.H.S.S. payments they might even yet become a permanent feature of life in the Valleys.

And then, perhaps, the workers would get themselves organised and rise again. Perhaps.

He walked on into the strike centre where Glynmor was on the telephone quarrelling while Stan Swansea was fiddling with the knobs of the wireless trying to pick up the Welsh midday news. `For a moment Glynmor's angry voice was competing with that of the news announcer when Glynmor slammed the 'phone down onto its rest.

'Terry Thomas, a prop forward with the Penrhos rugby club, who has been on the verge of international honours, has returned to his work down the local mine,' the news announcer said. 'Half the committee have now resigned rather than pick a scab for the team.'

'More scabs,' said Emlyn softly, pulling up a chair next to Glynmor and sitting down on it. 'Soon the world will be full of just Tories and scabs. That'll be nice, won't it? A real heaven on earth that'll be. A world run by people who just care about nothing but themselves.'

'There's more bad news, Emlyn,' said Glynmor, still snorting after his row on the telephone.

'How can anything be worse than it already is?'

'There's two scabs going into Aberfan colliery.'

'Nothing could be worse than it is.'

'Emlyn, are you listening to me now? Just watch my lips. There's two bastard scabs going into the Aberfan pit.'

Then, as if to confirm Glynmor's words, the item came over on the news. 'We have a late report that two striking miners have reported to work at the Lewis Merthyr colliery in the Aberfan Valley,' the news announcer said. 'The police mounted one of the biggest security operations in their history to ensure the two men got through the picket lines and the latest reports from the N.C.B. say that twenty-one men have now returned to work in the pits of South Wales.'

Emlyn could feel his cheeks go taut and all at once he lost his breath, his old eyes looking straight at Glynmor as his mouth opened and closed while his lungs searched and squealed for more oxygen. 'When did you hear this?' he asked finally.

'Only just now. That's what that call was all about. Those two scabs are going into Aberfan. There's about three thousand policemen an' no bastard can get near them. You can't even blow your nose anywhere in that Valley without getting picked up. That was the lodge secretary in Lewis saying it's no good even trying to picket the place.'

'I never – *ever* – thought my ears would hear what you've just told me,' Emlyn said, his big finger-tips slowly kneading his chest around his heart. 'They're not happy just breaking up our church. Now they've come to piss over the altar too. They turn out three thousand policemen just so two scabs can go and piss over our altar. Wasn't the death of a hundred children enough for them?'

'They're saying there's no point trying to picket the place but we've got to do something 'aven't we Emlyn? We can't just let this one pass.'

'Of course we've got to send in a picket,' Emlyn roared. 'I don't care if they've got three million police around that pit an' we've only got half a dozen pickets. If we pass on this we pass on everything. I had an uncle once who got into one of those marathon mountain fights. Nearly four hours that fight lasted but he won in the end 'cos he never threw in the towel. If we let those scabs go into Aberfan without picketing the place we'll be deemed as having thrown in the towel.'

'How are we going to play it?'

He sat down on his chair again, kneading his chest as he turned his head sideways in thought. 'We'll send in the picket

444

the same way the miners did in the 1925 lock-out an' there were troops crawling through every Valley. We'll spend the night in the forest and go down the mountain to get to the pit. Let's just go with our own boys so there's no chance of it leaking out. We'll go tomorrow. Tell the boys we're going down the mountain the way they did it in 1925.'

'What about Jack Young?'

'What about him?'

'He'd be interested in this. Should we tell him?'

'No. Leave him out of it. Even if he does find out tell him he can't come. This is a special one for us. This is one just for our boys, not just some play-acting for the tele. There's enough of that going on around here.'

'I should be able to get Huw to come if there were no cameras around.'

'Might you? That would be superb.'

'You'd be surprised what we can talk to one another about. I'll 'ave a word with him tonight.'

'Superb. He was born on the morning of the Aberfan slide wasn't he? He's the child of all our sorrows is Huw; the boy acquainted with grief. It's just right. The boys are always saying how Huw used to seem to look after them. Aye. Tell the boys Huw Bungalow will be taking us down the mountain.'

'Hello, Jack. This is Oboe Parry. A lot of the boys are going off on a picket early tomorrow morning so I'm going back to work. I've phoned the pit manager an' he's offered to send a car.'

'No Oboe. You've got to do it proudly. I can't pay you if you take the pit car. I want to film you walking from the village to the pit. You've got to be seen to be courageous to show an example to others who might be thinking of going back to work.'

A long silence.

'I'll ring the manager again then. A good few of the boys won't be around tomorrow morning so there won't be too much aggravation an' the next day there'll be lots more going back.'

'Where are they going tomorrow?'

'They're going to try and picket those two going back to work in Aberfan but they won't get anywhere near them. They've brought in police from as far as Port Talbot and Swansea. But the boys don't want you to go with them anyway, if that's what you're thinking.'

'Why not?'

'Aberfan is an old grudge thing with them. They're out to prove something to themselves. It's sort of symbolic, if you know what I mean. They're saying they don't want any of the media around.'

'Ah well. Perhaps it's all working out for the best I've got a small microphone I want you to keep in your pocket when you walk to the pit in the morning. I'll drop it off at your place after it gets dark tonight.'

The dark, creaking forest was full of the sound of drips. They dropped from every branch and every pine needle; they seemed to slide down the trunks of the trees and make the very earth hiss like snakes at bay. The boys pulled up the collars of their windcheaters and donkey jackets but there was no avoiding all the drips as they waited for a dawn which did not seem to want to arrive. It was as if the whole world was full of tears, pouring down on them as steadily as summer rain.

As miners they had long been used to squatting in dark, puddled places – that's why so many of their fingers were bad with arthritis after all – but it was this constant enforced inactivity that was the hardest to take as just eleven of them remained as still as statues amidst the low brown curves of the dead ferns.

After the breast-beating and posturing of the early days of the strike, and the recent continual disappointments, it was perhaps not surprising that they could now only muster a small hard core of men prepared to spend a night in the middle of winter hiding in a damp, cold forest.

'I've got my boot stuck in this mud,' muttered Abdabs.

'Well, pull it out again,' advised Stan Swansea.

Silently but forcefully the dawn light began to disperse the shadows and thick banks of rain mists which hung from the branches of the pine trees like ghost hammocks. An owl hooted and there was the sound of something crashing through the undergrowth.

'Picking with rain is it?'

'No mun. That's haze for heat that is.'

'Looks like rain for rain to me.'

'There'll be sun mun. Just hold on an' watch.'

Way out on the edge of the forest Huw and Glynmor were

moving down alongside a barbed-wire fence. Huw stopped occasionally to point at a path or over at two policemen wearing black capes and standing with binoculars on the prow of a distant *cwm*.

Emlyn's flat cap moved around in the ferns just inside the cover of the forest as he watched father and son moving up and down trying to decide which path they were going to take down to the mine. Now Huw was standing on a dry stone wall to view the lie of the land, his shoes dancing as bits of the wall gave way beneath him. Emlyn marvelled at the relationship between Huw and Glynmor; the way that, these days, without words and very few actions, they seemed to be able to communicate fully with each other, sometimes with as little as a look or a raised finger. It was only since the start of the strike that Emlyn had fully seen that Huw had a bright and vibrant intelligence, something that saw, absorbed and interpreted everything around him. And he could see now, looking back, how it was only his niece, Maggie, who had seen this intelligence and beauty right from the beginning.

The dull coin of the sun was just peeping over the Valley wall when Huw gave a long whistle and waved the boys out of the forest. They came out one by one, stamping their feet and swinging their hands against their shoulders to get the circulation going, a burly bunch for the most part with huge bellies made from too much beer and too many chips. Some wore caps festooned with strike badges, others had ski-slope bobble caps and a few wore motor-bike helmets.

The pit was not yet visible from where they were standing silently but, just on over a twist in the Valley, was the grassed, smooth slope where once an underground water bomb had exploded and pitched a tip forward for almost a mile to engulf the school. There was the red-brick of the new community centre at the end of the slope, the circular shape of the Garden of Remembrance and, nestling in the belly of the valley, the little *twll* of the village itself with its grey slate roof and smoking chimney pots.

Glynmor swallowed hard as he looked down on the shadow-haunted village where, one wet morning of mists, he had seen all the flowers die and all the laughter disappear from the Valleys; where love and hope had been swept away by the killer black tide. This was the first time he had come back here

447

since the day of the disaster. In his mind's eye, he could still see the evil black tip after it had spilled its guts on the school; still see the wailing people digging down into that foul-smelling slurry with their bare hands.

A white electric cart was juddering past the community centre when the boys began walking again. Through the still, bare branches of the trees they could see the cemetery itself; their very own sacred burial ground where all those children who had been put to the sword had finally been laid to rest in a row of white marbled graves high up on the hill. It was the great silence of the Valley that was so remarkable, broken neither by the sound of a car nor the barking of a dog.

'I never thought I'd come back here looking for a few scabs,' Glynmor said to no one in particular as he looked over at the gravestones. 'Here of all places.'

' 'Ow can anyone scab?' asked Eggey.

'Well 'cos they're skint I s'pose.'

'Aye, but we'll not always be skint, will we?'

Huw, who had run off down into a copse, emerged again waving for the boys to follow him. They went down a twisting shale path and came out, high up on a mountain and overlooking the pit itself. There was still an hour to go before the start of the morning shift but, even so, every road and field around the mine was throned with enough police to have quelled the original Tonypandy riots.

There were police with dogs and police on horseback. Five police cars were slewed around the entrance while line after line of black boiler-suited officers, carrying riot truncheons and body shields, were marching out of the pit gates to take up their positions around the grass roundabout.

'*Duw*, there's fucking millions of 'em,' said Tom the Nutter as the boys, almost instinctively, moved closer together.

'No wonder so few of our lot turned up,' said Stan Swansea.

'Are we still going in?' asked Jones First Aid. 'Or shall we all just kill ourselves 'ere an' now an' be done with it?'

' 'Course we're going in,' said Glynmor. 'Look, there's none of them around the road at the bottom of the mountain here. What are you anyway? Men or mice?'

'Mice.'

'Don't be so soft. We're pickets from Bont. We're the draughts that can get in anywhere. So what are we?'

'Mice.'

It was hopeless with this bunch.

'You'd better stay here,' Glynmor told Emlyn. 'You're getting a bit too old to be running down the mountain and fighting with the police.'

'No fear. I'm going to be right there behind you. But tell me one thing now Glynmor before we go in.'

Glynmor's throat thickened with emotion as he looked out over to that dark slope and back at the old miner's face. 'What's that then, Emlyn?'

'Have you just farted?'

' 'Course I 'ave. You don't think I smell like this all day do you?'

The laughter helped to ease the tension as they all set off nervously down the mountain path.

Over in Bont, Oboe Parry's wife was sitting in front of her dressing table red-eyed and crying into lumps of Kleenex, as Oboe looked in on his children, touching their sleeping backs with his fingers before putting on his donkey jacket and stepping out into the terrace.

He had told no one, except his wife, that he was going to break the strike. But he was surprised and relieved, nevertheless, to see no one around except four policemen who had been told to keep discreetly off the streets and stand at the entrance to the gully down by the Hall. He walked past the Co-op and the gutted chip shop before coming out to the square and the start of the pit road.

High up on the Valley wall, in a small lay-by on the forest road, they were filming Oboe's long, lonely walk from his house to the mine. Thin slivers of mist swirled around, with just the odd sheep leaving off its munching to look up at him. A group of blackbirds flew silently over the village.

Inside the television van Jack Young was watching the pictures on his monitor, occasionally fiddling with the dials on his sound console to pick up the signal from the microphone in Oboe's top shirt pocket: the sound of heavy breathings and the steady pounding of Oboe's frightened heart. Other microphones were beamed down in the Valley picking up the quiet, early-morning noises: the birdsong, rattling of milk bottles and the distant hum of traffic.

Jack was not too dismayed that the pictures were so quiet and undramatic. Their very silence would make a perfect counterpoint to the pictures he would get tomorrow morning. Then, when word of Oboe's apostacy spread, all hell would break loose.

The boys' hob-nail boots slipped and slid over the thick wedges of shale as the group continued their descent into the Valley. A stray breeze picked up the whinnies and smells of the police horses. Over in a small *cwm* just next to them sat an exploded chapel with its roof gone and nettles growing out of the walls.

''Ow the 'ell am I s'posed to get down this with my bad leg an' all?'

'Why don't you take that bit of corrugated iron an' slide down?'

Huw had come back up the path and moved to the centre of the group as they grabbed hold of sapling ash trees, and one another, to steady themselves as they went down the steep slope. Yet, with Huw among them, they soon began moving with more confidence, complaining less and not being so hesitant, more willing to take chances as they stepped around the jagged rocks and slippery sheep droppings.

Even though they were about to face bigger opposition than they had ever seen before they had started to laugh and joke again. In some mysterious way it was as if Huw had managed to wrap them in a protective cocoon, within which they could come to no possible harm. Soon they had begun jumping and hopping along with all the unselfconscious nonchalance of children merely avoiding the cracks in the pavement.

Even lumbering old Emlyn felt a sudden lightness of movement as they went down the mountain, coming together the closer they got to the pit, with all the controlled and nerveless discipline of a Welsh rugby pack, snorting with ancient fire, ready to tear anything apart in their quest to get hold of a couple of scabs.

The sun had risen higher now, creating a thick silver strip of phosphorescence all along the high Valley wall, highlighting the tall, almost geometric shape of the killer tip and sending small waves of warmth breaking down the cold mountain slopes.

Outside the mouth of the Valley a Cardiff taxi was speeding along as three young miners cussed and cursed as they

450

shouldered a concrete pillar across a field. At one stage they had to stop to take a breather then passed the pillar over the fence before nearing the motorway. Now one of them left and ran away leaving the two miners to shoulder the pillar alone. They came out onto the motorway bridge and shouldered the pillar up onto the parapet, peering out into the drifting mists and waiting for the taxi.

'We'll go down there and then decide what to do,' said Glynmor pointing to a workman's shed in the mouth of the old slate quarry. Huw paused and looked up into the eye of the breaking sun. Something black broke out of it like a massive meteor and he stopped still, his eyes widening and his whole body trembling with fear.

All the boys had seen something dark sweep fleetingly over the Valley but thought it might have been the shadow of a plane crossing the face of the sun. But now Huw seemed to be belching and swallowing as if he had drunk something very gassy. His hands were shaking too and, in a matter of seconds, the boys too were sensing the same fear. All the earlier good feeling had ebbed out of them.

Huw's eyes were getting even wider as a huge dark mass rose out of the slopes of the killer tip to eclipse the sun. It did not have a recognisable shape but it did have the primitive beauty of naked terror, rising higher and yet higher, making the sunlight go blacker and yet blacker. It was as if a great chariot of shadow was moving across the Valley with the blurred outline of a man standing at its helm.

Glynmor put his arm across his son's shoulders and looked down into the Valley again. What was it? He thought he could hear the sound of singing. Or was it weeping? Yet all they could see were the continuing movements of the police with yet more wire-meshed vans pulling up outside the pit.

With their confidence gone all the boys now stood gazing down into the Valley with their mouths dry and silent. Tom the Nutter lit up a cigarette nervously. Just then a cry rang out down the brambled slopes. It was the most terrible cry that any of them had ever heard – the racked yell of a god unable to endure his torment any longer – and they were all very frightened indeed.

*

If indeed the cry was that of a god in undendurable pain then it could only have been at his anguish that his Valleys of love were now being swept by a storm of hate; that these ancient hills of coal had become the home of repression, scabs and murder. Just at that moment, the two young miners dropped the concrete pillar off the bridge and it went smashing down into the windscreen of the taxi passing underneath, killing the driver and making the car slew over onto the grass verge.

At precisely that moment also Oboe Parry walked in through the pit gates, being congratulated by the pit manager for becoming the first scab in the history of Bont. Even the NACODS men turned their backs on him as he walked down to the changing rooms.

At that moment, too, Maggie woke up with a start, looking up at the bedroom ceiling with her heart pounding against her chest like a madman in an asylum. She'd been having terrible nightmares of her Huw being drowned in the black slurry while out with Glynmor in Aberfan. She had not wanted him to go at all.

Maggie's dream instincts had indeed been uncanny since Huw was feeling as if he was drowning. He was struggling for breath with great black waves smashing over his mind, even loaming around inside his eyesight. Glynmor could hear him mewling with fear and held him tight as his body stiffened with some form of epileptic seizure. They laid him down on the ground as Emlyn put a rolled handkerchief into his dribbling mouth.

Down below in the Valley all was panic and commotion. Police cars sped off with alarms whooping and lights flashing. Someone glanced up the mountain from the pit gates and saw the boys from Bont. Immediately a detachment of boiler-suited police with riot truncheons began making their way up towards them.

The sight of the riot police was too much for the boys who turned and began scrambling back up the mountain leaving Emlyn and Glynmor to look after Huw. Glynmor was not at all sure what was going to happen when the police surrounded them even if it was clear that there was no point in trying to fight them.

'One of our boys has had a fit,' said Emlyn.

'It's Huw Bungalow isn't it?' asked one of the police. 'Come

452

on we'll help you down and get him home.'

Glynmor held him by the shoulders as the three of the policemen handed over their riot gear to the others and helped carry Huw down the slope.

They got a Tylorstown doctor to give Huw a check-up and, when he was pronounced merely exhausted, they drove back to Bont where Huw was put to bed. By this time, the murder of the taxi driver taking two scabs to work in the Aberfan Valley had led the national news bulletins. But, shocking though that was, it was not nearly as shocking as the news that waited for them on their own scrubbed slate doorsteps.

That morning Oboe Parry had broken the strike and become the first scab in the history of Bont.

Maggie stayed with Huw in his bedroom as Glynmor and Emlyn absorbed this, the latest stab in the back. They could have faced almost anything but this. They could not even manage to talk about it in any coherent, sensible way. Emlyn just kept on losing his breath and walking out through the kitchen door to stand breathing in the cold, damp air. Glynmor just sat on his fireside armchair gazing into the glowing coals and reflecting on what Jack London had once written about the scab: after God had finished making the rattlesnake, toad and vampire he took the leftovers and made the scab. But even that trenchant definition somehow didn't seem to sum up Oboe Parry.

'Did the doctor say anything about any medicine or tablets or anything?' asked Maggie when she came down again.

'No, he didn't say,' Glynmor replied, without looking up from the fire.

'Well did he say anything at all?'

'No, he didn't say.'

'Nothing? Nothing at all? There must have been something wrong with him. 'E's as white as a sheet he is.'

'He just said Huw must have fainted from exhaustion or fright or something. He said he didn't understand it either. But he said Huw's all right now. That's all I know as well, so leave us alone will you?'

'Well I'll tell you something for nothing. That boy is not going out on any picket line ever again. You can stick a thousand pickets on the mine here to keep out Oboe Parry but Huw's not going to be one of them. You've heard me have you?'

'I couldn't fail could I, with you shouting like some bastard fish wife? You do pick some nice times to rant and rave you do.'

She poked her tongue out at him and went back upstairs. Emlyn walked back into the room. 'You've got snowdrops coming up out the back,' he said. 'You know that, do you?'

'Aye.' Glynmor waved a hand around uselessly. 'There's daffodils coming up too. Huw planted them.'

Emlyn sat down in the chair on the other side of the fire and checked the time on his fob watch. He stretched his back and his whole large body seemed to groan with effort. 'I'm getting very tired, Glynmor. Not just tired, needing some sleep either. This is long-term tired I'm feeling now. This is treble-shift tiredness this is.'

'What are we going to do about Oboe?' Glynmor asked quietly without looking up from the fire. 'You know I could go down there an' rip the nose right off his face an' that's a fact.'

'No.'

'What do you mean "No?" '

'No,' Emlyn repeated again re-checking the time. 'This is not Belfast where you murder and destroy what you don't agree with. This is Welsh Wales and we've got to do this proper: the Welsh way. There's been one murder in the Welsh coalfields today and that's one too many. Feelings are running high. Sure as hell Oboe might get murdered too, if we're not careful.'

'Well I'd murder him happily enough if I could lay my hands on him. There'd be such a smile on my face as I was strangling the scab bastard.'

'Aye and you'd end up in prison. And for what? For some rotten scab who the coal board will look after because he's one of their own. No. We'll handle Oboe the way we've handled everything so far in the strike — through the community. Tonight every door will be knocked on and, in the morning, we'll all just stand out there and show him our shame. Let the television cameras come and see our shame too. Let's tell Jack Young what we're doing. He'll go for that, for sure. Let's call everyone out in the morning and show the world our shame.'

Glynmor had barely moved from his armchair all day and was still brooding in front of the fire when Maggie came down holding one of Huw's paintings in her hands. 'I've just found this under Huw's bed,' she said. 'Glynmor, it's terrible. It's the most depressing thing he's done.'

She passed it over to Glynmor. After he had looked at it he just closed his eyes and let out a long breath through his nose. The painting had an awesome power, a black sun hanging over a Valley with a huge black cross standing high on a slope. Every detail of the painting was black except long trickles running out of the base of the cross which were bright red, the colour of blood. Also every detail of the village in the belly of the Valley of Aberfan. There was the Community Hall and the Memorial Garden and the bleeding cross was sited just next to the mass graves of the children.

'It's Aberfan,' he said. 'It's how the Valley looked when we were there this morning.'

'But Huw's never been to Aberfan before. An' he must have done that painting weeks ago.'

'I don't care when he did it but that's Aberfan.'

Maggie just stood there, swallowing a little, before she spoke again. 'Glynmor, I want to leave here. Let's go tonight.'

'We can't.'

'Yes we can. I've made lots of new friends in places like Birmingham. We can go and stay with that Anne Stagg. You always liked her, didn't you? They're tidy people. You could get a job up there.'

'We can't, girl.'

'But why not? I'm frightened Glynmor. I don't know why but I'm getting terrible frightened. I just want to get Huw away from this place. He's getting mixed up in something and I don't understand it. Glynmor, I've never been so frightened. He's our only son. We've got to save him.'

'We can't.'

'Don't just sit there saying "We can't. We can't." Just tell me why not. Eh? Why not?'

His lips had gone dry and he swallowed hard. 'Girl, it's too late.' Now he was crying and looking up at her.

'What do you mean? What are you talking about? What's too late? You were only telling me the other day that nothing was too late. Now you're telling me it is. There's things going on here that are making me terrible frightened and I want to take Huw away out of it.' Tears were pouring down her cheeks too and, still standing, she kept wiping them away uselessly with her hand. 'He's all we've got Glynmor. We've got to try and save him. It can't be wrong to *try* and save your own son, now can it?'

'It's not wrong Maggie. But we're caught in something I can't explain. All I know for a fact is that it's too late and our Huw is wanted for something.'

'But wanted for what?'

'I don't know. I just feel this burden. I've got this understanding. There's nothing we can do. There's nowhere to run now.'

Chapter Twenty-Six

Once there were dinosaurs wandering the western landspill with pterodactyls screeching over darkling plains and brooding forests. But then came the Ice Age and the monsters were frozen into the forests and the pterodactyls packed into layers of antediluvian coal. With the Ice Age came the continual shunts of the glaciers which first shaped and dug the Valley, sculpturing the high smooth walls and running a mighty crack down a land later occupied by the Silurian tribe.

This Valley was a structural masterpiece, big and proud and yet as stable as the very sun. Geological movements were largely the result of man's ceaseless burrowing. For the most part, the walls of the Valley were as still and intact as that day when the giant hands of the glacier first began prising them apart.

Except that this morning, in the vague grey time which was neither night nor day, neither light nor dark, there were some ominous rumblings deep within the face of the southernmost Valley wall. Occasionally a few large rocks went tumbling and bouncing down the tall, frosted wall. They hit into other rocks with the loud empty cracking noises of walnuts being broken open, making the smaller rocks come hissing down around them; both the large cracks and the smaller hisses amplified by the great, fearful echo chamber of the Valley itself.

Such rumblings, distant but distinct, brought an added sense of menace to the atmosphere of Bont as the villagers filed out of their homes into the pre-dawn murk, some to stand on the pavement, others to walk up the road towards the pit. Even at such an unearthly hour, it was almost as if the whole village was on the move, as if they were presenting a huge Passion Play like those they stage for the tourists in the Bavarian Alps. But in this drama there were no speaking or acting parts, nor was there a tourist in sight. For this particular Passion Play the director had merely called on them to stand still in their winter clothes and silently mime the grief they felt at their betrayal.

There was more cracking and rumbling on the southern wall but now it had become so faint, so much a sound of the Valley itself, that there was just a great silence stretching down from the still reservoir. If you listened very carefully there was just the faint but distant echo of weeping which hung in the air, with trembling sorrow, like the sustained chord of an old Welsh harp.

The morning had begun to lift the corners of the night when Oboe Parry opened his front door and stepped out onto Bont Terrace. At first he did a double-take when he saw what was going on, almost running back into his house again. Directly over the road from him, a silent group of women stood looking at him from the opposite pavement.

But it was quickly apparent to him that there was no aggression or violence with them. Oboe Parry, strikebreaker, reckoned it was just a few of the women out nosey-parkering as he tried to lead the village back to work. There was never any violence in that Thelma Jones. You only had to look at her the wrong way and she did burst into tears.

Oboe stood there for a minute or two, waiting for other miners to come and join him. His historic walk the day before had made the *South Wales Echo*, albeit on page two what with the murder of the taxi driver – and he was hoping that, by the bravery of his example, others would now come and join him too. *Duw*, everyone was now that fed up with this strike and Scargill's bastard Red army.

But no one came. He was mildly surprised; there was an unusual number of people moving around for that time of day.

He remained standing there a while longer waiting for the dawn to come up higher. Jack Young had told him that they needed a lot more light than they had got yesterday and it wouldn't matter if he was a few minutes late for work, particularly as he only sat on his own in the canteen all day when he got there.

'Good morning, ladies,' he called out to the women standing on the other side of the road. Wherever possible, Jack had told him, Oboe should speak to someone so that the

458

microphone could pick up the exchanges. But the women said nothing and, very slowly, they all turned their backs on him.

A small cloud of cheeping blackbirds passed overhead as he walked on up the terrace. Here, yet more of the village was standing, both singly and in pairs, watching him break their strike. The thin sound of some orchestral music on the radio came trickling out of one of the houses. A front window was pulled shut.

Jack Young's cameraman was working from the top of the television van but it was still so dark the pictures were not as clear as he would have liked. Inside the van the director himself, with earphones on and nibbling a cream cracker, was watching Oboe's progress on his monitor.

'Don't worry too much about the light,' he was saying to the cameraman. 'Keep it general and shadowy. This is good mood stuff. Take in as many of the villagers' faces as you can but no ... don't linger. Keep panning now. That's nice. Good black and white that. There's marvellous black and white around here. In a minute – but not just yet – I'll want you to swing up to your right and start tracking down the mountain until you finish up in the square just by the clock. But hold it there for a bit ... that's good, that's very good ... '

Oboe's walk was being monitored electronically by someone else too. A police inspector was standing by the side of the Welfare Hall, and describing Oboe's progress on a short-wave radio down to three coaches with iron-meshed windows parked down by the river just next to Gnasher's yard. The coaches were full of policemen, all sitting quietly smoking or picking their noses as they listened to the inspector's words in between the bursts of static. 'He's coming up to the row of shops now. There's about thirty people standing around next to Lipton's – over.' *Hiss, crackle.* 'No one's saying a word to him but there's a few turning their backs. There's no sign of any punch-ups yet. Thank God – over.' *Hiss, crackle, crackle.*

The police had made informal contact with the N.U.M. lodge the night before. On being told what was going to happen, they had agreed to stay away as long as there was no violence. They insisted on being close at hand, however, since the strikebreaker had been publicised in the *Echo.* With passions running so high in the coalfields just now, this was clearly an incendiary situation which could go up at any second.

'Well, just keep your lads out of the way,' Emlyn had warned the inspector. 'There'll be no trouble if you stay out of the way.'

'We're not going to be looking for any trouble. We've had enough of that,' the inspector had assured him.

By now Oboe was sweating profusely. He had a thirst on him he wouldn't have sold for a quid. So this was that ancient Valley punishment he'd last seen used when he was a kid and someone had taken a wedding ring off a dead woman and tried to sell it.

It was effective enough, that was for sure. Cold hatred like this burned at your insides and made you worry for the safety of your children. He wouldn't have minded so much if the women had just bashed him with their handbags and been done with it. He would even have settled for a good thumping from one of the men. Anything but this. But he could hardly turn around and run home now, could he? Being seen as a coward around here was almost as bad as being seen as a scab.

He passed the shops and was surprised to find a yet larger crowd standing around the clock staring at him. Some had the hoods of their duffel coats pulled down so that he could not see their faces though he did recognise Therese Williams, Mrs Walsh, Betty Thomas and the two Pryce sisters from the big house up on the hill. Again he lifted his hand in a sort of greeting but again they turned their backs on him. He was particularly unhappy to see that Betty Thomas behaving like this. He had once laid his head on her bosom and wept after his Mam had died. There had even been a short courtship with that Therese Williams until the soft cow had gone off with that Trevor Black from Ynyshir. Who would go off with anyone from Ynyshir of all places?

And so here they all were, burning up the past that they had all enjoyed together. None of the bridges would be repaired after today. He knew that now.

Even the boys on the bench – Bits and Pieces, Curly and Idris – had got up early and were sitting there with their arms folded, pointedly staring at the leper who, sad and confused, shuffled across the square to the pit road. Who would have thought that those idiots would have turned against him too? Well, they'd brighten up soon enough when he gave them a few bob to buy some of their precious cider.

'Just keep very tight on his shoulders for a moment,' Jack Young said into his microphone as Oboe stopped to look up and around him at all the people dotted around the slopes leading down to the pit. 'Now pan out slowly, taking them all in. Beautiful, beautiful. Keep an eye on the way the sun is coming up over the pit. We'll pick that up later. Ah yes, that's good. That's very good.'

Jack had told Oboe to take his time about getting to the pit but the truth was that he could not have hurried, even if he had wanted to, since the continual shocks of seeing people he had known all his life come out at this time of the morning to shame him seemed to drain the strength out of his legs. He might even have been walking underwater or even trying to wade through a sea of jam. Phillip Tibbles and his brother Bert, were standing just near him and then there was Jackie Davies, Aunty Phyllis and her friend Enid. Even Gnasher and his skinhead staff were out on those slopes, arms folded as they looked down.

Oboe had never realised that anything could hurt so much. He began weeping quietly as he continued his savage walk. Some men would have dismissed such treatment with a laugh or a mock show of bravado, but such men would have not been from the Valleys. For him the scene had all the force and authority of the gallows at dawn. It spelt out the wholesale withdrawal of the love of the community which was the very blood of a Valley man; this was their way of giving him the mark of Cain and expelling him from the joy of their fellowship for ever.

It was all this silence that Oboe found the hardest to take. Here were women who he had spent all his life with – women who would talk about anything from a safety pin to an elephant – and they wouldn't say as much as boo, baa, bob's your arse to him. He wished they would shout something, anything at all, even if only to call him a fucking scab.

Now hot tears were running down his face and, looking down the long pit road, he saw the red and gold banner of the Bont lodge hoisted high outside the pit gate. Emlyn Kremlin would be standing there and so, doubtless, would that mad bastard Glynmor Jones. All the lodge boys would be standing around that banner ... Eggey, Dan, Dai, Abdabs, Tom the Nutter ... the Nutter owed him a pint too but there was no

461

chance of him ever getting that back now – unless it was poured over him one night in the Hall. And there'd be the women from the support group standing out there too ...

Oh Jesus ... oh Jesus ... he couldn't go on like this. This was a dull way of carrying on this was.

'Better get yourself out of the bus and ready for some action,' said the police inspector on his short-wave radio. 'We've got some trouble on our hands. I should have known that nothing could ever be peaceful at this end of the Valley. There's a few dozen coming over from Penrhos in the next valley. No. Well fuck me high and low – oh shit – there's fucking hundreds of them.

Maggie got up from her armchair and promptly sat down again. Now she was examining her feet and wondering if it was time to cut her toe-nails. She got up again and went out into the kitchen to peel potatoes for dinner, only to discover that she had peeled them two hours earlier. So she peeled some more just to keep herself occupied.

She was normally very placid, particularly first thing in the morning, but she kept bouncing about the place as if she was on a hot tin roof. Paranoid ideas dropped down from the walls and attacked her brain like midges. Glynmor was going to be locked up for murdering Oboe. Glynmor had been badly injured by the police. They were going to come knocking on her door at any second to tell her that Glynmor had been taken to hospital ... Glynmor ... Glynmor ...

The real truth of it was that she was feeling terribly guilty about not being out with Glynmor along with the rest of the village. But she had decided to stay home to make sure that Huw did not go out. Indeed she was so determined that Huw wasn't going anywhere she had hidden his clothes. Glynmor's weeping and telling her that it was all too late had shaken her rigid. She really would have wrapped Huw up in cotton wool if she could have.

She made Huw a cup of tea and took it upstairs only to find that he hadn't even touched the last one. He was just lying there miserably and staring into space, not even looking at her when she put the steaming tea down next to his bed. 'What's the matter my little *dwt*?' she asked picking up the cold one. 'Not thirsty are you?'

He pulled his bedclothes to one side and made as if to get up but she eased him back down onto the bed. 'You stay put now and have a good rest,' she soothed. 'You must be wanged out after yesterday you must. But you do look all right I must say. Beautiful as ever.'

Huw continued to gaze blankly into space, so she went back downstairs again where she stood at the front door looking up the hill. She could see some people, unfamiliar to her, picking up some rubble from the demolished chapel and running along the gulley in the direction of the mine. A few other strangers were running down the terraces picking up empty milk bottles from the doorsteps as they went. There was a shout and a bright burst of shattering glass. In the distance there was a dim rolling roar of a baying crowd and, almost without thinking, Maggie pulled her coat off the peg in the passage and ran towards the mine. Just past the square she heard even louder sounds of violent commotion and the long bank of people with their backs to her told her immediately that there was a lot of trouble brewing.

And if there was trouble around, she thought bitterly, you could be sure that her Glynmor would be in the middle of it somewhere.

Huw heard the noise also and had got out of bed to stand at his bedroom window to look towards the pit. A row of terraces and the Welfare Hall blocked out the crowds but the mine itself was visible enough tucked right at the end of the Valley with the sun rising behind the still wheel.

Huw continued to stare at the mine when the wheel seemed to eclipse the sun, making its blazing heart go dark. But then it was as if the wheel itself had caught fire. Large, bright flames were flickering around the foundry and out of the washery, burning the whole bottom of the sky in a great orange and yellow glow. Huw kept gazing at the wheel of fire when he heard a whistling sound which was a distress call crying out for help. It was the song of the cave telling him that one of the tribe was in pain.

He looked around his bedroom for his clothes.

'Just hold it there for a while on that crowd coming down the Valley wall,' Jack said into his microphone. 'When you get them and Oboe into focus together then pull in tight on Oboe and stay there. I'm getting some very strange noises from him. Not so long ago he seemed to be crying. Now he's whistling. That's what you do when the shit is running down your legs I suppose.'

Even from afar the Penrhos mob looked truly terrifying as they came scrambling down the jagged face of the Valley, screaming and shouting and throwing rocks like a tidal wave of ravening wolves and slavering hyenas. Even the earth seemed to thunder as their feet pounded down the slopes, some slipping and sliding on the loose rocks, screaming the wildest obscenities as they fell. There might have been three hundred of them in all; a raggle-taggle army of farting thugs, dog-breathed gypsies and glue-addled teenagers, all bearing down on Oboe Parry like a swarm of enraged bees come to destroy an imposter queen.

Glynmor, who had been standing near the lodge banner at the pit entrance, looked at Emlyn and said one name: 'Dan Bag O'Shit.'

Now it was as if the whole world was bearing down on Oboe who, in that lonely moment, suddenly understood what it must have been like to have been a murderer on his way to Tyburn.

The Penrhos mob was pouring down the Valley wall to get him. Line after line of boiler-suited police were running up the pit road to save him. Gnasher and the skinheads were dashing into the fray because they thought it would be good fun. The boys from the Bont lodge were running towards Oboe too, unsure why, but running anyway – as fast as their legs would carry them. Even the television van began edging closer to the centre of the conflict.

'I want C Group to break away and come up from the river side,' said the police inspector over his short-wave radio. 'There's going to be an almighty scrap so I want the C men to run a pincer movement right into them and take out the strikebreaker. Handcuff three of the miners to anything mobile you can find and retreat back to the village behind it. They won't throw rocks at their own.'

Many of the villagers who had been standing out to watch Oboe's walk to the mine were now backing off nervously as a Penrhos hand hoisted a rock which curled high in the air before clattering near Oboe's feet. He managed to sidestep the next rock but the next one caught him on the cheek followed by another which caught him flush on the top of his head making his vision swirl like shimmering dartboards.

Back at the start of the pit road a man stepped out from the gully behind the demolished chapel and flung a petrol bomb at one of the empty police coaches. He dashed back down the gully chased by the driver when the coach went up in a great *voom*! with a billowing pillar of smoke and flame climbing high into the sky.

'They're going to get him now. Just hold the camera on Oboe. Try and get in the pit as background but don't worry if you can't. Oh hello. That nutty kid has turned up. Track him. Track him.'

Unseen in all the commotion, Huw Bungalow, dressed only in boxer shorts, was pushing his way through the fighting crowds towards Oboe. A miner taking pity on him took off his overcoat and threw it on him. There was a great deal more pushing when Huw managed to grab Oboe's arm, trying to pull him down past a roll of barbed wire and into the shelter of one of the concrete drains which carried the excess water out of the nearby tip. But Oboe, with soaring dizziness and blood running into his eyes, did not recognise Huw and pulled his arm away. Huw grabbed at Oboe's arm again, now hanging on grimly as more rocks and milk bottles came thumping and smashing down all around them.

Glynmor, sweating and panting from his own run from the pit, spotted Huw and shouted a loud and useless warning to him just as the police and Penrhos mob converged on Oboe at about the same time. Glynmor literally dived over a riot shield to get at Huw and, from then on, all was bleeding and bloody confusion as the scrapping, rolling scrum of bodies surged up and down the road.

Back in Bont Terrace Maggie ran home and up the stairs, bursting open the bedroom door to find that Huw's bed was empty. 'Oh no,' she cried. 'Oh Huw, you haven't have you?'

The television van moved closer as the fighting continued. Glynmor lashed out with his fists again and again as he looked around for Huw. It was just then that he spotted the smiling buffoon face of Dan Bag O'Shit so he gave him a good smack in the chops instead. Then he caught the brown flash of a riot truncheon and a handcuff was snapped onto his wrist. A bundle of miners and police went cartwheeling past when Tom the Nutter was handcuffed also and a police helicopter came flying in low, the noise of its rotor blades smacking against the Valley walls like the sound of repeated machine gun fire.

A detachment of police, under the control of the helicopter, now came up on the river side of the road, cutting the brawling mob in a huge pincer movement while the rest of the police gathered together and rolled backwards in a series of retreating phalanxes.

The move had cut the heart out of the fighting though, more importantly, the police had secured their objective of rescuing Oboe Parry and setting up a barrier to protect their retreat. It was the most horrifying barrier imaginable. The television camera panned slowly across the silent motionless people and framed it squarely.

A roll of barbed-wire had been pulled across the road and three men were impaled on it. In the scuffling they had been pushed forward onto the cruel spikes so that their bodies and heads were masked with blood. One was Tom the Nutter, squealing like a pig since, the more he moved, the more the spikes cut into him. The other was a semi-conscious Glynmor who had given up trying to move and was just groaning thinly.

At the centre of them was Huw Bungalow, his arms handcuffed to the wire on either side of him and the blood pouring out of his back and buttocks in fast red rivulets onto the road. His borrowed overcoat flapped open with a hot sun blazing down on his thin misshapen body covered only by a pair of white boxer shorts. Sweat was bubbling on his brow as he looked up at a dark curdling sky. When he tried to move, a spasm of pain racked the whole of his body as more spikes drove into his flesh. A thin trickle of blood began slipping silently out of the side of his mouth.

There are 2,200 thunderstorms raging throughout the world at any one moment. That afternoon three came piling down into the Valley. Thunderheads ricocheted against one another in the pines and jagged lightning slashed the sky to pieces just above the reservoir. At one point the thunderheads were breaking so hard and often they could even be heard down on the deserted coal face, a mile below ground, where there were slight showers of loose coal sounding like handsful of sand being poured on corrugated iron. But it was the continual, driving rain which was the angriest and most bitter – coming down the Valley in giant swirling cartwheels, hammering on the rooftops of the terraces and swirling around the volcano walls like giant dodgem cars trying to find a way out.

Down in the intensive care unit in Ferndale, Maggie was sitting alone in a corridor smoking a cigarette. She had never been much of a smoker, rarely taking down the smoke but now she was coughing heavily when the smoke caught in the back of her throat. Occasionally she stood up and walked down to the window at the end of the corridor, wiping a hole in the condensation with her finger-tips, through which she could just make out the bulky squat shape of the Moriah Chapel and the Midland Bank in the teeming rain. She took another drag on her cigarette but it almost looked as if she was eating it, rather than smoking it, since her hand was shaking so much she could barely get the cigarette into her mouth.

'Would you like a cup of tea, Mrs Jones?' a nurse asked.

'No thanks. Is he, is he?'

'No. I'm afraid not. We'll let you know. You just take it easy now. Your husband rang as well. He says he's all right and he'll be down as fast as he can.'

Maggie walked down to the other end of the corridor but turned back when she saw all the crowds just standing out there in the rain. It was odd the way the whole village just seemed to stop – stopped working, stopped eating, stopped fighting, stopped everything – just to come down to Ferndale and stand in the rain; just to be there with her while she waited on Huw. They were in a strange, unruly mood too, she could tell, and she so hoped that they weren't going to do anything silly.

The air inside the hospital was so thick and warm that breathing was rather like eating small balls of candy floss. She took another cigarette out of her packet but threw it straight into a red bucket full of sand. Then she began the ritual of walking the length of the corridor and looking out of the window again. She could just make out the outline of her face in the glass ... haggard, drawn cheeks; trembling dry lips; dark, sunken eyes. It was funny how all this rain was the exact image of what she was feeling inside her; how there seemed to

467

be this wild uncontrollable weeping both in the skies and in her heart. Oh Huw, my baby …

'Mrs Jones? There's a man from the *Echo* here. He wants to know if you'll talk to him.'

'No. Yes. Ask him to come in for a minute would you?'

A small, red-faced Irishman introduced himself as Dan O'Neill. She remembered that he had once written well about Huw when he had gone missing.

'I haven't got too much to say,' she said hesitantly. 'But I was … ah … wondering if you could tell me what's going on back in the village.'

'What do you mean Mrs Jones?'

'Is there any trouble? Any more fighting with the police?'

'No. Everything's quiet and the police have withdrawn. But there's one woman, Daisy – your sister I think – who's taken the women's support group to the mine where they've set up a picket. They're even keeping the safety men out. I was wondering, Mrs Jones, if you had any comment on the way the police behaved?'

'Have you seen my Glynmor at all? I heard they knocked him about a bit after they arrested him but couldn't think of anything to charge him with in the end. He sent a message here saying he was all right.'

'I heard that too. They let him go right enough. He's fine now but they've taken the other one – Tom the Nutter I think they call him – into the Royal in Cardiff for observation. It's your Huw that was injured the worst.'

Maggie's lower lip quivered on the verge of tears. She plucked up the courage to make her big statement. 'Huw, as you may have heard, is in a critical coma,' she said in an unsteady voice. 'There's a lot of internal bleeding which may drown his lungs. But what I want to tell you is that – even if he dies – even if … there must be no bitterness, no more fighting with the police. Huw was a dove you see, Mr O'Neill. Oh, people were always making jokes about him having the brain of a small soap dish but he was a dove of peace. He never did anything violent or hateful. He got his injuries trying to protect a scab. A scab! That's the way he was. He just *could not* do anything violent or hateful so would you write an article in your newspaper asking that all this fighting must stop? And it must stop now. You'd do that for me would you Mr O'Neill?'

'That's no problem, Mrs Jones.'

'Good. That's very good.' Maggie was surprised at her lucidity and calm in front of the newspaperman. 'I've read some of your stuff in the *Echo*. It's very tidy too, as they'd say around here. You should go on one of the national newspapers.'

'I've done all that but now I like living in Cardiff.'

'Fancy that. I can't imagine anyone liking to live in Cardiff.'

That same day the members of the Energy Minister's coal committee in London were all served with champagne. For the first time in a year more than one million tonnes of coal had been delivered to coal board customers within the week.

There were now forty-six pits working normally, according to the N.C.B. The biggest return of the day was in Scotland where seventy-eight men went back to work. Now there were nearly 3,000 working there and qualifying for a tax-free bonus.

And so the biggest and most continuous mobilisation ever mounted against the government was floundering towards an end. 'The mineworkers' strike, as a living entity with some sap left in it, is over,' said the *Financial Times*. 'The final moves are of vital, perhaps paramount, importance: but they *are* the end game.'

Back in the Valley the storms continued unabated. The Bont women's support group had commandeered a portakabin to set up a base outside the pit and maintained a twenty-four hour picket. But, after the morning's violence, no one went anywhere near the place. For the first time in its history Bont Colliery was without safety cover of any kind.

In the intensive care unit that night Huw continued haemorrhaging. Specialists went back and forth with Maggie and Glynmor taking it in turns to sit outside his cubicle. 'I don't know that I can take this much more,' Maggie wailed, white-faced. 'There's all this pain in me. It's everywhere ... in my hands, my legs ... I can even feel it in my teeth ... Everywhere. Oh Glynmor where's the sense in all this? Where's the sense in it? This is all so dull. We should have gone away, we should. We could have saved him if we'd gone away instead of letting him get crucified outside that bastard pit. Oh that bastard pit of yours. I'd fill it in, I would. Fill it in now, if they'd let me. This bastard coal. This bastard pain.'

In spite of the rain the crowds kept coming to stand outside the hospital, right through the night they came surging up the road and gathering to look up at the lit window of the intensive care cubicle. Occasionally hymns went fluttering warmly through the dripping darkness, adding a ferocious bite to Maggie's pain, making her get up again and look out onto the singing street with the tears flowing down her cheeks. At one moment she thought she had spotted the face of John, the tramp from Cardiff, in the crowd. But, when she looked again, his face had gone and there was just the rain.

The one beneficial result from all these downpours was that the streets of Bont were washed almost clean of the rubbish left by the NALGO strike. Much of it was carried away down the swollen river whose littered torrents swept all before it.

In the roof of the Welfare Hall the surveyor's torch swept around the forest of rafters as he picked his way over the old lodge banners which had been wrapped up and folded on the floor. Rain was dripping through parts of the roof and gushing down through great holes in others. There was such a stiff smell of decay it could have been sliced up and packaged.

'This roof's leaking worse than ever,' said the surveyor.

'Aye, there's a few leaks,' admitted Max Million, the committee chairman, standing near the hatch door, unwilling to enter any further into the darker side of the kingdom of his responsibilities. 'But this place is good for another hundred years yet.'

'Mr Million, this place is not good for another hundred seconds. It may even be too late for me to get out of here now. There's been no work done up here at all, as you promised, and ...'

'Well, we've had a strike, you know. You've heard of the coal strike, I take it? We haven't had the money for anything since the strike began.'

'Yes, I do see that. But, look here, these rafters are so rotten they come away in your hands.' He took hold of one of the rafters and a large chunk came away in his hands. 'There could be a dance in here tonight and the whole lot would fall in. That would look nice in the papers wouldn't it? Just come over here and look Mr Million. Come on now. Look at this.'

Slowly, reluctantly, with low sighs, the committee chairman picked his way over the lodge banners to stand at the surveyor's side. By torchlight they both looked at the cobwebbed, rotten woodwork.

'I'm afraid, Mr Million, I have no other option but to close you down immediately until you put a new roof on this place.'

Way down in the Bont mine, the main roadway is dark and deserted with the trams standing empty on the rails leading to the cage. Every fifty yards pale yellow puddles of light sit in the murk, occasionally catching in the silica of the pale grey dust which, as soft as down, covers the ground all around the rail lines. There are footprints of boots in the downy dust and coloured oil in the brown pools. Just about the only sound that can be heard is the steady trickle of drips falling into the empty trams.

Further down into this moles' warren the long conveyor belts stand silent, with only the odd black pat moving away from the glare of the lights and sinking down into the dust. The very air has the damp chill of the tomb and the foul smell of the sewer. Occasionally the smell of piss or shit loiters in the darkness; a reminder that three shifts a day for almost a hundred years have pissed and shat just where they stood.

The old roadways and abandoned faces are still there, running off the main working roadway. Down these old faces the buckled steel girders and the shattered pit-props stand around like a forest in hell. In parts there is enough water seeping in to get half a dozen miners screaming for water notes. Sitting in one of the old refuge holes, there are three dusty tea jacks and one tommy-tin, as if, all these years later, they are still waiting patiently for the tea-break whistle.

The giant air-conditioners have been turned off now and, closer down towards the main face, the air is still and bad. There have been more squeezes on the great girders of the main roadway too, and the shattered Atlases of the hydraulic props will be unable to hold up the heavy earth much longer.

There are still pale yellow puddles of light everywhere, glinting on the steel rails and buckled girders, highlighting the

471

hollow coffins of the trams and the sloping floors of this long roadway to nowhere. The chill of the tomb becomes chillier and, in the very intensity of the silence, there comes the voices of the hard heading men and the whistling hum of the conveyors and the rattle of the passing journeys of coal. But the sounds do not last. They fade as quickly as they come and there is the long and endlessly patient silence of the tomb again.

Now – late, dark and still raining – yet more people are flooding into the small streets of Ferndale and there is an overwhelming gale of loss and desolation blowing hard around every corner. The hymn-singing has started again and it is the most sweetly beautiful, the most painfully sorrowing sound that anyone can ever remember hearing in their lifetime in the Valleys. It is the many-layered sound of bleeding, breaking hearts; the minor key sound of a people in pain because they know that the handicapped prince of the Valleys is dying up there in that hospital cubicle.

They understand all too clearly that his life is their life; that his death is their death too. More crowds come and now there is practically no room to move anywhere at all in the crush of bodies. They look up at the oblong of light waiting for the shutter to be drawn. A great wave of singing and prayer continues to collapse over the hospital as the sodden people keep struggling to rediscover their lost faith without which life has no meaning; the faith without which the communities will fully and finally collapse and only the locusts of crime will carry on feeding until the corpse has been picked clean.

And the nightmare is living and looming over them now as they wrestle with their souls in this rain-drenched night. With the loss of their pit the nightmare has already begun and hell on earth is with them with the death rays of television radiating every home from which dark, stooped figures will emerge under the cover of night to pull the bodies of their children out of the gutters ...

And they know it too. Their imaginative, insecure hearts know that the nightmare has begun just as clearly as they know that they are standing there looking up at an oblong of light and waiting for a death in the family.

On the coal face itself, water is dribbling out, making the coal

472

shine like black diamonds. This is Bont's main seam which was coaling so well until the strike brought production to a halt.

Sitting in front of the face is the giant Dosco, now but a sleeping giant, shackled by the long, still Panzer chains. The machine stands on the tracks with no men to service its multiple needs; nothing but a leaking electrical circuit out of which sparks are leaping and twirling like electronic acrobats in a darkened circus ring. There is a short red flash of fury and the incandescent sparks leap again. Some three feet away a thin flame of blue methane is hissing out of the coal face …

The rain kept pounding down into the Valley throughout the night with all the wrath of the prophets of old, making the reservoir as full as an egg, swelling the already swollen river until it burst its banks down by the Banana Tip. There was so much water flooding through the gullies the drains could no longer cope. Soggy rubbish dammed the pipes, making springs of muddy water burst up out of the gutters and overflow into the streets.

The torrents had been so ferocious they had unleashed a further round of small avalanches on the southernmost wall of the Valley, sending a landslip of stone down onto one of the outer fields of Billy Smiles' farm.

It was late afternoon and already getting dark when Billy went out with his dog and stick to examine the fall. But even in the full fury of the storm he could hear something harsh and siren in the air which almost made him cower with fright. He turned his head to look up into the rain and could just about make out two ravens curling around one another as they flew through the driving rain. All the time they were making the most terrible sobbing noises Billy had never heard.

The doctor lifted the stethoscope off Huw's chest and shook his head grimly. The blood had completely drained out of Glynmor's face and he just stood staring, unbelieving, at his sleeping son.

Maggie leaned across the bed and kissed Huw's cold cheek. 'So goodbye then, my darling son of the morning,' she said as soft and quiet as her tears. 'Sleep well, my beautiful angel.'

A nurse pulled down the shutter on Huw's cubicle and outside, in the still-crowded street, there was a loud collective cry of the most abject agony. The cry gave way to weeping and then to the gentle drumming of the rain. A hymn flared briefly, as warm as a bonfire on a cold night, before the voices fell silent again, too choked to even weep, let alone sing. The son of the morning had left them and it seemed to everyone present that the sunshine would never come to the Valleys again. In ones and twos the people peeled off home into the rain. A child's dummy was being swept along by the torrents in the gutter. Far away there was the distressed sound of a pit hooter. Now there were just a dozen people left in the road outside the hospital still looking up at the dark, shuttered cubicle almost as if they were wondering if they would ever see any light ever again.

Chapter Twenty-Seven

'It's gone that I do 'ave a terrible 'eadache on top of everything,' said Glynmor, gazing down into the fire-grate in which there was no fire.

'I've got a headache everywhere,' said Maggie. 'There's some tablets out in the kitchen. By the tea caddy I think they are.'

They were both sitting, still in their coats and with hands thrust down into their pockets, in their cold living room. Their desultory conversation was broken only by the ticking of the clock.

'Shall I make a fire, shall I?' he asked.

'If you like. I'm not fussed. We'll 'ave to go to bed sometime I s'pose but what for I can't think. I shouldn't think I'll ever sleep again.'

'Your eyes have gone a bright red girl. Come over 'ere. Let's 'ave a bit of a *cwtch*.'

'You come over 'ere,' she smiled, looking over at him with her sore eyes.

They squeezed in together on the same chair and the feel of his strong arms around her made her start crying again. She put her arm around his neck, squeezing so tight he had to shift his head away.

'Come on, let's go to bed,' he said. 'Bed is always the best when you're not feeling up to the mark.'

But when they got upstairs she was still so wit-wat she automatically went into Huw's bedroom to check, as was her nightly habit, that he was all right. Glynmor had almost to pull her into their own bedroom where she was now in such a useless state he had to take off her coat and undress her himself.

She didn't think that she could possibly have had any tears left but they kept coming anyway, even as they made hot and fevered love right through until dawn, hardly pausing for breath after each dance, just keeping going in a series of small explosions of passion like bare electric wires touching one another, taking it in turn to mount one another, their hip-bones banging and clashing and kissing so hard their teeth cut into their lips until they were squealing and panting for breath, but still not stopping even for a short rest as their wired-up bodies kept up their frantic search to bring some relief and healing to the other's.

He was every bit as lusty and crazy as her and it was strange how, in the midst of death, they learned the secrets of life and it took them their greatest and most terrible crisis to learn about the healing sacrament of sexual love; how this most exciting species of existence can also bring warm and powerful feelings of comfort to the deepest and most persistent pain.

It wasn't as if Maggie was feeling less pain, as their bodies continued battling through that night of iron. It was just that, through all this driving, almost relentless physicality, her body was slightly more able to bear the pain. And, in some strange way, the holy sacrament of sex enabled her to make some sense of the pain too. She had absorbed it deeper into her being. Her grief, which she would carry with her always, had become a more certain part of her continuity, of her very life.

Their bodies were so exhausted finally they could barely move and they slept the sleep they needed so badly. Maggie was sitting with Huw and Glynmor on the beach at Barry Island. Old men with their trousers rolled up were paddling around in the tiny brown waves and Huw was building sand castles. Glynmor, with a handkerchief knotted over his head, was snoring on a deckchair when there was a cry and a great black wave broke inside Maggie, collapsing over her mind and even beginning to fill up her very eyes until she was fighting for breath as her lungs began to fill up. She could never remember being so enveloped in so much darkness, crying out and opening her eyes to find herself sweating and trembling in Glynmor's soothing arms.

Huw Bungalow's funeral attracted the largest crowd to Bont that anyone could remember and they re-opened the Welfare Hall just for the day.

His coffin was placed in the Starlight Lounge and people drifted in and out to pay their last respects as Maggie and Glynmor sat together near the lounge door. No one actually spoke to the bereaved parents though a few did come over and touch Glynmor on the shoulder or squeeze Maggie's hand.

'Can you do something about this chair,' Maggie asked Glynmor.

'What's the matter with it?'

'I can't seem to stop it wobbling.'

She stood up as Glynmor took a beer mat off one of the tables, ripping it in two and stuffing it under one of the chair legs. 'That's better,' she said when she sat down again. 'That's what I've always hated about this place. The chairs and tables have always wobbled.'

'Who's that man over there?'

'Don't know. Never seen him before.'

The main street of the village was packed and the throng gasped, as if they still could not believe their eyes, when the coffin was carried out of the Hall doors. Brilliant, cold sunshine sparkled on the gilt coffin handles. As the Ferndale Brass Band struck up *Cwm Rhondda* parts of the crowd picked up the hymn while the cortège set off to walk the mile or so the cemetery with everyone stopping every hundred yards or so to change pallbearers. To be a pallbearer was always a mark of Valley respect and love. Those who were widely respected and loved had dozens of pallbearers who saw to it that they carried the coffin at least a part of the way, all changing again when the hymn changed. Huw had hundreds.

Every shop was closed and every curtain drawn. Occasionally a tearful housewife pushed through the crowds to reach out and touch the coffin. Yet more crowds stood out on the Valley slopes to watch from afar while dark clumps of people stood, black on blue, on the very rims of the volcano. Further up the mountains, past the reservoir, there were still white streaks of snow. Even today, at the beginning of March, the winter was still showing no sign of releasing the land.

As the cortège thinned out and unwound it began to be possible to see who was and who was not there. The Buffs, with their rows of medals clanking together as they marched, had turned up in force as had the Rechabites and the Hearts of Oak. Gnasher and the skinheads were also there as were the boys from the bench with Idris wearing the war medals which usually came out only on Days of Remembrance. There was a uniformed group from the Boys' Brigade and representatives of the Boy Scouts and Girl Guides. Even the police – after a few discreet inquiries – had sent a delegation albeit in plain clothes.

As he had in his life, Huw Bungalow had managed to bring everyone together in his death.

The most notable absentee was Oboe Parry and his family. Even on its last day of normal operations the Hall committee, in an emergency meeting, had blackballed the whole of the family and Brenda was so upset she took the children to go and live for a while with her sister in Port Talbot. Where Oboe had gone no one had a clue. Word had got around that Oboe had been wearing a microphone on the day he had broken a strike so, perhaps fortunately for Oboe's continuing health, he had disappeared too – as had Jack Young with his television crew. The lodge was still considering what to do about Jack Young since they'd had a Chinese whisper that Jack had put Oboe up to breaking the strike.

The cortège was met at the wrought-iron gates of the cemetery by the Rev. Bruce Davies, an Anglican from Peterston-super-Ely, who had come up for the funeral and lead them up to the grave itself. In spite of the sun, the wind was bitterly cold as it whipped down past the alabaster angels and grey stone urns. Three ropes were used to lower the coffin into the earth.

It had been agreed that, as Huw was of no particular faith, the funeral service should be informal and open to all with the Rev. Davies starting it by reading Psalm 139: 'If I take my flight to the frontiers of the morning or dwell at the limit of the western sea, even there will thy hand meet me ... '

Clumps of snowdrops and daffodils were scattered all over the cemetery; the delicate snowdrops quivering in the wind and the trumpets of the daffodils facing the sky in an avid embrace with the cold sun.

'Thou knowest me through and through: my body is no mystery to thee, how I was secretly kneaded into shape and patterned in the depths of the earth ... '

The Buffs scattered ivy leaves over the coffin and, with their arms linked, sang their brotherhood song. More crowds came moving into the cemetery off the road – the men with their caps in their hands and the red-eyed women with their scarfed heads bowed – as the bugler from the Boys' Brigade played *The Last Post*. 'In the midst of life we are in death,' the Rev. Davies read from the Order of the Burial of the Dead. 'Of whom may we seek succour, but of thee, O Lord, who for our sins are justly displeased …'

Throughout the reading, Glynmor was standing ramrod-erect, staring over the lines of tombstones at the grave of his best butty Jampots who they had buried nearly twenty years ago now, after that explosion down the mine. He remembered how upset he had been at Jampots' funeral which contrasted oddly with how he was feeling at the moment – as cold and hard as a stone on the mountain. He did not even look down at the coffin of his son and just stood there concentrating on nothing, feeling nothing, wanting nothing … almost as if what was going on all around him was some elaborate charade which had nothing to do with him at all. Whenever he did allow his thoughts to form it was as if he was somehow deep within a pit from which there was no escape.

Emlyn, for the miners, gave the graveside oration: 'In the old days the miner always relied on the canary when he was working underground,' he said in a rich, full voice which carried far in spite of the cold winds bustling past the gravestones and sweeping some of his words away. 'If the canary was quiet there was no gas. If it began wobbling in its cage it was time to walk out of the mine. If it fell off its perch it was time to run. The canary was always there, with its sweet song and delicate lungs, ready to lay down its life for us. The canary warned, protected and comforted us and today our canary has fallen off its perch. Today our very greatest canary has died and there is nowhere for us to run or hide. So we just come and stand here to give thanks for a life which was given to us … and then taken away.'

After the priest had read the Committal, mourners lined up to throw a handful of earth down onto the coffin. Some threw flowers and it was nearly an hour before everyone had filed past the open grave with the earth swooshing down in small bumps and soft showers as Maggie and Glynmor stood together looking out over the Valley.

When the burial had finished they had the customary do with beer and ham sandwiches down in the Hall but Maggie did not attend and neither did Glynmor. They went home together where she took off her coat and sat silently in front of the banked-up fire as Glynmor made the tea. 'There's no sugar. I can't find the sugar,' he shouted from the kitchen.

'It doesn't matter.'

'Where's the sugar?' he shouted again.

'I said it doesn't matter,' she said louder.

He brought in two large mugs setting them down by the grate, before warming his hands, still red raw with the cold, in the fire, now taking the poker to it and using the tongs to put on a few more lumps. He looked down on the floor just next to him – as if he had lost something – then began poking the fire again, making the small red flames leap and splutter in somersaults of sparks.

'You're going to poke the guts out of that the way you're going on,' she pointed out.

'It's this coal. Some of Gnasher's stuff isn't it? There doesn't seem to be any bottle left in it at all.'

Maggie sniffed as if her nose had begun running but stayed slumped in her chair, hands in the front pockets of her skirt. Her mouth was hanging open slightly and her bottom jaw was trembling. She had not eaten anything since the accident and had gone as thin as a lath. She was trying so hard not to cry since she was sure that, once she started, she would cry for ever.

The back boiler water system inside the chimney began clanking and hissing so Glynmor went out into the kitchen to run off some hot water. Someone knocked on the door but neither of them answered it.

'Should I peel some spuds for dinner?' Glynmor asked her.

'As you like. I'm not hungry.'

'You've got to eat girl.'

She put her head to one side and closed her eyes, as if she had fallen asleep. But always Huw was there. His face and his laughter and his walk came to her in the most vivid strokes in the darkness. It was as real as if he was still in the room – and only when she opened her eyes and looked around the room did she realise that, far from being there, this was the day of his funeral.

The house was still littered with Huw's bits and pieces; his painting stuff scattered in the corner of the living room, his clothes hung up neatly in his wardrobe, his blue suede shoes in the passage. They hardly helped much but there had been no attempt to tidy them away. Even his bed had been left crumpled and unmade, exactly as he had left it.

'Shall I go and buy a bottle or something?' Glynmor offered but she did not open her eyes, as if she was asleep.

There was a knock on the door and, leaving Maggie to sleep, Glynmor answered it. Gnasher stood there, awkward in his dark new suit.

'The word is they're putting the mockers on the pit for definite,' Gnasher said quietly. 'So when're we going to move?'

'Not for a few days yet.'

'Why wait a few days?'

''Cos I've got to talk to the boys first. We can't do it alone can we?'

'Anyway I want to hear an official announcement about the closure of the pit before we make a move. Then we go straight in. I've got plenty of boys. We could do it now.'

Maggie's eyes opened as she tried to hear what was being talked about. But she couldn't make out anything at all. 'What was that all about?' she asked, when Glynmor returned inside.

'Nothing.'

'That was a lot of talk about nothing.'

He walked across the living-room towards the kitchen and paused. 'The garden's in a mess. I'm going to give it a good dig.'

Maggie thought it an odd time to give the garden a good dig but she said nothing as he stripped off down to his vest. Still wearing his best trousers and only decent pair of shoes, he took a spade out of the shed and began turning over the frozen earth at the end of the garden.

But the earth, he soon found, was far too hard for a spade. He took out a mandril too and, quite soon, had broken up the stiff earth, turning it over and over again until there was a sheen of sweat on his muscular compact body, staining the back of his vest and dripping off his brow. It took him a good half an hour to work through the main vegetable patch and, when he had finished that, he decided to do it all over again. Discovering that the roots of a lilac tree had spread into the patch he chopped it down and uprooted the stump in less than ten minutes.

'I don't know what you've got against that poor tree. The poor dab has done nothing to you.'

A shadow fell over Glynmor's shoes and he looked up to see his sister-in-law Daisy. Her eyes were so puffed from crying she could barely see.

'I've come to say goodbye,' she said. 'I'm going up to London for a while.'

'Going off to save the world are you?'

'Well there's nothing left here to save,' she said, still too upset to catch the edge of his sarcasm. 'The strike is falling apart and I s'pose you've heard the best news? They've decided to close the pit. It's official. There were two surveyors here this morning.'

'When you say it's official what do you mean?'

'They've told the Press. Told them about the fire on the face. It'll be in the *Echo* tonight.'

He looked along the rows of gardens to the side of the Welfare Hall. Huge beards of silver ice had broken open the drainpipes; sections of roof guttering were hanging outwards and downwards, poised to fall off at any second. Every window frame was rotten, with the windows themselves broken around the latches by thieves and most of them nailed up with planks and pieces of hardboard. Two blackbirds, caught in the sun as they flew overhead, sent their shadows sliding across the broken tapestry.

'You don't seem very surprised by the news, Glynmor.'

He shrugged his shoulders. Nothing would surprise him after all they'd been through. 'I'd 'eard there'd been a fire in the Dosco. I thought they might make that the excuse to close the pit. Now that we've lost the strike an' all. They've been looking for some sort of excuse for long enough.' His abstracted manner turned into something brisk and businesslike. 'Look girl. I've got this garden to dig and you've got a bus to catch. Just keep in touch eh? 'Phone or write.'

'Would you come up to London if I could find you and Maggie some work?'

'What would London want with a miner with one thumb?'

'Glynmor, there's far funnier people than you up there. But you'll get redundancy. You could start a small business or something. It would be good for Maggie to get away from here.'

'I won't be getting any redundancy.'

'Don't be so soft. Of course you will. Everyone gets redundancy if a pit closes. What're you talking about?'

'You'd better be off, girl. 'Phone or write now.'

Far from lifting its teeth of ice out of the neck of the Valley, winter actually bit deeper that night, making it the coldest March night of the century. Parts of the river froze up, with small white horses of ice leaping up over the boulders and hanging over them in mid-air. Even the reservoir iced over, forcing the ducks to clamber out and join the sheep in foraging the bitter slopes for something in the way of food.

Tinker, the plumber, was on twenty-four hour call and was so busy he actually fell asleep while trying to fix the frozen ball cock on Aunty Phyllis' water tank. Up in Giro City Mr and Mrs Peter Betts, two old-age-pensioners, went to bed never to get up again, dying in one another's arms from hypothermia. That night also the Co-op was done again and the same gang also broke into Danny Kettle's house stealing the video, television, microwave and Danny's sheepdog.

Up on the snow-patched mountain, icy gusts of wind roamed the pine forests looking for a bit of warmth to kill. The huge detached eyeball of the full moon glowered down on the neat marching lines of the trees.

Deep within a thicket of pines there were the hoarse caws and flapping wings of a small group of ravens plundering the hanging corpse of Oboe Parry. They fought with one another and squealed in high fury as one sank his claws deep into Oboe's nose, tearing at his eyes which were already but torn, bloody sockets. The long curved daggers of their beaks sank into the flesh. Lumps had been torn out of his neck and cheeks until his face was a totally unrecognisable patchwork of rips and dangling slivers. Other birds had come to peck at his hands and others at his legs where the bones were already visible beneath his torn trouser legs. Only his steel-capped miner's boots had saved his feet.

The next morning the sun brought some warmth along in her shopping basket, melting the icicles and clearing away the last patches of snow. The ducks were able to go back into the reservoir and the boys were able to go and sit back on their bench to drink their cider.

'The strike's good an' fucked I 'eard,' said Curly, kicking his heels and staring down into the neck of the cider bottle. 'Scargill is still saying it's on but it sounds as if it's back to work for everyone next Monday.'

'Aye. Back to work for everyone but our boys. Bloody marvellous init? Everyone is going back except our boys who've got nowhere to go except the dole office.'

'A year Idris. They struck for a whole fucking year an' all they ended up doing was putting the boot into their own pit. It's those bastard women I blame. They stopped the safety there din' they? Those women should never 'ave been let out of the kitchen if you ask me.'

'Well, that's the modern age for you *mun*. Under this government everything you do to try an' make things better just makes them worse. It stands to reason donit? It's like when you've got a car that's going tidy. There's nothing wrong with it but you take it to a garage for a service an' what 'appens? It goes wrong.'

'I don't understand,' said Curly with his forehead wrinkling. 'What's that got to do with the pit around 'ere closing? It was always knackered wasn't it?'

'Why do I bother to try an' explain anything to a flea-brain like you? Eh? Why? When someone's got a bit of piss for a brain they don't understand anything. Listen. If something's working all right why tamper with it? Why not leave it well alone? I mean to say that clock over there has worked fine for nearly a whole hundred years so there's no point in interfering with it is there?'

'But it's not working all right is it?'

' 'Course it's working all right. They've thrown everything at that clock. Shoes, boots, fucking ladders. They've thrown milk bottles, gas cylinders, fucking car tyres ... an' it's never lost so much as a second.'

'But the clock's stopped, mun.'

They looked down at Idris' cider bottle and then both the old, unshaven faces turned together to look up at the clock face.

'That clock has stopped,' Idris said finally.

'I told you din I?'

'When did that happen then?'

'A few days ago. They came along in the middle of the night an' ripped out most of the machinery. For scrap I s'pose.

484

They must have done it at three o'clock … the way it's stopped there at three.'

It was just after one o'clock and thick curls of mist were floating down the Valley walls and over the row of shops when Maggie came walking back from the cemetery. Dressed all in black she looked a sad, stricken figure who seemed not to want to speak to or face anyone until, just as she was passing the chemist's, she heard a whistle and stopped, lifting up her head to look around.

She hurried over the road and stopped by the corner of the Post Office when her blood ran cold as she saw her Huw, dressed in all his Edwardian finery, standing in the doorway of the ironmongery shop just next to some old disused paraffin pumps. He was whistling at her with his eyes wide and full of loving mischief. A group of housewives were walking down the pavement chatting to one another when, just as they passed Huw, he seemed to disappear as if by a trick of mirrors.

Maggie crossed the road in a wide circle, never once taking her eyes off the ironmonger's when she stood in the doorway of the Betting Shop. The thick curls of mist were actually shrouding a few of the parked cars when the whistling began again. Her heart leaped and she looked along the row of shops spotting her Huw again standing outside Lipton's which had been shuttered and locked up for lunch. All around him were gaudy posters offering special unrepeatable prices on such as sugar and corned beef while, for a second, she thought that Huw was actually pointing out this week's special offer in trading stamps to her.

'Oh Huw *bach*,' she said, but making no move towards him as her heart kept chiming. 'Oh Huw baby *bach*. Just come over by here and let's have a *cwtch*.'

Huw disappeared again when the Cardiff bus drove past, dispersing the floating mists in its roaring, exhaust-fumed wake. Her eyes wandered down the row of shops again, from the corner cafe to the boarded-up chip shop, but there were just the small spills of litter over the pavements and a sheep walking past with its head cocked to one side. Just then she could feel Huw actually standing next to her. She could feel him breathing and chuckling softly and her whole body suddenly flooded with relief and joy. She knew, with a mother's impeccable intuition, that he had just come back to re-assure her that all was well with him; that the best was yet to be and that he was going to live with her in the Valleys for ever.

He continued chuckling softly – closer to her than her own shadow he seemed to be – and she just stood there, enjoying his warmth and listening to the hissing sounds of the opening doors of the bus as it stopped in the square. Just then Huw's presence seemed to drift away again and, unsure of what to do next, she remained standing in the doorway of the Betting Shop when the door itself opened, letting out a small gale of cigarette smoke and the excited ravings of a race commentator. Piper Prosser stepped out of the shop, walking past her and pausing to examine his betting slip, before striding away up the hill past the broken-jawed rubble of the Libanus Chapel.

She looked around the street again but knew that Huw had gone now. It had just been a short visit to tell her not to cry. She decided not to tell anyone – least of all Glynmor – about Huw's visit. It would be a secret she would share only with Huw. Already her leaden spirits had begun hang-gliding on beautiful winds.

When she returned home, however, she found Emlyn sitting in her armchair talking with Glynmor. A sharp glance from Glynmor told her to steer clear. The tracks of anguished tears were coming down her uncle's face. She went straight out into the kitchen to make some tea, keeping half an ear on what Emlyn was saying.

The Old Hewer was clearly shattered by the events of the times, unable to respond in any other way to the news that the South Wales N.U.M. had just decided to throw in the towel and go back to work, without any agreement with the N.C.B.

'Without any agreement! In all my time with the union I've never heard anything like it. There's been eighty locked up and seven hundred sacked for picketing offences. Are we just to throw them all to one side like so much dross? Can't we hold on for at least a few days and at least *try* for an amnesty for them? No, they can't wait another day. After a year on strike they can't wait for another day. And what really cuts into my heart is that the Welsh have done this. The Welsh, mind you, who've gone and pissed on their own comrades. And do you know who held out? Well Scargill held firm – as always – and Kent. Kent!

What great flame-throwers they've been in all this strike eh? Where the fuck is Kent anyway?'

Glynmor had never heard Emlyn swear before. He sat in silence as the lodge chairman – an old, saddened man – turned his ripped hands over and over, as if examining all the small blue scars, the miner's badges of slavery.

'They said they'd raise the future of Bont pit as soon as they got around the table with the N.C.B.,' Emlyn continued. 'But a union that can't fight for eight hundred sacked men can't fight for an axed pit. An' there's still coal down that pit too. Bags of it.'

'We could still get that coal out,' said Glynmor.

'Hindsight is always an exact science but what a story it all turned out to be, didn't it?' Emlyn said following the track of his own thoughts. 'What a story! We get stabbed in the back by Thatcher. Well, you'd only expect that wouldn't you? We got stabbed in the back by the Labour Party and that quisling Kinnock. We got stabbed by a television director and one of our own. Then our very own union comes along and stabs us in the front. And on top of that we go and lose the boy we all loved the most. Marvellous isn't it? You just couldn't make up a story like that could you? I never believed the day would come when I'd be ashamed to be a Welsh miner. But that day's come, it has. We never had much but we always had our decency, always cherished our pride.'

There was a short silence broken only when Maggie put the tea down next to them, taking her own and sitting at the table. It was Glynmor who spoke next.

'I might as well tell you now, Emlyn, that me and a few of the boys have decided to take over the pit. When the time's right we're going to take it over and work it ourselves.'

The fire fell in on itself. From somewhere out in the street, there was the thin sound of a tin can being kicked around. Emlyn picked up his tea and sipped it as he stared at Glynmor. 'I always knew you'd make a great disciple of mine,' Emlyn said. 'I knew it that night we spoke together in that chapel in Aberfan.'

Maggie looked out through the kitchen window at a blackbird swooping down and foraging for worms in the earth.

'We're not playing about either,' Glynmor went on. 'We think it's time we stood up an' did something. Strangely enough it was Gnasher who came to me with the idea. He says he can sell as much as we can dig out. We know we're going to be running against the law but we don't think there's any other option.'

'When are we going in then?'

'There's no timetable just at the moment. We want to think it through first. You're with us then?'

'Well aye mun. Well aye.'

Three days later the winter broke camp and spring came charging into the Valley.

It was one of those brilliant cloudless days with the sky as blue as a bruise and great tanks of sunshine trundling down the bracken slopes. Even the sheep looked whiter and the blackbirds seemed to sing nicer this spring morning. Mrs Pryce's cat crept out onto the corrugated roof of the garage to bask in the unaccustomed warmth.

There were thrilling whispers of the resurrection to be heard almost everywhere in Bont. They were there in the small, curled buds of Dai Swansea's roses. They were in the small brown trout flashing over the dreaming pebbles of the river. They were even in the sight of Ted John North up on a ladder and busy painting the rotten woodwork of the still-closed Welfare Hall. A bright red he was painting them. The boys always said that he had no taste but no one made any objection since almost any colour was better than the sickly, rotten colours which the Hall had come to wear like a tatty Oxfam shawl.

A large green van pulled up outside the Hall and the driver opened its back doors and proceeded to unload piles of books which he stacked in neat piles at the locked entrance to the Hall foyer. Whistling all the while he may have unloaded a few hundred when Ted John North came down his ladder. 'What do you think you're doing then?' asked Ted.

'Unloading these here books,' replied the driver as he continued bringing out stack after stack.

'Why's that then? Bit of bed-time reading for the sheep is it?'

The driver surveyed Ted with narrowing eyes wondering if he was talking to an idiot which, in a sense, he was. 'I'm unloading them 'cos I'm the delivery man,' he said slowly.

'They're books from the University library in Aberystwyth an' I've been told to deliver them here.'

'Why 'ere?'

'Because this is the address on my note,' the driver said with his patience ebbing away a bit more. 'The Welfare Hall, Bont. That's this place isn't it?'

'But this place has been closed f'r ages mun. There's been a bit of mischief with the roof so they've closed it down.'

They both turned and looked up at the roof before staring at one another whereupon the delivery man spoke again. 'I've got a few thousand books in there,' he said jerking his thumb towards the van. 'It's a whole library it is an' I've got to drop them off here before I pick up another load over in Bedwas to take back to Aberystwyth.'

Almost as if it was all his fault Ted looked down at his paint brush shame-faced. 'Well I'm very sorry I'm sure,' he said. 'But, as I said, the Hall is closed till further notice.'

Another sagging silence.

'If this Hall is closed down as you say,' the driver said finally, 'why the 'ell are you up that ladder painting it?'

'Oh I just got fed up with looking at it. There's a few of us been starting to do things around here. Phillip Tibbles, over by the chip shop, actually began sweeping the streets so I thought, well, I'll clean up the Hall a bit. I 'ad some spare paint an' decided to paint it.'

'So who's in charge of the Hall?'

'Well, the committee chairman is prob'ly at 'ome, I should think. 'E lives two streets away. Are there any names on that note of yours are there?'

They both fell to examining the delivery note, turning it over and finding the name Emlyn Thomas, chairman of Bont N.U.M., Bont Hall.

'That's Emlyn Kremlin,' Ted explained. ''E lives three streets away 'e do. I'll go get 'im if you like.'

Still holding his paint brush Ted John North ran off over the square only to return, some ten minutes later, with Emlyn and Glynmor.

'I've got three thousand books for you,' the driver said without further ado. 'Just sign 'ere an' help me unload them will you?'

'You've got the wrong place, mate,' said Glynmor as

489

Emlyn went over to examine the books that had already been unloaded. 'No one reads around 'ere. Most of them can't even read a betting slip.'

'Well I'm not taking them all the way back to Aberystwyth.'

Emlyn stooped down and picked up one of the books. *Keir Hardie: The Man and the Message* by Bruce Glasier, it said on the spine. He picked up another. *Labour and Unemployment* by Kenneth Brown. He opened the book carefully, almost as if it was a very valuable and extremely old document. Bont Miners' Library, it said on a slip pasted inside the jacket, followed by a list of regulations.

'Well blow me, blow me,' Emlyn kept repeating, picking up yet another book. *Prophets, Priests and Kings* by A.G. Gardiner. 'Glynmor. We've got our library back.'

'What library is that?'

'Our library mun. How many libraries do you think we 'ad?'

' 'Ow come?' asked Glynmor going over to him and taking the book out of his hand.

'I'll tell you 'ow come,' said Emlyn taking the book back off him. 'Because I rang up the university in Aberystwyth the other day. I'd 'ad a couple of drinks I do admit but I got the boss man an' said if we didn't get our library sent straight back I'd send the flying pickets of Bont up to deal with them.'

'I bet that got them all trembling in their beds.'

'Well they sent them, didn't they? They sent 'em. They may not look much but there's the whole mind and history of Bont in these books. An' we've got them back Glynmor. We've got them back.'

'This is all very well,' said the driver. 'But I've got to be over in Bedwas in an hour. Can we unload them now?'

'Yes, yes,' said Emlyn, more excited than he'd been for some time. 'We'll get the key to the Hall from Max. It's just so great to have these books back.'

Ted John North was despatched again to find Max Million while the driver, Glynmor and Emlyn continued to unload the books onto the pavement. Every now and then Emlyn, who had stripped down to his shirt and braces, would stop work to open the pages of an old, favoured work and give a little chuckle of delight. 'This one's brilliant Glynmor. He foresaw the curse of

490

monetarism decades before it came. And that one too. Superb writing.'

Half an hour later the chairman came up the hill to survey, with some dismay, the growing mountain of books on the pavement. 'Emlyn, I wouldn't like to break up your party but it's a new roof we want not an old library.'

'We'll get the roof mun. It's ideas we're short of, not money. An' there's ideas in these books, Max. There's ideas that'll blow your head off. Change your ideas and you'll change everything. New ideas will bring us a new roof Max. This place began dying the day we gave these books away.'

'Where are we going to store them then?' asked Max taking out a key.

'We'll take them down into our strike centre in the basement,' said Glynmor. 'At least there's no damp down there – till we get something organised.'

When they had finished unloading the books and duly signed the driver's delivery note, Emlyn was still happier than a small baby, carting great armsful of them down into the basement room where he kept re-arranging them in different piles.

'Look, these books have been looked after lovely,' he crooned. 'There's no dust on them. I can't smell any damp either. We'll have to get them catalogued proper. *Duw*, Glynmor it's like getting back your only son after you've lost him for twenty years. These books could save us yet 'cos, sure as eggs, nothing else will.'

'There's the little matter that this Hall is condemned,' Glynmor pointed out. 'You can't 'ave your readers coming in to learn about the fleas in Karl Marx's beard if the fucking roof is going to fall on their heads now can you?'

'Ah. But you don't know what I know Glynmor. There's something I haven't had a chance to discuss with you just yet. I've been talking with Gnasher about our plans to take the mine. He's a bright lad that Gnasher, more brains than I've ever given him credit for anyway. 'E says he could turn over a lot of money quite fast through his outlets when we take over the pit. An', as there'd be no chance of keeping it away from the law, he thought we should use the money to repair the Hall. See? It keeps our hands clean that way.'

'Brilliant. We need popular support and that would be

491

popular right enough. Brilliant. I always said Gnasher would go a long way.'

'No, you never.'

They continued re-arranging the books and discussing how much it would cost to put the Hall right when they noticed a man standing at the door. Glynmor recognised him immediate, as John Rees, the Worthy Primo of the Buffs. 'Well, well Emlyn,' Glynmor said in a mock-reverential tone. 'Down on your knees. It's the Worthy Primo.'

'Don't go giving me a hard time now Glynmor,' said Worthy Primo, looking around and almost acting nervously. 'I've come to tell you something you ought to know. It's supposed to be a Buff secret since we were under the sacred oath when we were told. But you've got to know.'

'Know what mun?' Emlyn asked.

Now Worthy Primo had gone very white indeed, looking around him furtively. All this Buff secrecy had clearly gone to his head. 'We 'ad a meeting of the Buffaloes over in Aberdare last night,' he said finally, almost dropping his voice to a whisper and moving further into the room. 'As I say I'm not supposed to tell you but you've got to know.'

'Got to know what?'

'John Walsh, the pit manager, is one of us an' he's heard about your plan for taking over the pit. Another Buff told him. Don't ask me who. I can't tell you that.'

'Shit!' exclaimed Glynmor.

'And what's far worse is that John Walsh has told us – all in the strictest secrecy, of course – that he's gone and told the police. What I've come to tell you is that the police have been making their own plans too an', tomorrow morning, they're going to move in an' take over the pit to secure it for the board.'

The mists became thicker that night with huge articulated trucks roaring up and down the road. From a distance it looked as if there might be three trucks working – or it might have been four – and they kept it up for hour after hour.

Glynmor and Emlyn had been busy too, knocking on doors and telling the boys it was time to move.

'Abdabs, we're taking the pit tonight.'

'Aye. I'll just get my boots on.'

'Jonesey, we're moving into the pit tonight.'

'Aye, aye. I'll bring my tea with me.'

By the time they had finished knocking on the doors they had roused some fifty men with a further hundred of them coming along through word of mouth.

And, come the sunshine dawn, there was a high wall of rocks and slurry over the road and all around the front of the pit. On top of the mound there was a hastily painted sign which said: PEOPLE'S PIT – KEEP OUT. The Bont lodge banner had been erected in front of the canteen.

Inside the canteen the men were milling about excitedly as Glynmor climbed onto a table to address them. 'Boys, boys ... all I want to say is that a working schedule will be drawn up this morning an' then we're going to dig every last cobble out of this pit ... '

The rest of his words were drowned in a great roar. 'Every last bastard cobble.'

Outside, on the pit road, police cars and vans were pulling up in front of the bank of slurry to see that their own occupation plans had been foiled by a far earlier bird. When a few officers tried to scale the bank they were driven back beneath a hail of rocks and lumps of coal. An inspector tried, unsuccessfully, to open negotiations over a loudhailer.

Maggie sat at her kitchen table drinking tea. They had discussed the plans to take the pit and this was one foray that she was more than content to let Glynmor and the boys handle alone. When she finished her tea she swilled out her cup in the bosh, using her finger to wipe around inside the cup before placing the cup and saucer on the draining board.

Then she put on her coat and walked up past the Libanus where a large crowd was already building up behind the police lines. She climbed up the high wall of the Valley, coming out onto a ledge where she could watch the comings and goings in the pit yard. She had told Glynmor where she would be and, from time to time during the course of the morning, he would pause and look up at her standing there with her hands in her pockets looking down at him.

Glynmor had been surprised at how calmly she had taken the news of the pit occupation but, rather the reverse, she was monumentally proud of him; pleased that, after all these years, he was just not just fighting for himself at last; pleased that he was honouring the spirit of their only son, Huw.

Maggie noticed that the inspector was back on his loudhailer again with Glynmor scrambling to the top of the mound where they had sunk a sort of trench. When the police had finished his list of demands Glynmor merely lifted his hand and gave him a V sign.

Maggie couldn't help smiling at that. Her Glynmor could always find something disgusting to do, no matter what the occasion. She felt another sort of smile inside her too and knew that Huw was close to all of them, laughing softly in the wind.

A police helicopter came swooping in over the volcano wall, briefly eclipsing the sun and making it go dark. Glynmor looked up at the helicopter and his smile faltered when it seemed to change shape, evolving into some sort of chariot of shadows with a man at its helm. Just behind the man some six ladies were singing with such awesome power that the hymn kept rolling down the Valley. The whole shape of the chariot was instinct with terror and beauty. There was lament and heartbreak in the man's voice as he cried out to his people to awake and turn back to the one true and living God. A wilderness of confusion and pain rolled around Glynmor's heart and he looked up at Maggie's face on the Valley slope. She was still looking down on him but, by now, the sun had gone so black they could not see one another at all.

ONE WINTER OF THE HOLY SPIRIT

Tom Davies

'The old Welsh blend of poetry and brutality, tenderness and tragedy, flesh and spirit . . . the whole story is permeated by the same sense of raw power' Michael Saward, Radio Four

It is the winter of 1904 and in Wales times are hard. But while Michael Evans, a cockle-gatherer on the sands of the Gower, believes the new socialism heralds a bright new future his girl, Beth, looks to the chapel for her answers.

Miner-turned-preacher Evan Roberts has single-handedly given birth to an extraordinary religious revival. The pubs are now empty, the chapels are full – and by Evan's side stands Beth, one of the chosen few.

While Beth lies out of reach, enmeshed in the hysteria of the movement, Michael slowly unveils her tragic past and learns of the terrible burden of her guilt. Aware of her vulnerability he offers her shelter in the aftermath of the Revival's storm – but she is a broken bird and he can nurture her back to life only if she will let him . . .

'compelling . . . often funny . . . a wonderful ear for the rhythms of Welsh speech' *Sunday Telegraph*

'a hauntingly tragic love story' *South Wales Evening Post*

'Only a Welshman could have written it . . . worthy of Dylan Thomas' *South Wales Argus*

Futura Publications
Fiction
0 7088 3054 4

All Futura Books are available at your bookshop or
newsagent, or can be ordered from the following address:
Futura Books, Cash Sales Department,
P.O. Box 11, Falmouth, Cornwall TR10 9EN.

Please send cheque or postal order (no currency), and
allow 60p for postage and packing for the first book
plus 25p for the second book and 15p for each additional
book ordered up to a maximum charge of £1.90 in U.K.

B.F.P.O. customers please allow 60p for
the first book, 25p for the second book plus 15p per
copy for the next 7 books, thereafter 9p per book

Overseas customers, including Eire, please allow £1.25
for postage and packing for the first book, 75p for the
second book and 28p for each subsequent title ordered.